THEY W[...]
OTHER [...]
WIT[...]

D0632499

JENNY TAGGART[...] Passion and [...] Need made her a survivor in a harsh, alien land.

ANDREW HAWLEY—Pledged to defend his country, he was forced to choose between his love of England and his love for Jenny.

LIEUTENANT JEREMIAH LEACH—A commission from the king was his license to command. He used it with a vengeful will and an ungovernable lust.

JOHNNY BUTCHER—More than love, he valued freedom, but forced to choose between Jenny and liberty, he'd be damned if he wouldn't steal them both.

THE EXILES

A turbulent saga of love and lust, of loyalty and betrayal on the raw Australian frontiers.

"GRIPPING, DRAMATIC—A SUPERB HISTORICAL NOVEL THAT DOES FOR AUSTRALIA WHAT *THE KENT FAMILY CHRONICLES* DOES FOR AMERICA!"
 —Dana Fuller Ross, author of *Wagons West*

Other books in THE AUSTRALIANS series
by William Stuart Long

THE
EXILES

WILLIAM STUART LONG

A DELL BOOK

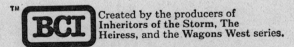

™ **BCI** Created by the producers of
Inheritors of the Storm, The
Heiress, and the Wagons West series.

Executive Producer: Lyle Kenyon Engel

Published by
Dell Publishing Co., Inc.
1 Dag Hammarskjold Plaza
New York, New York 10017

Produced by Lyle Kenyon Engel

While details of the maps in this book are accurate, they include additional information not known to the first settlers in order to provide the modern reader with a more complete picture of the area. The map of Sydney Cove, Port Jackson, is taken from an original drawn by Governor Arthur Phillip in March 1788.

Dell ® TM 681510, Dell Publishing Co., Inc.

ISBN: 0-440-12374-7

Printed in the United States of America
First U.S.A. printing—March 1980
Fourteenth U.S.A. printing—May 1985

Acknowledgments and Notes

The author acknowledges, with deep gratitude and appreciation, the help received in the writing of this novel from Lyle Kenyon Engel—on whose original concept it is based—and from his editorial staff at Book Creations, Incorporated, of Canaan, New York: Marla Ray Engel, Philip Rich, and Rebecca Rubin.

Also much appreciated has been the hard work done in the field of background and historical research by Vera Koenigswarter and May Scullion in Sydney, Australia; and in England, on the naval side, by Peter Gaston; and generally by the York Public Library staff, in providing research material.

The list of books consulted is too lengthy to be given in a brief acknowledgment but main sources were: *Sydney's First Four Years*—Captain Watkin Tench, 1793, reprinted by Angus & Robertson Pty. Ltd., 1961; *Phillip of Australia*—M. Barnard Eldershaw, Harrap, 1938; *Journal of a Voyage to New South Wales*—Dr. John White, 1790; *A Voyage to New South Wales*—George Barrington, Superintendent of Convicts, Dobson, Philadelphia, 1796; *A Picturesque Atlas of Australia*—Hon. Andrew Garran, Melbourne, 1886 (two volumes, kindly lent by Anthony Morris); *The First Twenty Years of Australia*—A. Bonwick, 1882; *The Convict Settlers of Australia*—L.L. Robson, Melbourne University Press, 1965.

Maps were made from copies obtained from various

sources, including the Mitchell Library, Sydney, by Vera Koenigswater, and ships' logs from the British Public Record Office and the National Maritime Museum by Peter Gaston,

Because this is written as a novel, a number of fictional characters have been created and superimposed on the narrative, but the basic story of Captain Arthur Phillip's voyage to Botany Bay and his governorship of the colony of Sydney is factually and historically accurate. When real life characters' actions, adventures, and misadventures are described, they are true and actually took place as nearly as possible as described, having regard for the novelist's obligation to tell a dramatic story against the factual background. The more unpleasant convicts have, however, in some instances, been given fictional names, lest offense be given to living descendants of First Fleeters.

The author spent eight years in Australia and served in the Australian Forces during World War II, later being transferred to the British XIV Army in Burma. The author traveled throughout the country, from Sydney to Perth, across the Nullabor Plain, and to Broome, Wyndham and Derby, Melbourne, Brisbane and Adelaide, with a spell in the islands, and on a station at Toowoomba.

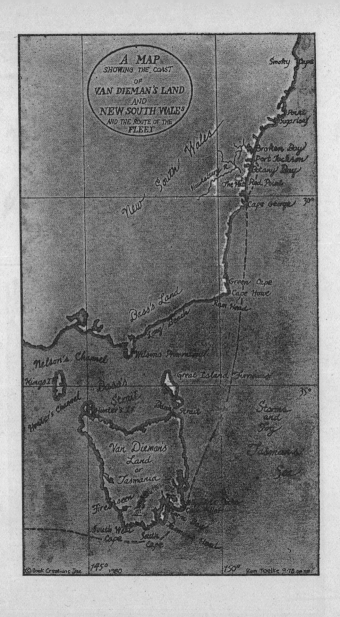

A MAP
SHOWING THE ROUTE OF THE
FIRST FLEET
from
England to Australia

Fleet sailed from Spithead ~ May 13, 1787
Tenerife June 3 ~ Corpus Christi Festival June 7
Fleet sailed for Rio June 10 ~ S.E. Trades picked up July 7
Rio de Janeiro August 6 ~ Officers entertained by Governor
Sailed Sept. 4 for Cape Town ~ Mutiny on Alexander Oct. 6
Fleet landed at Cape Town October 14
Sailed Nov. 12 ~ Phillip transferred to Supply ~ Nov. 16
Fleet divided off Kerguelen Is. December 13, 1787

The route of the Fleet is shown thus ·······
© Book Creations, Inc. 1980

1st division of fleet sight Van Diemen's Land Jan 2, 1788.
Severe storms Jan 17 ~ Phillip's squadron at Botany Bay Jan 18.
2nd division sighted mainland Jan 19.
2nd division led by H.M.S. Sirius reached Botany Bay Jan 20.
Phillip at Port Jackson January 21, 1788.
Arrival of Laperouse's squadron at Botany Bay Jan 24.
Phillip at Sydney Cove ~ January 25, 1788.
Flag hoisted and land claimed ~ fleet at anchor Jan 26.
The fleet in port is shown thus:

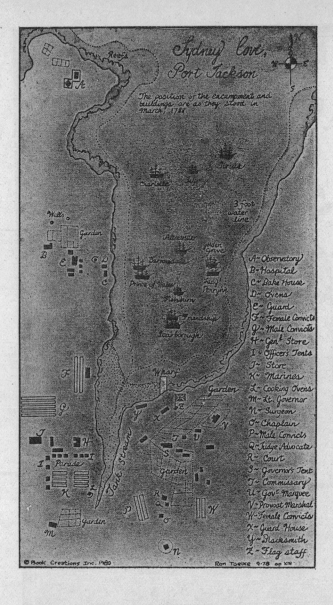

Sydney Cove,
Port Jackson

N

Reef's

The position of the encampment and
buildings are as they stood in
March, 1788.

3 foot
water
line

Sirius

Charlotte   *Supply*

Wells

Garden

Alexander

Borrowdale   *Golden Grove*

Prince of Wales   *Lady Penrhyn*

Fishburn

Friendship

Scarborough

A ~ Observatory
B ~ Hospital
C ~ Bake House
D ~ Ovens
E ~ Guard
F ~ Female Convicts
G ~ Male Convicts
H ~ Gen.l Store
I ~ Officer's Tents
J ~ Store
K ~ Marines
L ~ Cooking Ovens
M ~ Lt. Governor
N ~ Surgeon
O ~ Chaplain
P ~ Male Convicts
Q ~ Judge Advocate
R ~ Court
S ~ Governor's Tent
T ~ Commissary
U ~ Gov.r Marquee
V ~ Provost Marshal
W ~ Female Convicts
X ~ Guard House
Y ~ Blacksmith
Z ~ Flag staff

Wharf

Garden

Tank Stream

Parade

Garden

Garden

© Book Creations Inc. 1980   Ron Toelke 9-78 op XIV

FAREWELL
LONG WREKIN

CHAPTER I

The morning of September 29, 1781, dawned gray and overcast, with tendrils of damp mist swirling over the flat countryside surrounding the small Yorkshire market town of Milton Overblow. But as a watery sun rose to tinge the mist with pale reflected gold, all roads leading to the town soon became crowded with countryfolk in carts, on horseback, or on foot. It was the day of the Michaelmas Fair, traditionally reserved for the sale of horses and sheep, and many in the straggling procession on the road from Overdale drove flocks of sheep before them or had yearling horses tethered to the rear of their carts.

Their progress was, of necessity, slow, but few worried on this account. For the dale's farmers and small-holders and their families, the Michaelmas Fair was an occasion to which they looked forward from year to year. Clad in their best, their children with scrubbed faces and neatly combed hair, they contained their impatience, aware that the stalls and sideshows and the taprooms in the town would remain open until the last of the influx of visitors had spent his sale money and was compelled reluctantly to depart.

The party of horsemen who joined the road from the long tree-lined drive of Overdale Manor, however, was in no mood to brook delay. Led by the owner of the manor, Lord Braxton, on a handsome bay Thoroughbred, they cantered through a flock of sheep, scattering them and two families of walkers into the hedgerows with equal disdain. Only the rector of Overdale, a stout, elderly gentleman on a half-clipped cob, offered a breathless apology to the shepherd as he spurred after his patron, deeming it wise to shut his ears to the fellow's curses, which were, he knew, directed toward Lord Braxton rather than himself.

His lordship was far from popular either with his tenants or with the local farmers. He had no family ties with the county, for one thing. And for another, both his wealth and his title were of comparatively recent origin—the reward of naval service in the West Indies, where, if rumor were to be believed, he had shown more concern for the acquisition of prize money than for fighting his country's battles against the French and the American colonists. Nevertheless he had served with sufficient distinction under Admiral Rodney and his second-in-command, Rear Admiral Sir Samuel Hood, to merit the barony which had been conferred on him by a grateful sovereign. And now . . . Reverend Simeon Akeroyd gave vent to a sigh as he eased his sweating animal to a pace more suited to its age and sluggish temperament. Now, in retirement, the new Baron Braxton had purchased the lands and Manor of Overdale and had contrived to have himself appointed to the Magistrate's Bench as chairman.

Had this been all, the dalesfolk would probably have accepted him, the rector thought, as they accepted, with patient resignation, most of life's other vicissitudes, such as the harsh winters and the poor grazing which, combined with the ever increasing burden of high taxation necessitated by successive wars, came close to beggaring so many of them. The savage sentences Braxton imposed on petty criminals, the fines he exacted for minor breaches of the law—even the arrogance that characterized his dealings with those he considered his social inferiors—would have aroused no more than their unspoken resentment.

But the man was avaricious, and lately, with the aid of his lawyer, Thomas Slater, who was cast in the same mold, he had succeeded in obtaining eviction orders against several of his tenants by invoking the Enclosure Act, with the object of adding their land to his own considerable acreage. Under the act—a Tudor law that had never been rescinded—Lord Braxton demanded certain standards of husbandry that his predecessor, an amiable aristocrat, had not bothered to enforce, and the curtailment of the use of common land for grazing.

And this, patient and accustomed to injustice though they were, the dalesfolk would not suffer in silence. The average smallholder depended on the free use of common land, as had his father before him; sheep could find sustenance on hill and moor, but horses and cows could not. Bitterness against the new lord of the manor was building up to an alarming degree. There had been talk, among a few young hotheads, of paying the tyrant back in his own coin by pulling down the fences he had erected, and some of them had even considered violence against his person. As their spiritual counselor, the old rector had done all in his power to restrain them, warning them of the inevitable consequences of any such action, but most of them had been too angry to pay him heed. Only a week ago two fences on Braxton land had been torn down and the timber stolen under cover of darkness, and there had been a bungled attempt—attributed to footpads—to waylay his lordship's carriage as it returned late from town.

Fortunately for the culprits, the carriage had been empty and the coachman had met with no harm but . . . the Reverend Simeon Akeroyd sighed uneasily. It had been feared that Braxton's presence at the fair might provoke another futile act of retaliation, which had driven him, reluctantly, to ride over soon after dawn in order to attach himself to the manor party.

Lord Braxton had not welcomed him. He had Lawyer Slater in close attendance, and his rascally bailiff, Ned Waite, in addition to a one-time seaman known locally as "Gunner" O'Keefe, whom he employed as a groom and without whose escort he seldom stirred beyond the confines of his own walled garden. That he was bent on making trouble for some unfortunate seemed evident from his manner and the low-voiced exchanges with Thomas Slater as the small cavalcade formed up on the manor's graveled carriageway. But, apart from a disparaging remark concerning the ability of the rector's sorry nag to keep pace with his Thoroughbreds, he had raised no objection to his company, although . . . Simeon Akeroyd again buried his spurs in his mount's hairy sides . . . his lordship had made not the smallest effort to suit his speed to that of the poor animal. With relief the rector saw that Lord Braxton's party had, at last, drawn rein and, urged on by voice and heels, the cob broke into a shambling canter, to come to a halt, breathing heavily, beside the others on the road verge.

His relief was short-lived.

"That's t'fellow, me lord," he heard Bailiff Waite say. "That's t'Scotchman, over yonder. Taggart, he calls himself. 'Tis he lives by the west side o' Kirby Stray."

His pointing finger picked out a farm dray some fifty or sixty yards ahead of them, drawn by two well-matched Clydesdales, their brasses shining in the pale morning sunlight, their manes and tails decked with gaily colored ribbons in preparation for the fair. A man and a woman occupied the driving seat, with a child between them, and three young work horses, with haltered heads—obviously intended for the day's auction sale—followed behind.

Lord Braxton raised a hand to shade his eyes as he stared in the direction his bailiff had indicated. He asked, over his shoulder, addressing no one in particular, "Does he breed horses, this Taggart?"

The lawyer answered him. "Yes, my lord, so it seems—and he's said to be good at it. Certainly his animals fetch excellent prices when he puts them up for sale."

"He feeds 'em on the stray, me lord," Ned Waite put in, a hint of malice in his rough voice.

Slater cut him short with a warning glance at the rector.

Kirby Stray marched with the manor boundary to the west; it was prime grazing land, shared by the whole village of Kirby, but, by common consent, during the spring and summer months its use was re-

stricted to grazing by breeding mares and their foals
and a few household milk cows. The stray was one of
the present bones of contention between Braxton and
his tenants. The fences he had recently caused to be
set up there, timber posts and all, had vanished into
the night.

"You surely do not suppose, my lord," the rector
began, feeling it his duty to intervene on behalf of a
respected member of his congregation, "you *cannot*
suppose that Angus Taggart had aught to do with the
unfortunate episode of last week?"

"Unfortunate episode you call it, Parson?" Lord
Braxton exclaimed wrathfully. He transferred his
baleful gaze to the rector's face, eyeing him with contempt. "Plain theft, that's what it was—a deliberate
flouting of the law! I've a perfect right to keep the
damned smallholders' cattle off my grazing land unless
they pay me for it, as Slater will confirm. It's true,
isn't it, Thomas? I've title to the grazing?"

"You have indeed, my lord," Thomas Slater assured
him with servile eagerness. "The deeds are all legally
approved and filed." He took a large spotless linen
handkerchief from the pocket of his coat and blew his
long nose vigorously before embarking on an explanation of the finer legal points. Lord Braxton impatiently
waved him to silence.

"Why are you so sure that this fellow—what's his
name? This fellow Taggart hadn't anything to do with
the destruction of my fences, Parson? He had an axe to
grind, had he not? Needs grazing for his horses, don't
he? And needs it more than most, damme, seeing he
breeds 'em!"

It was true, Simeon Akeroyd thought sadly. But they
all needed Kirby Stray, poor Taggart was not the only
one. He knew, with virtual certainty, who had been

responsible for the tearing down of the fences, and the burden of his knowledge weighed heavily upon him. An innocent man could not be allowed to suffer for the misdeeds of others, yet . . . his eyes fell before the angry challenge of his patron's. Part of his stipend came from the manor tithes, he reminded himself wretchedly. It would behoove him to choose his words with care, lest they give offense for, heaven knew, his stipend was small enough.

He managed, stammering a little in his anxiety, "Angus Taggart is a decent, law-abiding man, my lord. He's not the sort of man who—well, who would stoop to clandestine law breaking. He'd not go behind your lordship's back. If he felt he had a legitimate grievance, I'm sure he would come out with it openly, my lord. Like all Scotsmen, he's proud and a mite stubborn, perhaps, but—"

"We'll see how proud he is," Braxton retorted with emphasis, "when he's faced with his accuser. Eh, Waite?" He glanced expectantly at his bailiff, who frowned as if the question had taken him by surprise and then nodded vigorously.

"Aye, me lord. 'Twas him I saw right enough. I'd take me oath on't."

"Then after him, man!" his employer ordered. "Tell him to pull off the road so that I can have a word with him."

"Have a care, my lord," Lawyer Slater murmured uneasily. "It won't do to antagonize the fellow until we have positive proof that he was involved."

"Oh, very well," Lord Braxton acknowledged. "You heard what Mister Slater said, Waite. No threats, understand—and mind your manners. Just tell Taggart I want to speak to him."

"Very good, your lordship." Ned Waite gathered up

his reins and trotted after the slowly moving wagon, careful—now that he was alone—to give a wide berth to a second flock of scrawny moorland sheep, which had spread itself across the narrow road. He even touched his cap to Taggart's pretty young wife when he drew abreast of the dray, the rector observed, and must have made his master's request civilly enough for, in response to it, Angus Taggart maneuvered his horses on to the road verge and pulled up. Handing the reins to his wife, he alighted and strode back to meet the oncoming horsemen, only pausing to lift a bleating ewe from his path.

He was a tall, solidly built man in his mid-thirties, with a dark, weatherbeaten face and a pair of friendly blue eyes. Dressed in brown homespun jacket and breeches, he wore his red hair tied in a neat queue, military style but unpowdered, and he made an oddly dignified figure as he halted to await Lord Braxton's approach. Ned Waite, who had prudently remained by the dray on the pretense of securing the horses, obeyed an imperious wave from his employer and returned, with obvious reluctance, on foot, dragging his own mount behind him through the milling sheep.

"You wish to speak with me, my lord?" Taggart inquired. His voice had a faint lilt to it, betraying his Highland ancestry and he spoke quietly, without aggression, as a man with a clear conscience and nothing to fear from what was evidently an unexpected summons. Recognizing the old rector, he smiled and gave him a polite greeting, which the rector returned.

"Your name is Taggart, is it not?" Lord Braxton intervened harshly.

"Aye, it is. Angus Taggart of Long Wrekin, by Kirby. I am one of your lordship's tenants."

"Of that I am well aware . . . and of the fact that

you breed horses, which you have had the effrontery to graze on my land. Is that not true, man?"

Angus Taggart stared at his questioner, his blue eyes first alarmed and then wary. "I graze my animals on the stray, sir, which is common land." He started to explain, quoting a local bylaw concerning grazing rights, but Lord Braxton would not let him finish.

"Tell this infernal fellow what *my* rights are, Slater. Tell him that unless grazing land is properly enclosed by fences—double fences, with a hawthorn hedge planted between 'em—by the date set by the commissioners, then all rights are forfeited."

Lawyer Slater, who was one of the Land Commission's solicitors, endeavored to obey him, but again Lord Braxton interrupted, his tone impatient.

"Oh, have done, Mister Slater, have done! He understands well enough, don't you, my man?"

"No, my lord, I do not," Taggart confessed. He looked acutely unhappy but he held his ground.

"Damme, you understand that *I* have done all that the law requires of me, surely? *I* have set up fences and had them uprooted in the night by cowardly scoundrels, afraid to show their faces in daylight like honest men. You know about *that*, I'll warrant!"

"Aye, my lord, I am knowing that it was done. But folk are in desperate need of that grazing—it will spell ruin for them if 'tis forbidden to them next spring."

"And it would also spell ruin for you, would it not?" Lord Braxton suggested. "Come now, Taggart—the truth!"

"Indeed it would," Taggart admitted, without hesitation. "My holding is marsh and moorland for the most part. I have just enough under the plow to feed my stock in winter, and for my neighbors it is the same.

Whereas for your lordship—" He thought better of what he had been about to say and left the sentence uncompleted, gesturing instead to the three young horses tethered to the back of his dray. "I cannot winter those, my lord, and they are the best I have. That is why I am taking them to sell at the fair."

Lord Braxton was smiling, his purpose achieved.

"He is condemned out of his own mouth, don't you agree, Mister Slater?" Ignoring the lawyer's warning headshake, he turned again to Angus Taggart. "My fellow Waite tells me that *you* were responsible for tearing down my fences, Taggart. That's so, isn't it, Waite?"

Thus appealed to, the bailiff inclined his close-cropped head. "Aye, me lord, me and O'Keefe." He exchanged a meaning glance with the ex-seaman, who bared his toothless gums in a wide grin of assent. "Sure, we seen him, your lordship, plain as could be. Diggin' up the fence posts, so he was, and loadin' 'em in his cart."

Taggart rounded on them, appalled. "You could not have seen me—I was not there! You're lying, Gunner— you know I had no hand in it." Despairingly, he appealed to the rector. "Mister Akeroyd, sir, will you not speak up for me?"

The old parson did his best, repeating the assessment of Angus Taggart's character that he had already supplied, but it was plain that Lord Braxton had no ears for him, and he lapsed into impotent silence as Waite, warming to his task, launched into a series of accusations. That these were unsubstantiated, save by the grinning O'Keefe, began at last to dawn on Taggart, and he said firmly, interrupting the bailiff's flow, "They offer no proof, my lord—it is their word against mine. And I swear to you that I had no knowledge of this affair until it was over and done. Indeed I spoke against it when the idea was first mooted and—" He broke off, realizing too late that he had revealed more than he had intended.

"Then you know the culprits?" Braxton suggested coldly.

"Not with certainty, my lord. Indeed, I—"

"You would be well advised to name them, Mister Taggart," Thomas Slater put in. "That is if you expect his lordship to believe that you had no hand in the affair."

"I cannot name them, sir," Taggart answered, tight lipped.

"Cannot . . . or will not, man?" Lord Braxton challenged.

"Then will not, if it pleases you," the Scotsman said defiantly. Slow to anger, his temper was at last aroused, and he added, with heat, "I am wishing I *had* been with them now. They had a right to do what they did—oh, not a legal right, perhaps, but before God, a moral one, with their livelihood at stake. Take that grazing from us, Lord Braxton, and we shall not be able to pay your rents, any of us." Once again, belatedly, he sensed that he had allowed his tongue to run away with him and fell silent. Braxton seized eagerly on his last admission.

"You may cease paying my rent now, Taggart. Give him formal notice, Mister Slater. I want him off my land within seven days—is that clear?"

"He is entitled to a quarter's notice," the lawyer demurred. "In writing, my lord."

"Then see that he gets it, damn your eyes!" Braxton ordered. He was about to turn away when Angus Taggart, pale but determined, laid a hand on his horse's rein.

"My tenancy is a yearly one, my lord."

"Is it, by thunder! And what do you pay me, eh?"

Taggart made an effort to control himself. "Six guineas for the land and two for the cottage, my lord."

"That's little enough. What's to stop me doubling your rent, my fine fellow? You'd sing a different tune then, I guarantee." Lawyer Slater caught his eye and shook his head warningly, but Lord Braxton was undeterred. "Ah, so he has a lease, has he? Well, no matter. As his landlord, is it not my duty under the Land Act to ensure that he farms productively?"

"That is a condition of his lease," the lawyer confirmed. "It is not provided for under the Act of—"

"If it's a condition of his lease, that will suffice. Very well, Taggart . . . you will, in future, put ten acres under wheat."

"My land will not grow wheat," Taggart protested, his face the picture of dismay. "It will just be throwing good money after bad. Even if I were able to clear the heather and bracken, there is rock only a few inches beneath the surface. And my horses—"

"Yes, indeed, there are your horses. Well, I won't be too hard on you, despite this matter of my fences." Lord Braxton, sensing victory, was almost jocular. The sheep had gone now and the road, for the moment, was clear. "Come, let us see what you have for sale, shall we? If they are any good, I'll take them off you at a fair price. That will buy you the seed you'll require and the implements."

Taggart's wife, a comely, fair-haired young woman, watched their approach nervously, gathering her child to her as if fearing that the little girl might be in danger. Braxton gave her a curt nod, which did nothing to reassure her, and then turned his attention to the horses.

"Run them out," he ordered. "I want to be sure they're sound in wind and limb."

Taggart stood mute, making no attempt to obey him, and Ned Waite slid from the saddle and, giving his reins to O'Keefe, freed the tether on the nearest of the young horses. They were crossbreds but clearly of good stock, and Lord Braxton eyed them appreciatively as the bailiff trotted them past him in turn. He was reputed to be a good judge of horseflesh, and it was evident, from his expression, that all three young animals pleased him.

"Are they broken to harness?" he asked. Taggart inclined his head in resentful silence. "Good! And to the plow? Speak up, man, I can't hear you!"

"Aye, the gelding is, not the others. . . ." The farmer met his wife's frightened gaze and added a sullen, "My lord." He was very white about the face, and his hands were shaking visibly. The old rector, taking pity on him and conscious that he had made a poor show of his defense, climbed stiffly down from his horse. O'Keefe relieved him of the animal, and he walked across to the far side of the dray where, for the moment, he was out of Lord Braxton's sight and hearing.

Rachel Taggart greeted his arrival with touching gratitude, and the child made room for him on the seat between them, a shy smile lighting her pinched, solemn little face.

"It's good of you to come, sir," Rachel Taggart said. She hesitated and then bade the child alight. "Walk about, Jenny love, and stretch your legs for a minute or two. Don't go too far, mind—stay where I can see you. And don't trouble your father just now—he's busy." When the little girl was out of earshot, walking sedately along the road verge, Rachel went on, her voice flat and controlled, "Angus is in trouble, isn't he?" It was more a statement than a question, and Simeon Akeroyd patted her hand awkwardly, having no choice but to confirm her fears.

"Yes, Rachel, I regret to say he is. But—"

"Serious trouble, Mister Akeroyd?" When he frowned, seeking the right words, she said vehemently, "I have to know, sir, else how can I help him? His lordship hasn't stopped us just to buy horses—he could do that at the fair."

"It's the matter of those fences he put up to enclose the stray, I'm afraid," the rector told her. "His lordship was extremely angry because they were pulled down and he—"

"But he cannot imagine Angus had aught to do with that!" Rachel protested.

"Bailiff Waite accused him of it, with that man they call the Gunner backing him up."

"Those two rogues!" Rachel was contemptuous. "And they say Gunner O'Keefe's not right in the head, Mister Akeroyd. Surely his lordship wouldn't take *their* word against my husband's?"

"I fear he seems inclined to, Rachel, my dear," the rector admitted reluctantly. "At all events he realizes that Angus knows who did destroy those fences and he's determined to force him to name them."

"Which he will not?"

"So far he has refused to. But. . . ." He told her the rest and saw the color drain from her cheeks as she took in the implications of what he was saying.

"*Ten* acres under wheat and that's—what did you call it, sir?"

"A condition of the lease. It means that Angus must fulfill it or lose his tenancy and that, I fear, can be enforced by law. But you will have a year's grace, I think. Perhaps in a year, Rachel, it might be possible."

"No." There were tears in the soft brown eyes, and Rachel made no attempt to hide them. "No, it will not, Mister Akeroyd. We could not clear ten acres in time for sowing, even if we wanted to, and the land is poor . . . the work would just be wasted. Besides, what Angus knows are his horses, he needs all his time for them. And if we are to lose the grazing on the stray, even their number will have to be cut down." She caught her breath on a sigh. "He has worked so hard with them, and we were counting on a profit this year."

"I am sorry," the old rector said, overwhelmingly conscious of his own helplessness in the face of her distress. "I am truly sorry for you both. I'll do what I can, of course—I'll try to speak to his lordship, Rachel, but I fear he will not relent. Unless, of course—" he paused, eyeing her uncertainly.

She guessed what he was about to say and shook her head. "Angus will not betray his friends, sir, whatever it costs him and they . . . well, they may be too fearful of his lordship to come forward and admit what they've done. They'll help him, though, in any way they can—of that I'm sure." Rachel glanced over to see the child retracing her steps and, swiftly dabbing at her eyes with a corner of her skirt, she summoned a smile. "I'd best keep Jenny with me until his lordship's done with Angus. Poor little maid, we'd promised her a visit to the fair as a treat." She called, and the little girl came running.

"Are we going now, Mam?" she asked eagerly. "Are we going?"

"In a little," her mother promised. "Have patience, child." She was still smiling and seemingly quite composed, and the rector marveled at her sturdy courage. He clambered down from the dray and offered his hand to enable Jenny to regain her lofty perch.

"You are looking forward to the fair, are you not, my little one?" he suggested and the child beamed.

"Oh, yes, sir, I am," she assured him. "Dadda has promised he'll buy me a new bonnet, you see—a bonnet with blue ribbons on it, for Sunday best."

"I shall look to see you wearing it in Church next Sunday, then," the rector said. He turned to take leave of Rachel Taggart, feeling a lump rise in his throat. These were good people, he thought wretchedly, they did not deserve what Lord Braxton was endeavoring to do to them. But it was happening all over the country. Braxton was not the only landlord seeking to wrest the few acres from folk of the Taggarts' kind. Sheep were more profitable than people these days—and infinitely less trouble to the landowning gentry than tenant farmers, whose rents could not legally be increased.

As he took Rachel's hand in his, Simeon Akeroyd wished fervently that it lay within his power to offer her practical help instead of the vague promises and the words of dubious comfort he was mouthing now. But, he was bitterly aware, it did not. Poor clerics like himself had no power; his own living depended very largely on the goodwill of the lord of the manor, and he was old, far from robust in health, with a family to provide for and not too many years between himself and penniless retirement. He could pray, of course, pray to the merciful God he served, and. . . .

"His lordship's movin' on, y'r rev'rince." Gunner O'Keefe's hoarse Irish voice sounded in his ear. "If ye'll be so good as to get back on y'r horse now, I'll be obliged to ye."

He thrust the cob's rein into its owner's hand and,

without waiting for him to mount, trotted off, grinning as usual to himself.

"Thank you for talking to me, sir," Rachel Taggart said quietly. She got down, unasked, to hold the cob's head and, as the old rector swung himself stiff-limbed into the saddle, she added uncannily, as if she had read his earlier thoughts, "Do not concern yourself in this matter if it is likely to make trouble for you with his lordship, Mister Akeroyd. Angus would not want that, I know. He fought the king's battles when he was a soldier, as bravely as ever Lord Braxton did . . . and now he'll fight his own."

"I believe he will, my dear, with you beside him."

Ashamed of the relief he felt, Reverend Simeon Akeroyd dug his heels once more into his horse's sides and set off in pursuit of Lord Braxton. Over his shoulder, not trusting himself to look round, he gave the Taggarts a parting "God be with you!" that came from the heart.

Angus Taggart walked slowly back to the dray, leading his three young crossbreds. He did not speak but busied himself adjusting their tethers at the rear of the cart, and Rachel, sensing the black anger which still gripped him, wisely left him alone. She got back into her seat and said gently to Jenny, "Be a good lass now and don't ask your Dadda a lot of questions. Better still, go and lie down in the wagon—you were up early enough, you could sleep for a little. Here, take my shawl and wrap it round you."

Jenny studied her face with startled eyes, but she obediently took the shawl. "We are going to the fair, aren't we, Mam?" Her voice was anxious.

"Oh, yes, we're going, love," Rachel assured her, suddenly resolute. It might be the last fair they would ever go to in Milton, she thought, but it would take more than Lord Braxton to keep them away from this one. "Off you go and don't fret," she bade the child. "Dadda's coming."

Her husband seated himself at her side and took up the reins. They had driven for nearly a quarter of a mile in silence when he burst out furiously, "Well, have you nothing to say to me, woman—no questions to plague me with? Do you not care to know what his lordship was saying to me?"

"I was waiting for you to tell me in your own good time," Rachel answered with unaccustomed meekness.

"Hoping that my rage would cool? Well, it will not!"

"But you are not angry with me, surely?" Rachel's hand closed about his arm. She ventured a smile.

"No, no." She had struck the right note, and he was instantly contrite, pressing her hand against his side. "Not with you . . . with that unprincipled scoundrel Lord Braxton. You do not know what he is threatening, do you?"

"I do, Angus. The rector told me." She turned to face him. "I said that you would not yield to threats— I said that you would fight him."

"And so I will, wife! 'Twill be over my dead body that he will evict us, that I swear. I. . . ." He hesitated, reddening. "I was not letting him have the horses. I refused to sell them to him."

"You refused? Oh, Angus, was that wise? They are for sale, surely—does it matter who buys them?"

"Aye, at auction, for a fair price. He offered less than half their value, and Ned Waite claimed that the gelding was spavined. You know that's not true."

"Ned Waite is a wicked man," she observed. "And Gunner O'Keefe another."

" 'Twas they who started all this," Angus said indignantly. "They were telling his lordship that they saw me digging up the fence posts on the stray and loading them onto my cart! I am wishing now that I had been there, since I am to be blamed for it—and I told his lordship so, to his face." He repeated all that had been said and finished bitterly, "His lordship has no right to enclose the stray. If he is ordering more fences to be put up there, I shall be with the others when they are knocking them down."

"And I will help you," Rachel promised.

"Aye, I believe you would, lass." He gave her his slow, warm smile. "I did not tell him who the others were, Rachel. I refused, when he asked me. That is the reason for his threats."

"Yes, I know." They were on the outskirts of the town now, the crowd thickening and a medley of sound reaching them from the fairground. Rachel took off her kerchief, flattened it carefully on her knee, and then replaced it on her head, thrusting some unruly curls within its confines.

Angus gestured with his whip. "I will be letting the two of you off there, so that you may go round the stalls, whilst I am entering my animals for the auction. It should be over by half past three, four at the latest, and I will meet you where I put you down."

"And you will buy Jenny her bonnet," Rachel reminded him.

"As if she will be letting me forget! Let her choose the one she wants, and I will pay for it from my sale money." Angus laughed, his good humor restored. "I will grow that wheat, Rachel—I will grow it if it kills me. Braxton shall not have my land." He brought the dray to a standstill and roused the sleeping child with a playful poke from his whip. "Bestir yourself little lazy-bones! We are here."

Jenny tumbled out of the wagon, rubbing the sleep

from her eyes. Clinging eagerly to her mother's hand, she led her from stall to stall. The old cobbled market-place was gay with bunting, the stalls with their striped awnings displaying all manner of enticing wares. There were jugglers and acrobats, organ grinders with their grotesque little monkeys—even a dancing bear, in cap and muzzle, treading a clumsy measure at the end of its long chain.

For a while Rachel was caught up in the general bustle and excitement, exchanging greetings with neighbors and childhood friends from her own part of the dales and sharing Jenny's enjoyment as the little girl shrilled with delight at her first Punch and Judy show. They bought gingerbread and apples for their midday meal, munching them as they moved about amongst the cheerful, laughing crowd, and Jenny spent a long time choosing the bonnet her father was to buy for her, setting first one and then another on her curly head and tying and retying their bows beneath her chin.

But at last the choice was made, the bonnet set aside until they should return to claim it, and they continued their wandering between the stalls and the tented sideshows, footsore now and conscious of weariness as the excitement began to pall and the crowds to thin. Rachel had no pennies left to spend on sideshows or refreshment, and the memory of the earlier happenings of the day, which she had put resolutely from her mind, returned to plague her.

They were early at the agreed meeting place but, to her dismay, Rachel saw that Angus was before them. One glance at his face was enough, and her heart sank. With a whispered warning to Jenny to keep a still tongue in her head, she hurried toward him, somehow managing to smile.

"He bought the horses!" Angus flung at her. "Bought all three of them, damn him to hell! And for half what they should have fetched. *This* is what I got for them." He held out his hand, letting her see the coins that lay on his palm, letting her count them.

"You—you mean Lord Braxton?" Rachel stammered, shocked. He was right, she knew—the young horses should have sold for twice as much. "But how did he get them for so little?"

"Ned Waite was the only man to bid for them," Angus told her. His voice shook with the effort he made to contain his fury. "Not another soul opened his mouth. It was as if they had all been struck dumb—yet the bidding was brisk enough until my animals came up."

"Oh, Angus!" They looked at each other despairingly, the child momentarily forgotten.

"We had best go home," Angus said at last. "I have the wagon ready. Come, Jenny. . . ." He made to lift her on to his shoulders, but she eluded him, her eyes brimming with tears. "Ah, now, what ails you, my wee hen? I was thinking you would be tired and wanting your Dadda to ride you back to the wagon."

"But my bonnet. . . ." Jenny reminded him, a catch in her voice. "We chose it and it's beautiful, Dadda. Please . . . can you not buy it after all?"

Angus dropped to his knees beside her, gathering her to him. "You shall have your bonnet, my little love. Dadda promised you, did he not?"

She hid her tear-wet face against his broad chest, and her voice was muffled as she answered, "It has blue ribbons and I told the rector I would wear it to Church on Sunday."

"And so you shall," her father vowed. Meeting

Rachel's gaze over the child's bent head, he said vehemently, "He'll not make me break my word to my own lass. I'll buy her that bonnet if it's the last thing I ever do!"

CHAPTER II

Her Sunday bonnet was, as things turned out, the last present Jenny ever had from her father. Years later when the straw of which it was composed had long since disintegrated, she kept its tattered blue ribbon as a talisman, for the memories of past happiness that it invoked.

She knew and understood little of the events that led up to her father's death or of the persecution he endured during the long winter which followed the fair, but she guessed, from his stooped shoulders and weary gait, that he was hard put to it to manage the work of the farm and cope with his horses as well. He was out in all weathers, from dawn to dusk, endeavoring to clear the ten acres of rough scrubland that must be sown with wheat in the spring. Sometimes, her mother told her, a few of the neighbors helped, but mostly it was only she who aided him, as best she could, in the backbreaking task he had set himself. The heavy snow, which came with Christmas and continued well into the new year, was a relief to both of them, although neither put it into words.

Jenny saw more of them then, for they were compelled to keep to the house for days at a time, leaving it only in order to feed the horses or struggle through deep drifts to attend Church. She remembered the Christmas Eve carol service and the one on Christmas Day as highlights in that bleak winter, but she remembered, too, her father's angry distress when he returned to find the padlocked gate on the brood mares' shelter broken and two of the mares gone. He had recovered them by late evening, but one had foaled prematurely, and all his care could not save her puny offspring from the effects of many hours' exposure to a freezing wind.

With the coming of better weather, he was out again to tackle the last of the clearing, and he was proud and happy, Jenny recalled, when he was able to tell her mother that the land was ready for the plow. A fortnight later she and her mother accompanied him to Milton Overblow in the dray, to buy and bring back with them the sacks of seed. Neither mentioned it, but the child sensed, from the care with which her parents stowed the precious grain sacks in a locked outhouse, that their purchase had cost them most of their ready cash . . . there had been no shopping done in Milton Market, despite the tempting array of goods on the stalls and in the shops. That evening, the brood mares—now in an open paddock—again made their escape and when Angus Taggart returned with the haltered fugitives at midnight, it was to find the lock on the outhouse shattered and half the seed sacks ripped open and the rest dumped into the stream at the back of the paddock.

They salvaged what they could, Jenny helping them, but it was little enough; and her father's face was black as thunder when he shoveled the muddy, swollen heads of grain into his small work cart and went to sow it—some already sprouting—in the land he had prepared so laboriously to receive it. Miraculously, though, it came up and her mother wept with joy when, with Jenny beside her, she trudged up the steep hillside to see, for herself, the bright green shoots pushing up to cover the ridges of turned earth, where once there had been only bracken and rock.

"It is the answer to prayer," she told Jenny through her tears. "Not ten acres, it's true, but seven perhaps . . . and thanks be to God for it!"

May came, and June, and they were months of warm sunshine, with just enough rain to replenish the grazing and make the stray a picture. Lord Braxton's fences went up, were knocked down, erected again, and once more uprooted, both posts and rails smashed with axes and left where they lay, so that no charges of theft might be laid. This time, Angus aided his neighbors in the work of destruction. It was openly discussed, in the little ale house at the head of Wrekin Dale.

Once Angus came home from the ale house with an eye closed and blackened and the knuckles of both hands skinned, but Jenny noticed that her mother did not reproach him when he told her, with a sheepish smile, that Ned Waite had a broken jaw and Gunner O'Keefe, together with two more of his lordship's men, had fled and were unlikely to enter the portals of the Rose and Cushion again.

For a while an uneasy truce prevailed. The fences

on the stray were not repaired and the smallholders' cattle and horses grazed freely on the lush summer grass. But then came the night that Jenny would remember with heartbreak for as long as she lived . . . and it came without warning, when she and her parents were in bed. Her first inkling that something was wrong was when the sound of men's voices wakened her from sleep. The voices were soft, as if they were not intended to be heard and, when she went to the window, all she could see were shadowy figures, moving with silent purposefulness at the rear of her father's small wooden stable. He kept the Clydesdale workhorses there, together with their harness and his plow and carts, Jenny knew, and she peered out anxiously, wondering whether the men were there at her father's invitation and if he were with them. If so, there was no cause for alarm but. . . . She glimpsed a torch, suddenly flaming in the darkness, and then a second and a third and, panic-stricken, heard a bellow of crazy laughter and a voice she recognized.

Gunner O'Keefe. Jenny ran, barefoot and frightened, to rouse her parents. Her father was instantly alert, taking in her stammered warning as he hurled himself from the bed to don breeches and boots. But long before he reached the yard, the flimsy wooden building was ablaze from end to end and the men had gone, the distant thud of their horses' hoofs muted by the crackle of the flames.

"Water!" Angus shouted hoarsely. "Bring me all the buckets you can lay hands on, lass—and tell your mother to do the same. I must get those poor beasts out before they suffocate."

He was ripping his shirt from his back as he dashed into the burning stable, smashing down the door with his booted foot and, as Jenny and her mother filled buckets from the horse trough on the far side of the yard, they saw him emerge, gasping, with one of the Clydesdales. The terrified animal was whinnying and struggling and, despite the strip of cloth Angus had bound about its eyes, he could hardly hold it and he let it go, shouting something that Jenny could not hear. Then he went back into the smoke and flames, and moments later the roof of the stable caved in, a shower of sparks leaping skyward as the beams crashed down.

The second plow horse plunged to safety and galloped off, and Jenny, running with her bucket of water, saw that the smoldering remnant of her father's shirt covered the frightened creature's eyes. She waited, expecting her father to follow it but he did not and her mother pulled her back when, crying his name in an agony of fear, she tried to go in search of him.

Neighbors came to assist in fighting the fire and when it was out at last, two or three of the men ventured into the gutted shell of the building. After a long wait they carried out a scorched and blackened object which might have been a log, but was, in fact Angus Taggart's body.

Some of the women stayed with Rachel; another took Jenny away and, bedding her with her own brood, with rough, inarticulate pity, bade her sleep if she could. Frantically though she pleaded, the child was not allowed to return to her own home until the day of her father's funeral. Then, numb with grief, she walked at her mother's side through the little churchyard to the graveside, seeing only the scorched log as they lowered the coffin into the moist brown earth, unable to believe that it was her father whom they were laying to rest with so much somber pomp. The old rector's words of sympathy, uttered with genuine feeling, left her as numb as before, and when the neighbors gathered in her mother's kitchen to partake of the refreshment, which, it seemed, was customary on such occasions, Jenny could only stand in sullen silence, hoping and praying for them to go.

When, hours later, they did so and she was alone with her mother, she was still unable to find any words to say and she ran out into the darkness, unhappy and bitterly ashamed of what she knew was unmannerly behavior. It was not until the following day that her mother confided her plans for the future to her.

"I shall engage a hired man, Jenny, to work the land with me," Rachel said decisively. "There are plenty who would come, for their board and little more. And if we can get the workhorses back, I'm sure we shall manage. It's what your Dadda would have wanted—God rest his brave soul, he fought hard enough to keep Lord Braxton from claiming his land. And I'm not one to give up. We'll sell off what young stock there are and buy sheep, in their stead. . . . I was brought up on a sheep farm and I could manage a small flock well enough. But you will have to help me, lass, young as you are."

"I will, Mam!" Jenny promised. "Oh, gladly I will."

They made plans, both of them finding a new purpose in the planning but their dreams were short-lived. The two plow horses, which had cost Angus Taggart his life, never reappeared—they had vanished into the darkness and the darkness had, it seemed, swallowed them without trace. Exhaustive inquiries yielded nothing, and even the sale of all the young stock did not raise sufficient money to replace the missing animals and buy sheep as well.

It was, however, a visit from Lawyer Slater which

finally shattered all Rachel's brave hopes. He came to the point without preamble, not deigning to alight from his horse. "The tenancy was in your husband's name, Mistress Taggart, not in yours. With his demise all rights revert to Lord Braxton and his lordship wishes to take the holding for his own use. It is all, of course, perfectly legal. . . ." He quoted the provisions of the law, his tone stern and even a trifle threatening, as if he anticipated an argument. When Rachel offered none, he continued less aggressively. "His lordship does not wish to cause you undue hardship. I am to give you a month's notice, here and now, to vacate your—that is, to vacate Lord Braxton's cottage. It will be pulled down, one month from today—that is, to be precise, the thirtieth of July."

"And if I do not vacate?" Rachel asked, in a small voice. "What then, Mister Slater?"

"You will be forcibly evicted and your household goods seized," he informed her coldly. "My clerk will see that you receive your notice in writing, of course, and it will be duly recorded in the parish records. I give you good day, Mistress Taggart."

When he had gone, Rachel stumbled back into the cottage, white and trembling. But she did not weep, as Jenny had feared she might, and she answered the little girl's questions with patient forbearance. Then, donning a bonnet and shawl, she went to seek advice from some of her neighbors.

It was after midnight when she returned, and Jenny, who had been dozing, eyed her with sleepy bewilderment when she said, "I've made my mind up, Jenny lass. Wake up now and listen! We're going to London. They say there's plenty of work for honest folk there, with all the fine houses and the wealthy gentry always wanting servants."

"London?" Jenny echoed, shocked into wakefulness. "But London's such a long way away, Mam."
The prospect terrified her. "We'd never get there."

"We will," her mother assured her. "If we set our
minds to it."

"Could we not go to your folk instead? That would
not be so far and—"

"They've enough mouths to feed and a hard
enough time doing it. And I could not go back, not
now, not after all that's happened. I'd not be able to
hold my head up." Rachel bit back a sigh. "People
talk, you see, love, and besides there would be no work
there. My Dad and my brothers work the farm—we
should just be a burden to them and I'd not want
that."

"I don't want to go away from here," Jenny whispered, near to tears. "Oh, Mam, I don't want to!"

Her mother put a comforting arm about her, holding her close. "There, lass, don't take on so! I'll not
pretend to you—it will break my heart to leave this
place. But without your Dadda it could never be the
same, even if his lordship had let us stay. And perhaps
it will all turn out for the best. Who knows, we may
make our fortunes when we get to London!"

Her faith and her determination to make the best
of their situation dispelled Jenny's fears, and she
began to look forward to their coming journey and
the strange new sights they would see when they
reached London. In the few short weeks left to them
before their notice of eviction expired, Rachel was
busy, haggling with friends and neighbors over the
price of the household goods she had to sell and,
from the small sum she collected, making thrifty
provision for the journey. Stout shoes were purchased,
shawls and a new dress for each of them, so that they

might appear clean and respectable when their destination was reached.

There was little left of the sale money, when the day of their departure dawned but Rachel had made the acquaintance of a family named Hawley—facing eviction like themselves—during one of her shopping expeditions to Milton, and it was agreed that they should meet on the road and travel together for mutual comfort and protection. Soon after first light on the morning of July 30, they were ready to set out, all that was left of their worldly possessions tied up in neat bundles, to be borne on their backs. They had made their few farewells the previous day and there was nothing to detain them, but Rachel lingered, making excuses for the delay, until Lord Braxton's men arrived with axes and sledgehammers to begin the task of knocking down the cottage. The hateful Ned Waite was with them, and at the sight of him Rachel's courage deserted her. Gripping Jenny by the hand, she turned her back on them, choking down her sobs.

They ran from the place that had been home for them, ran until they were both breathless and spent. But the sound of crashing masonry had faded, and when a little later they sat down at the roadside to break their fast, Rachel was able to put a brave face on and talk eagerly about what might lie in store for them at the end of their journey.

They fell in with the Hawleys a few miles along the road, the first to greet them being Andrew, the aging couple's son. He was a tall, strapping fellow, with a ready laugh, and his gentleness belied his appearance, as Jenny quickly learned. But that appearance and his obvious strength saved the two families from much unpleasantness during the long journey, for few would-be predators cared to tackle so powerful a man. Time and again, although already carrying more than his fair share of their joint load, he would hoist Jenny onto his shoulders and carry her for the last weary miles before darkness brought them to a halt. The Hawleys had little money, and Rachel, anxious to save what she could of her own, raised no objection when it was suggested that they should sleep rough, rather than seek lodgings. Each night they built a fire by the roadside on which to cook whatever food they had managed to buy or beg, and when it was eaten, all five of them dossed down beneath the hedgerows, sheer exhaustion bringing easy and instant oblivion. Save when rain made the lighting of a fire impossible and filled the roadside ditches, they suffered little from exposure; all were accustomed to an outdoor life, and, in any event, the weather was kind to them.

As they came nearer to London, traffic on the road increased. The post chaises and carriages of the gentry galloped past them; the regular coaches plying to and fro between the capital and outlying towns were seen with increasing frequency, but for the most part the travelers were—like themselves—on foot. Almost all were also, like themselves, displaced country folk on their way to London to seek work or bound for the seaports, with the intention of migrating to the newly freed American colonies. With so many, begging for food became harder, the occupants of houses along the way less charitable, and Andrew, who until now had talked confidently of his chances of finding employment, became—after talking to some of the would-be emigrants—less sanguine.

"Maybe we ought to follow their example," he said to Rachel, lowering his voice so that his parents might not hear him. "I'd go, I'd not hesitate, were it not for my Mam and Dad. They're old and even coming to London is bad enough for them. But if I can't get work—"

"You *will* get work, Andrew," Rachel consoled him. "A fine big man like you—of course you will! Don't lose heart."

But her own spirits sank as the plodding crowds grew thicker and the householders, of whom they asked only water, ordered them angrily on their way. "Perhaps we should seek a ship to take us across the ocean," she confided to Jenny when yet another door was slammed in their faces, and they returned, empty-handed, to rejoin the Hawleys. "We're young and, thanks be to God, strong and healthy, but it seems we're not wanted here."

She changed her mind, however, to Jenny's inexpressible relief, when Andrew suggested that they should keep together, instead of separating, when they reached the city. "I talked with a fellow on the road back there," he added, "and he advised me to make for the fish market at Billingsgate. It seems they need porters, and he said with my size I'd be taken on at once. If I can earn a decent wage, then you and Jenny won't starve, Mistress Taggart, that I promise you."

"We have our savings," Rachel answered gratefully. "We'll pool them, Andrew, if we stay together."

"Good!" Andrew approved. He swung Jenny onto his great shoulders, once more the happy, laughing giant she had come to know and love. "Because Jenny and I are courting. She's promised to marry me when she's a woman grown, haven't you, my little love? Eh? Tell your Mam you're promised to me!"

Jenny clung to him, giggling at the absurd idea but liking it nonetheless. "Oh, yes," she cried. "I am,

Mam—truly. I'm going to marry Andrew when I'm grown up."

"He'll have a while to wait," Rachel said dryly, but her hand closed around Andrew's big one in wordless gratitude.

And so, pushed and jostled by the ever growing crowd, they entered London and made, as the rest were doing, for the river, Jenny walking with her mother now and Andrew protectively with his parents. As they crossed by the London Bridge footpath Jenny looked down curiously at the dirty gray water and then cried out in horror at what she saw. Tied up to the riverbank were long rows of rotting, dismasted ships— once, though she did not know it, proud two- and three-deckers of her country's Navy. A ghastly stench rose from them and a bedlam of moans and cries which, to the frightened child, seemed like the sounds of hell, of which Rector Akeroyd had spoken, more than once, in his sermons.

"Oh, Mam!" she faltered. "Mam, what *are* they? Can there be people inside, people who are crying out?"

A strange voice answered her, coming from a few paces to her rear. "Why, them's the Hulks, little missie. And there's people inside 'em all right—convicts, tha'sands o' convicts, awaitin' 'is Majesty's pleasure."

Jenny turned, to find a scrawny little scarecrow of a man in tattered clothing regarding her with bright, birdlike eyes. Rachel quickened her pace, seeking to avoid him, but he grinned at her with engaging friendliness.

"What's your 'urry, ma'am? Your little girlie arst me a question and I was tellin' 'er. From the country, are you?"

"Yes," Rachel agreed shortly but she, too, was appalled by the sounds emanating from the rotting ships, and, overcoming her mistrust of the odd little stranger, she asked, "Did you say convicts?"

"I did, ma'am," the little cockney confirmed. "They used ter transport 'em, see—to America, ter get rid of 'em. Used ter send 'em ter Maryland an' Virginia before the colonists up an' revolted. Now there ain't nowhere ter send 'em an' they 'as ter stow 'em somewhere, so. . . ." His thin hand gestured to the Hulks, the gesture at once pitying and derisive. "If their crimes ain't bad enough ter get 'em topped, that's where they finish up."

"Topped?" Rachel echoed, mystified and finding both his accent and his words well nigh incomprehensible.

"S'right. Appointment wiv' Jack Ketch on the nubbing cheat—'anging, ma'am," he explained, his grin widening. "Mind you, there ain't much yer *can't* get 'anged fer these days. Bein' a rank rider on the 'igh toby, dippin' if yer takes more'n a shilling, cuttin' hop-binds . . . even impersonatin' Egyptians." Her bewilderment clearly amused him, but he relented when he saw her shake her head helplessly. "Ridin' the 'igh toby—that's bein' a gennelman of the road, an 'ighwayman. A dip's a pickpocket, an' impersonatin' an Egyptian—why, that's givin' aht you're a Romany an' tellin' fortunes."

"I see, I . . . thank you," Rachel acknowledged. She moved on, gripping Jenny's hand firmly, hoping to shake him off, but the odd little man matched his limping gait to hers.

"You by yerselves, you an' the lass?" he inquired.

"No, of course we're not." Rachel shook her head. Some distance in front of them, she could see Andrew Hawley's tall figure, but the crowd was taking him away from her and he did not look round, clearly supposing that she and Jenny were following close at his heels. The sun was going down, she realized in sudden panic—if she lost sight of the Hawleys now, she might never find them again when darkness fell. She started to run, but the crowd impeded her and she was forced to halt.

"S'all right, I see the party you're after." The cockney voice was reassuring. "Where're they makin' for, anyway?"

"Billingsgate, I think," Rachel told him.

"Lookin' fer work then, is 'e? Well, 'e'll get it there right enough. 'Ow about you—you lookin' for work too?"

"Yes. But I'm not sure if—"

Her new acquaintance looked her up and down approvingly. He winked impudently at Jenny. "Fine lookin' woman, your ma, ain't she? Easy fer a pretty wench ter find work 'ere, yer know . . . but it ain't guttin' fish." There was no mistaking his implication, and Rachel reddened indignantly. "I want to go to Billingsgate, Mister—er—"

"Sparrow's the nyme, ma'am—Watt Sparrow at yer service." He swept her a mock bow. "An' your moniker?"

"My name, do you mean? It's Mistress Taggart."

"And I'm Jenny, Mister Sparrow," Jenny volunteered. She liked the perky, cheerful little man, although no more able to follow what he was saying than her mother appeared to be.

"Nah that's what I call a real pretty nyme," Watt Sparrow said with flattering enthusiasm. He relieved Rachel of her bundles before she could protest and, when she did so, shook his head at her reproachfully. "I'm only tryin' ter be of 'elp to yer, Mistress Taggart.

Seein' as you're from the country and don't know yer way round old London Town, why not let the li'l ole Cock Sparrow be yer guide? Born an' bred 'ere I was . . . *and* within the sound o' Bow Bells. Nah where is it yer want ter go . . . still Billingsgate, is it?"

"Yes." Rachel made an effort to assert herself. "That's where our friends are going, and as I told you—we're together."

"Not any more you ain't," Sparrow retorted. "Gorn, that's what they 'ave . . . gorn off an' left yer."

He was right, Rachel realized, looking about her wildly as panic returned. There was now no sign of Andrew Hawley, and unless she accepted this queer little man's offer of guidance, she would have no idea where to look for their late companions.

"How—how much will you charge?" she asked uncertainly. "To help us find them, I mean."

A swift gleam lit the dark, birdlike eyes. Then it faded and, hefting both bundles on to his shoulders, Sparrow smiled at her. "Cor love yer, there won't be no charge. Off we go then—foller me! Step out lively, we've a way ter go."

Rachel did her best but, with Jenny clinging to her hand and the crowd impeding her, she could not keep up with him. For a while she managed with Jenny's aid to keep him in sight but then he, too, vanished as Andrew Hawley had done, and she realized, despairingly, that she had lost him. She was reluctant, even now, to believe that his action had been deliberate or that he had set out to trick her but. . . . She halted in a shadowed doorway to draw breath, and Jenny whispered anxiously, "Oh, Mam, he's gone!"

Rachel's teeth closed about her lower lip in a vain

attempt to still its trembling. "And he has our bundles . . . the new dresses. But at least he hasn't got my purse." The small leather purse containing the few coins she had left was secured by a thong around her neck and hidden in the bosom of her dress. She reached for it, her fingers clumsy in their haste. The thong came away but the purse was no longer there, and through a mist of tears she saw that the thong had been neatly severed . . . yet she had felt nothing and had not the slightest idea of when, during her conversation with Watt Sparrow, he had stolen it. Yet it must have been he, it could have been no one else. Her first impulse had been not to trust him, but she had allowed herself to be taken in . . . had let him fool her, with his glib talk and his engaging smile. She looked down at her dirty, travel-stained dress and shivered.

Jenny's hand found hers in the darkness. "He didn't take *my* bundle, Mam," she offered consolingly. "I've still got my bonnet—the one Dadda bought me, with the blue ribbons on it, and my shawl. And—" She delved into the bandana-wrapped bundle she had carried so far and brought out her own small purse. "There's a sixpence in here, Mam—Mister Akeroyd gave it to me, to spend on the road. We could spend it now, couldn't we, on something to eat?"

Rachel hugged her, hiding her tear-wet face from the child's searching gaze. "We'll spend some of it, love," she agreed. "But I'm afraid it won't be enough to buy us a bed for the night. We shall have to sleep out again. Still, in daylight we ought to be able to find our way to Billingsgate easily enough and I expect the Hawleys will be there."

They found a baker's shop after a little searching

and bought two penny pies. Then, the pangs of hunger satisfied at least, lay down together in the doorway of a deserted warehouse and, wrapped in Jenny's shawl, composed themselves for sleep.

CHAPTER III

A strident voice wakened them, shrieking foul-mouthed abuse. Rachel opened her eyes, instinctively clutching Jenny's small cold hand. It was still dark, and, by the light of a flaring torch carried by a Negro boy of about her own child's age, she stared up at the strangest apparition she had yet seen.

The creature who was shrieking at her was, she supposed, a woman but so tall and shapeless that, to Rachel's shocked eyes, she seemed to be a vision from another world, sexless and obscene. She was, however, dressed in female clothing, which, although of some magnificence, was also filthy, the braid with which it was decorated green and tarnished, the brocaded skirt torn in several places.

"Who—who are you?" Rachel faltered, struggling up into a sitting position. "What do you want?"

The harridan did not answer her. Instead, with an incongruously booted foot, she aimed a kick in Jenny's direction and bade her stand up, so that she might be inspected. Jenny obeyed, still clinging to her mother's hand, and Rachel jumped to her feet, fiercely protective for all her fear of the alarming stranger.

"Leave her alone! Don't touch her, do you hear? You—"

"She's a plain little piece," the woman observed. A bony, clawlike hand gripped Jenny's hair, twisting her face round into the flickering torchlight. "But she has good bones. I daresay we could make something of her. Is she a virgin?"

Rachel was beside herself with indignation at such a question, delivered in a loud, hectoring voice for all the world to hear. She wrenched Jenny free of the old woman's grasp and planted her own strong and shapely body in front of her.

"We are respectable folk," she declared proudly. "I'll thank you to leave us be."

The old woman heard the unmistakable Yorkshire accent, and her raddled face relaxed a little, twisting itself into what was clearly intended to be a smile. "From the country, are you? From the North?"

"Yes. We—we only reached London today. And we had nowhere to sleep. We—"

"And no money, like as not?"

"It was stolen. A man, a horrid little man with a limp, calling himself Watt Sparrow, tricked me into letting him carry my bundle and then he—he vanished."

"London's a den of thieves," the old woman said indifferently. She motioned the boy to bring his torch closer and, in turn, subjected Rachel to a searching scrutiny. "I come from the North myself but you'd never guess that, would you? 'Course it was years ago and I was only a little mite, like that one there. You've come looking for work, I suppose?"

"Yes," Rachel admitted. Her fears had subsided now; the old woman, although unpleasant, seemed not unfriendly.

"I might be able to put you in the way of it. They like 'em young in these parts but I daresay if you moved up Holborn way, you'd find custom all right . . . and I'd take the child off your hands. Feed her, give you both a roof over your heads until you got yourself started. . . ."

Much of what she was saying passed over Rachel's head, and when the strange creature gestured invitingly to a building some distance down the street and suggested that she and Jenny might care to partake of a little refreshment, she gave her assent without hesitation. It had been cold in the warehouse gateway, the cobbled pavement hard and unyielding, after the country hedgerows to which she had become accustomed, and besides, the woman came from the North and that made a bond between them, however tenuous.

"Then come along," her new acquaintance urged. "There'll be a bite or two left over from our supper, more than likely, and you shall have a drop of something to warm you up."

She set off, a hand on the Negro boy's shoulder for support, and Rachel made to follow her, but Jenny held back. "I don't like her, Mam," she whispered. "She's a witch—a wicked witch, I'm sure she is."

"She has promised us something to eat, love," her mother reminded her. "And maybe she will let us sleep under her roof."

"I *am* hungry," Jenny conceded.

"Then don't look a gift horse in the mouth, lass." Rachel smiled wryly, for the expression had been one Angus had often used in the old, happy days which they had left behind them forever. "We can leave in the morning if we want to and go and look for the Hawleys."

The house into which the old woman led them was less a dwelling place than a warehouse, which had been converted for use as a dwelling, but it was warm, and, to Rachel's surprise, reasonably clean. A few old sticks of furniture were scattered, seemingly at random, about the floor, some of the beds occupied by shapeless, blanket-covered forms, whose faces she could not see, but most of the beds appeared to be empty and only a thin, slatternly girl with a pockmarked countenance roused herself in response to the old woman's harsh call.

"We've some more lodgers, Patty, just in from the country. Get them something to eat . . . and bring me a glass, a clean one, mind."

The girl obeyed in sullen silence, but the food she brought, on a single cracked plate, was wholesome and appetizing. There being no implements with which to cut the slices of cold meat, Rachel divided them with her fingers and gave Jenny hers on a thick wedge of freshly baked bread. The child fell on it ravenously and their strange hostess, leaning back in a huge, padded armchair, gave vent to a cackle of laughter.

"Ready for that, weren't you, little 'un? Well, there's plenty more where it came from, never fear." She filled the glass the girl brought her from a bottle she took from the shelf behind her and passed it to Rachel. "There, drink that up, my girl—it'll put fire in your veins. What's your name? Better know it, hadn't I, if you're going to join our happy band."

Rachel told her. She took a cautious sip of the contents of the glass and gasped as the raw spirit burned her throat. "Go on, finish it," the old woman urged. "Never mind if you aren't used to it, it'll do you good." Leaning forward, she tilted the glass so that Rachel was compelled to gulp down several mouthfuls of the fiery stuff. "Best cure in the world for any ills is gin, I can tell you. You drink it down now and see if I'm not right."

Anxious not to give offense to her benefactress, Rachel tipped back the glass. The effect, she realized, was wonderful. She felt warm, almost for the first time since she had left the cottage at Long Wrekin, and filled with new confidence in the future. "You are very kind, ma'am," she acknowledged. "So very, very kind. I will try to repay you. If you can find me a position, I'll work hard and—" Even to her own ears, her voice sounded slurred, and she took a deep breath, seeking to control it. "I had thought of going to—to Billingsgate. We have friends who went there but a—a domestic position would be better, very much better. I'm a good plain cook, ma'am, and my little girl . . . my little girl Jenny, she could help me, she could make herself useful. I'd want to keep her with me, you see, because I wouldn't want any harm to come to her. And in a place like London—"

The old woman rose from her creaking chair. Firmly, the clawlike fingers biting into Rachel's arm, she led her to one of the unoccupied beds at the far end of the long room and thrust her on to it. "In with your ma," she bade Jenny, and as the child made to unlace her boots, laughter again overcame her. "No harm'll come to you if you go to bed in your boots, my lass, so in with you!" To Rachel she added, her voice suddenly harsh, "Go to sleep, Rachel Taggart. We'll talk about your *position* in the morning."

It was not long after dawn when Jenny's urgent whisper roused Rachel from her drugged sleep. "Mam—" The child was shivering. "Mam, *look*!"

Rachel raised herself on one elbow, still a trifle stupefied, to see a straggling procession wending its way across the floor of their refuge to where the old woman who had befriended them sat, in queenly isolation, in her armchair. There was a table at her side, on which stood several small piles of coins and, as each member of the newly arrived procession reached the table, more coins were added to those already there. The old woman counted them, made a note in a ledger propped against her knees, and then, grudgingly, returned one or two to the outstretched hands of those who had brought them.

They were a motley crowd, Rachel's bemused brain registered, and all female—there was not a man among them. Many were children, ranging in age from seven or eight to, perhaps, twelve or fourteen, but their faces were painted in imitation of those of their elders, who stood patiently beside them, awaiting their turn to approach the table. All were well dressed but—like the old woman's—their finery was dirty and bedraggled, and the children, without exception, maintained an adult, disciplined silence. Only one, a bony little girl in a sprigged muslin gown, with a velvet pelisse draped about her shoulders attempted, after receiving the deduction from her payment, to question its amount.

"I earned every penny, Missus Morgan, strite I did. 'E was 'orrible . . . an' you know what 'e wanted me for. I made 'im pay double, like you said I was to,

an' yet you're only givin' me the usual. T'ain't fair—
I'm entitled to me third."

The old woman struck her a stinging blow across
the mouth and then, thinking better of it, counted two
extra coins into her palm.

"All right, Melba my dear—you're a good girl," she
conceded. "But you'd best go along to the quack when
you've broken your fast. Tell him who you were with
and he'll give you a potion, most likely."

Listening to this exchange, Rachel felt the blood
freeze in her veins. Although she had never encountered anything of the kind before, Mrs. Hawley and
others she had met on the journey had spoken of the
houses of child prostitution which were said to exist
in London and, until now, she had only half-believed
the tales they had told her. Now, however, she realized
her mistake . . . fool that she had been, to imagine
that a woman like Mrs. Morgan would be motivated
by goodwill toward Jenny and herself, as friendless
strangers in a strange and hostile city! Thrusting the
bedclothes from her, she looked round wildly, seeking
escape. Could she, dare she just walk out with her
child, owing for their night's lodging, their food
and . . . she bit back a sob. The gin she had consumed. She could not even offer to pay, since only
fourpence remained of Jenny's little hoard and they
would need that, if they were to eat that day.

To her heartfelt relief, the slatternly Patty came to
her rescue. "I bin watchin' you," she said, in a hoarse
undertone. "Didn't know what you was lettin' yerself
in for, comin' 'ere, did you, Missus Taggart?"

Rachel shuddered. "No. No, I swear to you I did
not. We must get away, we—"

"Wait," the girl cautioned. "She mustn't see you.
When she goes ter sup 'er mornin' choc'late, I'll spill

it in 'er lap and you make a run for it, while she ain't lookin'. But don't stay around 'ere and don't come back or she'll 'ave yer fer sure."

Rachel thanked her with tears in her eyes. "I can't give you anything, we've nothing to give except—" The precious pennies were in the pocket of her dress and she started to reach for them but Patty stopped her.

"I don't want nothin', Missus Taggart. And you'll need what you've got."

"But you may get into trouble. She'll know that you've helped us," Rachel began. "And—"

Patty shook her head. "She won't. She thinks I'm caw-handed and so I am, with 'er. An' I'm never out o' trouble, so it won't make no difference."

"Why do you stay with her? *Why*, Patty?"

The girl laughed. "My ma sold me to 'er, when I were seven year old. An' she pays me well. I gets three good meals a day *and* I don't 'ave to do no street-walkin', only look after 'er comforts. Too ugly for the streets, she reckons, but that'd be all I could do, if I left 'er. So . . . I stay. It ain't a bad life, when yer gets used to it." She patted Rachel's arm. " 'Sides, the pickaninny's my brat an' she dotes on 'im. Reckons folk'll think she's a grand lidy if she 'as a little black pageboy runnin' after 'er!" A shout from her mistress interrupted her confidences and she winked at Jenny, in no way put out. "Wants 'er choc'late . . . well, she's goin' ter get it right enough. Soon as you 'ear 'er yell out, you leg it, fast as you know 'ow. An' remember, don't come back—it'll be as much as your lives are worth if you do."

The escape went precisely as planned. Rachel and Jenny fled blindly through a maze of streets, seeking only to put the greatest possible distance between themselves and the house where they had spent the night. Finally, breathless, they came to a halt at the edge of a huge marketplace, crowded with stalls that were already open for business. Jenny said, wrinkling her nose as a strange, pungent odor was borne to them on the early morning breeze, "Mam, I think we're there. That must be Billingsgate . . . look, there's a man carrying fishes on his head!"

Rachel followed the direction of her excitedly pointing finger and cried her relief aloud. A long line of stalwart fish porters passed them as they neared the great market, each bearing a hundredweight of fish in his wide-brimmed "bobbing hat" and moving at a brisk jog trot.

"Maybe Andrew's with them," Jenny exclaimed, dancing from one foot to the other in her eagerness. "He's so big, we ought to be able to see him, Mam."

"Yes, we ought," Rachel agreed, her hopes rising. "And we have tongues in our heads, too, love. We can ask folk to direct us."

But neither their search nor their diffidently voiced inquiries yielded any trace or word of the Hawleys' whereabouts. After a while, some of the stallholders grew impatient and ordered them about their business, and, tired and hungry, and with darkness approaching, Rachel began to despair and Jenny was in tears. A white-haired costermonger, taking pity on them, beckoned the little girl to him and gave her a handful of bruised fruit before wheeling his barrow away. They left the market as darkness fell, ate their fruit under the shelter of a culvert, and, as they had on the evening of their arrival in the city, prepared to snatch what sleep they could on the hard stone pavement.

Scarcely had they settled down, however, than a toothless crone shuffled up to claim their resting place as her own. Her manner was so sinister and her curses so virulent that Rachel was compelled reluctantly to pay her the tuppence she demanded, in order that they might remain there. They passed a miserable night and wakened to find that it was raining and their clothing was soaked. Chilled and dejected, they continued their fruitless search for the Hawleys, and Rachel endeavored to find work in the market but without success. There was a number of children begging from stallholders and passersby—skinny, whining little creatures, some with hideous sores and others with crippled bodies and twisted limbs, who dragged themselves along with pitiful slowness, beseeching anyone who gave them a second glance to spare a copper. The kindly costermonger gave his spoiled fruit to some of them and had only two rotting apples for Jenny when she shyly approached him, but, touched by the bitter disappointment in her eyes as she turned away, he pressed a penny into her hand.

She thanked him politely and he shook his head over her sadly. "You're from the country, ain't you?" he suggested. "Well, take my advice, duck, and go back there, you and your Ma. London's no place for the likes of you."

Sharing the pie her penny had bought with Rachel, Jenny repeated what he had said. "Couldn't we go back, Mam . . . couldn't we? It's awful here."

"We'll give it a few more days, love," her mother said. "Tomorrow we'll go round the houses where the decent folk live, and I'll see if I can get a position in service, like I always meant to."

The foul-mouthed old crone came again to dispute possession of their shelter under the culvert but this time Rachel, in desperation, stood up to her and the old woman departed empty-handed and vowing vengeance. That her threat was no idle one became all too evident when she crept back, in the darkness, and endeavored to snatch Jenny from her mother's arms. Rachel, roused from sleep by the child's terrified cries, fought the hateful creature off with the ferocity of a tigress but Jenny's shawl was lost in the struggle, and when the crone vanished with it, they clung together in shivering wakefulness for what remained of the night.

Next day they made for the city, but Rachel's quest for employment met with no more success than at Billingsgate. She rang the doorbells or tapped gently on the polished brass knockers of upwards of a dozen respectable-looking houses but was ordered contemptuously away by the servants who answered her summons, few of whom even gave her the chance to state her business. Faint from weariness and lack of food, Jenny lagged, weeping, behind her and finally, unable any longer to bear her plaintive whimpering, Rachel went into a baker's shop and flung her last two coppers down on the counter.

"Please," she said, "give us what you can for that."

The baker's wife, a stout, apple-cheeked woman in a spotless white apron, eyed her in speculative silence for a moment and then asked quietly, "Are you from Yorkshire, lass?" Her own voice sounded homely and familiar, and, hearing it, Rachel had to fight back the tears.

"Aye," she answered, slipping back easily into the dales speech of her childhood. "That I am, missus."

"And wishing you were back there, unless I'm much mistaken . . . just as I often wish myself." The woman smothered a sigh and would have said more but her husband, a thin, glum-faced man, whose face and arms were covered with a thick coating of flour, came in from the bakehouse and interrupted her.

"That's the last batch," he announced, mopping the sweat from his face with the back of his hand. "And we'll sell it all, I don't doubt, when the crowds start coming back. It's wonderful what a hanging does to put an edge on folks' appetite." He noticed Rachel then, with Jenny clinging to her skirt, and his expression changed to one of thinly veiled suspicion. "More beggars, wife?" he accused. "And I suppose you're feeding them?"

His wife shook her head. In a single swift movement she swept the two coppers from the counter into her till and from the laden shelf at her back took two freshly baked meat pies, a loaf, two apple turnovers, and a Yorkshire "lardy cake," wrapped them neatly, and gave them to Rachel. "These are all paid for," she snapped. "And your dinner's on the table."

Rachel started to thank her, but the baker's wife put a plump finger to her lips. She said, when her husband stumped off into the back premises, muttering aggrievedly to himself, "He meant no offense, lass —he's out of sorts. Wanted to go to the hanging instead of slaving away at his ovens. But like he said, trade's always brisk after a hanging and there's a big crowd watching today, with two of them being strung up."

"Two of them?" Rachel stared at her uncomprehendingly.

"Oh, aye, love—two of the most notorious highway robbers in the country, Logan and the one who used to call hisself Red Brannigan. Irishmen, they say and—" Again an impatient bellow from her husband interrupted her. "He's wanting his dinner," she apologized. "I'll have to lock up while he's having it."

Out in the street once more, Rachel looked around for a place where they could enjoy part, at least, of the generous supply of food they had been given. People were starting to drift back from the spectacle they had witnessed but as yet only in small numbers, and she found a flight of stone steps, leading to a shuttered public building of some kind, where they could eat and watch the passing throng.

Seated at the top of the steps, they both fell with relish on the pies. Rachel had intended to keep the rest for their evening meal but Jenny pleaded so hard for a taste of the lardy cake that she gave in, and between them they finished it.

"Mam—Mam, look . . . quick!" Jenny grabbed her arm. "Down there, where the folk are waiting outside the baker's!" She was tense with excitement. "It's that man, the little man who stole our bundles, truly it is . . and, Mam, he's *stealing*! I saw him take a man's watch from his pocket."

The child was right, Rachel saw. The little man with the limp was darting about among the people below, never pausing for more than the moment or two it took his thieving fingers to do their work. He was a common pickpocket, she thought indignantly, a sneak thief. It was because he had stolen their clean clothes and their money that she and Jenny had endured the degradation of the streets.

She got to her feet, clutching at Jenny's arm.

"Yes, it *is* him and no mistake. Jenny love, we're going to follow him, see where he goes and then—" She bit her lip, uncertain of what she could do, in the circumstances. Appeal to his better nature, perhaps—plead with him to give back their possessions? Or accuse him and give him in charge? He deserved to be punished for what he had done and there was a law against stealing—had he not told her so himself? Thieves were sent to the Hulks, even hanged, as those two highwaymen had been hanged this morning, and perhaps the threat of such a fate would scare him into restoring their property—if he still had it. He might have sold or pawned the dresses of course, but in that case he should at least hand over the money he had obtained for them.

"Mam, he's going—come on!" Jenny tugged at her mother's hand. "We'll have to hurry if we're to catch him." At the end of the narrow street into which he had turned, an inn sign creaked in the slight breeze, and Rachel saw him cross the pavement, still whistling, and enter the establishment.

She hesitated, her courage momentarily failing but Jenny looked up at her in surprise. "He went in there, Mam, didn't you see? It's an alehouse, that's what the sign means, doesn't it? Look, it's got three funny-looking clowns painted on it, like Punch and Judy, only there are three of them."

Rachel peered at the sign, spelling out the name of the inn slowly, letter by letter. "The Three Fools— that's what it's called, Jenny."

Jenny was all impatience, intent only on bringing their chase to a successful conclusion. "If he's in there, he can't run away, Mam. I remember his name now— it's Watt Sparrow. And he is a thief—I *saw* him take that man's watch. Let's go in, Mam, and tell him he must give us our bundle back."

Conscious of a sick feeling in the pit of her stomach, Rachel pushed open the door of the alehouse. After the sunlight outside, the taproom was dark and dismal, with a single candle on the bar, which was presided over by a formidable-looking woman of uncertain age wearing a voluminous and very dirty apron and smoking a clay pipe. At first there appeared to be no sign of Watt Sparrow, but then, when her eyes became accustomed to the dimness, Rachel saw him on the far side of the room. He was seated at a table, with a tankard beside him and a collection of small articles spread out in front of him—the result of his morning's thieving, seemingly, since it included a heavy silver timepiece and several linen handkerchiefs. His companion—to whom he appeared to be endeavoring to sell his stolen haul—was seated with his face in the shadows and all that Rachel could see was a vast belly, spanned by a watch and chain and adorned by a brocade waistcoat, of which several of the buttons were undone, in order, she could only suppose, to give him ease.

Taking her courage in both hands, she walked purposefully up to the table and, heedless of the consequences, made her accusation in a loud, clear voice, addressing Sparrow by name. He turned in his seat to regard her at first with bewilderment and then in smiling recognition as his eyes lit on Jenny.

"Why, if it ain't Missus Taggart . . . Missus Taggart an' Jenny! Well, this is a surprise . . . what c'n I do for you, ma'am?"

The sheer effrontery of the question roused Rachel to a fury of which, hitherto, she had never imagined herself capable. All the humiliation she had suffered at the hands of the old harridan who called herself Mrs. Morgan, all the hunger and discomfort she and Jenny had experienced since their arrival in London added fuel to the fire of her anger. She laid it, fairly and squarely, at Watt Sparrow's door and as she told of it she pointed an accusing finger at him, defying him to deny his guilt.

"That watch," she ended, picking up the silver timepiece and thrusting it under his nose. "You stole it—we saw you, Jenny and I, not twenty minutes since!"

"Well, now, Mistress Taggart," a gentle voice reproved her. "I think you should keep a rein on your tongue. The walls have ears, you know, and the Robin Redbreasts listen at all of them." Sparrow's companion leaned forward and she saw his face for the first time, astonished at what she saw. It was a round, hairless face, benign and almost cherubic, with a mouth that many women would have envied for its shape and color and a pair of kindly brown eyes, which regarded her now with evident sympathy. The stranger's voice was educated and he was dressed as a gentleman, with a jacket that matched the expensive waistcoat and an elegantly powdered wig. "Is this true, Watt Sparrow?" he demanded of the little pickpocket before Rachel could speak. "Did you indeed rob this poor woman and her child of all their earthly possessions?"

Sparrow squirmed uneasily, as if tempted to refute Rachel's accusations, but finally he nodded. "Force of 'abit, it was, guv'nor, strite. If I'd thought, I'd 'ave left 'em be."

A hulking fellow in a leather apron laid a powerful hand on the little cockney's shoulder.

"I've nowt agin' you dippin' in rich folks' pockets," he growled menacingly. "But w'en it comes ter preyin' on poor innocents the like o' these two, I'm tempted ter give yer a taste o' yer own medicine, Sparrow, and that's the truth!"

"Come now, Joshua, we will settle this without violence," Sparrow's companion intervened. He motioned Rachel to seat herself beside him and called out

to the woman behind the bar to bring her a glass of
porter. "And some milk," he added. "Yes, a glass of
milk for the little girl."

Rachel's brief anger faded. Awed by his presence
and his air of authority, she sat in silence, the porter
untouched on the table in front of her amid the clut-
ter of trinkets Watt Sparrow had deposited there.

"I am Doctor Fry, Mistress Taggart," her bewigged
host informed her. "Watt Sparrow shall make repa-
ration to you, as well as offering you his most profuse
apologies. That's so, is it not, Mister Sparrow?"

"If you say so, guv'nor," Watt Sparrow agreed
glumly. "They c'n 'ave their dresses back anyway—I
couldn't get nothin' for 'em so they're still at my
place."

"And their money?" Dr. Fry persisted.

The little pickpocket shrugged his contempt. "They
only 'ad a few coppers. And—"

"There were fifteen shillings in my purse," Rachel
interrupted, finding her tongue again. "You took that
as well, you know you did."

"Is that a fact, Sparrow?" Dr. Fry's tone was stern.

Again the little man seemed disposed to argue but,
as before, thought better of it. "Yeh, it's a fact," he
admitted. "But I ain't got fifteen shillin', guv, unless
you was ter buy that there silver 'unter orf me. It's
worth a coupla guineas at least—look at it fer yerself."

Dr. Fry did so, holding the silver watch delicately
in his plump, well-manicured hands, opening its back
and holding it to his ear before slipping it into his
own pocket.

"Very well," he said. "Two guineas—but one will
go to Mistress Taggart. Here you are, my dear." He
placed a gold coin on the table in front of Rachel
and tossed another deftly in Watt Sparrow's direction.

"What ab'art the rest o' the stuff?" Sparrow wanted to know. "Them clys are made o' good linen, guv."

"Cut along now and bring Mistress Taggart's dresses here—and no dawdling on the way, you understand? I shall expect you back in thirty minutes."

To Rachel's surprise the little cockney obeyed without demur. A dark-faced man with a twisted back shuffled up to the table with a brimming beaker of milk and grinned at Jenny in friendly fashion as he put it into her hands. "There you are, me little duck— that's strite from the cow, that is, just like the doctor ordered, ain't that so, Doctor Fry?"

"That is indeed so, Nick, my good fellow," Dr. Fry affirmed. "And since you are here, you may refill *my* glass . . . but not, I hasten to add, straight from the cow, if you please."

The man addressed as Nick roared with laughter as he reached for the doctor's tankard and shambled off with it to the bar. Left alone with Rachel and Jenny, Dr. Fry subjected each of them in turn to a thoughtful scrutiny.

"You said, did you not, that you were seeking employment, Mistress Taggart? One gathers, from your rejection of the—er—the offer made to you by Mistress Morgan, that you have work of a different nature in mind? Might I ask what it is?"

Rachel flushed under his searching gaze. "Anything, sir, so long as it's respectable and honest. I'm used to hard work. I . . . that is, I was hoping to get a domestic position, living in, where I could keep the little girl with me and—"

"And protect her from the evils of London," Dr. Fry finished for her. "A laudable desire, Mistress Taggart, and I fancy I may be able to assist you to achieve it. Doll—" He beckoned to the woman behind the bar. "Come over here, will you please? I have a proposition to put to you."

The woman set down her clay pipe and crossed over to join them, wiping her moist hands on her apron. Looking at close quarters, Rachel judged her to be younger than she had at first supposed—perhaps about forty. She had reddish hair and she possessed good features; indeed as a young girl she might even have been handsome, although too tall and strongly built ever to have been able to lay claim to real beauty.

"Yes, Doctor?" she said pleasantly enough. "What's the proposition?"

Dr. Fry ignored the question. "This is Doll Prunty, my dear," he told Rachel. "Mistress of this fine tavern, with her husband Nick, whose acquaintance you have already made." He gestured to the cripple. "And these two are the Taggarts, Doll—little Jenny and her mother, Rachel. As I understand the situation, Rachel is seeking domestic employment and is, so she assures me, an honest country wench who is willing to work hard, in return for board and lodging for herself and the child and, I imagine, a modest wage. Would she, perhaps, fill the bill for you?"

Mrs. Prunty considered, a frown creasing her brow as she studied Rachel with even more care than the doctor himself had shown. She asked a number of questions concerning Rachel's marital status and experience, where she had come from, and what wage she expected, her tone crisp and businesslike but uncritical. Glancing at Jenny, her face softened and she smiled.

"Do you want to work with your ma, duck?"

Jenny dropped her a curtsy, as she had been brought up to do when addressed by her elders. "Oh, yes, please, ma'am," she answered eagerly. "If you'll have me."

The curtsy and her prompt response overcame Doll Prunty's lingering doubts. "That's settled, then," she announced briskly. "You can start in the morning, and I'll give you a room and a meal tonight. It'll be hard work," she added. "But better than the streets, that I will promise." Over Jenny's bent head, she nodded at Dr. Fry, the nod seeming to express, if not gratitude, at least approval.

Rachel, who had no reason to doubt his altruism, thanked him with tears in her eyes, but, heaving himself to his feet, the stout doctor cut short her stammered protestations.

"If we cannot give aid and comfort to our fellow human beings when they are down on their luck, Missus Taggart, we do not deserve that the good Lord above should look upon us with favor," he proclaimed unctuously. "Think nothing of it—I am glad to have been of help to you and the little one. But now—" He took the stolen timepiece from his pocket and studied it, clicking his tongue with annoyance when he realized that it had stopped. "Sparrow is an unmitigated scoundrel—he has cheated me of two guineas! Unfortunately I have another appointment to keep or I would give him a piece of my mind. However, I trust he will bring back your dresses . . . if he should not, you may safely leave him to me. He deserves to be reported to the Robin Redbreasts but I have to confess to a sneaking fondness for the little rogue. My hat, Nick, if you please."

The crippled tavern keeper hobbled over with the fashionable beaver, but instead of donning it, the doctor scooped up the trinkets Watt Sparrow had been trying to sell to him and placed them in the hat. He tucked it under his arm in a single neat movement and made for the door.

"I shall be here at my usual time tomorrow, Doll," he said. "Good evening to you!"

When he had gone, Doll Prunty emitted a dry chuckle.

"Gives himself airs, don't he, considering what his trade is!"

Rachel was puzzled. "But isn't he a physician, Mistress Prunty? I thought he said his name was Doctor Fry?"

"Lor' love you, he was once but that was a long time ago. He got into trouble with the medical authorities —over bodies for dissection—and they revoked his license. Now he's one of the biggest fences in London . . . one of the richest too, I shouldn't wonder."

Rachel stared at her blankly, still somewhat at a loss, and Jenny asked, "Please, ma'am, what is a Robin Redbreast? And how can Doctor Fry be a—a fence?"

"Oh, my!" Doll Prunty collapsed in a gale of laughter. "You are a pair of innocents, aren't you? A Robin Redbreast is a Bow Street Runner, my little one, and you want to keep clear of *them*. I can see I'll have to teach you a thing or two, you and your ma. But you needn't start learning tonight . . . there'll be time enough for that. Cut along to the kitchen now, both of you, and get your suppers, and then I'll show you where you're to sleep."

They went, obediently thankful that for the first time since leaving home they were to have a safe roof over their heads.

CHAPTER IV

Rachel settled remarkably quickly to her new life. It was, as Doll Prunty had warned her, a hard-working life, and as she slaved in the dark basement kitchen, scrubbed floors, and waited on customers in the tap-room of the Three Fools, she suffered the pangs of homesickness and wished many times that she could return to her native Yorkshire.

But there were compensations. Doll was a hard woman, brought up in the East End streets, and she ruled the tavern with a rod of iron, giving her friendship sparingly. She gave it to Rachel after only a few weeks and in many acts of kindness—which she was at pains to conceal or make light of—demonstrated her affection for Jenny and her sincere liking for her new maid-of-all-work.

Rachel had made it plain, from the outset, that she

was a respectable woman, unlike the trollops who touted for customers among the tavern's clientele. In spite of this she found it far from easy to avoid unwelcome attentions from some of them when the drink was flowing.

The Three Fools was a regular meeting place for thieves and highway robbers, pimps, coiners and receivers of stolen property, and the first lesson Rachel learned when Doll, true to her promise, started to "teach her a thing or two" was to shut her eyes and ears to what was going on around her. For all they made no secret of their names and the "profession" they followed, none of the Three Fools' regulars had anything to fear from informants. There was, Rachel learned, honor among thieves and a strict code of conduct to which all were required to subscribe.

She kept Jenny apart, protecting her fiercely from association with all save Dr. Fry. He was on a different —and superior—footing where Rachel was concerned, and she never thought of him as a criminal and, indeed, found it almost impossible to believe that anything he did might be outside the law. For his part the obese doctor took a great fancy to Jenny and, finding her intelligent and eager to learn, amused himself during his leisure hours by teaching her to read, write, and cipher. He taught her manners, too, making her pour tea for him, practice her curtsy, and recite poetry to him in one of the tavern's upper rooms, which he rented for the purpose and insisted on calling "the schoolroom." Jenny was forbidden to enter the taproom—Rachel was quite adamant on this point and Doll supported her—and even the courtyard was declared out of bounds to her after darkness fell. When not required in the schoolroom by Dr. Fry, she worked in the kitchen, watched over by her mother and Doll, and given the lightest of tasks which childless and indulgent Doll could devise for her.

"If the doctor's trying to make a lady of her," Doll argued, "it's no use us undoing his good work by spoiling her hands, is it? And she's shaping well—who knows but she'll turn out to be quite a beauty, given the chance."

Rachel was happy for her child. She watched her grow with increasing pride as the months passed and then the years, and she herself became haggard and stoop-shouldered from her endless toil. Jenny did not turn into the beauty Doll had predicted, but she was tall for her age and certainly not ill-favored, with her father's red hair and his laughing blue eyes, her manners such that she could hold her own in any company. And, although she had been brought up among rogues and vagabonds, her childish innocence had been preserved . . . poor dead Angus would have no reason to reproach her on that score—wherever he now was.

Rachel sighed and closed her eyes, ignoring the great mountain of vegetables on the kitchen table waiting to be prepared. Vainly she tried to recall her husband's face, the sound of his voice; but his memory, she realized, had faded. She had mourned him for almost four years and those years, heaven knew, had taken their toll on her . . . all too soon, she would be old. Rachel got wearily to her feet and crossed to the square of cracked mirror which hung on the door of the kitchen.

She was glumly studying her image when Doll Prunty came bustling in.

"Why, what's to do?" she demanded. "You look as if you'd lost a guinea and found fourpence!"

"Yes, that's just how I do feel," Rachel admitted.

"Doll, all these years I've guarded my virtue as if—oh, as if it were something of value. But now . . . now I doubt if I'd even have to fight for it."

"Go into the taproom and see, my girl!" Doll advised, laughing. She made a coarse jest and then, seeing that Rachel meant what she had said, put an arm round her in understanding sympathy. "It's the spring," Doll told her. She took a bottle from the top of the dresser, uncorked it, and splashed two generous measures of gin into two of the fine bone china cups kept exclusively for Dr. Fry's use. "Cheer up, lass, you're not dead yet, you know! And"—a thoughtful frown puckered her brow—"there's a fellow you might fancy in the taproom with the doctor right this minute. He's from the North and he's come with a reputation. Made things too hot for himself on the roads up there, they say, so he's come to try his luck on the heath."

A highwayman, Rachel thought, only mildly interested. It was a precarious profession; no woman with a grain of sense would look for a husband or even a lover among their ranks. But if he was from the North . . . she gulped her gin, feeling suddenly reckless.

"No harm in having a look at him, I suppose. What's his name, Doll?"

"Captain Harry Wilkes. He—"

"*Captain?*" Rachel's brief elation faded. "A captain wouldn't look at me."

"Lor' love yer, that's only what he calls himself," Doll assured her. "I'm willing to wager he's never been in the army—or the navy, come to that. But he's a big handsome fellow, something after the stamp of your Angus, from what you've told me . . . *and* he has red hair."

"I look a fright, Doll. And I've not done those vegetables yet—" Rachel began nervously.

Doll studied her, head on one side. "In my closet,"
she said, "you'll find that green dress I bought from
the doctor . . . toward the back it is, behind Nick's
cape. Cut along upstairs now and put it on . . . you'll
look a treat in it."

"But you've never worn it," Rachel objected, deeply
touched. "I couldn't. It's kind of you but—"

Doll swore at her in mock anger. "You can and you
will, my girl. We'll have another little drop o' that
gin just to put a bit of heart into us and then I'll do
these greens and you go and get yourself into that
dress and show yourself to the gallant captain!" She
raised her cup in salute. "You're still a fine-looking
wench, Rachel," she said with conviction. "And in
that dress even Doctor Fry is liable to get ideas about
you, you see if he doesn't!"

Rachel, heartened by her words as much as by the
gin, went upstairs in search of the dress. It was an
elegant, beautifully cut gown and, to her delight, it
fitted her reasonably well, requiring only a stitch or
two to ease it round waist and bosom. She was so
pleased by her appearance wearing it that she climbed
to Jenny's attic bedroom in order to display herself to
her daughter, and the girl's "Oh, Mam, you look beautiful!" set the seal on her confidence.

There was a cockfight that evening in the neighbor-
hood, and the taproom, when she reached it, proved to
be deserted, save for Nick Prunty, dozing behind the
bar, and Dr. Fry seated at his usual table with the new
arrival.

Both turned at her approach, the doctor's jaw dropping in astonishment, but then, recovering himself, he

did the honors, a gleam of suppressed amusement in his dark eyes.

Captain Wilkes rose to his feet, smiling, to bow over her hand, and if he noticed its work-worn roughness, he gave no sign of having done so. He was, as Doll had said, a big, handsome man, with bold blue eyes and tanned skin, smelling pleasantly of tobacco and leather, and Rachel warmed at once to his unmistakable Yorkshire accent, faint though it was. They talked of places she had known and then of people, and when he told her, with a wealth of exaggerated—and probably untruthful—detail, that one of the carriages he had waylaid on the York road had been Lord Braxton's, he won her heart completely.

Dr. Fry departed, as usual, before the evening influx of customers, but Rachel, obeying Doll's signal, remained with the captain, and Nick saw to it that their glasses were never left empty. Word of the notorious captain's presence had spread, and the regulars, eager to make his acquaintance, crowded round the table, vying for his notice. One in particular, a good-looking young scapegrace named Ned Munday, who sometimes worked the crowds with Watt Sparrow, was so insistent in his approach that Captain Wilkes had, perforce, to speak to him. He did so harshly, annoyed by the youth's insolence, but quite unabashed, Ned offered his services in any capacity.

"I've ridden the heath," he boasted. "And most of the turnpikes out of London. I'd make myself useful, Captain . . . you'd not regret it, I swear."

"When I need a stableboy, I'll tell you," Wilkes returned contemptuously. "I don't ride with any but grown men—and then only those I can trust. Stick to your cly-faking and leave me be. You can see I'm occupied, can't you?" He winked at Rachel, well in his cups by now but clearly enjoying himself and not entirely averse to the stir he was causing.

"With that slut?" Ned Munday countered maliciously. "You don't know who she is, do you, Captain? Well, I'll tell you . . . she's Mistress Prunty's skivvy *and* she has a daughter near enough my age. Why—" Despite the drink he had consumed, Captain Wilkes moved with catlike speed. He was on his feet, and his fist caught the gangling Munday squarely on the point of the chin, felling him like a log.

"Oblige me by removing the body," he said, addressing no one in particular, and half a dozen of his admirers, laughing in drunken delight, picked up the dazed and angry youth and threw him out into the courtyard.

Rachel, her cheeks burning with shame, made to leave their table but Wilkes's slim brown hand closed about her arm, keeping her beside him. "Nay, don't go, lass. The night's still young and I've a few ideas as to how I'd like to spend the rest of it. And," he added softly, "that's with you, if you'll have me."

She faced him wretchedly, her lower lip trembling.

"It's true, what Ned Munday told you, Captain Wilkes. I *am* Doll Prunty's skivvy and my daughter's coming on fifteen."

"What of it?" he demanded, smiling. "You're a Yorkshire lass and a mighty well favored one, if I'm any judge." His fingers caressed her arm, traveling upwards to cup her breast, and she felt suddenly excited, drawn to him as, long ago, she had been drawn to her husband, Angus. Hastily she looked away, fearing that he might read the desire in her eyes. "Who d'you suppose I am, Rachel Taggart?" He laughed, suppressing a hiccough. "I was born and brought up on a farm, just like you were—aye, and driven from it in much the same manner as yourself. 'Tis nowt to be ashamed of, lass. The only real difference between us is that you chose to skivvy for your living and I took to the road."

"Yes, but—" Rachel continued to avert her gaze, still uncertain of him.

"Doctor Fry told me all about you, before I ever clapped eyes on you," he reproached her. "He said you weren't a trollop."

"Did he?" she looked up at him then, relieved.

"Aye, he did . . . but not the half of it and that's God's truth. Come, we'll have another drink and then I'll bed you, lass. 'Tis what I want and I reckon it's what you want too."

Their drinks finished, he accompanied her upstairs to her bedroom and took her, with practiced skill and evident pleasure, and she responded with a passion that delighted them both. Later, as they lay naked in each other's arms, Harry Wilkes said decisively, "I want you for my woman, Rachel. I had a good haul before I came down here so I shan't need to go on the road for a while. Can you arrange matters with the Pruntys? Get them to give us their best room, for a start, and hire another woman for their work . . . I'll not have you skivvying while you're with me, understand?"

Doll Prunty fell in with these plans with enthusiasm when Rachel broached them to her. "Well!" she exclaimed with satisfaction. "That's just what I hoped would happen and I'm glad . . . you've deserved it, girl. We'll clear out the first floor front for you and the captain—you'll be snug enough in there."

"What can I do about Jenny?" Rachel asked. "I wouldn't want her to know, Doll."

"She's bound to," Doll retorted practically. "You

can't keep a thing like this from her, no matter what you do. But she's not a child now. Best tell her, Rachel, rather than let her find out by chance . . . that'd hurt her far more."

Aware that this was sage advice, Rachel could not bring herself to take it, putting off from day to day the moment when she would have to tell her daughter the truth and resorting to every subterfuge she could devise in order to keep this from her. She was happy, happier than she had been for years and, blissfully unaware that Jenny would inevitably notice the change in her, she continued to procrastinate.

Harry Wilkes was generous and he insisted on keeping her in style. He bought her clothes and jewelry, took her with him to nearby eating houses and demanded that she drink with him in the taproom of the Three Fools each evening. Having released her from servitude, he wanted to free Jenny also and to deck her out in finery, so that she might do them both credit. In his more optimistic moments he talked of adopting her and was at a loss to understand Rachel's obstinate refusal to allow him to do anything for her child. She was in love and could refuse him little else but, where Jenny was concerned, she remained quite adamant and even Dr. Fry failed to persuade her to change her mind. Instead, out of affection for his young protégée but with extreme reluctance, he agreed to take Jenny with him on one of his mysterious journeys to the South Coast, on Rachel's assurance that she would break the news to her daughter when they returned.

They were away for the better part of fourteen days, during which time Rachel and her lover moved into their new quarters in the Three Fools's "first floor front," but despite the doctor's urging, Rachel still seemed unwilling to adhere to her promise.

"I'll tell the lass in my own good time, Doctor," she said firmly. "It will come as a shock to her, I know, so I want to break it gently."

In the end it was Ned Munday who, prompted by malice, revealed the truth, and he did it anything but gently. He sidled into the kitchen one evening when Jenny was alone, ostensibly to bring her a present. Since the episode in the taproom, when Captain Wilkes had made him an object of ridicule, he had been slyly endeavoring to insinuate himself into Jenny's good graces, and she, attracted by his youthful good looks, had not discouraged his advances. He came up behind her now, crossing the big, dimly lit kitchen on tiptoe and, putting both hands over her eyes, he challenged her to guess his identity.

"It's Ned," she scoffed. "Ned Munday . . . as if anyone else would have such great cold hands!"

"Ah, but you don't know what's in 'em, do you? There—feast your eyes on that!" He opened his hand to display an exquisitely enameled locket, set in a circle of small brilliants. "'Tis for you, Jenny—a present to remember me by." He tried to slip it round her neck but the chain from which it hung had been broken and Jenny rounded on him reproachfully.

"Ned, you stole it!"

"No, I didn't then. I bought it specially for you."

"I don't believe you—where would *you* get money to buy anything as expensive as this, for pity's sake?" Her tone was scornful. "Do you think I'm soft in the head?"

"Oh, very well then," Ned conceded, ruffled but determined to impress her. "I stole it. Held up a carriage on the heath last night if you want to know. One of the grand ladies was wearing it, and I scared her so much, she tore it from her neck to give to me."

"Take it back, Ned," Jenny pleaded. "You know I can't keep it if it's stolen."

" 'Course you can if you hide it. Put it under your dress—I'll show you where, shall I?" Jenny pushed his questing hands away, and he reddened resentfully. "All right, do it yourself . . . but keep it, Jenny. No one'll know you've got it if you don't tell 'em. You like it, don't you?"

"Yes, of course I do—it's beautiful." She studied the locket, admiring the craftsmanship that had gone into its making and, for all her pretense of scorn, she was touched that Ned should want her to have it. He could have counted on three or four guineas, at least, from Dr. Fry but . . . there was her mother. A long time ago her mother had warned her that she must never, in any circumstances, accept stolen property, no matter who offered it. The ban even included the doctor. . . she sighed regretfully and thrust the locket into Ned's hand.

"I can't keep it. I'm truly sorry, Ned—it was kind of you but . . . my mam won't allow me to take anything that's been stolen."

"Your mam hasn't a leg to stand on, not anymore. *She* takes plenty from her fancy man and where did he get the gold he spends on her? Ain't he on the high toby?"

"What do you mean—her fancy man?" Jenny asked.

Ned told her, with brutal frankness, sparing her nothing in the telling, and she listened in stunned silence. When he had done, she said with what dignity she could muster, "It's not true—Mam would have told me if it was. Get out of my sight, Ned Munday! I'll have no more to do with you, do you hear? You're a liar and a bag of wind. I wouldn't take your locket if you—why, if you went on your knees and begged me to!"

"I shan't do that," Ned told her sullenly. "But if you think I'm a liar, why don't you go up and take a peek into that fine bedroom in the front of the house? Your ma's moved in there while you've been away, and her fancy man with her. They—" He broke off, feeling a twinge of conscience when he looked into the girl's chalk-white face. "I'll go," he finished lamely. "But I want you to keep this." He laid the locket on the littered table. "Watt Sparrow will mend the chain for you if you ask him."

When he had gone, Jenny slumped into Doll Prunty's old chair and buried her face in her hands. She recalled her mother's visit to her, in the borrowed dress, with the reek of gin on her breath . . . hadn't that been the night when Captain Wilkes had first made his appearance in the Three Fools? And there was no denying that her mother had changed since his advent; she had started to take pains with her appearance, to use paint and powder on her face and . . . Jenny bit back a sob. And also to drink. She and Mrs. Prunty had often taken a glass or two, together, in this kitchen but they worked hard and Doll had called it, laughingly, their medicine.

It was different now, though. Her mother wasn't drinking with Doll Prunty in the kitchen—she was drinking in the taproom with Captain Wilkes. Jenny got to her feet, seeing the locket through a blur of tears, and almost as if it were an act of defiance, she picked it up and thrust it into the front of her dress. What did it matter if it had been stolen? Ned had stolen it for her, he had said he wanted her to keep it, and perhaps, after all, he had been telling her the truth.

She picked up a candle and, moving quietly lest either of the Pruntys should hear and attempt to stop her, she climbed the stairs. The sound of subdued laughter came from behind the door of the room she sought—a woman's voice, slightly slurred, cried out in mock protest and then a man's, easily recognizable as that of Captain Wilkes, demanded a drink.

"The bottle's not dead yet but I'm nigh to it, woman! Fetch me it here if you're expecting me to—"

Jenny pushed open the door then and stood there as if turned to stone. Captain Wilkes lay stretched full length on the disheveled bed and her mother was in the act of returning to it, a half-empty bottle in her hand. Both were naked. They turned, almost as one, to face the open door, and the captain, to Jenny's horror, started to swear at her. Her mother said nothing for a long moment; then, in tears, she let the bottle fall and, with both arms outstretched, stumbled unsteadily toward her daughter, seeking to take her into her embrace.

"It's—it's not what it seems, Jenny love. The captain and I . . . oh, lass, I would have told you long ago but I—"

"But you didn't, Mam," Jenny whispered. The accusation and all it implied hung between them, like a tangible thing, a barrier that neither of them could cross.

"You don't understand, child," Rachel managed at last. She was shivering, and Captain Wilkes passed her a sheet, still swearing under his breath. He reached for his shirt, dragged it over his head and fumbled about him for his breeches. "I'll leave you to settle things between you," he told Rachel. "I'll be in the taproom if you want me."

Left alone, mother and child stared at each other in hurtful silence. It was as if they were strangers, Jenny thought sadly, with no words that would bridge the gulf that had opened up so suddenly to hold them apart. Still shivering despite the sheet draped about her, Rachel retreated to the bed.

"You shouldn't have come up here," she said, seeking to reassert her authority. "That was—that was wrong, and you know it. If you are—if you're shocked, I'm sorry. But it isn't what you think, Jenny, truly it's not. I'm no wanton, you must believe that. I—I love him."

"More than you loved my father?" Jenny asked with a bitterness she could not hide. "Have you ceased to mourn *him*?"

"Four years is a long time to mourn any man," her mother answered. Without conscious thought she picked up the bottle. "I'll tell you about it, I'll explain but I—my mouth is dry, Jenny. I . . . he's made me very happy, you know, and I'm not an old woman. I have a right to a little happiness and you shouldn't begrudge me that—I've worked hard enough for it . . . and for you. I've sacrificed myself for you all these years, God knows I have, but you're forgetting that, aren't you? And when your father was alive I—" she was weeping, the bottle opened now, its contents slopping over as, with trembling hands, she attempted to pour herself a measure. "When your father was alive, I bore with what he did—I let him defy Lord Braxton and it lost us our home. It lost us everything we had. . . ."

Jenny watched her in heartbroken disgust, trying to shut her ears to what she was saying, yet unable to tear herself away. It was Doll Prunty who led her from the room at last; Doll, with the clay pipe clamped firmly between her teeth, holding her in strong arms and half carrying her up to her own small room beneath the eaves.

"There now, my lamb," she rasped. "Don't take on so. Your ma's not done anything wrong. She's a good, decent woman, and I daresay she ought to have told you, but we all make mistakes. She was only trying to spare you because she feared you might be hurt. But you've got to grow up, lass, you've got to understand that life's all ups and downs. Folk die but life goes on. I don't doubt your dad was a fine man, but he's been dead these four years past—and the captain's a fine man, too. . . ." She talked on and Jenny listened, frozen and having no answer to what, nevertheless, she recognized as the truth.

Others talked to her in the days that followed, with equal truthfulness and varying degrees of compassion . . . Nick, Dr. Fry, Watt Sparrow, and even Captain Wilkes himself. Jenny listened to them all and promised dutifully to follow the counsel they gave her. Only in the presence of her mother was she withdrawn and silent, outwardly submissive but refusing to give her the answer she wanted, and Rachel, finally losing patience, slapped the girl's face unmercifully and then, dissolving into tears, resorted to the bottle for comfort.

The captain took matters into his own hands after that. "We'll take a room elsewhere," he told Doll Prunty, "if you can care for the little wench meantime. Her tantrums are upsetting Rachel and I'll not stand for it—besides, Rachel's drinking a lot more than is good for her. More than my purse will stand, if she carries on," he added wryly. "But maybe a few weeks' separation will bring them both to their senses. It's to be hoped it will, for I've a mind to cut my ties here and head for the West Country at the end of the month and if I go, I'll be taking Rachel with me. The lass, too, if she'll come."

Aware that it was on Dr. Fry's advice that he was contemplating a move, Doll raised no objections. "The lass has a place here, Captain," she answered placidly. "You make whatever plans you wish. You hadn't thought, I suppose—" she broke off, pursing her lips.

"Hadn't thought of what?" Captain Wilkes prompted, smiling.

"Well, 'tis no business of mine," Doll said. "But it did occur to me that if you were to wed Rachel, you'd find both of them easier to handle. Rachel's not normally one for the bottle—it's only since she took up with you that she's shown any liking for it."

He shrugged, his smile fading abruptly. "I expect you're right, Mistress Prunty—you usually are. And I'd wed Rachel tomorrow if I could. Unhappily, though, I've a wife living, somewhere in Yorkshire . . . and Rachel knows I have. But we'll just have to make the best of it, I reckon."

He left, with Rachel, next day, and Jenny was told, somewhat tartly by Doll Prunty, that they had taken rooms in a lodging house on the other side of the river, at Blackfriars. "'Tis you drove your ma away, my girl—you and no one else, so don't you forget it. I'm counting on you to mend your ways . . . and that means buckling down to your work and seeing less o' that young good-for-nothing Ned Munday. Don't imagine I haven't seen him sneaking about when he thought my back was turned, because I have. And he's no good, Jenny lass, not for you. Give him his marching orders."

"All right, Mistress Prunty," Jenny agreed. She had no great liking for Ned Munday but, having called him a liar when he had told her the truth, she had felt guilty on his account. Besides, there was the locket he had given her. In the sanctuary of her own small room later that evening, she took it from its hiding place and sat for a long time with the gleaming trinket in her hand, admiring its beauty and glorying in its ownership.

She possessed no miniature portrait to put inside it, no precious souvenir or lock of hair but . . . there was the blue ribbon from the bonnet her father had bought her in the market at Milton Overblow, the day of the fair. Since the chain was broken, she would hang it from the ribbon and . . . yes, put a snippet from the now faded silk inside the glass of the locket so as to preserve what was left of its color. It should be her talisman, her lucky charm, she decided, and she would keep it forever to remind her—not of Ned Munday—but of her father. Just because her mother had taken a fancy man and ceased to mourn for him was no reason why she, his daughter, should be equally heartless.

Dr. Fry, when she carried his tea tray in to him, had a newspaper spread out on the table and he had his glasses on, studying one of the inner pages with rapt attention. He lifted the paper with an impatient grunt so that she might set his tray down and, ignoring her dutiful curtsy, said with unusual brusqueness, "All right, Jenny—pour out a cup for me and then make yourself scarce. I've no time for your lesson this morning."

Jenny obeyed. It was inadvisable to question any of the doctor's demands or decisions, she was aware, but her lower lip trembled, in spite of the effort she made to hide her disappointment, and seeing this, he relented, putting the folded newspaper into her hands.

"Your eyes are younger than mine, child. You may read me that passage aloud before you go." He indicated the column with a plump finger. "Start at the beginning and read slowly."

Jenny started to read. "The headline is 'Daring Holdup in Richmond Park,' and it says: 'On Wednesday evening last, the Marquis of Danbury held a reception at his Richmond home, attended by some eighty distinguished guests. Most took their departure at about eleven in the evening and four carriages were held up, in turn, as they drove through the park. It was a foggy night and the miscreants could not be identified but there were three of them, all well mounted, and one of the victims—who hails from the North—gave it as his firm opinion that the notorious Captain Wilkes was of their number—'" she broke off, with a stifled gasp.

"Go on, go on," Dr. Fry urged impatiently.

"Yes, sir." Jenny read on, in the clear, expressionless tone he had taught her to employ when reading aloud. "'As our readers may recall, we published only last week a report that the villain responsible for spreading terror on the Yorkshire roads—to wit, the so-called Captain Wilkes—had been seen in London recently. A substantial reward for information leading to his capture, already offered by the Lord Mayor and Aldermen of York, has now been augmented by our own city sheriff, and the Marquis of Danbury has stated that he will add one hundred guineas to this sum, provided the property stolen from his guests can subsequently be recovered—'" Again, unable to contain herself, Jenny broke off, staring up at Dr. Fry with frightened eyes. "Oh, sir, does that mean he'll be taken?"

"So you're concerned for him, are you, little minx, in spite of all your tantrums?" The doctor smiled then and, when she nodded shamefacedly, gently patted her bent head. "Don't fret, my child—however high a price they put on his head, Harry Wilkes will be safe enough here. Now go on reading, if you please . . . there's a list of the jewelry they took and from whom it was taken, and I want to take some notes—ah, just in case."

Jenny read out the list and Dr. Fry scribbled busily in his notebook. When it was complete, he dismissed her, and she returned, somewhat disconsolately, to the kitchen. Doll set her to work, and, as she plied her vegetable knife with the absentminded skill of long practice, she repeated as much as she could remember of the newspaper report. Doll's brow furrowed as she listened, but, like Dr. Fry, she pooh-poohed any suggestion that the size of the reward offered might tempt any of their own, tight-knit community to play the informer.

"Harry Wilkes is among friends here, lass—no one will give him away. It's a pity he had to go back to the road so soon but"—she shrugged—"you can't live the way he's been living and expect the money to last. Put them spuds on to boil as quick as you can and then watch the spit for me while I go and tell Nick. Likely he'll know already but maybe he'll want the captain's horse moved for a few days where it's less likely to be noticed."

She hurried off, and Jenny, left with the responsibility of preparing dinner, forgot her anxiety for her mother's fancy man in the bustle of preparation. Ned Munday came sidling in in his usual furtive manner, but mindful of Doll's instructions, she gave him short shrift and he departed sullenly, reproaching her for her ingratitude and threatening to reclaim the locket unless she showed him more respect.

It was that evening when disaster struck. Jenny, as usual, was in the kitchen, and the first intimation she had that anything was wrong was when she heard a commotion coming from the taproom. But there were often brawls and strong differences of opinion among the tavern's customers and she thought little of it until, to her stunned astonishment, Dr. Fry appeared in the kitchen. In all the years she had known him, the fastidious old doctor had never entered what he was pleased to refer to as "the nether regions," and the fact that he had done so now filled her with sickening fear.

"Doctor Fry . . . please sir, is there anything wrong?" she asked anxiously. "Is it—is it Missus Prunty? She's not been taken ill, has she?"

The doctor shook his head. He crossed to Doll Prunty's battered old chair, lowered his ungainly bulk into it, and then summoned Jenny to his side.

"Child," he said with unexpected gentleness as she came to him, "you must prepare yourself for a shock. An informer led the constables to Captain Wilkes's lodging an hour or so ago, and they bore him off in chains to Newgate. He'll be up before the Bench in the morning."

Jenny gulped, momentarily deprived of speech.

"And my . . . mam?" she managed at last.

"Arrested with him, I'm afraid . . . and charged with harboring a fugitive from justice. They surprised him in her bed. There, Jenny child—" He drew her to him, seating her on his knee as if she were indeed a child. "Cry if you want to. But you can rest assured that I shall do everything I can for them . . . we all will. It's a pity I'm a trifle short of cash at the moment but Harry Wilkes isn't. We'll see to it that your mother is provided for until she's brought to trial and—"

Jenny scarcely heard him. "Doctor Fry," she faltered. "What is the penalty for harboring?"

He hesitated in the act of taking his own fine cambric handkerchief from his pocket with the intention of offering it to her but, seeing that she was dry-eyed, he contented himself with patting her hand consolingly.

"It's a hanging offense, Jenny," he told her with reluctance when she repeated the question. "The same penalty as for highway robbery. Wilkes will hang, I fear, now they've caught him, but in your mother's case, it's just possible that we may contrive to have her sentence commuted to life imprisonment or transportation."

She looked up at him in shocked disbelief, and he sighed, holding out the handkerchief. "There, child, there . . . you—"

"I'm all right, sir." Jenny slipped from his knee, and studying her white, resolute face, Dr. Fry knew, in that moment, that little Jenny Taggart was being compelled to grapple with problems that even a grown woman would have found daunting . . . and it said much for her courage that his proffered handkerchief was ignored.

CHAPTER V

The arrest of the notorious Captain Wilkes caused a sensation. The newspapers announced it in banner headlines, all London was agog, awaiting his trial and inevitable sentence, and the pamphleteers were busy, preparing the story of his exploits and illustrating their lurid prose with sketches of him, masked and mounted on a fine gray horse, a pistol in his hand.

The result of their labors, offered for a penny in marketplaces and on the streets, enjoyed a brisk sale, and already the pie merchants, costermongers, and barrow boys, as well as the cutpurses and pickpockets, were making eager plans to attend the hanging. It promised to attract the biggest crowd of the year and bets as to the final number were being offered and freely accepted, although no accurate measure for deciding the number present had yet been devised.

Harry Wilkes himself, with a well-filled purse to ensure favorable treatment, was confined in a part of Newgate Prison known as the Master Side, where he was able to enjoy the luxury of a room to himself and have his meals and whatever drinks he required sent in from outside. But her mother, Jenny learned, had been taken to one of the dreaded Hulks—the ghastly, rotting prison ships moored on the river, which they had glimpsed on their first day in London as they tramped wearily across London Bridge in the wake of the Hawleys and Watt Sparrow.

Rachel's trial had been swift. Like her arrest, it had attracted none of the publicity accorded to that of the man she was accused of harboring, and Dr. Fry, who had made strenuous efforts to engage a lawyer to act in her defense, was not aware—until the actual day of the hearing—that it was taking place. The lawyer, without a proper brief and with no opportunity to speak to his client until she was about to go into court, had managed only to obtain a stay of execution, pending an appeal, when the death sentence was arbitrarily imposed. He had, however, made a successful appeal, and as the doctor had hoped it might be, the sentence had been commuted to one of imprisonment for fifteen years.

"We must get money to her," Doll Prunty told Jenny, when this news reached them, "because she will die if we don't. Those poor, lost souls on the Hulks die like flies if they can't afford to bribe the jailers, and without money she will have been put below decks."

"But where can we get money?" Jenny asked despairingly. "I can't ask the doctor for any more and—"

"Harry Wilkes will give us as much as we need,

without a doubt," Doll said with conviction. "He made a good killing that night in Richmond Park and he won't be able to spend it where he's going, poor fellow. The best plan will be if you go and ask him for it, Jenny. He'll trust you to take it to your ma, where he might not trust me. D'you think you can do it, lass, if I send Watt Sparrow along to look after you?"

Stifling her fears, Jenny nodded. "I'll do my best, Missus Prunty."

"All right, then." Doll gave her careful instructions and next morning, with Watt Sparrow acting as guide and escort, she made her way past St. Paul's Churchyard and the Old Bailey to Newgate. Sparrow, it soon became evident, knew his way about the prison and he confessed wryly that he had twice been incarcerated there. They skirted the elevated wooden platform on which the gallows was erected for executions and entered through the Debtors' Door. Crossing the open press yard, the little man told her that it was here that prisoners awaiting execution had their chains struck off and their arms pinioned, preparatory to mounting the scaffold. Gesturing to the barred windows that now faced them, he said grimly, "That's what they call the Common Side, Jenny. If you ain't got no cash ter pay yer way, that's where they stow yer, wiv' a few 'andfuls o' straw fer yer bed—if you're lucky, that is—an' bread an' water ter keep body an' soul tergether. An' you even 'ave ter fight fer that! But—" he shrugged, "the captain won't be there, o'course—'e'll be along this way, wiv' the nobs. Come on, me duck, just foller me, an' don't look too close, once we gits inside."

He took her hand, and she followed him blindly, sickened by the stench and terrified by the cries and

imprecations which were hurled at them through the
bars by creatures who, when she ventured to glance
at them, seemed scarcely human. On the Master Side,
however, it was very different and she almost sobbed
her relief when they reached it. A turnkey to whom,
as instructed by Doll, she gave sixpence, took them up
a dark flight of stone steps and, unlocking an iron-
bound door, waved them into the presence of Captain
Wilkes with a flourish.

The room, although hardly to be described as
pleasant with its heavily barred window and rough
stone floor, was clean and comfortably furnished with
a bed, a table, and several chairs. Captain Wilkes was
seated at the table, reading a newspaper, a bottle of
wine and several glasses at his elbow. He looked pale
but otherwise well enough and he greeted his visitors
cordially, wringing Watt Sparrow's hand and, to
Jenny's surprise, bestowing a kiss on her cheek. He
poured wine for them and then asked, his tone grave
and concerned, what news she had of her mother.

Jenny told him and saw his face contract in pain, as
if she had struck him. "Oh, dear God, I had not
thought to bring her to that! Poor lass, they had no
right to charge her—I told them she was innocent but
they would not listen, plague take them! They had
me, what more did they want? I'll give you money, of
course—all you want, Jenny, if you'll take it to her."

Jenny nodded, wordless. His manacled hands were
shaking, she saw, as he took a small leather purse from
about his neck and, pulling open the drawstring,
emptied its contents on to the table.

"I'll keep back only what I need, child," he said
in explanation, dividing the silver and the gold pieces
into two separate piles. "Don't give your mother gold
—they'd rob her of it, maybe even cut her throat to

get it. Let Watt here bargain with the jailers—he'll
know what to arrange, eh, Watty my lad?"

"You can rely on me, Captain," Watt Sparrow assured him.

"Then this for your trouble, friend." Harry Wilkes
flipped a gold half-guinea in Sparrow's direction. The
little man caught it deftly, grinned and, as deftly,
tossed it back onto the pile that the captain was re-
serving for his own use.

"I don't take nothin' fer helpin' me friends," he
asserted. "Pass that ter the gaffer, when yer mounts
the nubbing cheat, Captain, so's 'e'll give yer an
easy ride." He raised his glass in salute. "God bless
yer! You're a gennelman, Captain Wilkes, an' I'm
prah'd ter 'ave known yer!"

"Thank you, Watt," Wilkes acknowledged solemnly. Their eyes met over Jenny's bent head, and he
added softly, "It will be Monday, the governor told
me. I expect it'll be in the papers but see that the
doctor knows, will you? And . . . Rachel." He picked
up the little heap of silver coins and, replacing them
in his purse, gave the purse to Jenny. "I'd have wed
your mother, you know, child, if I'd been free. She
was a better wife to me than the one the good
Lord saddled me with and that's a fact—and the
irony of it is that, if she *had* been my wife, they
couldn't have charged her with harboring me!"

Jenny looked up at him, her throat tight, and
then, impulsively, she put her arms round his neck
and kissed him.

"Well, well!" he exclaimed with a return to his
old bravado. "What did I do to deserve that?" But he
hugged her, his cheek against hers, and to her surprise she tasted the salt bitterness of tears as the stubble of a sprouting beard brushed against her lips. But

he had recovered himself when he set her down, and as the turnkey's voice called out to warn him that the visitors' time was up, he asked brusquely, addressing Watt Sparrow rather than herself, "D'you know who informed on me?"

Watt hesitated and then shook his head. "I've heard no word, Captain."

"Oh, well, it's of no matter now, I suppose," the captain said. The jailer's key rasped in the lock, and he rose to his full, commanding height to take leave of them. "You'll be there, will you not, Watt lad?"

"I'll be there," Watt Sparrow promised.

"Good! Then you can bring the child . . . she shall see Captain Wilkes go to his end in style. It'll be something for her to tell her grandchildren, will it not?" His voice had a note of sarcasm so that Jenny wondered whether or not he meant her to attend his hanging but, when she asked Watt Sparrow as they descended the worn stone steps in the jailer's wake, the little man assured her with conviction that he did.

"Seein' yer ma can't, 'e wants you, duck. And 'e'll put on a show for the crowd, you see if 'e don't. It's in the tradition, see—a gennelman dies like a gennelman an' 'e'll want you ter tell yer ma."

Jenny was silent, trying vainly to digest the logic of this strange reasoning, as Watt Sparrow wove his way through a warren of mean back streets to the Thames Embankment. "'Ave ter brace yerself, you will, Jenny lass, when we gets ter the 'ulks," he warned her. "Newgate's bad, Gawd knows, but the 'ulks are worse. They say they're goin' ter transport most o' the poor souls they got chained up in them ships ter some place called Botany Bay—the men, anyways. If any o' them live long enough to be transported, that's ter say."

Jenny scarcely took in what he was saying. As they neared the line of anchored vessels, the terrible stench that she remembered from four years ago rose up to meet her and she shuddered, but Watt Sparrow's hand gripped her arm, urging her on.

"Yer ma's on board the *Kinsale*," he offered encouragingly. "An' that's 'er, see, at the foot o' them steps—the name's painted acrost 'er stern. Didn't take us long, did it, now? Lucky yer poor ma weren't packed orf ter Gravesend or Sheerness, like a lot of 'em are ... we'd 'ave bin all day gettin' down the river, never mind gettin' back. Better let me 'ave that purse now, lass, so's I c'n take care o' things."

Jenny gave him the purse and, frightened and anxious, followed him down the steps to a wooden jetty, guarded by a lounging sentry. Dismasted, her decks littered and filthy, the *Kinsale* showed little sign of her former glory. Built as a third-rate ship of the line over forty years before, she was by no means the oldest of the Hulks but she had been so severely damaged in a storm, not long after commissioning, that the Admiralty had deemed her beyond repair and had released her from the Navy to serve, first as a receiving ship and finally as a prison Hulk, when the demand for these increased.

Directed by the sentry to what had once been the captain's day cabin, Jenny looked about her nervously, while Watt Sparrow began negotiations with the warden. He was a small, unpleasant-looking individual, unshaven, and with one eye hidden behind a black patch. Lounging back in a padded armchair in his comfortable quarters, he regarded both his visitors balefully with his single eye and appeared disposed to send them packing, until Watt Sparrow produced one of the coins Captain Wilkes had given them. Letting it fall with a metallic ring on the tabletop, the little cockney made his wishes clear, and the warden became less truculent.

A second coin reduced him to eager willingness to serve them. He did not, he confessed, know Mistress Taggart's exact place of confinement but, as a newly convicted prisoner, without money, it was probable that she would be found on the orlop deck. They could see her, of course, since the girl was her daughter —he would summon one of his jailers to conduct them to the orlop and the man would be instructed to arrange her transfer to the upper gundeck forthwith. Prisoners on the upper gundeck enjoyed more ventilation, better food, and were more lightly chained; Mrs. Taggart would, undoubtedly, benefit from the exchange from her present quarters.

An underling, heavy-jowled and bestial in appearance, led them down through the cramped, 'tween-decks, to the orlop—the deck immediately above the hold. It was below the waterline and so dark that the "purser's glims," hanging from the overhead beams in cracked horn lanterns, scarcely penetrated the gloom. At first Jenny could see little; then as her eyes gradually became accustomed to the dimness she saw that rows of wooden bunks occupied what space was left by the slime-encrusted cable tiers—the oblong stowage space for the great coils of hempen cable by means of which, at sea, the ship's anchors had been raised or lowered. A noisome stench pervaded the whole dark, airless deck, emanating from the befouled bilge water in the hold below and from the occupants of the tiers of bunks—dirty, ragged skeletons, secured by leg and arm chains to iron rings driven into the planking. Their chains restricted their movements to a bare yard or two from the hard wooden couches to which they

were attached but most, Jenny saw, made no attempt
to move. They lay, inert and apathetic, viewing the
appearance of the jailer with indifference, if they
noticed it at all.

When passing the barred windows of Newgate's
Common Side, she and Watt Sparrow had attracted
curses and catcalls from the inmates, who had crowded
to the bars to stare at them and speculate as to their
purpose in entering the prison, but here . . . she
choked back a sob. Here it was as if all hope had gone
and death the only visitor they would welcome.

Watt Sparrow's fingers bit into the flesh of her arm.

"Yer ma, Jenny lass," he whispered hoarsely. "The
turnkey says she's at the end o' this row." He led her,
sick with the smell of fear and death, to the bunk
where her mother lay, as silent and apathetic as the
rest, and clad only in her shift. To Jenny's horrified
eyes she seemed to have aged by ten years, and when
at last they managed to rouse her, she stared at them
without recognition for a long time and then burst
into a torrent of sobs.

"They stole my clothes, Jenny—stripped me of
everything and took the money the doctor gave me.
It wasn't much, after I had paid the lawyer, but they
took it just the same. I . . . oh, God in heaven!" Her
voice broke and so softly that Jenny could hardly
make out the words, she added, "I wish they had
not . . . commuted my sentence. Hanging could be
. . . no worse than this."

The jailer intervened with gruff cordiality.

"On your feet, missus—we're shiftin' yer out of
here. It'll be a lot better where we're takin' yer, yer
see if it ain't." He unlocked the padlock securing the
leg irons and, with practiced skill, took the weight of
the chains by pulling the slack across his shoulder.

"Give 'er a hand, me bucko," he bade Sparrow. "And you take 'er other arm, lass."

Between them, not without difficulty, they lifted Rachel from her bunk. She was so weak, she could barely stand and, as they half carried, half led her between the rows of bunks, a dreadful wailing followed them, like no sound Jenny had ever heard. There was envy and despair in every face that met her gaze; she tried not to look at them, tried desperately to shut out the heartbreaking cries but it was impossible. Bony hands clutched at her sleeve, others were outstretched in supplication, and had it not been for Watt Sparrow's urging, she would have collapsed in a trembling heap on the unswept, evil-smelling deck boards.

They were almost at the foot of the companionway when a white-haired hag leaned forward, eyes bright with futile anger, to send a stream of yellow spittle coursing down Rachel's cheek. Jenny drew back in outraged horror, but her mother did not appear to be aware of what had happened or to hear the venomous curses the old woman hurled at her.

"Be'ave yerself, Molly," the jailer ordered harshly. With Rachel's chain wrapped round his fist, he struck Molly across the face and she fell back, screeching with pain. "Git your old man ter cross my palm with silver an' I'll shift _you_ up ter the gundeck," he advised and chuckled without rancor when the poor, crazed creature howled abuse at him. "Bin 'ere nigh on a year, old Molly 'as," he volunteered as they gained the comparative quiet of the lower gundeck. " 'Ad jail fever twice but some'ow she don't die. An' 'er old man's loaded wi' money and won't lift a finger ter 'elp 'er. Makes yer wonder, don't it?"

They reached the upper gundeck at last, and the

jailer took them to a vacant bunk on the port side. It was of the same construction as those they had seen below but it had been scrubbed and was furnished with a straw-filled palliasse and a worn blanket. An open porthole admitted a certain amount of light and air and even allowed a sight of the embankment, and there was a wood-burning stove, only a few feet from Rachel's bunk, on which two women were cooking something in an iron pot. The accommodation was crowded, even here, but the deck was clean and a strong smell of sulfur obliterated the worst of the stench from below.

The jailer secured Rachel's leg iron to a running chain, pointing out, almost with pride, the range of movement this made possible. He accepted sixpence from Watt Sparrow and added, ingratiatingly, that for twice that sum, he would replace the prisoner's lost clothing from the slop chest and bring her a mug of porter. The little cockney shrugged ruefully but, after some argument, handed over the money and the jailer departed, whistling, to perform his errand.

"He's not the worst of them," Rachel said wearily. "He will keep his word." She permitted Jenny to help her onto the bunk and lay back, eyes closed, as if the effort had exhausted her last reserves of strength. Her cheeks had an unnatural flush, Jenny noticed, and her skin was dry and hot to the touch, but after a while when the jailer returned with a dress and shawl and the promised porter, she roused herself sufficiently to drink the porter.

"Was it Harry Wilkes who sent the money?" she asked, addressing Watt Sparrow.

"It was," Sparrow confirmed.

"Then you've seen him?"

"This morning, Missus Taggart. We went first to Newgate."

"He asked after you most tenderly, Mam," Jenny put in. As lucidly as she could, she described their visit, repeating what Captain Wilkes had said and was rewarded by the return of her mother's smile.

"He is a good man," Rachel said with quiet conviction. "A truly good man. But . . . he's been condemned, hasn't he?"

Jenny exchanged an anxious glance with Watt Sparrow, who inclined his balding head in regretful assent.

"Then they'll hang him." It was a statement of fact, not a question, made bravely and without tears. Rachel drew a long, unhappy breath and then asked, her voice still steady and controlled, "When, Watt—when is it to be?"

"Monday, he said . . . seems the governor told him. It ain't bin in the papers yet though." The little man hesitated, a frown creasing his brow. Then he added, his tone apologetic, "He wants Jenny to be there, Missus Taggart. I knows 'ow you've tried ter shield the lass, but—'e does want 'er, seeing as you—"

"Yes," Rachel said quietly. "She shall go . . . you will, won't you, Jenny? For my sake . . . to bid him good-bye and to say a prayer for his soul."

Feeling as if her heart had turned to stone, Jenny nodded. It would be hideous having to watch Captain Wilkes die. Her mother's fancy man, her mother's lover but . . . was her mother not sentenced to fifteen years, perhaps even to transportation to some unknown land, half the world away, simply because she had been with her lover when the constables had taken him?

Her resolution hardened. "I'll go, Mam," she promised. "And I'll say a prayer for him."

"That's my lass," her mother acknowledged. "That's my Jenny." The rift between them, Jenny thought, was healed . . . or almost healed, and she was thankful that it was so.

"They batten down the 'atches at dusk," Watt Sparrow reminded her. "We'll best git ourselves ashore, Jenny girl." He gave her the purse. "Tell yer ma ter keep this well 'idden," he advised, lowering his voice. " 'Cause they'll put 'er back on the orlop deck if she can't pay 'er way. That'll last 'er for a while, but she won't 'ave ter let anyone take it orf 'er."

Rachel took the purse and, slipping the string about her neck, she concealed both carefully beneath her shift.

"Harry Wilkes is a good man," she whispered and suddenly her control deserted her and, burying her face in her hands, she wept. "Leave me be, child," she ordered fiercely as Jenny bent to kiss her. "Leave me be."

"Come on, me duck," Sparrow said, holding out his hand. "We've done all we can."

They emerged onto the open deck to find the warden by the gangway. He was drunk and he stood, a bottle in his hand, swaying unsteadily as if to the motion of a ship at sea. Recognizing Watt Sparrow, he hailed him with exaggerated amiability.

"Everything arranged to your satisfaction, friend?"

Watt Sparrow thanked him. "Missus Taggart is more comfortable now, sir. But she ain't well, she—"

"I'll have the surgeon look at her next time 'e calls," the warden volunteered. He laid a restraining hand on the little man's shoulder. "Been meanin' ter ask yer—ain't she Cap'n Wilkes's woman, your party?"

Sparrow nodded. Jenny opened her mouth to speak

but he flashed her a warning glance. "That's so, matey," he admitted.

"Ah!" The fat warden put his bottle to his lips, took a liberal gulp, and then passed it hospitably to Sparrow. "Help yourself—thersh plenny more where that came from." He grinned, as the little cockney availed himself of the unexpected invitation. "If your Missus Taggart ish the cap'n's woman, then you don't need ter fret about 'er whilst she's in *my* care. I'll see as she's treated right. They die 'ere, y'know, die in the 'undreds and the gov'ment don't care . . . but I'll look after Missus Taggart." With some difficulty, swaying as he did so, he took a pamphlet from his breeches' pocket and waved it triumphantly in front of Jenny. It was, she saw, one of the many currently on sale, in which the captain's exploits on the road were described in lavish detail.

Watt Sparrow repeated his thanks and made to return the bottle. "Keep it, cock, keep it!" The warden belched loudly and, leaning heavily on Sparrow's shoulder, said something in a confidential undertone which Jenny did not catch. She saw him recoil, then nod as if in reluctant agreement, and the warden let them go. When they were safely back on dry land, she asked him what the man had said, but he evaded the question, hurrying her along through the darkening streets as if fearing that the devil were after them.

At the door of the Three Fools, she asked him again and he sighed. "Well, yer can't be a child all yer life, I s'pose, and wiv' yer ma gone, who's ter say as you should? 'E arst me ter put in a word for 'im ter yer ma, that's all. 'E fancies 'er, see, on account of 'er 'aving bin the captain's light o'love."

Jenny stared at him, wide-eyed with horror and dismay.

"That dirty fat old man, Watt? Oh, no! Why the captain's not even—not even dead yet!"

"It'll be up ter yer ma, ducky," Watt Sparrow returned philosophically. "An' come Monday, the poor captain *will* be dead, 'cause they'll top 'im at eight o'clock sharp, that's fer bleedin' sure. 'E won't get no reprieve—them on the 'igh toby never does. An' yer ma'll be on 'er own then—she'll 'ave ter look out fer 'erself, won't she?"

He smiled, patted her hand gently, and made off into the swiftly gathering darkness without another word.

CHAPTER VI

By dawn on Monday morning the crowd that had assembled to witness the execution of Captain Harry Wilkes was unparalleled, being, according to the best calculation, nearly forty thousand.

Some people had waited all night, in order to secure the best vantage points, and although it was barely light when Jenny and Watt Sparrow entered Newgate Street, scarcely an inch of ground in view of the scaffold was unoccupied. But Watt was an old hand; he led her through backyards and through the graveyard of St. Paul's to a dismal cobbled lane, dignified with the name Green Arbor, and there assisted her to seat herself on the wall of a city merchant's warehouse. She was not alone; the wall already had its full complement, but Jenny managed to gain a place, the people good-naturedly making room for her when Watt told them her name.

"Take care now, lass," he warned. "There'll be folk trampled underfoot and suffocated in the crush, if any more try ter git in. You stay where you are an' I'll be back ter fetch yer when it's over."

"Oh, Watt, couldn't you stay?" Jenny pleaded, but he shook his head at her reproachfully.

"I got work ter do, Jenny—you know that. Got me livin' to earn an' a mob like this, why it's better nor a carnival! I can't afford ter miss the chance, 'cause they ain't all common folk 'ere today—the gentry's come along too." He smiled at her and produced a neatly folded square of cambric, smelling sweetly of lavender, and clearly—until a few minutes ago— the property of a lady of quality. Thrusting it into her hand, he whispered hoarsely, "I nicked this fer you, me duck, so's you c'n wave it to the captain when 'e gits up onto the scaffold. 'E'll expect yer ter tell 'im good-bye, fer yer ma's sake."

He was gone, his small, limping figure soon lost in the crowd, and Jenny, seeking to follow his movements, was able, with now practiced eyes, to pick out a number of other dips working the crowd—among them Ned Munday. He recognized her, gave her an impudent wink, and continued about his business. Time passed and the crowds increased, with gin peddlers, pamphleteers, barrow-boys, and costermongers shouting their wares, and the pie-men, their baskets balanced on their heads, doing a profitable trade with the hungry spectators. By seven thirty, with thousands crushed into the narrow streets, the pressure had become so great that many people became terrified and sought vainly to escape, and Jenny saw two women, one with a baby in her arms, fall beneath the feet of the surging mob, their shrill cries abruptly stifled as the mob engulfed them.

A young man, in the sober black of a cleric, who was seated on the wall a few yards away, started to pray aloud, and some of the people near enough to hear him joined in his prayer, pity and alarm mingled in their voices.

Encouraged, the young cleric urged them to pray for the soul of the man so soon to meet his end.

"That notorious malefactor, Captain Wilkes, my friends!" he proclaimed loudly. "Let us pray that he may repent of his wickedness even at this, his last hour on earth, so that he may find resurrection and eternal life, through the merciful forgiveness of our Heavenly Father!"

His crusading zeal was rewarded by an enthusiastic response, and mindful of her promise to her mother, Jenny added her voice to the rest, a lump in her throat as it was borne on her that this was, indeed, the last hour that Captain Harry Wilkes would spend on earth.

There was a stir in the crowd as the gate of the prison started to swing open. The crowd was held back by the marshals and constables lining the route to the scaffold and a half-troop of dragoons made their appearance, trotting out from a side street, with sabers drawn, to aid in controlling the mob.

Order restored at the cost of a few broken heads, the prison gate opened fully, and preceded by the sheriffs and followed by the governor and his officers and two city aldermen, the condemned man was led out. A priest walked beside him, intoning from the prayer book he carried, but Harry Wilkes paid him scant attention.

He was elegantly attired in a brass-buttoned cut-away coat, sprigged waistcoat, breeches, and boots, with his hair dressed in a queue, and he walked with a firm step, pausing to speak to friends and well-wishers in the crowd or to bow in acknowledgment of the cheers they accorded him. Only the fact that his wrists were pinioned in front of him and his arms tightly bound distinguished him from those who surrounded him; his manner was, if anything, more composed than theirs, and when he turned in her direction, Jenny saw that he was smiling. She waved the spotless white handkerchief Watt Sparrow had provided for the purpose but could not tell whether or not he had seen her, for he turned again to bow to a section of the crowd on the opposite side and the cheering was redoubled.

Reaching the foot of the scaffold, he hesitated for a moment and then ascended to the platform with a light step, the priest following closely behind him. The waiting multitude fell silent in expectation of a speech, and Captain Wilkes did not disappoint them. In a loud, clear voice, he thanked them for their presence and their support.

"I go to my death with fortitude and in the hope of divine forgiveness, for in very truth, I swear that I took no man's life from him but only the purses of such as could well afford to lose them. Aye, and from some that scarce noticed their loss!" The mob roared their approval and he went on, gravely now, "My trial was fair. I acknowledge my guilt on account of the charges laid against me, for which transgressions I must now pay the penalty demanded by the law. And . . ." He paused, but as the hangman moved tentatively toward him he shook his head. "What's your haste, friend? 'Tis I who am facing eternity, not you!"

Again there were guffaws and some subdued applause; not all had heard his sally but, when those who had repeated it, the mob's appreciation was plain.

Wilkes held up his bound hands. "I forgive all who ever did me an injury," he shouted. "Save only one— the Judas who sold me for his own gain. If that man is watching now, let him beware my dying curse . . . I leave it with him and he must live with it, till he, too, meets his end!"

There was a stunned hush as the crowd took in the meaning of his words and then a wild burst of cheering and cries of "God bless you!" and "Farewell, Captain!"

Harry Wilkes nodded to the executioner. The man bowed his head, accepted the gold piece from his prisoner's pinioned hands and deftly slipped noose and cap over his neatly dressed hair. The next instant it was over; the bolt was drawn and Wilkes's big body hung suspended and, after a brief struggle, motionless, as beneath the drop the hangman's assistant hauled on his legs.

"He died well," a gentleman observed dispassionately. "I shall bid for a piece of the rope."

"I too," the young cleric echoed, to Jenny's shocked surprise. "So long as it doesn't go for more than sixpence the inch."

Jenny put her hands over her ears. It would be an hour, she knew, before Captain Wilkes's body was cut down; until then the crowd would not disperse. Then there would be a rush by the superstitious to touch it, before it was borne away to St. Bartholomew's Hospital for the anatomical instruction of the medical students, and the barber-surgeon's apprentices, who walked the wards there in order to acquire professional proficiency. Then, too, the hangman and his assistants would auction the rope . . . she drew a sobbing breath, wishing that she might leave the scene now, at once, without having to witness Captain Wilkes's final humiliating exit. But Watt Sparrow had bidden her wait, and in so vast a press of people it would be folly to disobey him.

Jenny again glimpsed Ned Munday taking advantage of the turmoil to ply his trade. He worked briskly but without Watt Sparrow's practiced skill, and as she watched him coming nearer and nearer to her vantage point, she became anxious, for he was taking risks, and with the densely packed crowd hemming him in, he would, she realized, have little chance of escape should one of his victims become aware that he had been robbed.

She tried to signal to him to desist, but as before, a confident wink was his only answer. His hand went out, someone jostled him, and a red-faced man in a green overcoat, whose purse he had just lifted, spun round with a bellow of rage.

"Stop thief! Stop thief! There he goes, the villain!" He was pointing at Ned, and heads turned in the crowd as others identified the big gangling youth as the one accused. Ned made frantic efforts to evade capture but the cries of "Stop, thief!" followed him and he could make little progress. Then, as if suddenly recalling Jenny's presence, he changed direction and ran toward her. Instinctively, her only conscious thought the awareness of his danger, she slid down from the wall and pushed through the back of the crowd to meet him.

He was breathless and spent when he gained her side, the sweat standing in beads on his brow and upper lip, and she sensed his fear as if it were a living thing, reaching out tentacles to encompass her as well as himself.

"Over the wall, Ned!" she bade him. "There's a path—it leads to the graveyard, I think. You—"

"I'm going," he told her. "But keep this for me, will you? I daren't let them catch me with it."

He was gone, vaulting easily over the wall, before Jenny realized with dismay that the object he had thrust into her outstretched hand was the purse he had just stolen.

To her horror she heard a voice cry out from behind her, "That young girl has your purse, sir . . . I saw the thieving rogue pass it to her before he fled!" The voice was that of the young clergyman who had led them in prayer, Jenny recognized. She found herself surrounded, and as she looked from one to another of the hostile faces, she knew that she could expect no mercy from any of them . . . and least of all from the young cleric, who now held her in a viselike grip.

"Well?" he demanded coldly. "Do you deny that you have this gentleman's purse?"

Dumbly she shook her head, and he wrenched her around to face the owner of the purse. "Yield it up then." Jenny took the offending article from its hiding place and gave it to him, and he said triumphantly, "You see I was right, sir—the cutpurse *did* give it to her. She's his accomplice, no doubt, mere chit though she is . . . is that not so, wench?"

"No, sir," Jenny denied. "He gave it to me when he was running from you, but I'm not his accomplice. You saw me, sir, surely, when you invited prayers for Captain Wilkes's salvation . . . I have been seated on the wall close by you all morning. And—"

But the clergyman was not listening. Officiously he held out the purse and invited the owner to identify it as his property.

"Indeed yes, this is mine, and I am deeply indebted to you, young sir, for enabling me to recover it." The red face was smiling now, in pleasure and relief. "I'm from out of town and I have my night's lodging to pay for. If you will give it to me, I need trouble you no more, I—"

"Your pardon, sir, but the purse will be required as evidence when a charge is laid against the girl," the parson objected. "The thief has made his escape but I am sure that she can name him . . . is that not so, girl?"

Jenny repeated her headshake. "I am not his accomplice, sir, truly I am not. I beg you to believe me." She made her appeal to the owner of the purse, and he responded as she had hoped he would.

"I want no trouble, reverend sir—I have my money back now and I am prepared to accept the girl's word. After all if she has been sitting within sight of you all morning, she cannot have been aiding the pickpocket, can she?"

Several voices contradicted this assumption, some claiming to have seen the wink Ned gave her and all insisting that they had seen her jump from the wall and go to meet the thief, who had then—in their plain sight—slipped the purse to her.

"I want no trouble, gentlemen," he repeated. "And my wife will be awaiting my return to our hostelry with some anxiety if I am unduly delayed. We are due to leave London tomorrow morning by the stage. It's a question of time, you understand, I. . . ."

Another gentleman joined them at this juncture. He said smoothly, "The matter need take very little of your time, my good sir. It would seem that the girl has been caught red-handed in unlawful possession of your purse . . . that is so, is it not?" A chorus of voices confirmed his supposition. He gestured with a languid hand to the gallows. "As soon as they cut the malefactor's body down, the crowds will disperse, and then, sir, if you and the reverend gentleman accompany me to substantiate the charges against her, the girl can be taken into custody and—"

"Accompany you . . . where, sir?" the red-faced man wanted to know.

"Why, to Bow Street, sir. The magistrates sit there until eight of the clock. We will take a cab and the matter can be disposed of within the hour, so far as you are concerned. My name is Vickers, sir, and I am an officer of the court. If I inform their worships that you have pressing business elsewhere and must depart from the city tomorrow morning, the girl can be put up before them and an order made before the court closes."

"And my property will then be restored to me?" The red-faced man, his countenance redder than before, pointed, with some embarrassment, to the purse, which the young clergyman still retained. "Without it I cannot settle my score at the hostelry, as I explained to the reverend gentleman before you joined us. But he—"

"I told him it would be required as evidence," the clergyman put in. "I am right, am I not, Mister Vickers?"

"Indeed you are." Mr. Vickers was quick to take the point. "Then I take it the purse contains a considerable sum, Mister—er . . . what is your name, sir?"

"Clay, sir—Ephraim Clay of Maidenhead."

Mr. Vickers held out his hand for the purse. Feeling its weight, he observed shrewdly, "A very considerable sum . . . yes, indeed! May I ask you how much, Mister Clay?"

Ephraim Clay looked acutely unhappy. He glanced at Jenny and then swiftly away. "Tell me, sir, as an officer of the law—is it not a hanging matter, if the theft be of greater value than one shilling?"

"I—I did not steal the purse," Jenny faltered, appealing once more to the red-faced man. "I do beg you to believe me, Mister Clay. I am not a thief, sir, I—"

The lawyer ignored her. "Larceny of property worth more than one shilling is a capital offense, Mister Clay—and, my dear sir, it is your civic duty to take action against this girl if she has robbed you of *any* sum of money."

"She is very young. I have a daughter of her age. Poor child, she—"

"The law takes no cognizance of sex or age, sir," Vickers stated coldly, and a bakery owner came to his support.

"There are whores of her age, Mister Clay—aye, and younger! London is full of them. Those who steal from my shop are children, perdition take them . . . they're brought up to steal, taught how to do it by their parents. It's got to be stamped out, sir, so that honest folk can make a living."

"Then I may count on *you* to give evidence, sir?" Mr. Vickers inquired. He still had not opened the purse, Jenny realized, so perhaps, God willing, he might not do so.

"*Please*, sir," she whispered. "I didn't steal your purse. I'm not a thief, I—I would have given it back to you."

"Would you?" He looked searchingly into her face. "What is your name, girl?"

It was the first time anyone had asked her name,

Jenny thought bitterly as she supplied it, and was puzzled when she saw Ephraim Clay's ruddy face drain of its hectic color.

"That is my little girl's name," he confessed, visibly shaken. "And you are not unlike her, you—" he was interrupted by the Reverend Thorne.

"They are cutting down Wilkes's cadaver," he announced. "When the mob thins, we shall be able to make our way to Holborn—there is a hackney stand on the corner."

Mr. Clay, suddenly spurred into action, stepped forward and snatched his purse from the lawyer's hand.

"You asked me how much this contains, Mister Vickers," he said. "Well, sir, I will tell you—precisely eleven pence in copper coin! That is why it feels so heavy. You are no doubt aware that, where I come from, farm laborers refer to our pennies as cartwheels, and complain that their size and weight wear holes in their pockets."

Mr. Vickers, to Jenny's chagrin, threw back his head and laughed. "Your compassion does you credit, my dear Mister Clay—indeed it does. But it is, I assure you, misplaced. And on a legal point, my friend, you have stated before witnesses that you intend to settle your score at your hostelry with the contents of the purse. Do you seriously expect me to believe that you would settle it with pennies—come, sir, you must take me for a fool!"

Poor Clay stammered in confusion, and Jenny's brief hopes faded when, pressed by the lawyer, he admitted that he would be unwilling to swear, on oath, that his stolen purse contained only coppers. But he continued manfully to argue when, after walking to Holborn, they secured a hackney carriage to take them to Bow Street, and finally the lawyer, losing patience, suggested a compromise.

"Since you are the injured party, Mister Clay, I will bow to your sentiments. The charge shall be receiving and the sum involved one shilling and three-pence, provided these two gentlemen are willing to agree . . . which I think they are?"

The baker and the cleric inclined their heads, but Mr. Clay was still not satisfied. "But the sentence will be the same, will it not?"

"Indeed, sir, since it is arbitrary, that is inevitable. But I will, if you wish, myself represent the girl and enter an appeal for it to be commuted." He smiled and Jenny shivered involuntarily at the chill ruthlessness in his voice. "My fee, sir, will be two of the golden guineas from your purse."

Ephraim Clay took the coins from his purse and dropped them into Vickers's extended hand without further protest. To Jenny he said gruffly, when the hackney carriage pulled up outside the courthouse, "I have done what I can for you, girl. God grant it may be enough!"

She did not see him again. After a wait of over two hours in a cell filled to capacity with male and female malefactors of all ages, she was brought up before the magistrates and committed for trial.

Two days later a high court judge sentenced her to death by hanging and, in a weary voice, directed that she be taken to Newgate Prison to await execution. It was, Jenny remembered, her fifteenth birthday.

CHAPTER VII

Together with three other condemned prisoners, Jenny was taken to Newgate. It was, she reflected bitterly, very different from her first sight of the place, when Watt Sparrow had been her escort . . . was it, could it possibly have been only six days ago?

Then he had warned her not to look into the Common Side, lest the sights she saw there come as too great a shock to her. Now, shocked or not, she must not only look, she must enter its dreaded confines and, like her mother, endure the hideous discomfort of being chained, of being harshly ordered hither and thither by constables and jailers, and know—since no reprieve had yet been granted to her—that her only escape would be along the road that Captain Wilkes had traveled.

She was numb with fear, so stunned by all that had

happened to her as to be barely capable of coherent thought, and cowed, by the brutality of those in whose charge she had been, to an extent that rendered her mute and utterly defenseless. When the turnkey detailed to receive newly arrived prisoners asked her, not unkindly, if she had money to "pay her way," she could only shake her head in cringing silence, and dismissing her as probably imbecile, he drove her in front of him, as he might have driven an animal to slaughter, into a dark passageway between rows of locked cell doors. At its end he opened the gate of what appeared to Jenny's terrified eyes to be an animal cage, furnished only with scattered bales of straw and some low wooden platforms on which were crouched creatures so vile in appearance that at first sight they bore little resemblance to women or even to human beings. The floor was filthy, littered with soiled rags, and the remains of food. Here and there were motionless, huddled forms exhibiting no sign of life, even when one of the other inmates tripped or stumbled against them.

A ragged slattern, nursing a suckling child at her breast, was the first to observe and draw attention to Jenny's arrival in their midst. Her hoarse cry was echoed by a dozen others and the next moment Jenny found herself surrounded by a mob of shrieking harpies, who encircled her, their hands outstretched demanding "Garnish! Garnish!" in clamorous chorus.

Bewildered, she shrank from them. "Please . . . what do you want? I . . . don't understand."

From behind her a deep voice offered blasphemous enlightenment, and she turned, startled, to see that the voice belonged to a monstrous hag, seated alone on one of the low platforms, a blackened clay pipe clenched between her teeth. She was obscenely fat—

stomach, legs, and ankles swollen to gross proportions, her eyes almost lost in the rolls of flesh that covered her face—but she was, Jenny's bemused mind took in, the only one who was respectably dressed. Her gown of black velvet had outmoded panniers on either side of its skirt but it was clean, as were the white muslin kerchief about her neck and the mob cap crowning her head, from beneath which a few strands of lank, graying hair had been permitted to straggle.

"They ask only their due," the old woman repeated when Jenny continued to stare at her uncomprehendingly. "Where are your wits, girl? You don't get the run o' this place until you pays them their garnish . . . you've got a sye buck, haven't you?"

"No," Jenny faltered. "No, I—I have nothing."

"Nothing, is it? Not even a brown?"

"No, truly. Please, I—"

"Enough o' the gabbin', Meg," one of the women put in impatiently. "The snivelin' little chit's tellin' the truth—look at 'er! Too scared ter say boo to a goose. We'll take 'er duds fer payment—an I'll 'ave 'er shawl fer a start. Mine's mockered, I c'n do wiv it."

They were on her, tearing at her clothing with rapacious hands, and Jenny cried her fear aloud. The woman who had demanded her shawl seized it from her and draped it round her own stooped shoulders, twirling about in high delight to display it to others less fortunate, and they, in turn, endeavored to snatch it from her. The old woman, whom she had addressed as Meg, shouted at them to stop and, when they did so, held out an imperious hand.

"Give me the shawl, Hannah," she commanded, and the stoop-shouldered woman hesitated for a moment, swearing under her breath, and then sullenly took it off and tossed it onto the wooden platform.

" 'Tis a good shawl," she whined. "And I was needin' it, Meg—I was in sore need of it. Why—"

"A plague on you," old Meg returned, unmoved. She looked at Jenny who, stripped now to her shift, just as her mother had been, had slipped to her knees on the filthy, littered floor, weeping in hopeless despair. Meg's small bright eyes lit on the locket, which the others had been too excited to notice, and as Jenny belatedly tried to conceal it in the sagging front of her shift, the old hag was on her feet, and moving with unexpected speed, she made a grab at the ribbon from which it was suspended. The ribbon broke, the locket went tinkling to the floor, and before Jenny could retrieve it, Meg kicked it out of her reach.

"Well now, my pretty little *burick*!" she exclaimed. "What flam have you been tryin' to deceive me with, eh? So you've got nothin' indeed! *This* ain't nothin', not by a long chalk it ain't." Her swollen fingers closed about the locket, and she held it up, inviting the others to inspect her find. They clustered around, excited and envious, and the woman known as Hannah attempted to wrest the prize from her.

"You took the shawl, Auld Meg . . . you took my shawl off me. This is mine."

"Damn your body and eyes, you sneaking *didicoi*!" Auld Meg caught her a stinging blow across the mouth, but Hannah refused to relinquish the locket, and they struggled for its possession, screaming abuse at each other, with the rest gleefully cheering them on.

Suddenly Jenny could bear no more, and a sort of madness seized her. The locket contained the small scrap of blue ribbon that was now her last precious link with the happier days of the past and the father she had loved, and no matter what they did to her, she would not let them rob her of that. She flung herself at Hannah like a wild animal, clawing at her face, and the woman, taken by surprise, fell back with a cry of alarm, leaving the locket in Meg's hand.

Meg cackled with delight and made to retreat to her platform, dangling the locket from its torn ribbon as if challenging Jenny to pit her frail strength against her own vast bulk, taunting her with foul-mouthed suggestions as to how and from whom she had acquired it. But, reaching the platform, she stumbled, and Jenny was on her before the ungainly old hag could recover her balance.

"Give it to me!" the girl pleaded. "It's mine—give it back to me!"

Her small hands closed about Auld Meg's, seeking, in a frenzy of despair, to force them open, but when the woman ignored her plea, she buried her teeth in the fat white fingers. Her teeth grated on bone, and with a cry of pain the creature let the locket fall and staggered back to her seat, clasping her bleeding fingers to her bosom. No one else moved as Jenny bent down to pick up the locket; there was a shocked silence, broken only by Meg's outraged cries, and then Hannah whimpered, "The little hellion's mad—stark, starin' mad!"

A hubbub of voices echoed the accusation. The women formed a circle around her but none approached her, and Hannah, her earlier quarrel with Meg forgotten, clambered up onto the platform to examine the injury, clucking her tongue in sympathetic concern.

"The devil take her—look what she's done to Auld Meg's finger! Bitten it to the bone, she has." She drew

Jenny's shawl about her thin shoulders and faced her furiously. "What's the hell-cat bein' topped for—murder? She'll murder us if we ain't careful, and that's God's truth! Well, you whore's get . . . what have they sent you in here for, eh? Tell us, you sneaking little doxy!"

"Leave her be." Meg's voice, harsh and authoritative, broke into the tirade. "It don't do to rouse her kind, so just leave her be. I'll have my own back on 'er when the time's ripe."

They obeyed her, and the circle that had hemmed her in, to Jenny's heartfelt relief, melted away, the women still chattering excitedly among themselves.

Left alone, Jenny's anger faded into sick despair, and like some wounded creature of the wild, she crept into a dark corner of her malodorous prison and lay down, her face buried in her hands and her body shaken by sobs. None of the women came near her, and even when the jailer brought a blackened caldron of evil-smelling gruel and some crusts of bread for their evening meal, she made no attempt to join in the snarling rush, which, it seemed, was a necessary prelude to obtaining her share.

Meg's share was carried to her by Hannah, and the jailer, when he returned to remove the caldron, brought with him a bottle, which also found its way into Meg's hands. Within half an hour she and her cronies had drunk themselves into a state of noisy good humor, crowding round the platform on which a single candle provided them with a glimmer of light, toasting each other and emitting peals of cackling laughter, as Meg and Hannah continued to wrangle over the stolen shawl. It passed from one to the other but finally, following an outburst, the shawl ended in Auld Meg's possession, and Hannah, expelled from her place on the platform, was forced to slink away empty-handed, muttering curses in an excess of maudlin fury.

When, at last, the candle spluttered into extinction and loud snores succeeded the shrieks of laughter, Jenny endeavored to compose herself for sleep, but scarcely had she gathered a few wisps of straw to ward off the chill of the damp stone floor than a thin, dark-haired girl edged up to her, a finger to her lips.

"I saved you something to eat," she whispered. "But I didn't dare bring it till Auld Meg was asleep." She thrust a coarse earthenware bowl into Jenny's hands. The gruel was cold, the bread iron-hard and moldy, but it was food, and under the other girl's urging, Jenny—whose last meal had been taken twenty-four hours previously—eagerly choked it down.

"Thank you," she said. "Oh, thank you for that."

"You stood up to the old bag," the slatternly girl returned admiringly.

"I had to," Jenny confessed. "I couldn't let her steal my locket. I had to make her give it back to me."

"All the same, you'd have been wiser not to, my girl. Meg rules the roost here, and all the others do as she says. They'll have it in for you. If you'll take my advice, you'll pay the jailer his lucre first thing to-morrow morning and get yourself moved."

"But I haven't any money, I—"

"You have the locket. Give him that, it'll be more than enough to buy you a place on the Master Side, with food and bedding and some fresh clothes. Believe me"—the girl's tone was grave—"it will be more than your life's worth to stay here. They'll starve you, if they don't do anything worse."

Jenny's cold fingers closed about the locket. "I—I can't. It's all I have, it means a lot to me, you see."

"More than your life?" her companion asked starkly.

"No, but . . . I'm under sentence of death and—"

"Not for murder?"

"Oh, no—for receiving stolen property. I—"

"You'll be reprieved," the older girl told her confidently. "I was—it's a change of policy. Women convicted of minor offenses are to be transported, not hanged. That's what they say anyhow. You have an appeal lodged?"

Jenny thought of Lawyer Vickers and stifled a sigh. Despite the generous fee paid to him on her behalf by the man Ned had robbed, Mr. Vickers had said little in her defense in court, and she could not be certain that he had lodged an appeal against her sentence.

"I think so. I'm not sure. You see—"

"Better make sure," the other girl advised her. She had an educated voice, Jenny realized, for all her slatternly appearance and her concern seemed to be genuine. "Have you no relatives, no friends who will help you?"

"I have friends," Jenny confirmed. "But they weren't in court. They—" She felt tears welling in her eyes. The absence of Dr. Fry and Doll Prunty—and even that of Watt Sparrow—had worried and wounded her more than she cared to admit. "They probably did not know what happened to me . . . everything happened so quickly and there was no way I could get word to them." She explained the circumstances of her arrest and trial, and the other girl nodded her understanding.

"Yes, that's all too often the case," she said thoughtfully. "What's your name, lass?"

"Jenny—Jenny Taggart."

"Well, Jenny, if you'll take my advice, you'll strike a bargain with the jailer for that locket of yours—he'll get word to your friends for you. Then at least they can make sure that an appeal is lodged on your behalf. Do it first thing tomorrow, before Meg's awake." The girl got to her feet.

"Couldn't you stay?" Jenny asked shyly.

"No—I have my place over there. But you are welcome to share it with me . . . with us." In the dim light Jenny saw that a smile was curving her lips. She led the way to the opposite corner of the prison ward and halted by a bundle of straw that had been roughly fashioned into a crib, on which lay a tiny morsel of humanity, wrapped in a shawl. "My son," the older girl whispered. "He is the reason why I am here and why, much as I might wish to, I cannot call upon *my* family and friends to help me." She offered no other explanation but lay down, her arm in a protective circle around the sleeping child. "Try to sleep, Jenny," she added gently. "There is plenty of straw for all three of us."

Next morning Jenny was roused by the jailer shaking her shoulder. He said, before she could speak, "You've friends come ter visit you. They sent this in for yer." He draped a shawl, which she recognized as Doll Prunty's, around her shoulders, and Jenny's heart leapt. So they had not forgotten her, they had come, at last, to help her . . . she was on her feet in an instant, hugging Doll's familiar shawl about her shivering body.

"Looks as if they guessed right, don't it, sendin' you that in advance, so ter speak?" The jailer grinned. "You need it . . . old blubber n' guts 'as bin up to 'er tricks again. Well, we'll see about that." There was malice in his voice, and as he led Jenny past the

platform on which Auld Meg still snored, he aimed a
kick at her. She stirred, raised herself on one elbow,
and regarded him with bleary-eyed resentment.

"Let a body sleep, can't yer, Jack Foley?" she
grumbled. "If a body can't get peace ter sleep in
clink, where can she get it? Take yerself off, yer mean
chiseler an'—" She caught sight of Jenny then, and
her voice rose to an angry bellow. "Hey, where're you
takin' that snivelin' little piece o' hempseed? Ter keep
'er appointment wi' Jack Ketch, is it?"

"No, it ain't," the turnkey snapped, enjoying her
rage. "I'm takin' 'er acrost ter the Master Side, that's
where I'm takin' 'er, you old tabby! An' not before
time, by the looks o' things. You're a wicked old
woman, Meg—a real wicked old woman, d'yer know
that? *You'll* end up on the nubbing cheat if yer don't
mend yer ways!"

Meg affected not to have heard him. She scrambled
up and stood looking down at Jenny with hate in
her eyes.

"If you think you've got away from me, then you'd
better think again! I shan't forget what you done, I
shan't *never* forget. I got this ter remember you by,
ain't I?" She held up her hand with its swollen, blood-
caked fingers and delivered herself of a string of
blasphemous oaths. Jenny cowered away from her,
clinging to the jailer for protection and feeling the
terror of the previous night return.

"Stow yer gab, Meg," the turnkey admonished. He
picked Jenny up in his arms and carried her outside.
As the door of the ward clanged shut behind him, he
set her down, shaking his head in wonder as he looked
at her.

"Gawd, lass, small you may be but you 'aven't 'arf
stirred up Auld Meg! I reckon yer friends 'ave come

i' the nick o' time . . . she'd 'ave 'ad your guts fer garters if you'd 'ad ter stay in there much longer. What did yer do ter the old tabby?"

Jenny's teeth were chattering so badly that she could not answer him. He took her by the arm, still shaking his head in bewilderment, and led her through to the Master Side. Reaching the flight of stone steps that, so short a time ago, she had climbed on her way to visit Captain Wilkes, her strength failed her and the turnkey had again to carry her. "There, now, my little lass, don't take on so," he besought her. "Yer friends 'ave paid yer dues—thirteen shillings an' a stever—yer'll live i' the lap o' luxury from now on. An' they brought food for yer an' fresh clothes, an' I'm ter see as you gets beddin' an' candles an' a decent meal each an' every day. What more can you ask?"

"Where are they, where are my friends, Mister Foley?" Jenny managed when, at last, he set her down in a cell that was a replica of the one Harry Wilkes had occupied.

Jailer Foley gestured to the clothing laid out on the wooden bed. "I'll bring 'em up, lass, don't you worry. But if I was you, I'd get meself into that clean clobber there before you sees 'em. Wouldn't want a fine gennelman like Doctor Fry ter think as we've bin neglectin' yer, would yer now?"

So Dr. Fry had come . . . Jenny's heart lifted. When the jailer had gone, she donned the dress—also one of Doll's, she recognized. It was several sizes too large for her but it was clean and warm and she felt very much better as her trembling fingers set its voluminous skirt to rights.

When Dr. Fry entered the cell a few minutes later, Watt Sparrow was with him, and Jenny, unable to contain her pleasure and relief at the sight of them, burst into tears. The doctor, as he had been wont to do when she was a child, sat down and took her on to his knee, soothing and comforting her with almost womanly tenderness. Watt poured out a glass of wine from the well-filled basket they had brought with them and held it to her lips, coaxing her to drink it and refusing to put the glass down until the last drop was gone.

"We would have been here long before this, Jenny, my poor child," the doctor said, "had we known of your plight. But alas we did not . . . we imagined you safely in the country with the Pruntys."

"In the country? The Pruntys are in the country, sir?" Jenny could scarcely believe that she had heard him aright.

He inclined his head, exchanging a meaningful look with Watt Sparrow before replying. "It was thought advisable for them to absent themselves for a while, my dear. A Red—that is, a Bow Street officer had been making inquiries concerning our poor friend Captain Wilkes's sojourn at the Three Fools. So Doll's uncle took charge, and they left on the night of the hanging . . . taking you with them, we supposed. It was not until Doll sent word, asking me to look after you, that we realized you were *not* with them. And then Sparrow here dragged the story of your misadventures from the unspeakable Ned Munday. That's so, is it not, Sparrow?"

The little man nodded. His tone was angry as he took up the story. "Aye, that I did. First off all the young rogue would say was that 'e'd been on the run when 'e seen yer an' that you'd 'elped 'im make 'is getaway. Worse . . . 'e swore you'd gone back ter the Three Fools wiv'aht waitin' fer me ter take yer, so I didn't worry, see? An' I kept away from the Three Fools meself fer a day or so, till the heat cooled, so to speak, an' I didn't know no different."

Under the gentle prompting of Dr. Fry, the sorry tale came out, and Watt Sparrow swore under his breath.

He said, with some satisfaction, "O'course, I went after Ned then—one or two of us did—an' we give 'im the drubbin' 'e deserved, the caw-handed young chiseler! Didn't come ter see after you, did 'e, lass?"

"No," Jenny confessed. "No, he didn't. But I suppose he was afraid to, in case anyone recognized him." But that, she knew in her heart, was not the reason why Ned had not lifted a hand to help her. He had been afraid, of course, but afraid for his own skin and prepared to let her take the punishment he had merited if it meant that he could go free. "You didn't hurt him, did you, Watt? Not badly, I mean?"

The little cockney shrugged. "We only give 'im what 'e deserved, Jenny."

Dr. Fry confirmed his claim. "Munday committed the cardinal sin when he saved himself at your expense, Jenny. I've told you before, my dear, there is honor among thieves. The underworld has its own code of conduct, and Munday has been ostracized . . . sooner or later, someone will inform on him and that will be the end of it."

Seeing Jenny's distress at this harsh prophecy, Dr. Fry took her hand in his. "All this talk of the despicable Munday has made me forget the good news I have for you."

"*Good* news? Oh, Doctor, have I been reprieved?"

He smiled, patting the hand he held. "You have, my child. Your sentence has been commuted to transportation for"—he eyed her searchingly before continuing—"transportation for life, Jenny child, to New South Wales."

For a moment she could not speak. The girl in the prison ward had spoken of transportation, she recalled, and Dr. Fry had mentioned it before. But for life, for the whole of her life was she to be sent thousands of miles away from England, to an unknown land, peopled only by savages? She drew a sobbing breath. "Oh, Doctor, *must* I go? Isn't there anything that you could do? I'd be so thankful— Doctor, I'd work for you all my days, truly I would, to repay the debt. If only you will help me, sir, I—"

"My poor child," the doctor said. "It does not lie within my power, alas. I wish, with all my heart, that it did." He dealt with her as kindly as he could, at pains to point out that transportation, even to an unknown place, was preferable to its alternative of life imprisonment in England. "There are too many unfortunates confined in prisons throughout the country and in the Hulks, Jenny. Since the American Revolution, convicts cannot be sent out there, and the result is gross overcrowding here, with thousands dying because of the conditions in which they are kept. You saw what they were like in the Hulks when you visited your mother, did you not?"

"Yes," Jenny admitted shamefacedly.

Dr. Fry went on. "The government, in a laudable desire to effect economies"—there was a note of cynicism in his deep voice—"believes that it will be advantageous to establish a colony in New South Wales, without robbing Great Britain of her inhabitants, by dispatching convicts to lay the foundations of a new settlement there." He sighed. "They aim, I have heard on reliable authority, to send a fleet of close on a dozen ships, including naval vessels, transports, and storeships, under the command of a captain of the Royal Navy named Arthur Phillip, who is designated governor. Some seven or eight hundred convicted persons are to sail with him and the ships are now being fitted out."

"When, Doctor?" Jenny's throat ached with unshed tears but she forced herself to ask the question calmly. "When is it to be? When will they sail?" Her heart turned to stone when he answered pityingly, "In May, child, or so my inquiries elicited. The ships are at Plymouth and a number of convicts already on board."

Watt Sparrow, his small, thin face puckered into a smile, did his best to restore her spirits.

"I've 'eard tell as New Sath Wales is a beautiful place, Jenny lass—wot they calls a tropical paradise, wiv' flowers an' palm trees an' the like. An' the place the ships is makin' for is called Botany Bay, on account o' the flowers, see? It'll be a new life for you, me little duck. Cheer up, me lass—it ain't the end o' the world."

"It will be," Jenny whispered. "Oh, Watt, it will be! Without any of you, without Mam, and Doll, and Nick . . . without Doctor Fry." Her brave pretense of calm was shattered, and tears overwhelmed her.

Dr. Fry, who had long prided himself on his imperturbability in any circumstances, took refuge in a fit of coughing before hoarsely requesting Watt Sparrow to pour him a glass of wine.

"This waif," he confessed, "is breaking my heart, Sparrow—and damme, I never imagined I had a heart to break!" He swallowed the wine as if the taste were bitter and added savagely, "Perdition take the government of this country and may Sydney and Nepean rot in hell!"

Jenny clung to him, her frail body racked by sobs.

VOYAGE
TO THE UNKNOWN

CHAPTER VIII

The thirty covered wagons had been drawn up in Newgate's east courtyard since the previous night; now, with their teams of horses harnessed to their shafts, they awaited the convicts sentenced to transportation, whom they had been hired to convey to Portsmouth.

The turnkey roused Jenny before dawn and told her brusquely that she must descend to the yard.

"Take what you own," he advised. "But guard it well, for there'll be no difference 'twixt Master an' Common Side in them wagons—nor in the transports neither, I shouldn't reckon."

She shrank from him in nameless fear, newly wakened from sleep, and he eyed her pityingly as he poured a tankard of wine from one of Dr. Fry's bottles and thrust it into her hand.

"Best drink it, lass, whilst you've the chance. If you take it in among the mob, they'll rob you of it, sure's fate."

Jenny obeyed him, managing a few sips of the wine, but her teeth were chattering and she set the tankard down, pushing it and the half-finished bottle across the table toward him. "Please . . . have them for yourself if you want them, I . . . as a token of my—my thanks."

The jailer grinned. He drained the tankard, wiped his mouth with the back of his hand, and, tucking the bottle under his arm, made for the door. "I'll give you five minutes to dress—then I'll come for you. Make haste now!"

Shivering, she donned Doll Prunty's dress and shawl, careful to tuck her locket out of sight, and with her other few possessions wrapped in a neckerchief, when the jailer returned, stumbled after him down the cold stone steps, making a brave effort to fight down her tears.

"How long will it take us to get to—to wherever the ships are?" she asked him, when he halted to unlock the door into the yard.

"You'll be going to Portsmouth," he answered. "And that's a tidy way but I dunno how long it'll take. A coupla days, maybe. The Botany Bay Fleet's at Spithead, they say. Nah then, me lass. . . ." He became brisk and, grasping her arm, led her to where half a dozen other women were waiting to enter one of the wagons. Like herself, they came from the Master Side and wore only leg irons, but peering ahead of them, Jenny saw that all were having to submit to having manacles affixed to their wrists, to which chains were attached. When it came to her turn, the nearest wagon was full and she was pushed unceremoniously toward the next, being the first to clamber into its dark, malodorous interior. A jailer pushed her to its far end, deftly threading the end of her chain through a ringbolt on the straw-covered floor, on which she found herself compelled to crouch like an animal, held fast by the chain.

Other women—all strangers, Auld Meg was not one of them she saw with sick relief—were hustled in after her, many of them half-naked or in rags and two with small children wailing piteously in their arms. All, with the exception of the children, were chained, and when the doors of the wagon clanged shut, they set up a loud clamor, complaining of discomfort and over-crowding.

It was hot and airless, and the stench of unwashed bodies soon became well nigh unbearable; the straw on which she lay was dirty and verminous, the noisy grief of her companions so infectious that she found herself weeping with them, unable to control her emotion. They were afraid and she sensed their fear, as if it were a living thing, there to add to the torment of their long, unhappy journey.

They left London behind, and through the slats Jenny was able to catch tantalizing glimpses of open country, of trees and hedgerows, peacefully grazing cattle and sunlit grass. She raised herself with difficulty on one elbow, staring out, her heart close to breaking, and from behind her a voice croaked bitterly, "Look well on it, child, for we'll not see its like again. We're looking our last on England, heaven help us!"

The realization that this was the truth struck Jenny with the force of a physical blow. She let her head fall onto her manacled hands and wept soundlessly, too numb with despair even to rouse herself when, at noon, the wagon creaked to a halt and a man's voice proclaimed with gruff cheerfulness, "Grub's up, me lassies! Courtesy o' Cap'n Phillip of 'is Majesty's Navy . . . the same as is ter be yer guv'nor when yer gets ter Botany Bay!"

"A pox on Captain Phillip," a red-haired woman retorted savagely. "He don't care no more for the likes o' us than any of 'em do—let 'im rot in hell, I say!"

Captain Arthur Phillip, Royal Navy, appointed captain-general of the expedition to Botany Bay and governor of the new settlement to be established there, sat stiffly in the First Lord's anteroom at the Admiralty awaiting, with what patience he could muster, Admiral Lord Howe's summons.

Since hoisting his broad pennant on board his flagship, H.M.S. *Sirius,* at the beginning of May, Arthur Phillip had spent ten days in London. In that time he had called on as many government ministers and pleaded his case with twice that number of their under secretaries and department heads. From some he had contrived to wring a few minor concessions and promises—which might or might not be kept—but most of them had been interested only in learning the date of his departure.

Sir Evan Nepean, under secretary to Viscount Sydney at the home office, was, he knew, at this moment closeted with the first lord. He had been present during his own abortive interview with Lord Sydney the previous day and was now, no doubt, engaged in supplying the first lord with details of all that had passed between them . . . his complaints, Phillip thought bitterly, and his reluctance to sail until these had been rectified. Perhaps he would be wasting his breath if he repeated them, but Lord Howe was a seaman and therefore more likely to understand and sympathize with his problems than the civilian representatives of a parsimonious government, whose sole purpose was, it seemed, to rid themselves of him at the lowest conceivable cost.

At all events Admiral Howe was his last hope—the Botany Bay Fleet was at Spithead, and Phillip was aware that he could delay the sailing of his eleven ill-equipped ships no longer. Once his crews received their arrears of pay and the last batch of convicts from Newgate were delivered, he would have to get under way. . . .

"Sir—Commodore Phillip. . . ." It was the flag lieutenant, courteous and impeccably uniformed. "His lordship will see you now, if you will be so good as to step this way, sir."

He was announced and, greetings exchanged, waved to a chair opposite the one occupied by Sir Evan Nepean. The First Lord, however, did not seat himself; he continued to pace the narrow confines of carpeted floor between his desk and the window—a sign, which Phillip recognized with a sinking heart, of his displeasure.

A tall man, of impressive presence, the admiral was beloved of all the seamen who had ever served under his command, but he had a reputation for taciturnity, and his dark-complexioned face—which had earned him the lower deck nickname of Black Dick—wore a morose expression that, together with his restless pacing, boded ill for the success of Phillip's mission. Nepean, on the other hand, was smiling, although he did not look entirely at ease, and when Phillip seated himself, the under secretary avoided his gaze, fixing his own on one of the seascapes hanging on the wall, his plump fingers fidgeting nervously with his watch fob.

"Sir Evan tells me you're not satisfied with—ah—the manner in which the ships under your command have been equipped and supplied." Lord Howe halted, to regard his visitor from beneath frowning brows. "I'll thank you to tell me why, Mister Phillip. You've had four months to prepare for sea, damme! What do you lack?"

The list of his needs was so lengthy and daunting that Captain Phillip hesitated before starting to detail the more urgent of them, but remembering the appalling conditions in which his unwilling passengers were confined in the holds of his six badly found transport vessels, he plunged in.

"We lack medical supplies, my lord, and antiscorbutics. I have asked repeatedly for essence of malt and lime juice and received only what will suffice for His Majesty's ships under my command. Your lordship may not be aware that the convicted felons I am to carry to Botany Bay were sent to me without clothing—and this includes many of the women, of whom there are almost two hundred. They have been battened down in the holds while the ships lay in the river, some of them for four months, my lord, and they have been permitted no fresh provisions. There are serious outbreaks of fever among them. On board the *Alexander*, my chief surgeon, Doctor White, reports that over half the male convicts are afflicted, and he fears a wholesale outbreak, unless the sanitation of their quarters can be improved. He has requested oil of tar from the dockyard, fresh vegetables and wine for the sick but—"

Lord Howe interrupted brusquely, "Were these convicts not suffering from jail fever when they boarded the transports?"

"A number were, my lord," Arthur Phillip admitted unhappily.

He had besought Lord Sydney to order that only fit and healthy prisoners might be sent to him—if he were to found a settlement in Botany Bay at the end of his eight-month voyage, it was madness to take out the aged and the infirm. Yet these formed an inordinately high proportion of the unfortunates now languishing in the overcrowded holds of the hired Indiamen at Spithead.

He had asked for men with skills to be selected from among the convicts sentenced to deportation; he had particularly specified that he would need artisans and carpenters, farmers and gardeners to build huts and enclosures, clear ground, plant crops, and care for cattle, but instead they had sent him, quite indiscriminately, the scum of the jails—pickpockets, footpads, and coiners, without regard for their fitness to fill the role of pioneers. He had begged for women with even rudimentary training in nursing and dressmaking but they had sent him unclothed whores, many suffering from venereal disease and a number in the last stages of pregnancy. And virtually all were town dwellers, hailing from the stews and bawdy houses, the slums and rookeries of London. . . .

He started to explain and then broke off, conscious that Nepean was glowering at him, and that the admiral, who was in no way responsible for the selection of his wretched passengers, was about to tell him so, with a wealth of righteous indignation. He hastily changed his tack.

"My lord, we are deficient in ordnance stores. My requisition for small-shot for my marines has not been filled. The men have only what they carried in their packs and cartouche boxes on joining. The six-pounder guns on iron carriages I was promised by Sir Charles Middleton—eight weeks ago, my lord—have not been delivered. I anticipate that these will be needed for our defense when we land, should the native Indians—whose presence in considerable numbers was reported by the late Captain Cook—prove hostile toward us."

Admiral Howe looked shocked for a moment and then recovered himself. "Requisition small-shot for your immediate needs from your escorting frigate—the *Hyaena*—before you part company with her. And you shall have authority to purchase the ordnance stores you are deficient in at Rio or the Cape. You already have authority to provision and buy livestock in Capetown, have you not? Then buy your musket balls there . . . damme, Captain Phillip, you're not likely to require many until you land in New South Wales, are you?"

He had only four companies of marines—two hundred officers and men—distributed among the transports, to mount guard over some five hundred eighty male felons, Phillip thought, but he shook his powdered head, his face carefully impassive. The convicts would not know that their guards were virtually unarmed, and, he supposed cynically, the civilian masters of the Indiamen need not be told, lest they demand that the prisoners be kept in irons below deck throughout the voyage. He drew a deep breath.

"I am to be responsible for the lives of close on eight hundred unhappy souls, my lord, and I deem it my duty to deliver them to their destination in good health and spirits, so that they may lay the foundations of the colony His Majesty's government has commanded me to set up in New South Wales."

Sir Evan Nepean was unable to control his impatience any longer. "Bear in mind, sir," he said harshly, his round face suffused with angry color, "that these 'unhappy souls' are criminals, of whom their country is desirous to be rid. They are not embarking on a sea voyage for their health, 'pon my soul! You have been chosen to command the Botany Bay Expedition, my dear Captain Phillip, because his lordship and I and, indeed, Lord Sydney, have the utmost faith in your ability to overcome such minor inconveniences as may arise. And I daresay you've exaggerated some of these, as time will prove . . . although your keen sense of responsibility does you credit. I should, however, remind you that the settlement you are to found will be what, I believe, one of the newspapers called 'A Colony of Disgracefuls.' His Majesty's government has no great hope that it will even be able to repay the heavy cost of its establishment, but if you can render it self-supporting within twelve months of your landing, you will, sir, have discharged the most important of your responsibilities."

Lord Howe referred him to the controller, Sir Charles Middleton, and dismissed him, a wintry smile belying the conventional good wishes he offered. Phillip had a brief and somewhat acrimonious interview with the controller and boarded the mail coach to Portsmouth with Middleton's assertion that he would be glad to see the end of "this disagreeable and troublesome business" still ringing in his ears.

Seated in the stuffy interior of the vehicle, with his eyes closed, he thought long and hard about the voyage on which he was about to embark and about the myriad problems facing him, which somehow he must contrive to overcome. His fleet, collected piece-meal, was by no means well suited for a voyage into the unknown but he could expect, he now knew, no further help from either the government or the admiralty.

The three storeships and the six transports for the convicts had been chartered from the East India Company, and only one was of more than four hundred tons burthen. Manned by merchant crews, their eventual destination was China, where it was intended that they should load with tea for the return voyage. The transports—*Alexander, Lady Penrhyn, Charlotte, Scarborough, Friendship,* and *Prince of Wales* —had all been fitted out as temporary troop transports, by the provision of two-tiered wooden bunks in their holds. To guard against mutiny or any escape attempts by their convict passengers, a number of additional precautions had been taken, in the form of strong bulkheads dividing the 'tween decks, and cross-bar bolts and locks on the hatches, where sentinels were posted in pairs.

During the months of waiting, he himself had ordered the provision of barricades on the upper decks, abaft the mainmast, to enable the convicts to exercise in daylight and in the fresh air, which, he hoped, when they got to sea, might lead to an improvement in their health. The ships' masters, to a man, had disapproved of these orders, particularly where the women were concerned, and to overcome their objections, the bulk of the marines—whom he had intended originally to carry on board his flagship —had had to be transferred to the transports, to act as guards. And his marines were men, Phillip reflected ruefully. However well-disciplined, they had the same lusts and desires as other men and were just as liable

to be corrupted by women convicts of doubtful virtue
as were the merchant seamen . . . more so, perhaps,
since they were required to watch over the women's
quarters and stand sentry over the hatchways at night.
One ship, the *Lady Penrhyn*, carried female convicts
only; the rest were divided, in small batches, among
the other ships—the *Alexander* being excepted, because of the sickness that had broken out among her
one hundred ninety male prisoners.

The transfer of the marines had reduced his flagship to a total company of a hundred sixty officers
and men, and although officially designated a ship of
war, H.M.S. *Sirius*, her commander was fully aware,
represented yet another example of government parsimony. She was of six hundred tons burthen and had
been built as a victualler for the East India Company
and named the *Berwick*, but had been accidentally set
on fire before completion. Burned to the waterline,
the admiralty had purchased her bottom cheaply and
fitted her out with the refuse of the yards . . . so badly
that after only two voyages to the West Indies and
America she had been returned to the dockyard for
a complete overhaul. Now renamed *Sirius*, with
twenty guns hurriedly put on board her, she was considered adequate for the defense of the convoy and of
the proposed settlement at Botany Bay but . . .
Phillip sighed deeply. She would have to be, since she
and the little brig *Supply*—of eight guns, one hundred
seventy tons, and a crew of fifty—were the only
naval vessels under his command and the only ships
he would be permitted to retain, once the landing of
people and stores had been completed, seven or eight
months hence.

Leaning back in the swaying coach, he found himself wondering how many of the twelve hundred-odd

souls about to embark—less than half of them willingly—on this ill-planned venture could hope to survive it, himself included. At least, he consoled himself, he had some good, reliable officers who, God willing, would share the heavy burden of his responsibility. His second-in-command, John Hunter, at forty-eight, only a year younger than himself, had been given post rank on appointment to the *Sirius*. Hunter's patron was Lord Howe and there were those who had expressed surprise because the first lord had not obtained command of the expedition for him. But Hunter himself had made it clear, from the day of joining, that he was satisfied to serve in a subordinate capacity, and Arthur Phillip reflected thankfully that he could wish for no more loyal second. John Hunter had been given a dormant commission, appointing him acting governor in the event of his own illness or death, and this pleased them both, since neither had any great liking for the officer named as lieutenant governor, Major Robert Ross, the Marine Corps commandant.

And it was not service prejudice alone that dictated his feelings towards Ross, Phillip told himself. The man was pompous, aggravating, and absurdly jealous of his dignity, full of querulous complaints and overbearing in manner . . . and his pessimism concerning the expedition's chances of success was undermining morale. It was having a bad effect even on his own officers and men, and indeed, the commandant's only friend appeared to be his second-in-command, Captain James Campbell. Ross's two best officers, Captains Watkin Tench and David Collins—the latter appointed judge-advocate of the new colony—both efficient and likeable young men, were already at loggerheads with him; his junior subalterns and the rank and file cordially detested him.

But to weigh in the balance against the marine commandant were his naval officers, the majority of whom he himself had chosen—Henry Lidgett Ball, commanding the *Supply*; William Bradley, first lieutenant of the *Sirius*; and her second lieutenant, Philip Gidley King . . . Phillip smiled. Although only thirty, King was his closest friend; they had served together in his last command, the *Europe*, and King was, as he had anticipated, proving a tower of strength. So, too, were his naval secretary, Midshipman Henry Brewer, and the colony's surgeon-general designate, Dr. John White. Sharing his concern for the unfortunate convicts, all three had done battle with the purveyors, the contractors' representatives, the dockyard and prison authorities, and their efforts, in the teeth of official opposition, had wrought considerable improvement in the convicts' conditions and supplies.

The chaplain, Reverend Richard Johnson, who might have been expected to lend his support to their humanitarian endeavors, had, on the other hand, exhibited more concern for the souls of his unhappy charges than for their bodily suffering. In his mid-thirties and a nonconformist of passionate conviction, Reverend Johnson had preached eloquent sermons on board the various transports but had indignantly refused to descend to the holds, for fear of catching an infection from their wretched occupants. He and his acid-tongued wife had elected to travel in the store-ship *Golden Grove*, which carried no convicts, but they complained almost as much as Major Ross of their own conditions and discomfort, and the chaplain had taken offense when, with the best of intentions,

Phillip had requested him to stress the need for moral rectitude when preaching to the women convicts on board the *Lady Penrhyn*, rather than seek for converts to his faith.

But . . . Reverend Johnson had been, like Major Ross, a nominee of Lord Sydney's, and both, according to His Majesty's secretary of state for home affairs, were keen agriculturists and, on this account alone, would be of inestimable value to the new colony. Personal acquaintance had caused him to doubt this assertion, particularly in Ross's case but . . . Captain Phillip's head drooped. Lulled by the motion of the coach, he slept. . . .

Unaware that they had been occupying their commodore's anxious thoughts during his journey from London, Major Ross and the chaplain were engaged in an altercation in the flagship's wardroom.

"I tell you, Major," Reverend Johnson said indignantly, "it must have occurred when I was on board the *Scarborough* this afternoon. I was reading aloud from *Pilgrim's Progress* to some of the convicts, and the money and my watch simply vanished! The watch is a fine silver one, engraved with my initials. I"—he passed an agitated hand through his thinning, unpowdered hair—"it was a gift from my patron at Medbury. I prize it very highly, sir."

The marine commandant, sipping a glass of claret, eyed him with lofty condescension, his glance calculated to assert his own undoubted social superiority and High Church persuasion. Like the chaplain, he was married, but with the exception of his eldest son —who had accompanied him as a volunteer—he had chosen to leave his wife and family behind and go alone to the new colony. Robert Ross was a tall, thin man with a pinched, humorless face and a receding chin, whose uniform, although well pressed, was shabby and hung on him a trifle untidily as if it had been tailored originally for a stouter figure.

"I know my duty, Mister Johnson," Ross snapped. "And you may assure your—er—wife that I will do it, whoever is or is not on board this ship." Again he made to turn away, as if to seek more congenial company, and this time the chaplain, abashed, made no attempt to detain him.

Next morning, following the ceremonial hoisting of colors, he received a summons to attend Major Ross on deck. A sergeant and two private marines were standing stiffly to attention at the commandant's back, a fettered prisoner cringing between them, of whom the chaplain could see little, save that he was small and clad in rags.

"Is this your watch, sir?" Major Ross questioned crisply.

The silver hunter, offered for his inspection on the sergeant's extended palm, was indeed his, and Richard Johnson claimed it with immense relief. He started to voice his thanks but the major waved him to silence with an imperiously raised hand. There was an odd gleam of something resembling pleasure in his cold eyes as he turned to the men guarding the prisoner. "Seize him up, Sergeant," he ordered. "Is the surgeon present?"

"I'm here, sir." Johnson saw young Assistant Surgeon Lowes step forward. He did not hear all that passed between the two officers but, catching the words "two hundred lashes," he recoiled in horror, and his horror grew when he obtained his first clear look at the quaking prisoner. The thief was hardly more than a boy, puny and undersized, Johnson saw as the marines stripped him of his shirt and started to drag him to the grating, which had been rigged at the midship's gangway.

"Sir . . . Parson-sir, don't let 'em flog me!" The wretched boy was appealing to him for mercy, the chaplain realized. They had pinioned his wrists and he held them out in piteous entreaty, the tears streaming down his pale, twitching face. "I didn't mean no 'arm, sir. I'd of given the watch back to yer, honest. Stop them, sir, please . . . they'll kill me if yer don't!"

Reverend Johnson looked about him helplessly. Because the punishment was being meted out to a convict, the ship's company had not been mustered to witness it, and the officer of the watch—by ill chance, the master, Morton, who seldom asserted himself—was pacing the weather side of the quarterdeck, his gaze carefully averted from what was going on. It was evident that he had no intention of intervening. Johnson braced himself and approached Major Ross, nervously licking his lips.

"There is no necessity, Major, to punish this boy so severely on my account. I have my watch back, and the money does not matter. Surely, sir, a dozen strokes would suffice to teach him a lesson?"

"The matter," Ross told him icily, "does not rest with you, sir— *I* have ordered his punishment, and it will be carried out."

"But two hundred lashes . . . that is excessive! It— it could kill the unfortunate fellow."

"It will serve as an example to the rest," Ross retorted. "The surgeon has examined the fellow and pronounced him fit to receive punishment." He motioned to one of his marines, a husky corporal, who took the cat-o'-nine-tails from its red baize tag and, after tentatively running the knotted thongs through his fingers, went to position himself to the left of the prisoner. Opposite him a youthful drummer waited, drumsticks raised, his face devoid of expression.

The wretched prisoner renewed his pleas for mercy, addressing them now to Major Ross, but the commandant ignored him. "Do your duty, Corporal," he ordered, and turning again to the chaplain, he said with thinly veiled contempt, "Don't stay, Mister Johnson, if you have no stomach for such matters. Your presence is not required."

As a man of God and a civilian, Reverend Johnson would have given a good deal to have taken him at his word and absented himself from the unpleasant scene but Ross's contempt had stung him. He stayed, his stomach heaving as the lash descended on the pickpocket's bare back, wringing a high-pitched shriek of agony from him and raising a line of red weals across the tautly stretched skin.

To the monotonous beat of the single drum and the drum major's stentorian bellow as he counted the strokes, the flogging was administered. After the first dozen lashes, the unfortunate convict ceased to scream and only low moans escaped him. The corporal was relieved; a bucket of salt water was flung over the barely conscious prisoner, and at a nod from Major Ross the flogging was continued.

Three times Reverend Johnson attempted to intervene but he was curtly told to stand aside. "It is for the surgeon to say when he has taken enough. Be so good as to remain silent, sir."

Finally, to the chaplain's sick relief, the young assistant surgeon overcame his awe of the overbearing Ross and called a halt to the proceedings. The drum was silenced, the man with the cat mopped his brow, and the drum major severed the ropes at the top of the grating, his expression revealing nothing of his feelings.

Dr. Lowes bent over the slumped body of the young thief, but the chaplain did not wait to hear his verdict, knowing what it would be. Fighting down his rising nausea, he descended to his cabin and there fell to his knees, to pray long and earnestly for guidance.

Lieutenant King was on watch when Captain Phillip was piped on board his flagship. The side party dismissed, King stood, hat in hand, studying his face anxiously.

"Judging by the gravity of your expression, sir, you fared no better than usual?" he suggested.

"No better," his commander confirmed wryly. "The anxiety of the government to rid themselves of our cargo is equalled only by the fear that it is costing more than anyone bargained for when the idea of this expedition was first mooted! Even my good friend George Rose, at the treasury, was unable to convince them otherwise. And as to the home office. . . ." he spread his hands in a gesture of weary resignation. "Both Sydney and Nepean are resolved that our unhappy women in the *Lady Penrhyn* shall enter the new world in the same state of nakedness as they entered this one! I am to clothe them from the stores of this ship, with no guarantee that the Board of Admiralty will replace or even pay for what we are compelled to avail ourselves of! And the females, God help them, are to hide their nakedness in seamen's frocks and canvas trousers from the slop chest! I am to have the essence of malt I have so often solicited, but only in sufficient quantity for the seamen and marines."

"But, sir, how could you—" Lieutenant King began

and then broke off, color creeping up under the tan of his cheeks. "Forgive me, I mean no reproach. I know how hard you have tried."

"Yes, my dear boy," his captain answered wryly, "but it is akin to beating one's head against the proverbial brick wall—or as our evangelic chaplain would put it, extracting blood from a stone. They simply do not care whether the convicts live or die, and their solicitude where the rest of us are concerned appears no better than lukewarm. The first lord reminded me that I have been over four months fitting out and the only question any of the others asked me was how soon I could put to sea. Sir Evan Nepean—by what cannot have been chance—was with Lord Howe when I called upon him at the admiralty." He supplied details of the interview, his voice flat and bleak.

"What of our guns, sir—the ten six-pounders for use ashore?" King asked. "After all, we do not know what reception we may expect from the natives. Sir Joseph Banks warned that they might oppose our landing at Botany Bay, did he not?"

"That has been conveniently forgotten, my dear fellow," Arthur Phillip told him cynically. "It is taken for granted that we shall have no dispute with the natives, whose friendship we are to cultivate by making them gifts of mirrors and beads when we encounter them. We are to sail without the six-pounders *and* without my requisition for small-shot. The first lord gave me, in lieu, authority to purchase them in Rio or at the Cape, along with provisions and livestock. Furthermore the convicts' papers, setting out their crimes and the duration of their sentences—for which I have pleaded until I am hoarse—are to be given, not to me, but to the masters of the transports, on Lord

Sydney's insistence. They will be delivered to me after our landing."

"But you are appointed governor!" King exclaimed.

"Aye . . . with power of life or death over them," Phillip agreed. "With authority to reduce or increase their sentences, command their labor, grant them land, flog, or hang them. Nevertheless I am not to be entrusted with their papers, since responsibility for them on the voyage isn't mine but the contractors. However"—he smiled, without amusement—"the two hundred pounds of portable soup I requested is to be sent to the *Fishbourne* without fail."

Sensing that beneath the cloak of cynicism his commander was near to despair, Philip King did his best to divert him. He was a good raconteur, and by dint of outrageous exaggeration he was able to bring a genuine smile to the older man's lips. With a wealth of humorous detail he described Surgeon White's latest successful brush with the port victualling yard and the chaplain's less successful endeavor to arouse interest in the "good books" he had brought with him by reading aloud to an audience of illiterates on board the *Scarborough.*

Talk of the chaplain led to the incident with the watch.

"The watch was found, and the culprit was given two hundred lashes," King was saying. "He—"

"Two hundred lashes?" Captain Phillip put in, an edge to his voice. "By whose orders was he flogged?"

"Why, by Major Ross's sir. That is—"

"In future, Mister King, all punishments for serious offenses will be ordered by myself and the punishment carried out on board this ship and in my presence," Phillip told him with controlled anger. "See that my orders in this respect are made known to all commanding officers and ships' masters, if you please."

"Aye, aye, sir," Lieutenant King acknowledged. He hesitated, eyeing his commander uncertainly. Close friends though they were, he had not anticipated the outburst his last remark had provoked. Arthur Phillip was a humane and kindly man but a stern disciplinarian who in the past had never shown the slightest reluctance to order a flogging when it was deserved and necessary.

"Did the convict survive his punishment?" the captain asked in a quieter tone.

King shook his head. "He was dead when they cut him down, sir."

"You see why I must keep such matters in my own hands. These poor wretches are mere bags of bones— they've been confined in the Hulks and prisons for years, some of them on starvation rations, without adequate exercise. Dammit, a puff of wind is enough to blow them to kingdom come! I'll flog them if I have to but I will *not* award the same number of lashes as I would order for a healthy seaman. If we are to found a settlement with the poor devils they've seen fit to give us for the purpose, we must endeavor to deliver them alive and capable of performing the manual labor we shall require of them, don't you agree?"

"Yes, indeed, sir," King assured him. The captain clapped an affectionate hand on his shoulder. "Don't imagine I'm blaming you, my dear boy. It's just that . . . oh, plague take it, I'm tired, Philip!" He consulted his pocket watch and sighed. "Is there anything else I should be informed of before I go below? I don't doubt that the conscientious Brewer will have a mountain of paperwork requiring my attention, and I should like to dispose of it before dinner. Captain Hunter is dining with me but—" He smiled ruefully. "Good-hearted fellow that he is, he's inclined to hide vexatious matters from me in the hope of sparing my feelings."

Philip King considered the question, as anxious as Hunter to spare his commander's feelings if he could. Finally he answered, with some reluctance, "Well, sir, the provost marshal departed without asking leave, and it's my opinion that he has no intention of sailing with us. And five seamen ran from the *Fishbourne*—there's much dissatisfaction among the merchant seamen, sir, because they've received only their river pay and they complain that the masters have refused them advances, so that they are unable to outfit themselves for the voyage."

"Is that true, do you suppose?" Phillip asked wearily.

"I rather think it may be, sir."

"Then look into the matter tomorrow, will you please? Our seamen will receive their pay—it's only right that the merchant seamen should also, and I was assured that it's been sent. But we'll have to keep a close watch on them once they're paid—the last thing we want is liquor smuggled on board the transports. See that a reliable lieutenant is in command of the guard boat at all times, Mister King."

"Aye, aye, sir." Lieutenant King hesitated again, and then seeing that his captain was about to go below, he said uneasily, "There is one other matter, sir—your marine servant."

"Hawley, d'you mean?" Captain Phillip's dark brows rose in astonishment. "What of him—he's not in trouble, surely? A steady, reliable man, Hawley, and an excellent servant."

"He's not in trouble, sir," King assured him. "But. . . ." He avoided Phillip's eye. "Major Ross had him transferred to the *Charlotte*. I chose a man to replace Hawley—Dodd, sir, Edward Dodd. He volunteered, sir, and I'm sure he'll serve you well."

Arthur Phillip said nothing but inwardly he was fuming. It was only a pinprick, he reminded himself, and Dodd was an excellent man who had worked for him on his small farm in the New Forest during the years when he had been on half pay. But depriving him of Hawley was another example of the marine commandant's spite, and he was fairly certain, it had been done with the deliberate intention of causing him annoyance.

On May 12 he gave the long awaited signal to his fleet to sail. The seamen's pay had been delivered, together with the long-awaited supply of essence of malt, but the six-pounder cannon, clothing for the women convicts, and the promised portable soup had not.

Next morning, just before six, the whole fleet was under sail, and he was able to note in his journal: "The weather being fine and wind easterly, proceeded through the Needles with a fresh leading breeze," the transport *Charlotte* under tow by the escorting frigate *Hyaena*.

The eight-month-long voyage to the unknown had begun.

CHAPTER IX

Jenny had been sent on board the *Charlotte* when the wagons had finally passed through the streets of Portsmouth, reviled by a catcalling mob of virtuous citizens. Heavily chained, like all the rest, she had been respectably clad in Doll Prunty's dress and shawl, but no sooner had she entered the women convicts' quarters in the hold of the transport than an ugly struggle broke out among her fellow prisoners, all intent on seizing possession of her clothing.

She had resisted them for as long as she could, but sheer exhaustion had eventually compelled her to surrender first the shawl and then the torn remnants of her dress, and now, as the *Charlotte* pitched sickeningly in a rising sea off the Needles, she lay half-naked and shivering in the dark, airless hold.

The *Charlotte*, of three hundred forty-five tons

burthen, was an old ship and a notoriously poor sailer. Crowded on board her were her crew of thirty seamen, the guard of forty-two marines, eighty-six male and twenty female convicts—two with children. Thick bulkheads, said to be filled with nails to add to their weight and strength, separated the male convicts' part of the hold from that occupied by the women, and prior to sailing, so strict a watch had been kept that none had attempted to invade the women's quarters. Now, however, Jenny realized with a swift stirring of alarm, the situation had changed. Men's voices sounded from close at hand, booted feet thudded on the deck planking, and to shrieks of drunken laughter from a handful of the younger women who had gathered beneath it, the hatch cover was raised.

Two uniformed figures descended, bearing a small cask between them, and one, holding it above his head, announced invitingly, "Rum, my lassies! Who's for a nip o' rum?"

There was a concerted rush toward him. Some of the women, who had already formed attachments to members of the crew, had been steadily drinking the liquor smuggled to them earlier by the seamen in return for favors.

"Hold hard now, hold hard!" one of the men admonished. "There's plenty for everyone—but one good turn deserves another, don't it?"

Jenny tried vainly to shut her ears to their voices and to the obscene banter they exchanged as more men came slithering down the hatchway. Some, she knew from their attire, were convicts, but most of the invaders were marines—the same scarlet-coated martinets who, until now, had stood sentinel over them, permitting no liberties.

She turned to a frail, sickly woman in her fifties, trying to rest. Sarah Dow was a widow, so bowed down by grief and the shame of her present situation that she lay listlessly on her bunk, refusing food and, Jenny had sensed, praying for death to release her. All in their way had tried to show her kindness, even the most hard-bitten of them, but Sarah did not respond and, after a while, they had left her alone.

She lay now, as always, her face turned to the bulkhead to which her bunk was attached, paying no attention to the hubbub around her, the flimsy shawl, which the other women, out of pity, had permitted her to retain, wrapped closely about her small motionless body. Jenny watched her anxiously, hoping that, if they both kept silent, they would be left unmolested. But this hope faded when one of the male convicts, a hulking Irishman, came stumbling drunkenly between the two rows of bunks, shouting blasphemies at the marine who had deprived him of one of the young prostitutes.

"Sure an' didn't I pay ye a whole two shillings to get in here, yer black-hearted scoundrel?" he shouted angrily. "Am'n't I to get a woman for me money then?" He saw Jenny then and put out his hands to take her, but she warded him off, and her push sent him staggering against the opposite row of bunks. Observing the still figure of Sarah Dow on the bunk in front of him, he let out a whoop of triumph and hurled himself upon her, only to recoil in bemused horror when he touched her.

"Sweet Mother o' Jaysus!" he exclaimed in a strangled voice. "Holy God, 'tis a corpse there, not a woman! A corpse, d'ye hear me . . . an' stone cold, God rest her soul."

He crossed himself and beat a swift retreat to the

hatchway, calling out a panic-stricken warning to the rest of them to follow him before it was too late. Most of them ignored him, apparently deaf to his outraged cries or caring nothing for them, and Jenny, summoning all her courage, crossed to the bunk he had so hurriedly vacated, unable to believe that what he said might be true. But he was right, she realized when her trembling fingers encountered cold flesh . . . Sarah Dow had found the escape she had sought.

Sick with shock and pity, Jenny stood there, wondering what she should do or even whether she dared ask for help from any of the other women. Clearly it would be useless to appeal to the men, most of whom —marine and convict alike—were by this time as drunk as the Irishman had been. Uncertainly she started to move toward the hatchway when, from behind her, a voice said harshly, "Leave the old woman be and get back to your bunk, girl. It'll be time enough to report her death in the morning, understand? We don't want any officers poking their noses down here now. Having a party in the cabin, they are —that's how the lobsters got in here, so it wouldn't do to disturb 'em, would it?"

"Oh, but surely . . ." Jenny began, her heart pounding in sudden fear as she recognized the voice as that of a woman who was known as Mrs. Davis. She was said to have been a brothel keeper and to have been sentenced for manslaughter; better educated than most of the others, she was a big, red-haired woman, of whom they all went in awe, careful not to cross or offend her. Mrs. Davis had money and she spent it freely, keeping herself and her particular cronies well supplied with liquor smuggled from the shore or brought, in the guise of farewell gifts, by some of her numerous visitors from London.

Jenny had held herself aloof from the Davis circle, aware, in the light of unhappy experience, what joining it would be likely to entail, and to her intense relief the woman, finding that her tentative overtures met with no response, had abandoned them without apparent rancor. Now, however, she was revealed in her true colors. Gripping Jenny by the shoulders, she spun her around and, holding her firmly at arm's length, peered menacingly into her face.

"Understand this, Jenny Taggart," she threatened. "We'll have no stool pigeons here. Unless you want your pretty little throat cut, you'll see nothing and hear nothing—an' above all, you'll say nothing. The poor lobsters can be flogged if they're found in here with us after the hatches are battened down—and the good Lord alone knows what they'll do to the convicts. Hang 'em, I shouldn't wonder! So I want no puling little girls running to the officers with complaints or tall tales—is that clear? Whether you choose to keep your virtue or whether you don't is your affair . . . all I ask is that you keep a still tongue in your head."

Jenny shrank from the cold menace in her eyes, aware that her threat was no idle one. "I won't complain, Mrs. Davis—truly I won't. You can trust me. I won't say a word to anyone."

"If you'll take my advice, girl, you'll do what Betsy Lucas did—find yourself a good man who'll take care of you. Because *I* can't control the ones who come down here, least of all when they've a few drinks inside 'em. You'd better understand that too." Mrs. Davis laughed. "What's more, I don't reckon to risk *my* neck by trying. Get back in your bunk. And here, take this to cover yourself with." She jerked the shawl from Sarah Dow's stiffening body and thrust it into

Jenny's arms. "It'll keep the cold out—and the men away, if you're lucky." She stumped off, leaving Jenny, more frightened than ever, to cry herself to sleep.

On May 14 the eleven ships of the Botany Bay Fleet were clear of the Isle of Wight but the fine leading breeze, which had carried them past the Needles under all sail, shifted as they entered the Channel and began steadily to rise, whipping up a following sea.

On the *Sirius*'s quarterdeck Captain Phillip stood with his second-in-command, Captain John Hunter, both with their telescopes raised as they watched the convoy's response to the flagship's signal to tack and prepare to shorten sail. On the lee side the first lieutenant, William Bradley, paced impatiently up and down as, in obedience to the boatswain's stentorian bellow and the shrilling of his mates' silver calls, the waisters and the afterguard of seamen and marines went to their stations, ready to man the sheets and braces, and the topmen stood by, awaiting the order to go aloft when the time came to take in sail.

Bradley was an experienced and competent officer, Phillip knew, and he gave his own ship scant attention, concentrating on the handling of the transports, as the first lieutenant bawled orders through his speaking-trumpet, which were promptly and efficiently carried out. This was not the case with all the transports. Even allowing for their smaller crews, both the *Friendship* and the *Scarborough* had taken much longer than he liked to send down their topgallant masts and yards earlier that morning when it had first started to blow.

Hunter, who had also been watching the *Friendship*, sighed. A broad-shouldered, stolid, and somewhat forthright man, he did not suffer fools gladly.

"I'd have felt happier concerning this voyage were all our ships King's ships, sir."

"You've shepherded merchant convoys before," Phillip pointed out.

"But not with human cargoes, sir. Speaking for myself, I should not fancy being battened down in the holds of one of those old Indiamen. Least of all"— Hunter gestured to the wallowing *Friendship*—"in hers!"

Phillip frowned. "I intend to permit the poor wretches to exercise and dry their bedding on deck as soon as the weather moderates," he stated decisively. "Whatever objections the masters raise! And by the Lord Harry, they shall pump out their bilges too, at the first opportunity! I swear I can smell the *Alexander* from here."

"Major Ross will probably raise more objections than the masters," Hunter suggested dryly. "Ross considers guarding convicts in the nature of an insult to the corps . . . he told me so, very forcibly, last evening."

"Helm's alee, sir!" the *Sirius*'s quartermaster sang out. Instinctively Captain Phillip lowered his glass to look up at the sails above his head. He saw them commence to shiver as Bradley ordered the head and fore-sheets let go and wind spilled out of the jibs. The ship's blunt bow started to come round and the first lieutenant waited, judging his moment, and then shouted a succession of orders to the hands manning the braces and to the man at the wheel.

The booted feet of the marines thudded on the deck planking as the after yards were braced round and the cautionary shout of "Head braces!" sent the waisters scurrying to the weather side. Few of them had ever been to sea before; they had been gathered by the press or sent—in fetters, like the convicts—from the assize courts as unwilling volunteers, and it took a few blows from the petty officers' rope "starters" to hasten them on their way.

Aided by the pressure of the wind on the foresail—still braced for the previous tack—and the pull of the reversed rudder, Lieutenant Bradley brought the wind gradually broader on the larboard bow, and with the aftersails filling, he bellowed, "Let go and haul!" The forward tacks were let fly, the head yards braced round, and with her helm righted, the *Sirius* gathered way, settling to a monotonous pitching on the new tack.

As the day wore on, the wind rose to gale force, and the ships, under double-reefed topsails and storm staysails, took a severe battering. During the night, as Captain Phillip had anticipated, they failed to keep station, and it took until noon of the following day for the escort frigate, *Hyaena*, and the brig-sloop, *Supply*, to round up the stragglers, the *Charlotte* having to be taken in tow. Phillip, losing patience with them, signaled each ship in turn to come within hail of the *Sirius*, so that the masters might make their reports by speaking-trumpet and receive their sailing orders.

None mentioned the convicts in their reports; questioned, each gave the same reply—the hatches were battened down, sentries posted, and the prisoners, female as well as male, still in fetters and giving no trouble.

"They're all prostrate from seasickness, I don't doubt," Captain Hunter commented as the transport *Scarborough* delivered the same laconic answer; her master, the black-bearded John Marshall, was more concerned over a split foresail than for the plight of his two hundred male prisoners who, like the rest, were giving him no trouble.

By midday on May 16 the fleet had cleared the Channel, but with the glass still falling and the wind as strong as ever, there was little change in conditions. On the morning of Monday the twenty-first, her duty done, the *Hyaena* signaled "Good-bye and good luck" and set course for home, watched with bitter envy by the pressed men and defiantly cheered by the older hands. Phillip, grateful for the small-shot and other deficiencies in his supplies her captain had been persuaded to make up, responded with "Thank you and good-bye." The frigate came about and was soon lost to sight in the gray, storm-wracked distance.

Within two hours of the ship's departure the wind veered and dropped, bringing a welcome improvement in the weather, and Phillip gave the order that all convicts were to be released from their fetters and permitted on deck. His order brought the expected objections, signal hoist after signal hoist fluttering from the masts of the transport, but he refused to rescind the order, and after some considerable delay Hunter drew his attention to a small knot of ragged figures, emerging on to the *Charlotte*'s deck from the midship's hatchway. Phillip smothered an exclamation and turned his glass on them.

The convicts were under heavy guard—the scarlet jackets of a dozen marines first caught his eye—but he saw that their fetters had been removed and that they had plenty of room in which to exercise between the barricades he had caused to be erected for the purpose. Few of them, however, were able to take advantage of their new freedom. They staggered this way and that, clinging to each other for support and seemingly half-blinded by the sudden transition from the airless darkness of the hold to the bright sunlight of the open deck. Even at so great a distance their prison pallor could clearly be seen, and Phillip's glass revealed also that almost all were emaciated and that few could boast of being adequately clothed.

"We shall be fortunate," he said grimly. "We shall be very fortunate indeed, John, if we are able to keep even half of those poor wretches alive to see the end of this voyage. And they are the material with which we must build a new colony, God help us! It will be their labor on which we shall be dependent for our survival . . . damme, the masters must be made to understand that they are not commanding slave ships on a fast passage from Africa to the West Indies! Our destination is half the world away. . . ." There was a sudden commotion on the lee side of the quarterdeck, and Phillip broke off as he heard Lieutenant King, who had the watch, raise his voice in indignant argument.

"It's Major Ross," Hunter warned, his dark brows meeting in a forbidding scowl.

"I desire to speak to Captain Phillip," Ross said, his tone curt. "Kindly convey my compliments to him, Mister King, and inform him that the matter is urgent."

Arthur Phillip lowered his glass and turned to face the tall, advancing figure of the marine commandant. "Carry on, Mister King," he said formally and then, with icy politeness as Ross, dwarfing him by a good eight inches, came to a halt in front of him. "I am at your service, Major Ross. Is anything amiss, pray?"

Ross's complaints were much as Captain Hunter had predicted they would be—his marines, he asserted aggressively, were soldiers and not prison guards. It was an insult to the corps to employ them as such.

"They may furnish sentinels when the convicts are confined to their quarters below deck or when they are at exercise—provided they're fettered and exercised in batches. But to expect them to stand guard over mobs like those—" He gestured resentfully in the direction of the *Charlotte* and the cluster of scarlet jackets gathered around the planking barricades. "Damme, sir, those prisoners aren't in irons, and it's taking half a score of my men to see they don't get up to anything! It's not right, Captain Phillip—'pon my soul it's not!"

Phillip listened courteously and, with equal courtesy, attempted to explain his reasons for ordering the convicts' fetters to be struck off, but the marine commandant continued to argue, two bright spots of angry color rising to burn in his thin cheeks as he spoke.

"I don't want my men in contact with the women, sir. They're diseased and, damme, sir, they're whores—"

Captain Hunter interrupted him. "Signal from the *Scarborough*, sir," he said, his voice oddly flat. "She's coming within hail to report an attempted mutiny."

Captain Phillip stared at him in shocked disbelief. He forestalled Major Ross's self-righteous comments by dispatching a midshipman for his speaking-trumpet, and with the easy grace of an accomplished seaman, he ascended swiftly into the mizzen shrouds, as the *Scarborough* maneuvered to within hailing distance alongside.

The bearded master, John Marshall, was on his quarterdeck, speaking-trumpet in hand, and Phillip addressed him with studied calm.

"You wish to report an attempted mutiny, Captain Marshall . . . or the threat of one?" The *Scarborough*'s upper deck was deserted, save for the men of the duty watch, he saw, and two marine sentries, posted in front of the midship's hatch. "Well, Captain?"

"Why . . . the threat, sir," Marshall shouted back. "I learned of it before an attempt could be made. The convicts—"

"You have not yet released your convicts from their fetters, to exercise on deck?" Phillip put in.

"Indeed I have not!" Marshall retorted indignantly. "That would be madness in the circumstances! Devil take it, Captain Phillip, with one of your blasted pipe clays—that is, one of your marines a party to it, I can't take chances!" Marshall's language became blasphemous, and Phillip sharply cut him short.

"You say a marine is involved, sir?"

"Aye, that I do, sir. A private marine, name of Knight. Caught him red-handed, trying to release two felons from the hold. It was their intention to steal one of my boats and make their escape."

"Have you placed the miscreants under arrest?" Phillip demanded, maintaining his calm.

"That I have, sir," Marshall assured him. "Will you take 'em off my ship?"

"Bring-to, Captain Marshall," Phillip ordered. "I'll send a boat across to you at once." He descended to the deck, to be confronted by a white-faced major of marines.

"One of *my* men involved in an attempted mutiny?" Ross grated, almost beside himself with fury. "That is not possible, Captain Phillip—it simply is not possible! The master of the *Scarborough* is a damned rogue! He's lying, sir, lying—though God knows why. He—"

"I'd be obliged, Major Ross, if you would go across to the *Scarborough* in person," Captain Phillip said, an edge to his voice. "Captain Hunter will accompany you. . . ." He paused to exchange a meaning glance with his second-in-command and then added coldly, "A full investigation must be made to ascertain the truth of this unhappy affair and enable me to punish the culprits, whoever they may be."

Robert Ross made a visible effort to control himself, but his gray, slightly protuberant eyes were still angry. "Certainly, Captain Phillip," he managed.

"It is quite likely," Captain Phillip went on, "that prolonged confinement in fetters below deck, in the conditions we have recently experienced, drove the prisoners to desperation. That is why I am anxious that they shall be permitted fresh air and exercise on the decks of transports. No good purpose can be served by brutalizing them or treating them so inhumanely as to rob them of all hope." He again glanced at Hunter. "Be so good, if you please, Captain Hunter, as to see that my orders in this respect are obeyed by the master of the *Scarborough* forthwith."

A boat was called away, and with Hunter and Ross in the stern sheets, it pulled across to the *Scarborough*. The boat returned, barely half an hour later, with two fettered convicts and a private marine, whose wrists were also pinioned, crouching between the thwarts.

Phillip suppressed a sigh, but his spirits lifted a little when he saw that a crowd of newly released convicts was being herded onto the transport's upper deck, supervised by the bearded master himself.

To Lieutenant King he observed, with a wry smile, "I have long believed, Philip, that if men are treated like animals, they will behave like animals. Render their lives so unendurable that death seems preferable, and then, damme, they will risk their lives in an attempt to escape! But"—he gestured to the approaching boat—"I shall be compelled to make an example of those two poor devils, and Major Ross, without doubt, will give his fellow a bloody back—if he doesn't insist on hanging him! For the honor of the Marine Corps and in the interests of discipline, an example must be made there too. But these are the rules we live by and they leave us no choice." He shrugged resignedly.

King eyed him sympathetically. "What do you wish done with the prisoners, sir?"

"Have them confined in irons in the brig. I'll sentence the convicts when I deal with defaulters tomorrow. A couple of dozen lashes should suffice in their condition." Captain Phillip started to move away and then halted. "Oh, and pass the word for the purser to attend me in my day cabin, if you please. Those convicts are all in rags, plague take it—I shall have to raid our slop chest to clothe them decently!"

"Aye, aye, sir," King acknowledged. The boat came alongside, and he hurried to the entry port to receive the prisoners, the master-at-arms at his heels. Private Knight, he saw, was a boy of perhaps eighteen.

Jenny lost all count of time as she lay huddled and shaking with cold on the hard wooden planks of her bunk. The *Charlotte*, wallowing in the tow of the frigate *Hyaena*, or tossing, under storm canvas, several miles astern of the fleet, had reduced all her passengers and a number of her crew to the shivering miseries of seasickness, from which there was no relief.

Airless and lit only by two swaying horn lanterns, the hold was a foul-smelling place of horror, where it was impossible to distinguish daylight from darkness; for the women in its noisome confines, the first ten days of the voyage were well-nigh unendurable. They were securely battened down, and with sentries posted at the hatchways day and night, they received no visits, not even from the seamen.

Then, when most of them had yielded to black despair, the storm abated, and an officer, with two seamen and a guard of marines, flung up the hatch cover and announced that, on orders from the commodore, all convicts were to be released from their fetters and permitted on deck for exercise.

The removal of their fetters was followed by the arrival of bundles of rough but warm clothing from the *Sirius*'s slop chest. But, despite these humane attempts to lessen their ordeal, most of the women were, at first, too weak to take advantage of their new freedom, and two who did returned with the horrifying tale of having seen a man hanged at the flagship's yardarm.

"They say it was for mutiny," one of the women stated. "An' that the poor codger was a lobsterback marine. But two o' the convicts that was in it, they only got two dozen lashes apiece, 'cause Cap'n Phillip reckoned they was driven to it, bein' kept below in chains durin' the storm. So you'd all better get up an' exercise, afore you gets driven ter mutiny!"

Laughter greeted this sally but none of the others roused themselves. Jenny made an attempt but it was not until the following day that she found the strength to struggle up to the open deck.

It was as she stood there, drawing great gulps of blessed fresh air into her lungs, that the miracle happened. As if in a dream, she heard a voice whose familiarity bridged the gap of years and saw Andrew Hawley's tall, unmistakable figure come striding across the deck toward her.

She made to cry out to him in happy recognition, but the impulse was instantly stifled when she took in the fact that he was in uniform, with smartly pipe-clayed accoutrements and a corporal's stripes on the sleeve of his scarlet jacket. He was a marine, a Johnny-toe-the-liner, a lobsterback . . . Andrew Hawley, whom she and her mother had lost in the crowd and vainly sought for all those years ago in Billingsgate market *was a Marine*! Jenny felt tears come to ache in her throat. She started to turn away, ashamed to let him see her thus, dirty and disheveled, clad in a coarse seaman's jersey and the shawl that had once belonged to poor dead Sarah Dow, from beneath which protruded the stiff folds of a canvas smock.

But she had left her flight too late. The *Charlotte*'s laboring bows plunged deep into the trough of a white-crested Atlantic roller, and as she shuddered back onto an even keel Jenny was flung violently against the barricade. She picked herself up, wincing with the pain of her skinned knees, and Andrew Hawley came to a halt on the other side of the barrier, offering a big hand to assist her to rise.

"Are you hurt?" he inquired, and Jenny shrank from the pity in his eyes.

"No," she lied. "I'm not hurt, thank you."

He subjected her to a faintly puzzled scrutiny as if, for him too, a faint memory still lingered. But recognition did not come and he asked cautiously, "Do you know a lass named Jenny Taggart? I'm told she's with you."

His mention of her name was too much. Numbly, not looking at him, Jenny said, "Andrew, it's me—I—I'm Jenny Taggart."

He was visibly taken aback, but recovering himself,

he put out a hand to grasp hers. "It's been a long time, Jenny. But you knew me . . . you remembered."

"Yes," she answered. "Of course I did—you haven't changed. But I have, I'm the one who's changed."

"You've grown up. I remember you as a little lass— a fine, brave little lass who took the road with us from Yorkshire. I mind carrying you pickaback when you tired." He paused, frowning, in an effort to fit the details into place. "Aye, we planned to keep together, didn't we, you and your mam, but we lost you on the way into London. What happened to you, Jenny?"

She told him the story, forcing back her tears.

Andrew Hawley expelled his breath in a long-drawn sigh. "My mam took ill that very night," he said. "We took her to Saint Bartholomew's Hospital and we waited there, hoping against hope that the doctors would be able to save her, but she was too far gone, they said. She was dead within a week, God rest her."

"Oh, Andrew, I'm sorry." Jenny was genuinely distressed.

"The journey was too much for her, Jenny—the walking, the sleeping out. They told us it was pneumonia. But they were very good." Andrew smiled, the slow, gentle smile she remembered, and her heart contracted. "The almoner took an interest in us, and my dad being an old soldier, he got him into Chelsea Hospital as an in-pensioner. It was the best for him— he was too old to go on working. And seeing he was taken care of, I made up my mind to emigrate. I made for the docks, thinking to work my passage in a ship going to America. But"—he shrugged ruefully—"a recruiting sergeant in one of the riverside taverns plied a couple of us with drinks and the next thing we knew, we'd taken the king's shilling and enlisted in the Marines. I—" He broke off abruptly as a young officer emerged from the forward hatch to stand looking about him aggressively, as if seeking to find fault with the men on duty there. "Lieutenant Leach," Andrew said, lowering his voice. "Fancies himself as a taut hand, that young gentleman does, and it won't pay me to provoke him. I'll have to leave you, Jenny . . . but I'll see you again, lass."

He drew himself up to his full, impressive height and marched stiffly over to where the marine officer was standing, to come to attention in front of him with an impeccable salute.

"Ah, Corporal . . . Corporal Hawley, is it not?" Leach was a slim youth, with a pale, bony face and cold blue eyes, and he spoke with an affected drawl. He was the junior of the marine officers and, Andrew suspected, a trifle unsure of himself on that account. He had not been on the original list of volunteers for the New South Wales settlement and rumor had it that his reason for seeking inclusion in the contingent, only a few weeks before sailing, had been for the sole purpose of escaping from his creditors.

Standing rigidly at attention, Andrew eyed him warily.

"Aye, sir," he confirmed, since a reply appeared to be expected of him. "I'm Corporal Hawley, sir."

"Recently transferred from the flagship, I believe," Leach drawled. "By the commandant, in order to improve the discipline on board this ship . . . that's so, is it not, Corporal?"

"Major Ross had me transferred, sir," Andrew said woodenly. "I wasn't told for what reason."

"Well, *I'll* tell you, Corporal Hawley. You were specially recommended as a sober, reliable man who could be depended upon to ensure that the rank and file of the Marine Corps did *not* indulge in undue intimacy with the women convicts. They are whores, Corporal, filthy, diseased strumpets, the sweepings of the London brothels . . . you know that, don't you?"

Andrew reddened, but four years under iron discipline had taught him the folly of attempting to contradict an officer, so he remained silent, staring ahead of him, his expression carefully blank. It was to be hoped that poor little Jenny Taggart had left the deck or at least was too far away for Lieutenant Leach's unpleasant assertions to be audible. He risked a glance in the direction of the barricade and was relieved to see no sign of her, but Leach pounced on his lapse with sadistic pleasure.

"Ah, I see I was right—the sober, reliable Corporal Hawley was, as I suspected, holding converse with one of the whores before I came on deck! What sort of example is that to set for the men under your command, Hawley, eh? Answer me, man!"

Andrew's face remained blank but he could not prevent the rush of angry color to his cheeks. Aware that he had given himself away, he wondered whether to admit the truth or endeavor to deny his previous acquaintance with Jenny. Finally he said, "The girl fell, sir, when the ship rolled. I feared she might have injured herself and so I went to her aid."

"Your duty is to guard the prisoners, Corporal," the young officer reminded him harshly. "Not to aid them when they fall. I've heard rumors, you know, and I'm not a fool. It's said that these abandoned wretches are regularly visited during the hours of darkness by the seamen and male convicts. Tell me, do the marines visit them also? Or do they merely turn a blind eye when fetters are removed and hatch covers unbolted?"

"I've no knowledge of such things, sir," Andrew said. It was a partial truth, for he had been careful not to be within sight or sound of the women's quarters on such occasions as Leach had described. For one of his rank, he was only too well aware, it was wiser and safer not to intervene. But the picture the drawling young officer had conjured up was not a pleasant one and he found himself wondering whether Jenny Taggart was like the rest.

"I take leave to doubt your ignorance of what is going on, Corporal," Leach remarked accusingly. "But I shall be watching you, so have a care. Those stripes of yours won't spare you from a flogging if I find you are neglecting your duty. That's understood? All right then—you're dismissed."

"Sir!" Andrew acknowledged. He saluted and thankfully left the deck.

Later, on the mess deck, he sought advice from his immediate superior, Sergeant Tom Jenkins, who was a veteran of Rodney's naval actions in the West Indies and of the American war. Proud of his service and his calling, the marine sergeant was a fine-looking, white-haired man, respected by his officers and popular with the rank and file. His wife had accompanied him, their intention being to take advantage of the land grants that would be offered to free settlers in the new colony so that they might spend the evening of their days farming their own land.

The veteran listened in thoughtful silence to Andrew's account of his meeting with Jenny and its consequences, and then, puffing at his stained old clay pipe, he delivered judgment. "Your little Jenny Taggart's no wanton, my lad—and I have that on the best authority." He chuckled. "From Missus Davis, as it happens, and she should know, if anyone does. A couple of days ago she approached me and asked my help to have the lass found other quarters.

Said she feared for her life if she was left below with
the rest of 'em . . . and made it plain as a pikestaff
why. So you need have no doubts as to the girl's virtue, Corporal Hawley."

Andrew flushed uncomfortably but he felt relieved.
Sergeant Jenkins went on, affecting not to notice his
embarrassment. "Missus Davis asked me, if I couldn't
have her moved, whether I could find a decent,
reliable man who'd take care of her and make sure
she wasn't harmed. She reckoned an officer might fill
the bill and—"

"You need look no further than me, Sergeant," Andrew put in impulsively. "What's more, I'd marry
her, if I could obtain the major's permission, and do
what you're planning to do—apply for a land grant.
Why, I'd—"

"Not so fast, my lad, not so fast!" the old sergeant
admonished him. "The girl's a convict . . . you'd not
be given permission to wed her. Certainly not until
she's served her sentence or gained remission, and
you've your time to serve in the corps, don't forget."

"You didn't speak of her to any of the officers, did
you, Sergeant?"

Tom Jenkins was an honest and truthful man; he
hesitated, considering the question, and then replied
to it truthfully. "It so happens I did, yes. Missus
Davis is a hard old biddy, but she seemed truly worried about the lass. And we don't want trouble with
the women—you know that as well as I do."

"Which of them did you speak to?" Andrew demanded angrily. "Which of the officers?"

"I don't have to tell you that, Corporal Hawley,"
Jenkins reminded him, his tone sharp.

"No, Sergeant." Andrew controlled himself with a

visible effort. "But I'd be obliged if you'd tell me one thing, just to set my mind at rest."

Sergeant Jenkins tapped out his pipe and, taking a broken-bladed knife from his pocket, scraped the burned shreds of tobacco from its bowl with meticulous care. The operation, deliberately drawn out, afforded him time to think. He had expected no such complications as this when he had acceded to Mary Davis's request—indeed he had been grateful to the woman for coming to him, realizing that she would not have done so had the girl not been in real danger. Mrs. Davis's motives had not been entirely altruistic, the sergeant was fully aware; she wanted to be rid of the girl simply because, unlike the rest of them, Jenny Taggart was not of easy virtue. She was respectable and . . . she might talk out of turn, which wouldn't suit Mrs. Davis's book at all.

There was also the danger, which they both recognized, that a man, with drink inside him, might force his attentions on the girl, and if the man happened to be one of his marines, there could be very serious trouble indeed.

He sighed, continuing to occupy himself with his pipe, while studying Andrew Hawley's face covertly and attempting to assess his feelings. Hawley was a good lad, a credit to the corps, but he was young and impulsive and must be handled carefully. It was a pity he hadn't known of the lad's involvement with Jenny Taggart sooner; a pity, certainly, that he hadn't known of it before he had spoken of her to Lieutenant Leach. It had seemed a possible solution to the problem at the time, since Leach had asked about a woman, specifying that she must be virtuous or, failing that, young and reasonably good-looking. And, here as elsewhere, there was one law for the officers and another for the men—an officer could take any woman he liked to his quarters and keep her there throughout the voyage, if he wished to, and nothing would be said. The rank and file did so at their peril.

"Sergeant," Andrew Hawley prompted with more than a hint of impatience. "I have to know which of the officers you spoke to concerning Jenny Taggart. I—" He swallowed hard. "Was it Leach, Sergeant?"

"And why should you suppose it might be Lieutenant Leach, Corporal?" Jenkins asked quietly.

"I don't know—I hoped it wasn't, that's all. I . . . well, I had a bit of a run-in with him on deck during the afternoon watch. He saw me talking to the girl." Andrew repeated what the youthful Lieutenant Leach had said to him, his anger rising again as he recalled the arrogance of that affected, drawling voice and the unfounded accusations Leach had made.

"You'll be well advised to watch your step, my lad," Sergeant Jenkins told him severely, "unless you want a bloody back. There aren't too many officers the like of Captain Phillip, you know."

"I know that well. But—*was* it Leach?"

"Mister Leach asked about a woman. Not any woman in particular. He said if I could find him a clean-living girl to attend to his needs, do his laundry and mending and suchlike, he would be obliged to me. He—"

"He's not having Jenny Taggart!" Andrew exclaimed hotly. "The filthy, lying young hypocrite . . . laundry and mending indeed! That's the last thing he wants, plague take him. Why—"

"It's lucky for you that I'm a mite deaf, Corporal Hawley," the old sergeant observed dryly. "I didn't hear what you just said."

"But, Sergeant—"

"Don't try my patience any further, lad," Jenkins warned.

"I'm sorry, Sergeant. But will you help me or help Jenny Taggart, at least? Don't let that young— please, Sergeant, don't let Mister Leach get his hands on her. I'll protect her, I swear I will. Couldn't you find another girl to do Mister Leach's washing for him?"

The old sergeant permitted himself a rueful smile. "I'll have no trouble doing that—they all want officers, if they can get 'em. And I'll do what I can for your little lass, so long as I have your word that you'll leave the matter in my hands. It's for your sake as well as hers, Hawley."

Aware that he was right, Andrew gave his agreement with only a slight hesitation.

Having achieved as much as he could reasonably hope for, Andrew was about to return to his own mess when the sergeant, in the act of refilling his pipe, waved to him to wait. "There's one other matter I've just remembered concerning your little lass, Hawley. You spoke of her mother, did you not? Was she with you when you made the journey to London?"

"Aye, she was," Andrew confirmed. "Her name was Rachel, if I remember rightly—Missus Rachel Taggart."

Sergeant Jenkins lit his pipe. When it was going to his satisfaction, he said flatly, "The mother's with us, too—on board the *Friendship*. Did the girl tell you that?"

Shocked, Andrew shook his head. "No, she didn't. Poor souls, fancy them both being deported . . . they must have had it hard, after we separated. I wonder why Jenny didn't tell me?"

"Maybe she doesn't know," Jenkins suggested.

Andrew bade Sergeant Jenkins a thoughtful good-night and retired to his hammock.

Next day Jenkins approached his detachment commander, Captain Tench. Both were Welshmen, and although Watkin Tench was barely half his age, the old sergeant had conceived a warm liking for him, a sentiment that was returned in full measure. Cultivated and charming, Tench was a good professional soldier, with a strong sense of duty, and aware that the plight of the women convicts was a matter of much concern to him, Jenkins came to the point without preamble.

"The girl could be in real danger, sir," he ended. "And if anything did happen to her down in the hold, I couldn't answer for what young Hawley would do. And he's got the makings of a first rate N.C.O., sir, given a few more years' service. It'd be a pity if he was allowed to go wrong."

"Can you be certain he won't, Jenkins, if I place the girl in your care?" the captain asked shrewdly.

"I'd do my best, sir," Jenkins assured him.

"Well, then, your request is granted, Sergeant. And if you should have any trouble with Hawley. . . ." Tench smiled. "He was Captain Phillip's servant, you know, and I understand the captain was sorry to lose him. I feel sure, in the circumstances, there would be no objection raised if he were returned to the *Sirius*, so if you feel it advisable, be so good as to tell me."

"I will, sir," the sergeant promised.

An hour later he released Jenny from the hold and himself escorted her to the small cabin on the after part of the main deck, which, until now, he had shared with his wife. Olwyn Jenkins was a small buxom woman, of a talkative and friendly nature, whose first reaction to the suggestion that she should share her cramped quarters with a convict girl had been anything but favorable. Her husband had had eventually to insist that his orders required her to do so, and she had submitted resentfully after a lengthy argument, with the result that, when Jenny entered the cabin, she was met with cold hostility. Gradually, however, the little Welshwoman's resentment gave place to pity, and deeming it then expedient to leave them alone together, Tom Jenkins excused himself on the plea of duties awaiting him, confident that Jenny's diffident gratitude and good manners would eventually win his wife's approval.

His hopes were realized. Returning some hours later, he found them the best of friends, and Jenny, washed and dressed in a borrowed gown, greeted him with tears of happiness.

"I don't know how to thank you both, Sergeant Jenkins," she whispered. "Truly I—I don't. Mistress Jenkins has given me this dress and shoes and I—I can hold my head up again. I can even let Andrew Hawley look at me now without feeling ashamed."

"Now there's foolishness!" Olwyn Jenkins exclaimed. "Of what are you ashamed, my poor lamb? That they put chains on you, is it, and then ordered you into the hold with thieves and wantons for company?" She held out her arms, and with Jenny in her warm embrace, she rounded on her husband, to reproach him bitterly in their native Welsh for the injustice the girl had suffered and the conditions in which she had been confined in the *Charlotte*'s foul-smelling hold. Ending her tirade in English, she said vehemently, "She is nothing but a child, look you, Thomas! A sweet, innocent child . . . praise be to God that those evil whores did not corrupt her, as well they might have done!"

Sergeant Jenkins gave her no answer but he was smiling quietly to himself as he went in search of a hammock to sling in the senior petty officers' mess. Time enough to tell the girl about her mother when she had settled down and recovered her spirits, he decided. His kindly, cheerful Olwyn had taken the poor waif to her heart, as he had hoped she would, and could be trusted to care for her as if she were her own, if he knew anything about her.

He felt for his pipe. The fleet was still some two weeks' sailing from the first port of call—at Tenerife, in the Canaries—and two weeks would give her time to recover.

CHAPTER X

A signal from the *Friendship* urgently requesting his services sent Surgeon John White on a long pull across from the *Charlotte*, in a choppy sea, as the sun was setting in a blaze of unexpected glory.

Captain Meredith, of the Marine Corps, met him at the entry port with the grim news that the ship's young surgeon, Dr. Arndell, required his assistance with an amputation.

"It's one of our fellows, Doctor," Meredith added. "Corporal Baker . . . the damned fool ought to have known better, of course, but. . . ." He shrugged his broad shoulders helplessly. His breath, Dr. White noticed, smelled strongly of alcohol, but he walked quite steadily as he led the way below.

"What happened?" the senior surgeon asked curiously. "Did the man fall from the rigging?"

"Lord, no—the idiot shot himself in the foot with his own musket," Meredith answered disgustedly. "He's in here." He stood aside at the entrance to the ship's sick bay to permit White to pass him.

Thomas Arndell greeted his arrival with a relief he made no attempt to hide. He was recently qualified but an intelligent and conscientious young man and he had made all the necessary preparations for the operation. His instruments—a bone saw, two well-honed knives, and a supply of needles—were set out, with a tub of melted tar with which to cauterize the wound ready on hand. The patient, a husky fellow of about five-and-twenty, lay on the table, a tourniquet applied to the upper part of his injured leg, and straps about his arms and body that, when tightened, would effectively prevent him from struggling while the amputation was in progress. He had been well primed with rum and he looked up at Dr. White with bleary-eyed indifference as the surgeon bent over the table to inspect his shattered foot.

"I suppose he'll have to lose his foot, sir," Arndell said after apologizing for having requested his colleague's aid at so inconvenient an hour. "But I thought there just might be a chance of saving it and —well, I hoped you would not mind my asking your opinion."

"I'm glad you did, Thomas," Dr. White assured him. He probed with skilled fingers at the ugly wound, and young Arndell went on gravely, "It was the most extraordinary thing. The ball entered, as you can see, at an angle. It shattered the metatarsals but they turned it, and the ball, although spent, still had force enough to go right through a harness cask of beef, about eight inches behind where Baker was standing, and kill a couple of geese, penned up on the far side! I wouldn't have believed it if I hadn't seen it with my own eyes, sir, honestly."

"Quite extraordinary," John White agreed abstractedly as he continued to probe. A few days before, he had had to pronounce Private Daniel Knight dead of judicial hanging, and only this morning, he recalled, he had been witness to the slow, unhappy demise of a convict named Ishmael Coleman on board the *Charlotte*. Coleman was only in his late forties but he had looked twice that age; he had been one of those loaded onto one of the other transports at Deptford, and close on four months spent in the dark confines of the hold—preceded by a year in Newgate—had robbed him of all desire to go on living. In any event, the surgeon reminded himself, the poor devil's sentence was for life, and as he had recorded in his medical journal: "Ishmael Coleman, worn out by lowness of spirit and debility brought on by long and close confinement, resigned his breath without a pang."

It was not the first time he had written those words and it would, he knew, not be the last but . . . he looked down at the strong young body of Corporal Baker and reached a decision.

"Thomas, it will almost certainly take two or three months of constant care," he said, "but I believe we can save this man's foot and have him walking again. Let's get to work, shall we?"

"Gladly, sir," young Dr. Arndell agreed.

It took them two hours, and when it was over, both surgeons were summoned to the hold, where a woman convict was reported to be in labor. It was the first birth to take place during the voyage, and Dr. White was sickened and disillusioned by the callous lack of compassion shown by all save a few of the *Friend-*

ship's female convicts. Three of them helped with the difficult delivery of Isabella Lawson's puny infant; the rest, he saw to his disgust, were unpleasantly drunk and concerned only with a quarrel that had broken out between a dropsical old harridan in a velvet dress and a foul-mouthed pair of younger women disputing the possession of some articles of clothing. Their voices, screeching obscenities from the far side of the hold, drowned the cries of the newly born child and the stifled moans of the mother, and Dr. White's stern demands for an end to their bickering fell on deaf ears.

"They're a bad lot in this ship," Arndell told him ruefully. "The seamen smuggle liquor to them, and the master turns a blind eye to it. That revolting creature"—he jerked his head in the direction of the velvet-clad harridan—"is the cause of most of the trouble. I wish there were some way of separating them but, alas, there is not, since the sick bay has to be retained for the use of the ship's company and the marines. There's not even a spare cabin I can move this poor soul into." He looked down at the white, exhausted face of the young mother and sighed as he held the child up for her inspection. "You have a daughter, Isabella—a pretty little daughter!"

The mother said nothing, and John White was shocked by the naked pain in her eyes.

"Don't worry, Doctor, we will take care of them both." One of the women who had helped with the delivery took the baby into her embrace. She was slim and dark, Dr. White saw, and she spoke, to his surprise, in an educated voice. He would have asked her name, questioned her as to her circumstances, but as if sensing his intentions, she moved away from him before he could do so. He was tired and he did not attempt to go after her; with Arndell at his side he made for the hatch ladder, stifling a yawn, as the sentry raised the lantern to illuminate the rungs. Its rays fell briefly on the face of a woman of middle age, lying hunched on a bunk he was passing, and he was reminded, as he looked at her, of the face of Ishmael Coleman. There was the same uncomprehending despair written on it, the same hopelessness as if she, too, had lost all will to live.

"That is one I am anxious about, sir," Arndell said, following the direction of his gaze. "Her name is Rachel Taggart. She had jail fever when she came on board—transferred from the Hulks—and I hoped she would improve when we put to sea. Unhappily she has not, but. . . ." He, too, yawned. "I'll not trouble you to examine her now—you've done more than enough for one night."

"We both have, Thomas," Dr. White suggested wryly. "But I shall speak to Captain Phillip and ask whether he'll consent to some rearrangement of the women's accommodations. Clearly it would be an act of humanity if we were able to segregate the well-behaved and the sick from those evil creatures."

"Indeed it would, Dr. White," Thomas Arndell said feelingly.

It was already dawn, White realized, and it had been a long night. But they had brought a new life into the world and, God willing, had saved a fit young soldier from becoming a cripple. He dried his hands and reached into his pocket for his hip flask. James Meredith, he thought cynically, was not the only one driven to the bottle to drown his sorrows, and he could scarcely blame the women in the dark, foul-smelling hold for seeking the same temporary forgetfulness. He took a few sips of the raw spirit and then passed the flask to young Arndell, who, after a moment's hesitation, accepted it.

Two days and nights of thick fog were succeeded by two of heavy, airless calm, with thunder growling in the distance. But on June 2 a favorable wind sprang up, and by nightfall on the third the whole fleet came to anchor in the Santa Cruz Roads.

For Jenny, basking in the affection of the childless Olwyn Jenkins, the days passed happily. She was clean, warm, and well fed and, above all, free of the fear and degradation of the women convicts' quarters, and life began to take on new hope and purpose. It was no matter that the weather was misty, that the famous peak invisible, and that she was not permitted to go ashore. The island of Tenerife, seen from the *Charlotte*'s deck, appeared to be no more than a heap of rocks, piled one upon another and cut into deep ridges, with a small town of white-painted houses huddled beneath them.

Captain Phillip and his senior officers paid official calls on the Spanish governor, which were formally returned, and permission having been granted for the fleet to water and purchase fresh provisions, the diet of all—including the convicts—dramatically improved. Fresh beef was issued instead of the normal salt tack, newly-baked bread appeared on the mess tables, and quantities of green figs, pumpkins, and onions were taken on board and doled out as rations.

The women convicts appeared in factory-woven dresses bought for them by the seamen, and casks of local wine were smuggled into their quarters, with no attempt being made to prevent the traffic in the absence of most of the officers, who were granted shore leave.

Initially, still adopting as humane a policy toward them as he could, Captain Phillip ordered the hatches to be opened and the convicts to exercise on deck during the hours permitted to them when the ships were at sea. A man from the *Alexander,* however, contrived to make his escape in a stolen boat, and following his recapture, all the prisoners were again battened down in the holds. This did not unduly worry the women on board the *Charlotte,* who continued to receive their normal flow of visitors and were, it seemed, amply supplied with liquor by the affluent Mrs. Davis to enable them to while away the daylight hours when the ships' companies were at work, watering and victualing and manning boats.

Jenny, listening to the sounds of revelry which issued from the hold, was thankful to be free.

She had been permitted to see very little of Andrew Hawley, save under the supervision of one or the other of her new guardians, but he had made it plain that is was his intention to court her honorably, and this knowledge added much to her growing happiness. Andrew was as she remembered him from their journey to London—a kindly gentle giant, seeking in every way he could to shield and protect her, and she delighted in his quiet, inarticulate devotion. His own life was not easy. For no reason that Jenny could understand, he had incurred the enmity of Lieutenant Leach . . . although, Sergeant Jenkins admitted grimly, he was not alone in this.

Jeremiah Leach was already bidding fair to make himself the most unpopular officer in the fleet, not only with the men under his command but also with the *Charlotte*'s convicts and the civilian seamen. He did not go ashore with the others, pleading his inability to afford such distractions as they indulged in, and the easygoing Captain Tench—his immediate superior—was apparently only too pleased to leave him in charge, so that he himself might be free to dine at the governor's residence and explore the island.

Leach took full advantage of the opportunity to exercise his brief authority. The marines were paraded for inspection, in full marching order, twice in one day; men whose kit did not meet his exacting standards were not permitted to go off duty until all deficiencies had been rectified. For Andrew Hawley in particular he reserved the bulk of his spite.

"You've to take it, lad," Sergeant Jenkins warned, when Andrew, white with barely suppressed rage, joined him on the mess deck after the second of Leach's lengthy inspections. "He's an officer, he holds the king's commission, and when he gives you an order, you've no choice but to carry it out. If you stand up to him, he won't rest until he's broken you—he's that kind. Thank God," he added piously, "there aren't too many of his kind in the corps."

"No, Sergeant. But—" Andrew controlled himself. He went on flatly, "This morning, at the end of the forenoon watch, I was detailed to supervise the ration issue to the male convicts. There were fresh provisions —fruit, a whole stack of it, and soft bread—and the poor sods were clamoring for it. I had 'em lined up, ready, when along comes Mister Leach. 'Oh,' he says, very haughtylike, 'there's to be no issue of fresh provisions to these prisoners.'"

"No fresh provisions?" Sergeant Jenkins echoed, startled out of his stoic calm. "But they're entitled to them, on Captain Phillip's orders! Did Mister Leach give any reason why he was countermanding that order?"

"Aye, he did. Said he had good reason to believe that they were planning an escape."

"And were they?"

"It was the first I heard of it—and I was guard commander last night." Andrew shrugged.

"I'll try to have a quiet word with Captain Tench," Jenkins promised. "But in the meantime, my lad, you just keep a still tongue in your head and carry out any orders you're given . . . understand?"

Andrew did his best, but the following day— Thursday, June 7—the religious festival of Corpus Christi was celebrated in Santa Cruz. As usual all officers were granted shore leave but Captain Phillip forbade the masters of the transports to send boats ashore with loading or working parties, lest any misunderstandings should arise with the townspeople. The *Charlotte*'s seamen, in common with the rest, were ordered to remain on board, and anticipating a day to be spent carousing with the women, the seamen had brought out extra casks of the local wine to the ship and had hidden them on the mess decks.

Lieutenant Leach, waiting only until his seniors and most of the ship's officers had departed for the shore, ordered the hatches closed and padlocked and then paraded the marine guard. As ill luck would have it, Andrew Hawley was guard commander, and Leach's expression bore witness to his pleasure in this fact as he issued his instructions.

"Take an armed party below, Corporal Hawley," he commanded. "And make a thorough search of the seamen's messes. I have reason to suppose that illicit supplies of liquor, intended for the convicts, have been concealed there. You will seize and bring to me on deck any that you find . . . at once, understand?

If you meet with resistance, use what force is necessary to quell it."

Andrew acknowledged the order, wooden-faced. He detailed his search party but sent a man to summon Sergeant Jenkins and, filled with apprehension, led the rest below. The seamen, clearly expecting no interference from their own officers, had made only a cursory attempt to hide their supplies, and the search party found them without difficulty. Sullenly they watched the marines manhandle the casks from their temporary concealment, but when Andrew gave the order to take them on deck, the seamen's mood turned ugly.

"Bloody lobsters!" a powerfully built member of the carpenter's crew shouted accusingly. "What in hell d'ye think you're doing?"

"Obeying my orders, friend," Andrew returned.

"An' who give 'em you? That little bastard lootenant, was it?" The carpenter turned to his shipmates. "Are we standin' for this, boys? Are we lettin' these sodding Johnnie-toe-the-liners rob us of our liquor?"

A concerted roar of fury answered him.

"Bloody-back sodjers! Stinkin' pipe clays!"

"Bastard officers! Let 'em rot, I say!"

An elderly quartermaster, anxious to prevent the two sides from coming to blows, grasped Andrew by the arm. "Tell the officer you didn't find no liquor here, Corporal," he suggested breathlessly. "There'll be hell ter pay if you don't. Why—"

The suggestion, which Andrew would gladly have acted upon, came too late. Three angry seamen flung themselves on one of the marines and bore him to the ground; other blows were exchanged, and pandemonium broke out. Inwardly cursing Leach for leaving him to bear the brunt of the unpopular order, Andrew formed his party into line in front of the disputed wine casks and bade them fix bayonets. Faced by a wall of cold steel, the seamen drew back, venting their rage and frustration in blasphemy.

"I'll leave you a couple of casks!" Andrew yelled. "But see and hide 'em properly this time!" Out of the corner of his eye he saw Sergeant Jenkins and one of the ship's officers approaching; he gestured to them, and the quartermaster, divining his meaning, grabbed the nearest cask and rolled it out of sight. A second and a third followed it. Order restored, the marines were permitted to pick up the rest and retreat with them to the foot of the hatchway. As they were taking the casks on deck, Sergeant Jenkins came to a halt at Andrew's side.

"Lieutenant Leach?" he asked, in a low, controlled voice, ignoring the jeers that greeted him.

"Aye," Andrew returned with bitterness. "Who else? I reckon he means to dump the stuff over the side, too, when we take it on deck, damn his eyes!"

"The sergeant major's gone to have a word with him," Jenkins said. He sighed and then, mindful of discipline, drew himself up and ordered curtly, "On deck with you, Corporal Hawley—I'll be behind you."

But once again intervention came too late. When they gained the deck, it was to see the first of the wine casks being upended and its contents poured into the murky waters of the harbor. The senior sergeant of the company, a tough, battle-hardened veteran of the American war, stood silent and red of face, and Jenkins went to join him. After a brief, whispered exchange, the sergeant major stumped off, taking two men with him, and Jenkins marched across to where

Lieutenant Leach was standing, giving him an impeccable salute.

Andrew did not hear what he said, but Leach's reply, delivered in a loud, hectoring tone, carried to every man at the gangway. "Another word, Sergeant, and I will have you placed under arrest and charged with dereliction of duty! The sergeant major has been instructed to make a search of the women convicts' quarters, and the women will be brought on deck and held under guard while the search is in progress. You will be responsible for seeing that they hold no communication with the ship's company." He gestured to the men gathered around the wine casks. "I want all illicit supplies of liquor tipped overboard *now*, is that clear? Then jump to it!"

The marine search party reluctantly obeyed him. As the last cask was emptied the women convicts emerged onto the barricaded section of the afterdeck, and, evidently informed of what was going on and fearing for their own liquor supplies, they set up a furious clamor. High-pitched voices screamed abuse and obscenities at Lieutenant Leach, and he reddened resentfully; finally, with what dignity he could muster in the face of their noisy accusations, he retired to his own quarters, leaving Sergeant Jenkins in charge.

Mrs. Davis was the last to come on deck and she did not mince words when she saw that Leach had gone. Her complaints concerning his behavior, made at the pitch of her lungs to the unhappy Jenkins, were plainly audible to his wife and Jenny as they, too, came up on deck to take the air.

"He's a bad 'un," Mrs. Davis stated, when the sergeant had managed to calm her a little. "Three girls I've sent him, Sergeant, and they've all come back in a shocking state, refusing to have anything more to do with him. I tell you, if you won't report him to Captain Tench and the ship's master, *I* will! I'll cook his goose for him, if it's the last thing I do, the bullying young rogue!"

"He can claim that he's only been doing his duty," Sergeant Jenkins told her wryly. "Liquor is not allowed to be brought on board by the ship's company, Missus Davis. And it is strictly forbidden to male and female convicts, as you well know."

"Then what is to be done, Sergeant?" Mrs. Davis demanded. "Have we to suffer him, all the way to Botany Bay then?"

"I can have a word with Captain Tench, unofficiallylike," the sergeant offered. "If I let him know what has been going on, he will put matters right. But in his own time and in his own way, so long as we don't make an issue of it, understand? If you go complaining to the master, you will cook everybody's goose, for then it will have to be reported to Captain Phillip. And whatever they do to Mister Leach, *you* are liable to be battened down under hatches for the rest of the voyage, the lot of you—and the chains put on you again, more than likely. As for myself—" he shrugged—"I could expect a court-martial for allowing you too much freedom—dereliction of duty, they would call it. Mister Leach has already accused me of that, Missus Davis."

She paled. "Is that the truth, Sergeant?"

"It's the truth," the old sergeant declared emphatically.

Mrs. Davis sighed. "You know what's wrong with him, don't you? He wants the little lass you have taken under your wing and. . . ." she lowered her voice and Jenny did not catch the rest of what she said, but Olwyn Jenkins, sensing trouble for her husband, whispered urgently, "Go below to the cabin, *cariad*, and stay there till I come for you. I must speak to Tom before he has to go out with the guardboat, see . . . but take care, you understand? Go straight to the cabin; now there's a good girl."

Jenny obeyed without question. Andrew Hawley was pacing up and down in front of the midships hatchway, talking to one of the armed sentries Lieutenant Leach had posted there, and seeing her, he offered his escort.

"The seamen are in an ugly mood," he told her. "And since we can't keep *them* battened down, maybe I'd better come with you."

She let him take her arm a trifle nervously, but passing a group of angry seamen on the main mess deck, she was glad of his stalwart figure beside her when the men hurled abuse at them, interspersed with jeering accusations.

When they reached the tiny cabin she shared now with Olwyn Jenkins, he said, red with embarrassment, "As soon as ever I can get permission, I'd like to wed you, Jenny, if you'll have me."

She looked up into his strong, honest face, and her heart lifted. He was a good man, she told herself, and she would be fortunate indeed if he made her his wife. With a man like Andrew beside her, she knew the new colony would hold few terrors for her; they could make a home, farm the land he would be given, raise crops and sheep, perhaps, and . . . children too, children whose lot might be happier than their own. She would bear Andrew sons to inherit his land and they—

"Well, Jenny, love," Andrew urged. "What do you say? Will you have me?"

Jenny caught her breath on a sob. "Oh, gladly, Andrew," she answered. "I—I'm proud that you should ask me, that you should want me to marry you. But there's my sentence . . . it's a life sentence, you know. Will you be given permission to marry a convict?"

"I'll not rest until I am, lass," Andrew vowed. "If the commandant won't give it to me, I'll appeal to Captain Phillip."

Hope dawned, dispelling the nightmare fears that had haunted her for so long, and Jenny's eyes were shining as she looked up into Andrew's smiling face. He raised to his lips the hand he held and then, his smile widening, gestured to the curtain that hung at the entrance to the Jenkinses' tiny cabin.

"Go inside, Jenny. If we're to wed, I can claim a kiss, surely? A kiss to plight our troth, eh?" He followed her in and, letting the curtain fall behind him, took her into his arms. "I've not been one for the women, not till now," he told her softly. "But I'll love you, lass, and I'll be good to you, that I promise."

His mouth found hers, gently at first and then demandingly, and Jenny clung to him, her heart thudding like a wild thing in her breast, as a sudden wave of eager desire swept over her. In the old days, when she had lived and worked at the Three Fools tavern, Ned Munday had snatched a kiss or two when he came on her unawares, but Ned's kisses had engendered no emotion save, perhaps, disgust. He was no innocent, as he had frequently boasted, and he bestowed his attentions freely on any girl who did not slap his face or send him packing.

But this . . . this surely must be love, Jenny thought, bemused by the wonder of it, as Andrew's big hand tenderly cupped her small immature breast and then moved to trace the curve of her neck, her chin, the contours of her small erect body. In that moment of revelation she would willingly have surrendered her virtue to him had he asked this of her, and as if sensing her weakness and fearing to match it with his own, he put her from him, grimly resolute.

"Our time will come, Jenny," he said thickly. "You're mine and I love you, lass, and before God, it tears my heart out to leave you. But if my absence is reported to that young blackguard Leach, I shall be in real trouble. And trouble's the last thing I want just now." He bent to kiss the top of her head, holding her at arm's length, his hands not steady. "If we're to have any chance of . . ." The words died on his lips as, from the deck outside, Lieutenant Leach's voice bawled his name.

No liquor had been found in the women's quarters, and suspecting that the search had not been thorough, Jeremiah Leach was in a towering rage when he entered the *Charlotte*'s main cabin.

Normally used as a mess for both the sea and marine officers, the cabin was deserted except for the young fourth mate and the two stewards, whose duty it was to wait on the officers. The mate, after a glance at Leach's grimly set face, excused himself hurriedly on the plea of impending watch-keeping duties, and the senior steward—having no such excuse—came resignedly to ask Leach his pleasure. The steward had been dozing in his pantry, anticipating no calls for his services, since virtually all the officers were ashore, and he came in his shirtsleeves instead of the starched white uniform jacket he was supposed to wear. Leach scowled at him and brusquely ordered him to fetch a bottle of brandy.

"See that you're properly dressed when you serve it," he added, "or I'll report you to the purser."

The steward did not acknowledge the order. He donned his tight-fitting jacket and brought the brandy and a glass, setting both down with deliberate clumsiness.

"This is the last bottle in your name, sir," he said. "I can arrange to have a dozen supplied by one of the local merchants before we sail, if you wish. But I shall require payment, if you please—in advance, sir."

"Damn your eyes, I'll pay you when I see the stuff! And when I've tasted it—I'm not being chiseled by you or any of those rogues of merchants in Santa Cruz. I want good brandy, understand?" Leach's tone was deliberately offensive.

"It will not be inferior to what you brought with you, sir," the steward said pointedly and returned to his pantry.

"Insolent swine!" Leach muttered. He slopped a generous measure of the brandy his father had given him into the bulbous glass and drank it distastefully. It *was* inferior stuff; his father had purchased it cheaply from a friend in the trade, like the rest of the supplies he had provided for the voyage, anxious only to see the back of him. Damnation take him! He was the eldest son, Leach reminded himself, and his father wasn't poor by any stretch of the imagination, yet he had been sent into exile—which was what this voyage amounted to—with virtually no money and no promise of any in the future either . . . unless, as his father had put it, he "made good."

"This is your chance, Jeremiah," the old man had told him on the eve of his departure. "And I would advise you to take it, because frankly if you do not,

I shall wash my hands of you and make your brother Francis my heir."

Jeremiah Leach swore softly to himself and poured another measure of brandy into his glass, surprised and a trifle shocked to see that the bottle was now half-empty—and it was his last bottle, too, if the rascally steward was to be believed. But he felt better, considerably better than when he had decided to seek refuge in the cabin until the women convicts had settled down and the seamen had ceased whining about the liquor he had confiscated. Jenkins, he knew, could handle them. He held no brief for the old sergeant, who frequently overstepped the bounds of his authority, but the man's experience and the respect with which he was regarded—by the seamen and convicts, as well as by his own marines—rendered him useful at times.

There was still the matter of the girl, however . . . what was her name? Taggart, Jenny Taggart. Did Jenkins and the virtuous Corporal Hawley know that, however pure and unsullied they imagined her to be, she had a mother, a convict like herself, on board the *Friendship*? He had found this out by pure chance only a few days ago, when the *Friendship*'s surgeon, Dr. Arndell, had visited his colleague, Dr. White, on the *Charlotte*. After the manner of medical men, the two surgeons had fallen to discussing their more serious cases and Arndell had mentioned a Mrs. Rachel Taggart, whom he twice had had to bleed.

Leach smiled to himself. A few pertinent questions on his part had elicited the information he required concerning Rachel Taggart, and he had hugged his new knowledge to himself, waiting an opportunity to put it to use. The girl might not know that her mother was gravely ill, and if he told her and arranged for her to be transferred to the *Friendship*, that would remove her from the Jenkinses' clutches and place her in his debt. And, after that, what was to prevent his asking for a transfer to the *Friendship* himself, at Rio, perhaps, which would be the fleet's next port of call? He . . . Leach hiccoughed, slowly sipping the last of his brandy. The damned stuff was making him deucedly sleepy and he had told Sergeant Jenkins that he would make an inspection of the convicts' quarters and the sentries at five bells, and it must be nearly that now but . . . oh, to hell with it! Jenkins could wait—it would keep him on his toes. He would snatch a quick cat nap and then go on deck. He hiccoughed again and let his heavy lids fall. . . .

"Mister Leach—bestir yourself, for God's sake!" Someone was shaking him, none too gently, and Leach opened his eyes to find the fourth mate glaring down at him.

"W'assa matter?" he demanded thickly.

"My seamen are refusing to obey orders," the young mate informed him wrathfully. "They claim you stole their liquor without authority and dumped it in the harbor. If we have a mutiny on our hands, Mister Leach, the blame will be yours, not mine, and I want their grievances settled before the captain returns from the shore."

"How the devil d'you expect me to settle their infernal grievances?" Leach countered. "They'd no right to have the liquor in the first place, and in any event I can't get it back for them, can I?"

"A couple of guineas would settle it," the mate answered coldly. "That's what they say it cost them. And I think you'd be wise to pay up, Mister Leach, because if I log the men's refusal to attend to their duties, Captain Phillip will have to be informed. Threatened mutiny is a grave matter, you know."

Leach blustered, but he had finally to agree to the young mate's suggestion. Together they went to where the seamen had gathered, in a sullen mob, on the mess deck, and almost speechless with fury, Leach gave them the money. The ironic cheer with which they received it added fuel to the flames of his wrath, and he launched into a tirade concerning their lack of discipline, unable to restrain himself.

"If you were marines, I'd have the hides off the lot of you for this," he shouted. "And if this were a king's ship, you'd be hanged!"

"It ain't a king's ship, thanks be to heaven," one of the seamen snarled. "But if you think all your plaguey lobsters are so well disciplined, step below and poke yer nose into the sergeant's cabin, why don't yer? There's one of 'em there with 'is woman and it ain't the sergeant. A two-striper 'e is—'ave the 'ide off yer own kind, mister, an' leave us honest seamen be!"

Hawley, Leach thought . . . by God, it was Hawley, as he had suspected, it had to be. The virtuous Hawley, who had been sent from the *Sirius*, by Captain Phillip himself, to improve the discipline of the *Charlotte*'s marines! Hawley and, of course, the Taggart girl . . . he drew in his breath sharply.

The seamen dispersed to go about their duties once more. Several voices were raised in angry protest against the man who had spoken up about Hawley, but Jeremiah Leach ignored them. He made for the hatchway and then halted. Better not to be alone when he confronted Hawley. He retraced his steps and, with an imperious gesture, summoned two of the sentries to his side.

"Follow me, both of you," he ordered, and with the

men clumping after him, he flung himself down the forehatch, shouting Hawley's name.

The corporal emerged at once from the Jenkinses' small curtained cabin space to stand rigidly to attention in front of it. His uniform, Leach noticed with disappointment was correctly buttoned and he carried his musket, as standing orders required of him when on duty.

"You are absent from your post," he accused. "Are you alone, Corporal Hawley?"

"I have been absent from my post for ten minutes, sir," Hawley answered, with his usual woodenness. "Sergeant Jenkins was in charge of the upper deck guard, sir, and I—"

"I asked if you were alone, Corporal. Speak up, man! You came below with one of the female convicts, did you not?"

"Mistress Jenkins sent the girl she is caring for below, sir. I escorted her to the cabin and—"

"Then where the devil is she?" Lench asked harshly.

"I am here, Mister Leach." Jenny drew back the curtain. Standing at Andrew Hawley's side, she held her head high and did not flinch from the officer's angry scrutiny. Jeremiah Leach had not seen her at close quarters before, and although he saw her now through the fumes of the brandy he had consumed, he realized that she possessed a dignity and a youthful innocence he had not expected to find in any convict girl. He was momentarily taken aback and even conscious of a fleeting pity, but pity was swiftly succeeded by resentment when Corporal Hawley started to explain that the girl was his intended wife.

"I'm aware of your intentions, Corporal," he snapped. "But you, it would seem, aren't aware that you require permission to marry—and you'll not be given permission to wed a convict. You might as well make up your mind to *that*, my man, because it's the truth."

"I can wait until the lass earns her remission, sir," Hawley returned. His complacency infuriated Leach. It was an example of the fellow's dumb insolence, he thought—absent from his post, and now, far from apologizing, he was smugly claiming that he had a right to accompany the girl below because he had proposed marriage to her. There was no doubt that Corporal Hawley needed to be taught a sharp lesson, one he wouldn't forget in a hurry.

"She'll not find it easy to earn her remission," he said. "With her mother a convicted felon, as well as herself! Had you taken that fact into consideration, Hawley?" Satisfied from the corporal's sudden pallor that he had succeeded in striking him on the raw, Leach turned to face the girl. "Your name's Taggart, is it not, Jennifer Taggart?"

"I . . . yes, sir. But—"

"Is your mother's name Rachel Taggart?" Leach put in quickly. The girl nodded, started to speak, and then thought better of it, so he went on, "Rachel Taggart is one of the women on board the *Friendship*— sentenced to transportation for life, I understand. And according to Doctor Arndell, the *Friendship*'s surgeon, she is gravely ill but—it comes as a shock to you, evidently. Weren't you told?"

"No. No, I wasn't told." Jenny was so stunned by this news that she could hardly speak. She looked at Andrew in mute distress, her eyes pleading with him to deny that he had known of her mother's presence on board the *Friendship*, and when he did not deny it, she bit back a sob.

"Why didn't you tell me, Andrew—if you knew, why didn't you tell me?"

"We thought to spare you, Jenny. We—"

"But if she's gravely ill, I must go to her. She's my mother, they'll surely let me look after her, will they not?" Jenny's question was addressed to Andrew, but Leach answered it with well-simulated compassion as Andrew shook his head helplessly.

"I'll do all in my power to help you, Jenny. Transfers from one ship to another are not easily arranged, but in the circumstances and perhaps on Doctor Arndell's recommendation, yours might be permitted."

Jenny thanked him, her small face draining of color. She avoided Andrew's gaze, and Leach called him sharply to attention. "Return to your post, Corporal Hawley," he ordered. "And take these two men with you. I shall have to report your dereliction of duty to Captain Tench, of course, but let us hope, for your sake, that he may take a lenient view of your conduct. You are dismissed."

Andrew held his ground. "I'll not leave without the lass, sir," he declared stubbornly. "With your permission, I will take her with me. Mistress Jenkins is on deck, sir, and—"

Leach cut him short. "Are you refusing to obey an order from a superior officer, Corporal?" he challenged. "I doubt if Captain Tench will take a lenient view of *that*!"

The two marines he had brought with him, who had hitherto maintained a disciplined silence, muttered warnings under their breath, and the elder of the two, a grizzled veteran like Jenkins, stepped to Andrew's side and gripped his arm urgently. "Come on, Corporal," he advised. "He'll have you just where he wants you if you don't, lad."

Leach affected not to have heard him. "Well, Hawley, are you looking for a flogging?"

"You can flog me if you like, Mister Leach," Andrew interrupted, his voice dangerously quiet. "But you'll not lay a hand on my girl, on this ship or any other."

"I've no designs on any whore, you insolent swine!" Leach flung at him.

He was enjoying himself, sensing that at last he had penetrated the thick skin of the big, obstinate corporal, who had defied him for so long with his mulish refusal to respond to provocation. The girl no longer mattered; she was simply a weapon to be used against the upstart who had dared to claim her—a weapon to which, it was becoming increasingly evident, Hawley was vulnerable. And she had not moved; she was still standing at Hawley's side, looking at him with tear-filled eyes, unable to comprehend to what straits she had brought him. Or, come to that, herself . . . he could send her back to the hold with the other women, have her put in irons if he wished and tell Tench, when he returned to the ship, that he had caught her whoring with one of his marines. Tench would believe him without question and, as a conscientious officer, would almost certainly approve of the punishment and throw in a flogging for Hawley for good measure.

Leach suppressed a hiccough. He had drunk rather a lot, he reminded himself, and perhaps the drink was making him reckless because there was the earlier brush with the seamen to be taken into consideration. Captain Tench would certainly be told about that and might be less inclined to take his word concerning Hawley and the girl if he thought Leach had been deliberately stirring up trouble. So it would behoove him to go carefully, and indeed, the threat alone might suffice.

He uttered it, addressing the girl in a hectoring tone and causing her to shrink from him in terror. It was enough to break the iron control Hawley had imposed on himself.

He said hoarsely, "The deck's this way, sir. If you'll be good enough to precede me, I'll take whatever's coming to me for failing to obey my orders and being absent from my post. But the rest is not true, and you know it's not."

"Isn't it?" Leach taunted. "Are you sure, Corporal? Do you have witnesses to prove it?"

For answer Hawley thrust his musket into the grasp of the man beside him and, deaf to his shout of alarm, took Leach by the shoulders and propelled him forcibly toward the hatchway. Caught off balance, the young officer stumbled, and he was on his knees when he struck the lower rung of the hatchway ladder.

He picked himself up, breathing heavily, a thin trickle of blood at the corner of his mouth, and Olwyn Jenkins, in the act of descending from the deck above, stood there transfixed at the sight of him. Then, misunderstanding the implications of his presence outside her cabin, she rushed protectively to Jenny's defense, gathering the girl to her like a flustered mother hen.

"Leave the child alone, Mister Leach!" she bade him accusingly. "She is in my charge and not for the likes of yourself or for your pleasure, do you understand?"

Leach rounded on her, almost beside himself with fury. "Hold your tongue, woman! You saw what happened, dammit—this man struck me, and that's a court-martial offense! You two. . . ." The men he had brought with him stiffened to attention, avoiding his angry gaze, their faces white with shock. "Corporal Hawley is under arrest, charged with striking a superior officer," he told them. "Take him away—he's to be held under close guard until Captain Tench returns to the ship."

Jenny watched the four scarlet-uniformed figures vanish up the hatchway, one of the sentries gripping Andrew's arm with obvious reluctance. She felt sick with dismay and would have fainted, but Olwyn Jenkins, an arm about her shoulders, led her back into the cabin and gently helped her to lie down on the lower bunk. A few probing questions, softly voiced, elicited the whole pitiful story from the sobbing girl, and the motherly Welshwoman held her in comforting arms, letting her weep.

"What—what will they do to him, Mistress Jenkins?" Jenny asked, forcing her trembling lips to frame the question. "Will they—will they flog him?"

They would more likely hang him, Olwyn Jenkins thought grimly; if it came to a court-martial, no other sentence could be passed, should the charge be proved. Striking an officer was the most serious crime a soldier could commit in time of peace, and the death sentence, she knew, was arbitrary. "*Did* Andrew strike him?" she questioned gently. "Did he, Jenny?"

Jenny shook her head. "Oh, no," she asserted tearfully. "He kept his temper until Mister Leach said I was a whore and that he would have me sent back to the—the other whores and order me to be chained as a punishment. Then Andrew took him by the shoulders, that's all he did, and tried to make him go on deck, but he stumbled and fell against the ladder. He was drunk, Mistress Jenkins. I—I could smell it on his breath. The two marines who came with him—they saw what happened and they must have known Mister Leach was drunk. Surely they'll speak up for Andrew, will they not?"

It was probable that they would, Olwyn thought, if her Tom had a word with them. And there were the seamen, too—they had gone to Tom with their complaints of Lieutenant Leach's conduct, which was why she had had to delay her own return to the cabin. She answered Jenny evasively, still seeking to comfort her. It was a thousand pities that Tom had had to go out with the guard boat but . . . he would be back, God willing, before Captain Tench was. And nothing could or would be done until Captain Tench returned to the ship.

"Is it true about my mother?" Jenny whispered suddenly. "Mister Leach said she was on board the *Friendship* and that she was gravely ill."

Olwyn Jenkins admitted reluctantly that it was true.

"Tom said she was listed as being in the *Friendship*, *cariad*, but he did not tell me she was ill. Mister Leach may have lied—" she broke off, clicking her tongue with annoyance at the slip she had made. "He may have made that up, child, to—well, to frighten you."

"If Mam is ill," the girl said wretchedly, "it's my duty to go to her, to help her if I can. I shall have to ask to be transferred to the *Friendship*, Mistress Jenkins."

"Yes," Olwyn conceded, her mouth tight. "I suppose you will, my lamb—but we will make sure first. If you were to be transferred, you would be put back with the women convicts in the hold, you know. There would be no escaping that."

"I know," Jenny said and shivered. "But she is my mam and if she needs me, I—I *must* go to her."

Captain Tench returned to the *Charlotte* later that evening, to be met by Jeremiah Leach at the entry port. They were closeted together in Tench's cabin for about an hour, following which the marine captain sent for Sergeant Jenkins, and in his presence Andrew Hawley was interrogated. Next day he continued his inquiries. Shore leave had been canceled preparatory to sailing and there remained much to be done on board all the ships, but Watkin Tench devoted the morning to a careful search for the truth. Jenny was questioned, kindly and with no attempt to wring any damaging admissions from her. Tench was formal in his manner but courteous, and she left his presence feeling reassured, although he had given no hint of his own view of the events that had led to Andrew's arrest.

The day dragged on; she walked the deck with Olwyn at their accustomed hour, and together they watched a boat being lowered, which conveyed Captain Tench to the *Sirius*, accompanied by Sergeant Jenkins. It returned, an hour later, with Major Ross seated in the stern sheets with Tench, and the investigation was resumed in the *Charlotte*'s main-deck cabin, with the old sergeant still in attendence.

Jenny continued to fret until she watched a boat being lowered and saw Lieutenant Leach step into it, his kit being piled in after him by two grinning seamen. As the boat pulled away, heading for the *Alexander*, the convict women exercising on their barricaded deck raised a derisive cheer, and some of them, running to the rail, screeched obscene insults at the departing officer. Leach did not look up, pretending not to hear them, but his face was brick-red, and seeing this, the women doubled their cheers.

"There's justice now," Olwyn Jenkins observed shrewdly. "And Major Ross will *know* it is when he hears that!"

The marine commandant appeared in person a few minutes later to stand at the entry port at the head of a small procession. His boat was called alongside; he shook hands formally with Captain Tench, both of them smiling and seeming on the best of terms, and Jenny's hopes rose, only to be dashed again when she recognized Andrew's tall figure standing stiffly between two marine guards. He entered the boat, and with Major Ross in the stern sheets as before, the bowman shoved off and the naval crew bent to their oars.

"He is being taken to the *Sirius*," Olwyn said and sighed. "I am afraid that means he has not got off scot-free, Jenny. But maybe it will just be a flogging, so do not break your heart over it, my lamb. He is strong—it will do him no lasting harm, see."

Her husband confirmed her supposition when he came on deck. "Reduced to the ranks and three dozen lashes for being absent from his post without permission," Sergeant Jenkins told them. "And he's transferred back to the *Sirius*, Jenny lass. But he'll have the ear of Captain Phillip there, and I don't doubt he'll request permission to wed you, when the time is ripe for him to do so. Mister Leach is worse off than he is really—the *Alexander* is a tub and she's carrying all the known troublemakers among the male convicts and the sickliest of them too. Let him play the tyrant there, if he likes—he'll get no change out of them!"

CHAPTER XI

The fleet sailed at daybreak next morning—Sunday, June 10—but the light breeze that had carried them out of Santa Cruz Roads failed by evening, and for two days the ships were becalmed, lying almost motionless on a glassy sea. On the thirteenth the northeast trade wind found them and the calm was succeeded by heavy seas.

The chaplain, who had been rowed across to the *Lady Penrhyn* to conduct divine service on board, found himself an unwilling guest when a signal from the *Sirius* forbade ship-to-ship visits by boat during bad weather because of the risks involved and the delay caused when a boat got into difficulty. Deprived of his own comfortable cabin on board the *Golden Grove* and the devoted care of his wife, Reverend Johnson—at the best of times, a poor enough sailor —was soon reduced to a state of querulous misery.

The hatches were seldom closed; the sentries were lax, permitting access to the women by day, as well as by night, to the merchant seamen as well as the marines.

The limit, so far as Reverend Johnson was concerned, was reached on the second morning of his enforced stay when he came on deck to find an almost carnival atmosphere prevailing. The women were gathered on the forecastle, laughing and wildly excited, as half a dozen grotesque figures were hauled over the bows, led by an apparition festooned with false hair and trailing what seemed to be seaweed. The apparition wore a paper crown and clutched a wooden trident in its right hand, and the shrieks were redoubled when, in pagan parody, asserting that it was King Neptune, the strange figure pranced across the deck, claiming kisses from the women as it passed.

"I am Neptune, King of the Deep, and this ship is crossing the equinoctial line into my kingdom!" the loud voice proclaimed. "All who enter for the first time must pay tribute! Rum and sugar from the master, and the ship's name shall be entered in my log!"

Unbeknownst to the scandalized chaplain, crossing the line with passengers was an occasion for horseplay and high spirits, to lessen the tedium of a long voyage—even when the passengers were convicted felons. A canvas pool was rigged, bilge-water pumped into it, and the younger members of the ship's company—including officers and marines—were lined up beside it by the older hands, posing as Neptune's nymphs and Nereids, their faces daubed with red ocher. Each unwilling victim was seated on a stool, his countenance lathered with a nauseous mixture of tar and tallow, and after this had been scraped off with the aid of a two-foot length of wood shaped like a razor, the stool was deftly upended and Neptune's new subject given a ducking.

Captain Sever, Reverend Johnson observed—far from disapproving of the proceedings—was presiding over a barrel of rum from which, a foolishly indulgent grin on his round, red face, he was refreshing the various participants in the tomfoolery. True, the convict women were only present in the role of spectators, although two of them, scantily clad and laughing uproariously, had allowed themselves to be seized by four of the revelers.

The time had come to intervene. The chaplain thrust his way toward the captain, but before he could voice his disapproval, Sever himself ordered the women released. Their captors obeyed with drunken reluctance; then, to Reverend Johnson's speechless horror, they turned on him, grasping him firmly by both arms.

One of them, an Irishman and, inevitably, a Catholic for he addressed him as Father, exclaimed delightedly, "Ah, now, his rev'rince won't have crossed the line, so he won't! Ye'll be wantin' ter pay homage to King Neptune, will you not, Father? Down on yer knees then!"

Ignoring his protests, they forced him to kneel and then, without respect for his cloth, picked him up bodily and dumped him on to the ducking stool. Reverend Johnson, deeply affronted by what he deemed an assault on his dignity, could no longer contain himself. In a voice like thunder he silenced the women, who were now screeching with ribald laughter, and all four of the men who held him stood back, releasing their grasp of his arms. Neptune—revealed beneath the beard and the imitation seaweed as the first mate—said quietly, "It's a custom of the sea, Mister Johnson . . . there's no harm in it."

He was interrupted in midsentence by a roar from Captain Sever. Without warning, the blunt bow of one of the other ships loomed out of the mist, so close that Reverend Johnson drew in his breath in horror, certain that she must run foul of them. Both ships were under jibs and topsails; the newcomer had her forecourse set and she was moving swiftly through the heaving swell, her bowsprit jutting skywards and seemingly about to strike the *Lady Penrhyn*'s mizzen shrouds.

Disaster was averted by the speed of reaction displayed by Sever's crew. Neptune flung down his trident and hurled himself across the deck, and Richard Johnson was knocked down by the rush of men who followed him. The master himself took the wheel; officers and seamen hauled round the braces as the marines, abandoning the clamorous women, pounded aft, the thud of their booted feet drowning the cries of the women. The chaplain was no seaman; he had no idea of what they had done, but as he picked himself up from the deck and saw a widening expanse of water between the two ships, he breathed a prayer of thankfulness to his Maker.

A little later the brig-rigged sloop *Supply* came within hail and he heard a somewhat acrimonious exchange between her commander and the *Lady Penrhyn*'s master, which, to his hurt surprise, ended with a request from Captain Sever for a boat to be sent to take off the chaplain. Permission being granted by the *Sirius*, the boat rowed across the choppy water, and, soaked to the skin and decidedly out of temper, Richard Johnson was returned to the *Golden Grove* and his anxious wife.

That afternoon Captain Phillip and Hunter were discussing the morning's escapades and near tragedy when Phillip paused and sighed. "I don't much like the way the glass is behaving. Unless I'm much mistaken, we'll be in for some dirty weather before we make port at Rio . . . and our water may run short if we're delayed on passage. I think we should send Ball to Saint Iago in the *Supply*, to ascertain whether it's possible for the convoy to enter Port Praia to replenish stocks, what do you say? It may be three weeks or more before we can hope to pick up the southeast trades."

Hunter inclined his head. "I'll inform Captain Ball, sir."

The Cape Verde Islands were sighted on the eighteenth in poor visibility, and the following day, the *Supply* was ordered to go ahead, but with a heavy beam swell running and the wind capricious, she experienced so much difficulty in her attempt to work into Port Praia Bay that Phillip recalled her. There was now nothing for it but to set course for Rio de Janeiro and ration water for drinking and cooking purposes very strictly.

Conditions were far from pleasant for the next three weeks. Close, warm weather alternated with squalls and lashing rain or fierce thunderstorms, with lightning flashing across the dark, ominous skies. At times the convoy wallowed in the pounding seas; at others the ships were becalmed on a mist-shrouded ocean, and more than once they were compelled to heave-to, under bare poles, until the wind subsided.

The worst storm erupted on the night of July 5

and with little warning, save the distant mutter of thunder to the southeast and a sudden plummeting of the glass. Lieutenant King had the middle watch on board the *Sirius*; he came on deck a few minutes before midnight to relieve the master Morton and was surprised to find the ship still carrying unreefed topsails, forecourse, and jibs, despite the rising wind.

Morton made his report a trifle sullenly. He was a small wizened man, in poor health and, in King's critical opinion, unreliable and inefficient. Guessing that he had been below for part, at least, of his watch, leaving a midshipman in charge, the lieutenant taxed him with it and received a shamefaced assent.

"Devil take it, Mister Morton!" King swore. "I ought to log you for that!" He turned away in disgust.

Captain Hunter came on deck a few minutes later, a pea jacket over his nightshirt and his bare feet thrust into sea boots. The storm struck with a crash of thunder, sounding as if it were directly overhead, and in the vivid flash of lightning that followed, both officers looked up anxiously at the topmen laying out on the upper yards. Both watches were working; they had managed to furl the jibs and get the forecourse in as Lieutenant King directed the men at the braces and the two quartermasters fought the kicking wheel. Rain lashed down with tropical fury; the ship heeled drunkenly, burying her bows in a monstrous wave that crashed over the forecastle. The men striving to regain the deck from the jib boom had to cling for dear life to any support they could find.

Captain Hunter roared, "Mind your weather helm, quartermaster!" and an instant later, with a crack like that of the discharge of a signal cannon, the main topsail split and the ship's head flew up into the wind.

On the yard, which was braced well in, young Alan Harper was leaning over, endeavoring to secure the reef beckets when the wildly flapping canvas of the split topsail struck him a stinging blow across the face. Temporarily blinded and the breath knocked out of him, his bare feet lost their grip on the foot-rope, and suddenly he was swinging by his hands, the weight of his body dragging him down. On either side of him the other maintopmen battled with the torn sail, unaware of his predicament, and the howling wind bore his faint cries soundlessly away.

To his horror, as he hung there, a series of lightning flashes illuminated another ship of the fleet, the *Alexander*, and as his mesmerized gaze went to her he saw clearly and unmistakably a body go hurtling down from her upper rigging.

It was then, as the initial shock passed, that Harper realized that, but for the grace of God, he himself would be in the same awful situation. Clinging tenaciously to the lashing of the yard, he felt desperately afraid and conscious of his lack of experience. He had been in storms before but nothing like this, in so large a ship. He offered up a prayer, not daring to look down and feeling his hands start to slip. Oh, God, why didn't one of the other men come to his aid? Could they not see what straits he was in? Rain poured down on him, on his upturned face, as his legs flailed this way and that, seeking a foothold which would take some of the strain from his weakening arms.

And then, just as he knew that he could hold on no longer to the chafing rope, an authoritative voice bade him take heart. A hand gripped his arm from above. Sobbing his thankfulness, he held on grimly and felt someone grasp his other arm. As they hauled him back onto the yard and his feet at last found the footrope, he glimpsed a boat being lowered from the *Alexander*, obviously to look for the lost seaman.

It was not until he reached the comparative safety of the deck that Harper identified the man responsible for his rescue as the officer of the watch, Lieutenant King, who made the descent with him. He started to stammer his thanks, but King brushed them aside and told him curtly to carry on—and that, he saw from the activity on deck, meant going aloft again, to bend a new topsail. He obeyed, with a sinking heart. . . .

The storm had taken its toll, but two days later the southeast trades put an end to anxiety, and with greatly improved weather the spirits of all swiftly rose.

Once again the convicts were permitted on deck to exercise and an order went out from the *Sirius* that the bilges of the transports were to be pumped out to lessen the danger of sickness resulting from the tainted effluvia that had accumulated during the storms and high seas.

Many of the convicts were ill, and Jenny worried incessantly about her mother in the crowded hold of the *Friendship*, for it had become very hot, and with drinking water strictly rationed to three pints per head a day, conditions for the women convicts in particular were very trying.

Olwyn Jenkins, recognizing the torment of conscience the girl was enduring, no longer sought to persuade her to remain in the *Charlotte* but sadly promised to give her what aid she could to obtain a transfer to her mother's ship in Rio. The kindly Mrs. Jenkins's sadness sprang from rumors concerning the lack of discipline on board the *Friendship*. It was said that the male convicts had broken down the barriers that separated their quarters from those of the women, that there was constant fighting among both men and women, and that two of the marine sergeants on board had been threatened with court-martial on charges of unsoldierly conduct, from which only Major Ross's intervention had saved them.

But, much as she would have liked to, Olwyn Jenkins said nothing of this to Jenny. If the child had made up her mind, such rumors—whether or not they were true—would not change it.

A few days later Dr. White, who was traveling in the *Charlotte*, was summoned to the *Alexander* where a fresh outbreak of fever among the convicts threatened calamity. There was a strong sea running, and the fleet hove-to to permit him to take a boat across to the stricken transport. After spending some hours on board, the surgeon's boat pulled across to the *Sirius*, and shortly afterwards, one of the flagship's boats went alongside the *Alexander*, whose crew was next observed frantically pumping and swilling out her bilges.

Surgeon White took advantage of the enforced delay to visit two of the other transports, including the *Friendship*, and Jenny, watching the coming and going with mounting excitement, begged Sergeant Jenkins to inquire from him, on his return, if there was any news of her mother's condition. It was with mixed emotions that she learned there was none. Dr. White's call had been to examine a sick officer and he had seen none of the convicts. All he could say was that only one death had been reported to him and the victim was an elderly male convict who had been dying when he came on board.

A letter from Andrew, delivered by one of the boat's crew, relieved Jenny's anxiety on his account. The letter was brief, scrawled on a torn scrap of paper, but it told her that he had suffered only mild discomfort from his flogging—reduced to two dozen lashes by Captain Phillip—and that he had returned to duty.

The fleet got under way once more and on August 5 dropped anchor off Cape Frio at the mouth of Rio de Janeiro harbor.

Captain Phillip sent Lieutenant King ashore with greetings to Rio's Portuguese governor and viceroy, Dom Luis Velasque de Concierge, and with instructions to obtain official permission for the fleet to enter harbor and revictual. This being readily granted, King returned, bearing a gift of fruit for his commander.

"Dom Luis was most cordial, sir," he reported. "And he asked me particularly to tell you that your valuable service to his country's navy, during the Spanish war, has not been forgotten. He is anxious to serve you in any way he can."

"Excellent!" Phillip approved. "Then we will make our formal entry tomorrow morning."

"Aye, aye, sir. Er . . . the fruit's very good, sir."

"Is it?" Arthur Phillip smiled and selected an orange from the profusion in front of him. "Did you ask the viceroy if he could sell us the musket balls we need?"

"I hinted at our need in that respect, sir. But both His Excellency and his interpreter seemed so astonished, I hardly liked to pursue the matter."

"Small wonder he was surprised!" The captain laughed mirthlessly. "Who would believe that any government would send a convoy of felons halfway round the world with a scant two hundred marines to guard them, and they lacking the wherewithal to fire their muskets!

"Oh, by the by, it has been brought to my notice

that fruit and vegetables—purchased by some of our
people from the boats that have had the enterprise to
row out to us—have been paid for with counterfeit
quarter-dollar pieces. Doctor White informs me that
the spurious coins are the work of a certain Thomas
Barrett, who is a convict in the *Charlotte*. I've done all
in my power to ensure that the boatmen are reim-
bursed and—ah—the position explained to them. I
think they're satisfied, but you had better have Mister
Barrett sent across to me. I'll deal with the miscreant
at once and where the boatmen can see justice being
meted out to him."

"Aye, aye, sir," Philip King acknowledged. "Er—
did Barrett do his coining on board the *Charlotte*?"

"The doctor assured me he did, with some assistance." Captain Phillip permitted himself a frosty
smile. "He displayed great ingenuity, making his coins
out of old buckles, buttons purloined from the jollies'
jackets, and a number of spoons, also stolen. I *pleaded*
with Sydney and Nepean to give me farmers and carpenters and builders and, instead, I'm given coiners
and forgers! I don't doubt that Barrett is very skilled
at his trade, but of what use will he be in the new
colony? Damme, I've a mind to send him back, with
some of the aged and the sick and the infirm!"

"Unless he can cast musket balls, sir," King put in
with a boyish grin. They both laughed with rueful
amusement. Then Captain Phillip said, "Better have
the fellow sent across. We'll flog him first and then put
the question to him, eh?"

The fleet made its formal entry into Rio de Janeiro
Harbor at 1:30 P.M. on Monday, August 6, the
Sirius, wearing the commodore's pennant at the main,
making the customary thirteen-gun salute as she
passed the fort of Santa Cruz and came to anchor

abreast of a substantial stone jetty. The clouds, which had hung low over the town of St. Sebastian since dawn, rolled back with dramatic suddenness to reveal clusters of white-painted buildings circling the bay, with a breathtaking backdrop of mountains reaching skywards from the water's edge.

When Captain Phillip and his senior officers were rowed ashore, they found an official party awaiting their arrival in the wide, tree-shaded square behind the landing stage. First to step forward was a brilliantly uniformed dignitary of the viceregal court, with an escort of military officers and—since none of them spoke English—a somberly garbed friar to act as interpreter.

Compliments were exchanged; the two parties bowed to each other, and indicating that they should follow him, the friar gestured with a plump hand toward the far side of the cobbled square. His English was more picturesque than accurate, the speech of welcome he delivered of greater length than its original, but his round, sallow face was wreathed in smiles and his manner effusively friendly.

Addressing Phillip as "Your Excellency" he announced solemnly, "Our city and our people extend the hand of friendship to a tried and trusted ally. Your Excellency and your officers are free to go wheresoever you wish, in São Sebastião or the surrounding countryside. His Excellency the viceroy charged me to tell you that no guard will be set on your ships but guides will be furnished, should any of Your Excellency's people desire their services."

Behind him, as he attempted to make suitable reply to this hospitable invitation, Phillip heard Major Ross observe, "I had always heard that Brazil did not welcome strangers and that to display even the mildest interest in the mineral wealth of the country was to court arrest or even death. But," his tone was acid, "it would appear not to be so. To what, I wonder, do we owe our welcome?"

"We owe it to the commodore, Major," Lieutenant King said with finality. "His services to Portugal during the war with Spain have not been forgotten. His Excellency the viceroy told me so yesterday."

As the party approached the entrance to the palace a magnificently accoutred guard turned out bearing their colors, which were laid at Phillip's feet as a signal mark of respect and honor. A military band struck up a stirring martial air and marched in front of them to the inner courtyard of the palace.

The palace proved something of a disappointment. A long, low, stone edifice, with balconied windows, its architecture differed little from that of the buildings that neighbored it, and it seemed wholly to lack the magnificence of the two churches they had passed on their way. The reception room, in which they awaited the viceroy's summons, was sparsely furnished with a few hard-backed chairs and half a dozen card tables, its walls adorned with portraits of former Portuguese monarchs in faded gilt frames.

"No opulence here," Major Ross stated disparagingly. "For all their military pomp! I wonder how long we're to be kept cooling our heels before His Brazilian Excellency sees fit to welcome us in person?"

Ross was in querulous ill humor and, to Captain Phillip's embarrassment, bent on disparaging the city, the people who had watched their landing with such uninhibited interest, and his present surroundings. Both Hunter and King endeavored to counter his acid comments in the hearing of the friendly friar, but he persisted and was only shamed into silence when after some delay they were ushered into a sumptuously furnished banquet hall and the viceroy, after embracing Phillip, shook hands with each member of his party.

The corpulent viceroy was much as King had described him, but he was a gracious host and he kept an exceptionally fine table. With Phillip seated at his right hand and the friar standing at his back to interpret for them, he reiterated the promises already made and expressed an affable curiosity concerning the purpose of the voyage on which the eleven British ships had embarked.

"Your Excellency may, of course, purchase any supplies of which you are in need," the friar said on Dom Luis's behalf. "From musket balls to fresh meat, rum, the wine of the country, vegetables, and fruit . . . you have only to make your requirements known. Repairs can also be made to your ships—we have men skilled in such work."

Phillip thanked him gravely. His four years' service in the Portuguese Navy had given him more than a smattering of the language, but he spoke in English, and after a brief consultation with his patron the friar went on, "Dom Luis understands that Your Excellency is commissioned to found a new colony in the southern hemisphere. Is this to be in the land claimed for His Britannic Majesty by the much lamented Captain Cook, who was also received here at the start of his voyage?"

"Yes, that is so," Phillip confirmed. He did not betray his understanding when he heard the viceroy say, under his breath, "Terra Australis del Espirito Santo, named thus by our great Portuguese navigator Fernandez de Quiros almost two hundred years ago! Yet now the Dutch and the English lay claim to it and the

French cast envious eyes in the same direction." Instead, his face carefully devoid of expression, he answered as noncommittally as he could more questions put to him by the friar concerning the site of the new colony, its extent and location, and its present inhabitants.

"You have women on board your ships, Commodore? And men, some of them in chains?"

"Yes. They are felons, condemned to transportation from England, most of them for the term of their natural lives."

There was pity in the viceroy's dark eyes as the interpreter translated. "Then it will be a penal settlement, such as your government formerly maintained in North America? Your passengers are convicts?"

"Yes," Phillip was compelled to admit.

"They are many? Many women?"

"One hundred and ninety are women. Five hundred and sixty are male."

Once again there was a consultation between the viceroy and his interpreter, and then, beaming, the kindly friar announced, "Dom Luis will have a collection made, in order that they may be supplied with comforts. Priests of the Church will, with your consent, Commodore, visit the ships to ascertain what they stand in need of . . . also our surgeon general, Senhor Ildefonso."

It was impossible to refuse such well-intentioned offers, and with a good grace Arthur Phillip accepted them.

He took cordial leave of Dom Luis and was gratified to find during the ensuing three weeks that every promise made by the viceroy was kept to the letter. The supplies were delivered—fresh beef and mutton, coffee, rum for the ships' companies, wine, fruit of every kind, and the small-shot for the marines. Repairs were made to several of the ships, including the *Sirius*, which was partly recaulked, the recent storms through which she had passed having revealed serious neglect on the part of the dockyard that had been entrusted with her fitting out.

The officers found St. Sebastian an enchanting place, its people hospitable and eager to make their acquaintance, and free to go ashore whenever they wished, they took full advantage of the opportunity to visit and explore the city and its mountainous surroundings. Only Major Ross and the chaplain held aloof; Captain Phillip was feted wherever he went and, renewing old acquaintances in the city, admitted —to John Hunter's secret amusement—that this was not his first visit to Rio.

"I was here ten years ago, in command of a seventy-four of His Portuguese Majesty's Navy, the *Dom Pedro*. But I did not for a moment suppose that anyone here would remember me—I was here for so short a stay."

But remember him they did, and the guards at the viceroy's palace continued to honor him by laying their colors at his feet whenever he called on official business.

For the convicts, too, the stay in Rio de Janeiro was a welcome change. The gifts of palatable foods and medical comforts donated to them through the good offices of the viceroy and his surgeon general improved their health and raised their spirits to an unprecedented level.

They saw the town of St. Sebastian only from their barricaded exercise decks but were close enough to catch glimpses of flower-decked shrines, fine baroque churches, and colorfully dressed people moving about the steep, cobbled streets on foot, on horseback, and in sedan chairs. There were occasional religious festivals, with long processions of clergy wending their way through excitedly cheering crowds; many of the churches were illuminated at night; and there were two spectacular firework displays lasting till dawn. The plight of the convicts excited great pity, and passing boats showered them with oranges, for which no payment was ever asked.

Negro slaves, imported from Africa, did virtually all the manual work of the port, and the arrival of a snow, which dropped anchor alongside the *Lady Penrhyn* laden with heavily manacled African natives, roused the noisy sympathy of the women convicts—ironically under the circumstances since a number of them were also in chains.

On board the *Charlotte*, Jenny again begged Sergeant Jenkins to ask the surgeon for news of her mother, but the days passed, and Dr. White, his hands always full, was too busy—or, she began to fear, too forgetful—to take heed of her request. Finally, in desperation, she approached him herself, and he assured her that there were no cases of serious illness on board the *Friendship*.

"They are an unruly lot, the *Friendship*'s women," he warned her when she diffidently mentioned her wish to be transferred. "Why, only a few days ago Major Ross had to have four of them flogged for persistent insolence and fighting. Flogging, as a punishment for even female felons of the worst kind, is not lightly ordered—but there was no other way in which they could be controlled. During our passage from Tenerife more than half of them had to be chained, and the male convicts broke into their quarters—at their invitation, it would seem. So if you will take my advice, my child, you will stay where you are. You've no complaint of your treatment on board this ship, have you?"

"Oh, no, sir," Jenny answered. "None at all."

"You enjoy a privileged position, under Mistress Jenkins's care," the surgeon reminded her. "If you went to the *Friendship*, your privileges would be lost. And," he added gravely, "unless it is your desire to follow the way of life that most of them seem to have adopted, you could well be at some risk. They are violent and quarrelsome women of the worst type, Jenny."

"But if my mother is with them, sir, she may be in need of my help and—and protection. She is not a criminal—she is respectable. And she's my mother, sir. I owe her a duty," Jenny persisted.

The kindly doctor eyed her with a flicker of wry amusement in his eyes. "Your protection, child, would avail her little in such company! But"—he smiled—"it might be possible to arrange for your mother to be transferred to this ship. I believe that Captain Phillip has some such idea in mind—that is to say, he's mentioned that some of the best behaved of the *Friendship*'s women should be exchanged for half a dozen of ours who have given trouble. I will see what I can do in that regard. What is your mother's name?"

"Taggart, sir—Rachel Taggart," Jenny supplied, her eyes shining. "If you could speak to Captain Phillip on my mother's behalf, I should be truly grateful to you, sir. I am sure my mother's behavior will have been good—she is not one to quarrel or to seek the company of men promiscuously. She is the widow of a soldier, sir—a sergeant who served in the American war and was awarded a pension."

"I'll do my best," Surgeon White promised.

Two days later Olwyn Jenkins was summoned to attend him and when she returned to the cabin they shared, Jenny saw that she was deeply distressed.

"What is it?" she asked. "Oh, Mistress Jenkins, tell me please . . . what is wrong?"

CHAPTER XII

Olwyn Jenkins said, with a reluctance she could not hide, "Surgeon White has been to the *Friendship*, *cariad*, and he inquired about your mother, as you asked him to. He—I don't know how to tell you, my lamb. It is bad news, I am afraid—very bad news."

Jenny stared at her, conscious of a sick sensation in the pit of her stomach as she recalled Lieutenant Leach's taunting words to her, when he had hinted that her mother was gravely ill. "She's not . . . oh, Mistress Jenkins, my mam didn't die, did she, on the way here? Is that what you're trying to tell me? Is she dead?"

Olwyn shook her graying head. "No. She had recovered from her illness. But she—she suffered an accident, a fall, they claim, and she's like to die of it. She—"

"Then I must go to her!" Jenny cried, stricken. "I *have* to go to her, Mistress Jenkins. Please, I—"

Olwyn held out comforting arms to enfold her. "Child, you don't understand. The women in that ship are cruel, wicked creatures, always fighting among themselves. They claim your poor mam's fall was an accident, but Doctor White believes otherwise. He thinks that they set on her, that they beat her and caused her fall, only they will not admit it. If you go to her, my lamb, you will be in danger too, don't you see?"

Jenny's teeth closed about her lower lip, seeking vainly to quell its trembling. "Cannot my mam be brought to this ship, to the *Charlotte*? Surgeon White said it might be possible. He said—"

"She cannot be moved, my lamb—it is her back, you see. They fear it is broken and they dare not even try to lift her from her bunk in the hold."

Jenny freed herself from her benefactress's embrace.

"Dear Mistress Jenkins, I'm not ungrateful, truly I'm not—I owe you so much, more than I can ever repay. But you do understand, don't you—I cannot stay here when my mother is at the mercy of those women in the *Friendship*, helpless and in pain—dying perhaps. I must go to her. I. . . ." She controlled herself and added resolutely, "If I petition Captain Phillip, surely he won't refuse to let me go?"

Olwyn shook her head sadly. "He will not refuse you, *cariad*. He is coming to inspect all the ships of the fleet this afternoon, Surgeon White says. When he boards the *Charlotte*, you can make your request to him."

It was well on into the afternoon before the procession of boats, led by that of the *Sirius* flying the commodore's blue pennant, came alongside the

Charlotte and the inspection party prepared to disembark. The proper ceremonial for their reception was observed; the marine guard formed up at the entry port and presented arms to the roll of drums, the officers standing with drawn swords in front of them. From the deck above, Jenny had her first clear sight of the man who was to control the destiny of the new settlement and that of every man, woman, and child who would compose it.

She saw a slim, bewigged figure in a shabby blue uniform coat, with stooped shoulders and a tired, careworn face. Beside the tall, erect Major Ross, who followed him from the boat, Captain Phillip looked small and oddly insignificant; yet within minutes of his arrival every soul on board the *Charlotte* was conscious of his presence and those within earshot were hanging on his every word. He inspected the convicts' quarters, paying particular attention to the condition of the bilge water, and then with both male and female convicts gathered on deck to hear him, he addressed them in stern tones, exhorting them to be of good behavior in their own best interests.

"It gives me no pleasure to order floggings," he told them. "Least of all do I wish to see women whipped and chained. Nevertheless, if I am compelled to punish all or any of you, I shall do my duty, in the hope that you may thus be persuaded to mend your ways and earn remission by good conduct and a true desire to reform. Your fate is in your own hands, and each and every one of you should heed my warning. Merit my approval and you may depend upon it that I shall be just and merciful in all my dealings with you."

A few subdued cheers greeted his words but they were spasmodic, and the majority of both men and women heard him in disbelieving silence, their faces sullen and unresponsive. Captain Phillip sighed audibly and turned away.

"There is a girl you wish me to see, Doctor White?" he said. The surgeon beckoned Jenny forward. She approached nervously, her mouth dry, and instinctively dropping him a curtsy, she saw his expression relax.

"You have been well brought up, child," he suggested. "What is it you want? To join your mother in the *Friendship*, is that it?"

"Yes, if you please, sir," Jenny managed. She started to explain but the captain cut her short, his smile kindly. "Surgeon White has told me the circumstances and I have every sympathy with your desire to be with your mother in her hour of need . . . indeed, I applaud you for it. I must, however, be certain that you know what joining her will entail. If I transfer you—your name's Jenny Taggart, is it not?—if I transfer you to the *Friendship*, Jenny, you will not be able to return to this ship once we have sailed—and I plan to sail within the next two or three days. It will take us five or six weeks to reach the Cape. You will have to remain in the *Friendship* during our passage—you understand that, do you not?"

"Yes, sir," Jenny answered, looking up to meet his searching gaze. "I understand."

"And you still wish to be transferred?"

"Yes, sir, if you please."

A brand for the burning, Phillip thought regretfully—he was delivering this poor child to the flames.

Captain Phillip squared his shoulders, as if bracing himself. "Your request is granted," he said brusquely, and to Watkin Tench, hovering at his elbow, "See that this girl is sent across to the *Friendship* with the others, Captain Tench, if you please. And . . ." he paused, frowning, until Jenny, after stammering her thanks, had retreated out of earshot, and then asked, "Is that not the girl Hawley was involved with in that unfortunate business with young Leach?"

"Yes, that's right, sir," Tench confirmed. He added, "Hawley's a good man and an excellent soldier, sir."

"I'm aware of that, my dear Tench," Captain Phillip returned. "He's also the best servant I've ever had. All the same"—he lowered his voice, as Major Ross started to cross the deck toward him—"I fear I shall have to dispense with his services for the second time because it would, I think, be best if he were sent back to England with the other invalids in the *Diana*."

"Invalids, sir?" Tench questioned blankly. The master of the *Sirius* and two young midshipmen had been invalided, he was aware, and passages home in the British whaling ship *Diana* arranged for them. "But Hawley's not sick, sir. is he? That is . . . er. . . ." Light dawned and he exclaimed, "Oh, I see! You mean for his own good?"

"You said yourself he's an excellent soldier," Phillip reminded him dryly. "It would be a loss to the service if his promising military career were blighted over a woman, as I am sure you'll agree. It's a pity about the girl, but she's a convict, transported for life, so. . . ." He shrugged and made to move on. Watkin Tench, after a momentary hesitation, followed him as Major Ross said officiously, "Concerning the matter of my fellows' meat ration, Captain Phillip, I do deem it essential that when fresh beef is included, they should have priority over the convicts. . . ."

Their voices faded, and Jenny, unaware that the brief exchange between the fleet's commodore and Captain Tench was to take Andrew Hawley away from her, went to acquaint Olwyn Jenkins with the news of her impending transfer to the *Friendship* and to make her farewells.

"We shall be there when we reach Botany Bay," Olwyn said, "God willing. Remember, *cariad*, seek us out if you need our help. There will be a place for you in whatever home we make there. And may God have you in His keeping always, my poor sweet lamb!"

Jenny clung to her, unable to speak, but when the summons came for her to join the other women convicts in the *Friendship*'s boat, she answered it dry-eyed and resolute. There were five others with her, all of them chained and sullen, and they eyed her with overt hostility as Sergeant Jenkins handed her into the boat, wishing her well in a glum tone that carried little conviction.

"Why no clinkers for the sergeant's pet?" one of the women demanded of the marine guard, holding her manacled hands aloft. When the man did not answer her, she lapsed into a baleful silence that boded ill for Jenny's future in her company. Reaching the *Friendship*, all six of them were hustled unceremoniously into the fetid confines of the hold, their chains struck off, and the hatch cover closed and barred behind them. In the dim light of the spluttering lanterns Jenny looked about her, seeking a friendly face in the hope of being directed to her mother's bunk, but all the faces appeared as hostile as that of the woman who had complained because she was unfettered, and the hubbub of raised voices held more menace than welcome.

Recalling what Olwyn Jenkins had told her of the circumstances surrounding her mother's fall, she shivered. Had any of these women set upon and beaten one of their own? Had they really intended to injure or even kill a fellow unfortunate, or had the fall been, as they had apparently claimed, an accident for which no one was to blame? It was unlikely that they would admit it, she knew, but surely some of them had found it in their hearts to take pity on her mother in her helplessness, to care for her, now that she could no longer care for herself? Or were they just waiting for their purpose to be achieved and for Rachel to die? She bit back a sob and took a few uncertain paces into the evil-smelling darkness, and then, as if in answer to her unspoken prayer, she was able to make out a girl in a ragged dress bending over one of the bunks, a cup of water in her hand.

The bunk's occupant was covered by a blanket, with only the face visible, and at first, so terribly changed was it, she did not recognize it as her mother's. Her face was thin and deathly pale, and pain had etched deep lines around the bloodless lips and half-closed eyes, and Rachel Taggart looked, in that first moment, more like the grandmother Jenny remembered from her childhood than the mother she had come to seek.

She crossed on dragging feet to the bunk, and the girl, who had been spooning water with patient gentleness into the sick woman's mouth, turned to look at her in shocked surprise. "You!" she exclaimed. "I had not thought to set eyes on you again. But . . . are you Jenny by any happy chance? Missus Taggart keeps crying out for Jenny, poor soul, as if her heart would break."

The voice, Jenny realized, was vaguely familiar, educated and pleasant . . . where had she heard it before? Memory stirred . . . this was the girl who had taken pity on her that first dreadful night in Newgate's Common Side when Auld Meg and her cronies had attempted to steal her locket. The girl with the baby, who had advised her to sell the locket to the jailer. . . .

"*Are* you Jenny?" the girl asked with weary insistence. "Because if you are, she needs you sorely. Make yourself known to her for mercy's sake!"

"Yes," Jenny managed. "Yes, I'm Jenny," she said and dropped to her knees beside the bunk, reaching out a trembling hand to touch her mother's white, shuttered face. "Mam—Mam, I'm here. I've come to —to look after you, Mam."

At first there was no response; then Rachel's eyes opened, to stare without recognition into her daughter's face. It was a long moment before recognition dawned; then a smile of great happiness spread across Rachel's ravaged countenance and her lips pursed to form a single word. "Jenny!"

Jenny leaned across to kiss her cheek, and Rachel repeated her name in a hushed whisper. Then her eyes closed and she lapsed once more into unconsciousness. The girl who had helped her to drink set down the cup and, grasping Jenny's arm, led her to the bunk beyond, gesturing to her to seat herself on its bare wooden slats.

"Your mother will sleep now," she said. "She's not in so much pain as she was, and I did manage to give her nearly half a cup of water. Doctor Arndell says that is all we can do for her—see that she has as much water as she will swallow and keep her clean and warm." With brisk, impersonal efficiency, she explained what care was required and added, "Doctor Arndell has been very good—he's given her opiates and he visits her twice a day. But I wish she could have been moved. Down here, with these other women, it is difficult to care for her properly. They don't interfere but they don't help much either, with a few exceptions. And two of those who did have been transferred to the *Charlotte* as a reward for good behavior. That's where you've come from, isn't it?"

"Yes," Jenny confirmed.

"Willingly?" the other girl asked.

"Oh, yes," Jenny assured her. "I heard that my mother was here and then I heard about her—her fall. It was my duty to be with her but it wasn't easy to obtain permission to be transferred. In the end I appealed to Captain Phillip himself and he gave orders to send me here. At least I can relieve you of Mam's care and—"

"I did not ask to be relieved."

"Yes, but. . . ." In Newgate this girl had been nursing an infant, a little scrap not long born, whom she had cradled in a bale of straw. "There's your baby, isn't there? I mean, if you have him to look after, you—"

"My baby is dead," the older girl interrupted harshly. "He died of a fever before we ever left England." Jenny attempted to express her sympathy, but her companion brushed this aside, almost with contempt. " 'Twas better he did die, poor little mortal. What would there have been for him in Botany Bay, with his mother condemned to spend the rest of her life there . . . tell me that! Oh, I was heartbroken when it happened . . . he was all I had and I loved him. But when I came to ponder on it— why then I was thankful, for his sake and his father's, that he was spared this awful voyage to nowhere."

Jenny was silent, unable to find words with which to answer her, and the silence grew until, turning to glance covertly at the other girl's face, she saw that it was wet with tears. "You—you never told me your name," she ventured, thinking to distract her. "What is it?"

"Amelia—Amelia Bishop. That's what I'm known as. I—most people call me Melia."

Sensing that this was not her real surname, Jenny did not pursue the subject. Instead she started to thank her for her kindness to her mother, but again her thanks were brushed aside, as her sympathy had been.

"You were a fool to come here, Jenny," Melia told her. "You haven't learned much, have you? Didn't spend long enough in Newgate's Common Side, I suppose . . . they moved you to the Master Side after only one night if my memory's not at fault and"—she felt the cloth of Jenny's dress and shook her head almost sadly—"and you had it easy on board the *Charlotte*, judging by this gown."

"Yes, I—I was moved out of the hold. I shared a cabin with the wife of a sergeant of marines." Jenny explained the reasons for her good fortune and saw that Amelia Bishop was regarding her in incredulous astonishment.

"And you *asked* to be transferred to this ship? You even petitioned Captain Phillip to have you sent here?"

Jenny flushed. "Yes, because of Mam—because of my mother. What else could I do? If it had been your mother and you had been in my place, would you not have done the same?"

Melia's face froze. "No," she stated bitterly. "No. If it had been *my* mother, I'd have let her rot in hell before I'd lift a finger to help her!"

Once again silence fell between them, a constrained and hurtful silence that Jenny hesitated to break, but finally she said, her tone defiant, "My mother was asking for me, calling my name—you said so, didn't you? And she *was* happy that I came."

She was quite unprepared for the storm of rage her words provoked. Melia rounded on her, her voice harsh with strain. "Well, you've seen your precious mam, you've made her happy . . . let that be enough! *I'll* take care of her for as long as she has to live—and it won't be for long, you can see that for yourself, unless you're more of a blind little fool than I take you for. Petition the master or Doctor Arndell or Captain Phillip himself and get back to your cozy berth with the sergeant's wife—go back to the *Charlotte*, Jenny Taggart, before we sail. If you stay here, you'll be making the greatest mistake of your life, believe me!"

"But why?" Jenny stammered, completely taken aback. "I don't understand. If my mam is dying, *if* she is, I must stay with her, not leave her with—with a stranger. It's kind of you and I'm grateful but I can't desert her. I can't leave her here with these women!"

Melia's swiftly roused anger faded. "All right," she said flatly. "You'll have to know the truth and it will hurt. Your mam's fall was no accident, Jenny. It was deliberate—these women, as you call them, intended to kill her. They—"

"I know," Jenny put in quickly. "Olwyn Jenkins told me."

"You knew and you still came?"

"I had to. They said it couldn't be proved, you see, and I was afraid of what . . . well, of leaving her alone with them."

The older girl's eyes widened in what seemed at once to be surprise and a certain grudging admiration.

"They won't touch her now, Jenny—they don't need to."

"But why did they—" Jenny swallowed hard, having to force herself to ask the question. "Why did they want to kill her? What did she—what could she do to them?"

"Nothing. She was ill for most of the voyage. But she had money—gold—and she wouldn't give it to them."

Captain Wilkes's money, Jenny thought dully. Or could it have been? Hadn't he emptied his purse of silver, fearing to send her gold? She shuddered. Perhaps Dr. Fry had given her some sovereigns for the voyage . . . she bit back a sob, her fingers closing instinctively over the locket concealed, as always, in the bosom of her dress.

Melia went on, still in the same flat, expressionless voice, "In the hold of this ship, you are back in Newgate, Jenny, in the ward they first sent you to . . . or you might as well be, because they are all here. They—"

"Oh, but—" Suddenly Jenny felt icy fingers of fear coursing down her spine. "Do you mean that Auld Meg is here, Auld Meg and that gypsy woman Hannah? The ones who—" She could not go on.

"Yes, they're here. Auld Meg rules the roost on board this ship as she did in Newgate. They won't have seen you yet because they're sleeping, but they won't have forgotten you, I fear. Meg still bears the scars you inflicted on her, and when she's in her cups, she whines about the hellion who caused her so much pain. Pain and humiliation, Jenny—" Melia's hand closed about Jenny's and she added, lowering her voice to a whisper, "You bested her in front of the others, and that's something she'll never forgive.

That's why you must go back to the *Charlotte*, don't you see? Auld Meg is a very dangerous enemy and you"—her tone was again faintly contemptuous—"you are still an innocent child, Jenny Taggart. God knows how you've preserved your innocence but you have. And you'll be no match for Meg."

Jenny did not answer her. There were moments during the long and sleepless night that followed when she found her courage failing her and would have given anything in the world to be able to return to the cabin she had shared with Olwyn Jenkins in the *Charlotte* and to the stalwart protection Andrew Hawley's devotion had afforded her.

These women—urged on, no doubt, by Meg—had tried to take her mother's life and had almost succeeded . . . but they could not be punished, since nothing could be proved against them. No matter what it cost her, she could not desert her mother now. Let Meg and her cronies do what they would, she was going to stay at her mother's side until the end.

Rachel called to her by name, and when she went to give her the water for which she had asked, Jenny was greeted with a radiant, welcoming smile.

"It's so good . . . to have you with me . . . again, Jenny love," her mother whispered shakily. "So good . . . you'll stay, won't you? You won't leave me . . . now we've . . . found each other."

"I won't leave you, Mam," Jenny promised. "I'll never leave you again." She fetched water and a cloth and gently washed her mother's face and hands. Amelia joined her, pointing out almost harshly that the injured woman had other less pleasant needs. She said, when these had been attended to, "Well, are you going or staying?"

"I'm staying," Jenny told her without hesitation.

"You're a fool," the older girl returned. "Meg knows you're here—they've told her. She'll be along."

Auld Meg made her appearance half an hour later. She was, as she had been in Newgate, well and cleanly dressed, but her raddled cheeks were more puffed than ever and it was clearly an effort for her to move her vast, ungainly body between the narrow spaces that separated the bunks. Hannah and some of the others followed her, tittering among themselves at the prospect of her meeting with the hellcat who had defied her, but if they expected violence, they were disappointed.

Meg halted by Rachel's bunk, breathing heavily, and in silence held out her scarred fingers for Jenny's inspection.

"Go on, Meg!" Hannah urged. "Give the snivelin' little doxy the drubbin' she deserves! Give it to 'er and if yer want an 'and, I'm wiv' yer!"

Auld Meg, for answer, struck her a stinging blow across the mouth with her uninjured hand. To Jenny she said, with calculated venom, "So *you've* turned up again, like a bad penny! Well, I 'aven't fergotten yer, Jenny Taggart, an' I won't never fergit what you done, 'cause I've got these fingers ter remind me. I'll 'ave yer for it, make no mistake, but we got plenty o' time, ain't we? Not 'arf way there by all accounts. So you c'n sweat an' shake, never knowin' what hour o' the day or night I'm comin' ter get yer. But get yer I will an' wiv' this. . . ." There was a razor tucked into the sleeve of her elegant velvet dress, and she permitted Jenny a glimpse of it before sliding it back into concealment. "When I've finished wiv' yer there won't be a man as'll look at yer—not even one o' them black savages they say are waitin' fer us at Botany Bay! Carve yer up, I will, an' carve yer good!" She laughed and, removing the stained clay pipe from her mouth, pursed her lips and directed a stream of spittle into Jenny's face. The girl retreated, trembling, her newfound courage deserting her, and Amelia Bishop thrust forward to place herself between them.

"Have done, Meg," she pleaded. "Leave her be—she's enough on her plate caring for her mother, hasn't she?"

Meg grunted and then, to Jenny's amazement nodded.

"There's plenty o' time," she repeated. "Like I said, she can sweat. But you won't save 'er, Melia, an' yer'd best not try if you've any sense. All right, the rest o' yer—the show's over. Fetch me a glass o' that rum the kind folk on shore sent us—I'm parched an' me mouth's like the bottom o' a parrot's cage!"

Hannah scurried off to obey this command, and Jenny said wonderingly, "She *listened* to you, Melia—she let you stand up for me!"

Melia smiled, an odd, secretive little smile that did not reach her eyes. "Meg knows I have this," she answered quietly, and lifting her skirt, she displayed the hilt of a small dagger, tucked into her knee garter. "It's as good a weapon as her razor, and what's more, the old wretch knows I'll use it if she tries me too far, so she leaves me be. You may count on it, Jenny Taggart, if she attempts to make good her threats against you."

Jenny was comforted, if not wholly relieved, but she slept little and only dared to close her eyes when Auld Meg and her boon companions were drinking or, as was their habit, when they were visited during the hours of darkness by members of the crew. In harbor, permission to exercise on the open deck was restricted to the well behaved and trustworthy, and on Major Ross's instructions the privilege had been withdrawn from the *Friendship*'s women. But, although this meant that all were confined below, none of the women interfered with either Melia or herself. To Jenny's intense relief they were left to do what little could be done for poor, suffering Rachel who, as day succeeded day, began gradually to lose her slender hold on life.

The ship's surgeon, Dr. Thomas Arndell, was a kindly, conscientious young man and he gave the sick woman every attention, while holding out little hope of her recovery.

"Her back is broke, you see," he told Jenny. "But she is happy to have you with her, and you've become an excellent nurse. All I can do, I'm afraid, is supply her with laudanum so that she can be kept free of pain. If she lives, it will be thanks to the care you and Amelia are giving her. Once we sail, however, it will not be so easy to spare her suffering, and if we should run into bad weather. . . ." He spread his hands resignedly. "Our time is nearly at an end—they say that the commodore intends to give the order for sailing within a few days, so . . . we shall just have to do the best we can, lass, when the time comes."

The time came all too soon. On Tuesday, September 4 the fleet sailed for the Cape of Good Hope, the passage estimated by James Keltie—newly promoted master of the *Sirius* in place of the invalided Morton—likely to take five weeks, granted favorable winds and fair weather.

For the first two days after leaving Rio de Janeiro the weather was calm and pleasant. With the ships under easy sail and the sun shining, the hatches were again opened and the convicts permitted to take exercise on the open decks of all the transports.

With most of the *Friendship*'s women once more free to take the air, a girl of Jenny's own age, who had been transferred from the *Charlotte* with her as punishment for striking an officer, came shyly to offer her help in caring for Rachel. She had, it seemed, incurred Auld Meg's wrath, and although she played her full part in nursing the dying woman, it became evident from the way she clung to them that she had allied herself with Jenny and Melia for protection, rather than a desire to make herself useful.

She was a strange girl, Jenny thought, years older in worldly experience even than Melia, cynical and disillusioned, yet oddly cheerful, accepting hardship as her lot and seldom complaining—as most of the others did unceasingly—of the poor food and the restrictions on their freedom. Asked her name, she replied simply that it was Polly, giving no surname, and when Melia pressed her, she countered tartly, "I'll give you mine when you admit to yours!"

On the third day wild weather set in, dark with rain clouds and bitterly cold. For the injured Rachel the ship's heavy pitching and tossing was agony, and it took the combined efforts of her three nurses to hold her tortured body in some semblance of steadiness on her bunk. Toward dawn, the wind moderated, and when, after Dr. Arndell had administered a strong opiate, Rachel slept at last, the three exhausted girls huddled together on Jenny's bunk, sipping in turn from a mug of rum supplied by the kindly young surgeon. The raw spirit warmed them, and to Jenny's surprise it also had the effect of loosening Polly's tongue.

"You don't care much for your ma, do you, Melia?" she suggested. "Not the way Jenny does, I mean."

Melia shook her head reluctantly, and Polly went on in a low, bitter voice, "No more do I. My ma sold me when I was eight years old, for ten shillings and a bottle of this stuff." She held up the mug, the gesture derisive. "The truth is—I don't know my surname, I wasn't never told. I was just called Polly, and whenever I had to have a surname, I used Missus Morgan's —she was the one who bought me, see. A right old harridan *she* was and no error! Used to employ— that's what she called it—more'n a score of us. We was sent on the streets most of the time, but now and then she'd hire us out, like for what she claimed were special parties." Observing Jenny's look of bewilderment, she explained in horrifying detail what such parties had entailed. "Shocked you, have I?" she demanded cynically.

"No," Jenny denied. "Of course not." But the memory of the night she and her mother had spent in Mrs. Morgan's house returned with sudden clarity, and her tone was lacking in conviction. From what horrors had the girl called Patty saved them . . . she shivered and Polly laughed.

"You don't hardly know how you're born, do you, Jenny?" she accused. "Still I s'pose that's 'cause you had a mother to bring you up—a mother who cared and brought you up to be respectable. Learned you to read and write, too, didn't she? And yet you're both of you here, you and your ma! What were you done for, Jenny?"

"For receiving stolen goods," Jenny answered. "From a pickpocket."

"And you got *caught*? Oh, my! What about your ma?" Melia attempted to silence her, but Polly persisted. "I want to know what brings respectable folk down to this, what gets 'em deported as common criminals, same as me. I used to think that if my ma hadn't sold me, maybe I'd have been different, but now I ain't so sure. What *did* your ma do, Jenny?"

Jenny's cheeks burned as she told her mother's story, confining it to a few brief and bitter words.

"Oh, poor soul!" Melia drew in her breath sharply. "They hanged Captain Wilkes, didn't they?"

"Yes," Jenny said with a catch in her voice as she willed herself not to remember the tall figure walking so jauntily through the excitedly cheering crowds to the waiting gallows. But the vision persisted; she heard his voice, clear and with a tremor. "*I forgive all who ever did me an injury—save only one, the Judas who sold me for his own gain!*" To that man, whoever he was, Harry Wilkes had bequeathed his dying curse—a curse which, it seemed, had reached out to encompass not only the Judas but also her mother and herself. If Polly was seeking a reason for their downfall, she need look no further than the man who had betrayed Captain Wilkes to the constables and pocketed the reward. All their misfortunes stemmed from that betrayal and—

". . . a kind of badger game," Polly was saying, pursuing her own train of thought. "They call it the Cross Biting Law and it's rare, oh, it's rare! My partner was the Roistering Boy and while it lasted, we were in clover. Better than the streets and old Ma Morgan's special parties, I can tell you. 'Sides, when she employed you, she took her cut—two-thirds of what we made, never mind how we made it, that was her share. You didn't dare keep a deaner back; she always knew if you did, and it'd mean a beating and not even a crust to eat all day. Is it any wonder I quit, soon as I could?"

"No," Melia echoed sympathetically. "It's no wonder you did, Polly."

The girl talked on, describing her arrest and trial but her words washed over Jenny's head, most of them in any case incomprehensible. Melia listened, offering an occasional comment, but as always she kept her own counsel, and even when Polly invited her confidence, she remained evasive, giving no hint of the reason or reasons for her own harsh sentence and revealing nothing of her own past.

After a while weariness and the effects of the rum sent them to sleep, and when Jenny awakened, it was to the shocked realization that the storm had returned and that her mother was crying out in pain. She jumped up, and Melia followed her from the bunk above, to begin anew the exhausting struggle against the ship's wild pitching.

The gale continued for the better part of a week and often, so steep were the waves that buffeted the *Friendship*'s straining timbers, that no other ship of the fleet could be seen and it seemed that she was alone in a wilderness of tossing water. Sails split and yards carried away, the ship started to take in water and the pumps had to be manned, day and night. In the dampness of the foul-smelling hold, the women fell swift victims to seasickness and dysentery, and only the knowledge that her mother's life depended on it kept Jenny, stricken but determined, at her side.

At least, while the storm lasted, she was free of any danger that Auld Meg might endeavor to implement her threat, for in common with the rest Meg lay inert and helpless on her bunk, moaning her discomfiture aloud. The deck was forbidden to them, the hatches battened down, and only Dr. Arndell ventured into their quarters to stay for the few minutes it took him to dispense Rachel's laudanum and then depart, coughing and retching from the stench rising from the bilges, his duty done. More than once Jenny caught a strong whiff of liquor on his breath and guessed that he had had to fortify himself before coming below. The marine guards, including their commander, Captain Meredith, appeared far from sober when they made their daily—but cursory—inspection from the top of the hatchway, and all were deaf to the women's pleas and complaints, their only concession being a cask of Brazilian rum, which was lowered on a rope and gleefully seized upon by Hannah.

That Rachel survived was a miracle. She was now too weak to lift her head from the rough pillow Melia had contrived for her, and although she whispered Jenny's name in her few moments of wakefulness, the girl sensed that this was rather from habit than recognition. At times she spoke her husband's name and talked of the farm and the horses as if she had never left the home and the people she had loved, and as her mind wandered back into the past she smiled and seemed happy and at peace.

"We'll go to the Michaelmas Fair, Jenny."

"Yes, Mam," Jenny responded. "That's what we'll do—we'll go to the fair—you and Dadda and me." But with the howling of the wind and the swish of water in the flooded hold she could not be sure whether or not her mother had heard her and was thankful when, at last, she drifted again into unconsciousness.

A lull came on September 14, and the scattered fleet was reunited. The hatches were opened, the pumps started to make headway, and on deck, under a watery sun, soaked bedding and salt-encrusted garments were hung on improvised lines to dry, while below decks strenuous efforts were made to purify the air in the holds and rid them of vermin.

The following Sunday the chaplain came over by boat to conduct divine service on board the *Friendship* and still filled with missionary zeal he embarked on a lengthy sermon. The convicts listened restively and the flow of his eloquence was rudely interrupted by Auld Meg, who shouted drunken obscenities in so loud a voice that Captain Meredith ordered her to be taken below and put in chains.

Auld Meg was still drunk and in a smoldering rage when Jenny ventured back to attend her mother, but chained to her bunk, the old woman could do little more than reiterate her threats in a sullen tirade, which the girl affected not to hear.

"Forget her," Melia advised, her tone contemptuous. "She's almost as weak as your poor mother. She can't stand upright and with all that drink inside her, she's incapable of walking more than a couple of steps without keeling over. She won't touch you—she can't, Jenny, even if Captain Meredith tells them to unfetter her. And he's more likely to order her a whipping, after the way she behaved."

That night, with the sea as calm as a millpond, there were visitors to the women's quarters again, and more drink found its way to the hold. Polly abandoned her vigil by Rachel's bunk with a brief "See you later" and went to join the rest in a noisy celebration, which continued for most of the night, Meg's voice and her cackling laugh sounding louder and more raucous than ever as she drank herself into a better humor.

With the coming of daylight the men left the hold to return to their duties, the hatch cover clanged shut behind them and a welcome silence fell. Jenny dropped into an uneasy doze, kneeling beside her mother's bunk, her head resting on the blanket that covered Rachel, and she dreamed of the fair at Milton Overblow, with its friendly, happy crowds and the stalls and sideshows, the Punch and Judy, the dancing bears and . . . her father leading off the young horses he had come to sell. In her dream he turned to smile at her, holding out his arms, and as she had in childhood, she ran to him, eager and unafraid, to be lifted high up onto his shoulders, his deep, amused laughter ringing in her ears.

"Oh, Dadda, Dadda," she whispered, clinging to him. "I'm so glad to see you! So *glad*. . . ."

But he smelled of rum. She recognized the sickly sweet smell and was puzzled . . . her father was a Scot and his drink was whiskey, when he could afford the luxury, and ale when he could not. Jenny wrinkled her nostrils . . . the smell was strong and unmistakable. And her father's hands suddenly tightened about her, gripping her shoulders, digging into them. She woke, startled, still feeling the hands that tightened their grasp so painfully that she cried out in sudden terror, realizing that this was no dream.

The hands were real—fat, swollen hands with clinking chains attached to them . . . *Auld Meg's hands!* Jenny cried out again, but the chain slashed viciously across her face. One of the hands covered her mouth, stifling any further sound she might utter, and she felt the cold pressure of razor-sharp steel against her throat.

"I told yer I'd get yer, didn't I, yer chiselin' little peck o' hempseed!" Meg exulted. "Well, the time's come—I'm gonna mark yer an' mark yer good! When I've done, even yer own ma won't reckernize yer! Don't move nah or I'll slit yer gizzard. An' it's no use hollerin'—there's not one of 'em will help yer. They know better'n to go against me, the pack of 'em, 'cause I'd serve 'em like I served yer ma an' they ain't fools!"

Meg was wheezing loudly. Clearly it had been an effort for her to drag her huge, dropsical body along the narrow space between the bunks without rousing any of their sleeping occupants and Jenny drew hope from this. In silent desperation she fought to free herself and to resist Meg's efforts to haul her bodily from her mother's side, but, breathless or not, the old woman was immensely strong, and her weight began to tell as Jenny's struggles became weaker.

The razor bit into her cheek, laying it open. She felt no pain, only an anger so intense that it transcended fear. Meg had crippled her mother, on her own admission . . . cruel, wicked old woman that she was, Meg had sought to kill poor Rachel, and now God only knew what she would do to her, to them both. Jenny was conscious of the salty taste of blood on her lips, seeping beneath Meg's fingers, and she fought back despairingly.

The fingers slipped, and she managed to cry out again, and this time, by some miracle, Rachel heard the cry. With the last ounce of her failing strength, she reached out to grab the chain encircling Meg's wrist, jerking it so hard that the razor was dislodged from her grasp. The old hag stooped down, cursing, to retrieve her weapon, and as she did so Melia wakened and called urgently from her upper bunk.

"Jenny—catch this! And *use* it or she'll murder you both!"

The small dagger she carried in her stocking was flung in Jenny's direction. She caught it and stared dazedly at the long, bright blade, scarcely conscious of what it was or what her possession of it might lead to, but then Auld Meg recovered her razor and, screeching like a mad woman, turned to vent her fury on the helpless Rachel. Roused from her trance, Jenny gave vent to a piercing cry, like that of some small animal cornered by a predator and forced, at last, to stand at bay. She grasped the dagger in both hands and plunged it into Meg's straining, unprotected back. It sank to the hilt in yielding flesh, and the old woman slid to the deck, her high-pitched shriek of agony abruptly strangled as if by some unseen hand, as her head struck the iron support on which Rachel's bunk rested.

When Melia jumped down and managed, with difficulty, to turn her onto her back, Meg's lips were stained with blood-flecked froth, her eyes wide and blankly staring.

"She's dead," Melia said, in an awed voice. "Jenny —she's *dead*!"

It was the only warning she had time to give, for the next moment the other women came tumbling from their bunks, shrilly demanding to know what was going on and why their sleep had been disturbed. At the sight of Meg's lifeless body they halted, stunned and horrified. Someone took a lantern down from its hook and brought it across, holding it so that its beam illuminated the contorted face.

"It's Auld Meg!" Eliza Dudgeon, one of the most quarrelsome of Meg's cronies, exclaimed incredulously. "She's killed—murdered!"

"She can't be dead, not Meg. Why, she—"

"She's dead all right," Hannah stated and turned

red-rimmed, accusing eyes on Jenny. "An' this—this mealy-mouthed little gallows' bait done it! *She* killed Auld Meg!"

Jenny met the accusing eyes without flinching. Her calm was the calm of shock; she still had not fully taken in what had happened or what she had done. It was as if her dream—her happy dream of her father at the Milton Overblow Fair—had turned into a nightmare, and she stood there, facing them all, a hand protectively clasping her mother's limp one, waiting for the nightmare to end and reality to return.

Hannah burst into a torrent of weeping. "I allus said she'd kill someone! From the first minute I clapped eyes on 'er I knew. An' now she's gone an' done fer poor Meg, the scurvy little scab!"

Polly thrust through the press of muttering women and gestured to the open razor, to which Meg's dead fingers still clung.

"It was either her or them," she said scornfully. "Are you all blind—can't you see Jenny's face? Auld Meg swore she'd carve her up, you heard her, and she tried—she tried all right! It wasn't enough to do what she done to Jenny's ma . . . she had to have a go at Jenny too. She asked for it, if anybody ever did, but Jenny bested her . . . a slip of a girl bested that old bag of wind, and I say good riddance!"

"That's right enough," one of the older women agreed. She glanced uncertainly at the wailing Hannah, then she moved to Jenny's side and, with the damp cloth used for Rachel's toilet, wiped the congealing blood from the girl's cheek. "Meg was a bad 'un an' no mistake. She had it coming—we all know what she done to poor Rachel, don't we?"

Melia said quietly, "I threw Jenny my knife. I saw what Meg was up to, and I told her to use it. She had no choice—Meg would have cut both their throats, given the chance."

There was a murmur of assent. "What're we goin' to do?" a tall, pale-faced girl known as Charlotte asked, frowning. "We can't report it . . . we can't tell them, can we? Jenny will be in trouble if we do."

"Put 'er back on 'er bunk an' let the sawbones find 'er," Eliza Dudgeon suggested. "Gawd knows we've had deaths enough in this hell hole an' nobody worried about 'em. My guess is that Doc Arndell won't even ask the reason why—'e'll just pernounce 'er a goner an' put 'er over the side. It don't matter to 'im how she died. It don't matter ter no one when it's a convict."

Jenny said nothing. Their arguments held no meaning for her, and even when Hannah objected to Eliza's practical suggestion, claiming vehemently that she was a murderess and ought to swing for it, she was conscious of no fear, still less of any feeling of guilt. While they tugged and heaved Meg's great, obese body back onto her own bunk and secured her fettered wrists to it once more, she watched them with a strange indifference, as if what they did had ceased to be any concern of hers. Only when Polly touched her arm and said, with gruff pity, "Your ma's in a bad way, Jenny," did she waken from her state of frozen apathy and, with a stifled sob, drop to her knees beside the bunk.

Rachel was barely conscious, her breathing labored and shallow, but as Jenny's hand closed over hers, she opened her eyes and her lips twitched into the semblance of a smile. "I'm going home, Jenny love," she whispered, her voice so faint that Jenny could only just make out what she said. "To . . . Long

Wrekin. Your . . . dadda's waiting for me . . . there."

She did not speak again, and when Surgeon Arndell came to the hold just before midday, he pronounced her dead. Her body, with that of Auld Meg, was consigned to the deep, the ship's master reading a brief extract from the burial service over them both. The surgeon, as Eliza Dudgeon had anticipated, made no examination and did not seek to ascertain the cause of death in either case.

To Jenny, as he put two stitches in her lacerated cheek, he said kindly, "Her sufferings are over. She bore them bravely but there was no chance that she could recover. Don't grieve for her, lass—she's better off where she is, and you did all you could to care for her. You've no cause to reproach yourself." He tied off the stitches and returned the needle to the lapel of his coat, inspecting his handiwork with a critical eye. "This will heal and the scar will fade . . . no cause for anxiety on that account, either, because I'll not ask you how it happened. Better if I don't, eh?"

Jenny thanked him, avoiding his eyes, and he sighed. "There's another storm brewing up, devil take it! I'll have some rum sent down to you. Drown your sorrows, lass, as I intend to, before it strikes us."

That night the wind rose again with redoubled fury, the *Friendship* heaved and tossed as the waves washed over her. Just before dawn, the ship hove-to and there was much shouting and thudding of bare feet on the deck. The women listened apprehensively, some of them fearing that the ship might be about to go down, with themselves abandoned in the hold, and even the seasick staggered, somehow, to the hatch, to beat on it frantically and demand that they be released.

Jenny, sunk in her own private grief, continued to

lie where she was, and when the general anxiety was ended and the ship underway again, Eliza and Charlotte paused at her side to remark on her courage.

"You're a strange one," Eliza observed. "First you stand up to Auld Meg an' beat 'er at 'er own game an' next you stay as cool as can be, when the rest o' us are crazed with fear! How did *you* know it was a poor sailor washed overboard, an' them sending a boat ter look for 'im?"

"Was that what it was?" Jenny forced herself to ask.

Both women nodded. "So they told us. A lad who come 'ere from the *Sirius*, name of Harper, it was. They couldn't find the poor wretch," Charlotte said. She shrugged. "He drowned, Jenny, an' now I s'pose he's knocking on the door of Davy Jones's locker an' askin' your ma ter let him in."

"An' Auld Meg, as like as not, is tellin' 'im it'll cost 'im," Eliza finished, with a deep, booming laugh. "Oh, perdition take this scurvy ship!" She clutched her stomach as the ship rolled, and belched painfully. "I've puked all I can an' that's the gospel truth! Gawd grant we make land soon; whether it's the Cape or bleedin' Botany Bay, I don't give a tinker's cuss! All I know is I can't stand much more o' this!"

"There's some of Doctor Arndell's rum left," Jenny offered, indicating the small straw-covered cask the surgeon had sent her in the guise of medical comforts.

"Don't you want it?" Charlotte demanded, surprised.

Eliza chuckled. "Don't look a gift hoss in the mouth, woman! Our little Jenny's the cool one—she don't suffer from this 'ere mally de mare that afflicts us common folk. An' she ain't selfish, like old blubber an' guts used ter be. Lend us a daddle, Charlotte, an' we'll take this afore she changes 'er mind!"

When they had gone, happily carrying the precious cask, Melia leaned down from her upper bunk. "Jenny, my girl," she said pointedly. "Those two, Eliza and Charlotte, were Meg's slaves—she bullied them unmercifully! Whatever she asked of them, they did and—unlike Hannah—they never crossed her. Now they're looking up to *you.*"

"To me?" Jenny echoed dully, unable to believe it. "Oh, Melia, they're not! They couldn't be."

"But they are," Melia assured her gravely. "You bested Auld Meg, you rid them of her and that gives you the right to take her place, if you want to . . . that's the law they live by and understand. They're in awe of you, Jenny, and perhaps a little afraid."

"But I—"

"I know what you're thinking," Melia put in. "You're barely more than a child and Meg was an evil old woman who was up to every trick in the book. She led them a terrible life and they hated her, don't you see? Any of them would have done for her—even Hannah—if they could have found the courage to stand up to her. But they couldn't and you could. You *did!*"

"Yes," Jenny conceded wretchedly. "I killed her—I *murdered* her, Melia. I—" her voice broke. "I can't feel proud of that. I don't know what came over me . . . a sort of madness, I think. Like the time when I bit her fingers. Only this time I killed her. I—"

She had hated the vile old hag, she thought—hated her so intensely that she had wanted her dead. Not only for her cruelty to Rachel but for the threat she had posed and . . . Jenny bit her lip. For the fear that threat had induced in herself . . . for had there not been times when she had seen herself in Rachel's place, crippled at Meg's hands, helpless and in pain? Her hand went to her slashed cheek and she choked on a sob, frightened now of the vision of herself that her imagination conjured up.

"Auld Meg deserved to die," Melia said with firm conviction, as if Jenny had spoken her thoughts aloud. "You *must* not blame yourself. She would have killed you without a second thought . . . and cut your poor mother's throat if you hadn't stopped her. You know she would—that was what she had come to do." She clambered down from her upper bunk and, bracing herself against the rolling of the ship, came to sit by Jenny's side. "I share the responsibility for Meg's death," she pointed out earnestly. "I threw you my knife—I told you to use it, didn't I?"

"Yes, but—would *you* have used it?"

Melia hesitated, her smooth brow puckered. Then she smiled. "In your situation, Jenny, of course I would. If there had been time, it could well have been my hand that struck her. I'm sorry now that it wasn't if you are going to take all the guilt upon yourself. It was a very brave thing to do, and the others admire you for it, truly they do, you'll see. Certainly not one of them blames you . . . you had no choice, Jenny."

Jenny derived some consolation from her words, but as day followed day and the continuing gale-force winds and stormy seas reduced them all to abject misery, her conscience never ceased to torment her. Her sense of guilt returned, as the initial shock of what had happened wore off, and she slept fitfully, haunted by dreams in which Auld Meg and even her mother constantly reproached her. She had, she realized sadly, learned the last lesson that this awful life had to teach her, and in plumbing the depths of human fear and degradation, she had now left her childhood and its cherished memories forever behind her.

She could not hide her guilt from God, but perhaps in His infinite mercy and wisdom He would permit her to atone for it. In the new, strange land to which the storm-tossed ships were carrying them, she would build a new life, a good life, and as long as she lived she would never forget the lesson Meg's death had taught her. On her knees she prayed for forgiveness.

Jeremiah Leach stood on the *Alexander*'s heaving upper deck and cursed the day that Major Ross had so peremptorily and unjustly ordered him to transfer to her.

The *Alexander* was not a happy ship. Before making port in Rio, a convict named Carben had been hanged from the yardarm for attempting to escape and a marine, found guilty of passing counterfeit coins, had been given two hundred lashes, from which he had died. These two deaths, on top of those from natural causes among the convicts, had cast a gloom over the whole ship.

There were nearly two hundred male convicts confined in the hold, and they had begun the voyage in a sickly state, which had been in no way improved by the master's neglect of the hygienic precautions observed by the rest of the fleet. His failure regularly to pump out his ship's bilges had already earned him a stiff reprimand from Captain Phillip, but even that had not caused him to mend his ways. The foul fumes rising from the tainted bilge water had triggered off an outbreak of dysentery from which no one was immune, and since the ship left Rio the stench below decks had become well-nigh unbearable. It was almost as bad in the cabins as in the hold.

Leach started to pace the deck, bracing himself against the ship's heavy roll, drawing in gulps of fresh air as he glumly watched the sun go down. He had missed dinner because the master had insulted him, and the rum he had taken to compensate for the loss of the meal had turned to acid in his stomach. The rum was cheap local stuff, but thanks to his father's penny-pinching meanness—the devil take it—he had been unable to afford anything else, and no one in the cabin had offered him so much as a taste of their more than adequate supply of liquor. The ship's officers weren't gentlemen, of course—least of all the master, Captain Sinclair. He was a taciturn, hard-drinking Scotsman, given to spying on his men and punishing them for the most minor offenses by reducing their rations or docking their pay. As a result the *Alexander*'s seamen were insolent and resentful; they did not put their backs into their work and their sail-handling was lubberly and, at times, even dangerous.

Worse, in Jeremiah Leach's view, was the effect the seamen's lack of discipline was having on the marines. Admittedly he himself—on account of that infernal business with Corporal Hawley and the Taggart girl —had come to the *Alexander* under a slight cloud. But that, Leach told himself angrily, was no reason for the company commander Shea and his second-in-command Nellow to cold shoulder him as they had. And the ship's disgustingly unhealthy condition, about which he had repeatedly complained, seemed to worry them not at all. Indeed, they had laughed at him for complaining, and when he did so, they had held him up to ridicule in front of Captain Sinclair, whose in-

sults had culminated in the bestowal of a nickname.
Mister La-di-dah . . . the swine had addressed him
so publicly in the cabin, and now his officers, unprincipled toadies that they were, used it behind his
back, though not always out of his hearing. Leach
swore in angry frustration and continued pacing. The
ship's blunt bow drove into a mountainous wave,
failed to rise above it, and she plunged shuddering
into the trough, knocking him off balance. When he
scrambled to his feet again, it was to find the deck
awash. Useless to go below, he knew; his cabin would
be damp, his bedding soaked, and in any case he had
to inspect the convicts' quarters with the sergeant of
the guard before they were battened down for the
night.

Leach grasped the rope lifeline, which had been
rigged to enable the seamen to move about the deck
in bad weather, and cautiously made for the forehatch.
He would not wait for the damned sergeant, he decided. He would make his inspection now and then
go to the main cabin to see if the officer's steward
could produce something for him to eat. There was
always a sentry on duty at the hatch who could act as
his escort, and although there was no sign of him,
he was probably skulking behind the shelter of the
hatch cover, out of the wind . . . clearly not anticipating the arrival of the inspection party so early.

He groped his way forward, having some difficulty
in keeping his feet, only to see, to his fury, that the
hatchway was unguarded. The marine sentry who
should have been there was leaning over the bulwark
on the lee side, puking his heart out, his musket—
which he must have dropped in his haste—slithering
across the deck toward the scuppers.

Holding fast to the lifeline, Leach went in pursuit

of him, to grasp him by his pipe-clayed crossbelt and roughly jerk him upright.

"Get back to your post, you scoundrel! And that musket will have to be dried and reprimed. Attend to it at once, d'you hear?"

The sentry was young, little more than a boy, and he was obviously frightened out of his wits by the realization that an officer had witnessed his momentary lapse. He reached with shaking hands for the musket and, his face deathly pale, managed to stagger unsteadily back to his post.

"I—I beg pardon, sir. It's the motion, the pitching . . . I had to throw up, sir, and I thought. . . ." He gulped, once again overcome by an uncontrollable wave of nausea. "Sir, I can't—" the scant remaining contents of his tortured stomach sullied the deck at Leach's feet, splattering his boot toes. The boy retreated, mouthing an apology.

"Why, you filthy oaf!" Jeremiah Leach fumed. "Damn your eyes, just look what you've done! My boots, damn it—look at my boots!"

A sudden strong gust of wind carried his words away but the sentry understood their meaning. "I'll clean them, sir," he offered. "Please, sir, if you'll just wait, I—" He looked wildly about him in the fading light, seeking the means to fulfill his promise. Finding none, he dropped to his knees on the deck, still holding the musket, and with his free hand he started to wipe the stains from Leach's boot toes, muttering unintelligibly as he did so.

At that moment a freak wave struck the *Alexander* head on. She met it with a jarring lurch, and as tons of icy water came crashing over her forecastle she heeled over, the scuppers on her lee side awash. A bellowed order from the officer on watch to the two men at the wheel brought her head around, but for the young marine sentry the order came too late . . . and for Jeremiah Leach it was almost too late. He had a grip on the lifeline, and it held firm, despite the fact that the sentry was flung violently against his legs.

"Sir . . . help me, for God's sake! Save me, please!" Leach heard the boy's frantic cry, saw his extended hand reaching out above the frothing water, and instinctively he made a grab for it. For a moment or two he was able to support them both, but then the dead weight of the boy's body became too much, and he knew that unless he could break free of it, they would both be washed overboard. He wrenched his fingers from the other's convulsive grasp, compelled to use his feet to kick himself free, and as he regained his hold with both hands on the taut line he glimpsed the sentry's body, in its sodden scarlet jacket, strike the top of the lee bulwark and then vanish into the dark, seething water.

Voices sounded near at hand, men pounded across the deck toward him, the sergeant of the guard and a marine carried him to the shelter of the hatchway where he lay gasping, his head reeling and his mouth full of water.

"Did I see one of your men go over the side?" It was the officer of the watch, anxious and impatient, standing over him in dripping oilskins.

Leach dragged himself up. "Yes, the sentry. For pity's sake isn't there anything you can do?" He wondered fleetingly whether any of them could have seen his struggle to rid himself of the sentry's dead weight and then decided that it was impossible. "I tried to save the poor devil. I had a grip on him for a few seconds but I couldn't keep hold of him. He just slipped away—there was nothing I could do."

"You'd a pretty near shave yourself, sir," the sergeant observed.

"Yes," Leach agreed. "I suppose I had."

The officer of the watch grunted and answered his first question. "I expect the captain will lower a boat, Mister Leach. But there's not a hope in hell of finding the lad in this."

Then he was gone, to Leach's relief, his stentorian voice bellowing orders through a speaking-tube, sending the seamen of the duty watch into a flurry of frenzied activity. Captain Sinclair came on deck, foul-tempered as always, cursing everyone in sight and shouting his own orders. The ship hove-to, a boat was lowered into the raging sea and a signal cannon was fired to warn the other ships of the fleet. For close on two hours the *Alexander*'s boat continued the search, while the ship herself and those of her consorts that had heard her signal stood by, wallowing in the storm-wracked darkness and taking in water as the towering waves washed over them.

But as the officer of the watch had predicted the search was in vain. The boat was recovered and hoisted inboard; the exhausted crew went shivering below, and Leach, who with Captain Shea and Lieutenant Nellow had waited on deck for their return, thankfully followed their example.

Both Shea and Nellow had accepted his story of the accident without question. Indeed, both had praised him for his attempt at rescue, and when he descended at last to the comparative warmth of the main cabin, Leach found the atmosphere perceptibly more friendly. Shea pressed a glass of brandy on him, from his own supply; the surgeon made him strip off his wet jacket and brought a blanket to wrap round him; the mess stewards bustled around serving hot toddy; and even the master, when at last he joined them, expressed qualified approval of his conduct.

On the plea of indisposition Leach managed to avoid the hated duty of inspecting the convicts' quarters for the next three days, taking the place of Robert Nellow—on whom the duty devolved—at the whist table in the evenings. He even won enough from them to purchase a bottle of good brandy, and his luck held, for on the first day that he resumed his inspection duty he learned of a threatened mutiny among the convicts.

One of them, a man named Parr, who had been a merchant's clerk, having apparently lost faith in the would-be mutineers' chance of success, took him aside and revealed the plot to him in full and convincing detail. In a state of considerable excitement Leach brought the man out of the hold under guard and hurried to the cabin to report to Captain Shea.

"He says that some of the seamen are involved, sir, and the plan is for them to take over the ship on Sunday when they're brought on deck for divine service. The seamen are to lay hands on as many of our fellows' muskets as they can and pass them out to the convicts."

Shea frowned. "Does he know how many seamen are in the plot?" he asked. "Does he know who they are?"

"I brought him with me, sir," Leach answered eagerly, "anticipating that you'd want to question him and hear his story for yourself. He's outside in the passageway—shall I have him brought in?"

Parr was brought in and questioned exhaustively. He was a small, inoffensive-looking man and he was nervous, but his story carried conviction. After obtaining the assurance that he would not be sent back to the hold, where, he maintained, his life would be in danger, he named the ringleaders and, seemingly without hesitation also supplied the names of four of the *Alexander*'s seamen.

"They're men of bad character, sir," he added earnestly. "One of them—the one they call Ted Burns—is related to the convict Sharp, sir, and they cooked up the scheme between them. Some of the others ... well, they resent the fact that there are women on board the other ships but none on this ship, sir. That and the sickness and . . . well, sir, the state of their quarters. It's all built up to an extent where they've ceased to reason, you see, and I thought I'd have to report it to save bloodshed. Even if they failed to take the ship, sir, they could kill some of your men in the attempt."

Shea nodded gravely. He asked a few more questions, and then, having despatched one of the mess stewards to summon the master, he thanked Parr for the good sense he had displayed. "I'll see that Captain Phillip is informed of your conduct, which will not, I am sure, go unrewarded. You'll have to tell the master all you've told me and then I shall have you sent below to the marines quarters, where you will remain under guard until this matter is settled."

Captain Sinclair came reluctantly, his pea jacket worn unbuttoned over his nightshirt and his breath smelling strongly of whiskey. At first he indignantly refused to believe the accusations against his seamen but, when Parr named them, he was forced to admit that, as the one-time clerk had claimed, they were men of bad character.

"I'll see them masel', Captain Shea," he decided, rising ponderously to his feet. "And if they are mixed up i' this, I'll gie all four o' them tae Captain Phillip tae hang or flog, as he sees fit. But he'll need tae replace them for I'm short o' hands as it is." He was stumping wrathfully away when he spied Leach, and fixing the young marine officer with a critical eye, he said coldly, "Oh, aye, 'twas you reported this affair, was it not, Mister La-di-dah? Weel now, 'tis tae be hoped Captain Phillip will gie you credit for your zeal and devotion tae duty. And if he should find he's needin' ye on board his flagship i' the future, it wull no' break my hairt, I'm tellin' ye!"

Leach was dumbfounded. There was silence for a moment after the master had taken himself off, and then he burst out resentfully, "That was . . . devil take him, that was unjust! He had no right to speak to me like that."

"He's not overly fond of you, my boy," Nellow suggested, with a malicious grin. "And he's drunk just enough whiskey to cause him to tell you so . . . *in vino veritas*, you understand. Frankly, Leach, if I were in your shoes, I'd take his advice and apply to be transferred to the *Sirius*. You—"

"God rot you, Nellow, I'll see you in hell before I do!" Leach protested in a choked voice. He had expected praise for his alertness, gratitude even . . . damn it, hadn't he saved the ship and her drunken sot of a master from an armed attack by the convicts supported by some of his own seamen? Yet here was Nellow goading him without the smallest justification . . . he fell back on offended dignity. "I will thank you to apologize for that remark—" he began, but Captain Shea cut him short.

"That's enough," he snapped. "You acted correctly,

Leach, and I'm certain Captain Phillip will approve of your zeal when I make my report to him tomorrow morning. There's nothing more to be done tonight, so you might as well turn in." Leach accepted his dismissal without argument, and when he had gone, Shea eyed his second-in-command reproachfully. "You shouldn't bait him, Rob. He has a lot to learn, I know, and he's arrogant and touchy. But he did behave pretty well when that poor little devil of a sentry went over the side."

"I'm not so sure he did," Robert Nellow objected.

"What on earth do you mean?" Shea demanded, puzzled.

Nellow shrugged, his craggy face puckered into a thoughtful frown. "I wasn't going to tell you—because there's no proof, John—but Sergeant Knight, who's an honest, reliable fellow, said that when he came on deck the evening the lad was washed overboard, he saw—or thought he saw—the boy kneeling at Leach's feet. Leach had hold of the lifeline but the sentry, Dixon, hadn't . . . and he had his musket in one hand, which would have been quite enough to throw him off balance, when that freak wave struck us."

"Leach didn't mention that," Shea demurred.

"Quite. He wouldn't, would he?"

Shea recalled what Watkin Tench had told him, in confidence, concerning Leach's behavior before he had been transferred from the *Charlotte*. Tench was a kindly, easy-going fellow, who seldom spoke ill of anyone, but he had said that Second-Lieutenant Leach should be watched because he had almost caused a mutiny among the *Charlotte*'s seamen.

"Another thing," Nellow said, his frown deepening. "You know you asked me to take over Leach's inspection duty after his ducking? Well, quite a few of the convicts expressed the hope that they had seen the back of our young fellermelad. He wouldn't listen to their complaints, they said. I didn't set much store by that—they're always complaining about something. But—in view of what Knight has told us and old Sinclair's attitude, if the opportunity offers, why not get rid of the little swine?"

"Send him to the *Sirius*, you mean? He'll have to go as a witness with Parr, of course. Only—" Shea hesitated.

"Why not request them to keep him? Let the commandant take him in hand."

Captain Shea's expression relaxed. "That's not half a bad idea, Rob."

Next morning, Sunday, October 7, Jeremiah Leach found himself, for the second time, in a boat with his kit piled up beside him and without any clear idea of why his transfer should have been ordered.

CHAPTER XIII

At dawn on Saturday, October 13, land was sighted, and to the cheers of all those permitted on deck, at seven o'clock that evening the ships dropped anchor in Table Bay beneath the great humped shadow of Table Mountain.

Next morning the *Sirius* fired a thirteen-gun salute, to which the fort replied, signaling that the port was open, and by noon Captain Phillip and Lieutenant King were on their way ashore to call on the Dutch governor and seek permission to purchase victuals and supplies.

For the women in the *Friendship*'s hold the voyage from Rio de Janeiro had been a time of severe trial. Due to a succession of storms the hold had been feet deep in swirling water, bedding and clothes alike were saturated most of the time, drinking water strictly rationed and, in addition to the all-prevailing seasickness, both male and female convicts had begun again to fall victims to dysentery and scurvy. They wept with joy to see the land, and Jenny with them, anticipating a change from their monotonous diet of salt meat and dried peas and an end to the shortage of fresh water.

But, for no reason that they could understand, there was a delay of almost a week before bread and a small trickle of fresh meat and fruit were delivered, and the commodore and Lieutenant King paid two more visits to the governor before the situation improved. On the twenty-third Dr. Arndell informed the women that an order had at last been issued by the governor, Mynheer van Graaf, permitting his contractors to supply the Botany Bay fleet with all its requirements.

From then on, a steady stream of supplies of all kinds rendered the problem of stowage increasingly acute, for it was not only grain, meat, and water that arrived on board—there were livestock, purchased by Captain Phillip for the colony and by the officers for themselves, for which space had somehow to be found.

Lowing cattle, sheep, pigs, goats, crates of hens, and even a number of horses were herded on board and confined in pens on the decks, and even when it seemed that there was no more room for a single cask of water or crate of poultry, these continued to arrive on the quay to await the boats that would row them out to the anchored ships. The Dutch were avaricious and their prices excessively high, the officers claimed, but they went on buying, and it was without surprise that Jenny heard—again from the ship's surgeon— that it had been decided to remove the women from the hold of the *Friendship* and put sheep there in their stead.

"You'll be accommodated in one of the other transports," Dr. Arndell told her and added, smiling, "I imagine you would like to go back to your friends and your cozy berth in the *Charlotte*, would you not? I can arrange it—your behavior has been exemplary, Jenny, and you have set a good example to the others. You're entitled to your reward."

But Jenny, clearly to his astonishment, shook her head. Sergeant Jenkins had already made her the same offer, but she had refused and, even when Olwyn had obtained permission to visit her in the hope of persuading her to change her mind, she had remained adamant. It was, she thought regretfully, impossible now; while Auld Meg's death continued to weigh so heavily on her conscience, she could not face a return to the *Charlotte*, to Olwyn Jenkins's affectionate probing or even to her kindness. Besides, Andrew Hawley had been shipped back to England, Sergeant Jenkins had told her, and with his going she had lost her only chance of rehabilitating herself by making a respectable marriage.

"I will stay with the others, Doctor," she said firmly. "With my own kind, where I belong. I'm a convict, not a free woman—it is best that I keep my place."

The young doctor eyed her searchingly but did not question her decision, and on November 3 she was transferred with Melia, Polly, and four of the others to the *Lady Penrhyn*, the bunks they had occupied broken up, in order to make room for thirty Cape ewes.

The women of the *Lady Penrhyn* did not welcome the new arrivals. There had been some deaths, but their quarters were still cramped and overcrowded, and there were several children and a number of newborn babies, for whom no bunks were provided. They were a motley collection, more degraded even than those who had left the *Friendship*, and the ones who had formed attachments with the marine guards and the crew were ready to resent the newcomers, fearing their rivalry.

Eliza Dudgeon was soon involved in a fight. Pugnacious and strong, with red hair and the muscular body of a one-time circus performer, she displayed pity and kindness to those worse off than herself, but she possessed a savage temper, which the *Friendship*'s women had long ago learned better than to rouse. Mattie Denver, however, had ruled the *Lady Penrhyn*'s hold until the advent of the newcomers, and determined to maintain her supremacy, she chose the occasion of afternoon exercise to decide the issue.

Jenny never knew how the quarrel began, but shrill screams of contradictory encouragement and shouted abuse brought her from her bunk to join the ring that had formed round the two contestants.

"Go for 'er, Mattie! 'Ave 'er guts fer garters, why don't yer?" one of them yelled, and there was a chorus of voices urging her on as Mattie Denver tore savagely at Eliza's face with her fingernails. But, like Auld Meg, the ruler of the *Lady Penrhyn*'s women was a heavy drinker, and by dint of stealing from her cowed companions she was well dressed and proud of her appearance, which was crowned by an elegantly styled head of hair.

This afternoon Mattie had consumed more liquor than she normally did, and her gait was unsteady, many of the blows she aimed at Eliza falling wide of their mark, so that Eliza, using feet and fists to good effect, soon had her pinned against the barricade. Then quite by chance she made a grab for Eliza's hair and, jerking it roughly, forced the younger woman to her knees. Breathing hard, she aimed a kick at her opponent's stomach but this was too much for Charlotte, who plunged into the fight in defense of her friend, followed, to Jenny's shocked dismay, by Hannah. Both women fell upon Mattie Denver. In an instant her dress was torn from neck to hem, and as Eliza dazedly picked herself up the ring broke and the dreadful battle became a free-for-all.

The marine sentries, who had been watching from a distance with broad grins on their faces, now moved to intervene, and knowing that this would mean punishment for all of them, Jenny thrust a way into their midst.

"Stop it!" she cried desperately. "Do you want them to flog us? Eliza—Charlotte, leave her alone! Go below, quickly . . . the soldiers are coming."

They heard her, and Eliza and Charlotte came stumbling to her side; Hannah, deaf to the warning, was rolling on the deck beneath a press of bodies, but Jenny grasped her arm and dragged her free. At that moment Mattie Denver rose, swaying to her feet, and as she did so her elegant coiffure came tumbling from her head, revealing itself as the wig it was. There was a sudden titter of laughter, which rose to a full-throated roar from the advancing sentries, as they all turned to stare at the vision of an almost hairless head, surmounting the raddled, painted face of the discomfited Mattie Denver.

Peace was restored, but thereafter the seven from the *Friendship* segregated themselves from the rest as far as possible. They ate and slept and exercised in their own tight little group and spoke to the *Lady Penrhyn* women only when this was unavoidable. To her own surprise Jenny found herself elected as their leader and spokesman, and it was not until some days after their transfer that she learned of the reputation her companions had given her—one to be respected and left alone. Wrapped in her own self-imposed sense of guilt, she was content that this should be so, and when her sixteenth birthday came—unremarked by anyone save herself—she mentally recorded it as a milestone and the day when she finally became resigned to the role for which fate had cast her. It was, she knew, of little use to delude herself by making claim to respectability—she was a convicted felon, like all the rest.

On November 9 Captain Phillip and his senior officers, who had been lodging ashore, returned to their ships, and the last of the provisions were loaded. The signal for sailing was hoisted on the eleventh, but a contrary wind delayed them until midday on the twelfth when in warm sunshine and before a light breeze the last civilized port of call they would make was finally left behind them.

The most dangerous part of their voyage into the unknown had begun; virtually untraversed seas and an unexplored country awaited them at the end of it, from which, for many of them, there could be no return for the span of their natural lives. The passage from Rio to the Cape had been testing enough, but now they faced a journey that would take at least two months, in latitudes notorious for bad weather and on a course that would bring them close to the icy desolation of Antarctica, before steering eastwards to pick up the South Cape of Van Dieman's Land* and Captain Cook's anchorage in Adventure Bay.

Almost one hundred fifty years before, the Dutch explorer Abel Jansen Tasman had landed briefly there to lay claim on his country's behalf to the southeast land of Terra Australis, which he had named Van Dieman's Land after his patron—but he had been lost at sea in 1664 and the Dutch had never attempted to exploit their claim.

At first, after the fleet left the Cape, the winds were light and fitful, and with the ships rolling in a heavy swell the progress made was poor. On November 16 Captain Phillip decided to transfer to the sloop *Supply* and, leaving the rest of the convoy in the charge of Captain Hunter, take the three fastest transports— the *Alexander*, the *Friendship*, and the *Scarborough* —with him, with the intention of landing an advance party at Botany Bay to prepare a site for the new settlement.

"I shall need every skilled artisan we have among the convicts," he told Lieutenant Shortland, the naval agent. "All right"—as Shortland started to speak—"I know what you are about to tell me . . . there are few who can lay claim to such skills." He sighed in frustration. "Then we must make do with the fittest of them, and a large party of marines. Let me have your list first thing tomorrow, and we'll have the boats out and start transferring them. We must have some shelter in readiness for the women before we can put them ashore in Botany Bay, but I'm counting on a month's grace to enable adequate provision to be made."

*Now called Tasmania and an island—a fact which was not then known.

The transfers were duly carried out, the ships hove-to and the boats plying between them from dawn to dusk, but the calm persisted, and it was not until November 26 that the two divisions of the fleet parted company. Then, however, running before a brisk southeasterly, Captain Phillip signaled his squadron to make sail, and by sunset they were hull down.

From the deck of the *Lady Penrhyn* Jenny watched them go, conscious of a feeling of utter desolation. It grew steadily colder, and by mid-December the women in their thin, ragged clothing were suffering acutely. The weather became stormy with flurries of rain, alternating with a thick haze, and the wind carried them off course to the west. No other sail was sighted, and their only companions were whales and seabirds, of which there were a considerable number.

The water ration was reduced to three pints a day; it was impossible to wash clothes or dry them, and the *Lady Penrhyn* women complained incessantly. Punishment, ranging from flogging to having their heads shaved and confining them in chains, seemed to have little effect—they were unruly and prone to fighting among themselves—and Jenny, though she held herself aloof from their quarrels, began bitterly to regret having had to transfer to their ship.

The surgeon, Dr. Bowes, supplied them with medical comforts—mainly wine obtained at the Cape—and most of them drank themselves into a stupor each night, stealing without compunction from the sick, to whom the wine had been allocated. Visits from the seamen and marines took place whenever the prevailing weather conditions permitted, and even Polly, who had sought initially to join in their orgies, expressed herself disgusted by their wanton behavior and cease-less quarreling.

Sickness increased, deaths became almost common-place and births all too frequently ended in tragedy. Dr. Bowes, although no less conscientious in the performance of his duties than young Dr. Arndell had been, was less sympathetic, and his tendency to lecture his patients on their lack of morals made him unpopular with the majority, who nicknamed him Dr. Devil Dodger. They did not call him if it could be avoided, but one night in mid-December a girl named Dorcas Finnegan, who was barely seven-teen, went into a difficult labor.

She was a quiet, unobtrusive girl, well liked by the others mainly because she adopted a servile attitude toward them and gave them no trouble, seldom com-plaining whatever they asked her to do. But now, without warning, poor Dorcas filled the hold with agonized, despairing shrieks, and it being evident that she was struggling to give birth, they crowded around her, for once united in pity and eager to do what they could to help her.

"Best send for the sawbones," Eliza said, with the voice of experience after watching the girl's convulsive but unavailing attempts to obey the advice someone else had given her and "bear down." She gestured to the swollen body. "I reckin the baby's the wrong way 'round. She won't never born it with only us ter help her."

Melia went to kneel by the bunk, grasping the frightened girl's trembling, outstretched hands. "There, Dorcas," she whispered gently. "Don't strain anymore. We'll call Surgeon Bowes."

They called him, hammering on the padlocked hatch cover and shouting to the sentry, but it was almost two hours before he answered the summons. Dorcas was so weak by the time he descended to the hold that Jenny feared that she was dying, and Eliza, sharing her opinion, abused him roundly when at last he approached the distraught, sobbing girl.

In an angry mood, he ordered her to hold her tongue, but the others took up the cry, and he glared at them, keeping his temper with an almost visible effort.

"Be silent, plague take you! I can't deal with this in such a hubbub . . . stand aside and let me look at her! You there," he demanded of Jenny. "How long has she been in labor?" Jenny told him, and he pursed his lips, muttering to himself as he made his examination. "I'll have to fetch my instruments," he said, the examination over. "It's a breach presentation. And you'd better pray, if you know how. I think I can save the mother but I doubt if the infant will survive."

He hurried away in search of his instruments, and although he had spoken quietly, Dorcas must have caught his parting words for she set up a frightened whimpering.

"My baby—oh, my baby! It's not dead . . . tell me it's not dead! Oh, please . . . ." Her voice trailed off, and they all clustered around her, even Mattie Denver, seeking to console her.

"Give the poor soul a drop o' my rum—it'll put heart into her. Gawd knows she needs it."

The mother of a healthy little girl came to the end of the bunk, assuring her that the doctor had made a mistake; two of Mattie Denver's particular cronies brought the rum and a shawl, in which to wrap the baby when it should be delivered, while a third yielded up her own blanket.

"You'll need it," she said, "when this is over."

"Won't be long now, Dorcas child," another offered. "The doc'll be back any minute."

Listening to them, seeing the small but important sacrifices they were making, Jenny marveled at the transformation that had taken place. Hardened and normally unfeeling, quarrelsome and acquisitive, Dorcas's plight, her pain, and the fear she was enduring had touched their hearts. Her plight was common to all women, and suddenly they were united, their own concerns forgotten, if only momentarily, in a deeper concern for the terrified, helpless girl.

Dr. Bowes returned, and they stood back, making way for him. His tone, when he spoke, was harsh and impatient, as if he did not expect any of them to aid him, but they scurried this way and that in the dark confines of their prison, fetching him what he asked for without complaint. Jenny, enlisted to hold Dorcas's straining, pain-racked body still, was sickened by what he was doing; she shut her eyes, and Eliza, without a word, moved to take her place.

"I seen this sort o' thing before," she confided gruffly. "You ain't, so leave 'er ter me."

The baby was born at last, a puny, twisted little creature that uttered no sound.

"Dead," the surgeon stated. He shook his head as Eliza made to pick it up. "No use trying to revive it—been dead for hours. Wrap it in something and take it away." No one moved; then Melia, her face devoid of expression, did as he had asked. Several women, overcome by the sight, started to weep noisily, and the young surgeon turned on them in self-righteous scorn.

"For the Lord's sake, what are you creating such a fuss about? A baby with no father, born out of wedlock to a streetwalker . . . damned in the eyes of the Lord? The wages of sin are death, you hussies— and here's proof if you need it!"

A stunned silence greeted his words. Dr. Bowes restored his forceps to his bag, snapped it shut, and slowly rolled down the sleeves of his shirt over his bloodstained forearms. He gave instructions for the care Dorcas would require and left them with a curt promise to see her again next morning.

Jenny, with Melia, Eliza, and Charlotte, did what they could for the exhausted Dorcas but she was heartbroken by the loss of her child, and despite all their attempts to console her she slipped into unconsciousness from which it was impossible to rouse her. When Dr. Bowes returned just before ten, he pronounced her dead with a lack of feeling that caused Eliza's temper to flare.

Mouthing bitter accusations, she struck him a stinging blow across the face, and the surgeon, as angry as she, ordered her arrest.

"You'll get ten days in fetters, my girl!" he told her as the marine guard took her in charge. "And we'll have your head shaved to see if that'll teach you a lesson. Take her away . . . and get that body out of here while you're about it," he ordered the marines. "As for the rest of you . . . ." The surgeon paused, eyeing them balefully. "On your knees and pray to God to forgive you your sins—it's too wet for you to go on deck."

The open deck was forbidden to convicts in bad weather, and even when the rain ceased and the wind slackened, it was too cold to remain there for long. Nevertheless, after two days of being battened down in the hold with the women back to their old habits,

Jenny took every opportunity to exercise that she could, sometimes with Melia but more often alone.

Despite the desolation of the lowering gray skies and the wilderness of water that with its floating ice seemed to imprison the ship in a strange, lost world, there were seabirds in profusion to attract her attention. Jenny watched them, catching her first glimpse of the odd little low-flying creatures, known to seamen as Mother Carey's chickens, as they skimmed from wave top to wave top in the ship's wake, swifter even than the swallows she remembered from her childhood. Great numbers of albatross and petrels accompanied them, and each day whales could be seen—huge, cumbersome denizens of the deep, often alarmingly close at hand.

As Christmas approached, the cold increased and many of the animals on board died or were slaughtered for food. Even so, rations were short; the ship's company and the officers were as cold and almost as hungry as the convict women and disagreements were rife, as morale inevitably sank to a low ebb. Even the officers quarreled among themselves, and Mattie Denver, who was now seldom sober, was the victim of a drunken brawl three days before Christmas, in which not only her cronies among the women joined but also some of the seamen.

Polly, the unwitting cause of the outburst, came flying excitedly to where the little group of women from the *Friendship* had endeavored to isolate themselves, begging for their protection.

"I never did anything," she told Jenny indignantly. "But that old hag Hannah claims I stole her man from her. It wouldn't be difficult—look at her, scurvy old besom! A man's got to be blind drunk to cast his eye on her twice, and as for having anything else to do with her . . . well, I ask you! She's a right bag o' bones."

But the others, it seemed, had forgotten what had led to the argument. They traded insults and obscenities with the men, who retreated to the deck, evidently afraid that their officers might hear the uproar. When Mattie Denver attempted to pursue them, she lost her footing and was precipitated headfirst down the fore hatchway, to land with a sickening thud on the planking of the hold. Her wig saved her from serious injury. It was thick, the padded hair piled high on the top of her head, and when she picked herself up with the wig askew but seemingly none the worse for her fall, the women became convulsed with laughter. After a moment Mattie's resentful scowl faded, and she, too, joined in the laughter.

"Land's sakes!" she gasped. "The devil takes care o' his own, don't he? I'd never 'ave got up again if I 'adn't bin a mite tipsy. Here, give us a drink, one o' you, and let bygones be bygones . . . it's nigh on Christmas, ain't it? The season o' goodwill—well, let's just hope the captain remembers it!"

Christmas Eve was dark and gloomy, marked by an eclipse of the moon and very heavy seas, but on Christmas Day Captain Sever did remember. It was announced that he intended to make an issue of rum to everyone on board, and the women were summoned on deck to receive their issue, in addition to a small gift of soft sugar. The captain, a tall dignified figure, supervised the presentation himself, and when it was over, he read the lesson and led the singing of a Christmas hymn in a pleasant baritone. But, despite these well-intentioned attempts to raise their spirits, the women passed a miserable day that, for most of them, ended only when they had drunk themselves into insensibility.

"Christmas at home used to be so happy and exciting," Melia whispered in a rare moment of expansion, curled up at the foot of Jenny's bunk to enable them to share their blankets. "We began with prayers and my father reading the lesson, and then we had our presents, all piled up on the breakfast table in gay wrappings. We attended Church in the morning, and for dinner there was roast goose and pork and capon . . . such a feast as we had! And the house decorated with holly and mistletoe, and the servants—" Meeting Polly's wondering gaze, she broke off abruptly, flung down the wooden bowl of dry pea pudding she was making a brave pretense of eating, and, choking back a sob, climbed into her own bunk.

"Missus Morgan gave a party at Christmas, too," Polly said cynically. "For *her* servants . . . but it wasn't like that."

Jenny, her throat tight, remembered the last Christmas she had spent in the cottage at Long Wrekin when her father had been alive, the walk through the snow to listen to the rector's sermon, the blazing log fire that they had returned to, and her mother, with flour on her hands, taking a newly baked loaf from the oven to assuage their hunger until the leg of lamb should be cooked.

"Who knows," she offered, forcing herself to speak cheerfully, "what the new year will bring?"

"It won't be any different," Polly retorted. She reached for Melia's discarded bowl and scooped up its contents without relish. "It might even be worse, Jenny. So don't fool yourself."

As if to prove her words, the first day of the year 1788 was heralded by a severe gale. The ship rolled monotonously under storm staysails, with the seas crashing over her and the hold and 'tween decks flooded. After being washed out of their bunks by the rising water, Jenny and the rest were close to despair, but hopes rose a little when on January 7, the coast of Van Dieman's Land was sighted. They were still eight hundred miles from their destination, but after the hardships of the desolate miles they had traveled since leaving the Cape, the mere sight of land was cause for celebration.

At first it was obscured by a thick, impenetrable haze, but as they sailed closer in and the mists were dispersed, those who had braved the icy wind on deck were able to make out surf breaking on a rocky shore and a range of tree-grown hills in the background, which appeared to be capped with snow. At night the ships brought-to some five leagues from the coast, and flickering fires could be seen on the hill slopes and beaches, proof—if proof were needed—that the coastal area was inhabited.

They made sail next morning, and the women were in the depths of depression when the land was finally lost to sight. Food and fuel were running low, drinking water in short supply, and the fog that hemmed the ships in for two days was succeeded by one of the worst storms they had yet experienced. Lightning rent the somber night sky, thunder rolled; with daylight came a deluge of rain and a strong contrary wind, with hailstones the size of oranges bombarding the upper deck and the sea a welter of white, foaming water. Jenny lay listlessly on her bunk, knees hunched up to her chin in a vain attempt to keep warm, and her eyes closed, seeking sleep that would not come.

On the bunk above she heard Melia weeping, and her conscience pricking her, she sat up.

"Is there anything amiss, Melia?" she asked anxiously. It was not like Melia to show emotion; throughout the voyage, she had been stoically controlled and a veritable tower of strength, backing Jenny with unswerving loyalty in her dealings with the *Lady Penrhyn* women. But now, with the end almost in sight and Botany Bay not much more than a week's sailing away, she was weeping as if her heart would break.

"What is it, love?" Jenny persisted, and when Melia did not answer, she hoisted herself up onto the bunk above to put a sympathetic arm about the older girl's shaking shoulders.

"It's that hateful Doctor Bowes," Melia said. "He lectured me again as if I were no better than those abandoned wretches"—her gesture took in the drinkers at the opposite end of the hold who, as was their custom, were bickering noisily—"and he accused me of being hardened in my wickedness. But I'm not, Jenny. Before God, I swear I'm not!"

It was then, in a disjointed whisper, that Melia told her story.

She came, as Jenny had long supposed, from a well-to-do family whose name, even now, she was reluctant to divulge, and the story of her downfall was not new. A handsome young scapegrace had sought her hand when she was sixteen, but because he was penniless and without prospects, her father had frowned on the match and sent the young man packing. But Melia, imagining herself in love, had agreed to elope with him. He had an ensign's commission in the army purchased for him by a generous uncle. He had taken her to London, where they had spent his furlough at a lodging house in Bayswater Road. In the confident belief that, faced with their elopement, her father would consent not only to their marriage but also to make financial provision for them in the future, her lover had sold his commission and spent the proceeds, partly on riotous living but mainly on gambling.

The money had not lasted long. When it had finally run out, Melia had been pregnant with his child, and deeming this the moment to make his approach to her father, the young man had spent the last of his slender stock of guineas on the hire of a post chaise to take them to her home in Bodmin.

"When we reached the house," Melia said brokenly, "the blinds were all down and the curtains drawn. My father had died only two days before and my mother . . . my mother blamed me for his death. She said I had caused him so much shame and grief that it had destroyed him. She would not even allow me to stay so that I might attend his funeral. She—she sent us away, Jenny, empty-handed. My father was quite a rich man and I was the only child, but my mother would not give me a penny. She disowned me and told me I was never to show my face in the house again."

"What did you do?" Jenny asked, shocked by the realization that any woman of gentle breeding could behave so callously towards her own daughter.

Melia sighed. "We took the coach back to London, and Arnold left me with the landlady. He promised he would come back with the money to settle our score . . . but he didn't. He just vanished. And the landlady wanted her money so I—I went on the streets to get it for her. But it wasn't easy, and when I came to the last months of my time, even that wasn't possible, so she threw me out. I stole from an eating house Arnold and I used to patronize, because I was starving and the proprietor gave me in charge. My baby—my poor little dead baby—was born in Newgate."

Jenny hugged her, sick with pity, and she went on wryly, "Arnold married money, as he always meant to, and his new father-in-law must have purchased him a commission in the cavalry because he was married in uniform. The description of his wedding appeared in one of the newssheets—the landlady showed it to me, just before she threw me out, as proof that he wasn't coming back. It—it was a year ago today, his wedding, and by an odd coincidence, my mother married again on the same day. She—she married a business associate of my father's, Jenny, who was his best and oldest friend."

There was nothing Jenny could say, no consolation she could offer, and after a brief silence Melia turned to face her, dabbing at her tear-filled eyes. "I'll get over it," she asserted. "I—I thought I had, I thought I'd put it all behind me. And I *will*, truly I will . . . this is going to be a new life, and I'll try to begin it with a clean slate if you'll help me. Let's stick together, Jenny, you and me always—that's if you're willing, I mean."

"I'm willing," Jenny promised. She added, a catch in her voice, "Willing and . . . proud, Melia."

At eight o'clock on the morning of January 20, 1788, the *Sirius* led her convoy into Botany Bay to find the *Supply* and her three consorts already at anchor there.

The *Supply* dropped anchor off the point that Captain Cook had named Solander, at the wide entrance to Botany Bay at two fifteen on the afternoon of Friday, January 18, 1788, with her three consorts—

the *Scarborough, Friendship,* and *Alexander*—some two days' sail behind her.

Storms, fog, and strong contrary winds had delayed the advance division, but for the past four days the *Supply* had been within sight of the New South Wales coast, and Captain Phillip, his glass constantly to his eye, had subjected its steep, rocky shoreline and seemingly verdant woods to an anxious and searching scrutiny. A strong surf beat against the rocks, gulls and petrels wheeled above their dizzy heights, but of human life or habitation there appeared no sign.

It had been an arduous, uncomfortable, and at times perilous passage. The *Supply* was a small brig-rigged sloop of only one hundred sixty-eight tons burthen, and she labored badly in anything approaching heavy seas, with her narrow decks awash and her ancient timbers straining. Looking about him now as she rode at anchor in the bay that was their destination, Phillip breathed a silent prayer of thankfulness. Whatever lay ahead in the unknown land in which, twelve thousand miles from their homeland, they were required to establish a settlement, could not—surely could not—offer a greater challenge than the voyage had offered.

He said as much to Lieutenant King, who joined him at the rail with word that the boats were ready, but added wryly, "From what I can see of this place, it scarcely appears promising, does it? However, we must inspect its possibilities, so hoist away, Mister King. Let us hope the native inhabitants will not attempt to impede our landing or deter us from replenishing our water. You've armed the landing party, I trust?"

"Yes, sir," King assured him. "Seamen as well as

marines, with twenty rounds a man, sir. And the water casks are loaded."

The boats were hoisted out. As the men were debarking, Phillip turned to the *Supply*'s commander, Lieutenant Ball. "Should the transports arrive in my absence, Mister Ball, see that they anchor well offshore and permit no one to land. The bay's shallow, according to Captain Cook's chart, but we shall have to confirm that—it will render the landing of stores a most irksome task if they have to be ferried ashore by boat. Well"—he shrugged resignedly—"if we are not back by nightfall—or if you hear prolonged firing —send an armed party ashore in search of us."

"Aye, aye, sir," Henry Ball acknowledged. Hat in hand, he accompanied his commander to the entry port and watched him descend to his boat. Both crafts made for the north side of the bay, sounding as they went. First to gain the sandy beach was the boat carrying the marines, commanded by young Lieutenant Dawes, who put his men ashore in combat order, but no one appeared to contest their landing, and Phillip crossed the expanse of sand, with King at his side, both gazing about them with interest as they approached a belt of trees.

Sir Joseph Banks had waxed lyrical concerning this bay when he and the late James Cook had landed here almost eighteen years before, Phillip reminded himself. Cook had claimed it in the king's name, together with the whole of the unexplored eastern coast between the forty-third and the tenth degrees of southern latitude—a vast landmass that he had named New South Wales. In his report Cook had written of "deep black soil, capable of producing any kind of grain and at present producing, besides timber, as fine a meadow as ever was seen. . . ." The words were indelibly imprinted in his memory, he had read and thought of them so often. Phillip expelled his breath in a long-drawn sigh. He could see nothing that fitted Cook's description of Botany Bay.

The shore was a barren marsh beyond the sandy beach on which the *Supply*'s landing party had first set foot. As they progressed further inland they saw that the timber was stunted, and the grass, far from being lush and green as they had been led to expect, proved on examination to be coarse and spiny, growing in tussocks among rocks and sand dunes. And, although mid-January, it was hot, the air alive with myriads of insects while, among the trees, hundreds of brightly hued birds resembling small parrots darted this way and that, clearly disturbed by the intruders.

Unable to discern any sign of water, Phillip gave the order to retrace their steps, his face carefully expressionless. They returned abreast of the ship and there had their first encounter with a party of aborigines.

"Indians, sir!" King shouted in warning. "And they don't appear pleased to see us."

The Indians were of unprepossessing appearance, dark-skinned and bearded. Their naked bodies, Phillip observed, had been liberally daubed with mud, which had dried to a grayish dust, and their hair was ragged and unkempt. All were armed with spears and clubs, and they brandished these on the approach of the strangers, adopting a menacing pose and calling out in an unintelligible tongue, whose meaning was nevertheless quite plain.

"Stand back," Captain Phillip ordered. "We must endeavor to get on friendly terms with them if we can."

He advanced toward the threatening little group,

alone and unarmed, offering gifts of beads and a mirror, and making signs to indicate that he was seeking water. It was some time before he managed to disarm their suspicions, but finally, after motioning him to deposit his gifts on the ground, an old man with a hideously flattened face stepped forward and possessed himself of the trinkets. He then indicated that there was a stream in the opposite direction to the one in which they had been searching, and having inspected this and found its quality good, the *Supply* party filled their casks and rowed back to the ship.

Arthur Phillip spent an anxious and sleepless night, but he kept his own counsel. Next day, following the arrival of the three transports that had formed the advance division of the fleet, he continued his exploration with a larger party, in three boats, his anxiety and his disappointment growing. The weather was again hot, and they were plagued by clouds of flies and stinging insects, constantly watched, and occasionally menaced by parties of Indians who, in spite of the gifts they were offered, displayed no desire to establish friendly relations with the new arrivals.

They found two more small fresh-water streams but little else and, gathering at midday to eat a frugal meal of salt beef washed down with porter, made the discovery that the strange, gray-green leaves of the trees afforded scant shelter from the sun's heat but that their branches made excellent, pungent-smelling firewood.

King and Dawes led a party further inland than the main body had attempted to go, and after taking a long draft of his porter, Phillip King started to describe what they had seen.

"The soil was good, sir, a rich, dark-looking loam, and there seemed to be some quite good grazing land in the distance. Unhappily we could not descend the hill to examine it properly—about fifty Indians surrounded us and made signs to us to return to our boat. We tried to get them to accept the beads and ribbons we had, but they would have none of them, and when they started throwing spears at us, we thought it prudent to retire. All the same, sir, I don't think we should give up hope of this place altogether, because—"

Major Ross cut him short. He had arrived only that morning in the *Scarborough*, but already his feelings concerning the site of the proposed settlement were in no doubt. "Do you not, Mister King?" he challenged querulously. "Then I must beg to differ. In my view it would be a disaster if we attempt to set up the new colony here—our chances of survival will be slight indeed. There is insufficient water for our needs, and from my knowledge of agriculture this land will neither grow good crops nor feed livestock —and there appears to be little or no game. Besides" —he waved a deprecatory hand in the direction of the distant ships—"as a naval man, you surely cannot consider that this bay provides a safe or a satisfactory anchorage? The decision is not, of course, mine but. . . ." He broke off, avoiding Phillip's eye and then added pointedly, "I consider that it would be the height of irresponsibility to think of landing our people here."

Privately tempted to agree with this pessimistic opinion, Captain Phillip held his peace. He would, he decided, devote a day or two more to exploring Botany Bay since his orders had been to found the new settlement at the place where Cook and Sir Joseph Banks had landed. But a good harbor *was* essential —Ross was right on that score. Botany Bay, besides being shallow, was exposed to the southeast winds, which brought with them a heavy swell, and it was not large enough to provide shelter for all his eleven ships.

With the arrival of the *Sirius* and the second division of storeships and transports came a fresh sense of urgency. It was essential to set the artisans ashore so that a start might be made with the building of shelters and the erection of tents as soon as possible, since the month's grace Phillip had hoped for had been lost. Captain Hunter, at his request, joined the landing party, but their third day's exploration served only to increase Arthur Phillip's doubts and fears concerning Botany Bay as a site for the settlement. The swamp land was extensive and redolent of fever, a breeding ground for flies and mosquitoes—what had looked like lush green meadows from the deck of a ship was, in fact, moss and marsh grass on which cattle and sheep could not thrive. And there were a great many more aborigines than Cook's report had led him to expect. Indeed, Phillip reflected grimly, what he had now seen of the wooded slopes by which the bay was surrounded suggested a considerable number of human inhabitants and confirmed the dearth of fresh water and native game.

His commission as governor of New South Wales covered an immense area, and, he decided, with the responsibility for close on a thousand lives to be considered, it would behoove him to give more time to the search for a suitable site. He confided his decision to Hunter, and that evening after dinner on board the *Sirius* the two officers pored long and earnestly over their charts.

"I'm certain we'll be well advised to look elsewhere, John," Phillip said. He jabbed a slim finger on two inlets to the north, which Cook had named Port Jackson and Broken Bay. "Both these appear more promising, don't you agree?"

"Indeed I do," Hunter affirmed. "How about looking into Port Jackson tomorrow? It's not above eight or nine miles to the entrance. I can have a couple of longboats rigged and we can bring Mister Keltie along if you wish, to take soundings. And young Dawes, perhaps. Er"—he smiled—"Major Ross might remain in command here and begin preparations to disembark the working parties since I cannot."

"Excellent," Phillip approved. He echoed Hunter's smile. "Ross tends to be . . . how can I express it? Downright discouraging at times, does he not? And I must continue to hope that we can find a better site for our colony than this, or heaven help me, John, I'm lost!"

He spoke with seeming lightness, but understanding the strain under which he was laboring, John Hunter answered gruffly, "So are we all, sir! But God has brought us thus far safely—He will not fail us now."

"Let us pray that He will not," Phillip said gravely.

They set off on the morning of the twenty-first accompanied by a small party of marines commanded by Captain Collins. It was a warm and pleasant day with a brisk breeze, and, after sailing past frowning cliffs, they reached Port Jackson just after midday, to find themselves in the finest natural harbor any of them had ever seen. Its entrance was guarded by two rocky headlands—which Cook had marked simply as a boat harbor—and once past these, they saw the harbor unfold before them as a blue tranquil expanse of water winding away to the west, dotted with small islets, the high wooded shores by which it was contained terminating in sandy beaches and land-locked coves.

Phillip's heart lifted at the sight of it, and as they continued their exploration the officers who had accompanied him shared his pleasure and relief.

"A thousand sail of the line could ride at anchor here in perfect security," Hunter observed, his glass to his eye, "with a signal station on the headland there and, if need be, batteries mounted on both."

"Botany Bay bears no comparison," David Collins declared with conviction. "Why, I wonder, did Sir Joseph Banks commend it so highly, yet barely make mention of Port Jackson?"

"The late Captain Cook never put in here, sir," Keltie, the *Sirius*'s master told him. "The *Endeavour*'s people landed within a mile of that north headland there and did not even suspect there was a harbor here."

"It—it's like paradise, sir!" young William Dawes exclaimed, and Phillip, listening to these varied but unconflicting opinions, permitted himself a tight-lipped smile.

"Thanks be to Almighty God," he offered, his voice not quite steady, "that He has guided us here from the other side of the world!" Meeting Hunter's eye, his expression relaxed, and he added, "Here in paradise, with God's help, we will build our colony, John. It only remains for us to decide precisely where."

That decision was made, with the enthusiastic approval of the entire party, the following day when, after inspecting several arms and bays, a cove was found, some six miles inside the harbor and on its southern side. It possessed an excellent water supply in the form of a stream and anchorage for the fleet close inshore, with ample depth for the largest vessel within the confines of the cove.

Phillip and his party returned to Botany Bay to acquaint those who had remained there with the heartening news of their discovery.

Preparations to move to Port Jackson were well in hand next day when two strange sail were observed just outside the bay. The strangers were of considerable size, and speculation as to their nationality and intentions was rife throughout the British fleet. The most widely held belief was that they were French, and something akin to panic was caused when Major Ross suggested that Britain and France might again be at war and that the new arrivals were ships of war, come for the purpose of wresting the infant colony from the possession of its would-be settlers.

"We should beat to quarters, sir," he told Captain Hunter aggressively, "and endeavor to drive them off."

Hunter eyed him calmly. "They may just as easily be British, sir," he retorted.

"British? What makes you suppose anything of the kind, sir?" Ross demanded, bristling. "Why should British ships come after us?"

"With additional supplies, Major," Lieutenant King offered, a hint of a smile touching his lips. "The home government might have repented of its earlier parsimony. It's possible, is it not, sir?" he appealed to Phillip.

"Unlikely, I fear, Mister King," the captain answered. "They're French all right," he added as, finding the wind adverse for entering the bay, both ships stood off. "But peaceful Frenchmen on a voyage of discovery in the Pacific, who left Europe two years before we did and went round the Horn. I'll wager that is who they are—and that they'll be back as soon as the wind shifts to satisfy their curiosity concerning us. If my memory is not at fault, their commander is the Marquis de Lapérouse."

As a precaution, however, he postponed the fleet's departure, and when, early the following morning, the two strange ships reappeared, he sent the *Sirius*'s first lieutenant out to them by boat, to offer assistance in piloting them into the bay, should they wish to enter. William Bradley returned with confirmation that the ships were the *Boussole* and the *Astrolabe*, engaged in scientific observation and discovery, as Phillip had supposed, under the command of the Marquis de Lapérouse.

"Monsieur de Lapérouse wishes to enter the bay in order to take on wood and water, sir, and to make repairs to his boats, which were damaged in a storm," Bradley explained. "He was most friendly and hospitable, sir, and he told me that he had learned of our expedition when he touched at Kamchatka. I fancy he expected that our settlement would already be established, from the way he spoke."

Captain Phillip exchanged an amused glance with his second-in-command. "Did I not tell you that the noble marquis was curious, John? Well, we will leave him Botany Bay and show him every civility. I do not imagine there will be anything here to tempt His Gallic Majesty—although our own government will be relieved if Monsieur de Lapérouse so informs him, don't you think?"

Hunter nodded sagely. "That seems probable, sir."

"Then," Phillip decided, "we had better make for Port Jackson ourselves, as soon as he drops anchor. I will take the *Supply* there today and make formal claim to it . . . hoist the flag and post a guard, just

to be sure. You stay and do the honors and follow
us as soon as you can. Now that we have found the
place for our settlement, I am anxious to set our people
ashore with as little delay as possible."

The two French ships entered next morning.
Hunter paid a courtesy call on their commander and
then hoisted the signal for sailing. Led by the *Sirius*,
the British fleet weighed anchor and began at once
to work out of the bay. The passage, which took only
a few hours under a blue and cloudless sky, was en-
livened by the *Friendship* falling foul of the *Charlotte*
and the *Prince of Wales* as they were crossing the bar.
No damage was done, and with virtually everyone on
deck eager to glimpse the newly discovered harbor of
which they had heard so much, the whole fleet passed
between the headlands and, undeterred by the hostile shouts of natives on the shore, came to anchor in
the governor's chosen cove just before sunset.

The landing party from the *Supply*, consisting of
convict artisans, seamen, and marines, had been at
work since first light, clearing a camping ground beside the freshwater creek, which Phillip had earmarked for the settlement's future water supply. As
pleased with the new site and its surroundings as those
who had chosen it, the men worked with a will, cutting down timber, filling water casks, and erecting
a flagstaff. The air rang with the sound of axes; men
called out to each other cheerfully; there was much
coming and going between ship and shore, as tools
were landed and the Union Flag brought across
in readiness from the *Supply*'s signal locker.

Some of the convicts, with hopes of fresh meat as a
change from the monotonous salt tack, built a cooking fire at midday, but the three marines who had
been permitted to fare forth in search of game re-

turned empty-handed and disconsolate after a fruitless chase.

"All we seen was some o' them black fellows," one of them said glumly. "And they wasn't what you'd call friendly, not by a long chalk."

Enthusiasm flagged; all the men were weary long before evening. After being cooped up for months onboard ship, they had not regained their land legs, and toiling in the fierce heat of the sun rapidly reduced even the strongest to panting exhaustion. Observing this, Captain Phillip called a halt to the labor.

"They've done well enough for the first day," he told Lieutenant King, who had been assisting him to plan and mark out the site for the encampment. "They can rest for an hour, and then I want the ship's company and the marines to form up round the flagstaff, ready to hoist the flag."

Just before sunset the parade assembled. With due ceremony the Union Flag was raised to the top of the flagstaff, and in his first official act as governor, Phillip named the site Sydney Cove, in honor of Viscount Sydney. The marines fired three volleys, and the officers present drank a loyal toast to His Majesty King George the Third, in whose august name the territory was formally claimed.

When the *Sirius* dropped anchor, it was to find the flag flying and the ceremony over. Captain Hunter punctiliously ordered the firing of a twenty-one-gun royal salute.

Lieutenant Leach, in attendance on Major Ross, was the first to witness his superior's intense displeasure at the realization that the ceremony of hoisting the flag had been conducted without waiting for his arrival. The marine commandant said nothing but the expression on his thin, high-boned face spoke volumes, and Leach ventured diffidently, "That was discourteous, sir. *You* are the lieutenant governor."

Ross did not reprove him; indeed for a moment he looked pleased because his discomfiture had been recognized and the reason for it understood. Then, recollecting Leach's rank, his expression hardened.

"One has always to be on one's guard against slights," he said sharply. "You have not served in the corps for very long, Jeremiah, but you will learn that there is a tendency, on the part of virtually all naval officers, to regard officers of the corps as their inferiors."

When Leach had been sent so ignominiously to the *Sirius,* he had felt that Captain Shea—egged on, no doubt, by Robert Nellow—had treated him harshly and unjustly. Both, of course, were officers of the corps, which made it even more unjust. But the commandant had proved to be a man very much after his own heart. Furthermore Major Ross had taken a liking to him, and since the feeling was mutual, Jeremiah Leach was happier than he had been since leaving England. The commandant had his eldest son on board, as a volunteer like himself, and although the boy was only fifteen and not yet officially commissioned, a warm friendship had grown up between them, and this, too, had caused the commandant to look upon him kindly.

Major Ross went on, riding his favorite hobbyhorse, "The honor of the corps must be the paramount consideration of all its officers at all times. But here, here on land, where my command becomes an independent one—" Ross sighed deeply. "Independent, that is to say, of all naval officers save Captain

Phillip, who is appointed governor, I cannot count on the complete loyalty of all my officers, Jeremiah."

Leach was startled. "Why on earth not, sir? I don't understand."

The major eyed him with sad, lackluster blue eyes.

"Because," he said resignedly, "they have been given civil appointments that may well conflict with their military duties . . . and their loyalties. Captain Collins, for example, is to serve as judge advocate—he has no legal training, but his word will be law in this settlement, and his responsibility to the governor, not to the corps." Ross added with a bitterness he could not hide, "No account has been taken of seniority. Captain Campbell, as no doubt you are aware, is many years senior to Captain Collins and would have been the better choice. And then there's young Dawes—apart from you and my boy John, the most junior of my officers—but *he* is to be entrusted with the task of establishing an observatory! That virtually removes him from my command."

"That seems unfair, sir, in the circumstances. I mean—" He reddened, seeking vainly for words.

"Unfair, you say?" Major Ross repeated his sigh. Once again he had to remind himself that Jeremiah Leach was only a second lieutenant, a mere boy, who could not be expected to comprehend the complexities of government appointments and the reasons behind them. And perhaps, in his frustration, he had let his tongue run away with him, said more than he had intended to say to anyone.

Robert Ross glanced searchingly at the boy beside him. It had been a relief to speak his mind, a release of the tension building up inside him—and this boy was loyal.

"Believe me, sir, nothing you may choose to tell me

will be repeated—not to anyone," Leach assured him.
"You may rely on me, sir."

Ross nodded, a frosty smile briefly touching his lips.
"Then I shall, Jeremiah—I shall rely on you implic-
itly. And—I shall be going ashore first thing tomorrow. You and my son will accompany me. See to it
that my marquee is unloaded, if you please, and detail
a party to set it up."

Leach came smartly to attention. "Very good, sir,"
he said. "Leave it to me, sir."

"FERTILE PLAINS . . ."

CHAPTER XIV

During the next ten days the work of setting up the new settlement went on apace. More male convicts were landed from the transports and formed into working parties under guard.

A blacksmith's forge was erected; stores, tents, and supplies of dockyard canvas brought ashore; the construction of a wharf begun; and pits dug for cooking ovens and fires. Work started at first light and went on until dark, with a short break at midday.

The ground was staked out according to the plan Captain Phillip had prepared, with the marines under canvas on the west side of the freshwater creek, the convicts in newly built huts on its eastern bank. A hospital, initially of canvas, was to be set up on the headland at the cove's western extremity between the marines' encampment and the point designated as the site for an observatory, when Lieutenant Dawes should bring the admiralty telescope and other scientific instruments ashore.

On the eastern extremity the plan called for a small fort, mounting two of the *Sirius*'s guns for defensive purposes, with the Government House—at present a large canvas marquee—erected a short distance to the rear of the landing wharf and flagstaff. Parties were sent to clear the land of trees in the area behind the governor's marquee in preparation for the construction of a government garden and fenced enclosures for the various livestock brought, with seed and young fruit trees and plants, from Capetown.

Inevitably there were setbacks, and Captain Phillip, while careful to preserve an outwardly confident and unruffled appearance, fumed inwardly when the home government's parsimony was again revealed in the poor quality of the tools provided for the settlement's use.

"The axes and spades," he complained to Hunter, "are the worst I have ever set eyes on—inferior even to those used as barter with the natives of the Pacific Islands!"

The convicts, with one or two notable exceptions, drove him close to despair. Mainly city dwellers untrained in manual labor, they displayed a sullen unwillingness to exert themselves in its performance. The primitive huts they built—four posts, with walls of tree branches roughly interlaced and smeared with clay and a thatch of palm leaves—were too flimsy to stand up to wind and weather, and the native timber, which burned so well, proved useless for building purposes.

Fresh meat was virtually unobtainable. Organized hunting parties were sent out daily, but they returned, weary and dispirited, to report a lack of edible game. A few of the native marsupials—called kangaroos by the Indians—were shot, with an occasional crow, but for the most part the salt beef and pork, on which they had been compelled to subsist for the past eight months, remained perforce a major part of their diet. The livestock was required for breeding and could not be slaughtered, so that the only fresh food available was fish, and some spinachlike plants and berries, which Dr. White had declared of some use in the treatment of scurvy.

The government garden—still only half cleared and littered with the stumps of the trees that had been felled—must be brought into production as quickly as was humanly possible, Captain Phillip decided. He put his servant, Edward Dodd, in charge and allotted him a large convict working party in the hope of hastening the initial planting, and since most of the officers had purchased livestock, fruit trees, and seed for their own use, he began allocating individual plots of land to any of them who asked for it.

It was a beginning and a very necessary one, for a great many of the male convicts landed to make up the settlement's labor force were suffering from the ravages of dysentery and scurvy and quite incapable of prolonged work. The marines, who were younger and fitter, were forbidden by their commandant to do more than provide guards, and Phillip had his first serious clash with Major Ross on this account, within a few days of landing.

"My men are soldiers, Captain Phillip," the marine officer informed him with icy dignity. "They are here to do duty as garrison troops and for the protection of the settlement. They will confine themselves to this duty. On no account will I permit them to act as superintendents of convict labor, and they cannot be expected to perform manual labor either—save when they are off duty. Then—since you have not seen fit to assign any convict working parties to my officers—I have given them leave to assist in the clearing and cultivation of land taken up by their officers. It will be on a strictly voluntary basis, of course, and their labor will be rewarded. That, sir, is my final word on this subject. I give you good day."

Without waiting for Phillip's reply, he stalked off, a stiff, unyielding figure, attended as always by his son and Lieutenant Leach.

"What in God's name can I do with the infernal fellow, John?" the new governor asked helplessly of his second-in-command. "Our seamen are working harder than the convicts, without a word of complaint, but Ross forbids his damned jollies to do the same! And we need every man we've got."

"Have your commission read, sir," Captain Hunter answered uncompromisingly. "It appoints you as governor and captain general and places Major Ross and his corps unequivocally under your command."

"I will," Arthur Phillip agreed. "But we must land all our people—including the women—before I can do so. And we're not ready for them, heaven help us!"

There were tents for the marines' families—twenty-eight wives and a score of children—but the hospital was, as yet, a mere shelter, contrived of green timber and interlaced branches plastered with clay, like the huts, with a thatch of cabbage palm, reinforced with old sailcloth. It let in the rain, and there were few blankets to cover the shivering sick, who huddled there in abject misery. The huts planned for the women were only half completed, their latrines not even begun . . . Phillip sighed.

His own marquee, which had cost £125 and had been specially designed to provide both living and official quarters, was not weatherproof, he reflected wryly, and the slightest breeze disturbed its stability. But until, by their own labor, the settlers could improve on all these things, discomfort and even hardship could not be avoided. It would mean, in the end, the survival only of the fittest and would apply to them all—officers, garrison troops, and convicts alike—when the ships and the seamen sailed away. And somehow he must bring this bitter and unpalatable truth home to them . . . again he expelled his breath in a long-drawn sigh and reached for pen and paper.

His brow deeply furrowed, he started to compose the address he would make to them after his commission as governor was read. It took him until well past midnight, working by the light of a spluttering candle, as sheets of rain beat against the leaking canvas of his marquee. . . .

On February 5, a fresh issue of clothing from the ships' slop chests was made to the women convicts and their disembarkation ordered for the following day.

First to be rowed ashore were the wives and families of the marines, most of whom had been given passage in the *Prince of Wales*, and they were followed by the fifty convict women from her hold. The *Lady Penrhyn*'s women—the largest contingent of female convicts, numbering close to a hundred, with half a dozen children and as many babes in arms—were kept waiting on deck for two hours before the boats were hoisted out and the first mate bawled an order to them to start loading.

Jenny held back at the end of a long, straggling line with Melia, Polly, Eliza, and Charlotte, and a trifle to her surprise, she recognized Auld Meg's once-devoted crony Hannah Jones come sidling across to join them.

"Reckon as I'll tag along of you," she said, not waiting for any of them to raise objections. "It don't look much o' a place, do it?" she added in a querulous tone, jerking her head in the direction of the shore and addressing no one in particular.

Jenny, who had been drinking in the beauty of the wooded shoreline, eagerly awaiting her release from the confines of the ship, eyed her reproachfully but made no reply. This cove—now called Sydney—was to be their home for the foreseeable future, and it would be as well to make the best of it and the comparative liberty they would enjoy once they landed. But . . . she bit back a sigh. They presented a strange picture of womanhood, she thought wryly —herself in a seaman's striped jersey and ticking trousers; Eliza and Charlotte in much the same garb, but with the incongruous addition of ragged shawls; Polly in a dress, but bare of foot; and Melia's slim, shapely body half-buried in a sailcloth tunic.

Yet, Hannah apart, all were in an optimistic mood, eager to get ashore and set about the task of home-making, which, as the first mate had been at pains to warn them, would constitute their first task.

"There aren't enough huts to accommodate you all," he had told them as they stood huddled on the deck watching the boats of the *Prince of Wales* pull toward the landing beach. "Not by a long chalk there aren't. So if you want 'em, I reckon you'll have to set to and build your own. And that means," he had added waspishly, "that you'll have to keep sober!"

The warning was lost on most of them, however. As she followed Melia into one of the overcrowded longboats Jenny saw that Mattie Denver and a number of others were very far from sober, although, for once, the effect of the liquor they had consumed had been to dampen, rather than raise, their spirits.

"I'd as soon 'ave stopped in me saltbox at the bleedin' Newgate as come 'ere," the gaunt-faced mother of one of the infants claimed bitterly as the boat neared the landing stage. Several of the others voiced noisy agreement.

"Them's *palm* trees, for Gawd's sake! I reckon they've brought us to India, not New South Wales!"

"It's hot enough ter be flamin' India. An' them black critters we seen paddlin' their canoes over in Botany Bay—they was Indians, wasn't they?"

"Aye . . . the kind that'll cut our throats whiles we're asleep. I wish we'd stayed in the ship."

"They'll try to make us work once they get us on dry land," Mattie Denver complained. She took a bottle from beneath the folds of her once elegant velvet gown and, ignoring the envious glances it attracted, sipped its contents thirstily. "Well, I for one won't build any huts, whatever they say. That's men's work."

Polly sniffed disgustedly. "Listen to them, Jenny," she invited. "They make me puke! *Anywhere's* better than Newgate, and dry land's better and safer than any plaguey ship."

The boat grounded, and the women splashed reluctantly ashore, to be lined up by one of the ship's officers, who counted them before handing them over to the marine guard.

"Fifty-two females, eight infants, Sergeant. Sign for 'em, will you?"

The sergeant did as he had been requested. "All right," he said briskly, motioning to two of his men. "Take 'em along to the camp quick as you can and get back here."

The women had to run the gauntlet of cheers and catcalls from the various working parties of male convicts they passed on their way to the camp, which had been prepared for their reception, and Jenny's heart sank as she took in the scene about her.

Everywhere stores were piled up, spilling out of their containers; cooking, she saw, was being done in the open, and the roughly cleared, sandy ground was covered by a layer of ash from the burned trunks of felled trees, some of which were still smoldering. The stumps and roots were being grubbed up by hand and without enthusiasm by gangs of half-naked convict laborers.

There had been a deluge of rain the previous day, and all the huts and shelters had sustained damage. In one of the animal pens the entire fence on one side had collapsed, and two sullen convicts, instead of attempting to repair it, were standing, arms akimbo, watching the cattle it was supposed to contain make an unhurried escape. A marine sentry, posted to guard both convicts and animals, yelled for help, but the men ignored him and came grinning to meet the party from the *Lady Penrhyn* with obscene suggestions and complete indifference to the fate of the cattle.

Memory stirred. Many had been the time, in her childhood, that she had aided her father to turn back his young horses when they had broken out of the paddock at Long Wrekin . . . and these poor creatures, Jenny told herself, would almost certainly die if they were not brought back to their pen.

"Come on!" she said to Polly. "If we haven't lost the use of our legs, let's turn them before they go too far."

Polly giggled, and the two of them ran, barefoot, across the sandy ground in pursuit of the straying cattle. They had rounded up all but two of them when, driven by contemptuous shouts from the other women, the convict herdsmen reluctantly joined the chase and the fugitives were herded back into the pen.

"Why not mend your fence?" Jenny flung at them as they halted, mopping their heated faces and cursing. "It'd be less trouble, surely, than having to run after the poor things."

She returned to the cheers of the women.

"Well done!" Eliza acclaimed sarcastically. "Perhaps things will improve now they've brought us ashore to show them how."

By evening, however, the majority were bitter and disillusioned by the conditions prevailing on shore. The shelters and huts provided for them were primitive in the extreme, and fighting broke out as the possession of the more advantageous dwelling places was contested and bickered over, the enforced discipline of shipboard life forgotten within hours of coming ashore. At dusk, when the day's work was over, some seamen entered the women's camp with casks of liquor, but scarcely had they set these down than they were engulfed by an army of male convicts who drove them back to their ships and seized the liquor they had brought with yells of unholy glee.

A great bonfire was built; more liquor appeared; and heavily outnumbered, the marine sentries were powerless to stem the tide, even had they desired to do so. Jenny, sitting with her companions in a corner of the canvas-covered shelter, was thankful to recognize Sergeant Jenkins in charge of a file of men with loaded muskets, advancing to the relief of the sentries.

"Thank heaven I've found you, lass!" The old sergeant greeted her tensely. "Things are getting out of hand and our orders are to evacuate the camp and take no further action. The governor offers protection to any women who want it, and they're to come with us now. Help me find any you think wish out of here, and we'll escort the lot of them to our lines. But hurry, Jenny my girl—there'll be murder done before long, you mark my words!"

"The children," Jenny said. "And the babies—I'll get them first, Sergeant."

To her astonishment it was not only the children, most of them without their mothers, but also some of the more hard-bitten of the *Lady Penrhyn*'s women who elected to come with her. In all about twenty of them snatched up the bawling infants and frightened toddlers and, behind a screen of marines with bayonets fixed, made their escape from the mob.

Her last sight of the women's camp was of a huge fire, fed with the timber of which the shelter had been constructed and surrounded by a drink-crazed mass of men and women, many of them naked, embracing, dancing, screaming, and fighting, lost to all reason and all restraint. Jenny shivered, scarcely able to believe the evidence of her own eyes and ears, and beside her a tough young marine let out his breath in a long sigh.

"We had the breaks for eight months, I suppose," he said softly, "when they was battened down below hatches and in chains. Now it's their turn, and they've waited long enough for it—I don't reckon the Angel Gabriel hisself could stop 'em. Certain sure we couldn't—they're like animals; they'd tear us limb from limb if we tried!"

They passed Captain Phillip and some of his officers on the way to the marine guard post, and Jenny, looking back, saw that the new governor's face was deathly pale and his shoulders despairingly hunched, as if the scene he was witnessing passed even his comprehension.

The next day, Thursday, February 7, 1788, Governor Phillip inaugurated the new colony. The convicts, subdued after their night-long orgy, were mustered on a freshly cleared patch of ground in front of the flag-pole at an early hour, and a roll was called. Then the marine battalion paraded under its officers and marched, with colors flying and the band playing, to take post opposite them, the third side of the hollow square being formed by a naval contingent from the *Sirius* and *Supply* and parties of seamen from the transports.

When all were assembled, Captain Phillip and his principal officers, in full dress uniform, took their places beneath the flag. The marine band struck up the national anthem and heads were respectfully bared. Then, with due solemnity, Captain Collins of the Marine Corps, appointed judge advocate, read the governor's commission, followed by the act of Parliament and letters patent constituting the Civil and Criminal Courts of Judicature for the territory.

Jenny listened to the deep, slow voice of the young judge advocate, not taking in much of what he said but impressed, nonetheless, by the pomp of the occasion and by the sonorous words he was uttering with such telling gravity.

The powers that had been conferred on Captain Phillip as governor and captain general sounded immense. His authority was to extend from the northern cape or extremity of the coast called Cape York, in the latitude of 10°37′ south, to the southern extremity of the territory of New South Wales, in the latitude of 43°39′ south, and of all the country inland, as far as the 135th degree of east longitude, including all islands in the Pacific Ocean within these specified latitudes.

He was empowered to summon General Courts-Martial; to appoint justices of the peace, coroners, constables, and other necessary officers; to pass judgment on criminals; to make grants of land; and— Jenny pricked up her ears as the judge advocate read: "Should His Excellency the governor see cause, he shall grant pardons to offenders convicted in the colony in all cases whatever, treason and willful murder excepted . . . and he has the authority to stay the execution of the law, until His Majesty's pleasure shall be known. . . ."

Captain Collins finished his reading, the marines fired three volleys, and in the hush that followed, the governor stepped forward to address the assembled convicts.

"You have now been particularly informed of the nature of the laws by which you are to be governed, and also of the power with which I am invested to put them into full execution," he told them, his voice stern. "There are among you, I am willing to believe, some who are not perfectly abandoned and who, I hope and trust, will make the intended use of the great indulgence and laxity their country has offered in sending them here. But"—he paused, studying the sea of faces before him with narrowed eyes—"at the same time there are many, I am sorry to add—by far the greater part—who are innate villains and people of the most abandoned principles. To punish these shall be my constant care, and in this duty I will ever be indefatigable, however distressing it may be to my feelings." His voice was like thunder. "You may have my sacred word of honor that, whenever you commit a fault, you shall be punished, and most severely. Lenity has been tried; to give it further trial would be in vain—I am no stranger to the use you make of every indulgence, I speak of what comes under my particular observation. I warn you again, therefore, that a vigorous execution of the law, whatever it may cost my personal feelings, shall follow closely upon the heels of every offender."

There was silence, complete and absolute, and Jenny, venturing a glance at some of the faces around her, saw that almost all were sullen and resentful. They would give only what was forced from them, she thought; all were hardened to punishment and expected little else. They had no dreams of the future, no dreams and little hope.

The governor, as if he had sensed their apathy, made an attempt to offer them hope. He spoke eloquently of the promise this new land held out, the opportunities it offered. "Here there are fertile plains, needing only the labors of the husbandman to produce in abundance the fairest and richest fruits. Here there are interminable pastures, the future home of flocks and herds innumerable. . . ."

But the majority were not listening or, perhaps, Jenny told herself, they could not bring themselves to believe that the fertile plains and the flocks and herds could ever belong to them—they had been too long deprived of liberty. Besides, most were towns-folk; they had no love of the land, since all they knew were the streets of cities, and after over eight months at sea in the appalling conditions they had endured, they were weary and sick, wanting only to find oblivion in such liquor as they could obtain or, when this was offered, in the pleasures of the flesh, as they had sought the previous night.

The governor brought his address to an abrupt con-clusion; the marines marched back to their own side of the creek, where they formed up, preparatory to his inspection, and there being nothing else for the con-victs to do, they dispersed, with a reluctance they made no attempt to hide, to rejoin their working parties. Some of the women followed them, but Jen-ny's little group remained, gathering around her in an expectant circle.

"Jenny," Melia said. "We've been thinking over what the captain—that is, the governor—said in his address. What it amounts to, really, is that he'll be willing to reward good behavior with remission."

Jenny nodded, conscious of a lifting of her spirits.

"Yes, I'm sure that was what he meant," she agreed.

"And all that talk of fertile plains needing only the labors of the husbandman to produce the richest fruits," Melia went on. She smiled wryly. "What *that* seems to amount to is that if we don't grow fruit and vegetables for ourselves, we'll probably starve. Well, you were brought up on a farm, weren't you? You know how to grow things and how to care for ani-mals."

"I used to know, Melia. But it's been a long time since I worked on my dadda's farm and—"

A chorus of voices cut her short. "You know a flamin' sight more than the rest of us put together," Eliza told her with conviction. "But if we all stick together and work a garden plot the way you tell us to, it'd help, wouldn't it? And they'll surely let us have a plot of land and some seed if they see we're willing to put some sweat into it."

Jenny looked at their faces, and seeing the determination in almost all of them, she again inclined her head in assent. Some of them, she knew, had walked the streets since childhood; others had picked pockets; and most of them knew, from bitter experience, what it meant to starve. But if they were willing to work. . . . "There are no plows," she reminded them. "We shall have to clear trees and grub up the roots before we can even begin, and then we'll have to use hoes. It won't be easy."

"We know that," Charlotte assured her gravely. She turned to the others. "Who else has ever worked on a farm?"

Only one woman answered her. Ann Inett was a quiet, handsome girl, who had traveled in one of the other ships but had attached herself to the group the previous evening. "I have," she admitted. "But I've volunteered to go to Norfolk Island when Mister King goes to found a settlement there. Sixteen of us are going in the *Supply*, and they say we're to leave next week. I'd work for a week, though, if it would help you to make a start."

"I'll see Sergeant Jenkins," Jenny promised. "And ask him to get us a plot of land. If we can get it before you sail, Ann, then your help will be very welcome."

No difficulties were put in their way. Tom Jenkins went to his company commander, Captain Tench, and twenty-four hours later Jenny, with Melia, Polly, and Ann Inett, were offered a choice of plots, and after inspecting these, they settled on one on high ground near the head of the next cove, to the east of the main colony. The officers had been allotted plots in this vicinity, to enable them to grow corn with which to feed their livestock, and Jenny, with a shrewdness born of painful experience, reasoned that their garden, once established, would be safer here than anywhere else, since the officers' presence would discourage predators.

There were other advantages too. The plot ran down to the sea at one end, which would make fishing a practical possibility; there was a small stream flowing down to a rocky pool between this and the neighboring holding, which would ensure both an adequate fresh water supply and drainage; and the trees were sparse, growing mainly on the seaward side, where they afforded some protection from the sun.

A working party of male convicts, under Sergeant Jenkins's stern supervision, did what clearing was necessary in a single day and departed, having, on Jenny's insistence, left the timber screen on the seaward side untouched. Here, with infinite labor and assisted only by the *Charlotte*'s carpenter and two seamen, pressed into service by Tom Jenkins, the women built themselves three small but sturdy huts, into which they all moved. The *Supply* sailed for Norfolk Island, robbing them of Ann Inett's valuable aid and advice, but the two seamen from the *Charlotte* remained and occupied one of the huts with Polly and Eliza, and because both were sober and hard-working men, Jenny could raise no objection to their new liaison. In any event Polly was happier than she had been throughout the voyage and her seaman set himself to the construction of tables and chairs for the whole community—beautiful pieces, fashioned with a craftsman's skill from wood he smuggled ashore from the *Charlotte*'s stores.

Not to be outdone, Eliza's new lover turned his attention to the sea, and thanks to his efforts with nets and fishing lines, crabs, lobsters, and a number of hard-skinned but edible fish were added to the weekly ration of salt meat, flour, dried peas, and now rancid butter, to which each settler—free or convict—was entitled.

If Jenny had any regrets during the first busy weeks, these were solely on the Jenkinses' account. Sergeant Jenkins, who had initially endeavored to persuade her to join himself and Olwyn, no longer mentioned that possibility. He was hurt, Jenny knew, and the kindly Olwyn even more so, but much as this realization grieved her, she was determined to make her life with the convicts and accept no help or privileges for herself from which they were excluded.

Olwyn Jenkins's only visit to the busy little community in the eastern cove served merely to widen the rift that had grown up between them. She departed in tears and did not come again. . . .

On February 11 the first sitting of the newly established Court of Criminal Jurisdiction took place, and the whole of the convict community awaited its outcome with trepidation.

The judge advocate, Captain Collins, sat with three of his fellow marine officers—Captains Shea and Meredith and Lieutenant Cresswell—and Captain Hunter and Lieutenants Bradley and Ball of the Royal Navy, all in full dress uniform. Addressing the court, Collins went to some pains to point out that military courts-martial were to be quite separate from the criminal and civil courts—the marine commandant had reserved the right for men serving in the corps to be tried for military offenses by their own officers. The Royal Navy would, of course, retain the same right, and although, due to their present circumstances, the same officers were liable to serve on all three courts, a distinction would nevertheless be drawn between them.

"The letters patent of the second of April, seventeen eighty-seven, gentlemen, require that a Court of Criminal Jurisdiction shall be convened from time to time by His Excellency the governor for the trial and punishment of treason, felony, or misdemeanor. All decisions of the court will be subject to review by His Excellency the governor," Collins went on. "My duties require me to preside over sittings of the criminal and civil courts and to advise all courts-martial on matters of law. I am also required to examine the depositions taken upon the committal of offenders, to prepare information upon which they are to be tried by this court, to examine witnesses, assist prisoners in their defense, make minutes of the trials, and to keep and take charge of all the records of the court."

Hunter asked, "The examination of witnesses will, presumably, be carried on by members of the court, as well as by yourself, as judge advocate?"

"Yes, sir, that is so," David Collins confirmed.

"And all judgments will be determined by a majority?"

"To the best of my understanding, yes, sir."

"Then I foresee no pitfalls," John Hunter decided. There were nods of assent, and he turned again to Collins. "Be so good as to proceed, sir."

"Certainly, sir," David Collins assented. A smile

lightened the gravity of his good-looking boyish face. "There are but three cases to hear, sir."

The first case was that of a convict by the name of Samuel Barsby, who was accused of attacking the marine drum major with a cooper's adz and of abusing men of the guard and and sentries on the day of the women's landing. Brought in under guard by Midshipman Brewer, newly appointed provost marshal, Barsby did not attempt to deny the charges. He pleaded guilty and, invited to make a plea in mitigation, hung his head. Eyes on the ground, he mumbled wretchedly, "I come out in the *Alexander*, sir. We'd not set eyes on a woman since we left England, none of us 'ad. When I seen them dolly-mops runnin' 'round loose, I went berserk, sir, an' that's the Gorspel truth. I don't rightly remember what I done, sir."

"But you did assault the drum major?" Captain Meredith asked sternly. "You remember that?"

"Yes, sir," Barsby admitted. "I'm sorry, sir."

He received his sentence of one hundred fifty lashes without complaint and was marched out.

The next case, Thomas Hill, also entered a plea of guilty to a charge of having stolen two-pennyworth of ship's biscuit from a fellow convict. His sentence— the first of many yet to come—was to be confined in irons for one week, on bread and water, on a small, rocky island adjacent to the cove.

The third and last of that day's hearing was the case of a man named William Cole. He, too, was charged with theft but it was evident, when he appeared in answer to the summons, that he was simpleminded. Grinning amiably at the officers of the court in their swords and sashes, he confessed to having purloined two wooden planks—government property intended for building purposes—but pressed by Captain Collins, he could offer no valid reason for having done so.

"I didn't want 'em, sir—not to do nothin' with, like. I just thought . . . well, they might come in 'andy."

He was taken out, still grinning, and the court conferred. "He cannot be acquitted, sir," David Collins said diffidently, "since he has admitted his crime. But—a recommendation to mercy, perhaps, addressed to the governor might serve."

Captain Hunter inclined his head. "Fifty lashes then, gentlemen, with a recommendation to mercy— do you agree?"

There were nods of assent, and the court rose.

News that the governor had remitted the sentence on William Cole spread like wildfire through the convict camps. Spirits rose, and they rose still higher when it became known that a marine named Bramwell, charged with breaking into the women's encampment and beating Elizabeth Needham, had been awarded and received two hundred lashes.

The results were far reaching and unhappy. Thefts increased, the marines were jeered at and taunted by the women in the main encampment, and seamen, attempting to enter it, were assaulted and driven back to their ships by gangs of male convicts. Major Ross, resenting the governor's apparent leniency toward the convicts, sought him out to record a furious protest on behalf of his men.

"Examples will, alas, have to be made," Phillip told David Collins. "It is unfortunate, and I regret the necessity, but these people understand nothing else. They regard leniency as weakness."

The second court, which sat on February 27, endeavored to put matters right.

Three convicts—Thomas Barrett, Henry Lovell, and Joseph Hall—found guilty of conspiracy to rob the government provision stores, were sentenced to death. The governor, after reviewing their cases, commuted the death sentences on Lovell and Hall to banishment, but confirmed that imposed on Barrett, who had been flogged for coining in Rio de Janeiro. Before the day was out, four more miscreants had received the death sentence for theft, and orders went out for the marine battalion and the entire convict community to assemble to witness the hangings.

With the rest Jenny took her place on one side of a hollow square, with the marines under arms facing them.

The gallows was a tall tree, beside which stood a sergeant of marines and two drummers who had been ordered to act as executioners, all three looking pale and apprehensive at the prospect of the task before them. Thomas Barrett—little more than a youth, despite the record he bore as a hardened criminal— was led to the foot of the tree, under guard, his arms bound, and a halter about his neck.

The chaplain, Reverend Richard Johnson, walked at his elbow, in surplice and cassock, reading from his prayer book, and a murmur went up from the watching crowd, which was swiftly silenced when the condemned man turned to address them.

His manner was defiant and his voice steady. "Well, maties and"—he bowed in the direction of the women—"*ladies* . . . they're goin' ter turn me off, as you can see. An' all things considered, I s'pose I'm gettin' me just deserts, 'cause I'm a monster of iniquity accordin' ter them as judged me. All right, I'm guilty an' I ain't quarrelin' wiv' me sentence. It's a just one, an' I was given a fair trial. But take heed o' my fate, friends—let my death be a warnin' to yer. If yer gotta go on the pinch, just make sure you ain't caught." The chaplain muttered something, eyeing him with evident distress, and Barrett grinned at him. "If it'll please yer then, Mister Devil-Dodger . . . I commend me soul ter Almighty Gawd an' may He have mercy on me." He turned to face his executioner, and whatever he said clearly upset the sergeant, from whose cheeks the last vestige of color drained.

The hanging was badly botched, and there were screams from the women and shouted abuse from the men as Barrett's struggling body twitched and twisted and the taut rope slowly strangled him. Governor Phillip, his face almost as white as the wretched sergeant's, ordered the other executions postponed until the following day.

Just before sunset the next day the convicts again assembled facing the gallows tree and the pipe-clayed marines. It was announced that the sentences on Daniel Gordon and John Williams would not be carried out, the governor having pardoned them. The two other condemned men, James Freeman and William Shearman, were led out, as Barrett had been, under escort, with the chaplain walking between them. Lieutenant Leach, Jenny saw, was in command of the escort. She had seen and heard little of him since coming ashore, greatly to her relief, and apart from a rumor that it had been he who had uncovered the plot to mutiny, hatched by the seamen and convicts in the *Alexander*, she knew nothing of his recent doings. Now, however, she glimpsed the expression on his face with something of a shock.

He was standing only a few yards from her, and she could see his face quite clearly enough to read in it an oddly gloating satisfaction, even pleasure, as if the ghastly spectacle he was about to witness were one to which he was looking forward with more than ordinary interest. The same sergeant who had proved so poor a hand as executioner the previous evening was, she realized, waiting once again to act in that capacity, and his misery—like Leach's pleasure—was written on his face.

James Freeman, a big, hulking fellow of indeterminate age, was standing beneath the ladder with the rope about his neck, when the newly appointed provost marshal, Midshipman Henry Brewer—a man of fifty, despite his lowly rank—marched up to him and appeared to put a question to him. Freeman's jaw dropped in ludicrous astonishment; he gulped, staring at the harsh-featured Brewer as if doubting what he had said, and the provost marshal repeated his question. This time the prisoner nodded in vigorous assent, and the marine sergeant, beads of perspiration on his brow, removed the noose and began to coil up the rope with shaking hands.

Midshipman Brewer took a speaking-trumpet from the pocket of his uniform coat and announced in stentorian tones that the condemned man, James Freeman, had been pardoned.

"This pardon is conditional on his performing the duty of common executioner for as long as he shall remain in this colony. By order of His Excellency the governor, the sentence on Daniel Gordon for the same crime is also commuted. He is to receive a free pardon, on account of his youth. William Shearman is sentenced to receive three hundred lashes with a cat-o'-nine-tails, to be inflicted forthwith, in lieu of hanging. John Williams is to suffer exile to the South Cape, at His Excellency the governor's command."

He lowered his speaking-trumpet and said, in his

normal voice to Leach, "See to it that your men do their duty, Mister Leach, if you please—there is a man to flog."

A subdued Leach snapped the order, and the sergeant and his two assistants triced the convict Shearman to their crossed pikes. The cat was brought, in its all-too-familiar red bag, and the two drummers, in turn, laid on one hundred fifty lashes. At that point, with the unhappy prisoner unconscious and his back reduced to a bleeding pulp, Surgeon White ordered the punishment to be halted.

"He can receive the remainder a week from today," the doctor told Leach. "Be so good as to have him taken to the custody of your guard."

The flogging over, the convicts were dismissed, and the marines marched off. Melia grasped Jenny's arm.

"It's always going to be the same, Jenny, isn't it?" she suggested disconsolately. "The punishments, the brutality . . . whatever we do, it's not going to change. However hard we slave over that garden of ours, it won't gain us our freedom, will it?"

"It will keep us from starvation," Jenny asserted stoutly. "And prevent us falling sick."

"If we can make anything grow," Melia demurred. "We've worked for days in the heat, scratching the ground with those miserable hoes, and hardly any of it is ready for planting—even if we had any seeds to plant."

"The seeds are coming," Jenny countered. "I've applied for them; I've asked for sufficient for half an acre. And," she added, "Captain Tench has told me that I can take the manure from his stock pen and—"

"Manure?" Melia looked at her incredulously. "Do you mean we're to grub it out ourselves? Oh, Jenny, have mercy—I can't face doing that, even for you!"

Jenny smiled. "All right," she said. "You can empty and reset the fish traps. But I'm going to collect that manure if I have to do it alone. Land can't produce crops if it isn't fertilized, and our land is going to produce wheat and vegetables. I promise you it is, even if it kills me!"

The manure was collected and spread during the next two days, and on the third day two male convicts delivered the promised seed. Jenny opened the first sack and stared at it in dismay, reminded painfully of a morning, long ago, when her father had found the seed for his wheat field scattered in the damp mud by Lord Braxton's men. As it had been then, the seed was swollen, and ants, so prevalent in the soil of the cove, were crawling all over it in the sack, feeding on the precious wheat germ. It would be useless to plant it.

"Please take this back to the store," she begged the men. "It's spoiled, it won't vegetate. I'll have to ask them to exchange it."

The men shook their heads and made to retreat. "Take it back yourself, wench," the elder of the two growled. "But you'll get nowt else—if this is spoiled, it's all spoiled. They reckon it got overheated on the voyage and then soaked in seawater—and them pesky ants have done the rest."

Was all their work to be for nothing? Jenny wondered as the men shambled off. She looked at the freshly tilled half acre of dark, sandy soil, and her resolution hardened. With the help of Polly and some of the others, she took the sacks of seeds back to the guarded store shed and, after much heated argument, obtained in their stead two sacks of maize and some wilted fig and orange saplings, which had barely survived their journey from the Cape.

The women planted these as the sun was setting, and Jenny, remembering the wheat her father and mother had sown with so much labor on the barren moorland at Long Wrekin, prayed silently as she worked.

"Oh, God, don't let them die! Please, God, let them bear fruit."

That night two of her little band of helpers deserted her to return to the main encampment, and a third, Ann French, who had been a tireless worker, escaped with her convict lover to seek asylum with Lapérouse's ships in Botany Bay.

CHAPTER XV

During the next six months Governor Phillip found himself virtually in isolation, his authority and his administrative ability constantly challenged not only by the convicts and the local aborigines but also, to his bitter chagrin, by a number of his own Marine Corps officers.

Nevertheless, it was a time marked by encouraging progress in building and some fruitful exploratory expeditions, undertaken by the loyal Captain Hunter with the crew of the *Sirius*, several of which he joined as relief from the burdens of office. The flagship's master, James Keltie, and her first lieutenant, William Bradley, assisted Hunter to survey and chart the harbor. Names were given and recorded so that each cove, inlet, and stream, as well as each small islet, became recognizable under such descriptive titles as Rushcutters Bay, Farm Cove, North Head and South Head, and Garden Island. The bare, rocky islet used for the punishment of the more recalcitrant of the convicts was named, by them, Pinchgut and—in ever more frequent occupation—it lived up to its name.

On shore in Sydney Cove itself the few trained artisans—including those borrowed from the ships, whose departure was imminent—were set to work on the erection of necessary public buildings. Saw pits were dug, a bakery set up, kilns prepared for the making of bricks, and blocks of freestone rock hacked out by convict working parties for use in the construction of the larger buildings.

Of necessity Phillip accorded first priority where labor and materials were concerned to the provision of a permanent hospital. His visit to the makeshift edifice set up soon after landing—made at Dr. White's urgent request—had shocked him profoundly. John White, excellent physician that he was, had done all in his power to make the place habitable, but the sheer number of patients requiring treatment had been overwhelming . . . Phillip sighed, remembering.

It had been raining when he had made his inspection, and he had seen for himself that the cabbage-palm thatch did not keep out the wet.

"We've procured some dockyard canvas, sir," the surgeon general told him, "and when this downpour slackens—if it ever does—I'll have it rigged over the thatch. But, as you can imagine, sir, lying here without blankets to cover them and with the rain coming in, patients who shouldn't die are dying. The convicts, and the women in particular, have very little resistance to disease—and I've very few medicines to give them, alas. They tend to abandon hope, sir."

Remembering the thin, scantily clad women in the larger of the two wards, the governor shivered. Their pale, resigned faces had haunted him for days after that first visit, for they bore no resemblance to the clamorous, foul-mouthed strumpets who had so disgusted him on board the transports and who continued to do so in the women's camp. In the wretched shelter of wattle and daub that was all the settlement had been able to provide for them, they had become objects of pity and they troubled his conscience, for he could not escape the conviction that he had failed them. His plan for the future called for a building eighty-four feet by twenty-four, with brick floors and a dispensary, but the bricks had yet to be made, shingles for the roof cut and shaped, and the men assigned to the task worked with disheartening slowness . . . while the number of sick, even among the marines, increased at an alarming rate.

Indeed, the governor reflected with a seaman's instinctive mistrust of the land, they had lost fewer of their people from disease during the voyage from Europe than, it seemed, they were losing now, with the colony only a few months old. Cases of scurvy were the most prevalent, and he urged that more effort be put into the growing of crops and, in particular, to clearing and sowing more land for the government garden, which was intended for communal use.

Most of the officers had their own garden plots and stock pens, and he endeavored vainly to encourage the convicts to work smaller plots for themselves, but they were indolent and apathetic, preferring—in the time when they were free from their compulsory public labor—to search for edible plants in the surrounding bush.

To one of these, a small purple-flowered vine of the sarsaparilla family, many became addicted, brewing from it a concoction they called sweet tea.

Food—or the lack of it—presented the most pressing problem. Most of the fish caught went to the hospital as, too, did any game shot; the rest, convict and military alike, had to make do with salt tack. The imported livestock earmarked for breeding died from the ravages of wild dogs, in storms, or from starvation; the crops did not flourish, there was little wild game, and the hostility of the aborigines was a constant menace. In accordance with his instructions Phillip had done all in his power to establish friendly relations with the dusky-skinned Indians, but the attitude of both marines and convicts to them rendered his efforts futile. The marines fired on them with little provocation, the convicts tricked them of their spears and stole their canoes, and the aborigines retaliated by murdering any white man who ventured alone into the trackless wastes where they lived.

The French, still conducting their scientific survey in Botany Bay, found their native neighbors so troublesome that, on more than one occasion, they fired the small cannon they had landed in order to protect themselves, and this inevitably added to the Indians' desire for vengeance on all white intruders.

The British and French officers, on the other hand, had established the most friendly of contacts, and Lapérouse had displayed so keen and sympathetic an interest in the trials of the new colony that it was with a sense of loss that Phillip saw them depart at the end of March.

There were other departures, too, as the transports prepared to sail for China, the *Scarborough*, the *Charlotte*, and the *Lady Penrhyn* being the first to go. A number of petitions from their seamen wishing to marry convict women and settle in the colony had, perforce, to be refused, since Phillip was bound by the ship owners' contract with the home government, which required him not to deplete their crews.

"These are men I would give much to keep," the governor confessed when Captain Collins brought the petitions to him. "And yet, alas, I must let them go. They are all skilled men and have been most useful in directing the convicts' work—which the commandant refuses to permit his marines to do. It scarcely seems sensible, does it, when I would happily have traded ten convicts—or even ten marines—for each of them? Half our carpenters were supplied by those ships, and we have sore need of carpenters, heaven knows!"

The return of the *Supply* from Norfolk Island lifted his flagging spirits a little. Besides good news of the settlement started there by Lieutenant King, her commander, Henry Ball, brought fifteen giant turtles caught on an island on his return route, to which—in honor of the first sea lord—he had given the name of Lord Howe Island. The turtles made a much appreciated change from the year-old salt beef and pork, of which everyone was by this time heartily sick. Phillip asked him about Norfolk Island.

"The island has an area of about thirteen square miles, sir," Ball reported. "It's high and thickly wooded—a veritable garden, overrun with the noblest pines, and the soil is a rich black loam. I dare to swear that crops will grow well in it. There's no grass but the animals we landed are doing well on the leaves of trees and shrubs. Fish are plentiful, and there are many varieties of birds—so tame, sir, that you can almost pluck them from the air. We had some difficulty making our first landing—the coast is rocky and dangerous and there's a heavy surf, even in calm weather. But Mister King crossed the island while we were putting our people and stores ashore, and he found a good landing place on the sou'west side, sir —a bay, protected by a reef, with an easy opening and calm water inside the reef. We hoisted our colors there on the sixth of March and named the bay Sydney, after this settlement, sir."

Phillip questioned him exhaustively and, when he had finished, offered warm congratulations on all that had been achieved. "I shall send you back with more people as soon as you are ready to sail, Captain Ball," he said and added, more to himself than to the *Supply*'s commander, "Unless we can harvest a crop here, we may all be forced to remove to Norfolk Island to save us from starvation. And somehow, despite their indolence, I must persuade the people I have here to exert themselves so that at least they have somewhere to shelter when the cold weather comes. The ships are leaving—they must now depend on their own efforts if they are to survive!"

Following the departure of the transports, building work continued, albeit more slowly. A site was chosen for Government House; the keel of a launch laid down; and construction of a landing wharf, a bridge over the creek, and a water-storage tank begun, with bricks now in plentiful supply. Had it not been for an unexpected delay in completing the marines' barracks in time for the onset of winter, the governor would have been satisfied. But the delay—which meant that the marines must remain under canvas throughout the cold weather—had been caused by their own Commandant Ross, who had set them to building a stone house for his personal use.

"I would not mind so much, John," Phillip said, unable to conceal his exasperation, when Hunter accepted an invitation to dine with him, "but the infernal fellow insisted that his men must receive extra pay if they were to build their own barracks, as well as convict working parties to assist them with the labor. I agreed because I really had no choice—their tents are ill-suited to withstand the cold and I don't want them falling sick. But now, because the damned barracks are still unroofed, due entirely to lack of effort on the part of his men, all Ross can suggest is that their tents should be reinforced with thatch to keep out the wet. Work that, if you please, he says can be done by convicts!" He waved an impatient hand at the walls of his own marquee, already showing patches of damp. "I could tell him that most of the canvas we brought with us is rotting and that thatch won't keep out the wet!"

Hunter stared at him in stunned astonishment. "Frankly, sir," he admitted, "I don't know how you've kept your temper with Major Ross for as long as you have—*I* couldn't have shown a fraction of your restraint. The man's pompous and devoid of charm and about as difficult a customer as I've ever come across. Besides, he's disloyal—he's done nothing but complain and criticize since we landed. Can't you find an excuse to send him home?"

"It may come to that," the governor returned grimly, "because my patience is wearing thin—dangerously thin! He doesn't know of your dormant commission, of course, so I suppose he imagines he'll succeed to the governorship if I'm incapacitated. Certainly he misses no opportunity to assert his authority, even at the expense of mine."

He continued to mull over the problem of Major

Ross's behavior long after Hunter left him to return to his ship, unhappily aware that there would have to be a confrontation between himself and the marine commandant before long.

Although he had accepted appointment as judge of the Admiralty Court and, like the chaplain, was a justice of the peace, Ross no longer deigned to sit as a member of the criminal court and—following a difference of opinion with the young judge advocate, David Collins—he had begun to raise objections to any of his officers doing so.

The marine officers were, on the whole, anxious to assist in any way they could, and they continued to attend the courts, despite strong hints from their commanding officer that, in his view, this was no part of their duty. Several of them took part in the exploratory expeditions—Captain Tench frequently and enthusiastically as leader—but, Phillip knew, even this did not meet with Ross's approval. That matters would soon come to a head, he did not doubt.

It came the following morning, heralded by a breathless Captain Collins, who burst into the living quarters of his marquee while he was still at breakfast.

"The commandant's on his way, sir," Collins announced. "With an ultimatum, I understand."

The governor pushed his plate away and eyed him gravely. "Perhaps," he invited, "you had better give me a full and detailed explanation."

"That was why I came at this unseemly hour, sir," Collins told him. "Er—I'll be as brief as I can. It goes back to the occasion in February, sir, when two men from the transports—the *Lady Penrhyn*'s carpenter and a lad from the *Prince of Wales*—were apprehended in the women's camp after tap-too by the guard. If you recall, sir, Major Ross ordered their summary punishment—they were driven from the camp, preceded by a drummer and a fifer playing the Rogues' March, and with the women reviling them. It caused some heartburning with the ships' masters, sir."

"I recall *that* all too clearly, David," the governor said ruefully, "since I had to deal with their complaints. They both claimed indignantly and, I fear, rightly that a number of marines, discovered in similar circumstances to their seamen, had gone unpunished on instructions from the commandant."

"Quite, sir," Collins confirmed. He took a sheaf of papers from a file he was carrying and laid it on the table in front of the governor. "This is a transcript of the trial of privates Hunt and Dempsey of the corps . . . you reviewed it the day before yesterday, sir, and you concurred with the court's findings and sentences."

Phillip glanced at the papers. The two marines, he remembered, had been engaged in a brawl, which had been witnessed by a score of male convicts, and the guard commander, Lieutenant Nellow, had placed them under arrest. There had been no question of their guilt; both men had been drunk, they had deserted their posts, and their quarrel had been public. At the court-martial, presided over by Captain Tench, they had been found guilty and sentenced each to two hundred lashes.

"Surely Major Ross cannot object to the court's findings? I'm aware that poor Nellow received a reprimand for arresting the men but—"

"He *does* object, sir," Collins said with emphasis. "He demanded that the findings be reversed. Watkin Tench and the other members of the court refused his demand, and . . . he's put them all under arrest, sir, and Nellow as well."

The marine commandant stormed in, his second-in-command, Captain Campbell, and the corps' adjutant, Lieutenant Long, at his heels. Ross was beside himself with fury, his narrow, bony face contorted, and his pale eyes ablaze. He came to the point without preamble, his manner barely within the bounds of civility as he poured out his grievances. There was a lengthy list of them, in which the chief stated it to be his own right exclusively to command, discipline, and punish the officers and men of the corps.

"I give you notice, Captain Phillip," he finished in a shaking voice, "that from this day forward, no officers under my command shall assist the civil government of this settlement by acting as justices of the peace."

Was the man going out of his mind? Phillip wondered wearily—had the long voyage and the strain that all of them were under in this cruelly inhospitable land finally proved too much for him?

That without the services of Ross's officers the criminal court could no longer function was self-evident. Phillip could not replace them with his own naval officers, for the *Supply* must sail again for Norfolk Island and the *Sirius* complete her survey . . . yet, without any legal means of trying and punishing transgressors, a colony of convicts would swiftly lapse into anarchy. He turned to glance at David Collins, fearing that his loyalties must be divided and expecting no help from him, and was pleasantly surprised when the judge advocate, politely yet very firmly, started to point out the probable consequences of his action to the angry commandant.

Ross, however, would have none of it. "I am in

command of the Marine Corps, damme!" he retorted. "And I will decide what duties the officers under my command are to perform. Do your duty, sir," Major Ross bade him sharply. "I have placed seven officers under arrest for their refusal to obey my orders. Convene a court-martial and try them on charges of insubordination and—and conspiracy and anything else you damned well please!"

The governor opened his mouth to speak, but Collins flashed him a warning glance. "I regret, Major, that I cannot do as you ask. A general court-martial on any officer cannot be convened without the prior knowledge and sanction of their lordships of the Board of Admiralty."

Ross's angular face became suffused with indignant color, and fearing that he would be unable to control himself and might, in his rage, give vent to an insult which, before witnesses, he could not condone, Governor Phillip hastily intervened.

"I will look into the matter, Major Ross," he promised, his tone carefully expressionless. "And see what has to be done. My concern, as governor, must be for the well-being of this settlement and you will realize, I am sure, that our judiciary having been established by Act of Parliament, the civil and criminal courts must continue to function. Justices appointed to them cannot be forcibly or unofficially prevented from administrating them, to the best of my knowledge. . . ." His questioning glance brought instant confirmation from Collins.

Taking a paper from his file, the young judge advocate read out the words of the act.

"As governor, Your Excellency has the power to appoint, remove, or—er—reinstate justices of the peace. And as captain general, sir, your powers are—"

Phillip silenced him with a raised hand. "Thank you, Captain Collins, I am aware of my powers as captain general. In the circumstances, therefore, I must ask you, Major Ross, whether you are willing, in the best interests of all concerned, to withdraw the charges you have made against Captain Tench and the members of his court who—"

"I am not, sir," Ross stated, his mouth a tight, hard line.

"Then I am compelled to overrule you, Major Ross," he said with icy dignity and, turning to the adjutant, who was looking distinctly unhappy, added in a tone that brooked no argument, "Kindly see that the arrested officers are released forthwith, Mister Long. The court's finding will stand, and they are to return to duty."

"Very good, Your Excellency," Long acknowledged and scurried off thankfully.

Ross said nothing. He gave David Collins a withering look and turned on his heel, thrusting Campbell before him, to leave the governor's marquee in ominous silence.

Phillip's greatest anxiety at this time was, however, the rapid inroads being made into the colony's food stores and the failure of the government garden to produce a crop to offset the shortage of flour. The livestock brought from the Cape—with the exception of the pigs and poultry—died like flies, and breeding results were disappointing. Of the government flock of seventy ewes, only one now remained alive and healthy, and the cattle had broken loose and vanished into the bush. As the weather became colder even the supply of fish diminished for no apparent reason.

A few of the officers' and some of the convicts' garden plots flourished, notably the one diligently worked by a dozen of the younger women, which the governor observed with approval, but, he was bitterly aware, it was no use deluding himself. He had close on a thousand mouths to feed, and unless more provisions were sent from England or he could procure flour and livestock from Batavia or the Cape to make up their losses, the colony would soon be facing the very real threat of starvation. He needed the *Sirius* and needed her desperately to explore the coast and search for rivers and grazing land, but if the home government failed him, as he grimly accepted that it probably would, he would be compelled to send Hunter to purchase supplies before the end of the year.

In the hope of avoiding this, he sent appeals to Sydney and Nepean by every ship which left the harbor, and aware that a year must elapse before he could expect any reply, he cut the ration of meat and flour. Scrupulously fair, as always, having made this decision, he added his private stock—brought out at his own expense—to the common store and himself drew no more than a single man's share of the dwindling supplies. He transferred Dodd and the best of his convict husbandmen to an area sixteen miles from the head of the cove, where the soil appeared better, naming it Rose Hill after Sir George Rose, the treasury official to whom he owed his appointment as governor. The last of the seed grain was planted there, and when the hard-working Dodd reported that it had germinated, every male convict with agricultural experience or inclination was sent to work the new land, with a strong body of marines, under Captain Meredith, to guard them. The government garden in Sydney Cove was given over to the cultivation of vegetables, to which it proved better suited.

But Phillip was still anxious, and his letters to Lord Sydney and Sir Evan Nepean reflected his anxiety. After explaining his plan to send the *Sirius* to the Cape if provisions from England failed to reach the colony by the end of the year, he wrote:

> The crops for two years to come cannot be depended on for more than will be necessary for seed and what the *Sirius* may procure can only be to breed from. . . .

> All the provisions we have to depend on until supplies arrive from England are in two wooden buildings, which are thatched. I am sensible of the risk but have no remedy. This country at present does not furnish the smallest resource except in fish, which has lately been so scarce that the natives find great difficulty in supporting themselves.

To Lord Sydney he wrote:

> Your lordship will, I presume, see the necessity of a regular supply of provisions for four or five years, and of clothing, shoes, and frocks in the greatest proportion. The necessary instruments for husbandry and for clearing the ground brought out with us will, with difficulty, be made to serve the time required for sending out a fresh supply. . . .

* * *

The last paragraph was an oft-repeated plea:

> In our present situation, I hope few convicts will be sent out for one year at least, except carpenters, masons and bricklayers, or farmers who can support themselves and assist in supporting others. Numbers of those now here are a burden and incapable of any hard labor, and unfortunately we have not proper people to superintend the labor even of those who are capable of being made useful. . . .

At the time of writing, the governor had before him a report from Dr. White that listed thirty-six marines and sixty-six convicts in hospital, with a further fifty-two unfit for work due to old age and chronic illness, and over fifty dead. But the hospital building was now complete; he found White pleased on this account, but anxious because there were still no blankets for his patients and his medical supplies were almost exhausted.

"We are still losing more than we should, sir," the surgeon general told him wryly. "And it's not only the aged and infirm who are dying—this week, sir, two healthy young men died from dysentery, one of them a marine. And we lost a child from pneumonia. I had no medicines to give them, except Cape wine . . . and that's in short supply."

He would have to send the *Sirius* back to the Cape before the year's end, Phillip knew. Men could not give of their best on the present depleted ration—of which Major Ross, on behalf of his marines, was already complaining—and the fear of starvation drove even the more honest of the convicts to steal. Undeterred by the threat of punishment, they plundered gardens, stole the precious livestock, and robbed the storehouses with almost monotonous regularity; many, who consumed their whole week's ration in two or three days, stole in order to survive—and few were caught. Rats ate the grain and contaminated other stores, and the predator ants—with which Sydney Cove abounded—destroyed what was left.

Reluctantly Phillip gave the order for the *Sirius* to be recaulked, in preparation for her long voyage.

"If the worse should come to the worst before you return here, John," he told Captain Hunter, "we shall have to remove the entire settlement to Norfolk Island, where there seems some hope of growing enough crops for survival, according to Henry Ball." He shook his head helplessly. "Damme, if only I could make these people understand that they must *work* for their subsistence and that stealing from our stores can only preserve one life at the sacrifice of another!"

"You cannot change their nature, Governor," Hunter reminded him. "The reason they are here is because they are rogues and vagabonds, most of them—and the women even worse. They lived by stealing at home—they know nothing else, with a few exceptions. Most of the exceptions are tradesmen or country folk, with a skill of some kind, are they not?"

The governor inclined his head. "Yes, I fear you're right. Punishment is no answer but . . . perhaps reward for honest endeavor might provide one. What do you think? I've tried to hold out inducements to them to marry, but only fourteen couples have taken advantage of my suggestion. And they continue to plague and provoke the wretched natives with whom, as God is my witness, John, I've tried to remain on terms of mutual friendship and cooperation. We've lost a dozen or more convicts at their hands—the fools wander off into the woods, and the Indians revenge themselves for past crimes committed against them by indulging in murder of the most horrible variety. But the convicts won't learn." He sighed, and Hunter, anxiously studying his lined and care-worn face, thought how much he had aged in the past six months and did not envy him his hopeless task.

"You have done all that any man could in this situation, sir," he said with sincerity.

Phillip made an effort at cheerfulness. "I have not tried reward. His Majesty's birthday on the fourth of June might be a fitting occasion. We'll light bonfires, and the band shall play, and dammit—we'll give a spirit issue to every member of the community, free and convict alike! They shall drink to His Majesty's health, and I'll send MacEntire and his fellows out to shoot kangaroos and emus, so that we may feast ourselves for once." He smiled broadly, warming to his subject. "And an amnesty shall be given to all those sentenced to banishment for minor crimes, for in truth I've nowhere to banish them to, save the islets in the harbor. Divine service in the open, with special prayers for the safety and well-being of the settlement . . . we'll make it a day to remember. I think it might lift morale, don't you?"

"An excellent idea," Hunter approved. "Why not lay the foundation stone of government house, while you're about it?"

"The foundation stone of a building that won't have the smallest chance of being completed for a year or more, unless Sir Evan Nepean can be prevailed upon to scour the English jails for artisans?" Phillip demurred. "Would that not be premature?"

"It might inspire hope."

"Yes, it might—if only in those who don't know or

recognize the precariousness of our situation." The governor's smile faded. "I want the hospital dispensary completed first and those infernal barracks for the marines. But . . . on the question of reward, John. As you know, I've granted some remissions for good behavior, but until these documents pertaining to the convicts' sentences are sent out to me, I've no idea of individual criminal records, or even of the duration of their sentences. That is apart from what they tell me themselves—and some of them, I'm fully aware, have lied to me."

"But not all of them, surely, Governor?" Hunter questioned. "They must know you will find out the truth when the documents do reach you."

"Oh, certainly," the governor agreed. "And I've made it abundantly clear that any who do lie will be punished with the utmost severity. Nevertheless, I dare not overdo the remissions—it would be seen as weakness. No"—he frowned thoughtfully—"I was thinking of some kind of public expression of approbation on His Majesty's birthday, for those whose work for the common good are deserving of recognition. I want to hold them up as an example to the idle and the work-shy."

"Do you have any particular people in mind?"

Phillip nodded. "Yes—Bloodworthy for his work at the brick kilns, MacEntire for his hunting . . . mind you, hunting's MacEntire's trade, he was sentenced for poaching. And there are the women who've worked so hard and so successfully on their plot east of the cove. There are only about a dozen of them but their leader—who incidentally is a girl of about sixteen—was brought up on a farm. She has put the rest of us to shame—even the good Dodd admits it. She's grown a small crop of maize and has vegetables ready to harvest, and she's established some of the fruit trees we brought from the Cape. Dodd lost his."

Hunter smiled. "She must be a young woman of strong character. What's the name of your paragon, sir?"

"Damme, I can't recall her name—but David Collins or Brewer will know it." Phillip crossed to the flap of canvas that separated his office in the marquee from that of the judge advocate and, lifting this, called out his inquiry. Both Collins and Brewer were in the office, and they looked at one another in some astonishment.

"Then you've heard, sir?" Collins suggested. He rose, a sheaf of papers in his hand, and, motioning Brewer to accompany him, entered the governor's sanctum.

"Heard what?" Governor Phillip demanded.

"Why, about the girl Jenny Taggart, sir. The one you were asking about."

"Certainly I have, my dear fellow. And as I was telling Captain Hunter, I feel that her achievement in that garden plot she's been working deserves recognition." He enlarged on his idea for some form of public recognition to be accorded during the king's birthday celebrations and broke off suddenly, as memory returned. "Damme, John," he said to Hunter. "That's the girl my servant Hawley wanted to marry . . . Jenny Taggart. I remember her name now. There had been some trouble before we made Rio, between Lieutenant Leach and Hawley, which involved the girl. I sent Hawley home with the invalids, to keep him out of further trouble—which seems to have been an error on my part, as matters have turned out. Hawley was a damned good man and I

could have done with him here—he was brought up
on a farm."

"Forgive me, sir," Collins put in unhappily. "I'm
afraid the girl's in trouble—serious trouble, sir. Provost Marshal Brewer has the full report, sir."

Brewer nodded. "The Taggart girl attacked one of
the marines, sir—Private Bulmore—with a hoe, the
night before last. She injured him quite severely, sir.
One of the other women, Hannah Jones, called the
guard, and Taggart was put under arrest. She claimed
that Private Bulmore and two others of the corps
were stealing from her garden plot and that they were
armed, sir . . . but they all denied that. They denied
it on oath, sir, before the military court and—"

"You mean the girl's been tried?" Phillip interrupted sharply. "And by a military court?"

"Yes, sir," Collins answered. He consulted some
papers he had brought with him. "Major Ross convened a court-martial on Private Bulmore, and he
presided, with Captain Campbell and Captain Meredith, lieutenants Long and Furzer and second-lieu-
tenants Faddy and Clarke as members, sir. Second
Lieutenant Leach was commander of the guard on the
night in question, and he gave evidence that only
the men composing the guard had muskets."

"Leach?" Governor Phillip echoed, frowning.

"Yes, sir." Collins again consulted his papers. "The
court found Private Jake Bulmore not guilty and discharged him to hospital. They then examined the girl
Taggart, in the capacity of civil justices and found
her guilty on two charges. These were of causing
grievous bodily harm to Private Bulmore by making
an unprovoked assault on him, and—er—perjury, sir."
He offered Phillip the papers. "The evidence is given
in detail here, sir, and the trial took place yesterday

forenoon. Mister Brewer has just delivered the trial transcript to me. I wasn't present and I'd just started to read the transcript when you called out to me. But—" He hesitated. "The trial was a trifle irregular and the sentence caused me some concern, so I was about to bring the matter to your notice."

The governor eyed him in frowning question, and the judge advocate exchanged another glance with Midshipman Brewer before answering it. "The girl was sentenced to a week on Pinchgut, sir," he said at last. "And Mister Brewer—that is. . . ."

"I took her there yesterday afternoon, sir," Brewer confirmed. "In view of the fact that she's a female, sir, I thought it my duty to inform Captain Collins and request him to bring it to your attention if he felt, as I did, sir, that you should be informed. And some of the women—Taggart's fellow workers in the garden— are begging you to give them a hearing, sir."

The gray-haired Brewer was not easily shocked, Phillip thought, but there could be no doubt that he was considerably shocked now . . . as well he might be.

"I'll see the women—including Taggart—here this evening," the governor said. His voice was quiet but it had a distinct edge to it as he added, "And the marines concerned are to be brought to me at once. And, if you please, Mister Brewer, send a boat out to Pinchgut immediately to release the girl Taggart."

"Aye, aye, sir," Brewer acknowledged with alacrity. "I'll attend to it myself."

"Well," the governor went on in his normal, calm manner, "we had better try to finalize our plans for celebrating His Majesty's birthday, had we not? I wonder what effect it might have upon the Indians, if we were to invite a few of them to join the celebrations?"

"That, sir," Hunter exclaimed, with a guffaw of laughter, "is an idea worthy of the commandant of the Marine Corps! You cannot make a silk purse out of a sow's ear, need I remind you?"

"Or an honest, hard-working citizen out of a convicted felon," Phillip said. "You need not remind me, John . . . it's a truth that is being continually hammered into my poor brain. And to think that, only a few minutes ago, I was beginning to doubt the wisdom of my decision to send my good servant Hawley home for his own protection! Ah, well, one lives and learns, does one not?"

After Hunter had taken his leave, the governor found himself thinking again of Corporal Hawley. In the interests of discipline, of course, he had had no choice but to reduce the unfortunate man to the ranks and send him back to England. But to what fate had he condemned Hawley with his attempt to play God?

Wearily he let his head fall into his outstretched hands and prayed silently.

In the Marine Corps barracks at Chatham, the object of the governor's thoughts, Private Andrew Hawley, was on guard duty. As he paced stiffly up and down in front of his sentry box his thoughts were angry and rebellious. Shore duty was what he most hated; discipline in the corps was strict and he longed for the active life of service in a ship at sea. It was a hard life, but it had its compensations—time passed swiftly and there was little leisure or time for regrets and recriminations.

But how different it might all have been if Captain Phillip had permitted him to continue the voyage to

Botany Bay. He could have married Jenny . . . indeed, he gritted his teeth, he *would* have married Jenny, whatever obstacles had been put in his way. Once married, they could have applied for a grant of land and settled down to the farming to which they had both been bred.

He had considered numerous plans that might enable him to go out to New South Wales, even now. He could desert, commit some crime that would cause him to be sentenced to deportation, or sign on as a seaman with one of the transports bound for the colony but . . . he halted in his measured pacing. Even the thought of deserting went against the grain—he was proud of the corps and, with a single exception, of his record. Besides, with war clouds looming, how could he run away? He had his duty, he had taken the oath of allegiance to King and Country. Even for little Jenny Taggart he would not break that oath. And would *she* wait for *him*?

A plague on it, he had no way of knowing. The Botany Bay Fleet had vanished from his ken, only official mail had been reported, and there was a dearth of information in the newspapers he had managed to obtain, all of which seemed solely concerned with the danger to peace posed by the revolution in France.

Andrew resumed his sentry-go, his booted feet stamping out his frustration.

CHAPTER XVI

Jenny crouched, shivering, on the narrow ledge of rock to which she had been shackled and gave herself up to despair. The settlement lay some four miles away, separated from her by the shark-infested waters of the harbor, so that—even if she had not been chained—she knew that escape from her desolate prison was impossible.

She had been numb with horror when Major Ross had pronounced sentence on her, aware of Pinchgut Island's terrible reputation. Men had gone mad there; none had ever forgotten the experience; and only one man, a strong swimmer, had attempted to gain the shore—an attempt that had resulted in his death, although no one knew whether at the hands of natives on the shore or by sharks before he reached it.

Her trial had been a parody. Only the marines'

evidence had been listened to, and they, of course, had backed each other up, swearing on oath that Bulmore had been unarmed. Certainly he had dropped his musket after she had hit him with her hoe, Jenny remembered, but not before he had threatened her with it when she and Hannah had caught him red-handed, plundering the garden of its hard-won harvest now coming at last to fruition.

But it had been Hannah's evidence, Hannah's utterly damning and distorted evidence, that had finally tipped the scales against her. Jenny bit back a sob. During the past six months, Hannah Jones had been—or had seemed to be—one of her staunchest supporters. A woman of the London streets, and now no longer young, Hannah had toiled harder than any of them and had become a skilled and knowledgeable gardener. She had foraged in the bush for edible plants and fruit bushes, had brought them back, planted, and nurtured them with a zeal not even Melia had equaled.

When Polly had drifted back to the main women's camp, saddened and angry because her seaman lover had been refused permission to wed her, Hannah had stayed. Even when their numbers had dwindled to fewer than a dozen, as others defected, Hannah had continued to work, and she had put a great deal of thought and effort into making their huts weather-proof and comfortable.

And yet . . . Hannah had gone screaming accusations to the guard when Bulmore fell and she had repeated her accusations in court. Had she, Jenny wondered bitterly, been biding her time, waiting until an opportunity should arise to avenge Auld Meg's death? Was anyone, even Hannah, capable of such treachery?

They had taken it in turns—ever since the garden had begun to produce enough to tempt the pilferers who abounded—to watch at nights, so as to preserve their precious three acres. The vegetables and the thin but healthy crop of Indian corn were destined, under the governor's rules, to be taken as a contribution to the common store, to be shared by all, and proud of their successful husbandry, the women had all agreed to keep a watch. And, because they were women and the majority of the thieves were men, they had also agreed that it would be prudent to arm themselves with hoes.

Rumor had it, indeed, that the marines were among the most persistent of the pilferers, and it was said that their commandant, far from punishing them for their predatory expeditions, had actually advised them to use their bayonets to defend themselves if they were molested.

Jenny looked down at her right arm. Melia had bound up the wound Bulmore's bayonet had made, but in spite of the fact that blood had soaked through the bandage, Major Ross had accused her sternly of lying when she had endeavored to draw his attention to the injury inflicted on her. And Lieutenant Leach had told the court that he had searched and found no musket and no bayonet anywhere in Bulmore's vicinity. He—Jenny shivered again in the chilly darkness—he had also suggested that the marine had come to the garden, not to steal but to—how had he put it? "To seek his accustomed pleasure with one of the whores there."

If only Sergeant Jenkins had been in command of the guard that night! Or Andrew . . . dear God, why had Andrew been sent back to England? To prevent him from marrying a convict, she could only suppose—just as Polly's handsome young sailor and Eliza's steady carpenter's mate had been sent back to the *Charlotte*, for all that they had both wanted to stay. Convict could marry convict but that was all, and Polly, hiding her heartbreak behind a defiant smile, now took any man who desired her and never came to the garden where once she had been happy.

Jenny shifted her position on the hard, unyielding rock, feeling the shackles chafe her ankles as she moved. Lights were springing up in the cove now, as bonfires were lit—outside the inflammable huts, by order of the governor—to cook the evening meal. She imagined Eliza stirring the blackened iron pot in which they made broth from bones, dried peas, and the outer leaves of the spinachlike plant that grew wild close to the shore, sometimes adding a hunk of salt meat from their ration to give it what Melia laughingly described as "body." And Melia herself, working their meager supply of flour into dough, which was cooked on a stone placed among the smoldering embers of the fire. Dipped into the broth, the bread improved its taste and kept hunger at bay for a few hours at least. Fish was a luxury now that winter had set in, but their crab and lobster traps still produced enough for a welcome change of diet, although half their catch went, by order, to the hospital.

But here, here on this lonely rock, there was nothing with which to assuage the pangs of hunger, save a small stone jar of water and a stale hunk of bread, contaminated by salt water during the row from Sydney Cove. That was the ration for twenty-four hours, Mr. Brewer had told her, and no prisoner sentenced to banishment on Pinchgut was permitted more. But in spite of his stern words and stiff, official attitude he had not treated her unkindly, Jenny recalled. Indeed, he had handed her out of the boat almost as if she were a lady, her chains looped over the arm of his shabby blue uniform coat, and had whispered, before parting from her, that he intended to report her case to the governor.

"I do not think he'll leave you here for long, lass. No woman has ever been sent out to Pinchgut before, and I trust you'll be the first . . . and the last. I wish I could leave you a blanket, but it's forbidden. Stay beneath the shelter of the rock if you can, and if it rains, shift over to the loo'ard side but be careful you don't get the chain fouled."

It was starting to rain now, Jenny realized, as a few icy drops struck her upturned face. Her dress, fashioned from some old seed sacks, was little protection, and careful not to catch the chain on the jagged rocks, she followed Mr. Brewer's advice and stumbled over to the lee side to crouch down once more under an overhanging boulder. Belatedly remembering that she had not brought her water and bread ration with her, she was compelled to retrace her difficult steps in search of them. By the time she had regained the shelter of the overhang, she was breathless and exhausted, her dress soaking, for the rain was coming down in torrents, and it was dark, with storm clouds blotting out the stars.

From where she now lay, she could see the northern shore and a few flickering native campfires springing up like glowworms among the trees. She had had little contact with the Indians, but the tales of their savagery had spread throughout the settlement and had deterred the majority of the convicts from any attempt to escape. True, Ann French, who had sought asylum with the ships of the Marquis de Lapérouse,

was believed to have been taken on board with her
lover—himself a Frenchman—but all the others who
had risked the journey through the bush to Botany
Bay had been refused. Many, making the return
journey to the encampment after dark, had never
reached it, and their bodies had been found, with
spear wounds or with their heads smashed by blows
from native clubs. The convict who had so carelessly
permitted the governor's cattle to escape, John Cor-
bett, had fled to avoid punishment, but he had returned in a state of mindless terror a week afterwards
to report that the Indians were cannibals who
roasted and ate their captives after subjecting them
to unspeakable torture.

Even those who claimed that China was a mere
one hundred fifty miles distant and that it could be
reached by heading inland toward the mountains became lost and, if the natives did not murder them,
returned starving and demoralized to the settlement,
to take whatever punishment was meted out to them.
The Indians, they said, were without exception hostile
and lacking in pity, and even a starving white man
need hope for no mercy from them. They—There was
a faint sound, which carried across the intervening
stretch of water, followed by the low murmur of
voices. Jenny froze into immobility, listening intently
and endeavoring to interpret the sounds.

There was a boat, coming steadily nearer to the
island, but its approach was stealthy. There was no
creak of rowlocks, no shouted word of command, as
there would have been from a naval boat, rowed by
seamen. This boat was gliding over the water, propelled by paddles which meant . . . her heart in her
mouth, she suppressed the temptation to scream. If it
was a native canoe, perhaps it would go past on what-

ever errand it was bent, without being aware of her presence, for surely the night was too dark and rain-obscured for them to see her. Unless, of course, they had watched Mr. Brewer's boat taking her out from the settlement long before darkness fell—unless they had watched him clamp on her shackles and were aware that she was chained and helpless, a woman alone. . . .

Shaking uncontrollably, Jenny hid her face in her hands and prayed that the Indians had not seen her, that they would go past, but when she opened her eyes again, she knew that her desperate prayer had gone unanswered. There was a shadow on the rain-whipped water, deeper than the faint shadows cast by the rock, and she glimpsed the canoe's outline, with three or four dark bodies seated in it, plying their paddles vigorously. They were still some distance off, but then, as suddenly as it had begun, the rain ceased, the clouds parted, and a watery moon reappeared to shed a soft, silvery glow over the still choppy water. A few minutes later the bow of the canoe grounded against the flat slab of rock that Mr. Brewer's boat had used as a landing stage, and two of its occupants stepped lightly ashore.

They padded toward her, and Jenny stared at them, speechless with terror. It was still too dark to see their faces clearly, but both carried spears and throwing sticks, and one appeared to be white-bearded and old, the other somewhat younger. They came to a halt five or six yards away and, making no attempt to touch or otherwise molest her, called out a soft but unintelligible greeting. Her mouth dry, Jenny forced her trembling lips into the semblance of a reply, and thus encouraged, the younger of the two came cautiously nearer and put out a hand to touch her chains. Ascertaining that it was these that held her imprisoned, he demonstrated the fact to his companion, and both shook their heads in bewilderment.

The younger of the two took up the slack of the chain and, exerting all his considerable strength, tried vainly to pull it from the iron ring by which it was attached to the rock. His right thumb, Jenny noticed, was without its top joint, and both his face and that of his bearded companion were heavily pockmarked. Still they offered her no violence; their voices were soft and friendly when they addressed her, and she began, at last, to lose her fear of them. Several times they gestured to their canoe as if inviting her to free herself and accompany them, but when she held up her manacled hands, they appeared to understand that, even had she wanted to, she could not accept their invitation. Despite this they did not go away. Instead, squatting on their haunches in front of her, the spears laid aside, they made strenuous efforts to communicate with her, to which she tried unsuccessfully to respond. Finally she pointed to herself and repeated her name, and after a while the younger one appeared to understand, for he said, very slowly, "Jen-nee . . . Jen-nee."

She nodded and he smiled at her warmly then, tapping his own dusky chest, announced triumphantly, "Ban-ee-lon!"

The older man, also smiling, followed his example, giving his name, as nearly as Jenny could make out as "Col-bee."

Then, with unexpected abruptness, they tired of their game. Both got to their feet and ran back to the canoe; Jenny heard the low hum of voices as they talked to the two who had remained there. Colbee stepped back into the canoe, and the youthful

Baneelon bent down to take something from it. A few moments later he padded back to her side and motioned to her to hold out her hand. She did so, and he placed some round, dark objects in her palm, indicating by lifting his own hand to his mouth that she should eat them.

Jenny tasted one of the objects uncertainly, but it was meat, and she ate it hungrily, finding it appetizing. Baneelon's teeth gleamed whitely as he smiled before again returning to the canoe. This time he laid three wild figs beside her and, his arm raised in farewell, took his leave of her.

The soft splash of skillfully wielded paddles faded gradually into the distance, and she was once more alone, but oddly heartened by their visit and their kindness. She ate the figs and, after a while, drifted into an uneasy doze.

When she awakened, it was daylight—a chill, gray daylight, with all about her shrouded in misty curtains of rain. She sat up, shivering, and, looking down dazedly at the chains on her wrists, found herself wondering whether it had all been a dream. . . .

Private Robert Sibley of the Marine Corps sat on the far side of the tent, making a pretense of cleaning his musket but, in fact, listening apprehensively for the return from guard duty of the four men with whom he shared his hot, airless quarters.

He had bunked with the other four on board the *Prince of Wales* transport on the voyage to Botany Bay. They were in the same company and they had slept and wakened in this tent together since the landing at Sydney Cove, so that, he supposed glumly, he could claim them as his closest friends. Yet now—now that he knew them for what they were—he wished wretchedly that he had never set eyes on any of them . . . least of all on Joe Hunt. Or, come to that, on the oafish, foul-mouthed madman Jake Bulmore, with his womanizing and his drinking, who had so nearly landed him in the hottest water he had ever been in.

Sibley drew a deep breath and expelled it slowly, his hands moving the oiled cloth up and down the already well-oiled barrel of his musket without conscious thought, all his senses concentrated on the sounds reaching him from outside.

He would hear them coming, of course, for they would, as usual, be drunk as owls—when Joe Hunt was assigned to guard the commissariat store on the government wharf, he used his key, and they all helped themselves to anything they fancied, from liquor to meat or rice or flour. That they would be found out sooner or later Sibley was convinced—hell, that rogue of a convict locksmith, who had made the key, wasn't to be trusted—he would squeal his pesky head off at the first sign of trouble. And there *would* be trouble when Zachariah Clark, the commissary's assistant, woke up to what was going on and made an inventory of his stores.

Joe would be in for it then and no mistake, for he was a marked man, after his crazy fight with Dempsey . . . he had been let off the two hundred lashes Captain Tench had awarded him for that little episode, but only because the commandant had intervened and refused to confirm the sentence. Besides . . . hearing the sound of approaching footsteps, Sibley tensed. But the footsteps passed by, and he let himself relax again, still working on his musket.

Could he, he asked himself, dare he request to be posted to the Rose Hill detachment or to Norfolk

Island without Joe Hunt suspecting what his reasons really were? Joe would give him a drubbing, if he ever found out, no doubt of that—the whole bunch of them would turn on him but . . . somehow he had to get away from them because, if he didn't, they would embroil him in another of their escapades. And next time he might not be so lucky as he had been when he and Joe and Jake Bulmore had raided the women's garden. He had been able to slip away—at Joe's behest, as it happened, not because he had run out on them. Joe had thrust the bloodstained bayonet into his hand and hissed, "Get rid of it—go on, the bleeding guard's coming!" and he had taken to his heels, thankfully, and done as he was told.

But, holy hell, he hadn't liked it. He hadn't fancied the idea of the raid—the women had slaved away at that garden of theirs for months—and he had felt sorry for the little slip of a lass who had stood up to Jake Bulmore's bayonet, defying him to lay a hand on her and giving as good as she got when he had lunged at her.

Sibley closed his eyes, trying vainly to shut out the scene from his memory. Jake, lying there, his head bleeding, cursing, and swearing fit to bust himself, and making out that he had been hurt far worse than, in fact, he had. And, partly because of that but mainly because they had all lied about what had taken place, the little lass had been sentenced to a week on bloody Pinchgut . . . a woman, on that bleak, unprotected rock! He shivered involuntarily. She would be there now—he had watched the boat take her out, he . . . a voice, stridently shouting obscenities, broke abruptly and unpleasantly into his thoughts. He heard a roar of laughter, unmistakably Joe Hunt's, and his fingers tightened instinctively on the butt of the musket and then relaxed again.

He ought to stand up to them—damn them to hell—they were a rotten bunch, a lot worse than some of the poor devils of convicts, if the truth were known. But . . . he passed his tongue over lips that had suddenly gone dry. It wasn't only that he was scared of them, he reflected miserably, he owed them a good deal, too. They had taken care of him when he had first joined the corps, shown him the ropes, stood up for him, and kept him supplied with food and liquor and 'baccy. He had taken these things, knowing where they came from—he hadn't ever refused them—and he had grabbed Jake Bulmore's bayonet and hidden it, when Joe had told him to, and at the Taggart girl's trial, he had kept his mouth shut, as Joe had also said he must. Which made him one of them, however little he wanted to be. . . .

They erupted into the tent, laughing and in high good humor, their faces flushed in the flickering light of the whale-oil lamp.

"The watch—the sodding convict watch!" Joe Hunt exclaimed. "Came right past us, they did, clasping their cudgels and marching in step, like they was soldiers . . . I wish you'd bin there, Rob, me old son. There was I, with me key in the storehouse padlock and the bloody door half open. I challenges them, bold as brass, and they gives me the old heave-ho and off they goes. Never saw a thing."

They were unloading their booty, Sibley saw, and his eyes widened in shocked surprise.

"Joe, you want to be careful with that convict watch," he warned. "They—"

"They won't try to touch us," Hunt retorted. "An' s'pose they was to, the major would soon sort it out.

A' insult to the corps, convicts makin' unfounded accusations against us clean livin', well-disciplined sojers . . . they wouldn't have a hope in hell. Jus' get theirselves bloody backs, more likely. Look what the major done when me an' Demp had that punchup! 'Shake hands, my lads,' he said and that were the end o' it." He grinned at Private Dempsey with maudlin affection and then picked up the small wooden keg of government rum they had brought with them, splashed a lavish tot into a beaker, and gave it to Sibley. "Com on, Rob boy—you've got a bit o' catchin' up to do afore we sets out on our little jaunt. Drink it down!"

Sibley took a quick gulp of the liquor, then another, his heart sinking. What fresh devilry were they planning, he wondered uneasily—a plague on them, why could they not toe the line for once, keep within bounds?

"Jaunt?" he echoed hollowly. "I don't want to go out now—it's late. I'm going to get my head down and—"

"Mealy-mouthed young toad!" Dempsey sneered. "I don't know why you wastes any time on 'im, Joe."

"Young Rob's all right," Hunt defended. He reached for the rum keg and held it poised over Sibley's beaker. "Go on," he invited. "There's plenty more where this come from. An' you're comin' with us, like allus, ain't you?"

Sibley drained his beaker and let Hunt refill it.

"Where are you going?" he asked nervously. The rum was rapidly going to his head, and his resolution was faltering, as it invariably did, when Joe Hunt put pressure on him. After all, he told himself, he owed Joe a lot.

Dempsey cackled with laughter. "We're goin' ter

finish off what we started, cock—even the score for ole Jakie. Think of 'im, poor codger, a-lying in the 'orspital wiv' 'is 'ead all bashed in by that crazy little strumpet! All 'e wanted was a quick kiss an' cuddle, an' she 'ad ter go for 'im wiv' an 'oe!'

Young Sibley swallowed hard. "You can't mean you're going back to the women's garden?" he said, aghast. Ignoring the laughing Dempsey, he appealed to Hunt. "Joe, you must be out of your mind even to think about it. The blooming watch'll be down on us like a ton of bricks if we go anywhere near those women. They—"

Hunt closed one eye in an elaborate wink. "They won't—it's all bin seen to. Keelan an' his bully boys'll be off on a nice li'l wild goose chase by the time we gets there."

"Yes, but"—despairingly Sibley took another swig from his beaker—"how do you know it's going to be all right?"

"'Cause the idea come from on high, matey," Hunt told him, grinning. "Not officially, mind—it were just an 'int, like. But a nod's as good as a wink, ain't it? Right, then—sup up now an' let's be on our way." He picked up Sibley's musket and threw it to him. "Fix bay'nets, boys—they're a right doughty mob, them women. But all we need to do is threaten 'em—no comin' to blows. You got that, Demp me son?"

Dempsey's rejoinder was obscene and had them all laughing, and they continued to laugh, like a pack of schoolboys bent on mischief, as they set off at a brisk pace, skirting the parade ground and the officers' tents. Two of them had hatchets tucked into their belts, and Ted Ricketts, Sibley saw, had brought the blackened spade they used for cooking, in addition to his musket.

The women's garden was bathed in silvery moonlight when they reached it, their huts silent and in darkness. Hunt put a finger to his lips, motioning them to give the huts a wide berth, and then belied his own caution by hiccoughing loudly.

"We ain't pinchin' nothin', boys," he told them. "So's they can't accuse us o' theft. But we'll make darned sure as there ain't nothin' left for anyone else to pinch, understand? Right, then—go to it!"

They did, Sibley with them, laughing and fooling with the rest. He felt light-headed and without any qualms of conscience as he hacked and slashed at the rows of growing crops, thrusting his bayonet into some trellised vines while, a few yards away, Ricketts dug up marble-sized potatoes with the spade he had brought and, giggling, kicked them and stamped on them with gleeful abandon.

The women heard the racket and came running out with shrill cries of alarm, but Hunt and Dempsey met them with fixed bayonets and mocking taunts, and they backed away, white-faced and frightened.

"Git back ter your beds!" Dempsey yelled at them. "We'll be 'appy ter join you when we've done what we're at!"

But they did not take his jeering advice; they stood huddled together weeping, and listening to their sobs, Sibley became once more aware of the twinges of conscience. He had not drunk as much as the others—he had not had time—and as the effect of the rum wore off he found himself wishing that he had not listened to Joe Hunt. He lowered his mud-stained musket—hell, why had he bothered to clean it?—and looked over at the little knot of women, his throat tight. They were watching months of back-breaking toil being destroyed, seeing their hopes wantonly shattered, but they were afraid to make a move to stop it, because one of their number—one who had had the guts to try—had been sentenced to a week on Pinchgut Island for her pains.

Pityingly he went to them and ushered them back to the huts. "There's nothing you can do," he told them. "Nothing. But I'll see the lads don't molest you. I'll stay on guard till they've finished."

No one spoke, but still sobbing, they obeyed him.

The following afternoon, heralded by the shouted orders of Midshipman Brewer and the sound of oars creaking in their rowlocks, a boat from the *Sirius* came to Pinchgut Island.

Henry Brewer stepped ashore. He said, with his accustomed gruffness, "By order of His Excellency the governor . . . you are to be released and pardoned, it being deemed that you have suffered sufficient punishment for—" Feeling the frozen chill of Jenny's thin arms as he unlocked the shackles, he broke off, his mouth tight, and started to chafe her hands. "Why, you poor child!" he exclaimed with a swift change of tone, and taking off his threadbare boat cloak, he wrapped it around her and carried her to the boat.

She sat beside him in the stern sheets, stiff with cold, and he put an arm about her shoulders.

"Was it a terrible ordeal?" he asked after a while, as the seamen settled to their oars.

Unable to stop shivering, Jenny inclined her head. She started to tell him about the visit from the natives, but seeing from his expression that he did not believe her, she ended flatly, "Perhaps it was a dream, Mister Brewer. I—I'm not sure, I . . . it seemed very real."

"It was a nightmare," Brewer said positively. "Understandable when you were alone and frightened."

He hesitated and then took a flask from his pocket and offered it to her. "Rum," he explained with a wry grin. "And I shouldn't be giving it to you but . . . it'll probably do you more good than the wild figs of your nightmare, my lass, so swallow it down. His Excellency wishes to see you and the other women who were concerned in the unhappy—ah—affray with the soldiers."

Jenny stared at him aghast. "The governor wishes to see us . . . to see *me*, Mister Brewer? But I thought you said that I was to be pardoned?"

"I anticipated his verdict," the provost marshal confessed. "But don't worry, I am confident that you will be. At all events you will not be sent back to Pinchgut—that is not a punishment for women." He added softly, "Take heart, Jenny Taggart! The governor thinks so highly of the work you and your companions have done on that plot of yours that he spoke of according you public recognition. He may change his mind on that score, in view of what has happened but . . . your conviction will be quashed, I'll warrant, and you'll hear no more of it."

He proved, to Jenny's heartfelt relief, to be right, although the brief interview with the governor left her still very conscious of the social and judicial gap between those who were convicted felons and those who, like the marine officers, represented authority.

Captain Collins told her curtly that her sentence had been commuted because the marine Bulmore had admitted, in the hospital—where he now was—that he had been drunk and, on that account, might have attempted to molest her.

"He cannot recall having done so," the judge advocate said, "and he continues to deny that he was armed or that he went to your plot with any intention of stealing from it. The female convict Hannah Jones has not changed her evidence. She claims to have known and been closely associated with you for over eighteen months, and, as you are aware, she stated on oath that you have a violent and ungovernable temper that has led you, on a number of occasions, to assault your fellow convicts. However. . . ." His expression was wary as he looked at her, Jenny noticed, as if her appearance and manner were not what he had expected, but he did not relax the sternness of his tone as he ended, "His Excellency has decided to give you the benefit of such doubt as exists, in view of your previous good conduct and the work you have done here since landing in the settlement. Your punishment, ordered by the criminal court, will be remitted. Now I'll take you to him."

The governor was seated at his desk when Jenny entered at Captain Collins's heels, and he, too, eyed her with some surprise when she dropped him a curtsy and then stood facing him, her head held high. In the ill-fitting sack dress and worn shawl, her hair flowing loose and unkempt from her twenty-four hours on Pinchgut, she looked, she was aware, very much like the kind of woman Hannah had suggested she was. Many hours of exposure to the sun had tanned her skin to a healthy brown, but her hands were ingrained with dirt, the nails cracked and broken, and her bare feet must have appeared, to the governor's fastidious eyes, even more filthy and uncared for than her hands . . . Jenny bit back a sigh.

"So you are Jenny Taggart," Captain Phillip observed thoughtfully. "And you are very young, are you not?"

"I'm almost seventeen, sir . . . Your Excellency."

"And your sentence—your original sentence—was for how long?"

"For life, sir."

"And your crime?" the governor persisted.

"I was convicted of receiving stolen property, sir," Jenny told him. "In London."

"But you are of country stock, I believe?"

"Yes, sir. My father was a smallholder in Yorkshire. He had been a soldier, sir—a sergeant in His Majesty's Forty-second Foot. But then—" Jenny broke off, flushing, afraid that she had said too much, but the governor gestured to her to continue. Under his quiet scrutiny she stammered out the story of her father's death and the seizure of his land, which had forced her mother and herself to make the long journey to London.

"Your mother was also sentenced to deportation, was she not?" Phillip questioned. "And she died on board the *Friendship* during the voyage here?" Jenny nodded. "I gave you permission to transfer from the *Charlotte* so that you could take care of her—in Rio de Janeiro, I recall. For what crime was she convicted?"

Jenny answered reluctantly. "She—for harboring a highwayman . . . Captain Harry Wilkes, sir. He was good to her, to us both, but they hanged him, and my mother was sent to the Hulks. My mother was a respectable woman, sir. She—" Again fearing that she had told him too much, Jenny broke off in confusion. But she had a right to defend her mother, she thought defiantly, a right and . . . a duty.

Governor Phillip was silent, reading through a small pile of legal documents spread out on the desk in front of him, his thin dark brows meeting in a pensive frown. His face was devoid of expression, and try as she would, Jenny could not guess what he was thinking. She waited, with a patience born of resignation, wondering—since he recalled her petition to transfer to the *Friendship*—whether he remembered that he had sent Andrew Hawley back to England and why he had done so. But she was too much in awe of him to ask, and when he shuffled the papers he had been reading into order and looked up at her again, she saw with dismay that his expression had hardened. He lectured her about her violent and ungovernable temper, warning her sternly that she must learn to control herself.

"You made a good start here," he said. "I spoke to some of those who have assisted you in your gardening, and they gave you a good character—with a single exception. The woman who gave evidence against you in court—Hannah Jones. Because she was with you when you made this—this unfortunate assault on Private Bulmore, which she says was unprovoked, I am bound to take notice of her statement. Tell me, child—has Hannah Jones any reason to bear a grudge against you?"

Jenny bit her lip, seeking vainly to still its trembling. She said, in a small voice, "Yes, sir, she has. I'd rather not say why."

The governor did not press her for reasons. He sighed heavily. "I had it in mind to reward your good start by giving you remission of part of your sentence, but, in view of this unhappy episode, I cannot now consider doing so. Remission must be earned by continued good behavior, Jenny Taggart. Bear that in mind. My advice to you is that you marry a good, steady man who—"

"A convict, sir?" Jenny challenged with a bitterness she could not hide.

The governor's nod of dismissal was cold. "A convict with only a short sentence to run," he suggested. "I could then make a grant of land to both of you, and if your conduct merited my favorable consideration, you could both gain remission and become free settlers. That would be a goal to work for, would it not?"

Would it? Jenny asked herself miserably . . . could this harsh, unfruitful land ever become home to her? Perhaps with Andrew it might have, but Governor Phillip had made that impossible when he had sent Andrew back to England . . . she lowered her gaze and answered with pretended submissiveness, "Yes, sir."

She had meant to tell him of the visit of the two natives and of their unexpected kindness to her when they had found her marooned on Pinchgut Island but she was outside his marquee now and could not go back. In any case Mr. Brewer had not believed her account; he had told her that it had been a nightmare, brought on by loneliness and fear, and perhaps that was what it had been. The natives were savages, intent only on murdering any white settler who crossed their path . . . their kindness was out of character, so that clearly she must have dreamed of it. It would be best to speak of the matter to no one, she decided—not even to Melia who, no doubt, would be as skeptical as Mr. Brewer had been.

Melia and the others were waiting for her, gathered in their nightly vigil by the open cooking fire. They all seemed subdued and unhappy, and Melia's eyes were red from weeping. Hannah was not there, and Eliza said, when they had all expressed relief at Jenny's return from Pinchgut, "She knows better than to show her face here again, the scurvy old hag! She's gone back to the main camp and good riddance, I say!"

Deftly she tossed one of the cakes of dough that Melia had prepared on to the blackened slab of stone that served them for a griddle and jerked her head in the direction of the cooking pot. "Fish, Jenny," she announced proudly. "Three prime leatherjackets Charlotte caught in the nets. We kept them all to celebrate your return from Pinchgut because we reckoned you deserved them more than that Bulmore in the hospital, the lying swine!"

They ate with enjoyment, all striving to appear cheerful and in good heart, but sensing that their gaiety was forced, Jenny asked bluntly, when the meal was over, "There's something wrong, isn't there? What are you trying to keep from me?"

Melia got up. She said wearily, "You had better come and see for yourself, Jenny," and led the way to their garden.

Even in the moonlight the devastation there was plainly to be seen. The maize lay trampled into the sandy soil, all the half-ripened heads—unseasonable yet almost ready to harvest—torn from their roots. The immature fruit trees were slashed to ribbons, the potatoes and the single row of pumpkins had vanished, and where the carefully hoarded manure had been there was now a small pool of stagnant water, from which a vile stench emanated.

"Who?" Jenny asked, her throat tight. "The soldiers?"

"Yes," Melia confirmed. "They came last night, after it got dark—seven or eight of them. And they taunted us when we tried to stop them, saying we wouldn't dare attack them unless we wanted to end up on Pinchgut with you. They were all armed, of course, with bayonets fixed to their muskets, and there was nothing we could do. We just had to stand and watch them."

Jenny drew a deep, uneven breath, feeling as if she were choking. The governor had lectured her concerning her violent temper, her loss of control, she thought, with newborn cynicism. Her attempt to protect the garden from the thieving Bulmore had lost her the chance of remission, and now his comrades, not content with seeing her sentenced to a week on Pinchgut, had destroyed all that she and the others had worked for in a senseless act of revenge.

"We'll have to set to and clear up the mess," she said grimly. "First thing tomorrow, all of us, Melia! I'll apply for more seed. At least we shall be planting it at the right time in this topsy-turvy place—they say the summer's coming and maize needs sun to ripen. And I'll speak to Sergeant Jenkins about his men— he'll know how to stop them from doing anything like this again."

"Is it worth it?" Melia retorted. "Is it worth even trying to do it all again?"

"It's worth it," Jenny said, with deep conviction. "If we're going to survive here, we've got to work the land—we've got to! And I'm not going to be beaten by stupid, drunken fools like Bulmore and his kind. If we've got to spend the rest of our lives in this place, let's try to make it a place where we can be happy and needn't starve."

The others stared at her in astonishment. "Jenny's been listening to the governor!" Charlotte exclaimed derisively. They laughed, and Eliza, down to earth as always, put an arm affectionately around the girl's thin shoulders.

"You're nawt but a slip of a lass," she said. "But you've more guts than all the rest of us put together, haven't you? And you're right, what's more—we don't have any choice, really, except to clean up this mess and start again. Well, I for one am with you, lass."

Next morning Polly and two of the younger women, who had earlier deserted to the main camp, came to rejoin them. By noon a small party of seamen from the *Sirius* had volunteered their help, and Tom Jenkins, with two of his fellow sergeants, brought sacks of seed corn from the government store and, stripped to their shirt-sleeves, worked until dark, digging in the leaves of the first crop, mixed with wood ash, to serve as fertilizer. Within a week most of the hard work had been done and the resowing completed.

The king's birthday was duly celebrated on June 4, and true to his promise, the governor made it an occasion. A royal salute was fired by the *Sirius* from her anchorage; Holy Communion was celebrated by the chaplain in one of the officers' marquees, and this was followed by an open-air service, at which prayers were offered for the future prosperity and well-being of the colony. The marine band played, the corps paraded for inspection, and the governor entertained all his officers to luncheon. In the evening bonfires were lit, and although MacEntire, the government huntsman, was able only to shoot four kangaroos, some sheep and pigs were slaughtered and the whole community feasted on fresh meat and drank to the king's health in spirits, the ugly specter of famine banished for that day at least.

It returned, all too soon, to haunt those in authority and cause Governor Phillip deep concern. The most serious shortage was of flour, and even with the ration drastically reduced, the commissariat officers reported that present stocks would be exhausted in six months. Repairs to the *Sirius*, such as they were, being completed, Phillip knew that he could delay her sailing to the Cape for fresh supplies no longer, and he ordered Captain Hunter to prepare for sea.

"I can ill do without you and your noble fellows, John," he told his second-in-command, as they discussed plans for the voyage. "But there's no help for it—explorations and surveys must be held in abeyance. As it is, you'll have to take the Cape Horn route if you sail at this season of the year, so that I cannot anticipate your return to the colony in under six months." He sighed in bitter frustration. "It will be a long wait, John my friend. God alone knows if we shall survive it."

Hunter echoed his sigh. "I'll make all the speed I can, sir," he promised, studying the governor's pinched, unhappy face with a concern he could not hide. The infernal Ross was, he was aware, tormenting Phillip. The thefts of livestock and vegetables from the settlement's gardens were by no means all committed by the convicts, but Ross would hear no word against his men—indeed, he was believed actively to encourage them in their depredations.

Hunter cleared his throat and asked quietly, "You are sending the *Golden Grove* to Norfolk Island with a batch of convicts, are you not?"

"Yes, she'll call there on her way to China," Phillip confirmed, "With about fifty convicts and five-and-twenty of Major Ross's fellows. It will ease our supply problem a little. I may send more, I haven't yet made up my mind."

"Why don't you send Ross with them?" Hunter suggested bluntly. "You've considered that possibility, I imagine?"

Phillip eyed him somberly. "The thought—even the

desire—has occurred to me, I admit. But I could not
send him while Philip King is in charge—and King
is doing too fine a job at Norfolk for me to recall him.
But . . . I shall bear the thought in mind, you may
rest assured. In the meantime"—he smiled—"I intend
to concentrate all our agricultural resources at Rose
Hill. Brewer, who's been inspecting it with Bloodworthy, talks of the establishment of a brick kiln—
there's good clay there, it seems, and the land's more
fertile than it is here. So we shall build more huts and
a barrack, perhaps even a hospital at Rose Hill, John,
during your absence, and I'll confine myself to growing vines in the government garden. Ah. . . ." His
smile widened. "Major Ross is keen on taking land
there for himself, and he's become an enthusiastic
agriculturalist—so I shall not stand in his way."

With that, John Hunter had to be satisfied. The
Sirius departed on her long voyage on October 2, the
Supply and the storeship *Golden Grove* sailed for
Norfolk Island, and for the first time since the arrival
of the convict fleet, the great harbor of Port Jackson
was empty of shipping.

July and August had been cold and wet, September
and October were much milder, and by November,
with the temperature approaching the seventies and
the sun shining in a blue, cloudless sky, the prospects
for the harvest were good, particularly at Rose Hill,
where Edward Dodd had performed miracles, despite
the apathy of his convict labor force.

Governor Phillip's hopes were rekindled. There
must soon appear the storeships from England, for
which he had sent so many urgent requests to Lord
Sydney and Sir Evan Nepean. With its stores replenished, the colony could survive, he told himself. True,

there was still sickness but, Dr. White and his able young assistant surgeons had found antiscorbutic herbs and fruits growing wild, to which all but the most obstinate cases eventually yielded, and these were now being grown in the hospital garden. Honest toil in the warm spring sunshine had done wonders for the health of most of the convicts—the women included.

More serious, in the governor's eyes, was an outbreak of smallpox among the aborigines, the origin of which was a mystery, for there were no cases of the disease in the settlement. In yet another endeavor to create a more friendly spirit among the native inhabitants, Phillip sent two of his surgeons to treat those of the sufferers who would permit their approach, but they were few and the death toll heavy. The surgeons saved no lives, and they returned, compelled to admit defeat that, in part at least, they ascribed to their inability to make themselves understood.

"Until we can learn their language or are able to train one or two of them as interpreters, it's hopeless, sir," Dr. Arndell said after making his report. "They simply don't understand the instructions we give them and, the minute our backs are turned, they resort to some weird kind of witchcraft, with bones and incantations."

"Then," the governor returned briskly, "we had better set about capturing a couple of them, I think. If we treat and feed them well, and then send them back, perhaps they will speak favorably of us to their own people."

The idea—one that had been in his mind for some time—was put into effect when the *Supply* arrived back from Norfolk Island. Her commander, Henry

Ball, was instructed to take two boatloads of seamen and marines across the harbor to a sandy beach beyond the North Head, which, because so many male natives had been seen there, they had named Manly Cove. The party returned with a single captive.

"We lost the second fellow, I'm afraid, sir," Ball said apologetically. "We had managed to seize two of them, but about fifty or sixty of them attacked us with spears and stones. George Johnstone had to order his fellows to fire over their heads, and in the confusion the older of the two made his escape."

The captive Indian accepted his fate with dignified resignation. He was about thirty years old, as nearly as anyone could judge, short of stature but robustly made. George Johnstone's marines delivered him to the half-completed brick building that governor Phillip had recently started to use as his official residence; he displayed much interest in its construction and, freed of his bonds on the governor's instructions, entered it with his head held high and without apparent fear. Phillip received him kindly; offered him food, which he ate with enjoyment, but restricted himself to fish and duck, with salt meat, bread, and liquor being vehemently refused.

After the meal he submitted to being cleansed of the gray mud with which his body was daubed and he showed no resentment when his beard was shaved by one of the governor's servants and his hair cut short and searched for lice. When these were found, he proceeded to eat them with undisguised relish and, presented with a shirt and a pair of seaman's trousers, he readily donned them, his changed appearance— demonstrated by means of a mirror—seeming to please him.

Phillip, anxious to make a friend of him before

returning him to his own people, spent as much time as he could with the captive, aided by Captain Tench, who had set himself the task of learning the aborigines' language. Communication was difficult at first, and unable to discover his name, Tench addressed him as Manly, to which he answered, a puzzled expression on his dark, but by no means unintelligent face. He made great efforts to understand what was required of him and to comply with his captors' requests, displaying a dignified courtesy toward any women he encountered and a warm, uninhibited affection to the children who approached him when Watkin Tench took him on a tour of the settlement.

It was only when, to prevent his attempting prematurely to escape, Phillip assigned an elderly convict to act as his guardian and had one of his wrists fettered, that Manly became sullen and dejected . . . but as soon as the fetter was removed, he was again smiling and tractable.

After a week's stay he had settled down. He announced that his name was Arabanoo and, under the governor's gentle probing, began to give him and any other officers present what lessons he could in the language of his people. His appetite was enormous but only fresh food would satisfy him; as he had at the outset, he refused all salt meat and, his manners impeccable after very little tuition, he ate at the governor's table, consuming seven or eight pounds of fish at a sitting.

Tench marveled at the manner in which he learned to use a napkin and even to handle a knife and fork; his sole lapse, if a dinner party went on too long for his liking, was his tendency to stretch out on the floor and sleep, oblivious to what was going on around him. A warm mutual regard sprang up between the marine captain and the strangely civilized savage, and Tench was genuinely regretful when the governor decided that the time had come to permit Arabanoo to go back to his tribe.

"He's showing signs of restiveness, and it's important that we convince his people that we have not harmed him," Phillip said. "Perhaps, if we do, they will learn to trust us—and they must, if we are to live in peace together."

Next morning he set sail for North Head and Manly Cove in his cutter, accompanied by Tench and a small party of marines, with the Indian seated beside him in the stern sheets. On reaching the beach, however, his carefully laid plan met with an unexpected setback. Hailed by the captive from the boat, a number of Indians gathered cautiously around to converse with him, but when Phillip ordered his release and he splashed eagerly ashore, all turned their backs on him, making it clear that he was no longer welcome in their midst.

Poor Arabanoo wept and pleaded; his countrymen were deaf to his entreaties, and the unhappy captive, emitting piteous cries, had to be taken back to the settlement.

"We'll try again," the governor promised, seeking by signs to make his meaning clear, but Arabanoo continued to weep, his shaven head bowed as if in shame. A second attempt to restore him to his own kind, made two days later, met with no more success than the first. The gifts he had brought were treated with disdain; the Indians stood in silence, waiting for him to go.

It was rejection, complete and absolute, and seemingly aware that from henceforth his lot was cast with the white strangers who had abducted him, Arabanoo laid his hand in that of the governor and smilingly indicated his willingness to return to the settlement. He lived from then onward in a small wooden hut built specially for him and spent most of his waking moments in the company of Phillip and his officers, eating all his meals at Government House.

The harbor remained as empty as before. In the hope that a store ship might be on the way, Phillip ordered a lookout station to be set up on the South Head to signal the first appearance of a sail on the horizon, and at regular intervals he dispatched parties of marines to Botany Bay, in case the master of the eagerly expected vessel had put in there, unaware of the removal of the settlement to Port Jackson.

No one watched the signal mast at South Head more eagerly than the weary, anxious governor, but no sail was sighted, and as the year wore on to its conclusion and the temperature rose, all were hungry and despondent. The convicts were in rags, few had shoes, and even the marines paraded bare of foot, their scarlet coatees faded and threadbare, their morale at its lowest ebb.

"We must celebrate Christmas, David," Phillip said to Judge Advocate Collins, "and pray to God for our preservation, for, it seems, only God can help us now. I begin greatly to fear that the home government has forgotten us!"

Christmas came, in blazing sunshine and almost unbearable humidity, and although valiant efforts were made to celebrate the occasion, it was hard for people accustomed for most of their lives to snow-covered streets and overcast skies to reconcile themselves to a midday temperature of almost one hundred degrees. And, instead of the surfeit of food and drink that even the poor could somehow manage to consume—if only in memory—at home in England, there was just a meager ration of salt meat too long in the cask to be palatable, some fish and turtle meat, and a small issue of spirits with which to wash it down.

No tea, save that brewed from the native creeper and of which most of them were, by this time, more than a little tired—no crackling Yuletide logs, for what was the sense in lighting bonfires, when even the coming of darkness brought small relief from the heat?

The Christmas Eve service was attended by all, but the convicts' attendance was compulsory and the singing of hymns reflected the general resentment this order had caused. The men were weary of the endless toil, the women homesick and dispirited, and the rank and file of the marines—as well as some of their officers—could talk of little but their longing to be relieved.

For Jenny the Christmas of 1788—her first in the colony—was the saddest she had ever spent.

Olwyn Jenkins had fallen ill some three weeks earlier. Brave and uncomplaining, she had made light of her malaise, refusing obstinately to request the surgeon's attention or even to rest in her hut. By the time, driven by despair to overrule her, Sergeant Jenkins sought Jenny's aid to nurse her, Olwyn was coughing up blood and was unable to lift her head from the rolled-up cloak that served her as a pillow. Dr. Arndell, summoned at last, shook his head regretfully and gave her only a few days to live. There were no medicines to give her, for the hospital's supplies had been exhausted as long ago as September, and in any case, the conscientious young doctor admitted, nothing could have helped her.

She was weak but in no pain, save when her coughing racked her, and she welcomed Jenny's appearance in her hut as she would have welcomed that of a much loved daughter, making no mention of the coldness that had been between them since their landing. Jenny, contrite and tormented by her conscience, endeavored to explain the reason for her decision to live and work with the other convicts, but Olwyn brushed her stammered explanations aside.

"There, *cariad*, don't take on—you are here now, that is all that matters, isn't it? You have come, when I need you, and you are going to stay with me, aren't you now, until the Lord sees fit to call me to Him?"

Jenny inclined her head in unhappy assent, and Olwyn smiled at her, with some of her old warmth and pleasure.

"You are a good girl, like I always believed you were. And you have proved it. Tom has told me how hard you have worked on that garden of yours and what a fine example you have set to the rest of them. He says that even the governor has noticed and commended you for what you have done."

"Yes, but . . . I killed Auld Meg, Mistress Jenkins," Jenny said, anxious to make her understand. "That was why I could not make my home with you and Sergeant Jenkins, why I had to stay with the convicts. You see, I—"

"I see many things at this minute, Jenny," the sick woman put in, still smiling at her affectionately. "Clarity of vision, that's what the good Lord gives, when you are near to the end. And I have it now . . . I can see you, as clear as anything, my lamb. If you had not defended yourself against that terrible old woman in the *Friendship*, she would have killed you. It does not make you guilty of murder, child, if you fought her off to save your own life, without the intention to kill her."

Olwyn sank very rapidly, and it was evident that she did not mean to fight for survival. She was devoutly religious and, on this account, had no fear of death . . . indeed, there were times when Jenny wondered whether she were not seeking it, as a release from a life she now found unbearable.

"I am not cut out for pioneering," she remarked one evening when they were alone. "I did not imagine, when Tom said he was wanting to volunteer to come out here, that it would be like this. I pictured us on a little farm, like the one I was brought up on, with just the ordinary chores one has in such a place. I never imagined New South Wales would be different. But it is—it is a cruel place, Jenny, and it has not welcomed us. I shall be glad to leave it—or I should be, were it not for Tom. It is on Tom's account that I am worried . . . you will help him all you can, won't you, *cariad*? You will look out for him, when I am gone?"

Feeling tears ache in her throat, Jenny nodded wordlessly. Olwyn studied her face with anxious, feverbright eyes. "My Tom is a good man," she asserted and paused expectantly.

"Yes, I know he is," Jenny agreed. "I have much to thank him for—much to thank you both for, Mistress Jenkins." She bent forward to wipe the beads of sweat from Olwyn's brow, shocked to feel how hot it was. "You should try to sleep now," she urged. "You must not overtax your strength. I—I'll be here when you wake up."

But Olwyn was not to be put off. She closed her eyes for a moment or two, as if pausing to gather her failing strength, and then said, clasping Jenny's hand tightly between her own moist palms, "Tom will finish his time in the corps by April of next year, Jenny, and he has applied for a grant of land and permission to remain here as a free settler."

"Yes, Mistress Jenkins, he told me so." Guessing what Tom's wife was about to say, she busied herself with the only medicine Dr. Arndell had been able to provide for his patient—a leather-covered flask of Brazilian wine. Pouring some of this into a pewter beaker, she held it to the sick woman's lips, hoping to distract her.

Olwyn drank thirstily and then pushed the beaker away. "I know he is old enough to be your father, *cariad*," she said softly, "but he cares for you as much as I do and . . . as a free settler, my Tom could marry whom he wishes. If you were to wed him, Jenny, it would be—oh, what they call a marriage of convenience, see? You would be granted remission, I am sure of that, and the two of you, why you could work the land, couldn't you, together?"

Jenny did not answer. She felt the warm, embarrassed color that suffused her cheeks, and made to take the beaker and restore it to its place on the makeshift table on the far side of the hut, but Olwyn's fingers tightened about her hand.

"No, hear me out, my lamb. If Andrew had been here, I would not have made any such suggestion. But he is not here, Jenny—nor likely to be, for he has his time to serve. And you . . . why, you need a man to take care of you, as much as my poor Tom needs a woman, don't you?"

Perhaps she did, Jenny reflected and . . . had not the governor advised her to marry a good, steady man? A convict, with a short sentence to run. The governor had taken from her the one man she had loved and purposed to marry. She bit her lip fiercely, stilling the rebellious words she wanted to say, and forced herself to consider what Olwyn had proposed.

Marriage to a man as steady and respected as Tom Jenkins—a retired sergeant in the Marine Corps— would almost certainly lead to her emancipation long before her sentence, even with remission, had expired. And, as Olwyn had pointed out, it would be for them both a marriage of convenience. Tom would continue to treat her as a daughter and— She thought again of Andrew, recalling the details of his strong, tanned face, the sound of his voice, the touch of his hand. There had been no one else for her; unlike so many of the other women, she had not taken a lover, had not wanted to, and she had refused several proposals of marriage made to her by convicts. But, as Olwyn had reminded her, Andrew had been banished from her life—he was not here and it was unlikely in the extreme that he ever would be. She would be wise to forget him and—

Olwyn was suddenly seized with a terrible fit of coughing, and when the paroxysm was over, the front of her shift and the cloth Jenny had held to her mouth were both heavily stained with blood. She sipped a little more of the wine and, recovering her breath, returned obstinately to her theme.

"I'd not want to die knowing that my Tom would be left on his own, Jenny," she whispered painfully. "Or that he was maybe forced to turn to one of those wantons in the camp. But you are a good girl; he thinks the world of you. And with you he could be happy and content—you both would, with a farm of your own, just as Tom and I dreamed it would be when we set out. Tell me you'll not refuse him if he asks you to wed him, my sweet lamb?"

It was impossible to deny her the reassurance she sought. Jenny gave her word, holding her in her strong young arms and biting back the tears, as Olwyn wept her relief.

She died on New Year's Eve very peacefully, with Tom Jenkins at her side, slipping quietly into a sleep from which there was no awakening, and her husband mourned her passing as if, for him, no other woman had existed or ever would.

Jenny did what was necessary, attended the simple funeral service in the as yet almost empty graveyard at the extremity of the marines' camp, and returned, heavy of heart and alone, to the hut she shared with Melia and three of the others.

The garden had again been robbed, Melia told her, and Hannah Jones had returned, expressing contrition. That night—the first night of the year 1789—was one which Jenny had cause to remember, for it was then that her precious locket was stolen.

CHAPTER XVII

New Year's Day was hot and sultry, with scarcely the whisper of a breeze. The previous night's celebrations —the occasion for more liquor-induced than genuine gaiety—had gone on until the early hours, and after working all day in the garden by themselves, Jenny and Melia retired early to their hut. Eliza and Charlotte, who normally shared it with them, had not yet returned from the main camp, and accustomed by now to such periodic defections, neither remarked on their absence.

They had improved the wattle and daub huts by adding extra layers of clay to the walls and by replacing the original cabbage-palm leaves with a tightly packed thatch of rushes, which kept out all but the heaviest downpour. No glass was available for windows, but Melia, with infinite pains, had contrived two small latticed apertures with interlaced twigs and these served to let in the daylight. Their door was a flimsy framework of wood, with a square of sailcloth stretched across it. It was fastened in place by means of leather hinges attached to wooden pegs and, lacking any form of lock, was there rather in the interests of modesty than in the hope that it would deter an intruder.

Situated where they were, well away from the women's main camp, they had been troubled only by intruders bent on robbing the garden—none had attempted to enter the huts—and they had come, in consequence, to think of themselves as reasonably safe. Both were tired, and they settled down to sleep without indulging in conversation, lying down fully dressed, since nightclothes and candles were things of the past, dimly remembered but no longer consciously missed.

Jenny fell into a deep, dreamless sleep, untroubled by the distant rumbling of thunder and so accustomed, by this time, to the nocturnal sounds emanating from other parts of the camp that she hardly heard them. She was shocked into wakefulness when two sinewy hands closed about her throat, cutting the breath off from her lungs.

She struggled to sit up, to cry out to Melia, but the hands tightened their grasp, and turn and twist as she would, she could not break free of them. A cackling laugh sounded in her ears, a woman's voice muttered obscenities, and as a red mist blotted out her vision, one of the hands relaxed its grip to reach for the length of coarse ship's twine, by which—since its ribbon had long since rotted and distintegrated—the precious locket Ned Munday had given her was hung about her neck.

She felt the twine snap, heard as if from a very long way away Hannah's voice exclaim in blasphemous triumph, and then both hands clawed viciously at her bruised and aching throat, once again depriving her lungs of air. The red mist closed about her, and she lapsed into unconsciousness.

When her senses returned, the intruder had gone, and Melia, only a few feet away, slept on, oblivious. Gasping, Jenny sat up, the roof of the hut whirling about her in crazy circles, now receding, now seeming as if it were about to fall and crush her. She stumbled over to the door of the hut, drawing great gulps of warm night air into her straining lungs as she crouched there, too sick and giddy to stand upright. The tension eased at last. She dragged herself to her feet and, as memory returned, felt for the locket in the bosom of her dress, uncertain—until she had confirmed that it was missing—whether, like the visit of the Indians to Pinchgut Island, this, too, had been a nightmare.

After a while she reentered the hut and, groping for the cask of drinking water they kept there, stumbled against some unseen obstacle and wakened Melia.

"Jenny . . . is that you?" Melia sat up, startled. Glimpsing Jenny's white face in the moonlight, she cried out in alarm. "Is anything wrong? You look terrible, as if— Did someone try to break in?"

"It was Hannah. She—she tried to strangle me." Jenny's voice was a hoarse croak. "Melia, she stole my locket!"

"You must have imagined it." Melia came to her, wide-eyed and skeptical, until she saw the telltale imprint of clawing fingernails on the tanned skin of Jenny's throat. Even in the dimness the marks were clear enough. "Are you sure it was Hannah?" she questioned, still doubtful.

"I think it was—I heard her voice. And she knew about the locket . . . she knew how I treasured it."

"Yes, but—" Melia was examining the bruises. "Are you sure it wasn't a man?"

Jenny gulped down a sip of the water. "A man would have made sure," she managed painfully. "He'd have killed me."

"But why should Hannah try to kill you?" Melia wrung out a scrap of cloth in the water and laid it gently on Jenny's throat. "There—that may help to ease the pain if you hold it against the bruises." She sighed and returned to the subject of Hannah. "I wouldn't put it past her to want to steal that locket of yours, Jenny—it's a beautiful piece, and valuable too. But . . . I didn't think Hannah hated you. Enough to break in here and try to strangle you, I mean."

"She lied about what happened in the garden when we caught Bulmore robbing it," Jenny reminded her with bitterness. "Because he *was* armed and he did go for me with his bayonet—I've got a scar on my arm to prove it! I suppose she's trying to get back at me for Auld Meg but . . . she's waited so long, Melia. And no one can say she cared all that much for Meg, surely?"

"In a twisted sort of way, perhaps she did," Melia demurred. "But still, as you say, she's waited a long time, if that is behind it. And when she came back to us, she really did seem to be sorry that she had caused you to be sent to Pinchgut. *I* believed her, I must admit, and so did the others. Polly said she didn't realize what she was doing, and Eliza thinks she's going out of her mind. This place is enough to send anyone out of their mind. I . . . ." She hesitated.

"Are you going to report her for what she did to-night?"

Jenny shrugged. "What use would that be? I can't prove anything, and even if I could, having Hannah punished would help none of us, would it? I mean, if we appear to be causing trouble, they might send us back to the main camp—or even to Norfolk Island. I shall try to get my locket back but . . . we have to stick together, earn remission by good behavior, if we're ever to make anything of our life here. I want to be *free*, Melia—" she broke off. Until then she had told no one of Olwyn Jenkins's dying wish, but the need to confide in someone became suddenly overwhelming. Her voice still a painful whisper, she told Melia of her promise and saw that the older girl was regarding her in open-mouthed astonishment.

"But Sergeant Jenkins is a marine, Jenny!" she exclaimed. "Would they permit him to marry you?"

"When he's served his time, they would have to."

"But he's old enough to be your father!"

"I know. And that's how I think of him—or as an uncle, perhaps." Jenny smiled. "It wouldn't be a real marriage, Melia—Olwyn Jenkins, God rest her, knew that."

"You would get your freedom, as his wife," Melia pointed out, a faint hint of envy in her voice. "And you would be safe, you would be protected. But you're very young, Jenny—and you've never known love, have you?"

Jenny thought fleetingly of Andrew, and her resolution hardened. Of what use was it to think of Andrew now?

"No," she conceded. "But I'm not sure that I want to anymore. Other things seem more important out

here—things like freedom, having enough to eat, being treated with respect. What does love matter?"

"What indeed!" Melia echoed cynically. She let the
subject drop, but next day, when they were hoeing
side by side in the garden, she returned to it. "If you
are given the chance to marry Sergeant Jenkins, Jenny,
you should take it."

Jenny paused to wipe her damp face with the sleeve
of her dress. "Should I?"

"Yes," Melia said. "*I* would, in your place—even
if the man was old enough to be my grandfather! It
would be a small price to pay for an end to—to
degradation." She plied her hoe with sudden angry
vigor. "Hannah has gone again—did Eliza tell you?
So it must have been she who attacked you last night
. . . Eliza said she was behaving very oddly. I think
she must have gone out of her mind—and she's not
the only one, by all accounts. There's a rumor going
round that a woman from the main camp was stabbed
to death by the man she was living with. Eliza and
Polly were both full of it when they got back this
morning."

The rumor was soon confirmed. A male convict
named Ruglass had murdered one of the *Lady
Penrhyn* women, Ann Fowles. He was arrested and
made no attempt to deny his guilt; at his trial, two
days later, he preserved the same stoic indifference
to his fate, claiming only that Ann Fowles had been
unfaithful to him and—perhaps on this account—the
death sentence he had received was remitted to one
almost as bad, seven hundred lashes.

Jenny sought out Hannah Jones but could get
neither sense nor an admission from her. The old
hag screamed furiously that she had never set eyes
on the locket and created so great a furor that Jenny

was compelled to take flight, lest her hysterical threats
and accusations bring the other women of the camp
to join in the wordy battle.

"Bad cess to yer, yer little strumpet!" Hannah
shrieked after her. "I'll cook yer goose for yer, if it's
the last thing I do! And," she added vindictively,
"yer'd best watch out, 'cause Jake Bulmore's come aht
o' the 'orspital an' 'e's lookin' for yer, so's 'e can get
'is own back!"

Jenny shivered involuntarily but, turning her back
on the foul-mouthed old harridan, continued on her
way in silence, her head held high.

Rob Sibley was drunk when the disagreement
started, and it had become a full-fledged battle between Joe Hunt and Jake Bulmore before he had
collected his wits sufficiently to realize the danger.
Jake had been discharged from the hospital earlier
that day, still wearing a bandage on his head and
with a decided chip on his shoulder, and when he
joined them in their tent, they had all—himself included—gone out of their way to make him welcome.
Joe and Seamus O'Halloran had produced a keg of
rum from its hiding place, and it was prime stuff,
undiluted and surely, Sibley had supposed, just the
thing to help Jake drown his sorrows.

Instead he had become surly and morose, making
wild accusations against them all collectively and Joe
in particular, complaining of the pains in his head
and of what he claimed were untruthful statements
made about him to the commandant.

"Dropped me in it, you did, the lot of you, actin'
as if I was the only one that raided the women's
garden an' tryin' ter run off an' leave me when that

little hellcat come at me wiv' a bleedin' hoe. Bunch o' bloody narks, that's what you are an' no error!"

"Och, now, we're not, boyo," O'Halloran protested, and Dempsey, nettled, gave voice to angry obscenities.

"Pipe down, the lot of you!" Joe Hunt gritted. "Want ter bring the bleeding sergeants in 'ere, do yer? 'Cause you're goin' the best way about it, shootin' off yer mouths the way you are. If you've got a grouse, Jake Bulmore, we'll go down the cove aways an' have it out where no one can't overhear us."

"I got a grouse all right," Bulmore assured him. "But first off I want ter settle that little hellcat's hash, an' I'm countin' on you ter lend a daddle."

Sibley, listening with pained anxiety to their raised and angry voices, attempted to pour oil on troubled waters.

"We did their garden over good and proper, Jake," he said earnestly. "And she was given a spell on Pinchgut . . . that makes you even, surely? Anything more will only cause trouble for us."

But Jake Bulmore was not to be placated. He rounded on them all in blind fury, and Hunt, losing patience with him, jerked his head in the direction of the tent flap.

"Out!" he snarled, "the bunch o' you an' look lively!"

They followed him in a straggling procession, still trading accusations, with Sibley reluctantly bringing up the rear. Reaching the small deserted inlet—well out of earshot of their camping ground, which had become the traditional place for the settling of differences between them—Hunt halted and started to unbutton his frayed and faded tunic.

"Right!" he said truculently. "If this is what you're wantin', Jake, I'm yer man. Stand to yer mark!"

It was evident to Sibley and the others that he intended to make a fair fight of it, man to man, and they all stood back, forming a rough circle round them. Jake Bulmore, however, as if suddenly aware that he was in for a drubbing at the hands of the powerfully built Hunt, drew his bayonet and lunged at his opponent. Taken completely by surprise, Hunt nevertheless reacted swiftly, and the point of the bayonet—instead of striking him in the chest—caught him a glancing blow on the arm.

"The bastard's off his head!" he yelled. "Lend a hand, boys, for Gawd's sake, an' get that sticker off 'im!"

O'Halloran and Dempsey needed no second bidding. They hurled themselves on the swaggering Bulmore, wading into him with fists and boots, and Hunt, swearing triumphantly, grabbed the bayonet with his uninjured arm. Bulmore fought back, but he was no match for three of them, and when he fell before the weight of their onslaught, Tommy Ray—normally, in Sibley's estimation, the least aggressive of their bunch—rained blow after blow at him with a piece of driftwood, picked up on the shore a few moments earlier and fashioned into a cudgel.

They stood back at last, their fury spent, and Sibley, choking on a sob, thrust past them to drop to his knees beside their victim. His frantically searching fingers found no heartbeat; the battered, blood-soaked body was inert when, sick with dismay, he turned it over onto its back.

"Jesus God!" he cried, looking up at their white faces. "He's dead! Dead, I tell you!"

Joe Hunt was the first to return to sobriety. "He can't be!" he protested. "Out o' my way, Rob, an' let me look at 'im."

"He's dead," Sibley repeated. Sobs racked him as the horror of what they had done slowly sank in. "Joe, they—they'll hang us for this. We—"

"If they catch us," Joe Hunt gritted. "If they pin it on us . . . but I don't aim ter let 'em, Rob lad. Come on, lift 'im up . . . we'll dump 'im a bit further along, near where them women 'ave their fishnets. Let 'em think the women done 'im in . . . or the Injuns. Take 'old of 'is arm—an' you, Seamus, grab t'other. It won't take us above 'arf an hour all told, an' then we'll leg it back ter camp an' act like we ain't never left our tent."

They obeyed him, moving like sleepwalkers, in stunned and cowardly silence, prevented—by the untimely appearance of the convict watch—from leaving the body as near to the fishnets as Joe Hunt had planned.

The discovery of Private Bulmore's body, by the watch, created a major sensation in the settlement. Suspicion fell, at first, on the natives, but the Indian Arabanoo, called upon to act as interpreter, pointed out with irrefutable logic that his people killed with spears and that no spears or fish gigs had been found in the vicinity of the dead marine's body . . . whereas an alert convict constable of the watch had found a military bayonet, with blood on it, on the foreshore barely a quarter of a mile distant.

Next day, to the loudly expressed indignation of their commandant, five of Bulmore's comrades were arrested by Provost Marshal Brewer and charged with having caused his death. Tried by a court-martial composed of their own officers, with Major Ross presiding, all five were acquitted for lack of proof.

The marines were openly jeered at by the male

convicts, even the officers coming in for their share of scornful ribaldry, and the women made it known that the recently released men, who had been frequent visitors to the main camp, were no longer welcome there.

For Jenny the trial had been an ordeal she had not bargained for, since Major Ross—after questioning her in private—had endeavored to suggest that the injuries she had inflicted on the dead man with her hoe had been, in part, the cause of his demise. Hannah, summoned to repeat the evidence she had given at Jenny's own trial, had done so with venomous pleasure, and the knowledge that the governor had asked to see a transcript of the evidence added, Jenny was unhappily aware, another black mark against her name.

Sergeant Jenkins—whether as a result of this or for personal reasons, she had no means of knowing—was at pains to avoid her, and her cup of bitterness ran over when she learned, from Polly, that the sergeant had taken to visiting the women's camp, to be entertained by Mrs. Davis, the one-time brothelkeeper from the *Charlotte*.

To Melia she said bitterly, "It doesn't look as if I need have any qualms over breaking my promise to poor Olwyn now. If the sergeant seeks another wife, it will not be me he'll ask—and as for earning remission, why, I'd be a blind fool to hope for anything of the kind!"

But for all her blighted hopes she went on doggedly tending their garden, and it was with something approaching triumph that the harvest of maize was gathered, excelling in both quality and quantity the poor crop yielded by the replanted government farm in the cove. Cabbages, melons, and pumpkins were also growing well, and thanks to the vigilance of the night watch of convict constables, garden robberies were now less frequent.

The watch was a godsend to all the garden owners and, in particular, to Jenny and her hard-worked helpers, who had been badly dispirited following the ruin of their early crop by Bulmore's comrades. The men selected to act as constables were volunteers of good behavior, and armed with staves, they patroled from dusk to dawn under the command of a convict named Keelan. Pilferers were seized and hauled off to the marine guardhouse with scant ceremony, and any irregularities were reported the following day to the judge advocate, Captain Collins.

"That poor devil Keelan doesn't have an easy job though," Eliza stated with conviction when the women gathered around their cooking fire a few weeks after the discovery of Private Bulmore's body. "The governor warned him not to get into no disputes with seamen or lobsterbacks but"—she stirred the soup caldron, pausing to taste its contents critically—"if any of 'em are found in the convict lines after dark or if they gets caught red 'anded when engaged in stealin,' why then they has to be delivered to the guard'ouse, an' the watch has to lay such information concernin' their be'avior as'll enable their own officers to deal wiv' 'em. I'm quotin',"" she added, "from their instructions."

"Did Keelan tell you that?" Melia asked curiously.

Eliza nodded. "Aye, he did. More'n a mite worried, he was, the poor cuss. *We* know who does most o' the camp visitin' an' pilferin' around here, don't we?" There was a murmur of rueful assent, in which Jenny joined feelingly.

Eliza added some sliced pumpkin to the stewpot.

"Well, as you might expect," she went on, "one o' the first to be caught red 'anded was a jolly-boy. Lucky for Tich Keelan, he was on his own so he didn't put up much of a fight—jus' give in an' let 'isself be carted off to the guard'ouse. He weren't much concerned though. The major'd get him off, he reckoned—an' Keelan reckoned that too."

"And did the major get him off?" Jenny questioned. She suppressed a shiver, remembering Major Ross's cold gray eyes, the veiled threat in his voice as he had accused her of being responsible for Private Bulmore's death. *"You struck the poor fellow, did you not, Taggart? You struck him on the head with a hoe, wounding him grievously . . . and you wanted revenge for what you imagined his comrades did to your miserable little patch of land. . . ."*

Eliza snorted her contempt. "Get 'im off—'course he did!" she asserted. "An' not only that—he went to the governor. Keelan said he claimed as it was an insult to the corps o' marines for the governor to permit a convict to place a member o' His Majesty's Forces under arrest!"

There was a shocked silence. "But if a member of His Majesty's Forces is caught breakin' the law, it's only right for him to be put under arrest, ain't it?" Charlotte suggested belligerently, her dark eyes flashing.

"Not by a *convict*," Eliza said dryly. "Accordin' to the major. But the governor stood up for Keelan—he's an 'ard man, is Captain Phillip, but he's fair—you got ter give 'im that. An' he don't hold wiv' one law for us an' another for them sods o' lobsterbacks, not by a long chalk. Tich Keelan says as it's caused a right rumpus atween him an' Major 'Igh an' Mighty Ross. Well, all I can say is I hope the governor will stick to 'is guns . . . an' I'll wager our little Jenny feels the same as what I do!"

"Yes," Jenny confirmed, her voice not steady. "I do."

Opinion among the convicts was, however, sharply divided. The law abiding and those with cherished garden plots, most of whom had suffered at the hands of the major's men, were wholeheartedly in favor of the watch, and a petition was sent to the governor, requesting that the night patrols should be continued. Others, for less worthy reasons, held that the marine guard provided adequate protection during the hours of darkness and protested vehemently that no civilian patrol was necessary—least of all one composed of their fellow convicts. The loudest protests came from the main women's camp, where the marines were the most popular night visitors, since, now that the ships had gone, they were the source of the supply of illicit liquor, in exchange for which the idle and the abandoned eagerly sold themselves.

The petition and the controversy it stirred up was brought to a head barely a month later, when some marines in the act of robbing the spirit and tobacco store on the government wharf were surprised by a convict patrol. Wisely the convict constables called out the guard, and the arrests were made, with some reluctance, by the guard commander.

The story made the rounds, losing little of its drama in the telling. Polly came running from the women's camp, with Eliza and Charlotte hard on her heels, and the work Jenny had planned on the fishnets had to wait until all three had given a breathless and, at times, contradictory account of the night's happenings.

"There were seven of them in it," Polly said. "The

ones that did regular sentry duty at the store. One of them had a key made to fit the padlock on the door."

"That was Joe Hunt," Eliza supplied. "A rogue, if ever there was one! Got a convict locksmith to make it for 'im, eight months ago, they reckon. No wonder they was allus so free wiv' their liquor an' their 'baccy . . . they'd bin robbin' the store whenever any of 'em was on sentry-go. But Joe Hunt went an' bust the key in the lock an' the commissary seen it an' tipped off the watch. That was how they got caught, see? Keelan an' his lads was waitin' for 'em, when they tried ter get the broken key out."

"We haven't told you the best part, Jenny," Polly said excitedly. "The five who were tried for Bulmore's murder were in this gang! They got off then but they won't be so lucky this time, the rogues! And they call *us* felons!" She laughed derisively. "Major Ross won't be able to get them acquitted a second time, I'll take my oath!"

But would the black mark against her name be erased, Jenny wondered wryly—would Major Ross even remember the false accusations he had leveled against her concerning Private Bulmore's death? Would he even bother to withdraw them? This would be a blow to him, finding that some of his marines, whose honor he had defended so fiercely, were no better than the convicted thieves and murderers they were employed to guard.

Eliza was speaking and she made an effort to listen.

"They're to be tried Monday, all seven of 'em. I've heard that Joe Hunt has confessed and that he's goin' to turn King's evidence . . . in the hope that he'll be let off, I suppose, the yellow-livered coward! Well, I for one hope as they'll string him up. Thieving's one thing but ratting on your mates is another."

The other women echoed her sentiments, with varying degrees of indignation. Jenny, recalling all too
vividly Joe Hunt's cringing obsequiousness when faced
with his commanding officer's hectoring questions, remained silent. A villain he undoubtedly was, but now
that his villainy had been revealed, she could find it
in her heart to pity him, aware that he could expect
no mercy from the man to whom he had lied.

Major Ross was in his tent when Jeremiah Leach,
sent hot foot from the court to acquaint him with its
findings, entered and came rigidly to attention in
front of him.

"Well?" the commandant demanded hoarsely. "I
trust that justice was done?"

Leach, taken aback by the manner in which the
question was phrased, cleared his throat nervously,
uncertain how to answer it.

"Oh, devil take it, boy!" Ross snapped. "What was
their verdict?"

"Not guilty in the case of Sibley, sir. But—" Leach
braced himself for the expected storm. "The others
were found guilty on all charges, sir, with one member
of the court dissenting . . . Captain Campbell, sir."

The storm did not materialize. Keeping himself
under iron control, Major Ross asked, "Was the death
sentence imposed?"

"Yes, sir. Except in the case of Private Hunt. He's
to receive seven hundred lashes. Er—the sentences are
to be carried out within an hour of tap-too, sir."

"Then I had best prepare to attend," Ross said
stiffly. He consulted his pocket watch and permitted
himself a long-drawn sigh before asking for details of
the evidence. Leach supplied these with careful pre-

cision. "As you told the governor, sir, it's an insult to the corps—"

Major Ross cut him short. "So long as Captain Phillip is governor, such decisions are his, not mine, Jeremiah. I registered my protest, I can do no more."

"Er—yes, of course, sir." Once more Leach found himself floundering, anxious to please his commanding officer yet unable to fathom the way in which his mind was working. "It was Captain Collins's questioning of the witnesses that got the men convicted, sir," he ventured, knowing himself to be on relatively safe ground; Major Ross had developed an almost fanatical dislike of Judge Advocate Collins, so that any criticism of him was well received. Collins had damned himself in the commandant's eyes forever when, following the death of Captain Shea a month ago, he had refused Ross's offer of promotion in the corps and command of Shea's company, preferring to remain judge advocate and the governor's loyal right hand.

Leach's lips curved into a smile as he saw Major Ross rise to the bait. It always paid off to deprecate Collins, he reflected smugly, listening with half an ear to the familiar tirade. Shea's death, coupled with Collins's refusal of promotion, had left a vacancy into which both he and the major's son, young John Ross, had been enabled to step. "Little John" had obtained his commission, while he himself was now officially on the strength of the corps as a full lieutenant, and paid accordingly. So much for his brother Francis's hopes of ousting him as their father's heir, Leach thought, his smile widening. Prejudiced though he was, his father could not deny that he had "made good." And he should have no chance to deny it.

His thoughts were rudely interrupted when Major

Ross jumped to his feet. "They shall not be executed as soldiers of the corps, by God!" he exclaimed. "They shall be drummed out. Well, what the devil are you waiting for, boy? We shall have to act fast. Cut along to the camp—your legs are younger than mine. Tell Mister Long the battalion's to parade in half an hour, with drums and fifes, and the prisoners under guard. And have a runner sent to the court. I want all my officers on the parade ground immediately."

Jeremiah Leach stared at him uncomprehendingly for a moment and then, as his meaning sank in, he was off on his errand. Long, the adjutant, was in his canvas orderly room. He listened in frowning silence to the commandant's orders and then nodded.

"The major intends to drum them out, you say? Well, that's the best way, I suppose, for the honor of the corps. All right, Leach, I'll attend to it—you go and summon the members of the court."

The courts-martial were still held under canvas, pending the roofing of a half-finished building on which work had been temporarily suspended, and the officers who had tried and sentenced the seven marines were glumly refreshing themselves in the curtained-off section, which served as an anteroom when the court was in session. Although the raised voices were swiftly hushed as he entered, it was evident to Leach that a quarrel of recent origin had divided them.

Captain Campbell, second-in-command of the corps, stood with the quartermaster glaring at Captain Meredith, who glared back at him. Meredith had obviously been drinking heavily and was, in consequence, in an evil temper which he made no attempt to hide. Jeremiah Leach found himself wishing that the adjutant had not insisted on his acting as messenger. But, since there was no escape, he cleared his throat cautiously and, addressing Campbell, informed him of the commandant's order.

"What the devil are you gibbering about?" Meredith demanded aggressively before James Campbell could reply. "Speak up, Leach, for heaven's sake!"

Leach repeated the order, speaking with slow deliberation, as if his listener were hard of hearing, and then, with equal care, explained the reason for it. He despised Meredith, as much for his uncouth manners as for his drinking.

Campbell turned to Captain Meredith. "You heard the order, James—and it's to be carried out immediately."

James Meredith controlled his anger. He left the tent, walking quite soberly, and the others followed him. Leach fell into step with Lieutenant John Johnson.

"Our men are soldiers," Johnson grumbled. "If a soldier's condemned to death, he should be shot, not hanged like a common felon. And damme, our fellows are to be hanged by a convict hangman! That I don't hold with."

"For the blasted convicts the death penalty should be arbitrary," Furzer put in. "But not for the corps. The sentence should have been flogging for our men."

When they reached the parade ground, they found Captain Meredith's company already mustered and the fifes and drums about to march on. Leach left them, to take his place at Major Ross's back, with young John Ross, also acting as his father's aide. The commandant, busy discussing procedure with the adjutant and two of the senior noncommissioned officers, ignored them. The younger Ross whispered, a trifle apprehensively, "Father's in a state, Jeremiah. I've never seen him so put out. This"—he gestured

to the parade ground—"this is a calamity, isn't it?
A terrible insult to the corps."

"Yes," Leach agreed, "but your father knows how
to deal with the matter. If I were you," he added, not
unkindly, "I'd keep a still tongue in my head and
just do whatever he tells you to."

The boy shuddered. In his ill-fitting, faded uniform, he looked very young and frightened, turning
his head away as, led by the drums and fifes, the six
condemned men were marched onto the parade
ground, under the escort of ten of their comrades.
With the best part of one company at Rose Hill, there
were only about a hundred twenty marines on parade,
but they were formed into the usual hollow square
and made, despite their lack of numbers, a somber
and impressive display.

The prisoners, in full uniform, were marched into
the center of the square, the fifes and drums playing
the Rogues' March; then, as they came to a halt facing the commandant, Adjutant Long stepped forward
to read out the charges against them and the sentences
imposed. This done, he stood back, and the two
senior sergeants, who had been standing at the head
of the guard, advanced, saluted, and received the order
to do their duty. To the slow roll of the drums, they
went up to each prisoner in turn, removed his head-
gear and cut the buttons and insignia from his tunic.
Fetters were hammered onto their wrists and ankles,
and the adjutant read out the men's names, ending
with the stentorian announcement that all six were
discharged with ignominy from the Marine Corps.

The wretched prisoners stood like statues, and looking at their expressionless faces and downcast eyes,
Leach wondered what they were feeling. But worse
was to come. The two sergeants, their unhappy task

completed, returned to their platoons; the guard received the order to reverse arms, and led by the drums and fifes now playing the Dead March, the parade was formed into marching order, and the chaplain went to take his place beside the fettered prisoners, reading from his prayer book.

Beneath the gallows Freeman, the convict executioner, waited with his two assistants. The convicts were already assembled in serried ranks, the marine company took post facing them, and the prisoners were marched to the foot of the gallows to hear their sentences read again, this time by the provost marshal.

There were no speeches; the convicts did not shout the usual farewells. In an eerie silence the men were dispatched, in turn and without mishap, only the roll of drums, as each man mounted the ladder, broke the silence, and Leach, although he had witnessed many executions, found that the palms of his hands were moist as he watched. Beside him young John Ross was trembling, his face drained of color.

The sixth man, Hunt, who had turned King's evidence, was being triced up to the pikes. He was a big, powerfully built man but, Leach decided, studying his ashen face dispassionately, almost certainly a coward. His betrayal of his comrades proved that, and the first few lashes emphasized the fact. Hunt screamed as the tails of the cat bit into his flesh; he wept, crying out to the governor for mercy, and the convicts broke their silence. They yelled their derision, catcalling, mocking the writhing man as, to the beat of a single drum, the drum major called out the strokes, his voice harsh with barely suppressed anger.

John Ross grasped Leach's arm. "My—my father,

Jeremiah . . . do you see him? He's—oh, my God, he's weeping!"

They were tears of humiliation, Jeremiah Leach saw . . . and they were still coursing, unchecked, down the commandant's bony face when, after Private Hunt had received two hundred fifty of his seven hundred lashes, he was cut down, unconscious, his back flayed to a hideous, bleeding pulp.

The convicts were still jeering when, a hand on the hilt of his sword, Major Ross turned his own back on the ugly scene and stalked away.

Private Robert Sibley, dismissed at last from the parade, went stumbling blindly to the beach where the fight with Bulmore had taken place. Still clutching his musket in shaking hands, he crossed the sandy foreshore and walked, with only a momentary hesitation, into the water. It rose to his knees, to his waist, to his shoulders and still he went on, sobbing now in an inarticulate prayer for forgiveness. Joe had not implicated him, had given him his life, but the gift was worthless and he no longer wanted it. They had hanged his comrades, they would flog Joe Hunt to death—or cripple him if they did not kill him.

The blue calm waters of Cockle Cove, lit to transient gold by the sunset, closed over his head, and Rob Sibley did not struggle. He was long dead before the first of the cruising sharks started to tear at his limp, scarlet-clad body.

CHAPTER XVIII

A major battle between a party of convicts and a
large body of natives in the vicinity of Botany Bay
followed hard on the heels of the execution of the
marines. A handful of convict survivors fled back to
the camp to tell a tale of unprovoked attack made on
them by the Indians, and although the governor
doubted the truth of this claim, Captain Meredith
was sent out with a well-armed party to bring in the
dead and wounded.

The result was an order to the entire settlement—
only the officers being excepted—that any association
with the Indians was prohibited . . . an order which
Jenny unwittingly disobeyed on the very day that it
was brought into force.

She had taken to roaming the beaches to the east
of the cove in search of shellfish during the heat of

the day, when work in the garden was suspended, and had turned her enterprise to a not unprofitable concern. Her afternoon wanderings had the added advantage of providing solitude, since she went alone and seldom encountered anyone else at that hour.

The beach she frequented was hemmed in by towering rocks, and she enjoyed wading thigh-deep in the cool water and clambering over the rocks to search the pools for crabs and cockles. There was no surf, just a wide expanse of golden sand set against a backcloth of tree-grown cliffs, beneath whose shadow she could stretch out peacefully to rest when her collecting basket was full. The ever-present threat of starvation still hung over the settlement; rations of salt meat, flour, and rice had been cut and cut again, and any contribution to their depleted larder was, she knew, eagerly welcomed by her fellow garden-workers.

On this particular day she had garnered a basketful of edible crabs and one or two small fish and was making her way back across the sand, well satisfied with her catch, when to her dismay she saw a native canoe rounding the point. There were four men in the frail craft and they paddled rapidly into the cove, beached their canoe, and, armed with fish spears, started to clamber over the rocks as she had done, only a few minutes before, to search the pools for stranded fish. She was in shadow but they observed her footprints, on the damp sand, and two of them came running towards her at a rapid jog trot, following unerringly the trail she had left.

Jenny cowered back against a cleft in the rock, her heart pounding as she sought some means of eluding them, but they saw her. One of them called out to the others, and all four of them came to encircle her, cutting off any chance of escape with their menacing spears. It was then that she noticed the missing joint on the hand of one of the two who had tracked her down—the top joint of his right thumb had been severed—and, looking up into his dark, pockmarked face, she remembered the man who had given her food when she had been a prisoner on Pinchgut.

"Baneelon!" she exclaimed, in glad relief. And his companion was older, a stocky gray-beard, whose face also bore the telltale marks of smallpox. "Colbee!"

The expressions of both men relaxed in wide, flashing smiles. Baneelon stepped forward and pointed to her wrists, indicating by signs the chains she had worn when they had last encountered her, and Jenny echoed their smiles, no longer in the least afraid. They had shown her kindness, and she had supposed it a dream . . . a nightmare.

"Jen-nee!" the gray-beard cried after searching his memory. "Jen-nee—*dee-in*!"

Their companions were introduced, with voluble explanations that were quite unintelligible to Jenny, but all seemed friendly, and when, a little later, a smaller canoe entered the cove, containing a man and two women, they too were brought across the beach so that they could make themselves known to the white stranger. One of the women, young and shy, who gave her name as Barangeroo, appeared to be Baneelon's wife. They inspected Jenny's basket and shook their heads over it, clearly considering her catch a poor one, and Baneelon motioned her to accompany him to the edge of the cove.

Poised on a rock, he bit into the leathery contents of a cockleshell, chewed it and then spat it, with accurate aim, into the clear water below him, his fish gig held ready to strike. The handle of the weapon was of wood, Jenny saw, its prongs—three in number —barbed with what looked like bone. When some fish darted out from the shelter of the rocks to snap up the bait that had been offered, Baneelon, choosing his target carefully, plunged the barbed prongs into its swiftly moving body and withdrew it, vainly struggling, to gasp its life away at her feet.

He repeated this display with effortless skill, going from pool to pool, collecting cockles for bait as he moved nimbly across the rocks. Sometimes, if he had to throw his gig at a distant target, he let it drop into the water, and when it floated to the surface with the fish impaled on its prongs, he seated himself, cross-legged, and retrieved both prey and weapon with a long stick, hauling them in and taking great care not to wet his mud-daubed body in the process.

In the meantime the two women put out in their canoe to fish in the deeper water, not with gigs but with hook and line, and observing that they had had some success, the other men put out in their own canoe and, darting past the women's flimsy craft, proceeded to spear fish from a running shoal, to which, it seemed to Jenny, only their keen hunters' instinct could have led them.

Dusk was approaching when both canoes returned to the beach, and Jenny prepared to take her leave, but both Colbee and Baneelon motioned her to remain. The women carried a smoldering branch from their canoe to where she sat, set it down, and, feeding it with dry grass and twigs torn from a nearby eucalyptus tree, constructed a cooking fire, onto which they threw half their catch, uncleaned and with skins intact. After a while they poked out the slightly charred fish, tore off the skins with their teeth after rubbing away the outer scales, gutted each with a shell-bladed knife and returned them to the embers of the fire to finish cooking.

Despite the primitive method of preparation, the result was delicious, but it was dark before they had finished eating, and when Jenny began to show signs of anxiety, pointing in the direction of the settlement to indicate that she must return, they did not try to detain her. Colbee and the older of the two women went with her for part of the way, and when they finally parted from her, it was in friendship, their gestures clearly suggesting that they would welcome her return.

Back in her own small camp, Jenny did not tell the others of her adventure, and it was a week before she went back to the cove, to find it as devoid of life as it normally was. Next day, however, Baneelon and his wife made their appearance and, as before, permitted her to accompany them in their fishing. Their efforts were unsuccessful, and they abandoned them after barely an hour, instead going ashore to search for other game. A strange-looking animal was unearthed by Baneelon in the tall, spiny grass on top of the headland. He located its nest—a circle of grass lined with moss and downy fur—and secured the ratlike inhabitant by impaling it on the point of his spear.

Retracing their steps to the cove, Barangeroo fetched the smoldering branch, as before, from a pile of earth in the bow of the canoe. The fire was lit and the rat-like animal's carcass flung, hair and all, into the leaping flames.

"*Wurra*," Baneelon said, gesturing to it with satisfaction. "*Bud-ye-ree!*"

Unable to comprehend, Jenny smiled back at him

and then watched as Barangeroo neatly skinned and
gutted the half-cooked carcass as she had done with
the fish. To complete the cooking, she coated it with
damp mud and thrust it back into the embers, piling
these around and on top of the quickly hardening
clay. When it was done, a few taps with a club parted
the clay, and the perfectly cooked meal was ready.
Fresh meat had become a delicacy now seldom enjoyed by any of the settlers, and Jenny did full justice
to the repast, watched with indulgent amusement by
the two aborigines as she smacked her lips, as they
did, when it was finished.

From then on, defying the order, she went daily to
the cove, and two or three times a week, Colbee and
Baneelon came to visit her, with their wives and
other members of their tribe. To any strangers she
was invariably described, with expressive signs and
gestures, as the one who had been chained, Baneelon
making a great pantomime of it, groaning, rolling
his eyes, and pointing to Pinchgut Island, which
instantly won her the sympathy of the newcomers.

Jenny learned much from them, from the fashion-
ing of their fish gigs to the way the women spun the
bark of a particular shrub into fishing lines. Lines
and hooks were made by the women; spears, gigs,
shields, and clubs by the men, but both sexes used the
inside of their thighs or the soles of their feet as work-
boards, standing or seated cross-legged in order to do
so. Tree bark, branches, leaves, and rushes served
them for a multitude of purposes; trailing vines took
the place of rope; shells were used in the making of
knives, fish hooks, and drinking vessels. They made
their canoes and huts of bark and fashioned primitive
but effective birdtraps of reeds and interlaced twigs,
and ate, with apparent enjoyment, snakes and a va-

riety of insects—caterpillars being regarded as a particular delicacy.

Like the newly arrived white settlers, they were almost always hungry; they took what their barren land provided and somehow made it suffice by dint of moving on when the food supply in any one locality was exhausted. They had never attempted to grow crops, and Jenny's efforts to show them how met with polite interest but eventual indifference, Colbee making it plain to her that his tribe would be long gone before any seeds they planted were ready to harvest.

Her association with them came to an unexpectedly abrupt end with the advent of colder weather. She had noticed a vague restlessness among them, but communication was still difficult, although she had learned a few words of their language, and on the last day of April, when she went to the beach, it was to find only Colbee and Baneelon there. Colbee gave her a fish gig and, with smiles and gestures, gave her to understand that it was a parting present. They were leaving the area but would see her again when the warm weather returned.

Standing on the rocky headland of the cove, Jenny watched them paddle away, conscious of a strange sadness. She raised her hand high above her head in farewell, glimpsed an answering wave from Baneelon, and then, hearing the sound of approaching footsteps behind her, turned to find herself facing Lieutenant Leach.

Jeremiah Leach had come off guard and, after a busy night that had tried his temper sorely, was looking forward to breaking his fast when the woman convict sidled up to him, addressing him by name.

He recognized her as the woman who had given

evidence against Jenny Taggart, but affected ignorance, brushing her impatiently aside. She persisted, calling after him in whining tones, and finally, realizing that the men of the guard were watching with avid curiosity and straining their ears to hear what was being said, he motioned her to follow him to his tent. Once there he kept her cooling her heels outside while he washed and shaved, and then, when his servant had served him with the miserable mess of ship's biscuit soaked in broth—all that was left of his week's ration—he shouted to her to come in and state her business.

"I'm Hannah Jones, sir," the woman announced. "You remembers me, don't yer?"

Leach took a lengthy draft of porter and nodded. Her eyes, he saw, were fixed enviously on the bowl of congealing broth on the table in front of him, but the fact that she was hungry failed to arouse his sympathy. Damn it, he thought, everyone in the entire settlement was hungry, including himself—this unpleasant hag was no exception. Too idle to work, in all probability, and too old and ill-favored to earn an extra crust the way most of her wanton kind contrived to do—by selling themselves.

"Well?" he snapped irritably. "What do you want?"

"To do you a service, Mister Leach," the woman answered.

"What sort of service?" Leach sneered, wishing now that he had sent her packing. He spooned the tasteless mess of biscuit into his mouth, pleased when he saw her pass her tongue over her lips and then turn her head away, as if unable to watch him eating. But she stood her ground and did not go away. Instead, she asked, lowering her voice, "You ain't forgot the girl Jenny Taggart, 'ave yer, sir?"

Leach said nothing, but his interest quickened. Indeed he had not forgotten Jenny Taggart and did not require the recital he was treated to of the girl's obstinate refusal to admit that she had been the cause of Private Bulmore's death . . . a refusal which had also angered Major Ross a great deal.

"I was there, Mister Leach," Hannah stated. "I seen what she done wiv' me own eyes. An' we was shipmates, so ter speak, in the *Friendship* . . . a real bad 'un, she is, wiv' a hellish temper, as I've good cause ter know. But she looks that innercent, she's able ter get away wiv' it see? An'—"

"Come to the point, woman!" Leach bade her. "I've been on duty all night and I'm tired."

But Hannah Jones was not to be hurried. "Got you inter some sort o' trouble when she was in the *Charlotte* too, didn't she? Leastways, that's what they say. An' they say as you wanted her but *she* was wantin' ter get 'erself wed ter one o' yer lobsterbacks. An' he got 'isself a bloody back fer hittin' yer."

Leach reddened with embarrassment. God, was that infernal story known to the convicts—known and talked about? He said thickly, "I've never heard anything so ridiculous in my life! Where the devil did you get hold of such a pack of lies?"

"Lies, is it, sir? Oh, or'right, let it pass. But I was thinkin' . . . s'pose Taggart was breakin' the governor's orders, breakin' 'em regular, an' I knew she was, why . . . I'd be right ter report 'er, wouldn't I, sir?"

Jeremiah Leach shrugged, with well-simulated indifference. His cheeks were still burning, and the woman, he knew, had noticed it. "Report her, of course," he managed, "but not to me. The provost marshal or the judge advocate or the blasted watch might be concerned—I'm not. So off with you and stop wasting my time."

Hannah ignored his attempt to dismiss her. "Associatin' wiv' them Indians, Taggart is," she asserted, and satisfied that at last she had gained Leach's full attention, she gave him a detailed account of the girl's doings in the cove. Having described its precise location, she went on vindictively, "Goes there every arfternoon, she does—givin' aht as she's fishing. An' so she is, Mister Leach, along o' the Indians. Eats wiv' 'em, too . . . I know, 'cause I followed 'er, to see what she was up to."

"Then report her to the judge advocate. What she does isn't my affair," Leach said, but even to his own ears, the denial of his interest lacked conviction.

Hannah's pinched lips twisted into a smile. She took a small object from beneath her dress, removed its wrapping of leaves, and laid a pretty jeweled locket on the table for Leach's inspection.

"I fahn'd this, sir," she told him. "Belongs ter Taggart, it does . . . an' she sets great store by it. Must 'ave lost it, running around them pools wiv' the Indians. Or maybe one o' them tried ter steal it. I reckon as she'd give you 'most anythin' you wanted ter get this locket back and—not so fast, Mister Leach!" Leach made to pick up the locket, puzzled by the fact that it contained a small, faded strip of blue ribbon instead of the usual portrait miniature, but Hannah was before him, her bony fingers closing about it possessively. "Got a price, this 'as," she informed him, still smiling.

"All right—how much?" he asked harshly. "It's liquor you want, I suppose—well, I've only got issue rum."

"That'll do nicely, sir," Hannah assured him. She

drove a hard bargain but eventually she departed with what she had asked for, leaving Leach with the locket and the power—if he decided to use it—to bring Jenny Taggart to heel.

He lay down on his camp bed, but sleep eluded him, and after eating the usual miserable midday meal in the officers' mess tent, he set off for the cove, bringing two marines with him as escort. His original intention had been to go alone, but he thought better of it—for one thing, the natives might attack him if he went unattended, and for another, he would need witnesses to Jenny Taggart's misbehavior if any charges were to be brought against her.

He and his escort reached the cove in time to see that Hannah Jones's claim was well founded. From the cover of a clump of trees they watched the two Indians land from their canoe, saw them approach the girl waiting for them on the beach, and after a brief but obviously friendly exchange, witnessed their departure. When he had satisfied himself that they were unlikely to return and that there were no other natives in the vicinity, Leach ordered his escort back to camp and himself descended cautiously to the rocky shore. The girl was standing with her hand raised in farewell to the occupants of the swiftly moving canoe and she did not hear his approach.

Seeing her standing there, he felt all the old attraction she had had for him return. She was much better looking than she had appeared on board the *Charlotte*, despite the decorous clothing she had worn then. Now, for all she was clad in ragged sacking, she had the appearance of some young water nymph, rising from the sea to ensnare him, and Jeremiah Leach felt his heart quicken its beat. Gone was the prison pallor, gone the demurely downcast eyes—

with her hair flying loose and her skin tanned to a warm golden brown, the little waif from the *Charlotte* had become an infinitely desirable young woman.

He drew in his breath sharply and, momentarily forgetful of the underlying reason for his presence here, he said her name softly, almost with reverence, and not in the harsh tones he normally used to the convict women.

"Jenny! Jenny, you are lovely. . . ."

She turned to face him, dismayed but not afraid.

"Mister Leach . . . what are you doing here? Why have you come?"

"I came to look for you," Leach admitted. On impulse, still a trifle bemused by the change in her, he took the locket from the breast pocket of his jacket and held it out to her. "And to give this back to you. You lost it, didn't you?"

Jenny's eyes lit with glad surprise. "Yes, I did. That is—" The joy faded, to be succeeded by an expression he could not fathom, at once wary and somehow resentful. "So that's how you found me! You got this from Hannah, didn't you—from Hannah Jones? I suppose she must have followed me here."

Leach did not trouble to deny either assumption. "The woman told me she had found it on this beach. She claimed you had dropped it—running around with some Indians, she said. You've been associating with the Indians, haven't you?"

"Yes," Jenny confirmed. She offered no explanation, and Leach decided to press home his advantage.

"It is strictly forbidden for convicts to have any association with the Indians," he reminded her. "Surely you know that?"

"Yes, I know it. But I was doing no harm. I did

not steal from them or cheat them—they have been my friends, they and their wives. They—"

"Nevertheless," Leach put in sternly, "I could have you arrested and punished for it. You could be put in irons, banished to Norfolk Island—even flogged, Jenny, if I were so minded. But I'm not." He put out a hand to touch her cheek, then let it fall, his fingers gripping her shoulder, drawing her closer to him. She did not resist, but her slim body was stiff and rigid, her head held high in defiance.

"May I have my locket, if you please, sir?" she asked with cool politeness. "You said you had come to give it back to me."

"Ah, but not for nothing, my girl!" He laughed with rueful amusement. "Damn it, the bauble cost me a week's rum ration! The miserable hag who found it refused to part with it for less."

"She did not find it—she stole it from me," Jenny protested. "And it is mine, Mister Leach. The only thing of value that I have ever owned."

He hesitated, impressed for no reason that he could have explained, and then gave it to her, forcing a smile.

"Then take it, as a gift from me."

"Thank you." She took it from him. With a length of native-made fishing line deftly threaded through the eyelet hole, she secured the pretty trinket about her neck, tucking it out of sight beneath the coarse sacking of her dress, so that it fell into the hollow between her two firm, shapely young breasts.

Jeremiah Leach watched her, his pulses racing. He had taken several different women on board the *Charlotte*, and there had been others since their landing, whores from the camp, whose shamelessness had disgusted him once the desires of the flesh had been assuaged. Diseased creatures, many of them, who had walked the London streets since childhood, heavy drinkers, whose breath stank of the liquor they had consumed . . . some he had only beaten and obtained his satisfaction thus, without the need to bed them. But this girl was different. She was clean and healthy, her skin smelling of seawater and warm from the sun, her body lissome and strong. Clearly she was not of his class and could not be treated as such, but she had good manners, dignity, and courage. It was rumored that she had a hellion's temper—indeed, the wretched Bulmore had found that out to his cost, but . . . he licked at lips that had suddenly gone dry and reached out for her, his whole body tense with the lust to possess her.

"Am I to have no reward, Jenny?" he demanded hoarsely. "For the locket, for not reporting you—not even a kiss, to show your gratitude?"

She eluded his grasp, wary as some small creature of the wild facing a predator, and there was a native fish gig in her hand, he saw, held firmly—not threateningly, but there just the same, a barrier between them.

"You want more than a kiss, Mister Leach," she told him wryly. "And I am not a whore. Please . . . leave me be."

She was poised for instant flight; remembering Bulmore's discomfiture at her hands, Leach attempted blandishments.

"An officer's woman enjoys many privileges, Jenny . . . and I need a woman, to cook and care for my house when it is built. I'd see you didn't go without —Lord, that would be better than grubbing in that infernal garden of yours, wouldn't it? Living with whores in a filthy hut? What have you to lose . . . if you please me, I'll keep you as my woman, I swear I will. Hell, you're not a virgin, are you? What about Hawley? You—" Jenny took flight then, and cursing furiously, Jeremiah Leach went after her.

He brought her down among the rocks at the entrance to the cove, after a breathless chase. The fish gig struck him a glancing blow on the thigh before he could wrench it from her, and the pain from the slight wound it inflicted inflamed more than it hurt him. With his fists he beat her brutally into submission and, when she lay sobbing and at his mercy, he tore the sacking dress from her shrinking body and took his will of her with calculated cruelty, astonished but not ill-pleased to learn, as he did so, that she had indeed been virgin. . . .

It was almost dusk when Leach returned to the camp. He washed, changed his shirt and boots, refreshed himself with a glass of brandy, and then made his way to the tented office shared by the judge advocate and the provost marshal. It was better to be sure than sorry, he told himself—there was no knowing what that little vixen would accuse him of, when she regained her senses.

With the air of one regretfully undertaking a distasteful duty, he made a formal report to Midshipman Brewer.

Captain Collins, who had listened in silence, looked up from the papers piled in front of him when Leach came to the end of his recital. "The Taggart girl again," he observed. "That's odd . . . but you say you have witnesses, in addition to the girl's own admission?"

Leach nodded. "Yes—two of our fellows were with me. They'll confirm what I've told you. And—er—" he hesitated, sensing that Collins was not entirely convinced. "The girl tried to tell me that the Indians had offered her friendship, but as you'll see for yourselves if you call her in for questioning, her appearance doesn't bear out any such claim. It looked to me as if she'd been attacked by them—not that she's likely to admit that, of course. You know what these women are—whores and liars, the lot of them. But I imagine even the most depraved would draw the line at an Indian, don't you?"

His implication was plain, and David Collins's dark brows lifted in surprise. "According to Watkin Tench, who is rapidly becoming an expert on Indian behavior, they're not even remotely interested in our women," he objected mildly. "And certainly H. E.'s chap Arabanoo never looks twice at them. It's something to do with body odor, Tench says—we repel them as much as they repel us. So I honestly don't think that would be a reason for them to attack the girl."

"Well, she had one of their fish spears," Leach suggested hastily. "She probably stole it and they turned on her."

"That's possible," Collins conceded. "As you know it's the reason for the ban—the convicts *will* steal. We can't allow them to steal from the Indians if we're ever to get on good terms with them—and the governor's determined that we shall. With every stalk of wheat worth its weight in gold to us, he's afraid the Indians may try to burn our crops if the convicts make trouble."

"What will happen to the girl?" Leach asked curiously.

"If she has been associating with them, you mean? Well, she'll probably be sent to Norfolk Island—that's the present policy. Mister King needs more workers, and we don't need troublemakers." Collins nodded, in dismissal. "All right, Leach—thank you. We'll look into the matter."

"Where is the girl, Mister Leach?" Brewer inquired with unexpected sharpness. "You brought her back, did you not?"

"No, I—that is. . . ." Jeremiah Leach had not anticipated the question, and for a moment, he was disconcerted by it. But the Indians would be blamed for any injuries the wretched girl had suffered, he consoled himself, and he shrugged with calculated indifference. "She ran away from me and hid among the rocks. No doubt she'll make her way back before tap-too—she wasn't badly hurt."

When he had gone, Brewer exclaimed explosively, "I do not like that young man! And I don't trust him —if you'll pardon the vulgarity, sir—further than I can spit."

Collins eyed him thoughtfully. "Why not, Henry?"

"He has a very nasty reputation, especially with the women," Brewer asserted. "And he's a deuced poor liar. I don't believe the half of what he's just told us—the Taggart girl is one of the decent ones. Respectable and hardworking. She—"

"*Respectable?*" the judge advocate challenged dubiously. "I didn't think any of them were! And what about that business with the marine she went for with a hoe?"

"He was armed and thieving from her garden."

"All right but—"

"She's not a whore," Brewer said, with quiet conviction. "I hear things in my job, Captain Collins. The women who work with her in that garden think the world of Jenny Taggart, and they're a hard-bitten lot for the most part, not easily fooled. The worst they

say of her is that she has a fiery temper when she's
provoked—and a saint would be provoked ten times
a day in this place!"

"You like the girl, don't you?" Collins suggested.
"Wasn't she the one you rescued from Pinchgut a
while ago?"

Henry Brewer inclined his graying head. "Aye,
that's so. And she spun me some yarn about the natives
then—said two of them had brought her food. I didn't
believe it, told her she'd had a nightmare in fact,
because it's out of character for them, isn't it? But
then we never chained a woman on Pinchgut before
or since, did we? Maybe they *did* take pity on her and
she's seen them again."

"The same ones? That would be something of a
coincidence, would it not?"

"Well, maybe it taught her not to be afraid of
them, as most of the convicts are. If she made the
right approach, she could have got on friendly terms
with them, couldn't she?"

Captain Collins spread his hands helplessly. "And
landed herself in serious trouble as a result, Henry!
Because if she *has* been associating with the damned
Indians, she'll have to be sent to Norfolk Island.
H. E.'s quite adamant on that score—the convicts are
under no circumstances to have any dealings with
them. And if she tried to steal from them, as Leach
suggests, then I fear your little paragon will be in the
next batch the *Supply* takes to work for King." He
sighed, "I'd better question her, I suppose. But not
tonight; it's been a long day—how about tomorrow
morning?"

"I'll bring her in, sir," Brewer promised.

CHAPTER XIX

Long after tap-too had sounded, Jenny stumbled painfully back to the settlement, conscious of a humiliation so deep that she knew she could not face the others. She waited, hidden in the trees until, their evening meal over, the women started to make their way to the main camp, the sound of their voices—unbearably cheerful—drifting back to her hiding place.

Even when these sounds had faded into silence, she remained where she was, hoping that Melia might fall asleep, so that she could enter the hut they shared unheard and unquestioned, but finally pain and thirst overcame her scruples and she staggered dazedly across the moonlit clearing, seeking the only sanctuary she knew.

Melia was awake and anxious. "Jenny!" she ex-

claimed. "I've been worried about you. Sergeant
Jenkins has been asking for you and—" she broke off,
glimpsing in the dim light Jenny's bruised and bleeding face and the torn dress she was endeavoring to
hold about her. "Oh, God in heaven—what's happened to you?" She was on her feet, eyes wide with
horror. "Jenny, those natives—the ones you've been
fishing with—did *they* do this to you?"

Jenny shook her head wordlessly. She tried to pick
up the water pitcher, but her hands were shaking,
and Melia took it from her and held it to her lips.
When her thirst was at last assuaged, the older girl
helped her to discard the torn and bloodstained dress
and fetched a tattered shawl to wrap around her.

"Who, if it wasn't the Indians?" she asked, and
then, catching sight of the locket hanging from Jenny's
neck by its length of native-made fishing line, "Surely
it wasn't *Hannah*?"

"No, it wasn't Hannah. I. . . ." Jenny told her the
truth, in a broken, unhappy voice. "No one else is
to know," she whispered urgently. "No one except
you, Melia. And you're not to tell anyone—promise
me you won't. Please—I want your word."

"Very well," Melia agreed reluctantly. "But you
will report him, surely? You—"

"I couldn't bear the shame," Jenny said and clung
to her, sobbing and perilously near to breaking point.

"But that swine of a Leach will go unpunished if
you say nothing, Jenny," Melia objected.

"I don't care. The Lord can punish him. But if he
ever touches me again, I shall kill him . . . even if they
hang me for it!"

Melia looked down into the girl's ravaged face, believing her. She touched the bruises. "How will you
explain these? You cannot hide them."

"I fell," Jenny told her. Fiercely she bit back the tears. "I fell from the rocks when I was fishing—that's what I shall say. And you must bear me out, Melia."

Melia sighed. "And what of Sergeant Jenkins?"

"What of him?"

"I told you he was asking for you. Jenny, his time expires next month, and he's applying for a grant of land, as a free settler. He wants to apply also for permission to marry you and—"

"Did he tell you that?" Jenny's voice was low and full of pain.

"Yes," Melia said pityingly. "And he told me that he was getting over his wife's death. It hit him hard, but he's getting over it and he wants to fulfill her dying wish and marry you. It's a wonderful opportunity for you—a chance to be free, Jenny, and safe from swine like Lieutenant Leach. You—"

"I can't marry him now," Jenny returned. "Not after . . . what Leach did, not without telling him. And I couldn't tell him, I . . . couldn't tell him, Melia, if my life depended on it. And besides," she added with a hint of her old spirit, "I'm sure he'd much rather marry a woman nearer his own age, like Missus Davis. He's spent all his free time with her since Olwyn died, hasn't he?"

"She kept him supplied with liquor," Melia said dryly. "He's hardly been sober since his wife's death. It takes some men that way . . . didn't you know?" She dropped to her knees at Jenny's side and started gently to bathe her face, wiping off the bloodstains with a cloth wrung out in water. "And *I* spend my time patching you up, Jenny! I'll get some grease for these bruises, though I'm afraid it won't help much. That Leach is . . . God forgive him, he must be an animal to have used you so!"

Jenny shivered as the nightmare memories returned.
But she said nothing, her fingers closing convulsively
around the locket with its precious scrap of faded blue
ribbon at her breast. How long had it been, she wondered dully, since her father had bought her the
bonnet trimmed with that ribbon? How long since
Ned Munday had given her the locket as she worked
in Doll Prunty's kitchen at the Three Fools, with its
appetizing smells and a sirloin sizzling on the spit?

So long—she smiled wryly to herself—so long that
she could even think kindly of Ned, although it was
on his account that she was exiled here. Ned, for all
he was a common pickpocket, would not have used
her as Lieutenant Leach had done.

Melia noticed the smile and, unaware of the reason
for it, marveled at her courage. "Jenny," she urged.
"You don't have to tell Sergeant Jenkins anything.
Marry him for the advantages it will bring you."

"And if I should have a child," Jenny retorted
bitterly. "Could I expect that good and kindly man
to father Leach's bastard? Without even telling him?"

"There's no certainty that you will have a child."

"There's no certainty that I shall not, however
little I want it. Please, Melia, don't speak of what's
happened anymore," Jenny pleaded. "I fell from the
rocks when I was fishing—that's all anybody need
know."

"All right," Melia agreed. She deposited a light kiss
on Jenny's cheek, her own eyes filled with tears. "At
least," she offered comfortingly, "you can rest assured
that foul young swine of a Leach will not contradict
you. He dare not."

"Yes." Jenny lay back wearily and closed her eyes. "I
can be sure of that, thank God!"

But next day, when Provost Marshal Brewer came

to take her to the Government House marquee, it became evident that her hopes had been unfounded. Sick with disgust at Lieutenant Leach's perfidy, she submitted to being questioned concerning her association with the aborigines. She admitted this freely and made no counterclaims or accusations, a mixture of pride and shame setting a guard on her tongue.

Captain Collins was stern but not unkind, Midshipman Brewer openly sympathetic, urging her to tell the truth and seeming, despite her denials, to sense what the truth really was. Jenny did not yield to his persuasion, and even the threat of banishment to Norfolk Island failed to frighten her into changing her story.

"I did not steal from the Indians, sir," she told the judge advocate with quiet insistence. "They were my friends. Colbee and Baneelon and their wives taught me to fish and to hunt. They gave me the fish gig as a parting gift, because they're going away until the winter is over. And they didn't attack me. I fell from the rocks when I was fishing."

Neither of her interrogators could make her admit more than this, and finally they let her go. The tent flap fell shut behind her, and Collins expelled his breath in a frustrated sigh.

"Well, do you still believe her, Henry?" he demanded.

Henry Brewer frowned. "I'll put it like this, Captain Collins—I believe everything she said concerning her association with the Indians. I believe she *did* make friends with them . . . dammit, she even knows their names! But I don't reckon she's telling the truth about how she sustained her injuries, and by the same token I don't reckon Mister Leach is either."

Collins was silent as the implication of his words

sank in. "If you mean what I think you mean," he began, "then—"

"We'd never be able to prove it, sir," Brewer returned with a shrug. "And the girl doesn't want us to, for reasons of her own . . . pride, probably. I told you she was respectable. Maybe Norfolk Island will be the best place for her, for her own sake, even if she doesn't deserve to be sent there."

"Perhaps," Collins said. "But there's a fresh complication—it came in this morning." He hunted through his papers. "Yes, here we are. This is an application to the governor for permission to marry the Taggart girl. It's from Sergeant Thomas Jenkins of the Marine Corps, whose term of service expires this month. He intends to settle and he's applying for a grant of land. He's a widower—lost his wife at Christmas from a disease of the lungs. They both came out in the *Charlotte* with the Taggart girl and, it seems, they meant to adopt her if they could, before the wife died."

Brewer pursed his lips in a silent whistle of surprise. "Well, he can't marry her if she's banished to Norfolk Island, can he?"

"No," the judge advocate conceded, "he can't. But it will be up to the governor to decide—I can only submit the application and put the facts, as I know them, before him."

"Including Mister Leach's accusation?"

"And her denial, Henry. She denies that the Indians attacked her."

"Yes, sir, but—"

Collins repeated his sigh, with some exasperation. "She has made no accusations against Mister Leach, has she? And suppose you're wrong—suppose she did sustain those injuries at the hands of the Indians?"

"She would not be here," Brewer retorted. "Six full grown Indians and one little white girl of barely eighteen . . . she'd be dead as mutton, sir. She—" He was interrupted by a tumult of voices outside the marquee, and the marine sentry came rushing in to shout the news, almost inarticulate in his excitement.

"Sir—a ship's been sighted! Will you inform the governor, sir? They say she's the *Sirius* returned at last . . . thanks be to God, sir, she's safe!"

It was, indeed, the *Sirius*, and the entire settlement gathered to watch her work her way slowly into her accustomed anchorage.

Governor Phillip stood on the slight eminence in front of the Government House building with members of his staff. His seaman's eye, aided by a glass, was the first to see that her figurehead—a scarlet-and-gold-painted effigy of the Duke of Berwick—had been carried away and that her bowsprit was jury-rigged. As she came nearer even the uninitiated watchers remarked that she was lying very low in the water and that she answered sluggishly to her helm.

"Can she be overladen, sir?" Augustus Alt, the elderly government surveyor, asked curiously, shading short-sighted eyes from the glare reflected by the water.

The governor, without taking the glass from his own eye, gave him a positive denial. "No, not overladen, Mister Alt. Her timbers are strained—she's taking in water and her pumps are going. Captain Hunter, I fear, has had a difficult passage, but, please God, he will have brought us the means to prolong our survival for a few more months. And perhaps he may have news, garnered at the Cape, of storeships on their way to us from England."

Captain Hunter, hastening ashore, did indeed bring

this hoped-for news in mail picked up in Capetown. Sir Evan Nepean informed Governor Phillip that a man-of-war, H.M.S. *Guardian*, commanded by Lieutenant Riou of the Royal Navy, was being fitted out and might be expected to reach Sydney by the end of the year, carrying all the government supplies and livestock for which Phillip had asked.

"I was given to understand, sir," Hunter said, "that Sir Joseph Banks is to supervise the loading of garden plants and seeds and that the *Guardian* will carry a score of convict artisans and husbandmen, chosen particularly to meet your needs. The livestock will include deer and rabbits, as well as domestic animals, and the government will be sending supplies of medicines and clothing, in addition to tools, to replace all deficiencies."

The *Sirius* herself had brought four months' supply of flour for the hungry settlers, some livestock, and a year's provisions for her own ship's company . . . but, as the governor had feared, she had had a nightmare passage from the Cape.

Seated before a glowing fire in the recently completed brick-finished reception room of Government House and enjoying the luxury of tea, served in china cups from a silver teapot, the *Sirius*'s commander told of her narrow escape from disaster in a gale off Van Dieman's Land.

"We left the Cape on the twentieth of February, after fifty-one days in the port," John Hunter went on after describing the earlier part of the voyage at some length. "We followed the course of the fleet under your command, Governor, sailing southeasterly, but from the third day we ran into gale-force winds and heavy seas. . . ." He went into details, quoting from his charts and reporting the damage his ship had sustained to her masts and spars in the icy southern latitudes, constantly assailed by slashing squalls and threatened by the close proximity of enormous bergs.

With her bowsprit sprung and her figurehead carried away, she had been leaking badly when she sighted the coast of Van Dieman's Land and ran for shelter in Storm Bay.

Phillip gripped his hand warmly. "Rest assured that the people of this colony will be forever indebted to you, my dear John. Had the *Sirius* been lost, I do not believe there would be many of us left to greet the *Guardian*'s arrival at this year's end."

Hunter eyed him searchingly. "Are matters so bad then?"

The governor bowed his head. "We brought stores for two years with us, as you know . . . and they are well nigh exhausted."

"You've made progress with your building, though."

"Yes," Phillip agreed. "But that, too, is a miracle. A few good men make it possible. And I have hopes of the farm at Rose Hill—the excellent Dodd is saying that it will yield two hundred bushels of wheat, as well as maize and barley, when the time comes to harvest. But that will not be until December, alas. However, we're building a launch, which should be completed before then and will serve to carry supplies to and fro—including, God willing, our wheat. But we can't use it for food, John—it must be preserved for next season's sowing."

"I observed some gardens in the cove looking well," Hunter said.

"They require constant toil. The women led by the Taggart girl have done wonders with their plot, but they, too, poor souls, lose the fruit of their labor to thieves. However"—the governor's lined, anxious face relaxed in a smile—"Philip King makes good progress on Norfolk Island, where the crops *do* grow and the livestock flourishes and breeds."

"It's not been easy for you, has it, sir?" Hunter offered with gruff sympathy.

"It will be easier, now that you are here," Phillip admitted. "I want to extend our exploration of the surrounding country, John—examine and chart Broken Bay and follow the two river branches we have found. We've named them the Hawksbury and the Nepean, respectively, but I suspect that, in fact, they are not two separate rivers but one and the same. Wait—let me show you the map Captain Tench has made. A useful fellow, Tench—he and young Arndell have been on several expeditions with me . . . 'parties of pleasure,' as our friend Ross chooses to call them!"

Hunter made an expressive grimace. "You sound as if he's still a thorn in your side."

"Major Ross? Yes, indeed he is." Governor Phillip found the map he had been searching for and, moving the teacups, spread it out on the table between them. He pointed, mentioning each place by the name it had been given and offering a brief but graphic description of its location and prospects. "We must find land that will grow crops—it's vital that we should. And those mountains"—his pointing finger rested on the outlines Tench had tentatively sketched in—"I named them the Carmarthen Mountains, at Tench's suggestion, needless to say. We haven't managed to get within miles of them yet but—I want to take a closer look, John, try to find a way round or over them if I can. This coastal land is poor . . . we can't graze cattle on it or even sheep. But, as one goes further inland, the soil improves quite dramatically, so who knows what pastoral plains we may find on the far side of the range?"

Hunter studied the sketch map with growing interest.

"With my ship laid up, I'll be more than happy to join you on one of the—what did Ross call them? Parties of pleasure, was it not? When were you thinking of going?"

"Toward the end of June," Phillip said. "It's heavy going in hot weather and the insects are murderous. But, by June or July, it should be quite pleasant. Young Dawes is keen to join us too. You know"—he frowned—"both Tench and I are still puzzled as to why Sir Joseph Banks recommended Botany Bay so highly as the site for our settlement. Damn it, John, in the whole area of the coast for more than thirty miles we have not found two hundred acres that can be cultivated!"

Hunter grunted in sympathy and continued to study the map. "How about the Indians if we strike inland, sir?" he asked. "Are they likely to give us trouble?"

The governor smiled. "We've tamed one—probably you noticed him when you first came in, sleeping by the fire? His name is Arabanoo, and I'm hoping to use him as an interpreter, in order to avoid trouble. Poor devils, there's been an outbreak of smallpox among them and it's taking a heavy toll. We've tried to help; I've sent our surgeons to aid them, but they are still afraid of us. And the convicts make matters worse. It's impossible to prevent them stealing—they take their canoes, their spears, even their food sometimes, and, of course, the Indians retaliate. I have had to issue an order forbidding the convicts to associate with them." He rose, stifling a yawn, and Hunter rolled up the map, preparatory to taking his leave.

"I'll start unloading your supplies tomorrow, sir," he promised. "And then, with your permission, I'll careen the ship and see just how badly she's been damaged."

Phillip held out his hand. "It's good to have you back, John," he said with deep sincerity. "You and the ship . . . thank God you returned safely!"

"Amen to that, sir," Hunter echoed gravely.

THE SECOND FLEET—1790

CHAPTER XX

Jenny leaned on her hoe and looked about her with conscious pride at the fruits of a year's labor.

Fresh green spears of wheat, planted only in February, were already showing six inches above the ground; barley and maize were still further advanced, and a week ago the clearing and clod-molding of four more acres of virgin land had been completed, ready for a late sowing of whatever seed the government store could provide.

It had been a hard year, she reflected, but not an unhappy one, either for Tom Jenkins or herself. Work brought its own measure of contentment, as well as forgetfulness of past sorrows . . . and hope for the future. She smiled, as her gaze went to the small wattle and daub cabin some three hundred yards from where she stood. Smoke was rising from its brick chimney, and its sturdy, bleached clay walls gleamed white in the strong rays of the afternoon sun, reminding her of the cottage at Long Wrekin, for all it was so much smaller. The cabin had been the first task facing them, and they had toiled and sweated to build it, aided by the two elderly male convicts assigned to Tom as laborers . . . as she herself had been.

Jenny drew in her breath sharply. The governor, in his wisdom, had been responsible for that. He had put her on probation, instead of having her banished to Norfolk Island for which, she supposed, she should have been grateful—although at the time she had felt only bitterness at the terms of her probation. She must work for her prospective husband for a year, she had been sternly told, after which—if her conduct had been good—he was to be permitted to marry her and his grant of a hundred thirty acres of land would then, on her account, be increased to a hundred fifty.

She had played her part, Jenny reflected. The land they had taken, two miles from the government farm at Rose Hill, was good land, but it had been thickly wooded. The two elderly convicts, although willing enough, were unskilled and, indeed, incapable of heavy manual labor, so that most of the work of clearing had fallen on Tom and herself. They had felled trees, grubbed out roots, burned the dead wood, and dug in the ashes. After that had come the backbreaking toil of hand-hoeing, which she had done at first with Tom and the two convicts, next—when the convicts were withdrawn—with Tom, and finally alone when Tom had been laid low by an attack of dysentery.

But now, at last, the year was over. Tom Jenkins's second application for permission to make her his wife had been approved; they were to be married next

Sunday, when Reverend Richard Johnson came to Rose Hill to conduct his twice-monthly service of worship there. And she could have no regrets, Jenny thought as she resumed her hoeing. There was no more gentle, kindly man than Tom, no one—not even Dr. Fry—whom she could trust so completely or care for as warmly.

His attitude toward her had, as always, been fatherly; he was as he had been on board the *Charlotte*, save that now, missing Olwyn and with his health still impaired, he was dependent on her, rather than she on him. But that, she told herself, was as it should be. She was young and strong and she owed him a great deal—not least for the manner in which, respecting her confidence, he had never once spoken of the man who had defiled her or tried to learn his identity after she had told him the sorry story and begged for his forebearance. It was possible that he had guessed; Tom was no fool, but if he harbored any suspicions concerning Lieutenant Leach, he had never voiced them to her.

His leisure time, such as it was, he spent with Edward Dodd, the stout superintendent of the government farm, and with former cronies of the Rose Hill guard, in whose company he enjoyed a drink and a game of draughts in their recently completed barrack. Occasionally—as he had today—he joined them on a kangaroo shoot, usually contriving to return with meat of some kind for the pot, which made a welcome change from a diet of home-grown vegetables, on which they now largely subsisted. The ration of salt beef and pork had been drastically reduced; the supply was almost exhausted, and although as new settlers they were entitled to draw rations from the government store, on principle Tom refused to do so.

"There are those with emptier bellies than ours, lass," he said. "Let them have what there is. So long as our land produces cabbages and potatoes and I can still aim a musket and bring down a bird or two, we'll not starve."

Jenny smothered a sigh and glanced skyward, estimating the time from the sun's position. Tom liked to hunt; it took less out of him than the monotonous labor on the land, but she wished that they still had the convict laborers . . . Mr. Dodd might, perhaps, agree to let them have old Reuben White back, once his own planting was completed. Reuben had been slow but he had been reliable and trustworthy and could be left in charge when she and Tom were both absent. Even here there were thieves; the vegetable garden was sufficient temptation for some of the Rose Hill men to walk two miles in order to possess themselves of a sack of potatoes or a few pumpkins, so that the place could not be left unguarded after dark. Penalties for stealing were as severe as ever, but this did not deter the hungry, and here, of course, there was no watch to apprehend them.

The sun sank lower, and she continued conscientiously working until it set. Tom would not be back until the small hours, she knew—the most successful kangaroo hunts took place just after dusk, and this one, involving about a score of men, intended to venture further afield than the smaller parties usually did, in the hope of a big bag and a feast on Sunday. Some of Tom's friends were planning a wedding breakfast for them—the men, of course, not the women. Jenny shouldered her hoe and started to walk toward the cabin, tears coming unbidden to ache in her throat.

To the wives of the other married marines, she was

an outcast, a convicted felon and, as such, unaccept-
able in their tight-knit circle to which—however exemplary her conduct, now or in the future—she
would, she knew, never be admitted. There were only
twenty-five of them, married to rank-and-file soldiers,
but they bore the stamp of respectable womanhood,
whereas she was labeled a whore and worse. Jenny
wiped the sweat from her brow with the back of an
earth-stained hand, fiercely biting back the cowardly
tears. The fact that, for the past year, she had been
compelled to live with Tom as his assigned servant
could not, in their eyes, be put right now by marriage.

If Olwyn had lived, it might have been different,
she thought wryly; they would then, perhaps, have
accepted her as Tom's adopted daughter. But Olwyn
was dead, and although Tom Jenkins was old enough
to be her father, it occurred to none of them to see
him in that light. He was a man, she a convict whore,
condemned to cook and clean for him and work on
his land.

She entered the cabin, and for all her bitter
thoughts it was with a feeling of pride that she did
so. The cabin consisted of only two rooms; the larger,
a living room, in which she cooked and slept. Tom
had spent long hours contriving its furnishings, and
although these were primitive and confined to bare
necessities, he was clever with his hands and, in the
course of their construction, had begun to develop a
craftsman's skill. A table and four chairs occupied
the center of the room, the fourth chair being a rocker,
on which he had lavished much care and in which,
last thing at night, he liked to seat himself to enjoy
a pipe of tobacco—usually in the open doorway so
as to catch the cool evening breeze.

Jenny crossed to her cooking fire, tested the contents of the only iron pot she possessed, replenished the fire, and then carried Tom's rocking chair to the doorway to await his return.

It was lonely here in the evenings, and not for the first time she found herself missing the friendly chatter and companionship of her fellow women convicts in the garden at Sydney's Farm Cove. Only sixteen miles separated them—a journey made easy, now that the first settlement-built launch plied regularly between Sydney and the river mouth at Rose Hill—but convicts could seldom obtain permission for purely social visits.

She had last seen Melia three months ago, when Tom had taken her with him to deliver their small harvest of maize and barley to the main government store, and the time had been all too short—much of it spent, of necessity, in loading the seed and tools they were to take back with them. But Melia had promised to seek permission to come to Rose Hill for her wedding, and perhaps, since it was to take place on a Sunday—when no convicts were required to muster for public labor—her petition would be granted. If only, Jenny thought sadly, it were Andrew Hawley to whom she would make her marriage vows but . . . it was not and never could be. She forced her errant thoughts back to Melia and the garden women.

"We're still working the garden, as you can see," the older girl had said. "But somehow without you to direct us in husbandry—and bully us into keeping the weeds in check—it's not the same. Your loss is sorely felt, Jenny. But in spite of it," she had added unselfishly, "I'm glad for you. Once you are married to the good Sergeant Jenkins and working your own land, the governor will be certain to grant you remission."

Jenny hoped Melia was right. Wearily she sank into Tom's rocking chair and, setting it gently in motion, closed her eyes. She had not intended to fall asleep, but the long day's work had tired her, and within a few minutes of sitting down she had drifted into dreamless oblivion.

The sound of approaching footsteps awakened her. It was dark, she realized, starting up guiltily. Dear heaven, she must have slept for several hours, for the slim crescent moon was already high in the night sky. Tom would be returning to a long-dead fire and the cold remnants of the meal she had started to prepare for him. She was in the act of entering the cabin when something about the footsteps made her pause, instinctively scenting danger. Tom, she knew, would have come alone but the sounds she could hear were such as would be made by more than one man . . . and they were cautious, as were the lowered voices and the absence of lights. With the fire gone out, the cabin, too, was unlit, offering no guidance to approaching strangers, and as she stood uncertainly in its open doorway Jenny heard a muffled voice say impatiently, "God's teeth, where has that damned hut disappeared to? I thought you said it wasn't above two miles? We must have covered more than three!"

Someone stumbled on the uneven ground, and above the muttered curses, came the unmistakable sound of clinking chains. Convicts, Jenny's mind registered. These were men condemned to wear fetters for some recent crime and thus more likely to be bent on escape than on raiding her potato patch. Probably they meant to conceal themselves in the cabin until the hunt for them spread farther afield.

Her first instinct was to take to her heels and hide

from them but then, recalling the imminence of Tom's return, she hesitated. Unless she could warn him, he would blunder into them and, being armed, would deem it his duty to try to apprehend them. And he would be outnumbered—from the sounds, she judged that the party numbered at least four or five, and possibly more; they would be desperate, as all escapers were, seeking the road to China overland and preferring to brave its dangers than to endure the harsh and degrading punishment meted out to them by the settlement's criminal courts.

She started to inch her way around the far wall of the cabin, ears straining for any sound that might indicate that her escape was cut off. The voices were coming nearer, but they were coming from the front of the cabin, the metallic rattle of dragging chains suggesting a quickened pace.

"There's the hut!" a man's voice exclaimed in relief. "And it looks as if it's empty. Come on—let's get inside! I want rid of these sodding chains."

So that was what they were after, Jenny thought . . . they would know that Tom had tools, a hammer and a chisel. Perhaps all they wanted was to use these in order to free themselves of their fetters, and when they had succeeded in hacking them off, they would continue their flight. If she could intercept Tom, prevent him from trying to tackle them by himself, all might yet be well. The escapers would steal such provisions as they could carry, of course, but if left undisturbed, the chances were that they would not linger or do any irreparable damage either to the cabin or the crops.

She reached the far side of the cabin's rear and saw the men for the first time as indistinct but bulky shadows, approaching at a shambling run. They halted by the door, and she counted five of them, all apparently fettered, and two, at least, armed with clubs. The man who was in the lead reached the door, kicked the rocking chair on which she had been sleeping out of his path, and peered into the interior of the cabin. Satisfied that it was indeed empty, he went inside, and the other four followed him.

Jenny waited, her heart thudding, and then, when they did not reappear, she left her temporary hiding place to listen for a moment before making her own bid to escape. Voices sounded from inside the cabin; then she heard the jarring crack of metal on metal and knew that the convicts had found Tom's tools and, as she had anticipated, were using them to strike off their fetters. Taking advantage of the noise they were making, she started to run, but she had covered only a few yards when a tall figure loomed up in front of her and two muscular arms reached out to grab her around the waist.

"Not so fast!" her captor warned. "Reckon we'd best have a li'l talk 'afore you goes rushin' off, me lass."

He bent and lifted her off her feet, and struggle as she might, Jenny could not free herself. His face, she realized with a shock, was coal black, his fettered arms the same color, and he was well over six feet in height—a big, powerful Negro of whom, she recalled, she had heard numerous stories. A prodigious worker, he was also the settlement's most persistent escaper and was known as Caesar.

"Rest easy now," he admonished her. "Ah don't aim tuh hurt you none."

She ceased to fight against him, and he carried her, quite gently, into the cabin and set her down in front of the fireplace, which one of the convicts was replenishing with logs. They had found her small stock of candles too, Jenny saw, and by the light of two of these were engaged in knocking off each other's chains.

"Who've we got here?" a dark-haired man with a thin, sallow face demanded, eyeing Jenny with evident dismay.

"Jus' a li'l bird a-tryin' tuh fly de coop, Nat," Caesar told him imperturbably. "Ah reckoned as she'd be better inside hyah with us than runnin' off down tuh tell Mister Dodd where we're at."

"What's your name, wench?" the man addressed as Nat asked harshly. Jenny told him and he questioned her minutely as to Tom's whereabouts and the probable time of his return.

"He won't be alone," Jenny lied when her attempted evasions failed to convince him, but he brushed the implied threat aside.

"We're not staying longer than it takes to get these chains off," he retorted. "And to collect a few supplies to keep us going. You'll come to no harm if you keep a still tongue in your head. An' whilst we're taking what we need, you c'n heat up whatever grub you've got in that stewpot an' serve it to us, 'cause we ain't eaten all day and we're hungry. Brew us some sweet tea too while you're about it—go on, jump to it! There's no time to waste."

Jenny obeyed him. The man who had been stoking the fire yielded his place to her and stood eyeing her appraisingly as she set water to boil. He was a young man, by no means ill-favored despite his unshaven cheeks and long, unkempt hair. He had a reckless, devil-may-care air about him that accorded with the deep marks on wrists and ankles made by fetters worn over a long period—the sign, which she had come to recognize, of those who defied authority.

He and black Caesar were of a kind, she thought. No cage would hold them for long, no punishment dim their determination to find freedom, whatever the cost, and for all she knew that they intended to rob the cabin of the stocks that she and Tom, with so much toil, had managed to accumulate, Jenny could not but feel a certain sympathy for them—and even, in her heart, wish them well. It took courage to attempt escape; few made the attempt more than once.

The young man turned, to reply to a remark from one of the others, and she saw, beneath the tattered rags of his shirt, the unmistakable red weals of a recent flogging. She said nothing, deeming it prudent not to draw attention to herself, but as if sensing her unvoiced pity, the bold blue eyes sought hers again.

"They sentenced me to fetters for a year and four hundred lashes," he told her, his smile amused rather than abashed. "I took two hundred . . . what have I to lose?"

"You . . . nothing, I suppose. Except"—Jenny bent over the cooking pot, averting her gaze from his—"except your life. There's little food in the bush, and China is a very long way from here."

"Ah!" He laughed, ignoring a reproving growl from the man called Nat. "But we shall not stay in the bush for long, my pretty. I'm a seaman and I know how far it is to China—I've been there. We're intending to lay our hands on a boat and sail it to Timor. We—"

"Stow your gab, Johnny!" the leader of the party bade him sharply, his sallow face suffused with angry color. "D'you want the wench blabbing our plans all around Rose Hill?"

"But she's one of us, Nat. She—"

"She keeps house for a bloody soldier," Nat told him. "Knock Caesar's irons off, if you've nowt better to do, and then the two of you go outside and keep watch. And you, girl—make haste with our grub, unless you're wanting your old lobster to find us here."

Reminded of the danger to Tom, Jenny did as he had asked. She served the meal, such as it was, and all six men ate hungrily, wolfing down the broth with noisy appreciation. They filled two sacks with provisions, after they had eaten, Caesar and three of the others going outside to gather what growing vegetables they could find in the garden patch at the rear of the cabin.

Jenny was hard put to it not to cry out in angry protest, as she listened to them blundering about in the darkness, trampling down the young plants she had tended with so much care. But it would do no good to raise objections, she knew, and her teeth closed fiercely on her lower lip as she started to clear the mess they had left from the table, alert for any chance of escape, however slim.

The man known as Johnny watched her with narrowed, speculative eyes and, when Nat left the cabin in response to a low-voiced summons from one of Caesar's companions, he moved to her side and, grasping her arm, turned her to face him.

"Don't try to run off," he warned. "Nat's liable to turn very nasty if you do. Be patient—we shan't be here much longer."

"But what else do you want?" Jenny asked despairingly. "You've taken all we have." He did not answer and she studied his face anxiously in the flickering candlelight, conscious of the steely resolution behind the seemingly casual manner and the bold blue eyes.

Of superior breeding and education to Nat or any of the others who had escaped with him, he was, in his way, more ruthless than any of them, she decided . . . and infinitely more dangerous.

Where others might falter and fail, he would succeed by sheer audacity or count his life well lost in the attempt. And perhaps, against all the odds, he would make good his boast and sail a small boat to Timor.

She ventured an appeal, aware that time was passing. "Let me go, please. I won't give the alarm, I won't inform on you. But I—"

"You're trembling," he reproached her. "Hell's teeth, we intend you no harm, Jenny! We're not savages, just men who have been tried beyond endurance and are ready to risk everything to get away. We've robbed you, I know, but we will have to survive for maybe weeks in the bush before we can carry out our plans . . . and we've only taken what we need. So"—his fingers loosened their grip on her arm and gently stroked her cheek—"just you bide quiet as a mouse until we finish our business here and you'll suffer no hurt. You have Johnny Butcher's word on that and—"

Jenny cut him short. "Until you finish your business here?" she echoed in a strangled voice. "*What* business? What are they doing, Nat and the others . . . where have they gone?"

Johnny Butcher's expression hardened. "We need a musket," he answered brusquely. "They've gone to get one. Reuben White told us that the old lobster you work for kept his for shooting game and, since it's not here, he must have it on him. So Nat will—" He broke off at the sight of Jenny's white, stricken face. "For God's sake, what is he to you, the old lobster?"

"He . . . I owe him everything." Jenny choked on a sob. "I'm going to marry him. For pity's sake, you don't want bloodshed, do you? Tom Jenkins won't give up his musket just for the asking . . . he's a good man and he knows his duty. Please let me go—let me try to warn him, to stop him coming here." She was almost beside herself, sick with apprehension. Tom would be no match for five of them, and one of those five the giant Caesar . . . if they attempted to take him unawares, he would still put up a fight, she thought wretchedly. Oh, dear God, why hadn't she realized what they were going to do when they went out, leaving her here with Johnny Butcher? Why . . . Sharp and clear through the night air came the sound of a single shot. She wrenched herself free of Johnny's detaining hand and ran to the door of the cabin.

"It's too late now, lass." He was beside her, listening intently, his strong, lithe body taut as a steel spring. The sounds borne to them out of the darkness were confusing—a muffled cry, shouts, a brief silence, and then the pad-pad of running feet. Nat was the first to reach them, and Jenny saw, with dismay, that he was holding a musket triumphantly above his head.

"We had to clobber him," he announced breathlessly. "But we got it . . . and a couple o' ducks he was bringing home with him." He grinned. "They'll make good eating."

Jenny stared at him, appalled. Could they, for the sake of a musket and two scrawny marsh ducks, have callously left Tom out there in the darkness to die, she wondered bitterly . . . or had they only stunned him? Before her stiff lips could frame the question,

Johnny Butcher asked curtly, "You didn't kill him, did you?"

"I don't reckon we did," Nat denied. "Ask Caesar —he clubbed the old cuss. But hell, it was him or us, Johnny! As it was he loosed off one shot that only missed me by inches and then he tried to wade in with his fists. I'll say this for him—he's a game 'un right enough."

He moved closer and added something in a low voice, which Jenny could not hear. She guessed that it concerned herself and, terrified that they might decide that it was too dangerous to leave a witness of the night's happenings behind and force her to go with them, she broke away from Johnny's light grasp and plunged into the darkness. Fear lent wings to her feet, and with the advantage of knowing the land in the vicinity of the cabin so well, she had found concealment in an irrigation trench long before any of the men came in pursuit of her.

The search was half-hearted. Clearly, having obtained the weapon and the supplies they wanted, they were anxious to get away. Johnny called out to her that they were going, some ten minutes later, and— evidently as a salve to his conscience—passed on directions to enable her to find Tom.

She waited until the sound of their footsteps had receded into the distance and then began her own search. It proved harder than she had anticipated. She found the place where the ambush had been laid—the trampled heads of barley and Tom's discarded straw hat confirming the accuracy of the directions she had been given—but of Tom himself there was no sign. Her hopes rose; perhaps, after all, he had not been seriously hurt. If he had summoned strength enough to pick himself up and walk, then there was reason for hope. And if he could walk— or even crawl—being Tom, he would surely try to reach the cabin to make certain that she was safe. Had he not always protected her, to the best of his ability?

She called but there was no response, and stumbling with weariness, she started to retrace her steps, guided by the faint red glow of the cooking fire shining through the open doorway of the cabin.

Tom was there, seated in his favorite rocking chair, but the chair was not moving, and when she reached him, Jenny saw that his white hair was dark and matted with congealed blood, his face and the front of his shirt thickly spattered with scarlet stains.

With a stifled cry she dropped to her knees beside him, and he put out a hand, shakily, to clasp hers. "You're . . . safe, Jenny child . . . thanks be to God. I . . . was afraid for you."

"And I for you! Oh, Tom, are you badly hurt? What should I do for you?" The tears were streaming unchecked down Jenny's cheeks. She must help him, she thought desperately, cleanse his hideous wound, move him, if she could, to the fire's warmth. He needed a surgeon's aid, it was evident; perhaps, when she had attended to his more urgent needs, it would be best to go to Rose Hill to seek skilled help for him. She made to rise but his hand restrained her.

"No. They've . . . done for me, lass, and it . . . pains me too much to . . . move. Just . . . leave me be." His voice was a thin whisper of sound in the shadowed room, and the effort to speak was costing him dearly. But he made it. "Stay with me, Jenny . . . I must talk to you. About the . . . land. I want you . . . to have my land, as you would have done had we been wed."

She clasped his thin, work-roughened hand in both

her own, unable to find words for the anguish she felt. "Don't try to talk, Tom," she begged him. "And don't worry about the land. Unless I can share it with you, I don't want it. Let me fetch you a drink, something to cover you at least."

"A cup of water then," he conceded. "And pen and paper. You know . . . where they're kept, child."

Jenny obeyed him. Tom took two sips of the water, let her wrap his old uniform greatcoat about his knees, and then bade her to take up the pen and write to his dictation.

"Head it: 'The Last Will and Testament of Thomas Gareth Jenkins, late Sergeant in His Majesty's Corps of Marines.' Have you got that down?" His voice was stronger now, a note of urgency in it. "It is important."

Jenny set the ink pot on the floor in front of her and, with a sheet of paper resting on the Bible that had once been Olwyn's, wrote with numb fingers and an aching heart, until the stub of candle the convicts had left burning flickered into extinction and she could no longer make out the words she had penned. Tom had made out wills before, for men about to go into battle, and he knew the correct formula and the appropriate legal terms, but his strength was failing long before he came to the end of his own. And when, at his request, she held the paper for him to affix his signature to it, he could not write his name. With infinite pains, he scrawled a cross at the foot of the sheet and whispered faintly that she could write his name beneath it.

It did not matter, Jenny thought. She had been speaking the stark truth when she had told him that she did not want the land, unless he could share it with her . . . and that, she now recognized, was no longer possible, for Tom was dying. She stayed with him, cradling him in her arms throughout the endless night, doing what she could to ease his passing.

At times his mind drifted from reality, returning to Olwyn and past incidents in his military career, but at others he was lucid and aware of her presence, addressing his slow, faltering words to her with gratitude and warm affection. But, for most of the time, it was to Olwyn he spoke, and when the end came, her name was on his lips.

Jenny left the cabin at dawn and trudged wearily to Rose Hill. The report she made to Captain Meredith was brief and deliberately uninformative. Poor Tom was dead, she told herself, and the capture and punishment of Johnny Butcher and his fellow escapers could not bring him back . . . and, in any case, Captain Meredith, dull-eyed and apathetic after a night's drinking, did not press her for details.

She did not show him the will, knowing he would tell her that it was invalid, and since he seemed anxious only to rid himself of responsibility for her, she asked and was given permission to return to Sydney Cove.

Tom's funeral was attended by a file of marines, who fired the traditional volley over his grave, and when it was over, Jenny—on what was to have been her wedding day—made the sixteen-mile journey back to Sydney Cove in the home-built launch, which the convicts called The Lump, dry-eyed and resolute. But she was thankful for Melia's company and touched by the warmth of the welcome she received when, at dusk, Melia led her back to the cabin.

After the first few days it was as if she had never been away or dreamed, fleetingly, of freedom. . . .

*   *   *

Thaddeus Slack, one of the assistants to the commissary, was at work in his office, checking ration tallies, when he observed a thin, ill-clad convict hovering at the entrance to the main government store.

Slack, who had come out as a representative of the victualling contractors in the storeship *Borrowdale*, was instantly alert. He was a man who prided himself on his honesty and he had only recently been exonerated by the criminal court on charges of embezzlement and theft, brought against him by some of the convicts employed at the store. Convinced that his detractors had themselves been responsible for the crimes of which they had sought to accuse him, he had come to mistrust all convicts as a breed, and the sight of this hovering scarecrow roused him to instant fury.

"Devil take you, fellow!" he exclaimed suspiciously. "What d'you think you're doing here? The store is out of bounds to the likes of you, except at the times officially set aside for the issue of rations."

The man touched his forelock humbly as Slack came striding towards him, brandishing his quill like a cane.

"I'm not meanin' no 'arm, yer honor. I was looking for Mister Miller or Mister Clark, sir."

Andrew Miller was the commissary and Slack's own immediate superior, Zachariah Clark an assistant like himself. Slack bristled. "Well, they're not here. What d'you want with Mister Miller anyway? And who are you—what's your name? I haven't seen you before. You don't work here."

"Me name's Collington, sir." The shifty brown eyes avoided Thaddeus Slack's searching gaze. Their owner was painfully thin, his clothes mere rags that barely covered his skeletal frame, and taking pity on his evident wretchedness, the assistant commissary said in a kinder tone, "Well, what do you want of Mister Miller, eh, Collington? Was he expecting you?"

"Oh, no, sir," the man denied. "It's somethin' I found—I was wantin' his advice, in case . . . well, in case it was valuable like. But maybe you could 'elp me, sir." Without waiting for Slack's agreement, he fumbled among his rags and brought to light a still filthier rag, its four corners knotted to form a small sack. "If I could spread this out on your table, sir, you'd be able ter see it better."

With a certain ingrown reluctance Thaddeus Slack permitted him to enter his sanctuary. Collington opened the package and displayed a pile of what appeared, at first sight, to be earth, but as his bony fingers flattened out the pile Slack saw that it contained a number of small particles of stone or ore, which gleamed dully when he turned them over and the light from the door caught them.

"Well. . . ." The assistant commissary was still suspicious. "Are you trying to tell me you've found gold?" Another convict, a fellow named Daly, had made this same claim during the first year of their arrival in Sydney Cove, he reminded himself. Daly had brought news of his discovery to Captain Campbell of the marines and had endeavored to bargain for a free pardon and his passage back to England in exchange for disclosing the location of his supposed gold mine. But Campbell and later Lieutenant Johnstone, searching on the governor's instructions, had revealed it for the fabrication it was—and Daly had received a flogging for his pains.

Yet all the same . . . Slack picked up one of the fragments, frowning as he subjected it to a careful inspection. It was not beyond the bounds of possibility that there might be gold buried beneath the surface of this godforsaken land, although the convicts, ever eager to embrace any project which might be turned to their own advantage, had made false claims often enough in the past. Men had come in from the bush—escapers particularly—insisting that they had found new rivers, valuable ores, and sites where limestone, chalk, and even marble might be quarried, and singularly few had spoken the truth.

"It's gold all right, Mister Slack," Collington said earnestly as if sensing his doubts. "I 'ad one o' me mates test it—'e used ter be a goldsmith afore 'e was sent out 'ere. I'll call 'im in, if yer like, so's 'e can vouch fer it. 'E come with me, see, and—"

"No." Thaddeus Slack shook his head, his dark brows gathered in a frown. Before suffering the indignities of a trial in the criminal court, he might have risked keeping this to himself, he thought, but now . . . now it simply was not worth the risk entailed. Some of the convicts had it in for him; this could be a fresh ploy of theirs, another attempt on their part to blacken his name. They hated him, he was aware, as men would in a community that was on starvation rations, seeing him as the custodian of the supplies of food and drink they all coveted and unable—or unwilling—to admit that his ration was exactly the same as theirs. Or come to that, the same as the governor's, for Captain Phillip drew no more, each week, from the public store than the humblest convict. If their flour was cut by a pound or more, so was his.

Slack settled his stout frame more firmly in his chair and reached for the lists he had been checking. "Go away, Collington—and take that stuff with you," he ordered brusquely. "I want nothing to do with it, d'you hear?"

"You're makin' a mistake, sir," the old convict whined. " 'Cause it won't cost yer nothin' ter come along with me an' see fer yerself. Mister Miller'd come," he added provocatively, "if I told 'im, like I intended."

Perhaps Andrew Miller would, Slack reflected uneasily. "How far is it?" he asked, careful to sound distant and noncommittal.

"Only a few miles, yer honor. Five, maybe six miles, that's all. I'll fetch me mate in, so's 'e can bear me out. Like I said, sir, 'e used ter be a goldsmith . . . an' 'e's just 'ere, waitin' on me ter call 'im." With remarkable agility for one in his seemingly debilitated state, Collington whisked out of the office, to return a few moments later with a big, powerfully built man, who wore a stained leather apron over his threadbare clothes. Slack recognized him as one of the blacksmith's helpers, but before he could recall his name or anything about him, the big man drew a knife from beneath his apron and, as Collington kicked the door of the office shut, he held the blade menacingly to the assistant commissary's throat.

It was a plot, Thaddeus Slack thought, panic-stricken—an ingenious plot to kill him. The government store was always under guard—damn it, there was a sentry not twenty yards away, well within earshot. He opened his mouth to call for help, and the knife came closer. "Not a sound," the big blacksmith warned. "You just do what we tell you an' you'll suffer no hurt." He moved around, taking up a position to the rear of Slack's chair, and lowered his knife until its point was pressing against the man's rib cage. The weapon was sharp; it passed easily through the cloth of his coat, and Slack winced as he felt it strike bone.

"Half an inch higher," the one-time goldsmith added, "and it'll go right through to your heart, I reckon."

"What do you want of me?" Slack asked, endeavoring to conceal his fears but wretchedly aware that he was trembling.

Collington gave him a gap-toothed smile. "Why, 'ere's what we want, Mister Slack." He laid a requisition form in front of the assistant commissary. "All set out, ready fer you ter sign, see? Stores ter be transferred ter Rose 'Ill."

"But good heavens—" Thaddeus Slack read the list in mounting disbelief. "Two men can't carry all this! You'd need a score at least." He gulped, yielding to the threat they posed. "I'll let you have a couple of sacks of flour and a cask of salt pork and write them off as spoiled. I can do that, I—"

The smith laughed unpleasantly. "I don't doubt you can, mister. But we want what's listed on that there paper, every last pound of it, or you don't live to fake any more requisitions. And you don't need to concern yourself about how we'll carry the stuff— we've got the boys ready and waiting, just as soon as you put your name on that paper." In response to his nod, Collington thrust quill and inkpot across the table. The knife was pressed painfully into the unhappy commissary's chest as a big hand gripped his shoulder, drawing him upright and onto its point. He suppressed an outraged cry, feeling the warm blood start to flow. If only Andrew Miller had been here, but of course. when he was needed, he had taken the day off to join a hunting party, plague take him! No doubt these miserable villains had been aware of his absence—they would never have dared come into the store, with their knives and their threats, unless they had known they would find him by himself. He tried to get to his feet but his captor pushed him back into his chair.

"We got nothin' ter lose if we cut yer throat," Collington reminded him. "The sentry won't notice nothin' 'cause we'll lock the door after us an' go out givin' you a real civil good-bye. You'll not be found till tomorrow mornin', when Mister Miller comes with 'is key."

"You won't get your provisions. You—"

" 'Course we will—we'll 'elp ourselves." The convict put the quill into Slack's shaking hand. "Sign it, Mister Slack, if yer want ter go on living."

If they took all the stores listed on the requisition form, it would leave the reserves of flour and meat seriously depleted, and they were low enough already, heaven knew. The loss could not be hidden or written off, unless he could somehow persuade them to take less. Licking his dry lips, Thaddeus Slack tried despairingly to make them understand. They would have to settle for much less if they carried out their threat and killed him—the sentry might not realize what had happened but he would certainly not permit a score of convicts to invade the store without authority, still less would he stand idly by while they walked out carrying sacks of precious flour and casks of meat and biscuit. He would call out the guard and they would all be put under arrest. The two men listened, grinning, as this was pointed out to them.

"All right, so we'll 'ave ter clobber the bloody lobsterback," Collington conceded. "But that's why we want you ter sign on that there bit o' paper, Mister

Slack. Do that an' you'll save yer hide, an' the sentry won't be none the wiser. Makes sense, don't it?"

Reluctantly Thaddeus Slack had to admit that it did. He forced his trembling fingers to grasp the quill and scrawled his signature on the requisition.

Collington pocketed the form. "On yer feet," he ordered brusquely. "An' tell the lobster he's ter let our mates inter the store."

With the knife against his back, Slack obeyed. For a moment, as he faced the sentry from barely twenty paces away, he was tempted to summon the man to his aid but the blacksmith's hoarse whisper banished the thought.

"This would be in your ribs long before that soldier-boy could collect his wits, Mister Slack," the big convict asserted. "And I'm sticking to you like a leech till we're in the clear, understand?"

A prod from the knife gave painful emphasis to his words. Then some fifteen or sixteen other convicts came crowding into the store, and Thaddeus Slack knew that he had let slip his last chance of preventing the robbery. He watched impotently as they helped themselves to sacks of flour, rice, and peas and then began on the casks of salt tack, splitting them open and loading their contents into sacks, which were lighter and less awkward to carry. They were careful to take only what had been specified on the requisition he had signed, he observed with a sinking heart— this was, clearly, a well-planned theft, and they were adhering without argument to Collington's instructions.

"That's the lot," the convict announced at last, a hint of triumph in his voice. "Out wiv' yer, me lucky lads! We'll be diggin' up that gold in no time, you see if we ain't. An' you're comin' along too,

Mister Slack, just ter make sure we ain't stopped by the guard."

They would also make sure that he was implicated in their infernal plot, Slack reasoned despairingly—and implicated to his neck so that, for his own sake, he would not dare to report what they had done. His signature alone on that requisition form would suffice to bring fresh charges of embezzlement against him, were they to produce it. And his presence in their ranks, as they marched off with their booty, would get him hanged, as like as not, for it would be his word against theirs . . . the word of one man, already suspect, against many, allied to the sentry's evidence and, no doubt, that of the guard.

He trudged miserably along, the knife still pressing into his back, and as he had feared they would the rogues went to some pains to ensure that the guard saw them. Quite properly they were stopped, and he was compelled to permit the guard commander a sight of the requisition form, with its damning signature, the whispered warning from the man walking behind him still ringing in his ears.

"One word out of you and you're a dead man, Mister Slack. And if that means the rest of us get topped—well, you'll be the first. You can bet on that."

Shamefully he said no word, hoping that the guard commander might sense, from the glumness of his expression, that all was not as it should be. But the officer, Lieutenant Johnstone, merely glanced at the requisition and gave him a nod of acknowledgment. He had the authority to distribute government stores; it was not Johnstone's duty to inquire for what purpose, and in any case the store at Rose Hill was regularly supplied from Sydney Cove and convict working parties employed to load the sacks and casks on board the *Lump*. They headed for the Rose Hill wharf now, a shambling line of ragged, unshaven men bowed down under the burdens they carried, but once out of sight of the guard, their demeanor changed. They straightened up and began to laugh and joke among themselves, delighted with the success of the deception they had practiced.

"Cor, we fooled 'em, didn't we?"

"Never suspicioned a thing, the bloody officer, not wiv' the assistant bloody commissary along!"

"Trust ole Jim Collington ter think that one out! Got brains, has ole Jim an' no mistake."

Collington silenced them abruptly. "We got a way ter go yet, lads. Blindfold Mister Slack, Tom."

Blindfolded and with his hands tied behind his back, poor Slack had little idea of which direction the gold-seekers took. He thought they headed south, toward Botany Bay, but all he knew for certain was that they were in thick bush country and that the way was long and rough. Along with his sense of direction he lost all count of time also and could only guess that they had been walking for three hours when, without warning, they came to a halt. He heard the lap of water and some shouted oaths, as some of the men splashed about, evidently searching for a boat hidden among the mangroves. They found it after a while and started loading it with the stolen provisions, talking in low voices just out of his hearing.

He began to tremble, fearing that, now having almost reached their destination, they would kill him so as to avoid any chance of betrayal, but to his heartfelt relief, Collington kept his word.

"We're off now, Mister Slack," he said without rancor. "But we can't let yer go, understand, not right away, 'cause we need a bit o' time. So we'll dump yer back along the trail aways, with yer 'ands tied an' the blindfold on. I don't reckon it'll take yer above an 'arf hour ter get yer 'ands free, and then it's a three-hour slog back ter Sydney Cove. You'll likely get there afore dark, if you 'urry."

"But for God's sake," Thaddeus Slack protested, "I'll be at the mercy of any passing Indians—alone, without weapons! You can't leave me like this— untie my hands, at least, I beg you."

"Sorry I can't oblige," the convict answered without contrition. "You'll just 'ave ter take yer chances wiv' the Indians, same as we will. But if we find gold an' the guv'nor lets us buy our passages back to England out o' gratitude fer makin' this a rich colony —why, you'll get your share, mister, don't worry. Couldn't 'ave done it wiv'out your 'elp, could we?" He laughed and, bending down, loosened the knots binding the assistant commissary's wrists. "There, that's the best I can do for yer. An' if you'll take my advice, Mister Slack, you'll find out some way o' cookin' your books at the store when yer gets back, so's ter cover what we've taken. No one ain't goin' ter believe you 'ad no 'and in it if you try ter give us away . . . not wiv' *your* record they ain't. Lieutenant Johnstone seen yer wiv' us, don't ferget."

He was not likely to forget, Slack thought bitterly, as he started to struggle with the rope around his wrists. The splash of oars told him that the men were on their way; the sound of their voices faded, and he was alone, the silence broken only by the harsh screech of a native bird and the buzz of wings about his sweat-damp face as a horde of mosquitoes attacked him.

Despite Collington's gesture of slackening his bonds, it took him much longer than the estimated half hour to free himself from them. He pulled the blindfold from around his eyes and, blinking in the strong sunlight, sought to orientate himself. Pausing only to slake his thirst at a small stream, he set off, finding tracks in the sandy soil that the men had left, which acted as a heaven-sent guide to his faltering footsteps.

He pressed doggedly on, his whole body aching and soaked in perspiration and the blood pounding in his ears. He led too sedentary a life, he told himself resentfully, working on inventories and requisition lists all day instead of taking time off, as Mr. Miller did, to go hunting and enjoying himself with the garrison officers.

The sun was sinking when, to his horror, Slack glimpsed a party of Indians through a gap in the trees to his left. They were coming toward him quite slowly, but he did not wait to ascertain whether they were hostile or friendly. Seized by blind panic, he took to his heels and ran in the opposite direction, careless of where he went and intent only on avoiding them. He heard them shout, then the pounding of feet as two of them came after him, still shouting something unintelligible in their own language.

Expecting momentarily to receive a spear in his back, he looked around and then, seeing his two pursuers, plunged on, gasping with effort, his legs feeling like lead. But fear lent him strength; he kept ahead of the running natives and then, without warning, was brought to a halt when he found himself knee-deep in swampy ground. The weight of his body bore him down and his floundering struggles only resulted in his sinking deeper into the morass. Soon it reached to his waist, and terror-stricken, he implored the men from whom he had been fleeing to come to his aid.

"Help me! For the love of God . . . help me!"

The aborigines heard, and understanding his predicament if not his words, both flung themselves flat on the deceptively green surface of the marsh, and one, inching toward him, held out the shaft of his spear, grunting instructions to him to remain still. Instead, too frightened to do so, he renewed his struggles in a vain attempt to grasp the out-held spear shaft and felt it slither from his reach as he sank still lower in the treacherous mud.

It covered his arms, his shoulders, his mouth, choking the breath from him and silencing his desperate cries. A tree branch, torn down by one of the Indians, bridged the gap between them, but it came too late. Slowly, inexorably the morass closed over his head, and he vanished from their sight. They rose and, their dark faces expressionless, padded away without a backward glance.

On the morning of April 5 Captain Tench reported to the governor that the flag had been hoisted by the naval watch on South Head. Since the departure, a month earlier, of both the *Sirius* and the *Supply* for Norfolk Island, the harbor had been empty and Phillip had almost given up hope of seeing the arrival of the long and anxiously awaited *Guardian* with her promised stores.

The settlement was nearer to starvation than it had ever been; the unaccountable disappearance of the assistant commissary, Thaddeus Slack, with a party of escaping convicts and a large quantity of meat and flour, had shaken the governor to the depths of his being. The convicts had, it was true, given themselves up when the food they had stolen ran out, but their denial of any part in the unfortunate Slack murder had not been believed. The criminal court had ordered the ringleaders to be hanged and the rest flogged, but that, alas, Phillip thought, could not replace the stores they had squandered—or bring Slack back to life. Or even ensure that his body was given Christian burial, since it had not been found.

He sighed regretfully. He had been driven of necessity to send some two hundred convicts and two companies of marines in the *Sirius* to Norfolk Island where, at least, the crops and livestock were flourishing sufficiently well to sustain a virtually doubled population. He had also summoned Lieutenant King to return, intending to dispatch him to England to make a personal plea for an end to the home government's neglect and, with relief and a clear conscience, had sent Major Ross to act as lieutenant governor of Norfolk Island in his stead. The *Sirius* was to return with King and then make the voyage to China to purchase the most desperately needed supplies.

When Watkin Tench informed him of the signal flying on South Head, Phillip said, "Not, I fear, the *Guardian*, Tench . . . but rather Captain Hunter who is now, it would seem, our last hope. Could you make her out?"

Tench shook his head. "I went to the observatory, sir, to make certain that the flag *was* flying before reporting to you but"—he sighed, his despondency matching the governor's—"all I could make out, with Dawes's large telescope, was a single solitary being who, after hoisting the signal, was strolling about in most leisurely fashion, sir, unmoved by what he saw."

Only the return of one of the colony's own ships could produce such indifference on the part of the watch, Phillip thought wryly—the sight of a strange sail would have brought every man racing to the lookout point, eager to cheer her into port. They had waited and prayed for over two years now for the sight of the storeships . . . and their prayers had been in vain. But it would be churlish not to bid Philip King welcome.

He forced a smile. "I'll take a boat down the harbor to meet them," he said. "It's the least Mister King deserves of me, I think. Do you wish to accompany us?"

"Thank you, sir—yes," the marine officer answered readily.

The governor's launch—a trim craft, under sail, which he used for exploration—put off from the jetty and, well handled by her coxswain, had covered some two miles at a spanking pace when a boat was sighted, pulling round from the north shore. Both Phillip and Tench put their glasses to their eyes.

"The *Supply*'s longboat," the governor said. "And Henry Ball's on board her, with King." He gestured to the helmsman, and as the two boats closed the distance between them, the *Supply*'s commander was seen to spread his hands in a strange, despairing gesture.

"Sir," Tench exclaimed, a catch in his voice. "Prepare yourself for bad news!"

Phillip was silent, his face drained of color. What, he wondered bitterly, could have happened, what fresh disaster had now befallen them? The *Supply* had returned, Ball was there but . . . what of the *Sirius*? The launch's sail was backed, the longboat drew alongside, and his worst fears were realized when Henry Ball informed him gravely that the *Sirius* had been wrecked on Norfolk Island seventeen days before.

"No lives were lost, sir," Ball added. "And we saved most of the supplies. But the *Sirius* is a total loss—she was driven onto the reef in Sydney Bay."

Ross had been anxious to be set ashore, so when

Hunter couldn't enter Sydney Bay on the safer south side, he agreed to steer for a farther bay. It proved disastrous. The *Sirius* drifted near a reef.

King continued with his report, "They, of course, made every endeavor to stand off, but the wind being dead onshore, sir, and the ship being out of trim and working unusually bad, she would not go about. Then, sir, just as she was coming to the wind, she tailed the ground with the after part of her keel and with two sends of the vast surf that runs there, she was thrown completely on the reef. Captain Hunter did all in his power to save her—he let go both anchors and stoppered the cable securely, and though it failed to ride her clear, it caused her to go stern foremost onto the rocks. A most happy circumstance, sir, for she lay with her bow opposed to the sea. Had she been broadside on, it is more than probable that she would have been dashed to pieces and every soul have perished before any help could have reached them."

"How did you get them off?" Phillip asked.

Both King and Ball supplied the details. Hunter and his ship's company, having cut away her masts, had rigged a breaches buoy, and with assistance from those on shore, the *Sirius*'s people had been dragged, in pairs, through the surf, which at times broke over their heads.

"Many of them were half drowned and considerably bruised and knocked about," King said. "Captain Hunter was the last to leave her, and he was knocked off the grating we were using to float them across and flung onto the rocks. We feared we had lost him, sir, but he managed to return his grip on the line and finally came safe ashore. We were all night at the rescue, and I have to say, sir, that a number of the convicts were of material assistance and displayed considerable courage, both on that night and later when the weather moderated and we brought off the cargo and livestock. I have a list of their names, sir, should you feel that some recognition is due to them."

"Certainly," Phillip agreed. He was reeling from the news of the disaster, and disaster it was, especially for his own people, rather than for the now almost self-supporting settlement on Norfolk Island. It was his people who would starve. Without the *Sirius* to convey them to Norfolk Island, he could not—should the worse come to the worst and no storeships arrive from England—remove more than a handful of them from Sydney Cove now. And he could no longer send to China for the provisions needed to keep them alive, since the only ship he had to send was the little brig *Supply*, of less than a hundred seventy tons burthen.

He said, breaking into King's continued account of the wreck, "I shall assemble all my officers in council this evening, gentlemen. The situation here is now of such gravity that I cannot, alone, decide what is to be done."

In all the years King had known him, he could not recall an occasion when Arthur Phillip had failed to act decisively or to rely on his own judgment, however serious the situation. The past two years as governor of this ill-starred colony had tried even Phillip to the limit of his endurance.

"I'll do anything in my power to help," King offered with heartfelt sympathy, and Ball, equally concerned, echoed his offer of aid.

"You may, between you, be the means of our salvation," the governor answered. "But I can no longer take the burden of responsibility solely on my shoulders, for I am driven to despair when our precious stores of provisions are robbed by the very people I am trying to keep from starvation. How soon can you make the *Supply* ready for sea, Henry?"

Henry Ball's hesitation was momentary. He thought of his battered, leaky little ship and his overworked crew and then asked quietly, "For how long a voyage, sir?"

"To Batavia," Phillip told him.

"Within eight or ten days, sir, if I can have the services of some caulkers. But, sir, you know the ship—I've little space to carry stores."

"You will have to hire a vessel from the Dutch to carry the stores, Henry . . . as cheaply as you can, of course." He turned to Philip King. "And you, my dear boy, will take passage from Batavia in a Dutch vessel and return to England, as we originally planned, to plead our cause as only one fully conversant with our situation can." King nodded a trifle glumly and he paused, expelling his breath in a long-drawn, unhappy sigh. "And I shall give you my letter of resignation, Philip, to deliver in person to Lord Sydney."

Again both officers stared at him aghast. "Not that, sir, surely," King began in a shocked voice. "Without you . . . dear God!"

The governor returned his gaze sadly. "Oh, I will stay at my post till the end. It is only a gesture, an expression of my feelings, if you will. But I hope it may advance our cause and stress its extreme urgency to those who have the power to alleviate our distress. Well"—he nodded to his coxswain—"it will take you at least six months to accomplish your mission. I shall call for the commissary's report on all our remaining stocks but I can tell you, without fear of contradiction, that we have less than will sustain us for six months. We shall be required to cut the rations of all still further—and men cannot work on what they are receiving now."

He stressed these inescapable facts later in the day when the council of officers assembled in response to his summons. It was agreed that the ration must be reduced to two-and-one-half pounds of flour, two pounds of salt pork, one pint of peas, and one pound of rice per head a week, and the marines' ration of rum halved. The governor donated the last of his private supply—three hundredweight of flour—to the public stock and ordered the convicts' compulsory hours of labor to end at one P.M. instead of at sundown.

This settled, Phillip outlined his plan to dispatch the *Supply* to Batavia, and the council gave it unanimous agreement. It was, nonetheless, with a heavy heart that he watched the brig weigh anchor on April 17, with Lieutenant King taking passage in her. She was the settlement's last hope . . . and he prayed, with something approaching desperation, that no harm might befall her.

After her departure, there was nothing to be done save wait and endeavor to make the last of the government stores suffice to ward off starvation. The meager rations were issued under guard; volunteers were called for to assist in fishing for the common good, all boats were commandeered, and even the officers were pressed into service to man them. Each day parties of convicts and marines went out into the bush to hunt for game; crows and wild dogs were amongst the most prized items in the pitifully small bags they brought in—the occasional kangaroo a cause for celebration.

The days passed, with wild storms to mark the end of April, and the first three days of June were wet and windy—but on the morning of June 3 the wind dropped, and in the middle of the afternoon a report came from the observatory that the signal to denote that a ship had been sighted was flying from South Head. The news passed like magic from end to end of the settlement. In a torrent of rain a great crowd gathered at every vantage point on the shore, and officers, crowding into the observatory with telescopes, shouted out that the naval watch on South Head was cheering.

The governor, standing in the midst of an excited throng of his officers, was soon able to make out that the ship was a large one, flying British colors. The wind rose again with redoubled fury as she began to work her way into the harbor, and Phillip's heart sank as he followed her progress through the observatory telescope.

"Sir." Watkin Tench was at his side, with David Collins and the surgeon, John White, with him, all three looking as apprehensive as he felt himself. "If she were to founder now, I could not vouch for my continued sanity."

"Nor I for mine," Phillip confessed, his throat tight. "We'll take a boat out and pilot her in and be damned to waiting in suspense!"

Because of the squally weather they took an oared launch in preference to the sailing cutter, but in spite of this both officers and crew were soon soaked to the skin as the wind-whipped water of the harbor buffeted and washed over their frail craft. The oarsmen pulled with a will, and Tench and Collins cheered them on until they came close enough to discern the name LADY JULIANA, LONDON painted across her stern.

Disillusionment followed all too swiftly and bitter disappointment stifled their cheers. This was no supply ship but a convict transport, with two hundred twenty-five women felons on board, carrying supplies only for that number.

From her master, the governor learned that three more transports were to be expected, and that the *Guardian*—the warship that had been carrying the supplies of meat, flour, medicines, tools, and clothing for which he had so often pleaded—had struck an iceberg four hundred leagues from the Cape the previous December. She had limped back to port, weeks later, rudderless and with the loss of half her crew, and it had been possible to salvage only a small part of her cargo. The little that there was had been divided among the other ships, the *Lady Juliana*'s share being seventy-five barrels of flour. And over a thousand convicts, under sentence of transportation, had left England in the second fleet.

In the unhappy conviction that fate had dealt him a mortal blow, Governor Phillip left his officers on board to glean news of the outside world and collect mail, and he himself returned in his boat to Sydney Cove amid the still cheering throng of people, waiting to welcome the ship from home.

CHAPTER XXI

Jeremiah Leach returned from a shooting expedition without any wild game to show for his efforts but with the unexpected bonus of two escaped convicts, stumbled upon quite by chance in the area to the east of Botany Bay.

There had been six men in the escapers' party, and four had contrived to get away, but thanks to the alertness of the marines who had accompanied him, Leach had been able to arrest a giant Negro known as Caesar. The other man, who gave his name as James Clarke, had been wounded in a brush with the Indians and, unable to run, had offered no resistance to his captors.

Feeling pleased with himself, Leach handed both prisoners over to the guard, elated to learn from the guard commander of the arrival of the *Lady Juliana* from England, three days before. "She's brought over two hundred women convicts," Lieutenant Poulden informed him with a wry grimace. "Most of them aged and infirm, by all accounts. But she also brought mail, and I fancy I saw a letter addressed to you."

Leach went eagerly in search of his letter, but his mood changed to one of shocked dismay when he read it. It was from his father, and although it began "My dear Jeremiah," the paternal advice it contained was anything but pleasing. After telling him that there had been a revolution in France that had led to the fall of the Bastille and wholesale anarchy throughout the country, the letter continued:

You will, I trust, now have established yourself in the colony and, by sober and zealous application to your military duties, will have merited the approbation of your superiors.

It is announced in the newspapers here that the fleet, which is to carry a thousand more convicted felons to do the work of the settlement, will also carry an advance party of officers and men of the New South Wales Corps, newly formed for service in the colony.

Inquiries I have made have elicited the fact that, whilst this corps is intended for the relief of the present garrison in which you, Jeremiah, have the honor of serving, no let or hindrance will be placed in the way of any officer already in New South Wales who may be desirous of transferring to the new corps. Furthermore, my good friend at the admiralty, Mr. Low, has informed me privily that grants of land will be made, on generous terms, to officers who apply to transfer their commissions to the New South Wales Corps and who subsequently elect to remain in the colony.

In my considered opinion, this is the best step for you to take, and as an inducement to you to take it, I will remit funds to you to enable you to purchase livestock from the Cape of Good Hope—which, according to Mr. Low, is all that you will require to set you up.

Your brother, Francis, has now entered my business as a full partner, having applied himself in exemplary fashion during the past two years to his clerkship, and it would be a churlish return to him for his hard work were I to retain a share in it for you—although you are his elder.

Lest you may think that I am doing you an injustice, Jeremiah, I would remind you of the considerable sums I was called upon to expend in settlement of the debts you incurred before leaving this country and of the cost, which I also met, of equipping you for your voyage to Botany Bay.

There was more, on these lines, but Jeremiah Leach crushed the flimsy pages between his fists in sudden fury. Damn his sanctimonious eyes, and damn Francis for the conniving little swine that he was! Not only were they robbing him of his inheritance, between them, they were condemning him to stay here, in this godforsaken place.

And his father had not sent him any funds, oh no, just a vague promise to do so. He hadn't even committed himself as to how much he was prepared to remit, had he? Leach hastily smoothed out the crumpled paper, seeking to reassure himself on this point at least but, of course, the old skinflint had been careful, as always, not to specify a sum.

A postscript written at the foot of the page caught his eye—a few lines of spidery writing, scribbled diagonally across what was already written there, so as to save the cost of postage.

He turned it over, holding it close to the candle he had lit, and read:

> Major Francis Grose is, I understand, to command the newly raised corps, transferring from H.M.'s 96th Regiment and coming out this year. But taking passage in the *Neptune* is a young officer recently appointed to the corps, Lieutenant John Macarthur, with his wife and child. Pray introduce yourself to Mr. Macarthur when he arrives and cite, as claim to his acquaintance, the good Mr. Low, who is well known to him. . . .

Jeremiah Leach's mouth tightened. The devil could take Major Grose and Mr. and Mrs. Macarthur and fly with them wherever the fancy might take him. All his efforts to earn the approbation of his present commandant had been in vain, he reflected resentfully. Despite the friendship with young John, which he had painstakingly cultivated, Major Ross hadn't even taken him to Norfolk Island. And he wanted to go—God, how he wanted to go—for on Norfolk Island at least they weren't on starvation rations, as everyone was in Sydney.

Leach swore, loudly and blasphemously, caring little who might hear him, as he thrust his father's letter into the pocket of his threadbare jacket. He was so infernally hungry, he told himself, that he would willingly give the promised remittance for just one meal that he could enjoy. A dinner of fresh, succulent roast pork for instance . . . the sort of meal, dammit, that his father and Francis sat down to every day. Did they, did anyone in England, know that this miserable colony was facing famine? Clearly the reports in the English papers that his father had mentioned must be inaccurate and misleading, otherwise why in heaven's name had more convicts been sent out? And—

His servant came in. "Message from Captain Collins, sir. He'd like a word with you about the two convicts you brought in. He—"

"Did he say when?" Leach snapped irritably.

The servant eyed him warily, knowing his uncertain temper. "Right away, sir," he ventured. "That is, before you dine. I've brought your shaving water, sir."

Grumbling, Leach removed his eight-day growth of stubble, changed his worn, sweat-soaked shirt for a freshly laundered but no less worn one, and walked through the windy darkness to Government House. He was kept waiting; Captain Collins, the orderly sergeant told him, was in conference with the governor and the master of the *Lady Juliana* but would not be long.

He was pacing impatiently up and down the small anteroom when the governor's native interpreter came in, walking arrogantly ahead of the convict servant assigned to guard and care for him. The first so-called interpreter, Arabanoo, had died of smallpox nearly a year ago, and of the two other Indians who had been taken captive in his place on the governor's instructions, one had contrived to escape. The man who remained, a husky, scarred fellow of about twenty-five, was known as Baneelon, and in Leach's view the governor's treatment of him verged on an almost insane indulgence.

Baneelon had a fondness for spirits and a seemingly insatiable appetite, both of which were gratified. Officers might go hungry or be deprived of their full spirit ration, but the Indian was given anything he desired. He took tea and dined at the governor's table and, to augment the miserable ration of salt meat on which everyone else had to exist, he was given quantities of fish from the public catch and a share of the turtles occasionally brought to Sydney by the *Supply*.

Since his capture, which he had accepted as philosophically as had Arabanoo before him, Baneelon had picked up a fair smattering of English. He wore European clothes, save for shoes, and went where he would unfettered and unrestrained, treating his convict guard as a servant and addressing the governor as father in his native tongue.

Leach disliked him as, indeed, he disliked and mistrusted the entire race, but Baneelon, to whom all his captors were now friends, approached him with a broad smile of welcome and both hands extended, clearly with the intention of embracing him. Furious at the creature's familiarity, Leach evaded his embrace, giving him only a curt greeting, and Baneelon's smile faded abruptly.

He turned to look at the sergeant of the guard in mute question, and the old sergeant put a sympathetic arm about his shoulders and said reproachfully, "You've no call to treat Baneelon that way, Mister Leach. He's like a child, you see, and his feelings are easily hurt."

"He's a filthy savage!" Leach retorted. "And I can tell you this, Sergeant—if I were the governor, *I* wouldn't give him houseroom. Certainly I wouldn't give him four times as much food as any of us are allowed."

"Well, sir," the sergeant suggested diplomatically, "that's policy. The governor doesn't want the Indians to know how badly off we are for food. If this lad were made to live on our rations, he might tell his people and encourage them to attack us in force, knowing us to be too weak to put up much of a fight against 'em. Anyway"—he beamed with obvious affection at Baneelon—"this one's a wily rogue if ever there was one! Laps it up, he does—very different from poor old Arabanoo. More spunk to him, if you take my meaning, and I reckon, from the way he behaved when he first come here, that he'd had some contact with our people. Convicts, maybe, and women convicts at that. Kept asking for one he called Jenny and looked for her too for quite a while. But he never did find her and now he's given up asking, as if . . . Why, sir, what's the matter? You've gone as white as a sheet!"

Leach swiftly recovered his composure, furious with himself for having, even momentarily, allowed his feelings to show. There must be a dozen Jennies among the women convicts, he thought, and in any event he had nothing to fear from this ugly black specimen of humanity. Even if he *had* been the one with whom Jenny Taggart had been on friendly terms, he had seen nothing. The natives with whom she had been talking had been long gone from the beach before he had descended to it, and Jenny Taggart had made no complaint against him—the little fool had gone off to Rose Hill with old Jenkins, and he hadn't set eyes on her for nearly a year.

He said grimly to the sergeant, "It's hunger, I expect. I've been out in the woods, shooting, for over a week, and on the diet we're expected to live on, who doesn't look as if he's at death's door? All we managed to bag were a few scrawny crows and one duck. Why—"

He was interrupted by Baneelon. The Indian stepped up to him, shaking off the kindly sergeant's arm, and said slowly and distinctly, "Jen-nee . . . where Jen-nee go? You see Jen-nee?"

This time Leach had his emotions under stern control.

"I've no idea, my black friend," he returned, his tone deliberately condescending. "I don't know anyone called Jenny, so how can I tell you where she's gone?"

Baneelon reverted to his own language. "Wee-ree!" he exclaimed and, after a lengthy but quite incomprehensible tirade, he put his dark face close to Leach's and spat out angrily, "Go-nin Pa-ta!"

"What the devil's he talking about, Sergeant?" Leach demanded, taken aback by the aborigine's vehemence.

"Well, sir," the sergeant answered apologetically. "I'm afraid he's saying that he doesn't much care for you. I only know a little of their lingo but I know that wee-ree means bad and—er—that last name he called you is—well, it's not too polite, sir. God knows what's set him off—maybe he heard me talking about Jenny. But don't you worry your head about it, Mister Leach—he gets turns like this sometimes and there's one way to calm him down." He grinned at Baneelon's convict guard. "Better give him a dose of his medicine, eh, Jack?"

The convict nodded. He took a pewter beaker from the shelf behind him; the sergeant poured a generous measure of the governor's Madeira into it and handed the beaker to Baneelon. To Jeremiah Leach's barely suppressed disgust, the aborigine raised the beaker in one black hand and solemnly offered a toast.

"Long live King George!" he exclaimed and downed the wine with lip-smacking relish.

Leach gave the now grinning black fellow an icy stare, and then, to his relief, Provost Marshal Brewer invited him to enter the judge advocate's office.

"Sorry to have kept you, Leach," Captain Collins greeted him, waving him to a chair. "But I want a word with you about those two escapers you brought in. That is"—he referred to a note on his table—"James Clarke and the West Indian John Caesar, who both absconded from Rose Hill. Where exactly did you run across them?"

Leach told him all he could.

"You didn't notice whether they had any supplies with them?" Brewer persisted. "Sacks of vegetables and flour? Or . . ." he paused, "a musket, by any chance?"

Leach considered the question and then repeated his headshake. "No, I didn't. As I told you, it was dusk. They might have had, of course. The four who eluded us could have legged it with almost anything and we wouldn't have spotted what they had. We were all pretty well done up, you know—we didn't pursue them. Most escapers come back to the settlement and give themselves up, don't they, when they're hungry?" He frowned, as the full significance of Brewer's question sank in. "Hell . . . you asked if they had a musket! What makes you think they had?"

David Collins answered him. "There have been a number of escapes from Rose Hill recently. One party raided a settler's hut, robbed his garden, and then ambushed him, for the purpose of stealing his musket." He sighed. "The settler in question was a time-expired sergeant of the corps—a very fine type of man by the name of Jenkins. Thomas Jenkins. I expect you knew

him, he came out here in the *Charlotte*. The poor
fellow died from the injuries these villains inflicted on
him, so naturally we are anxious to trace and bring
them to justice."

For the second time that evening Jeremiah Leach
was taken by surprise and visibly shaken. Sergeant
Jenkins dead, he thought. Well, be damned to him for
a self-righteous, awkward old swine!

"What about his wife?" he asked thickly. "He married some convict woman, did he not?"

Brewer said, a slight edge to his voice, "You mean
the Taggart girl? No, unhappily for her, poor Jenkins
died a few days before their wedding. She was with
him as his assigned servant for a year, on parole . . .
you know that, surely? *You* reported her for having
dealings with the Indians."

Leach could feel the betraying color creeping into
his cheeks, but he made an attempt at bluster. "No,"
he denied. "I don't recall that, Mister Brewer. Why
should I? It's a long time ago, and the girl's just a
convict whore, like all the rest, isn't she?"

Collins gathered up his papers and glanced at
Brewer, who rose at once. "We need not detain you
any longer, Leach. Thank you for your assistance."
Then, relenting, he smiled. "The master of the *Lady
Juliana* brought us one piece of good news. There's a
storeship on her way to us—the *Justinian*—as well as
the convict transports. And if she gets here before
the convicts, we may well know what it's like to eat
till our stomachs are full again! It's a good augury,
don't you think?"

Perhaps, Jeremiah Leach thought as he made his
way back to his quarters, though he was sure no
good would come to him from it. It never did.

* * *

The storeship *Justinian* entered the harbor on the morning of June 20. She had made a fast passage from Falmouth in just under five months, and with her arrival the immediate threat of famine receded from the colony. Those in authority were well aware that the threat could return, but the *Justinian*'s cargo had won them time, and the meat and flour rations were restored in full the day after she had dropped anchor in Sydney Cove.

Reverend Johnson conducted prayers of thanksgiving at a service attended by the newly landed women convicts from the *Lady Juliana,* and in common with the rest, Jenny joined fervently in the prayers.

She had found some changes on her return to the garden. Polly had married a pleasant young convict named John Williams who—a carpenter by trade—had built a separate hut for himself and his new wife and improved those inhabited by the other women by the addition of shingled roofs and brick chimneys. Polly was happily pregnant, and she talked optimistically of taking land at Rose Hill when her new husband should have served his seven-year sentence.

"The good Lord saw fit to send us here, against all our wishes," she told Jenny with a smile, "and supposing there must be a purpose in it, Will and I reckon we might as well make a life here. There'll be no going back, will there, for the likes of us?"

Eliza and Charlotte, although clinging to the hope of an eventual return to England, were also contemplating matrimony—both to seamen of the *Sirius*.

"Seein' as my man's stuck on Norfolk Island for the time bein', I'm stayin' faithful to him," Eliza announced philosophically, "in the belief that he'll be back here just as soon as there's a ship ter send for the

Sirius's people. So you can count on me an' Charlotte, Jenny m'dear, when you start puttin' our garden ter rights again. An' I'll tell you straight—you've not come back 'afore time, lass. The crops have bin a real disappointment this past twelvemonth. Only the 'baccy's done well—an' you can't eat bloomin' 'baccy, can you?" She cast a reproachful glance at Melia, who defended herself with spirit.

"All right, so the tobacco *was* my idea," she admitted. "I thought we'd be able to trade it for meat and flour. But then the commissary made that an offense, if you please! The whole crop has to be sold to the government store and there's talk that we'll be forbidden to grow any at all in future. Yet it's the one thing, apart from liquor, that the men crave for!"

"Hannah used to trade it for us," Charlotte put in. "But since she died, we've done ourselves no good with the stuff."

"Did you say Hannah was *dead*?" Jenny exclaimed, startled by this news, yet not a little relieved to hear it.

Eliza answered, without remorse, "Yes—she died two months ago, the thieving old hag! Natural causes, Doctor Arndell reckoned . . . but she drank herself to death, Jenny, if you want to know the truth. Not here," she added hastily. "In the main camp. She ran out on us when they stopped us from trading our 'baccy. None of us saw hide or hair of her after that, and I expect you can guess why, can't you?"

She could indeed, Jenny thought wryly. Her finger closed instinctively about the locket Ned Munday had given her. Even that, she had good reason to suppose, Hannah had sold to Lieutenant Leach for part of his liquor ration, caring little for the consequences of her action to herself or anyone else.

"Hannah is no loss to us," Melia observed later

when they were alone together, "but we shall need two or three more reliable workers, Jenny, if we're to bring the garden up to scratch again. Perhaps when the other transports get here, we shall be able to find some women who have worked on farms in the country. Or . . ." she hesitated, eyeing Jenny searchingly from beneath lowered brows, "or men."

"But I thought," Jenny began uncertainly. "I thought we—that is—"

"I know what you thought," Melia interrupted, her tone suddenly harsh. "But I have got over Arnold, Jenny—just as you've got over Andrew Hawley—and I'm lonely. Perhaps it's seeing Polly and that good young Will of hers or perhaps"—her voice softened —"perhaps it's because of the baby she is expecting, I don't know. But she's right about one thing—there will be no going back to England for us, will there? It is foolish to hope."

Was it, Jenny wondered, was it foolish to hope that one day she might see Andrew again? And had she, as Melia supposed, "got over" him? She thought fleetingly of Johnny Butcher and his companions, who had dreamed of making their escape by sailing to Timor, and then inclined her head in assent. It *was* both foolish and useless to hope that any of them would ever see England again or that Andrew would go on caring enough for her to contrive a posting to New South Wales. Had she not admitted as much when she had agreed to marry poor Tom?

Melia went on thoughtfully, "Polly and Will plan to settle. Eliza and Charlotte will probably do the same, if their sailors are not permitted to take them back to England. I should like children, Jenny, and a decent man. There are not many I'd set my cap at here at present but"—she smiled—"who knows what the second fleet will bring?"

Excitement in the colony ran high as the arrival of the three transports was hourly anticipated. A sail was sighted from the South Head on the twenty-third, only to vanish again before a contrary wind. But three days later the flag was hoisted and the transport *Surprise* entered the harbor amid scenes of wild rejoicing on shore, and she was followed, on the twenty-eighth by the *Neptune* and the *Scarborough*.

First ashore were two companies of the New South Wales Corps, who landed in good order and, met by the band of the Marine Corps, were inspected by the governor before being marched off to the spacious barracks built by the marines. No convicts were landed for two days, during which time tents were set up in front of the hospital and a large marquee—intended to serve as a portable hospital—was sent ashore from the *Justinian*.

These preparations and an order for the women to assemble on the west side of the cove to give what aid they could to the new arrivals should, Jenny thought, have warned them what to expect . . . but it did not. Even when the first boats put off from the *Neptune* and it was seen that their human cargo was hoisted into them like so many sacks of provisions, those on shore were not anticipating the horrors that met their eyes when the boats grounded.

The poor wretches who found the strength to stumble ashore were filthy, emaciated, and half-naked, and after staggering for a pace or two along the newly completed stone jetty, they collapsed, begging for food and water, unable to walk farther. Those who came after them were in an even worse state, too weak to clamber from their boats, and the sailors dumped them unceremoniously on the ground and put off back to their ship. The first woman Jenny approached with her cannister of water was like a ghost, her skin covered with hideous sores and her bones showing through as if she were a living skeleton. She gulped a few sips of water and then fell back, exhausted, and when Jenny and Melia tried to lift her, it was to realize that she was dead.

"Oh, dear God!" Melia whispered in a shocked voice. "What have they done to them?"

It was a question they were all to ask, again and again as, sick with pity, they met the boats plying between ship and shore. Male convicts from the settlement formed working parties, with litters, to carry those who could not walk to the hospital; the women, Jenny among them, supported others and bore them, tottering with weakness, to shelter and fed them broth and hot sweet tea. Even the marines, paraded to guard the disembarkation, obtained permission from their officers to break ranks and go to the aid of some of the helpless wretches.

The landing had been just over an hour in progress when the governor, with a face like thunder, was seen putting off to the *Neptune* in his cutter. Those on shore, who observed him and guessed the purpose of his visit to the transport, shouted out to him that he should order the master hanged, and the cry was taken up by hundreds of shocked and vengeful voices.

Phillip himself was filled with a sick anger that transcended any emotion he had previously experienced. To David Collins, who had elected to accompany him, he said only, "You hear what they're saying? Dear God, I wish I *could* order all these villains hanged! I would give the order without hesitation . . . but my powers are limited, are they not?"

Collins inclined his head in tight-lipped silence.

Captain Trail was not on deck when the cutter came alongside the *Neptune*'s dingy hull and the bowman hooked onto her starboard chains, but he came speedily in response to the governor's stentorian demand for his immediate presence. He was a thin, gaunt-faced man in his late forties, his ill-fitting wig askew and his blue cloth jacket unbuttoned, as if he had donned both in response to a summons that had taken him by surprise. Wearing no hat, he contented himself with the mere suggestion of a bow in lieu of the salute that Phillip's rank required, and asked aggressively, "To what do I owe this honor, sir?"

His accent was thick and uneducated, and his breath reeked of rum; the governor eyed him distastefully and said, his tone calculated to cut like a whiplash, "I came to tell you in person, Captain Trail, that you are the most callous and unmitigated rogue it has ever been my misfortune to encounter! You have perpetrated crimes against humanity that pass belief —by God, sir, they are calling out to me on shore that I should have you hanged!"

Captain Trail retreated a pace before the blazing rage in the governor's eyes. "I'm at a loss to understand your outburst, sir," he blustered. "Of what am I being accused? Is it my fault that the scurvy felons I was charged to transport to your penal colony were sent on board my ship with jail fever and worse, so that they could not stand the rigors of the voyage?"

"It is your fault that the unhappy wretches are in the last stages of starvation," Phillip told him. "They are dying as you put them ashore. In God's name, Captain, have you no spark of human compassion? These are *English* men and women."

"They are felons, sir. And those from the other ships are no better. They—"

"Most of the dead and dying are from this ship, Captain," Phillip said coldly. "How many did you undertake to transport?"

Trail's thin face was drenched with sweat. He shook his head resentfully. "About five hundred. A hundred and fifty died on passage—damme, sir, they were sick when they came on board!"

"There will be twice that number dead before this day is out—and you shall be held accountable for every one, I promise you, Captain Trail. In England, if not here." The governor turned to Collins and added, in a carefully controlled voice, "I wish this man to be held under arrest on board his ship, Captain Collins. He is not to be permitted to set foot ashore. The government paid you seventeen pounds sterling a head to feed each convict you carried, Captain Trail. I brought out seven hundred and seventy-five in the first fleet to sail here and lost only twenty-four on passage—yet they were victualed for considerably less than you received."

"You can't keep me here, you can't stop me from coming ashore," Trail began furiously. "You may be the governor of this blasted place but you—"

"As governor, I have the required authority," Phillip asserted. He laid a hand on Collins's arm. "We will visit the other ships, David."

But still the boats went from ships to shore, from the *Scarborough* now and the *Surprise*, to unload more pale-visaged, unhappy souls, blinking with red-rimmed eyes in the strong sun, as if, for them, it was their first glimpse of daylight since the start of their long, cruel voyage. The women from the *Lady Juliana* —although their passage had lasted ten months—had been fit and healthy, but these poor people, who had left England only in January, were like ghosts long dead.

And still they came. By now the hospital was full and could contain no more; the thirty tents pitched beside it and all the adjacent huts were overflowing.

"We'll have to take some of the poor souls to our huts," Jenny said despairingly. "At least until they've had the new marquee set up. We can't just leave them on the bare ground to die."

She dropped to her knees beside the slumped form of a man who had managed to drag himself a dozen yards toward her and was shocked to the depths of her being when the ragged creature raised his head and, in a hoarse voice, spoke her name.

"Jenny . . . Jenny Taggart! By all that's wonderful . . . it *is* you, isn't it?"

The bony, unshaven face, the sunken eyes, the tremulously smiling lips were unfamiliar to her and yet, she knew, this was no stranger. The locket she wore had escaped from the confines of her dress as she bent over him, and when his hand closed about it, she guessed who he was before he said thickly, "I gave you this . . . in the kitchen of the . . . Three Fools. Don't you . . . remember?"

"Ned—*Ned Munday*!" The tears that, throughout the horrors of the day, she had steeled herself not to shed, came coursing down her cheeks now as she looked at him. "Oh, Ned . . . poor, dear Ned . . . dear heaven, but you've been sorely used!" Tenderly she took him in her arms and held him close, and he clung to her, sobbing weakly.

Melia said, from behind her, "An old friend, Jenny?"

"Yes," Jenny confirmed shakily. "From my childhood. We must help him, Melia. He'll die if we don't. He—"

"Take his other arm," Melia interrupted. "We'll carry him to our hut."

Somehow, between them, with frequent pauses for him to rest, they managed to guide Ned's faltering footsteps to the hut. He was exhausted when they reached it and fell onto Jenny's rush couch, gasping for breath, his pallor alarming.

"He's pretty far gone, Jenny," Melia warned. "I don't think I ever saw a man of his age so thin and wasted. I'll make some sweet tea for him—that might revive him."

When she returned with the dark, steaming brew, she thrust the earthenware cup into Jenny's hand and said, with barely contained fury, "They are murderers on those ghastly ships, Jenny—murderers! Our people were right when they shouted out that the governor should hang the masters of them—they deserve no less for what they have made those poor souls suffer. It's . . . dear heaven, it's inhuman!"

Jenny held the earthenware cup to Ned Munday's bloodless lips and urged him gently to drink.

"One man whom I helped to the hospital told me the most terrible story," Melia went on. "He said they were given so little to eat that when one of their number died, the others left his body where it was so that they might go on drawing his ration. Imagine it—a stinking corpse left to lie with the living so that a single ration should not be taken from them! And he said that all the ships threw bodies overboard before they reached the cove. It . . . oh, God, it doesn't bear thinking about, does it?"

"But *why?*" Jenny questioned in utter bewilderment. "Why did they treat them so? Why did they starve them?"

Ned drank thirstily and then pushed the cup away. He answered her question with bitter cynicism. "They got word that the colony was short of food, so they starved us, in order to have surplus provisions to sell here . . . at a handsome profit to themselves. You'll see, when they open up for business in a day or so." A fit of coughing racked him, but when he had recovered his breath, he continued in a painful whisper, "I was . . . in the *Neptune*. Her master, Captain Trail . . . used to command a slave-trader plying to the . . . Caribbean, and he knows his filthy business well. He robbed us of everything we had . . . even our clothing and our shoes. We had to buy . . . extra food from him . . . to stay alive. There were over five hundred of us . . . when we sailed from the Thames. I doubt if . . . half that number will live to join your settlement, Jenny."

Jenny stared at him incredulously. She glanced at Melia and saw her own shocked disbelief mirrored in the older girl's eyes.

"You'll see for yourselves," Ned muttered, as if resenting the fact that they could doubt him, "when the swine set up shop here with what they stole from us." He swore under his breath. "Look at me . . . am I not proof enough? Or must I die to convince you?" Then, as if losing interest, he lay back and closed his eyes. "A plague on it, I'm tired—too damned tired to care if I live or die. But I hope I'll live long enough to see that foul blackguard Trail swing."

Jenny cried out in distress, but Melia took her arm and led her out of earshot. "Let the poor fellow sleep," she advised. "It's the best thing for him—he's as weak as a kitten. What did you say his name was?"

"Ned Munday."

Melia eyed her thoughtfully. "I remember you telling me about Ned Munday. Was he not the one who escaped and left you with the purse he'd stolen —the one who caused you to be transported?" Her tone was dry.

"Yes," Jenny admitted reluctantly. "But it wasn't his fault—he didn't know that I'd be caught with the purse. And I don't bear a grudge against him, truly I don't. I know he's not much, but he reminds me of Mam and better times, and . . . and besides, Melia, I can't just let him die. You'll help me care for him, will you not?"

Melia smiled. "Yes, of course I will. You stay with him, Jenny, and I'll have some broth ready for when he wakes."

Jenny remained at Ned's side all that night. The other women came and went, but she did not stir and scarcely heard them when they spoke to her. All were deeply moved by the horrors they had witnessed during the disembarkation, and they could talk of little else. But to Jenny, keeping her silent vigil beside Ned Munday's couch, he was the only one who mattered. He was a link with the past, and the old memories returned as she wiped the sweat from his white, shuttered face and, when he cried out for water, gently held a beaker to his lips. Even remembering that aiding Ned's escape from the gentleman whose pocket he had picked had been the start of her troubles she knew, studying his gaunt, ashen face, that she did not want him to die.

That it would be a battle she was well aware, for he was, as Melia had said, as weak as a kitten, and she prayed—as she had prayed for Tom—that he might be spared. With the coming of daylight he wakened, and she was able to spoon some of Melia's meat broth into his mouth. He took it eagerly but, by the following evening, had developed a fever and lapsed into a state of delirium, which lasted for almost twenty-four hours. At times he struggled and lashed out so wildly that it took the combined efforts of Melia and Jenny to hold him down and prevent him from doing himself injury. From the hospital the other women brought despairing tales of the number of deaths among the new arrivals, over four hundred of whom were listed as patients. But the ships that had brought them in so terrible a state of sickness and malnutrition had, ironically, saved the colony itself from starvation.

Four hundred casks of beef and two hundred of pork had already been landed, Eliza reported, and flour was coming ashore in such quantities that soft bread was being baked for the first time in over a year, and the ration for all was restored to what it had been when they had originally landed in Sydney Cove. "The master of the *Neptune*'s been put under arrest," she added. "But the other masters have set up shop. You can buy shoes an' dresses an' liquor an' fresh meat, if you've the gelt to pay their prices."

"Shoes?" Melia echoed wistfully. "And *dresses*?"

"Aye," Eliza confirmed, her tone harsh. "An' all filched from the likes of your Ned Munday. Kept 'em chained below decks, they did, for most o' the voyage ... all of 'em, even the women. You'll have your work cut out pullin' him through, Jenny love. In a bad way, he is."

The crisis came that night. Although his emaciated body was burning with fever, Ned cried out constantly that he was cold, and his convulsive shivering could not be assuaged by the ragged garments in which they had wrapped him. They had no blankets, and in desperation Jenny lay down beside him and took him into her arms, praying that the warmth from her own healthy body might ease his torment. She held him as a mother might have held her child, and he lay with his head on her breast, at times sobbing helplessly and, at others, railing bitterly against those whom he believed to have brought about his downfall.

He spoke in disjointed whispers, mouthing accusations in thieves' cant, reliving the horrors of the voyage, and vowing vengeance on all who had maltreated him. Much of what he said was unintelligible, but Jenny heard enough to realize that his arrest had been —in his view, at least—the result of his having incurred the enmity of Dr. Fry . . . and she was shocked and dismayed when Ned asserted that she herself was the cause of the doctor's attitude toward him.

"Always had a soft spot for Jenny Taggart, the sodding old capon," Ned stated hoarsely, as if he were addressing a stranger. "And he took it hard when she was deported to Botany Bay. Spread the flam that I was to blame and lined up all the broggers against me, so's I couldn't pledge my loot. They bounced me from Rats' Castle and Field Lane, and there wasn't a flash house nor a bousing-ken north of the river where I dared show my face. Doctor Fry had 'em all sewn up. Him and Watt Sparrow, between 'em—getting even for Jenny Taggart and her mam, they claimed."

"But they wouldn't do that to you, Ned," Jenny protested. "Not on my account. They knew you weren't to blame. I told them so when they came to visit me in Newgate."

But Ned neither heard nor, it seemed, did he recognize her. After another bout with convulsive shivering, he clung to her fiercely and repeated, again and again, that his arrest had been contrived by one of Dr. Fry's cronies, who had informed the beadle of his presence in the notorious Rookery of St. Giles, with his unsold booty still concealed on his person.

Jenny felt a deep and abiding pity for him, tinged now with a sense of guilt, and she fought tenaciously for his life. It hung in the balance, even when his fever had abated, but then, very slowly, he began to gather strength and was able once again to take solid nourishment. With each day that passed, his appetite became keener, and for all that the full ration was restored and her own given almost entirely to him, she was hard put to it to feed him adequately.

Melia, Charlotte, and Eliza came to her aid, with soft bread and antiscorbutics begged from the hospital; they scoured the woods for sweet-tea berries, plundered their garden for immature vegetables, and Eliza risked the penalty of bartering tobacco in order to obtain illicit fish from boatmen in the public service.

Ned, able to hobble to the door of the hut and bask in the warm sunshine, which heralded the advent of spring, accepted the women's gifts as his right and, while shamelessly exerting his charm to wheedle still more from them, showed little gratitude for their kindly self-sacrifice and no inclination to shoulder even the lightest of their chores. As his health improved the gifts became fewer, and Jenny, try as she might to make excuses for him, found that his continual demands were a strain on the tolerance and friendship that hitherto the other women had shown her.

Eliza, outspoken as always, suggested that the time had come for Ned Munday to fend for himself.

"He'll make a slave out of you, Jenny, if you don't watch out," she warned. "An' get you into plenty of trouble, too, like as not. A real hard case, he is . . . the kind that won't never knuckle under nor try to make a go of things. The first time anyone crosses him, he'll hit back—whoever it is, a lobster or Governor Phillip hisself—an' you know what that'll mean. You've saved his life, you don't owe him nothin'. An' I don't reckon he's as sick as he makes out. Let him go to the hospital with the rest of 'em."

She was right on all counts, Jenny knew, and yet she could not bring herself to take Eliza's sensible advice. Fate had brought Ned back into her life, and now that he was here, she couldn't tear herself away from him. She did not deceive herself into believing she actually loved him, but he was the only link she had with her past . . . a past that was fading in her memory. Ned helped to keep that memory alive.

As soon as he was fit, Ned would be required to perform his daily quota of public labor, but, Jenny reflected unhappily, as Eliza had said he was the kind who would find it hard to knuckle under and accept the harsh discipline imposed on the convict workers. Even now, savagely resentful of the manner in which he had been treated during the voyage, he could talk of little save a burning desire to settle his score with those in authority and, in particular, with the *Neptune*'s master. The fact that Governor Phillip had announced that Captain Trail would be sent back to England to face trial and, in the meantime, that he would be kept under arrest on board his ship, mollified Ned not at all.

"The swine'll be laughing his sodding head off— for who's going to hang a ship's master in England if he's sent there for trial? Who's going to give evidence against him, for a start? Those who could testify to his crimes will all be here, like me, slaving their guts in this godforsaken place—unless they do something about it. And I'm going to, even if I swing for it! I'll slit Trail's gizzard if it's the last thing I do, Jenny—you can count on that. And be damned to your Governor Phillip and his empty promises! Plague take it, what else am I good for now? I can't even make love to you after what that bloody murderer did to me!"

It was useless to argue with him, Jenny thought resignedly, for he would not listen, and his ineffectual attempts to become her lover, to which she had reluctantly submitted in the hope that it would help his recovery, put an unbearable strain on his temper. But she would keep him out of trouble for as long as she could, she decided, and if it were a matter of feeding him, then she would do that too, at least until his health and strength were fully restored . . . and whether or not the other women were willing to help her. Had not Baneelon and Colbee taught her Indian hunting and fishing skills?

The day's work in the garden ended at midday, and leaving Ned dozing in the hut and Melia and Eliza preparing broth and doughcakes for their meal, Jenny set off for the cove where, over a year ago, she had cemented her friendship with the dark-skinned aborigines.

The memory of Lieutenant Leach's vicious assault on her lingered unpleasantly and caused her to look over her shoulder several times as she made her way along the familiar path and into the open country, but no one followed her, and when she reached the cove, it was to find it deserted. She clambered barefoot over the rocks, seeking cockles and then, her hooks and lines baited, she set them out as Baneelon had taught her, wishing that she still had Colbee's

fish gig for use in the shallower water. But her
efforts were rewarded in a catch of half a dozen
quite sizeable fish. Delightedly she gutted them and
loaded them into her plaited rush basket. She was
ready to return to the settlement when the splash of
paddles drew her attention to the cove's entrance.

A native canoe was approaching rapidly, but in the
fading light Jenny saw only that it contained a single
occupant—a man, clad in a white shirt. Some distance
off the point, a second canoe floated idly by, the three
Indians in it resting on their paddles, as if waiting for
the first. This, propelled by strong strokes of the occupant's shirt-sleeved arms, came alongside the rock on
which she was standing, and a familiar voice exclaimed
joyously, "Jen-*nee*!"

She recognized Baneelon but was astonished at the
change in him. He was freshly shaven, his frizzled hair
neatly trimmed and combed, and he wore, in addition
to the shirt, a pair of very English-looking breeches,
held up by a tooled leather belt. He surprised her
still more when he addressed her in halting but quite
intelligible English.

"Where you go?" he asked, holding out a hand to
grasp hers. "I look—I ask—not find Jen-nee."

She tried to explain, and he nodded, appearing to
understand, and then gestured in the direction of the
settlement. "I stay *Wee-rong* many days. Governor
good—*bud-ye-ree*. Him father—*been-ena*."

"Oh, Baneelon—is that where you got your clothes?"
Jenny pointed to his spotless shirt, smiling at the look
of pride on his dark, scarred face. "Did the governor
give them to you?"

"Governor, yes." Baneelon's smile abruptly faded.
"I run—not stay governor. Bad people come, very
sick."

"You mean you've run away?"

"Run away, yes. Go back people. You not tell?"

"No," Jenny assured him.

Baneelon indicated the second canoe. "Colbee . . . Barangeroo . . . Daringa!" Those were the names of their wives, Jenny recalled, his and Colbee's. She raised a hand in greeting, to which Colbee responded by lifting his paddle. He called out something in his own tongue that appeared to be a warning, for Baneelon, with a swift glance at the setting sun, made ready to depart. Then, glimpsing the contents of Jenny's basket, he grinned hugely. "Many fish . . . *bud-ye-ree!*"

There was a hint of envy in his voice and, on impulse, Jenny held the basket out to him. "Do you want some, Baneelon? Take what you need." She had, she reflected, learned the art of fishing from him; if he was hungry, then he had a right to her catch. Baneelon's grin widened. He selected three of the light-horsemen, laid them in the bow of his canoe and then, still grinning, stripped off his shirt and gave it to her. Before Jenny could thank him, he had gone, paddling with easy, skillful strokes to join Colbee and the two women. She looked at the shirt, feeling its texture; it was of fine linen—in all probability one of the governor's own—and Ned, she thought, would be pleased with such a gift to replace the ragged garment in which he had come ashore from the *Neptune*.

It was long after tap-too when she reached the settlement, to find a small agitated gathering about the cooking fire. A sudden, constrained silence greeted her arrival; the women avoided her gaze, and no one asked how she had fared with her fishing or came to take her basket from her as, in normal circumstances, they would eagerly have done.

Jenny set it down. "What has happened?" she asked dully. "What's wrong?" And then, guessing from Ned's absence, that whatever had upset them concerned him, "Is it Ned? Is he in trouble?"

Melia answered her. "Yes, I fear he is, Jenny—bad trouble. He slipped away, after you'd gone . . . none of us noticed him. Anyway we didn't think he could walk very far. But he did—and he stole a boat, apparently in an attempt to go out to the *Neptune.*"

"Oh, no!" Jenny's heart sank as she remembered Ned's threats, his avowed intention to take revenge on the *Neptune*'s master. "Did he get to the ship? Surely he was too weak to row out to her?"

"He was caught and arrested before he'd gone any distance," Melia said. "By Lieutenant Leach, Jenny . . . and he'll be tried tomorrow on a charge of attempting to escape. It will mean a week on Pinchgut, at the very least, if he doesn't earn himself a flogging. The fool! Fancy thinking he could get away with it in broad daylight!"

"He didn't tell them *why* he wanted to go on board the *Neptune*, did he?" Jenny questioned anxiously.

Melia shook her head. "No. But that won't save him from punishment. They'll send him to Pinchgut."

She proved to be right—Ned was duly sentenced to seven days on Pinchgut. He returned from his ordeal more dead than alive, and once again Jenny battled for his life, obstinately refusing to concede defeat or allow him to be sent to the hospital.

Weary from the work of hoeing freshly cleared land in readiness for planting, she went without sleep and virtually without food in the effort to save him, but it was a thankless task. In addition to the effects of exposure on the bleak rock and the wretched diet of bread and water, Ned was suffering from the rough handling of the soldiers who had arrested him, and he lapsed into apathy, refusing to make any effort to help himself.

For hour after hour Jenny sat with him, spooning broth or sweet tea into his mouth when he would consent to take it, sponging his bruised and sweat-drenched body to give him ease, dressing the suppurating wounds made by the musket butts of Leach's guard, and pleading with him to summon up the will to live.

"What is there to live for in this hellhole?" he demanded bitterly. "I'd as soon die as serve seven years with no hope of release or of ever getting back to England . . . and being treated worse than an animal!"

"Ned, you could earn remission," Jenny reminded him. "They're saying that authority has been sent out to the governor to remit even the sentences condemning us to transportation—the ones passed in England."

"We should still have to stay here, shouldn't we?" Ned demanded, his tone skeptical.

"Yes," Jenny conceded. "We'd have to stay. But the governor has promised that those who serve the colony well are to have their sentences reduced. They can become free settlers, Ned, working their own land."

Ned offered sourly, "Aye—but only after years of slavery, years of clearing barren land, building mud huts and roads to nowhere! That's what serving the colony means. Plague take it, I want no part of such a life and I'll be no man's slave!"

"It need not be like that, Ned—truly it need not."

"Oh, for God's sake, how else could it be?" Ned challenged, still skeptical. "I could take to the woods, I suppose, and—" He broke off, frowning. Deaf to

Jenny's exclamation of dismay, he went on, "Look, I talked to a Negro in the jailhouse. He'd been caught and was waiting for his second dose of two hundred lashes but he told me that he and five others had managed to survive in the woods for weeks. It was sheer ill luck that he was apprehended—his companions are still at large, and they're planning to steal a boat and escape by sea. To Timor or somewhere."

Caesar, Jenny's mind registered with a pang, Black Caesar. He had been caught, but the others, Johnny Butcher and the man they had called Nat, evidently had not. And if they were still at large and planning their escape by sea, then. . . .

"I've a mind to join them," Ned told her with something of his old arrogance. "They need help to steal the boat. And what have I to lose but my life?"

Jenny sought desperately for some way to convince him of the folly of attempting to escape. She remembered Polly and Will and said impulsively, "Convicts are offered encouragement to marry, Ned. If we married, we could apply for a grant of land. It would be small, only a few acres, but—" There was Tom's bequest to her, she thought, which might yet be proved—or the garden, when Eliza and Charlotte left to wed their seamen, as they would when the crew of the *Sirius* returned. "It wouldn't be slavery. And we—"

Ned cut her short. "You'd marry *me*?" He sat up, his eyes feverishly bright in his wan, pinched face. "In spite of what they've done to me? In spite of knowing, the devil take it, that I can't consummate any marriage? God, when I think of the women I've bedded, I could spew!"

The bitter humiliation in his voice touched Jenny to the heart. She slipped to her knees beside him, holding him close, raining kisses on his unshaven cheeks. All the affection she had felt for him in her childhood welled up inside her, and the futile fits of rage and jealousy his impotency had caused forgotten in her anxiety to comfort him.

"Dear Ned, it will not last forever, you know. It's because you've been starved. But you'll be strong again, strong and lusty, as you used to be . . . and gay and happy, even here. Don't throw your life away."

Ned's mouth found hers. He kissed her hungrily, his hands fondling her breasts as he drew her down beside him.

"By heaven, you're right!" he exclaimed suddenly. "You're right, Jenny . . . it didn't last forever. It's over, do you hear? Thanks be to God, it's over!"

He flung himself on her, tearing at her dress, and she felt his thin body harden against her, miraculously gathering strength and the purposefulness of desire.

"You're mine, Jenny!" he exulted, and as her dress parted under the assault of his impatient hands, he arched himself above her naked, trembling body, breathless and bathed in sweat, and imprisoned her beneath him. "You're mine and no one shall take you from me!"

CHAPTER XXII

Governor Phillip, awaiting the appearance of the boat that was to take him to the South Head on a tour of inspection, looked out across a harbor once more empty of ships and expelled his breath in a tired sigh.

He had sent the *Justinian* and the *Surprise* to Norfolk Island with urgently needed supplies at the end of July, and the *Scarborough* and the *Lady Juliana* had followed a week later, their destination Canton. Last to leave had been the *Neptune,* her departure delayed by the unseemly wrangling to which her rogue of a master had resorted in a vain attempt to avoid the civil trial that would await him when he reached England.

Donald Trail richly deserved whatever fate might be in store for him, the governor reflected grimly and found himself wishing, not for the first time, that the powers newly conferred on him by His Majesty's government had included the right to put the erstwhile slave trader on trial in the colony.

His launch came smartly around the point, with eight men at the oars and young Lieutenant Waterhouse in the stern sheets. David Collins came hurrying down to join him as the boat grounded on the sandy shore and the bowman splashed into the water to assist him to embark.

"They're making some sort of signal from the South Head, sir," Waterhouse told him when the boat was under way. "Not the 'sail sighted,' alas, sir," he added, anticipating Phillip's question, for the return of the little *Supply* from Batavia was being spoken of eagerly now. "To be honest, I couldn't make head nor tail of it but I think it may be from Captain Tench's party. You remember, sir, he and Captain Nepean and Doctor White were planning to put ashore at Manly and walk overland to Broken Bay."

The governor nodded. Tench and White, those two dedicated explorers, had enlisted the recently arrived Nicholas Nepean, a captain in the New South Wales Corps, as a partner in their expeditions to take the place of William Dawes, whose newly constructed observatory was now demanding most of his time.

"There's a rumor, sir, among the fishing parties that the whale that swamped poor young Jamie Ferguson's boat has been washed up dead on Manly Beach," Waterhouse went on. "I don't know if it's true or if it's the same whale, but Bryant was positive he'd seen the creature threshing about in some distress, three or four days ago."

Phillip's brows met in a thoughtful frown. "Let us hope it is the same dastardly monster," he returned feelingly. Poor young Ferguson, the midshipman son of the governor of Greenwich Hospital, had been drowned, with three marines, when on his way to the cove from the South Head lookout station, their unavailing struggle against the whale's attack witnessed helplessly by those on shore.

"The Mills of God, sir," David Collins observed wryly.

"Indeed," the governor agreed. "If the rumor is true and the whale *has* been washed onto Manly Beach, I imagine it will bring every Indian in the area there, seeking food. That is probably why the people on South Head are trying to signal us."

"Shall we make for Manly to find out, sir?" Waterhouse asked.

Phillip, his glass to his eye, gestured ahead of them. "There's a boat making for us now, fine on our starboard bow. We'll see what her cox'un has to say."

The coxswain made his report excitedly when the two boats came within hailing distance. He had landed the exploring party at Manly, and Captain Nepean had sent him back to intercept the governor.

"There's a dead whale on the beach, sir, in an 'orrible state o' putrefaction, and about two 'undred Indians carvin' it up. I reckon they mean to eat it." His tone was disapproving, and, with evident disgust, he indicated a tarpaulin-wrapped parcel lying on the thwart beside him. "That's some o' the flesh there, sir. That Indian you used to 'ave at Government 'ouse— the only they call Baneelon—'e sent it as a personal gift to you, sir."

Baneelon, the governor thought, so he had been accepted back by his people. The gift of the whale meat proved that, at least, he had not forgotten his time spent with the governor. Phillip was touched.

"Are the Indians hostile or friendly, cox'un?"

The seaman scratched his head. "It's hard to say, sir," he admitted. "That Baneelon and 'is mate, the feller they call Colbee—they're friendly enough, sir, and Baneelon, why 'e was askin' most kindly after Your Excellency's 'ealth. But the rest . . . well, they're all armed, and I wouldn't say as they was too 'appy about seein' us on the beach. Captain Tench ordered us to put off, sir, and land 'is party 'arf a mile along the shore from where they was gathered." He hesitated. "There was a lot o' talk, sir, between the Indians and our officers, concernin' fishin' gear the Indians claimed 'ad been stolen by convicts. They was demandin' hatchets in place of the stolen gear. That Indian boy Nanbaree was with us as interpreter and he said that if you was to come yourself, sir, then Baneelon would come back with you to Sydney Cove an' collect them hatchets."

A few hatchets would be a small price to pay for Baneelon's return and his continued friendship, the governor decided, and in any case he did not doubt the Indians' claim. The convicts robbed them at every opportunity, creating hostility and mistrust between the natives and themselves. He thanked Tench's coxswain and dismissed him and ordered Waterhouse to make for South Head.

"We'll pick up one or two muskets there," he said. "Just in case of trouble. But they can be kept out of sight, while I talk to Baneelon."

"Do you think you'll be able to persuade him to come back to us, sir?" Collins asked.

"Who knows, David?" The governor shrugged. "It's worth trying, I think. He and Colbee exert considerable influence with their people, and with their help, I am convinced that we can improve our relations

with the local tribes. You scarcely need me to tell you
that they've gone from bad to worse since Baneelon's
untimely departure."

They reached South Head after an hour's strenuous
pulling, and received by Midshipman Southwell and
his small party of naval signalers, the governor inspected the work done on the stone column that was
being erected as a guide to ships on their approach
to the harbor and took some light refreshment while
a search was made for spare weapons. Four muskets
and a pistol were found and stowed out of sight in
the launch, and the crew bent to their oars again,
as Lieutenant Waterhouse steered for Manly.

The scene on the beach when they came in sight
of it was much as Tench's coxswain had described,
save that there were now well in excess of two hundred
natives milling excitedly around the rotting carcass
of the whale, seemingly quite undeterred by the
foul stench that emanated from it. They displayed no
alarm at the approach of the launch, and the governor
instructed Waterhouse to set him ashore.

"Keep those muskets hidden," he warned and shook
his head firmly to David Collins's offer to accompany
him. "It will be best if I go alone, David. And don't
worry—once I've made contact with Baneelon, I shall
be in no danger."

He stepped confidently ashore and strode unhur-
riedly toward the nearest group, calling for Baneelon
by name. The Indians in general—and Baneelon in
particular—had always trusted him, and he had no
reason to fear. Baneelon appeared on the edge of the
throng but made no move to approach him. There
was, he saw, a startling change in the young native.
He was greatly emaciated, and in addition to a long

beard there was a recently healed scar above his left eye and a gaping wound in the fleshy part of one arm.

He replied sullenly to the governor's questions concerning his wounds, stating coldly that he had received them at Botany Bay.

When Colbee joined him, his manner became more friendly, and finally both men advanced with hands outstretched, leaving their spears behind them. Retaining his grasp of Phillip's hand, Baneelon inquired by name for the friends he had left behind him at Government House, speaking in broken English and imitating the voices and mannerisms of each, to the evident amusement of his companions. Seeing Lieutenant Waterhouse standing by the grounded launch, he rushed over and kissed him ostentatiously on both cheeks, roaring with laughter at the sensation his unexpected action caused.

Satisfied that their former good relations had been restored, the governor called for the provisions he had in the launch to be brought to him. They were scanty enough but included a bottle of wine, and when Collins uncorked it, he poured two glasses and offered one to Baneelon.

"The king!" he said solemnly.

"The king!" Baneelon echoed in high glee and, lifting his glass, poured its contents appreciatively into his mouth. Collins and Waterhouse distributed the rest of the provisions among those standing nearest to them. One man, presented with a hunk of salt pork, flung it down in disgust. Offered a seaman's knife, he tested its blade and accepted it reluctantly, turning to Baneelon to remonstrate with him at some length in his own language. A chorus of voices gave loud and angry support to whatever demands he had made.

Baneelon turned to Phillip, his tone suddenly aggressive.

"Him say want hatchets. Plenty hatchets."

"We have none with us, Baneelon," Phillip told him. Out of the corner of his eye he saw that two parties of natives, each about fifty strong, were moving slowly to the right and left of his own party, with the evident intention of surrounding them. Fearing that their retreat might be cut off, he motioned the crew of the launch, who had come up to join him, to return to their grounded craft. "Take no action unless I order it," he bade Waterhouse in a low voice. "But if they attack, put off at once without waiting for me."

"Come with us, sir," Waterhouse urged anxiously. "They're in an ugly mood, some of them."

The governor shook his head. "I'll try to talk to them. The last thing I want is to provoke an attack, and in any case they probably have a legitimate grievance." He laid his hand on Baneelon's shoulder and said with kindly firmness, "You come Weerong and I will give you hatchets for that Indian and his people. Tell him so. Tell him that men of his tribe may come to Weerong also."

"I not stay *Wee-rong, been-ena*," Baneelon objected.

Phillip smiled at him. "No. You may come or go, as you desire—any of you. Tell the others this."

Baneelon echoed his smile. "I come," he promised. "Soon . . . see Jen-nee, see *murree-mulla*, drink tea, drink toast to king. *Bud-ye-ree!*" He was using all the old, friendly words, Phillip noticed, relieved, and some of the tension drained out of him. An exchange of gifts, in accordance with native custom, ought now to be made in order to signify that mutual harmony had been restored. He pointed to the long, barbed spear that Baneelon had set down behind him and held out his hand for it, but, to his surprise, Baneelon jerked it out of his reach and ran off, to lay the weapon down at the feet of the squat, elderly man who had accepted the seaman's knife with so much reluctance.

A brief consultation took place between them, and David Collins murmured uneasily, "Do you not think, sir, that it would be advisable for you to return to the boat? With that surf running, it might take us a while to pull out of range of their spears."

Again the governor shook his head. He glanced across at the launch, which Waterhouse had prudently swung round, so that its bows were afloat, and said flatly, "They clearly believe that they have been wronged, and it is essential that I promise them redress. None of our people will be safe outside the bounds of the settlement until they learn to trust in us. Besides, if we turn tail and run from them now, they're likely to imagine that we're afraid of them, which would be inviting an attack."

They might also, he thought grimly, being in such overwhelming numbers, go in pursuit of Tench's small exploring party, with consequences too awful to contemplate. But at that moment Baneelon came striding back, bearing a throwing-stick and Phillip added reassuringly, sensing Collins's uneasiness. "It's all right, my dear David—look, he's bringing us a gift after all!"

Watching anxiously from the boat, Waterhouse saw Baneelon approach the governor and ceremoniously present the throwing-stick. He was too far away to hear what was said, but the approving smiles on the faces of the Indians in the immediate vicinity, as Phillip accepted the gift, stilled some of his fears. Honor seemingly satisfied and the crisis averted, he

waved to the men who were standing by, and who
were having difficulty in holding the launch steady
against the assault of the surf, to pull up; and they
hauled her just clear of the pounding waves. The
coxswain, crouched on the bottom boards with a
loaded musket, laid the weapon down and raised
himself on his elbows, the better to observe what was
going on, but Waterhouse bade him tersely, "Keep
out of sight, you damned fool—and that musket at
the ready!"

The coxswain obeyed him, startled by his vehemence.

Phillip looked about him and, seeing the smiling
faces, nodded his satisfaction. He was about to return
to the launch when, without warning, the man who
had the seaman's knife flung it from him and, with
a hoarse cry, inserted a lance into his own throwing-
stick. With the weapon aimed menacingly at the
governor, the Indian moved toward him, mouthing
threats in his own language, his flat, dark face contorted with fury.

Collins made to step between them, but Phillip
motioned him back. "Wait!" he commanded sharply.
"I'll deal with him. He hasn't understood, I fear."

Slowly, but without hesitation, he walked to meet
the angry native and, realizing that the man was
eyeing the sword he wore with visible apprehension,
he started to unbuckle it, with the intention of letting
it fall to the ground behind him. His action, far from
restoring confidence, added to the Indian's alarm. He
shouted something unintelligible in a high-pitched,
angry voice, and at once his fellow-tribesmen gathered
round, to form a semicircle at his back, their faces
reflecting their chief's pent-up rage.

The sudden, inexplicable change in their attitude

was startling. The black ranks swayed, pressing forward to meet the governor, Baneelon's earlier clowning and the laughter that had greeted it apparently forgotten. As he faced them Phillip was chillingly aware that if he displayed any fear, they would be upon him, tearing him limb from limb. He halted, forcing a smile, and, having discarded his sword, held out both hands to them in token of friendship. Baneelon had disappeared in the crowd. Deprived of his interpreter, Phillip did his best to make his would-be attackers understand that what they were doing was wrong, using the native tongue as well as his own.

For answer, there was a savage howl, and the man to whom he had given the knife drew back his throwing arm and, taking careful aim, sent his barbed spear viciously winging its way toward Phillip's heart. The governor had time only to make a half-turn, but the point of the spear missed his heart, burying itself instead in his right shoulder, just below the collarbone. It struck with such force that it went right through him, tearing muscle and sinew and causing him to sink to his knees, gasping with pain.

Knowing that to cry out would, in all likelihood, create a panic and bring his own men with their muskets rushing vengefully to his aid, he endured the pain in stoical silence. When Collins raced to his side, he dragged himself to his feet, leaning heavily on the younger man's arm, to see his assailant making off as fast as his legs would carry him, with a number of natives in pursuit.

A few more spears and one or two badly aimed rocks were thrown at them, but Collins placed himself protectively in front of Phillip, and these did no damage. A single musket shot rang out, as Waterhouse led six men of the boat party up the beach toward him, and somehow the governor summoned the strength to bawl an order to them to hold their fire.

"Get me . . . to the boat . . . if you can," he gasped to Collins and then, following the young judge advocate's unhappy glance, he became aware that the shaft of the spear was protruding from his chest, a dangerous, ten-foot-long impediment to his escape.

"I'll try to break it, sir," Waterhouse offered. He struggled manfully with the stout wood of the shaft, causing Phillip such agony that it took all the willpower he possessed not to scream at him to desist. At last the shaft snapped, and, with Collins and Waterhouse supporting him on either side, they retreated to the launch, two seamen bringing up the rear with loaded muskets. A hail of spears and stones followed them as they put off into the surf, but all fell short.

It was a five-mile row back to Sydney Cove, but with their governor's wound bleeding in alarming fashion, the men bent to their task with a will, and they accomplished the return journey in under two hours. Phillip, lying with his head pillowed on David Collins's knee while Waterhouse endeavored vainly to staunch the bleeding, endured the discomfort without complaint, occasionally lapsing into unconsciousness.

When at last they came alongside the landing stage and made ready to carry him to the hospital, he said faintly, "I am concerned for the safety . . . of Tench and Nepean . . . and Doctor White. They cannot . . . have gone far from Manly and . . . if those Indians are . . . looking for trouble . . . they must be stopped. Send out . . . a strong party . . . to find them. A . . . strong party, you understand?"

"Aye, aye, sir," Waterhouse acknowledged, pale and tight of lip. "They'll get what's coming to them, I promise you, sir, for what they did to you."

"No." Phillip raised himself painfully. "There are to be . . . no reprisals. I'm not . . . dead yet, Mister Waterhouse." To Collins he added, "And please see that . . . Baneelon and Colbee get the . . . hatchets, if they come for them, David. This . . . incident must not be allowed to . . . jeopardize our . . . good relations with the . . . Indians."

Within a week Phillip was back in his office, and following the safe return of the exploring party, Captain Tench volunteered to make contact with Baneelon and seek to persuade him to visit the settlement.

The negotiations were somewhat protracted, with promises given and received, but Tench stuck to his task, and finally, after leaving Lieutenant John Johnson as a hostage with the Indians and returning the stolen fishing gear to them, on October 7—a month after the attack on the governor—Baneelon consented to come to Sydney accompanied by Colbee and two others. On Phillip's instructions, they were treated as honored guests; food and wine were served to them, the hatchets and some freshly caught fish laid out for their inspection.

When the time approached for them to leave, Baneelon expressed sorrow for the attack, which, he said in a tone that carried conviction, had been the work of a man of another tribe, named Wileemarin, on whose behalf he begged the governor's forgiveness. As proof of Wilee-marin's contrition, he offered a parcel wrapped in tree bark, which, on being opened, Phillip saw with delight, contained his sword, undamaged and carefully cleaned.

When they had gone, escorted by Watkin Tench and young William Dawes, the governor said thoughtfully to David Collins, "You know, David, I truly believe that this marks a turning point in our relations with the Indians—thanks be to God! I should like them—and Baneelon and Colbee in particular—to feel that they may visit us whenever they feel so inclined, in the knowledge that no let or hindrance will be put in their way."

"I'm sure that would be an excellent thing, sir," Collins agreed. "But how can we make them understand?"

"Well—" The governor smiled. "I've been giving the matter some thought. Suppose we were to give them a place of their own in the settlement? A hut, for their exclusive use, situated close enough to the shore for them to reach it by canoe. In fact we might let them choose the site for themselves—what do you say?"

"I think it's a capital notion, sir," Collins approved, and then added wryly, "so long as we can stop the convicts' raiding the hut and stripping it bare!"

Phillip's smile faded. That, he thought unhappily, was the problem, and it would continue to be for as long as the home government refused to heed his oft-repeated requests for discrimination to be exercised in the selection of the convicts sent out to the colony.

He had studied the records of those he had brought out—delivered to him, at long last, by the ships of the second fleet. He thought glumly of the handful he had freed—Bloodworthy, of course, that excellent builder; six men of the convict watch; a dozen survivors from the ill-fated *Guardian*—all artisans or husbandmen—whose assistance when their ship was wrecked had earned them recommendations from the *Guardian*'s commander, Lieutenant Riou. And there were the garden women, led by little Jenny Taggart, whose original sentences he had reduced with, perhaps, just over a score of others . . . few enough, in all conscience, to encourage hope.

"We shall have to flog any who steal from the Indians," he said, his tone regretful. "In their presence perhaps. And as soon as the *Supply* returns—which, God willing, should be soon—we might send all persistent escapers to Norfolk Island. They'll be hard put to it to escape from there, and the threat of being transferred might act as a deterrent to others."

"I wonder how Major Ross is finding his sojourn as lieutenant governor," David Collins remarked, and Phillip glanced at him sharply.

"Waiting eagerly for his relief, I should suppose," he returned, his voice without expression. "As, God knows, am I, David."

"It will be a sad day for the colony when you go, sir."

"Will it? I sometimes wonder whether it will. Or if another man might have done better than I, in this situation. That is . . ." Phillip hesitated, conscious in that moment of how heavy the burden of responsibility had become, "that is the question that haunts me, David, because I cannot answer it."

It seemed that, perhaps, his faith was justified when, on October 18 the gallant little *Supply* returned from Batavia to a rapturous welcome from the entire settlement. Her commander, Lieutenant Ball, had brought what provisions and livestock his ship could carry, and, in addition, he told the governor that he had hired a Dutch snow, the *Waak-sam-heyd*, under the command of a Malay master named Detmer Smith, to deliver the remainder of the supplies of meat, flour, rice, and butter he had purchased from the Dutch.

"Smith is a rogue, sir," he confessed regretfully. "And the Dutch rapacious as ever in the matter of prices, but we had no option. There was a fever epidemic raging throughout the whole of Batavia—I lost five good men and I fear I haven't yet recovered from a dose of it myself. But . . . I put Mister Ormsby in charge of the *Waak-sam-heyd*, and pray heaven, she'll make port before the end of the year."

The snow, a sturdy, square-rigged vessel of three hundred tons burthen, arrived six weeks later, to the relief of all, for the colony was suffering from a drought, and even at Rose Hill the crops had suffered severely. But Philip was pleased with the progress made there when he and Henry Brewer—who had displayed an unexpected aptitude as an architect and land surveyor—made a tour of inspection a week before Christmas.

Twenty-seven new huts and a fine storehouse, one hundred feet by twenty-four feet, had been built in deep red brick, produced by the recently established kilns, and a wharf and a mile-long road between the settlement and the river were well on the way to completion. The hospital, although still only a thatched wooden shed, had been enlarged to provide accommodation for two hundred sick, a house for the chaplain was finished, and one for the judge advocate, which was to include a small courtroom, had been begun.

"The foundations of a house for Your Excellency have been laid," Brewer pointed out proudly. "It will be of lath and plaster forty-four feet long by sixteen feet wide, with a brick foundation and a tiled roof. And Bloodworthy and I have drawn up a plan for permanent barracks for the troops, sir, to be situated close to the wharf and the storehouse, to which wings for the officers can be added when we have the required labor."

Phillip congratulated him warmly. The labor situation had been improved by the addition of some good men from the second fleet and, as Brewer confirmed, by the superintendents sent out originally in the wrecked *Guardian*.

"They keep the convicts to their work, sir, and permit no idling but—" Brewer spread his hands in a gesture of helplessness. "If only more of them were skilled or were even desirous of learning skills, we could have a town here in six months."

The governor nodded in sympathetic understanding. "The sending out of the disordered and helpless clears the jails and may ease the parishes from which they are sent," he said bleakly. "But as a result this settlement will remain for years a burden to the mother country. It might have been different if the *Guardian* had reached us, but the one ship we needed went down. One cannot, alas, argue with fate, Henry."

"No, sir," Henry Brewer conceded. "But, all the same, one cannot help regretting what might have been."

Phillip found Edward Dodd in much the same state of mind. The superintendent of agriculture had done wonders, with two hundred acres in cultivation, a further two hundred newly planted, and cattle enclosures constructed, awaiting the arrival of the livestock to fill them. But the drought was causing him concern, the standard of work by the convict laborers left a great deal to be desired, and Dodd himself, stout and perspiring, looked anything but well.

"Each man, sir, is set the daily task of hoeing sixteen rods," he stated despondently. "And look, I beg you . . . the earth is barely scratched over! If we had

beasts to pull them, I could make plows and the toil
would be halved, with our yield doubled. As it is"—
he shrugged—"they perform their public work with
little heart, but their own gardens are a very different
matter. When they work for themselves, sir, even the
elderly and the infirm seem to be able to grow maize
and vegetables."

"Ah!" The governor's dark brows met in a pensive
pucker. "You've reminded me of an idea I had some
time ago, Mister Dodd, on which I should value your
opinion. I've considered granting up to thirty acres
to convicts of good behavior, who would be released
from their public labor and permitted to husband
their own land. They would require to be fed, of
course, but in return for meat and flour their crops
would be taken for the public use, in the same manner
as those of the free settlers. Would it show results, do
you suppose?"

"In this area, sir?" Dodd questioned.

"Yes—it is the best land we have available, is it
not?"

"Indeed it is, sir," Dodd agreed. "And I believe
such a policy would show good results, provided the
men selected are of the right sort. The danger would
be mainly from robberies, as Your Excellency well
knows. I think, sir," he concluded, "that if you permit
convicts to take up grants of land here, you would
have to allow them to defend their holdings, in the
same manner as free settlers. They—"

"You mean allow them muskets?" Phillip put in,
his frown deepening.

Brewer started to speak and then thought better of
it, as Dodd said emphatically, "I do, sir. Provided, as
I suggested, sir, that the men selected are the right
sort—men of proven good character."

"That will require considerable thought," the governor observed. "And I shall give it thought, Mister Dodd."

On the way back to Sydney they talked again of the problem of landholders defending their property. The incident of poor old Jenkins's murder brought Jenny Taggart to Henry Brewer's mind.

"She is a young woman of good character and she was devoted to Jenkins . . ." He started to recite Jenny Taggart's record and saw that Phillip was smiling at him, in unconcealed amusement.

"She has a good advocate in you, Henry!"

"Yes, sir," Henry Brewer admitted frankly. "She has. She's got courage and the ability to succeed, allied to the *will* and, from the day she landed, she has worked hard and without complaint. I truly believe, sir—" he met the governor's gaze squarely— "that in the absence of better material, the Taggart girl and the few who are like her represent the—the foundations on which this colony must be built."

Then their discussion moved to the New South Wales Corps. "Some of the officers leave a good deal to be desired," Phillip sighed.

He was thinking, in particular, of Lieutenant John Macarthur, Brewer knew, although he mentioned no names. Macarthur's young wife, Elizabeth, who had come out with him in the advance party of the New South Wales Corps, was pretty and charming; she had endeared herself to all, including the governor, whose table she frequently graced, but Macarthur himself was a very different proposition. Arrogant and opinionated, he had fought a duel with the master of the *Neptune* before the ship left Plymouth and this had led to the master's replacement by the infamous Captain Trail. Not content with this, Macarthur had quarreled with his detachment commander, the excellent and popular Captain Nepean, and this, finally, had led to his being transferred, with his wife and child, to the *Scarborough* when the fleet reached the Cape. Since landing in New South Wales, the two officers had not been on speaking terms with one another and the fact that Nepean had been granted one hundred twenty acres of land at Rose Hill and Macarthur only thirty at Farm Cove had led, Brewer was aware, to another bitter quarrel. But Nicholas Nepean was working his land with his entire company, whereas Macarthur. . . .

"I do not intend," the governor went on, his tone level, "to pander to the officers of the corps in their demands for land, Henry. All land grants must be utilized in order to grow food and raise livestock for the benefit of the colony as a whole. With that aim in mind, as I told Dodd, I shall regard with favor applications from convicts of good character and proven ability—even if their sentences have not expired or been remitted—as well as those from officers and men of the corps. But I shall give priority, since they have earned it, to seamen of the *Sirius* and the *Supply* and to any of the Marine Corps who wish to become settlers."

"Yes, sir," Brewer said, with warm approval. "I'm quite sure that is the right course to pursue."

Brewer and David Collins were in the Government House office, endeavoring to catch up with an accumulation of paperwork when Collins, sifting through a batch of applications for land grants, suddenly gave vent to a smothered exclamation.

"The deuce! Here's something that will be of interest to you, Henry. It's from your little convict paragon, Jenny Taggart. She's requesting thirty acres at Rose Hill, part of the holding of the late Sergeant Jenkins—the area exactly specified—and her application backed up by what purports to be poor old Jenkins's will. Unhappily, though, the will isn't signed. There's only a cross . . . but surely he could read and write, could he not?"

Henry Brewer rose and came to study the papers spread out on the judge advocate's table. He read the will with interest and only after he had subjected it to a careful scrutiny did he reply to Collins's question.

"Yes, Jenkins was literate, sir. But it states here that he dictated his will as he was dying and was too weak to sign it. That should not invalidate it, should it?"

"It isn't witnessed," Collins pointed out. He reread the application, frowning. "Taggart states that her application is made on behalf of herself and a prospective husband—one Edward William Munday, sentenced to seven years for theft—who came out here in the *Neptune*. Didn't he get a week on Pinchgut for trying to escape a little while ago?"

"Yes," Brewer confirmed. "And he would have been flogged had it not been for the fact that he was in poor physical condition."

"Hold hard," Collins interrupted. "There's something else, if I can lay my hands on it." He searched among the piled-up applications. "Yes, this is it. Quite a coincidence, it's an application for the *whole* of Jenkins's grant by—whom do you suppose?"

He made a wry grimace. "The application is from Lieutenant Macarthur, that's my guess."

David Collins shook his head. "No—not Macarthur. One of his bosom friends though—Lieutenant Leach, who recently transferred to the New South Wales

Corps. And *he* specifies the exact location of the land. Most of the applicants, as you also know, do not. An odd coincidence, don't you agree?"

Henry Brewer inclined his graying head. "Very odd indeed—and hardly justice, if he's awarded the whole grant." His words were mild enough, but his expression was truculent.

Collins smiled. "Well, it will be for the governor to decide," he said philosophically, starting to gather up the applications. "I *did* hear a rumor that Mister Leach was in line for a posting to Norfolk Island, as part of the relief garrison. Perhaps I should remind His Excellency—what do you think?"

Henry Brewer's expression did not alter. "In my view, sir, you would only be doing your duty as secretary were you to offer such a reminder." He added quietly, "I seem to recall that Mister Leach *applied* for Norfolk Island when Major Ross went there . . . possibly His Excellency will recollect the fact."

The governor, however, had matters of greater urgency on his mind when he returned, an hour later, with Captain Nepean.

His face was gray with fatigue, his shoulders stooped, and he said, gesturing to the pile of papers Collins had placed on his desk, "I cannot deal with these now, David. Nicholas has brought me the most distressing news from Rose Hill—the admirable, indispensable Dodd is dead!"

"The poor fellow was in bed, recovering from a bout of fever, when thieves raided his garden. He gave chase to the rogues, clad only in his nightshirt and, aided by some of my men, hunted them for several hours. But the effort proved too much for him—he collapsed and died before we could get him back to his house."

The governor slumped down in front of his desk and, sweeping the papers aside, buried his face in his hands. In a muffled voice, speaking more to himself than to either of the two officers, he burst out, "And I had dared to think that we had turned the corner at last! Merciful heaven, a drought, our precious crops in danger, and now we've lost Edward Dodd—the one man who might have saved them! God rest his noble soul . . . and damn theirs to perdition! There's not a man in this whole colony to take his place."

Collins touched Nepean's scarlet-clad arm and jerked his head in the direction of his own office. "We'd better leave His Excellency alone," he advised. "Dodd was his man—he brought him out with us in the *Sirius* and thought very highly of him."

"Is he really irreplaceable?" Nepean asked.

"Time will tell." David Collins mopped his brow, suddenly overwhelmingly conscious of the relentless heat. "We'll know when this drought ends. Dodd is the second key man we've lost—MacEntire, the government huntsman, was the other. The Indians wounded him in an ambush three weeks ago and Doctor White says he's dying."

Nicholas Nepean looked up quickly. "Yes, Tench was talking about that unfortunate incident. He said he led a punitive expedition in search of the culprits but could find no trace of them. It happened in the Botany Bay area, didn't it? It's strange because I was in that area with quite a small party at about the same time as the attack on MacEntire and I had no trouble."

"The Indians have always feared and disliked MacEntire," Brewer volunteered. "And probably with good reason. Even Baneelon wouldn't go near him or permit the fellow to lay a hand on him. But we know who the attacker is now—Baneelon named him as Pimelwi. The governor will probably send out a party to find and bring him in . . . or shoot him, if he eludes capture; Captain Tench has offered to lead it."

Nepean appeared surprised. "But I thought our much esteemed governor was against any action being taken against the Indians? He made no attempt to punish them for his own wounding, did he?"

Brewer and Collins exchanged glances. "If Mac-Entire dies, he will, Captain Nepean," Brewer stated with conviction. "He accepts that the time has come to teach them a lesson."

David Collins was silent for a moment. Then, a gleam in his eyes, he said emphatically, "And Pimelwi will be tried and hanged if he's brought in! It is, alas, the only way to make the Indians understand that we are here to stay."

CHAPTER XXIII

Jeremiah Leach was in no very pleasant frame of mind when he returned to his quarters, after an abortive interview with the governor, to find an invitation to dine with the Macarthurs awaiting him.

His temper cooled a little as he read it. From the first moment of making John Macarthur's acquaintance, he had recognized in him a kindred spirit, and the new arrival, anxious to learn all he could of the colony and its administration, had gone out of his way to foster their growing intimacy.

This evening, however, when he presented himself at the door of the small stone house overlooking Farm Cove—built originally for Lieutenant Clarke—with the hunk of bread in his pocket, which all dinner guests in Sydney were requested to provide for themselves—Leach knew that he was more in need of

advice than in a position to give it. He found John
Macarthur alone in the cramped living room and
barely listened to his apology for the absence of his
hostess before embarking on a recital of his own
pressing problems.

"I came early because I have to talk to you," he
explained. "Plague take it, John—I've been ordered
to Norfolk Island! It means that my application for
the land at Rose Hill will be rejected out of hand,
because I cannot persuade anyone to exchange post-
ings with me. And the governor won't listen—I've
just seen him. He says the matter doesn't concern him
and he cannot intervene on my behalf."

Lieutenant Macarthur subjected him to a faintly
chilling scrutiny and then, crossing to the unpolished
wooden table, which did duty as a sideboard, poured
a generous measure of brandy into a battered pewter
tankard and offered it to him.

"Drink that and you'll soon feel in a better humor,"
he suggested. "It's not the end of the world, my dear
fellow. They cannot send you to Norfolk for a while
in any case. Henry Ball is down with that fever he
picked up in Batavia, is he not?"

"Yes," Leach confirmed resentfully, "but the *Supply*'s master, Blackburn, has been ordered to take her
to Norfolk on the twenty-second, and I'm to sail with
her. I . . . and that assistant surgeon you brought out,
Wentworth, and a batch of blasted lifers and persistent
escapers from this colony."

"Why the haste?" Macarthur questioned.

"Oh, the governor wants Hunter and his people
from the *Sirius* brought back. They've been there for
about ten months, ever since the *Sirius* was wrecked.
And Phillip and Hunter are birds of a feather." Leach
gulped down his brandy, reddening a little under

John Macarthur's disapproving gaze. "I'm sorry . . . I needed that drink, John."

Macarthur picked up the tankard and refilled it without a word. Of medium height, he was possessed of a sharp-featured, intelligent face, shrewd dark eyes and a pendulous lower lip, which gave him at times a curiously sullen appearance. To Leach's disappointment, he seemed unmoved by the disaster that was threatening the plans they had recently made, and Leach said, taking the refilled tankard without acknowledgment, "The devil take it, John, if I don't get that land; we cannot share it, can we? And you'll not be given a grant unless you resign your commission in the corps."

"True," Macarthur conceded. From the room next door came the thin wailing of a child and then, raised very sweetly, the sound of a woman's voice offering the solace of a lullaby. His expression relaxed. "Elizabeth has a charming voice, has she not? And she is making fine progress with her piano lessons from Doctor Worgan."

Leach sipped his brandy, fuming inwardly. Macarthur's devotion to his wife and small son worried him—it was the one sign of weakness in an otherwise strong and ambitious character. Elizabeth Macarthur was a pleasant enough young woman, but she was excessively timid, and as a wife for John, in Leach's view, she fell short of perfection and occupied too much of his time and attention. The governor sought her company, admittedly, for dinners at Government House but. . . .

"Who will be granted that land," Macarthur demanded suddenly, "if your application is refused?"

"A bunch of convict whores," Leach answered resentfully. He told the new arrival about Jenny and the garden women. "She's petitioned for thirty acres —for herself and a young ne'er-do-well who came out in the *Neptune*. A convicted pickpocket named Munday, who's already made one attempt to escape. Damn it, Phillip *wants* to give them the land!"

Leach thought of Jenny Taggart, and his resentment increased. It was an infernal pity she had not been exiled to Norfolk Island, as she should have been, and, damn it, the height of injustice that he himself should have been ordered there now, just when he might have entered into partnership with John Macarthur. Even the little money promised by his father for purchasing livestock would have sufficed. John had a good head for business, without doubt. It had been his idea that they should pool their resources to enable them to bid for part of the next cargo of livestock and essential supplies that reached the colony. Rum, tobacco, and sheep, he had claimed, would be the means by which they could double their available capital.

But . . . Leach felt the sweat break out on his brow. If he were packed off to Norfolk Island, his chance would be lost—Macarthur would seek a partner elsewhere.

"I intend to relinquish my holding here," Macarthur stated, still thoughtful. He gestured disdainfully at the rough-hewn sandstone walls of the room in which they stood, with its shoddy, convict-made furniture. "I want something better than this hovel in which to bring up my family! And as for the land here . . . all I've raised on mine is a flock of scrawny chickens. I shall insist on sufficient land at Rose Hill to sustain my stock, build a fitting house there, and bide my time. Phillip will not be here for very much longer, you know."

Leach eyed him in astonishment. "You mean as governor?"

"Yes, that's what I mean. He's requested that he should be relieved—surely you knew?"

"I'd heard rumors," Leach admitted, "but I wasn't sure if they were true."

"They were . . . and are. He's going all right. And be damned to him for the blind, priggish fool he is!" Macarthur sneered. "Trying to make honest men of convicted felons by showing them favors, trying to make friends with bloodthirsty black savages and going out of his way to put the military officers at a disadvantage."

"Phillip's successor may be no less blind, John," Leach suggested uncertainly.

"He could scarcely be more so," Macarthur retorted. "And he might well be one of us. Wait till our commandant, Major Grose, arrives. Grose is no sluggard, and I'll warrant that he'll not stand by in silence and see his officers deprived of opportunities given so freely to convicts and arbitrarily refused to them."

His wife joined them at that moment, and he broke off to take her hand affectionately and commiserate with her when she complained wearily of the humid heat and their small son's reluctance to settle down for the night.

Leach endured the wretched meal of tough, tasteless fowl, imbibing freely of Macarthur's excellent claret and containing his impatience when the conversation turned, as always in Elizabeth's company, to her domestic difficulties, her newfound passion for the piano, and her fears for her son's health. She was pregnant and she looked ill and washed out, snapping at the maid who waited on them and paying her guest the minimum of attention, as she sat uncomfortably in her hard, straight-backed chair and picked distastefully at her food.

To his relief she excused herself soon after they had finished eating, and John Macarthur, having seen her to the bedroom, placed a brandy bottle and a cedarwood box on the table and offered hospitably, "Stay and smoke a pipe with me, Jeremiah." He smiled, opening the box of tobacco. "This is locally grown . . . and not too bad, in my opinion. It came from your so-called garden women, surreptitiously, of course. By coincidence I obtained it through the medium of the pickpocket you mentioned. What did you say his name was—Friday?"

"Munday," Leach supplied. He helped himself, crushing the dark, musty-smelling leaves into the bowl of his pipe.

"Munday is a rogue," Macarthur said flatly. He filled his own pipe, an odd little smile playing about his full lips. "It would not be difficult to discredit him. He's been assigned to work on the government fishing boats, he told me . . . information that was followed by his offer to supply my household with fish, also surreptitiously and at a price."

"Yes." Leach did not pretend to misunderstand him. "I take your point, John. But discrediting Munday will not help me—I'm due to sail in the plaguey *Supply* in less than a fortnight."

"I've been giving that matter some thought, my dear fellow." John Macarthur had his pipe going, and he leaned back, the long stem clamped between his teeth, to stare with narrowed eyes at the thin blue cloud of smoke rising ceilingward. "You could be taken ill, of course, but you would have to convince the surgeon that the complaint was genuine. That would not be impossible but—I've a better idea. Abbott tells me that he and Tench are taking a second party to search for the Indians who attacked that gamekeeper fellow to the north of Botany Bay. You could volunteer to accompany them, could you not?"

"Volunteer?" Leach was shocked out of his calm. "In heaven's name why should I? It's ghastly country north of the bay—full of swamps and sand flies and mosquitoes! And in this heat I've no desire to go anywhere near it."

John Macarthur laughed, his amusement tinged with malice. "Nothing is achieved without effort, Jeremiah. If you really want to avoid being posted to Norfolk Island . . . well, a punitive expedition to Botany Bay would afford you ample opportunity to contract a fever, would it not? Or to sustain a wound of an incapacitating nature—an Indian spear in the fleshy part of the leg, for example. You could hardly be sent to Norfolk Island if you were unfit to carry out your military duties, could you?"

His laughter suggested that he did not mean his outrageous idea to be taken seriously, but looking into his cold brown eyes, Leach was not sure.

"You're jesting with me!" he accused irritably. "What are Tench and Abbott going to think if I make myself a target for some infernal Indian's spear? And how the devil can I ensure that it strikes me in the fleshy part of the leg and not in my vitals?"

Macarthur regarded him with thinly veiled contempt. "Tench and Abbott cannot think anything if you are out of their sight," he said scornfully. "And I didn't suggest that an *Indian* should throw the spear, did I, my dear fellow?"

Again the implication was plain, and Jeremiah Leach gulped down his brandy, his irritation growing.

"Are you suggesting that *I* should inflict a wound on myself?" he demanded.

Macarthur shrugged. "Did I say that?"

"No. But you—"

"Surely, my dear Jeremiah, it depends on how much you want to stay here. And"—Macarthur set down his pipe and rose, ostentatiously smothering a yawn—"and how much you want to enter into partnership with me. Sleep on it, why don't you? And I will do likewise. I bid you goodnight, Jeremiah."

Next day Leach volunteered to accompany the expedition, and Tench readily accepted his offer.

"We'll be leaving at first light in the morning," he said. "Abbott, Prentice, and myself, and we're taking Sergeant Williams and the two convicts who were with MacEntire when he was attacked to act as guides. We'll proceed by boat to the peninsula at the head of Botany Bay and strike north from there, in the hope of deceiving the Indians, and then double back, under cover of darkness, to Pimelwi's village and try to take his people by surprise, if we can. You know our orders?"

Leach shrugged. "To apprehend what's his name—Pimelwi—and bring him back to the settlement for trial, that's all I know."

"The governor is resolved to make the Indians understand, once and for all, that they cannot attack and murder our people with impunity," Tench told him. "So if we fail to capture Pimelwi alive, he's to be shot and his head brought back, as proof of his execution. But no other Indians are to be fired on, save in self-defense; no molesting of women or theft of Indian property permitted. Is that clear to you?"

"Perfectly, sir," Leach acknowledged. "Thank you."

The party, consisting of four officers and thirty-six other ranks, set off at daybreak the following morning. The peninsula at the head of Botany Bay was reached without incident, but they were compelled to wait for the tide to ebb before they could cross the intervening arm of water at the ford, and it was dark when, leaving knapsacks and baggage on the bank with a small guard, they finally tackled the fording of the river beyond.

Leach, stumbling blindly through waist-high water, with his firelock and cartouche box held above his head, silently cursed Macarthur and his own impulsiveness. Watkin Tench, full of energy and zealous as always, took no heed of the fact that the rest of his party was greatly fatigued, and led them on for nearly an hour, until brought to a halt by a flooded creek, some sixty yards wide, which stood in their way. By the faint light of the newly risen moon it appeared a formidable obstacle, but Tench was undeterred.

"Damme!" he exclaimed. "This looked dry from the seaward and I supposed we could walk across without getting our feet wet." He summoned the guides, both big, hulking men, who had worked as game killers under MacEntire's direction, and consulted them as to the chances of their being able to cross.

"We'll lose a lot o' time, goin' 'round the 'ead o' the creek, sir," the elder of the two told him. "Might take us till daylight, an' if you're wantin' ter take them Injuns by surprise, it'd maybe mean we'd 'ave missed 'em."

"Yes—but is it safe to wade across?" Tench slapped at a stinging insect on his sweating cheek, and Leach listened to the exchange, wanting nothing so much as to hear his commander give the order to make camp. What the hell, he thought rebelliously, did it matter if they advanced on the Indian village tonight or tomorrow night? The Indians weren't going to vanish from their homes or— To his chagrin he heard Tench say, "Very well, we'll push on. Lead the way, Marlow. Mister Leach, you follow him, if you please—and have a care, all of you."

Leach obeyed with extreme reluctance, but his first few steps reassured him, and with the convict Marlow and a stout sergeant of the Grenadier Company, he made rapid progress for about thirty yards. Then, his heart in his mouth, he felt himself sinking almost waist-deep into glutinous mud, into which his struggles to free himself only caused him to sink deeper. He yelled out a warning, expecting Tench to come to his aid, but, instead, the expedition's leader merely directed the others to cross farther to the right. On all sides he could hear cries for help; the stout sergeant declared himself incapable of moving either backward or forward, and Marlow, although he said nothing, appeared to be in a similar predicament. Tench himself was floundering not far away; Ensign Prentice was half-buried in the clinging slime; and Lieutenant Abbott, who was with the rear guard, shouted something Leach could not hear and went running off toward the head of the creek.

The rear guard crossed without difficulty, to stand aimlessly on the farther bank, peering down at their struggling comrades but doing little to help them to extricate themselves from the morass. The noise they made, Leach thought irritably, was enough to scare off every Indian within earshot, and he shouted to Abbott to cut off some tree boughs and lay them across the swamp. He had used the device once before, when caught in quicksand, and to his heartfelt relief

Abbott and his party did as he had asked. By dint of building what amounted to a raft and throwing lopped-off branches to the trapped men to grasp, all were eventually able to drag themselves to the far bank, the sergeant being hauled in by means of a rope, which Marlow contrived to hurl to him, lying flat on his stomach on the raft.

It was a disastrous beginning to the expedition. All the men, rescuers as well as rescued, were exhausted, and the muskets of those who had sunk into the swamp were clogged and had to be cleaned of mud and slime before they could be rendered serviceable. Tench, however, insisted that they must push on to the village; he divided his small command into three parties, and about half an hour before sunrise all three detachments of weary, cursing men entered their objective to find it devoid of its inhabitants, the cooking fires cold.

Leach was so filled with rage that he could not trust himself to speak when Tench announced, after a brief consultation with the two guides, that they must retrace their steps to the river immediately.

"The tide will change in an hour, Marlow says, so we'll have to make a forced march and cross by the ford before it's flooded. If we don't, we shall be without food until evening, because all our baggage is on the peninsula."

In the glare of the rising sun they staggered back to the first ford, alternately running and walking at Tench's command, and reached it, more dead than alive, just before the tide turned. The baggage guard crossed to meet them as they slithered into the water of the second fording place and, relieved of their muskets by the men of the guard, they splashed disconsolately back to their starting point, to fling themselves down beside the campfire, too drained of energy even to curse.

Revived by food and drink and a few hours' sleep, Leach roused himself to the realization that, for all the hardships he had endured, he was no nearer a solution to his problem than he had been when he set out. Somehow, he knew, he would have to absent himself from the main body long enough to put Macarthur's plan into operation—*if* he did—but he was now even less enamored of it than he had been when John Macarthur had first suggested that he might attempt it...the whole idea was mad. Mad and dangerous, and he was sorely tempted to abandon it and, indeed, might well have done so had not Tench unexpectedly played into his hands.

"We're going on," the marine captain announced. "Recommencing our operations in the opposite direction from the route we followed last night." He went into details of the ground he intended to cover, and Leach listened glumly. He brightened, however, when Tench said, "I want you to take a couple of men back across the river to hold off any Indians who may try to double back to the village past our rear. Don't open fire on them unless you have to—the threat of your presence should be enough to deter them. Ah ... you'd better take Sergeant Williams and Corporal Clay, they're both pretty done up, and it will be easier for them than if they come with us. All right?"

"Certainly, sir," Leach assured him. It was fate, he thought as, half an hour later, he set off in obedience to his orders. Neither Williams nor Clay raised any objection when, having posted them at the point Tench had indicated, he announced his intention of reconnoitering the village by himself. He left them, seated contentedly on the riverbank, with their muskets across their knees and their heads drooping with weariness, and—careful this time to circle around the head of the creek—found himself, an hour and a half later, on the outskirts of the cluster of Indian huts that they had searched earlier without success.

Some broken spears and fish gigs had been left in one of the huts, and having satisfied himself that the village was still deserted, he entered the hut in search of a spear suitable for his purpose. He had decided on a method of wounding himself. Again fate was on his side—he found just what he was looking for in the shape of a spearhead, with two of its barbs broken and its shaft splintered some twelve or fourteen inches from the head. Leaving the rest where they lay, he emerged into the clearing in front of the huts and squatted down on his haunches to examine his find more closely. A sudden movement on the far side of the clearing caught his eye, and he froze.

There was no sound, but in the leaf-dappled shadows cast by the moon he saw—or imagined he saw—a deeper, more substantial shadow disengage itself and come gliding toward him. Leach's heart quickened its beat as a nameless fear gripped him. No white man moved so swiftly and silently, he told himself, and Williams and Clay would not have followed him. Damn it, it had to be an Indian! The fugitive Pimelwi, perhaps, or one of his murderous tribe, slinking back to the abandoned village by canoe, instead of overland as Tench had anticipated. He felt for his musket, letting the spearhead fall, his fingers groping for the cocking hammer. His powder might be damp, better perhaps if he— The shadow revealed itself, as a squat, dark-skinned figure stepped into a shaft of moonlight, head on one side, listening intently.

Leach did not recognize him; the light was too faint, and in any event one black fellow looked to him much like another. But he saw that the man—barely forty paces from the empty hut—was armed with spear and throwing stick, poised, ready for action, and clearly suspecting the presence of a stranger as he looked cautiously about him. Leach rose to his feet, the musket leveled. He had no conscious memory of discharging his piece, the crash of the discharge a meaningless sound, echoing in his ears, and it was not until he saw the Indian fall that he realized what he had done. The man lay for a moment where he had fallen, moaning softly, then he managed to get to his feet and shamble off, still clutching his spear and throwing stick and leaving a trail of blood behind him, a dark stain on the sand of the clearing.

Leach stood as if turned to stone, his smoking musket still to his shoulder. Then memory returned, slowly and with seeming reluctance, and he found himself shaking with silent laughter. The fates had, indeed, come down in his favor, he thought exultantly—no one, not even Captain Tench, would suspect that he was lying if he claimed that he had been wounded in an attack by a native of Pimelwi's tribe whom, in self-defense, he had fired on and hit.

He bent and picked up the broken spearhead, shuddering as he looked at it. He hadn't cleaned the plaguey thing, he remembered, but there was time. Sergeant Williams would have heard his shot—he and Clay would hurry, they were bound to, lest their officer were in danger. So . . . he frowned. He could allow himself half an hour, at least, to clean the spearhead and, as a precaution fire a second shot, to make certain that the stout grenadier sergeant was left in no doubt as to where his duty lay.

He reloaded his musket, primed it carefully, and fired. Then, using his handkerchief, he wiped the barbs with even more care, moistening the linen with spittle and even extending his cleaning operation to include the splintered spear shaft. When it was done, he stood with it in his hand, the sweat pouring off him as he realized that he could delay no longer—he must carry out Macarthur's plan now or abandon it completely and let them send him to Norfolk Island.

"Nothing is achieved without effort," John Macarthur had said. He took the broken spear in his right hand, raised it above his head, and, gritting his teeth, plunged its barbed tip into his thigh with all the force he could muster.

In the soporific calm of the riverbank, his head resting against the gnarled trunk of an ancient gum tree, Sergeant Williams slept the sleep of the physically spent, emitting an occasional snore from between his parted lips. Beside him, Corporal Clay struggled manfully against the almost overwhelming desire to follow the older man's example for he, too, was very tired, and night had brought little relief from the all-prevailing heat. Dimly, from somewhere in the distance, he heard the crack of a musket shot and he sat up, blinking.

"Sar'nt . . . Sar'nt Williams!"

Williams was instantly alert. "Yes, what is it?" Clay told him and he grunted. "How far away d'you reckon it was?"

"Hard ter tell. All I know is that it was faint. Maybe a couple o' miles distant. It was just the one shot."

Sergeant Williams spat, with great accuracy, into the dark, arching roots of the mangroves below him.

"Could it have bin from that village, the one we went to las' night?"

"It could 'ave, I s'pose, but I can't be sure." He hesitated and then asked, with a reluctance he made no attempt to hide, "Did we oughter go an' see if Mister Leach is all right, Sar'nt?"

"No call to do that," the sergeant decided, "if it was just the one shot. We've got our orders an' we'd best stick to 'em. The captain an' his party'll be back soon—we can report hearin' a shot an' let him say what we're ter do."

He composed himself once more for slumber, and after a few minutes Corporal Clay did the same. Neither of them heard the second shot. . . .

In the clearing in front of the native huts Jeremiah Leach looked down at his bleeding thigh and swore weakly. Holy hell, he asked himself, what had possessed him to jab that foul barb so deeply into his flesh? The pain was appalling, and he was losing more blood than he would have believed possible. Had he, without knowing it, cut through a vital blood vessel? He tried to shift the spearhead in the hope of easing the pain, but it was firmly implanted in the muscle of his thigh and the slightest movement increased the flow of blood, so he desisted, biting back a sob.

Williams and Clay should not be much longer, but the fools might have lost their way or gone floundering into the creek in their haste to get to him and . . . damn them to hell, he might bleed to death before they reached the village! He would have to put on a tourniquet because somehow the bleeding had to be stopped. His fingers clumsy in their haste, he took off his sweat-soaked neckerchief and bound it, as firmly as he could, about the upper part of his thigh. It had the desired result, and relieved by this small success, he took a swig from his canteen and settled down to wait with what patience he could muster.

No one came. He strained his ears, but there was no sound, save the beating of his own heart and the faint stirring of a breeze rustling the leaves of the trees on the edge of the clearing. He sat up, shuddering, and was shocked to see the gray lightening of the sky that heralded the dawn. Plague take those infernal, idle soldiers. Why hadn't they come? Hadn't they heard his shots—had the swine been asleep, *asleep on duty*? He would have them flogged if they had and see that their blasted stripes were taken from them if it was the last thing he did.

But . . . Tench and Abbott should be back at the ford by now. They would not fail him, even if his shots had gone unheard—Tench would realize that he was missing and send out a party to search for him. If he fired another shot, it would save time, would guide them to him. He felt about him for his musket, wishing now that he had reloaded it before thrusting that miserable spearhead into his leg.

He managed, at the cost of considerable pain, to ram ball and powder cartridge into the barrel, but the tourniquet loosened as a result of his exertions, the bleeding restarted, and he was compelled to abandon the loading in order to tighten it. He laid the musket down, swearing impotently, his whole body bathed in sweat and his hands shaking as he snatched at the sodden cloth.

It was at that moment that he looked up and, in the dim gray light, saw three Indians enter the clearing. The man in the center, apparently injured, was being supported by the other two, both of whom were armed. Guessing that the injured man was the one he had wounded, Leach yielded to panic, aware that if they saw him, they would almost certainly seek revenge. His musket was useless—he had time neither to prime nor to cock it—but he snatched it up and, using it as a crutch, took to his heels in an attempt to find concealment in the bush. His leg was stiff; he stumbled, measured his length on the sandy ground, dragged himself up, and hobbled on, gasping with pain.

The Indians heard him, and after only a momentary hesitation one of them slid his spear into his throwing stick and came padding after him, in swift, relentless pursuit. The spear, well aimed and deftly thrown, struck Leach between the shoulder blades, and he went crashing down, screaming his agony aloud.

Dawn was breaking when Watkin Tench's party returned to the river. They had struggled through thick bush for most of the night without seeing hide nor hair of their quarry, and the men were limp with fatigue, their sweating faces swollen from insect bites, and their spirits low. Tench received Sergeant Williams's report of the single musket shot with understandable dismay.

"That infernal young fool Leach!" he said to Abbott, keeping his voice low. "He's been out here long enough to know the danger of wandering about these woods by himself. We'll have to break our fast before we go look for him. These poor fellows cannot be expected to march any farther with empty bellies and, come to that, neither can we!"

The search party set off two hours later.

Jeremiah Leach was unconscious when they found him. He was lying face down in a pool of blood, and other bloodstains led across the clearing and into the bush, where they petered out, yielding no clue as to the whereabouts of the man or men who had fled, wounded, from the scene.

"The poor young devil is still alive," said Tench. "We had better break off that spear and carry him on a litter. I don't give much for his chances, although maybe the surgeons will contrive to patch him up, if we can get him back to the settlement in time. Damme! We should have got here sooner—it's my fault."

"We couldn't have, sir," Abbott told him flatly. He gestured to the tourniquet, on which the blood had now dried. "This happened hours ago—long before we got back to the river. In fact"—he knelt down by the injured man, gently turning him onto his side and peering down at the spearhead embedded in his thigh—"he was hit twice . . . look! He must have broken the shaft off this and then tried to staunch the bleeding with his neckcloth—and the second spear must have struck him as he was endeavoring to make his escape. My God, it's in deep! I'm afraid to try and break it."

"Leave it to Marlow," Tench advised. "He's an expert." He sent a soldier in search of the convict huntsman, who was working on the preparation of the litter, adding a sharp command to him to hurry.

Abbott moistened his handkerchief from his canteen and wiped Leach's ashen face and flaccid, blood-stained lips. "He's pretty far gone, I'm afraid. Well, at least he won't feel anything."

Marlow came striding up and Tench said, "Ah, good. See if you can snap this spear shaft off, lad, and then get Mister Leach onto the litter. Have a care how you do it."

Edward Abbott yielded his place to the convict, and the two officers moved out of earshot.

"Wasn't Leach under orders to sail with your advance party for Norfolk Island?" Tench asked curiously. "On the *Supply*'s next voyage there?"

Abbott nodded, his blue eyes troubled. "Yes, he was —though he was doing his damnedest to get one of us to exchange with him. He had some ploy in prospect with Johnny Boddice . . . er . . . that is John Macarthur, sir. I'm not sure what it was—a partnership in a land grant wangle, I think, or something of the kind. You know the governor's policy regarding our officers." He sighed. "Well, the poor fellow won't have to worry about going to Norfolk Island now, will he?"

"No, that he won't. He'll be deuced lucky if we can get him back to Sydney Cove." Watkin Tench picked up the discarded musket, his mouth tightly compressed. He had never liked Jeremiah Leach and he did not greatly care for his prospective partner either but . . . this was unfortunate and he found himself wondering why Leach should have chosen to go back to the village alone. Glory hunting or some less worthy motive, perhaps? There was no way of telling and, in any event, it was not up to him to delve any deeper.

But the governor, who set such store by the maintenance of good relations with the Indians, would be greatly displeased by what had happened. Undoubtedly it would mean another punitive expedition.

From somewhere in the bush at his back he heard the strange bird the natives called a kookaburra emit its high-pitched cackle, sounding for all the world like demented laughter, and suddenly irritated, Tench thought longingly of his impending return to England. Another nine months or perhaps a year of this and then . . . home. Home, God willing, before he became infected by this place and as demented as its infernal birds.

Marlow came to stand woodenly at his side, his dark, gypsy face devoid of expression. "The officer's dead, sir," he announced. "Shall we bring his body back with us?"

"His *body*? I . . . yes, we must bring it . . . him back for burial." Watkin Tench caught his breath and then said, "God rest his soul," his voice as flat as Marlow's had been.

Abbott glanced uneasily at the still figure on the litter and responded with a constrained "Amen."

CHAPTER XXIV

Jenny heard the news of Jeremiah Leach's death with curious indifference. Ned was now her sole concern, and his behavior was so erratic and unpredictable that she was kept in a state of constant anxiety. At first he had been an ardent lover, eager to please and acquiesce in anything she asked of him, but all too soon he began to take their relationship for granted, treating her with a casual possessiveness she found unbearably humiliating.

With the return of the *Supply* from Norfolk Island at the end of February, bearing Captain Hunter and the officers and men of the wrecked *Sirius*, Eliza and Charlotte achieved their hearts' desire. Their seamen, William Read and Robert Webb, obtained permission to wed them and each was granted one hundred twenty acres of land between Rose Hill and Mount

Prospect. With their departure, all the work of the
garden fell on Jenny and Melia. Ned, claiming that
he was fully employed on the government fishing
boats, did little to aid them, and to Jenny's chagrin
he seemed—despite the example set by Eliza and
Charlotte—more determined than ever to avoid the
ties of matrimony. Her application for part of the
land granted to Tom Jenkins depended on her marriage, and although she warned him that if she did
not marry, she would be forced to abandon her claim,
Ned was adamant.

"A plague on it, Jenny, I'm not cut out to be a
‚soil-grubber," he objected. "And if I wed you, that's
what I'll be condemned to, sure as fate, with no chance
of getting away from this damned hellhole! But I
am going to get away; I'm going to escape from here
if it kills me. I'd as soon be dead as spend the rest
of my days here, so you may as well make up your
mind to it!"

He was obsessed by the desire to escape, and unhappily, the work to which he had been assigned
served to encourage his hopes. Aware of Jenny's disapproval, he was secretive concerning his plans, but
from the occasional hints he let slip—or confided
to Melia—it was evident that there was a scheme
afoot among the fishery workers to steal a boat . . .
a scheme in which Ned was deeply involved.

Such attempts had been made in the past, but almost all had ended in failure, and Jenny was not
seriously alarmed on Ned's behalf until, going down
one evening in early March to watch the unloading
of the day's catch, she was shocked to see Johnny
Butcher in the crew of the first boat to tie up at the
wharf. He recognized her after a moment's frowning
scrutiny and raised a hand in greeting. Later, when

the unloading was completed and Will Bryant, the convict superintendent, dismissed his crew, he came strolling over to join her, a pleased smile curving his lips.

"Remember me, Jenny Taggart?"

Jenny had not set eyes on him since the night that he and his companions had raided Tom Jenkins's cabin, and she studied him with a certain hostility, noting the changes that time had wrought in him. His skin was deeply tanned and he still had an air of devil-may-care arrogance about him, but he was thin to the point of emaciation and the marks of fetters showed red-raw on his wrists and ankles, indicating that they had only lately been removed. Clearly he had been compelled to give himself up and had paid dearly for his few weeks of freedom in the bush.

"Well," he prompted. "Do you remember me?"

"Yes," Jenny admitted warily. "You're Johnny Butcher. I remember you—have I not cause?"

"Aye, that you have, lass. But you'll not hold it against me, will you?"

"Why should I not?"

"Because I'm begging your forgiveness," he offered gravely.

Of what use was it to bear a grudge? Jenny hesitated and then, with a reluctance she could not hide, shook her head. "You didn't get to Timor, did you?" she challenged, recalling the boastful claims he had made as justification for the raid and, when it came to that, for his companions' brutal attack on poor Tom. "You never made your escape, for all your bold talk, so it was all in vain. You—"

Johnny Butcher cut her short, his voice low and intense. "It was not in vain, Jenny—we're going to Timor, never fear. Our sailing had to be delayed because some of our plans went awry and we could not stay in the bush any longer. Starvation and those bloodthirsty Indians beat us. They killed Jack Mercer and Toby Locke, and Black Caesar and Jim Clarke were taken by the lobsterbacks so that only left Nat Lilley and me. We had to give ourselves up when we ran out of powder and shot—we had no choice."

"And you were flogged for your pains," Jenny suggested, still bitter. "Flogged and fettered! Yet you go on talking of escape."

He flashed her his arrogant smile. "We chose our moment to return—the governor declared an amnesty to celebrate the colony's third year. They kept us in fetters for a couple of months but they didn't flog us, praise be! And then Will Bryant had us assigned to his boat, all nice and legal. So we'll be going any day now, granted a modicum of luck. There's only one thing lacking now—a compass. But Will knows where he can lay hands on that."

"Will Bryant?" Jenny echoed incredulously. She thought of Ned and drew in her breath sharply. Was it with these madmen that Ned intended to make his bid for freedom, she wondered dully. Was he, too, mad enough to believe that he could reach Timor in a small boat, across three thousand miles of ocean? She had not supposed that any of the men who had raided Tom's small holding would be among the escapers and, least of all, that Will Bryant, the trusted convict whom the governor himself had appointed to superintend the fishery workers, would be party to the venture. "*Is* Will Bryant going with you?" she asked, a catch in her voice.

Johnny Butcher nodded. "Of course—he always was."

"But he's married—he has a wife and children here!"

"Aye, so he has . . . and he's bringing them with us."

"He must be out of his mind!" Jenny exclaimed, shocked. She hesitated, biting her lower lip. But she had to know, she told herself, and asked uncertainly, "And Ned—Ned Munday—is he going with you?"

His bold blue eyes met hers in thoughtful question, then he shook his head. "Not if I can help it. Oh, he wants to right enough, but I don't trust him to pull his weight. Munday's an idle rogue, unreliable and out only for himself—we can do without his kind. Although Will Bryant—" He broke off, frowning. "None of this will go any farther, will it, Jenny?"

"No," she assured him. "Of course not."

He beckoned her nearer, and she came, conscious of the strong magnetism he possessed. She had felt it, all those months ago, in the hut at Rose Hill, she remembered, but then her anxiety for poor Tom and her fear of Nat Lilley and his companions had deadened her response to it. Yet he had made an impression on her, even then; certainly she had never forgotten him and, had the circumstances been different, would have been pleased to see him again.

"Will is putting Munday to the test," Johnny told her, lowering his voice. "If he fails it, he'll not be coming with us."

"Putting him to the test? What do you mean?"

"I can't tell you that." His strong brown hand reached out to take hers, drawing her yet closer and, to her own surprise, setting her heart beating wildly. Confused, she attempted to free herself, but he kept her hand imprisoned, looking down into her face, his own suddenly grave and pensive. "Jenny, this is no madcap venture, I give you my word. We shall make it to Timor, never fear."

"But it's so far," she demurred. "How can you hope to go so far in a small boat?"

"Aye, three thousand miles. But"—Johnny's smile returned, mocking her doubts—"we shall have charts, a compass, and a quadrant, and I'm a fair hand at navigation, like I told you before. We'll be close enough to land for most of the passage to enable us to take our bearings and replenish our water and supplies. And we'll have a good boat, the best there is. It may take us three or four months but what's that, what are three thousand miles, if there's freedom at the end?"

Like Ned, Jenny thought wretchedly, whose only dream was of escape, Johnny Butcher did not care how high the risk was or count the cost of failure. He had paid it more than once already and now . . . now he was again putting his life in the balance. His life and Ned's, if they permitted Ned to join them—and, despite his opposition, she had little doubt that they would. Will Bryant was a friend of Ned's; test or no test—whatever that might entail—Bryant would speak up for Ned. He—

"Come with us, Jenny Taggart," Johnny suggested unexpectedly. "Why don't you? Mary Bryant would be glad of another girl's company. And as for me, why"—heedless of who might be watching them, he took her in his arms, his hard, muscular body pressed against hers—"I'd be for taking you—aye, that I would! I've fancied you since the first time we met."

"Oh, please!" Jenny struggled against him. "Let me go, I—let me go, Johnny!"

He laughed. "Nay, I'm serious—I mean it, lass. If it would set matters right for you, we could wed before we sail. Hell, what's there to lose? We'd get home from Timor—don't you want to go back to England?"

Breathless, she whispered, "Yes. But there's Ned. I . . . let me go. Please, I—"

He stiffened and released her. "What's Munday to you, plague take him? *I* asked you to join us, I offered to wed you, did I not?" His tone was harsh. A hand beneath her chin, he forced her to look at him. "Or did he ask you first, Jenny? Is that it?"

A wave of color flooded Jenny's cheeks. Ned hadn't asked her either to wed him or to join the escape attempt, she thought wretchedly. Until now she had supposed that no women were to be included. Tears came to ache in her throat, and it was all she could do to hold them back.

Johnny Butcher swore softly and vehemently, but then his anger faded. He laid his hands on her shoulders quite gently, and there was a gleam of what might have been pity in his blue eyes. "I thought his girl was the dark lass—the one they call Melia Bishop," he said. "She's been with him a time or two when we've been talking over plans with Will and the others."

Aware of this, Jenny nodded but said nothing, and he went on, "You made a grave error, choosing Ned Munday, Jenny. He's no good to you and I swear he never will be."

"I—I've known him a long time," Jenny managed. "Since we were children. And he came out here in the *Neptune*—I had to take care of him. He would have died if I hadn't."

"And you don't fancy the idea of him coming with us to Timor?" Johnny suggested. "You want him to stay?"

Did she? Jenny wondered. Did she really want Ned to stay? "I don't know," she confessed. "If he's made his mind up, I would not try to keep him here against his will. But for his sake—"

"You could settle it by coming in his stead, lass. There's still time, and I still want you." The look in his eyes told her that this, at least, was true, and for a moment she was tempted. What, after all was said and done, had she to lose? Was shipwreck more to be dreaded than the drudgery of this place? The new life she had tried so hard to build was still only a hope, growing fainter, and compared with this man, what had Ned to offer? Not even loyalty, it seemed, and certainly not love. Yet . . . Jenny drew in her breath sharply. It was Ned who dreamed of escape, not she. If she accepted Johnny Butcher's strange proposal, would she not be robbing Ned of the one chance he had?

She started to tell him so, but he silenced her with a raised hand. "Think on it, Jenny."

Without waiting for her reply, he turned on his heel and went striding purposefully away across the wharf.

In the hut he shared with Jenny, Ned took the locket from its hiding place and went to the door to examine it the better in daylight. It was a good piece, he decided, eyeing it critically, and she had cared for it well—not a single stone was missing from the circle of brilliants by which it was surrounded. He opened the frame carefully and removed the faded scrap of blue ribbon it contained—God knew why the little fool had chosen to frame so torn and tarnished a relic! Sentimental reasons, probably. He let the ribbon fall and was closing the delicate catch on the locket when Melia came to stand beside him, emitting a little gasp of dismay.

"Ned—that's Jenny's locket! The one thing above all others that she treasures. What are you doing with it?"

He thrust the locket quickly into the pocket of his trousers. "I gave it to her," he retorted defensively. "And I need it." He had not expected Melia or, indeed, Jenny herself to be here at this hour; normally they put in an hour's work at the fishnets just before sunset, prior to cooking the evening meal, and he was disconcerted, aware that Melia would reproach him if she were to guess his intentions.

"Why do you need it?" Melia asked. He shrugged, and she said accusingly, "You stole it, didn't you?"

"And if I did? I can put it to better use than Jenny does, plague take it!"

"What better use?" Melia persisted.

Net laughed and put an arm round her slim waist. He was aware of the attraction he had for her but aware also that Melia was ashamed of the feelings he could arouse in her, and was fiercely determined not to yield to them. She was a lady born, he thought derisively, and fastidious. No unwashed convict soil-grubber or drunken marine for the Lady Melia; but he himself, because he was always clean and well shaven and could ape the manners of the gentry when he chose, had a certain appeal, even to her. But she was loyal to Jenny, bound to her by the strong bonds of a friendship forged in adversity, and on the few occasions when he had ventured to take liberties with her, he had sensed her inner conflict. He could snatch a kiss and feel her hunger, her desire, but in an instant it was stifled; she would turn on him resentfully, and he, wise in the ways of women, would make a jest of it, pretend casualness and pass it off thus, leaving her feeling both guilty and unsatisfied.

He held her to him now, his mouth seeking hers, and for a moment she let herself relax against him, and desire flamed in them both, mutually and swiftly communicated. Then Melia thrust him away, her cheeks flaming, and Ned, in no way disconcerted, roared with unseemly laughter and left her to what, he knew, would be a torment of her conscience. At least, he told himself smugly, his ploy had caused her to forget the locket, and by the time she remembered it and told Jenny, it would be long gone.

Will Bryant was waiting for him in Cockle Cove, the skiff he kept for his own use drawn up on the sandy beach. He was a tall, good-looking man, a fisherman by trade, and anxious that they should not be observed, he came at once to the reason for their meeting.

"Here you are," he said and counted five gold sovereigns into Ned's hand. "That's the agreed price. But Detmer Smith's a slippery customer—make sure he doesn't cheat you." He issued crisp instructions to enable Ned to ascertain that the instrument he was to buy was in working order and added warningly, "Better do this right, Ned lad—we can't leave till we get that compass. And if you slip up, Johnny and Nat say you're out. They don't want to take you along with us anyway, as you very well know."

Ned nodded sullenly. "Bad cess to both the bastards then! Why don't you leave *them* behind?"

"Because Johnny's the navigator—the only one we've got," Bryant retorted impatiently. "I can handle boats but I can't plot a course to bleeding Timor. All right—off you go. Smith's expecting you, and Nat and Johnny will be waiting for you here when you get back. Give them the compass and the charts and then make yourself scarce—they'll take the skiff and stow it away."

Ned rowed out in the fast fading light to the anchorage. The Dutch snow, *Waak-sam-heyd*, had been chartered to take the officers and men of the wrecked *Sirius* to England, and the bargaining for this charter with her rapacious master had, he knew, kept her in the harbor for over three months. But it had been concluded at last, and now Detmer Smith was preparing to sail, making what money he could before he left the colony by supplying Will Bryant with the charts and navigating instruments needed for the voyage to Timor.

He had previously sold them a quadrant, some muskets and ammunition, and a few casks of salt tack and biscuit but, cunningly had withheld delivery of a compass until the last moment, in the hope of raising its price.

The *Waak-sam-heyd*—brig-rigged, with a trysail mast—was small and very dirty, and as Ned stepped on board, leaving his skiff secured to her midship chains, his nostrils wrinkled in distaste as a strong, pungent odor of cooking spices reached them, unpleasantly mingled with the stench from her bilges and the sickly sweet smell of rotting rice. The crew of the *Sirius* would not like the conditions they would find here, he thought maliciously, not after their spick-and-span bloody warship but . . . they'd lost her, so be damned to them! At least they were going home, leaving this accursed, famine-stricken place behind them.

Detmer Smith, a dark-faced man of mixed Malay and European ancestry, was in his cabin, engaged in the consumption of a large meal of curry when Ned was conducted into his presence by a slovenly Malay seaman. The compass and two tattered charts lay on the littered table beside him; he gestured to them but did not invite his visitor to sit down and partake of the meal, as Ned had hoped he might. Instead, his mouth full, he said in heavily accented English, "So . . . you bring money? All in order, as agreed?"

"Yes." Ned reached out to take possession of the compass, but a sinewy brown hand gripped his wrist.

"Pay first. Let me see gold."

"I've got it," Ned assured him. "But I have to look at the compass first, just to make sure." He glanced pointedly at the array of dishes spread over the table and then asked, in a more placatory tone, "You can spare me a few mouthfuls, can't you? I'm hungry."

Smith ignored the request and went on eating.

"Show me gold."

The colony had no currency; the gold sovereigns had been obtained, Ned knew, from the limited stocks hoarded by some of the wealthier convicts, who had bartered them in exchange for fish and other illicit foodstuffs that the fishermen had contrived to trade with various ships that, from time to time, entered the harbor. It had taken Bryant and his men nearly a year to lay their hands on the gold, and the five sovereigns he had been given, in order to conclude the bargain with Detmer Smith, represented the sum total of their remaining cash. Apart from a few forged silver dollars—which the Malay master had refused to accept—they would be penniless when they reached Timor, dependent on charity and with no means of paying for their further passage back to England. But if he could keep possession of the gold . . . Ned forced a smile. After all, he thought, had he not earned one of the coins from Lieutenant Macarthur, for supplying his household with fish and some stolen lambs?

He took the locket from his trouser pocket and laid it on the table.

"This is worth more than five sovereigns, Captain," he suggested ingratiatingly. "Take a look at it and you'll see. The diamonds are real."

Suspiciously the *Waak-sam-heyd*'s master examined the locket, and while he did so, Ned checked the compass, finding it, as nearly as he could judge, in good working order. Detmer Smith, it was evident, liked the locket, but even so, the subsequent bargaining took over an hour. It was concluded eventually by the addition of a single sovereign, and Smith emitted a loud belch and pushed his half-finished plate of curry contemptuously across the table.

"Eat," he invited. "I had enough. Then you go. If you caught with my compass, I say you steal . . . understand?"

Ned nodded. He wolfed down the curry ravenously and, returning to his skiff, rowed cautiously back through the darkness, the four remaining gold coins still in his pocket. Butcher and Lilley were waiting for him on the deserted beach with an impatience they made no attempt to conceal.

"Bleedin' hell, you took your time!" Lilley accused wrathfully. "Keepin' us 'ere 'arf the night, coolin' our 'eels an' the soddin' watch liable ter come along askin' questions any minute!"

"Wasn't my fault," Ned began. "I—"

"Did you get the compass?" Johnny Butcher put in.

"Yes, I got it and the charts. But that Detmer Smith's a downy cove right enough." Ned yielded up the compass and took the folded charts from the front of his sweat-soaked shirt. "They're ream, ain't they? I tested the compass like Will said."

Butcher studied the instrument, moving it this way

and that in his big hands. "Can't tell for sure in this light. It's a mite coopered, but I reckon it'll serve well enough. What took you so long?"

"The sodding little chiseler tried to gammon me," Ned returned, the lie coming as easily to his tongue as the thieves' jargon of the London streets. "He wanted more push than Will bargained for, and I had to talk him 'round. It wasn't easy, I can tell you —he's as crooked as two sticks. Still"—he grinned and slapped his thin stomach with satisfaction—"I ate fit to bust myself while I was doing it! It's a hell of a long time since I had a square meal like that inside me. Some sort of spiced meat it was, very tasty and—" Hearing the splash of oars, he broke off in sudden, instinctive alarm.

"The boat," Lilley said. "Now we'll find out. Stay right where you are, Munday—no skiving off!"

"I'm not going anywhere," Ned blustered. He waited, as the boat approached, puzzled but not seriously worried until he saw that it was rowed by four of the *Waak-sam-heyd*'s dark-skinned Malay seamen. It grounded and from it, to his dismay, stepped Billy Morton, one of the Timor party and, like Butcher, a one-time sailor who had served in East India Company ships. Clearly he had come from the Dutch snow, Ned thought, and must either have been on board during his lengthy interview with Detmer Smith or gone out to the *Waak-sam-heyd* very soon afterwards. He panicked and would have taken flight, but Lilley's hand grasped his arm.

"Not so fast," he cautioned. "What about it, Billy?"

"Like we thought, Nat. The young sod tried to cross us. Better search him—he's probably still got our money on him." Morton came stumping up the beach, and again Ned attempted to make a bid for freedom, but Johnny Butcher put out a foot and he measured his length on the sand. They had little difficulty in finding the four gold coins.

Nat Lilley went to work on Ned with his fists, brutally and without pity, while Johnny Butcher and Billy Morton stood watching, grinning and talking in low voices. The beating over, they picked Ned up and dumped him, bruised and sobbing, in the *Waak-sam-heyd*'s gig.

As the boat put out, Johnny Butcher called out derisively, "You can forget Timor, Munday! Captain Smith's going to keep you under wraps until we've gone and then he's going to report you as a stow-away . . . and I don't envy you!"

Ned, his cherished dream of escape abruptly shattered, cursed him savagely. Then the pain of the drubbing he had received caused him to spew up the meal he had so greatly enjoyed, and he wept, as one of the Malay oarsmen aimed a kick at his ribs. . . .

"It's to be tomorrow night, Billy," Johnny Butcher said as Morton fell into step beside Lilley and himself. "The *Supply*'s gone to Norfolk Island, so she can't be sent after us, and Detmer Smith reckons to sail Tuesday forenoon, Will says. Did he tell you any different?"

"No." Morton shook his head. "Tuesday forenoon it is." He jerked his head in the direction of the skiff Ned had used. "You taking that back or shall I?"

"I'll take it. I want to stow this compass where no one's likely to stumble over it—we can pick it up when we've got the cutter." He smiled in the darkness, his eyes suddenly bright with anticipation. "After all this time . . . we're really going to be on our way! Hard to believe, ain't it, Nat?"

Nat grinned back at him and swore softly.

"C'n you manage on yer own? I could do with gettin' me head down for an hour or two."

" 'Course I can," Johnny assured him. He laid the precious compass, with the charts, in the stern of the skiff and started to push it out. "Tell Will I've an errand to perform first thing in the morning, but I'll be with him in plenty of time for the night fishing." He closed one eye in an elaborate wink and then stepped into the boat, hearing the laughter that greeted his last remark.

"See she gives you a good time, Johnny boy!" Morton called after him. "It'll have to last you for a while . . . all the way to flaming Timor maybe!"

"Don't you be too sure of that," Johnny countered. He raised a casual hand in farewell and then bent to his oars.

Jenny was tending her fish traps at first light and, alone on the small sheltered beach below the garden, was so intent on repairing a damaged net that she did not hear the approaching footsteps until Johnny Butcher hailed her softly.

She sat back on her heels, looking up at him in surprise, which was swiftly succeeded by alarm. Ned had not returned that night, and although he had occasionally absented himself without explanation before, this time she sensed that all was not well. His theft of her locket—of which she had heard from Melia—had hurt her more than she had cared to admit, but guessing that it had to do with the escape attempt, she had been prepared to forgive it.

Unless . . . she caught her breath sharply, as Johnny gave her a sober good morning and seated himself beside her, his face grave and unsmiling.

"Is it Ned?" she asked wearily. "Has he got himself caught?"

"In a manner of speaking he has, aye."

"What do you mean?"

He shrugged. "He's no good, Jenny—no good for you. You're wasting your time on him. But you know that, don't you?"

"Perhaps. I . . . what has he done, Johnny?"

Johnny told her, in a few scornful words. "He's on board the *Waak-sam-heyd*. Detmer Smith, the master, will keep him till we've made our getaway, then he'll turn him in as a stowaway and—"

"And he'll be flogged for it," Jenny put in. "And lose his chance of remission."

"It's no more than he deserves, lass."

Perhaps it wasn't, Jenny thought dully. This, seemingly, had been the test Johnny had spoken of the previous day—they had set a trap for him, and Ned had fallen into it, from motives of what—greed, selfishness, a dyed-in-the-wool dishonesty? He had stolen her locket, took it from her hiding place when she was out working, with never a word of explanation or apology. Yet surely he must have known that, if he had asked her for it, she would have given it to him willingly and without question. She looked at Johnny Butcher, taking in the fact that he had shaved before coming to her and must have bathed in the sea too, for his face and body smelled salty and freshly clean.

"We're sailing tonight," he said. "It's been put forward. That's what I came to tell you, not about that damned rogue Munday. Come with us, Jenny." He reached out to take both her hands in his. "I can fix it with Will Bryant. And we can be wed in Timor since there's not going to be time for that here. I'd care for you, I swear it, just as if you were my wife."

He was everything Ned was not, Jenny told herself —trustworthy, strong, straightforward. Reckless, certainly, but with the cool courage to offset the recklessness; the competence and the determination to see even this desperate adventure through to its end . . . whatever that end might be. She shivered, thinking of the open boat, crowded with fugitives—Mary Bryant and her two small children, Nat Lilley, of whom she was afraid and . . . who were the others Melia had named? Billy Morton, Sam Bird, Jim Martin, Will Allen—all associates of Lilley's, except Morton, all hardened criminals, transported for life. And young Jim Cox, a decent lad, who had been planning to marry a girl in the main camp but who had recently joined them and intended to leave his girl behind when they sailed.

She tried to visualize what it would be like in such conditions and with such companions, sailing along an unknown coast peopled by hostile Indians, where they would be in peril of their lives each time they attempted to land. There would be storms—the storms had been bad enough when encountered in the ships of the Botany Bay fleet but in a small sailing boat, at the mercy of wind and current . . . she shivered again and felt Johnny's hands tighten about hers, as if seeking to make light of her fears.

"I'm wooing you, Jenny," he told her softly, "but there's not much time. I want you, lass, any way I can get you—I want you to come with me and not be afraid. Forget this place, forget that scoundrel Munday . . . we'll get to Timor, never doubt that. Don't you want to be free?"

It was a dream, Jenny thought—Ned's dream but not hers. She had never tried to escape, had toiled for three long years to make a life here, to build a home,

grow crops, as the governor had urged all of them
endeavor to do. The words of the speech he had
made came back to her unbidden, the pledges he had
made when he had inaugurated the colony more
than three years before. *"Here are fertile plains,
needing only the labors of the husbandman to produce in abundance the fairest and richest fruits. Here
are interminable pastures, the future home of flocks
and herds innumerable. . . ."*

She bit back a sob, her throat tight, and shook her
head. "No—no, I want to stay here, Johnny. I can't
go with you."

He stared at her, the blue eyes incredulous. "You
mean you don't want to see England again? You can't
mean that!"

What had England given her? Jenny thought rebelliously. A few years of happy childhood, then poverty,
drudgery, injustice—a cruel sentence for a crime she
had not committed, the awful degradation of Newgate, the final repudiation of exile as a convicted
felon . . . tears choking her, she said, "No, I don't
want to see England again. My life is here."

"With Munday?" Johnny Butcher's tone was harshly
angry. "I wanted to wed you," he flung at her in bitter
reproach, "but if you're Munday's whore, then you
can be mine!" He took her roughly in his arms, his
mouth bruisingly on hers, on her throat, her breasts,
her belly, seeking, demanding, his big, hard body
holding hers as if in a vise.

She struggled against him, breathless and afraid,
and then, almost against her will, found herself re-
sponding to his demands with a passionate urgency
that matched his and would suffer no denial. In that
moment there was no one else, the dawn world blotted
out, the whisper of a breeze, stirring the treetops be-

hind them, the only sound as he took possession o
her slender, compliant body with a completeness sh
had never known. In all her life she had experience
nothing even akin to this; Ned's lovemaking was swif
and selfish and left her unsatisfied more often tha
not, but Johnny Butcher, despite his initial roughness
was a skilled and tender lover, and she felt no guil
in the response he drew from her and none in th
manner of her surrender to him.

Had he asked her then, as they lay side by side o
the warm sand, their passion spent, she would hav
promised to follow him to the ends of the earth, fo
all her pangs of conscience on Ned's account and he
instinctive fear of his fellow escapers and the danger
ous voyage on which he was pledged to embark. Bu
he was silent, his expression inscrutable, the blue eye
avoiding hers and seemingly fixed on the sky, tinge
now with the golden glow of the sunrise.

Johnny got to his feet and, still silent, started t
buckle on his trousers. Watching him, seeing th
marks of the fetters on his wrists and ankles and th
scars of half a dozen brutal floggings on his back
Jenny stifled the impulse to beseech him to stay, t
abandon the escape attempt. There could be no lif
here for a man of Johnny Butcher's stamp, she knew
She must go with him or let him go—perhaps to hi
death, certainly forever, for even if the desperat
venture succeeded and they reached Timor, he woul
never come back.

She donned her rough sacking dress, waiting fo
him to break the silence. When at last he did so, hi
words had a contemptuous finality that made he
recoil, feeling as if he had struck her.

"That's it then—you can go back to your fancy man
after they've done flogging him, and the two of you

can slave your lives away in this wilderness! For all I care, you can rot here . . . you made your choice, did you not?" He kicked at the nets she had been mending and added, with conscious cruelty, "I could have loved you, Jenny—now, God help me, I just want to forget you ever existed. You're like all the rest, you—"

Jenny waited to hear no more. Sick with humiliation, she ran blindly into the growing crops, heedless of the destruction her flying feet caused to the trailing vines and the tender corn shoots, intent only on putting as great a distance as she could between herself and him.

The governor was at Observatory Point, watching the departure of the *Waak-sam-heyd* for England, with Captain Hunter and the officers and men of the *Sirius* on board, when David Collins brought him news of the escape of the fishery superintendent, his wife and children, and nine other male convicts.

"They stole your cutter, sir," the judge advocate admitted regretfully. "And—"

"*My* cutter? The devil take them for insolent rogues! And a plague on Bryant." Phillip's temper flared. He had planned to use the cutter in a week's time for exploration of the Broken Bay area, in conjunction with a landward expedition to survey the Hawkesbury River, and on this account the loss was a serious one. But he controlled himself and asked levelly, "When did this occur, David?"

"Last night, sir. Bryant and three of his fellows—all of them seamen—went out ostensibly for a few hours' night fishing, but instead of that, they took the cutter from her moorings, loaded her up, and sailed under cover of darkness." He expelled his breath in an exasperated sigh. "Henry Brewer's gone after them in the launch." He pointed, and the governor turned his glass onto the launch, which was tacking across the anchorage under a single lugsail.

"Damme, Bryant tried to escape before!" the governor exclaimed, remembering, "but because he was a good man, I gave him a second chance. You say he's taken his wife and children with him? Weren't the children born here?"

"Yes, sir—one is only a few months old." Collins hesitated. "The master of the *Waak-sam-heyd* found a stowaway on board and sent him ashore just before he weighed anchor . . . a convict named Munday, who came out in the *Neptune*. He's been working under Bryant, sir, and claims to be able to name the men who escaped. He says they intend to make for Timor. I put him under arrest and told the guard to hold him, as I thought you might wish to question him."

"I do indeed," Phillip said with emphasis. He snapped his glass shut and started to move down the slope. "I'll see him at once. There's nothing more to be done here now that, alas, the Siriuses have left us."

As he walked briskly in the direction of Government House, he was deep in thought. He would miss John Hunter—dear heaven, *how* he would miss that loyal and efficient officer! And the others, too—the ship's company: William Bradley, Keltie the master, young Southwell, and the talented Dr. Lowes who had all, in their various capacities, served the colony well.

Captain Hunter, it was true, had returned somewhat disgruntled from his enforced stay on Norfolk Island, and latterly had not been the best of company, with his alarming tales of Major Ross's tyrannical governorship. Predictably Ross had contrived to stir up ill feeling and make himself heartily disliked by the entire community, official and free, as well as convict.

A severe hurricane had wrought havoc with Norfolk's hitherto flourishing crops, and the delay in sending supplies by the *Justinian* and the *Surprise*, the previous August, had reduced the settlers there to the verge of starvation, which had not improved the situation. Yet he had cleared the ships as expeditiously as he could, the governor reflected, and he had sent all the provisions he could spare for their relief. Ross had no right to blame him for the delay, although, if John Hunter were to be believed, Ross *had* blamed him, publicly and often.

Phillip quickened his pace, in an effort to escape the torment of his conscience. The fact that he had transferred the marine commandant to Norfolk Island was on his mind and weighed heavily there, for all that the idea of doing so had come initially from Hunter. But, God willing, Philip King would soon be back to resume direction of the island's affairs, and Ross, when he returned to Sydney, would do so only briefly. He and his marines would be relieved by the New South Wales Corps and on their way back to England by the end of the year. He heaved an audible sigh, and David Collins, mistaking the reason for it, offered diffidently, "I can deal with the prisoner Munday for you, sir, if you wish."

The governor shook his head. "No, David, I want to hear what he has to say. He'll have to go to trial, of course, but. . . ." His tired eyes held a fugitive gleam of what might have been admiration as he added, "They have courage, the rascals who stole my cutter—one must grant them that. To take Timor as their objective is indeed courageous, if foolhardy."

They were in sight of Government House, now completed in pleasing red brick, with a second story above the public rooms, and he paused for a moment to gaze upon it with conscious pride. It would, he knew, be a wrench to leave when the time came, but come it would. He had written to Lord Sydney's successor, Lord Grenville, only two days ago, requesting once again to be relieved, and had dispatched the letter with Hunter in the *Waak-sam-heyd*. He had couched his letter in urgent terms, admitting to Grenville the truth he had concealed from everyone here —that he was ill. He had written:

> A complaint in the side, from which in more than two years, I have seldom been free, has impaired my health, and at times puts it out of my power to attend to the charge with which His Majesty has been pleased to honor me in the manner I wish and the state of the colony requires. . . .

He had asked only for a year's furlough in England, to enable him to recoup his strength and— He smiled to himself. This Colony of Disgracefuls was of supreme importance to him now; he had promised to return and resume his task as soon as his health would permit. Once Ross had gone and there was no likelihood of his taking over the reins, as lieutenant governor, he could take his furlough and, God willing, seek a cure for his malaise.

"Sir," Collins began uncertainly, as the governor continued to stand in silence, looking up at the building he had so often despaired of seeing completed. "Are you all right, sir?"

Phillip sighed. "I'm tired, David," he confessed.

"See this fellow Munday for me, will you please, and take a statement from him. I'll take a tub and rest for an hour but I'll be in my office at midday. You can report to me then."

He had fully recovered when the judge advocate, in obedience to these instructions, presented himself with his full report just after midday. After he laid the whole scheme out before Phillip, the governor swore softly.

"Munday insists that he was taken forcibly to the *Waak-sam-heyd* because Bryant and Butcher were afraid he'd betray them." Collins went on. "He says he had no intention of trying to stow away."

"D'you believe him, David?"

Collins shrugged. "He's a slimy young fellow and not above lying to save his skin but . . . on this occasion, I'm inclined to believe him. He had certainly been given a drubbing, sir, and his story seems to me to hold water. I suspect that he was originally one of the party and that he fell out with them, but there's no proof—indeed, sir, there's no case against him. With your permission I propose to release him."

Phillip, leafing through the papers in front of him, nodded his assent. "Very well. But he'd best not go back to work on the fishing boats. We shall have to set a guard on all the small boats in the harbor, David, to prevent this happening again— perhaps you would see that Captain Campbell is informed. And draw up new regulations to cover boats being taken out after sunset, with a list of authorized persons to be supplied to the guard commander."

"Very good, sir," the judge advocate promised. "I'll see to it at once. About Munday, sir—" He laid a second file of papers on the desk. "The Taggart girl has applied for a grant of land at Rose Hill, on condition of her marriage. It seems she's intending to marry this fellow Munday and"—he pointed to the date of the file—"we've had her application in for a while now, sir. As you can see, there was another application for this same plot of land, made by the late Lieutenant Leach."

"In partnership with John Macarthur!" Phillip exclaimed. He read on, frowning. "This is the land originally allocated to Sergeant Jenkins and . . . what's this, David?"

"Jenkins's will, sir. It's invalid unfortunately— poor old Jenkins died before he could sign it—but he wanted to leave the grant to Jenny Taggart. She worked on it with him, sir, for a year as his assigned servant."

"Then let her have the house and thirty acres," the governor decided. "She has earned her chance. Make the grant conditional on emancipation, and I will review her case in six months' time." Phillip appended his signature to the application.

"Yes, sir." David Collins started to gather up his papers. Henry Brewer would be pleased, he thought— old Henry had never lost faith in the Taggart girl. Thinking of Brewer, he wondered how the chase was faring, and the governor, as if divining his thoughts, said briskly, "Let me have word when Brewer gets back. I don't imagine he'll catch up with the cutter, unless they do something very foolish. Which"—a rueful smile played briefly about his lips and he gestured to the papers which Collins was restoring to their appropriate folders—"seems unlikely. Bryant's a good hand with boats, and I see from Butcher's dossier that he was a master's mate in the Bombay

Marine. I wish I'd known that before—we could have used him better than we did."

It was after midnight when Henry Brewer returned, to report an abortive hunt for the stolen cutter.

"They've got clear away, sir," he told the governor, whom he found still working at his desk. "But God help them if they try to make Timor!"

"Amen to that," Phillip said so quietly that Brewer was not sure if he had heard him aright.

"Sir?" he questioned, puzzled.

"I was thinking aloud, Henry. It's of no importance. Off you go and get some sleep—and thank you for your efforts."

"Aye, aye, sir," Brewer acknowledged.

From his house, fifty yards away, as he undressed and prepared to retire he saw that the whale-oil lamp in the governor's office was still burning.

CHAPTER XXV

The wind, gusting at gale force from the northeast, whipped the dark surface of the ocean to whitecapped fury. It sent showers of icy spray to drench the occupants of the heavily laden cutter, making a mockery of their weary attempts to keep their frail craft afloat.

The cutter—twenty-three feet long, with eight oars, a jib, and a dipping lugsail—had served Sydney's governor well enough for the purpose of surveying and charting the harbor of Port Jackson and the adjacent coastal area, Johnny Butcher thought sourly. But she was old, her timbers warped by the strong New Holland sun, and she was leaking badly, lying sluggishly low in the water, borne down by the weight of the supplies she carried, as well as by that of her human cargo.

There were eleven of them all told, counting Mary

Bryant and her two small children, who now lay huddled miserably on the bottom boards, prostrate with fear and seasickness. Not that some of the men were in much better shape. Seated in the stern and fighting the kicking tiller with all his remaining strength, Johnny Butcher studied the faces of his companions with narrowed eyes, wondering for how much longer he could count on their endurance. It was, by his reckoning, April 7 of the year 1791—ten days since he and his fellow convicts had stolen the governor's cutter and made their bid for freedom.

At first all had gone well. They had eluded the launch sent after them in pursuit, their moment well chosen to coincide with the departure for England of the only seagoing ship in the harbor, the Dutch snow *Waak-sam-heyd*, whose rascally master had, in any event, been privy to their plans and careful, because of the aid he had given them, to steer his course well clear of theirs. They had glimpsed his distant topsails and cheered as they vanished from sight. They had cheered again, in heady triumph, when Will Bryant had run up the cutter's dingy canvas and a brisk southerly breeze had set them on their way.

Will had hoisted his perky, two-year-old son onto his shoulders and the boy had cried out in delight to see the sails fill and the forbidding, rocky shoreline merge with the noon haze and then disappear, as if it had never been.

"A plague on that hellhole!" Nat Lilley had shouted, doling out rum from the *Waak-sam-heyd*'s cask with an all too lavish hand. "I'll give you a toast, boys—damnation to Governor Phillip an' his scurvy colony! We're well rid of 'em both!"

It was easily said and easy to believe, with the sea like a millpond, the wind in their favor, and the fumes of the potent Dutch spirit clouding their minds. The sense of freedom alone was heady enough after the years of captivity they had all endured, the floggings, the backbreaking forced labor, and the felon's chains. But it was three thousand miles to the destination they sought and . . . Johnny drew in his breath sharply, as a flurry of wind caught him unprepared, almost jerking the tiller from his grasp and bringing the boat's head around.

A deluge of water cascaded in over her stern before he could right her, and he yelled at the others frantically to look alive. "Bail, for God's sake! She'll be swamped if you don't!"

Nat Lilley swore at him resentfully but obeyed, kicking the man beside him into wakefulness. They had been bailing almost continuously throughout the day and taking their turn, for two hours at a time, at the oars, but now, exhausted, with darkness coming on, the perils they faced were being brought home to them with alarming clarity. And not before time, Johnny reflected wryly. Apart from Will Bryant, Billy Morton, and himself, none of the men were seamen. Their first and only experience of the sea had been the voyage from England, in the holds of Governor Phillip's convict transports. Bryant and Morton had been fishermen, and as for the woman, Bryant's wife. . . . He managed to bring the cutter's head into the wind again and glanced down at her with swift concern.

Poor young soul, she was scared out of her wits, clutching both children to her, her eyes wide with terror—yet she did not cry out, did not reproach him. She had courage, more guts than one or two of the men; her fear was for her babies rather than for herself.

"Johnny. . . ." Will Bryant was beside him, breathing hard, his ragged shirt clinging to him like a wet skin, soaked with sweat and seawater. He was a big man and as courageous and uncomplaining as his wife but he sounded defeated as he said, hands cupped about his mouth to make himself heard above the howl of the wind, "We'll have to put ashore."

"In darkness?" Johnny objected.

"Aye, in darkness—we've no choice. She'll sink if we don't."

He was right, Johnny knew. But if they were driven ashore onto rocks, they would lose the boat anyway and with it their precious supplies of food and water.

"We'll have to find a cove or an inlet," he said flatly, "and risk the Indians. But God knows how, in this."

The charts, which the master of the *Waak-sam-heyd* had sold them at so high a price, were innaccurate and unreliable, but he had glimpsed what appeared to be a wide bay before the light had faded, and the chart had shown it with an island near its northern arm. Both lay several miles astern of them now, but with this wind and the prevailing current they could drift back with only two men at the oars and the rest bailing, and if they missed the island in the darkness, the bay would afford them shelter and the chance of a sandy beach for their landing. It was the best they could hope for, and when he put the suggestion to Bryant, the one-time fisherman nodded.

"There'll be Indians in the bay, Will," Johnny warned him.

"We've got the muskets. An' they likely won't be out in this storm anyway, if they've any sense. Put her about, Johnny. We can run in with the jib."

Rain beat down on them as the cutter neared the

shore and the curtain of moisture blotted out all landmarks. Johnny heard, rather than saw, the surf beating against the seemingly never-ending cliffs and then, with heartfelt relief, spotted the break in the frothing line, where no rocks impeded their rushing passage. It was more by good luck than any attempt on his part at navigation that had brought him to the bay, and wind and current carried them in, to deposit the cutter with a shuddering lurch on the yielding sand he had prayed they might find within its sickle-shaped confines.

For a long moment no one moved. Then young Jamie Cox grabbed Morton by the shoulder, and the two of them went splashing ashore, ignoring his shout to them to help in pulling the boat up to the dry sand above the tide line.

"Lily-livered bastards!" Johnny shouted after them. He lifted Bryant's boy into his father's arms, Martin took the baby, and with the woman still lying motionless on the bottom boards, he and Nat Lilley, aided ineffectually by Bird and Allen, managed to drag the cutter clear of the water. It took the combined efforts of all the men to beach her to his satisfaction, and they came unwillingly, cursing him for his insistence. Bryant, he thought—a martinet when he had been fishing superintendent in Sydney—had lost his authority due to the presence of his wife and their two children for whom, it was evident, he was almost exclusively concerned.

He said as much, not troubling to choose his words with any care, when the big man came back to the cutter to carry his wife ashore.

"We've got to have order, Will, or we'll never make it to Timor. You're letting them get out of hand."

A trifle to his surprise, Will Bryant did not argue.

"Then take over, Johnny," he suggested. "I'll back you. You're the only real seaman among us, after all—the only one who can navigate." He shivered, plainly anxious to find shelter from the downpour. "I'm in an awkward position—they resent me, because I brought Mary and the little ones along. I daren't push them too hard on that account, don't you see?"

"Yes, but—"

"Leave it be," Bryant put in wearily, "till we've dried out and had a few hours' sleep. We'll put it to the others then."

Would he have been in the same position, Johnny asked himself, if Jenny Taggart had yielded to his persuasion and come with them also? Perhaps it was as well she had not. He shrugged and went to rig the cutter's spare jib so as to catch sufficient rainwater to top up their depleted casks, while the others spread out to search for shelter.

They found a shallow cave about two hundred yards from their stranded craft, unloaded the muskets and some provisions, and, unsuccessful in their efforts to light a fire, crouched there in sodden misery until daybreak, their hunger barely assuaged by the meager ration of crumbly biscuit and raw fish, which had been their diet for the past ten days.

With the coming of daylight, the rain ceased and their spirits rose. They were in an extensive natural harbor, its shores well wooded and ringed with wide, sandy beaches and what appeared to be a stream or a small river about half a mile from where they had taken shelter. Johnny, with the aid of Captain Detmer Smith's chart, put its position at between twenty-nine and thirty degrees of south latitude but, lacking a sextant, could not be certain and recorded it with a query in the log he was keeping.

The men, led by Nat Lilley, announced their intention of taking the muskets in order to hunt for game, and it did not take a warning glance from Will Bryant to put Johnny on his mettle. The moment had come, he knew, when he must assert himself or relinquish command of their perilous venture to Nat or anyone else who chose to seize it with, almost certainly, fatal consequences. He had spent weeks in the bush with Nat Lilley and knew him for what he was—a man of small intelligence, who acted on impulse and was incapable of planning ahead. And a man, too, who imposed his will on others with his fists. Johnny Butcher braced himself and held out his hand for the musket the older man had purloined.

"First things first, Nat," he said crisply. "The cutter has to be caulked. We'll need all the hands we've got for that job."

"We can't work on empty bellies," Nat retorted. "Find some wood an' get a fire goin' if you don't want to come with us. There's a river yonder—we'll maybe pot a few duck or a 'roo."

"And disturb a few Indians. We can't afford to linger here and the boat's our only means of escape, if we have to run for it. Besides, we'll need the muskets to defend ourselves with, if they attack us."

"Who says they'll attack us?" Nat's expression was ugly. "An' where *are* your scurvy Indians—no sign of 'em that I can see! Come on, lads!" He shouldered his musket and made to move away, but Johnny planted himself squarely in his path.

"Not till the cutter's repaired, Nat."

Nat swore at him. "You takin' on yourself ter give orders? Hell, I thought we was finished with all that when we left soddin' Sydney Cove behind us!" There was a murmur of approval from several of the other men.

"Johnny thinks 'he's back in the perishin' navy!" Jamie Cox taunted. "Anyways, Will Bryant's in charge, ain't he?"

Bryant moved to Johnny's side. He said curtly, "Not anymore. Johnny's the seaman—he's goin' to get us to Timor, where we'll be safe. We knew when we started out that we'd have to put up with some hardships, and hunger's one of 'em, so best make up your minds to that. As to the Indians—damn it to hell, Nat, this godforsaken country's swarmin' with Indians and just because we can't see 'em don't mean they're not here." He gestured to the abandoned cutter. "Johnny's right —that boat's our only means of escape, and we can't put to sea in her till she's caulked. So let's get on with it. First thing we'll need is a fire. If you're wantin' to look around, Nat, go an' look for wood."

"Like hell I will!" Nat returned sullenly. "That's woman's work—send your woman. Bin nothin' but a burden so far, with 'er pulin' an' pukin'. You said she'd pull 'er weight, didn't you? Only good fer one thing that I can see an' that's only fer your benefit. Why—"

Johnny hit him on the point of the jaw. Taken by surprise, Nat Lilley measured his length on the sand, the musket falling from his limp grasp. He scrambled up, cursing savagely and full of fight, to find himself looking into the muzzle of the weapon that was leveled unwaveringly at his heart.

"We'll settle this some other time," Johnny told him, his voice dangerously quiet. "In Timor, if you like. But now we have work to do, all of us, if we're ever going to get there. For a start let's get the boat unloaded and careened. That's man's work, so let's

see you tackle it, Nat my friend . . . and the rest of
you, buckle-to!"

Jim Martin's thin face split into a grin. "Aye, aye,
Cap'n," he acknowledged cheerfully. "Whatever you
say."

By midafternoon, with a small fire going to heat the
mixture of pitch and tallow Will Bryant had prepared,
the cutter's starboard-side seams had been paid and
Morton, who had some skill as a carpenter, had shaped
two lengths of hardwood with which to repair a
sprung plank in her stern. Pleased with the result of
their efforts, Johnny yielded at last to Nat Lilley's
demands for a chance to go hunting.

Lilley and Jamie were gone for barely half an hour.
They returned at a panic-stricken run, with Jamie Cox
in the lead, yelling out a warning.

"Indians—dozens of 'em! Look out!"

A shower of spears attested to the truth of his words.
With a smothered exclamation Will Bryant dashed
across to fling himself protectively in front of his wife,
Johnny seized a musket and fired at the advancing
mob of natives, and Nat, showing considerable courage, went down on one knee and used his own weapon
to stem their advance. No hits were scored, but the
discharge of the muskets clearly alarmed their attackers and they drew off, allowing time for the muskets
to be reloaded.

"There's a lot of the bastards," Nat said breathlessly, joining Johnny in the shelter of a rocky outcrop.
"A whole village, up there by the river mouth. I don't
reckon they've ever set eyes on a white man in their
lives. Me an' Jamie ran full tilt into a fishin' party—
we was lucky ter get back here, I can tell you."

They both looked at the island, clearly visible about
a mile offshore, at the northern side of the bay. They

had missed it in the rain-swept darkness the previous night but . . . Johnny got to his feet. It was where he had originally planned to come ashore, and if they pulled across to it now, in daylight, it would offer a safer refuge than the exposed beach, if the Indians renewed their attack. The repairs to the cutter weren't finished, but a few hours would see them completed and the craft seaworthy once more. He sighed and went to consult with Will Bryant, who agreed unhesitatingly that the island represented their best chance of survival.

"Some of our powder's damp, Johnny," the big fisherman added ruefully. "And with only four muskets between us, we haven't a hope in hell of holdin' them off if those Indians mean business. And if there's as many of the black swine as Nat reckons, they've only to rush us and it'll be all up."

With two of them standing guard, it took the other men almost an hour to get the cutter reloaded and back into the water. The natives, reinforced by a party from the village, gathered in a large menacing group at the edge of the trees, watching their preparations for departure and occasionally hurling spears and stones to hasten them on their way. Johnny's finger itched on the trigger of his musket, but none of the Indians came within range or attempted to interfere with the loading of the boat; all they wanted, it seemed, was for their unwelcome visitors to go away, and overtures of peace were pointedly ignored.

In appearance these people resembled the aborigines of the Sydney and Botany Bay areas—lithe, dark-skinned men, with unkempt hair and matted beards, their bodies liberally daubed with dried or drying mud. But they were infinitely more hostile, and it was a relief to climb on board the cutter at last and pull out into the bay. Despite the exhaustion they all felt, the Englishmen raised a ragged cheer as they bent to their oars, and hearing it, the Indians broke from cover to line the beach they had vacated, throwing stones and executing a savage victory dance, their lances and throwing sticks brandished above their heads.

In the cutter's bow Mary Bryant held her children to her in thin, protective arms. She shivered but, Johnny saw, she did not weep, and he was again reminded of Jenny Taggart, who had displayed the same resigned and dry-eyed courage the night that he and Lilley and the others had raided her hut. He smiled across at Mary Bryant over the bent heads of the men toiling at the oars, and after a moment's hesitation she smiled back shyly. By sunset they reached the island.

After passing an undisturbed night, they resumed work on the cutter's seams at daybreak. By noon, the caulking was finished, the boat as watertight as they could make her with the materials at their disposal and they again put to sea.

It became necessary to guard the rum and, within another twenty-four hours, tht water cask also. Cox and Lilley allied themselves with Bird and Morton in perverse attempts to elude Butcher's vigilance, and Johnny, overcome by the need for sleep, woke to find both casks empty and the four men aggressively drunk and spoiling for a fight.

He steered for the distant shore in angry silence, and, when they beached the cutter, ordered them curtly to go in search of water.

"Give us a couple o' muskets then," Lilley demanded. He looked about him, seeing green tree-filled hills beyond the beach, and grinned, without rancor. "That looks like kangaroo country ter me, Johnny old mate. We'll eat ternight an' we'll eat good!"

"Let him have 'em," Will Bryant advised. "We could do with a square meal, Johnny—we all could. And I don't see any Indian canoes." When the four men had gone, he carried his two children ashore, and leaving his wife with Martin and Allen to get a fire lighted, he and Johnny took the water casks and set off in the hope of finding a stream.

They found a partially dried up creek and, after much searching, the thin rivulet that fed it, but they had scarcely begun to fill the casks when, heralded by shouts and the discharge of a single musket, Lilley and his three companions went crashing through the bush a few hundred yards away. They were in pursuit of a wounded kangaroo and, as they emerged into a clearing in the trees, they brought it down, yelling and laughing in drunken triumph when Jamie Cox flung himself on it, battering it to death with the butt of his musket.

"Damn their eyes!" Johnny exclaimed ruefully. "If that don't bring the Indians, nothing will!" He lifted the refilled cask onto his shoulder and started after the noisy hunters, still cursing under his breath. Will Bryant followed him in apprehensive silence.

The Indians made their appearance when the kangaroo was half-cooked. Spears spattered the ground about the sizzling spit, and undeterred by the shot Will Bryant fired into their midst, fifty or sixty clay-daubed warriors advanced threateningly on the little group squatting beside the fire.

"Get the boat out!" Johnny shouted. "Leave them the 'roo—that's what they want!"

"No!" Nat Lilley was beside himself. He grabbed

the kangaroo's smoldering carcass and attempted to carry it to the boat, careless of burned hands and the aborigines' angry cries. Will Bryant and Jim Martin plucked the two children from the ground and ran with them, wailing, to the cutter, Mary and the others at their heels. Johnny put his musket to his shoulder and fired at one of the blacks, bringing him abruptly to a halt with blood pouring from a shattered arm. A well-aimed spear struck Lilley a glancing blow; he dropped the kangaroo, and Johnny kicked it toward the surging ranks of their attackers. As they fell upon it he seized Lilley about the waist and dragged him, still mouthing obscenities, to the boat.

Safe beyond the line of surf, they watched in bitter frustration as the blacks devoured their meal.

After the incident, they landed only when their water supply ran out, stayed on shore no longer than was necessary to replenish the casks and ate what fish they could catch from the boat in its raw state.

Two weeks later a strong current carried the cutter some twenty or thirty leagues offshore during the night, and the weary men woke to find that they were in sight of a small group of low-lying islands. These appeared to be uninhabited, but rendered cautious by the previous attacks they had suffered, they approached the largest of the group warily, subjecting its palm-fringed shores to a careful scrutiny.

"Not a sign of life that I can see," Will Bryant said at length. "Let's risk it, Johnny. We can't go on much longer the way we are."

They stayed for five days on the island, eating and recouping their strength. There was no fresh water spring, but pools of rainwater, formed after a sudden and welcome tropical downpour, enabled the casks to be refilled; turtles and turtle eggs fed them all to repletion and were dried and cooked, then loaded into the boat, together with as many coconuts as she would hold. Despite this comparative wealth of provisions and the general improvement in the whole party's health and spirits, they were reluctant to abandon the sanctuary they had found. It took threats, as well as persuasion on the part of Johnny and Will Bryant to get them back on board the cutter, and their sullen complaints were renewed when, later in the day, they were compelled to row for lengthy spells in order to offset the pull of the current. But the mainland coast was sighted just before sundown, and with a brisk breeze from the southeast, sail was set and the oarsmen able to snatch a few hours respite from their toil.

All went well for the next four days, and they made steady progress, always keeping the shore in sight. On the afternoon of the fifth day, however, the ominous clouding of the sky gave warning of a coming storm, and in an attempt to seek shelter from it before it struck, the cutter was driven onshore by a heavy surf.

With two men on each oar, Johnny fought desperately to keep the frail craft off the rocks which threatened to smash her to pieces. Blinded by spray, the tiller several times almost wrenched from his grasp, he managed somehow to steer her to safety, the pounding breakers flinging her, like a discarded toy, broadside on through a gap in the rocks and onto a patch of wet sand. There she grounded, her slender bowsprit snapped off at the cap and casks and coconuts spilling out into the receding water.

Most of the men would have run for dry land in panic but Johnny and Will Bryant, using fists and voices, made them drag the boat up and Bird and Martin, unbidden, waded waist-deep into the surf to salvage what they could of their lost cargo.

It was thirty-six hours before the storm abated, and apart from collecting rainwater, there was little they could do, save wait for it to blow over, but Mary Bryant showed her mettle by contriving to light a fire in a small rock cranny and serving hot turtle broth to the weary, disspirited men.

Fortune, at last, relented and smiled on them. No Indians made their appearance and Will and Billy Morton were able to go into the bush and, after some searching, find a hardwood sapling which would serve as a replacement for the cutter's shattered bowsprit. Without proper tools, it took most of the day to hack it down and finally to rig it but, after a cooked meal and an undisturbed night, they put to sea the following morning in good spirits, with sail set and a light offshore breeze, which later veered to the southeast.

The chart showed extensive coral reefs and dangerous shoal water, marked simply as such, but, Johnny decided, the cutter's light draft would permit her to go in safety where a larger vessel would fear to venture, and he continued to steer a course that kept them within easy reach of the shore during the hours of daylight. At night they came to anchor, save when the moon afforded sufficient light to enable him to steer clear of unexpected rocks and shallows, and when it was necessary to go ashore, they did so under cover of darkness, when the natives were less likely to dispute their landing. Drinking water became harder to find, however, and there was no rain, so that they were compelled to make do on a scanty ration, measured in sips, twice a day.

The two small children, for all Mary Bryant's selfless care and devotion, were a source of growing anxiety, visibly losing strength and weight and soon reduced to a state of silent apathy that was more alarming than their earlier fretful sobbing.

The weather continued fair and the winds mainly favorable, but as day succeeded day, with an endless sameness, tempers again became frayed, and fear and hunger generated a blind resentment directed, for the most part, against Johnny and the Bryants.

They had been at sea for almost five weeks when they passed, with no untoward difficulties, through the passage Captain Cook had named Endeavour Strait and entered the Gulf of Carpentaria. Penciling in their new westerly course in his log, Johnny was conscious of a sense of heady triumph, and the spirits of the whole party rose when the dawn of a new day showed them the mouth of a wide river as they closed the coast. Oars were willingly plied to take the cutter into it, and they tied up to the overhanging branches of a tree, a quarter of a mile from its entrance, to drink their fill at last.

"You done all right, Johnny boy," Nat Lilley conceded, slapping him on the back with something of his old affability. "How much longer is it goin' ter take us, eh? A week, maybe?"

"To get to Timor?" Johnny shrugged. "Awhile longer than that, even if we head straight across the gulf, Nat. And if the wind's southerly, we may be driven off course and have to beat back for a spell. It could take us another month—longer, perhaps."

Nat groaned. "We'll be bleedin' skeletons when we get there, plague take it! An' I thought our troubles was over!"

In fact, as they all came soon to realize, the worst of their troubles had yet to begin. The water casks refilled and their food supplies augmented by shellfish and several large seabirds they contrived to shoot, they set sail once more and, as Johnny had feared, were driven off course during the night, both wind and current conspiring against them. Daylight found them in sight of a group of islands fringed with palm trees, as one of their earlier refuges had been, and Johnny yielded to the concerted demands of his companions and steered toward the nearest of these. But they had scarcely approached within a mile of it when three large canoes, each under sail and manned by some twenty or thirty native oarsmen, put out to intercept them. The natives were armed with spears and what appeared to be bows and arrows, their dark faces daubed with brightly hued paint and wearing feathers in their hair.

Any hope that they might be friendly vanished as, having cleared the reef that circled the lagoon in which their canoes had lain in wait, they unloosed a shower of arrows in the cutter's direction. All fell short of their target, but the savage shouts and cries that had accompanied them made their intention all too plain, and the canoes, expertly handled, were gaining rapidly on the heavily laden cutter.

"Row for your lives, boys!" Johnny yelled, putting his tiller over. "If we can get to wind'ard of the swine, we may have a chance. Put your backs into it for God's sake!"

The men needed no second bidding. Weak and exhausted though they all were, they pulled on their heavy oars, and the pursuit finally slackened as they drew away.

They came to the verge of starvation during the last two weeks of their voyage, suffering from extremes of heat and cold and having to ride out a severe thunderstorm that had at least the advantage of providing them with rainwater when the drinking casks were all but empty. Will Bryant, hitherto one of the fittest, succumbed to an attack of fever that rendered him delirious for two days; the two children were sick and had difficulty in breathing, and Mary Bryant, brave and uncomplaining to the last, went for long hours without sleep, clasping both poor little creatures in her arms in an attempt to keep them warm. Johnny, hunched over his tiller, found that his legs had swollen to such an extent that he could only move them with difficulty, and the others complained of cramps in the stomach and constant nausea. But they kept on, for much of the time sunk into a state of semiconscious resignation from which it was well nigh impossible to rouse them.

Suddenly, almost without warning, their ordeal was over. They sighted land and encountered a Dutch trading schooner, whose captain, when Will Bryant hailed him, answered that the land they could see was, indeed, Timor. He took the waterlogged cutter in tow, passed water and food down to them, and next morning they found themselves in Coupang Bay.

"We've all got to stick to the same story," Johnny warned as they prepared to stumble ashore. "We are the sole survivors of the Indiaman *Merlin,* sunk off the New Holland coast on passage to Calcutta. Say as little as you can—let me do the talking."

The castaways were received with hospitable kindness by the residents of Coupang. It was a small town —little more than a fishing village, in fact, if the fort and the neat, white-painted houses of the Dutch garrison and officials were excepted. These circled the seafront and included a hospital, in which they were lodged, and the office of the United East India Company, the only two-story building in Coupang.

The Dutch Company officials listened to Johnny's

story and appeared to have no doubts concerning its truth; they marveled at the manner in which they had sailed their small craft in safety for so great a distance, and eagerly plied the English party with questions as to the route they had taken.

The company manager, who spoke a little English, asked frequently about the settlement at Sydney, and Johnny answered as evasively as he could, fearing to betray himself. The Dutchman volunteered, "Two years ago, one of your sea captains came here, as you did, in a small sailboat. His name was Bligh—Captain William Bligh of the English warship *Bounty,* whose crew had mutinied off what you call, I think, the Friendly Islands. He and, I understood, eighteen loyal officers and men were put off by the mutineers, and they made port here in much the same state as you yourselves have done, after a voyage of almost three months. We offered them hospitality, and they remained here from June until August to recoup their strength. But"—he sighed—"they did not all survive their ordeal, Mister Butcher. The grave of the botanist, Mister Nelson, is here, and some three or four others died after reaching Batavia. We must take good care of your party, must we not? For yours, like that of Captain Bligh, was a truly remarkable feat of navigational skill and endurance and greatly to be commended."

Johnny thanked him, made a trifle uneasy by his manner and by the constant spate of questions to which he was subjected. Did the man suspect? he wondered. Had any of them given him any reason to suppose that they were not what they had claimed to be?

The answer to his fears came only a few days later,

when the Dutch official came to the hospital with two armed soldiers at his heels.

"I regret exceedingly, Mister Butcher," he said without preamble, "but you and your party are to be held in house arrest by orders of His Excellency the governor. You will be handed over to the custody of the captain of the first English ship that calls here, as escaped convicts from the penal settlement at Sydney."

"Escaped convicts, sir?" Johnny echoed, sick with dismay but attempting to bluster. "Who says we are?"

"Two of your party, Mister Butcher," the Dutchman answered, "under the influence of drink, I fear, revealed the truth. I am truly sorry. But rest assured, you will be well treated whilst you remain here—also on our governor's orders. The soldiers will not interfere with you, unless, of course, you should attempt to leave here without permission."

He bowed and was gone. Johnny buried his head in his hands and wept.

CHAPTER XXVI

On July 9, 1791, the transport *Mary Ann* dropped anchor in Sydney Cove. She had a hundred forty female convicts on board, all in excellent health, and had made the passage from England in the record time of four months. In addition to provisions of meat and flour, she had brought supplies of clothing, and the news spread like wildfire throughout the colony that her master had informed the governor that a third fleet, carrying over two thousand convicts, was on its way out, escorted by His Majesty's ship *Gorgon*.

In Rose Hill—which, on the occasion of the king's birthday, had been renamed Parramatta—Jenny waited with mixed emotions for the ships to arrive. Settlement in the area had almost doubled, and with the influx of fresh labor, building was going on apace.

She and Melia, aided by Reuben White, the old convict who had returned to take charge of Tom Jenkins's
holding, had made repairs and additions to the cabin
and store sheds and brought another six acres into
production. But it had been hard, back-breaking work,
and the discovery that she was pregnant caused her
more anxiety than happiness.

At first she had been overjoyed when her application for a land grant was approved, but Ned's reaction
to it had swiftly soured her joy. The grant was in her
name, not his, and resentful on this account, he had
refused to have any part in it. How different it might
all have been, Jenny thought sadly, had Andrew Hawley been in Ned's place. She could have viewed the
future with confidence, could have gloried in her
pregnancy, but Ned seemed capable only of destroying
all her hopes.

"I told you I'd have none of your soil grubbing,
Jenny," he complained sourly, "and I meant what I
said. I'm staying with the fishing boats, and a plague
on your land grant. Work it yourself!"

Even when Captain Collins had told him that the
governor had ordered his removal from the boats, he
had sought for some means that would enable him to
remain in Sydney Cove. Parramatta, a slow, four- to
five-hour journey by water in the *Lump*, was an
obstacle to the escape he still dreamed of and it was
only when Jenny broke the news of her pregnancy to
him that he consented, with a bad grace, to join her.
But, to her distress, he would take no steps to legalize
their union.

"Hell, Jenny, we're married in the sight of God—
isn't that good enough for you!" he said in answer to
her diffident plea. "I'll be damned before I'll go crawl-

ing, cap in hand, to His sodding Excellency to beg permission to wed you."

A fresh cause for resentment came when he found himself assigned to work the thirty-acre grant in place of old Reuben, who, allotted a grant of his own, left the holding on the day of his arrival there. But, with the only alternative assignment to a road gang, of which he had had experience in Sydney, Ned gave in and, for a while, made an effort to compensate for Reuben's loss. Melia, who had begun by criticizing his lack of skill and initiative, had lately defended him and, to Jenny's complaints, said only, "Jenny, he's trying—give him a chance. We weren't all brought up on a farm like you."

"You weren't," Jenny agreed, "but you work ten times harder than Ned does."

Ned's coming had not brought her the happiness she had so fervently hoped for—rather it had caused the first serious rift in her long friendship with Melia, and the rift, despite all she could do to prevent it, was growing wider.

To make matters worse, for all her slowly thickening body and the weight of the coming child, Jenny toiled obstinately, as she always had, but with ever increasing weariness, too exhausted when night fell to do anything save sleep and often too spent even to eat when the day's work was over.

"You're no company," Ned grumbled. "It was better when we had that plaguey garden in the cove— at least there was plenty of help then and only a third of the land to work. We need another man here—old Reuben wasn't much good but he could dig ditches and cut corn. Damn it, I can't be expected to do all the heavy work; I'm not a blasted ox. Besides"—he grasped Melia's hand and grinning, bore it to his lips

—"Melia needs a man of her own, don't you, girl? A fine, lusty fellow who can do a few things Reuben couldn't. Hell, with two thousand to choose from, you ought to be able to find one to your taste—and they'll be here any day now, Melia, if the master of the *Mary Ann* wasn't out in his reckoning."

His forecast proved correct. Word that another transport, the *Matilda,* had reached Sydney on August 1 came to Parramatta two days later, when the first batch of her two hundred male convicts was sent up-river in the *Lump* to swell the agricultural community's growing labor force. Ned's jibe seemingly forgotten and both of them hungry for news of home, he and Melia set off together soon after dawn to meet the new arrivals. Jenny elected to stay where she was.

She was tying up vines in front of the cabin when she saw him coming slowly across the undulating ground above the creek, and for a moment she could scarcely believe the evidence of her own eyes. But there was no mistaking that odd little figure with the limping gait and the head cocked on one side, and her heart turned over at the sight of him. Dropping her pruning knife, she ran to meet him, calling his name in a choked voice. "Watt—Watt *Sparrow*—is it really you? It can't be—I must be dreaming!"

"It's me orl right, Jenny," he assured her as they clung together, laughing and weeping by turn. "Yer old Cock Sparrer in person. A mite battered an' a few years older an' not too 'appy to be 'ere. But you—" He held her at arm's length as he studied her with the bright, birdlike eyes she remembered so well. "A woman grown, my little Jenny! I'd never 'ave known you an' that's a fact. Mind, I come lookin' to find you, lass, an' they said you'd be 'ereabouts. Got yer own place, 'ave you? An' married, too . . . just fancy that!

Last time I seen you, you was just a slip o' a lass an' didn't 'ardly reach ter me shoulder."

He looked ill, Jenny realized. Ill and emaciated, his skin wrinkled and the color of old parchment. Evading the question concerning her marital status, she took his arm and led him to the cabin, seating him in front of the fire and fussing over him as she poked the embers to life and set the iron kettle on to boil.

"What was the voyage like, Watt? Bad?"

The little man shuddered. "It was a nightmare. The *Matilda*'s near as old as I am an' a whaling ship by rights. She stank o' blubber an' leaked something chronic. We was never dry in the 'old an' packed in so's we couldn't 'ardly move. We lost twenty-seven poor souls from fever an' landed gettin' on as many sick, out o' two hundred. Even the sodjers was goin' dahn wiv' it."

"You're sick, aren't you?" Jenny suggested gently. She brewed the sweet tea and put a beaker of it into his small bony hand.

He shook his head. "Nah, not me. Too fly fer that, lass—you know ole Watt. Weren't fly enough not ter get nabbed, though—an' at a toppin' too." He spoke ruefully. "But there it is—I got a mite caw-'anded in me old age an' since the doctor died, it ain't bin the same. Not the same at all, why—"

"The doctor *dead*?"

"A year since, lass—no, must be nearer two year, now I come ter reckon up. In 'is bed, though, very respectable, an' they give 'im a grand funeral . . . 'is family, that is. Very well connected, Doctor Fry was, though 'e never let on. . . ." He went into details concerning the doctor's family and his last illness, but Jenny was scarcely listening, tears blinding her as she mixed damper and set it to cook.

She choked on a sob. He had not written, and she had wondered why, had even felt hurt by the omission when the ships had come with mail at last and there had been nothing for her.

"I come across someone else as knew you, Jenny," Watt Sparrow said. "Quite a coincidence, that was. You remember the feller you was searchin' for, you an' yer ma, that day when you first come ter London? A big, tall lad as traveled wiv' yer from Yorkshire?"

"Andrew Hawley? Oh, yes, indeed I do!" Jenny drew a quick, uneven breath. "Do you mean—oh, Watt, did you meet Andrew Hawley?" She was hungry for news. "How was he?"

Watt's grin was rueful. " 'E went for a sojer, didn't 'e, Jenny? Well, that was 'ow I met 'im. One o' the escort, 'e was, takin' us downriver from Newgate ter join the *Matilda*. Said 'e'd volunteered fer the duty in the 'ope o' sendin' word ter you. When we was in the boat, on our way ter Gravesend, 'e called out, askin' if any of us knew you. An' o' course I spoke up. . . ." He talked on, and Jenny listened avidly, as he repeated all Andrew had told him of the circumstances of his own enforced return to England from Rio de Janeiro.

"Posted ter a ship called the *Pandora,* 'e said, and still wiv' 'is time ter serve. But 'e said I was ter send 'is good wishes ter you an' yer ma an' tell you as 'e'd not fergotten yer." The little man sipped his sweet tea appreciatively, the warmth of the fire restoring a little color to his thin cheeks. "This is a drop o' good stuff! What is it, Jenny?"

Jenny collected her scattered thoughts and somehow managed to speak normally, although she felt as if her heart were breaking. How different her life might have been had Andrew not been sent away from her. But. . . . "They call it Botany Bay brew or sweet tea. It's made from a berry that grows wild here." Deftly she turned the damper and saw Watt wrinkle his nose at the appetizing smell that rose from the heated stone. "And this is what we use for bread, when there's a government issue of flour in the ration."

She spoke briefly of conditions in the settlement as he ate hungrily, making light of the hardships lest she discourage him, and then asked about the Pruntys.

"They never come back, lass," Watt answered regretfully. "Stayed where they was, in the country. Took an inn, Taunton way. The doctor used ter stop there when 'e was on 'is travels an' 'e reckoned they was doin' all right. Doll's uncle took over the Three Fools but 'e was a surly ole curmudgeon an' wasn't liked. Lost most o' the trade Doll used ter 'ave." He sighed. "Times change, don't they? Is yer ma doin' as well as you've done?"

"No. She died on the way out here." Jenny offered no explanation, and after a quick glance at her face, Watt Sparrow asked for none.

"I'm sorry," he said. "She was a good woman, yer ma."

To change the subject she asked him if he had been assigned to a labor gang, and he admitted that, as she had suspected, he was officially on the sick list and had been ordered to report to the hospital when he reached Parramatta.

"They give me a couple o' weeks' grace. Reckoned as I wasn't fit fer 'ard labor, not yet awhile," he said wryly.

"I can apply for you to be assigned here, Watt," she offered. "If I say you're a relative, there won't be any objection—the hospital's always overcrowded, they'll be glad to have you off their hands." They were always glad to rid themselves of responsibility for the aged and the infirm, she thought bitterly, and Watt, for all his protestations, came into that category now. But she would feed him, care for him, restore him to health. She owed him almost as much as she had owed Dr. Fry. And Ned, surely, could not object, although there had been no love lost between them in the old days.

Watt was questioning her about her status, and she replied as fully as she could, explaining that she was to be considered for remission and, in the meantime, had been given a grant of land and leave to work it as a reward for good conduct.

"All we produce goes to the government store, and in return we're given rations, seed, and working tools, and we can grow vegetables for ourselves, and fruit too. We don't starve, Watt—the land is good here. Drought—months without rain—that's the big danger but we're not far from a good creek. The effect of the drought this summer was worse in Sydney Cove than it was here—even the Tank Stream almost dried up and all our vegetables withered."

"You're quite the little farmer, ain't you?" Watt suggested, his tone admiring.

"I was brought up on a farm," Jenny reminded him. She told him of her garden in Sydney Cove and of the women who had helped her to work it. "Eliza and Charlotte and Polly have married and received grants of their own, but Melia—Amelia Bishop—is here. And Ned too. You remember Ned Munday, don't you?"

Watt Sparrow's indulgent smile abruptly faded. He looked at her in shocked dismay. "Ned Munday's not —you're not married to him, are you, Jenny?"

"I—" She could feel the color rising to flood her cheeks as his gaze went to her swollen belly and then to the tips of her worn shoes, as if he were reluctant to look at her directly until his question was answered. "I'm not married to him, no. But I'm . . . his woman, Watt. The—the child will be his."

"You're goin' to 'ave 'is child and he ain't married you!" He was angry, although he did his best to hide it. "Is that your choice or 'is, lass?"

"It's . . . his," Jenny admitted. "He hasn't settled here; he hates this place and he's not happy. He dreams of escaping, you see—indeed he's tried to escape, and I fear he'll go on trying. So he won't tie himself to me or to anyone. He thinks marriage would trap him into staying here . . . and I suppose it might."

She thought of Johnny Butcher and recalled guiltily how close she herself had come to making an escape attempt with him. It had only needed a word and she would have taken her life in her hands and gone with him on that perilous, ill-conceived voyage to Timor in the governor's stolen cutter. Will Bryant's party had not been caught, it was true, and had not returned to Port Jackson, as so many did, defeated and driven back by stormy seas and starvation. They had simply vanished, as others had vanished before them.

Watt Sparrow got stiffly to his feet. "I'll need ter make tracks fer—what do they call the place? Parramatta, to the 'ospital. It's a goodish step an' I'll be liable ter lose meself if I wait till dark."

Sensing his disapproval, Jenny laid a hand on his arm. "You can stay here," she offered. "There's a hut that Reuben White used, and it's been empty since he left. Please don't go, Watt."

The little man hesitated and then shook his balding

head. "I'd best give it to yer straight, Jenny. I can't stay 'ere if Ned Munday's wiv' yer. There's bad blood between us—things 'e done that I can't never forgive."

"Not on my account, Watt," Jenny pleaded. "I know he got me arrested, but that's all forgiven and forgotten now. Ned didn't mean to let me be caught. He—"

"That's only part o' it, lass." Watt spoke with flat finality. "Gettin' you nabbed fer 'is botched-up dip was one thing, an' it was bad enough, 'cause 'e could 'ave cleared you if 'e'd come forward. But it ain't all. He . . . you won't like me fer sayin' this, Jenny, but I'm glad you ain't married ter Ned Munday. You'll find out what 'e is one day an' then you'll be glad too, believe me yer will."

"I don't want to believe you, Watt." Jenny bit her lip. "Truly I don't, I—"

"Nah, 'course yer don't. So it'll be best for all of us if I make meself scarce. But you'll know where I am, if yer should need me. Just say the word, my lass, an' I'll be 'ere."

There was pity in the little man's eyes as he looked at her, and conscious of his uneasiness, Jenny let him go. Ned had his faults. He had hurt her and would almost certainly go on hurting—and disappointing— her but . . . she went back to the fire and slumped down in front of it, staring into its glowing embers with tear-filled eyes.

For good or ill, he was her man; she had chosen her path and her life, with Ned to share that life, and there was no going back now. There was the child to consider. She touched her distended belly and smiled as she felt the movement under her hand. Watt would come around when he had had time to think matters over, and surely, if Ned were to ask him, he would change his mind and agree to join them.

It was no use having regrets; the past was the past. Dr. Fry, Andrew Hawley, her mother, Olwyn, and Tom were all in the past. But it was good to know that Andrew had not forgotten—from the depths of her heart, she wished him well.

She rose resolutely and went back to the vines.

Ned had found the visit to the main settlement at Parramatta both profitable and enjoyable. In addition to the newly arrived convicts, some seamen from the *Matilda* had come upriver, bringing illicit supplies of liquor and tobacco to trade for fresh fruit and vegetables and the favors of any women who expressed willingness to make an exchange.

Ned had contrived to add considerably to the stocks he had brought with him for barter, by the simple expedient of stealing from the smallholdings and gardens they had passed on their way, and in the face of Melia's shocked disapproval he had struck several good bargains.

A small cask of rum, a pair of good buckled shoes, a shirt, and a plug of ship's tobacco had been acquired in trade, and while Melia talked nostalgically of England with an aging scarecrow of a man from her hometown, Ned had put the time of waiting to good use by picking the pockets of the sailors from whom he had obtained the rum. The convicts were a poor lot, the majority of them old and ailing, and he quickly lost interest in them when it became evident that they had little of value to barter. And they had little news either, save that the war—of which so many conflicting rumors had reached Sydney—was over and the British fleet laid up, the crews paid off, and the officers on half pay.

Ned attached himself to a garrulous old seaman who told him that the government planned to ship convicts and provisions to New South Wales in regular, twice-yearly sailings and that the *Matilda* and three of her sister ships were going back to Van Dieman's Land as soon as they had unloaded and made repairs, to hunt whales.

"We seen hundreds of 'em off the coast," the old man said, his faded eyes holding a gleam of eager anticipation. "Blue fin, humpback, sperm—never bin hunted, I reckon, an' there for the taking. An' we found a fine harbor south o' here. . . ." He prattled on, and Ned listened with quickened interest when he learned that the *Matilda* was short of her full complement of seamen.

"I used to be at sea," he suggested tentatively. "And my sentence is nearly expired. . . . How about it, matey? D'you reckon your master would give me a berth?"

The old sailor eyed him thoughtfully. He did not challenge the lies, although it was possible, Ned decided, that he was not taken in by them. He drank from a flask of rum he carried, hiccoughed, and hospitably offered it to his companion. "Have a sup, lad," he invited.

"Thanks . . . and good health to you!" Ned gulped gratefully at the raw spirit and repeated his question.

"We can use a few good strong men," the old fellow admitted. "Ten or a dozen, maybe—an' no questions asked." He closed one eye in an elaborate wink. "Take us a few weeks to clear, but I'll send word. What's your name, lad?"

Ned told him, accepted another sup of rum, and,

feeling elated, went in search of Melia and the proceeds of his trading, which he had prudently hidden beneath some bushes at the edge of the track. He pressed on her the fine linen kerchief he had taken from one of the *Matilda*'s officers and had intended as a gift for Jenny.

"For you, m'lady," he said when they were out of sight of the new brick buildings of the settlement. He made a show of putting the kerchief about her slender neck. "There . . . it looks well."

"Where did you get it?" Melia asked, eyeing him uncertainly as he smoothed the linen over the coarse folds of her worn and oft-mended dress. "Tell me, Ned!"

He laughed. "Ask me no questions and you'll hear no lies." He deftly tied the ends and stood back to admire his handiwork, conscious, as always, of the challenge her aloofness posed. But she was not quite as aloof or careful as she normally was, and he felt his pulses quicken. "It suits you a treat. You're very beautiful, Melia—truly you are. How about a kiss to reward me for my pains?"

She sighed and was silent but she did not reprove him. They were still too close to the settlement, Ned decided; he hefted the cask onto his shoulder and, with his free hand, took her arm. "Best be on our way," he suggested, "in case those damned lobsters change their minds and start searching us. They're quite capable of it, plague take them—come on, let's put some distance between us and them."

Melia trudged along beside him, carrying the basket containing the shirt and shoes, and repeating snatches of what the old man from her hometown had told her, her voice charged with emotion.

"I'd give ten years of my life to be back there now,"

she said. "Imagine it, Ned—the green fields of England, the oak trees, and the hedgerows in place of this barren jungle and the creaking gum trees, which look as if they've been dead for centuries! To be able to ride on horseback or behind a carriage and pair, to dress decently again, to behave and be treated like a lady, instead of going barefoot and grubbing in the soil from sunrise to sunset, just for the means to keep alive. To eat fresh meat again, properly cooked and served—" Her voice broke on a sob. "He was a clerk, you know, the old man I was talking to—a clerk at Babcock's in the High Street. And he—he remembered my father."

It was the first time she had ever talked to Ned of her previous life and circumstances in any detail, and he listened as she recalled places and incidents, people she had known, things she had done as a child and a young woman. Her memories went far beyond his experience. He had ridden a horse, it was true, but never behind a carriage pair in the luxury of a chaise, and the only country he had known had been the heath and Richmond Park. For no reason that he could understand, this made her suddenly more desirable than she had ever been, and his longing to possess her became, in a strange way, a test of his manhood.

Reaching a clump of trees—creaking gum trees, Melia had scornfully called them—he halted and set the cask down beneath the gnarled and hollow trunk of one that did, indeed, look as if it had been dead for centuries.

"Let's take a rest," he suggested, adding persuasively, "and a drink wouldn't come amiss, would it?"

To his surprise she did not demur, letting him lift

the cask for her and drinking thirstily from its wide mouth.

Melia sat down beside him on the spiny grass. "Oh, Ned. . . ." Her eyes were filled with tears, he saw as he leaned toward her. "I can't go on, I can't stand this awful life any longer. The dirt, the drudgery— look at us, we're both filthy! Peasants, without shoes."

"That's easily remedied," Ned retorted. He reached into the basket for the shirt, stripping off his own and grinning, donned the buckled shoes, aware of the fine figure he cut, with his tanned skin and the muscles his toil on the land had given him. Rising, he swept her a bow. "M'lady, may I have the pleasure. . . ."

But Melia did not respond to his clowning. She said wretchedly, "I've served almost five years of my sentence and I expect I'll be given remission, but what is there to look forward to, to hope for? Remission will not mean that I can go home, will it? The only way I could pay for my passage would be if I sold myself to a ship's officer and—"

"You wouldn't do that, would you?" Ned protested, shocked. He dropped to his knees beside her, reaching for her hand. "Would you, Melia?"

Her tear-filled eyes were raised to his. "Why not?" she countered defiantly. "If it's the only alternative to staying here for the rest of my life? And what *is* my life? Jenny has you, but I have no one. You were right, Ned, I want a man of my own to—to make it even bearable. I—"

"Jenny doesn't own me," Ned told her thickly. He had known that it would come, that sooner or later she would turn to him but . . . now that the moment was here, he was half-afraid that she might still rebuff him. He hesitated, but the look in her eyes spurred him on. He kissed her hungrily, tearing off the kerchief he had tied so carefully about her neck, tasting the rum on her lips and tongue as a fiery echo of the fumes that were filling his brain and kindling desire in both of them.

"Ah, but you're lovely!" he exulted, feeling her slender body arch beneath him as his hands caressed her with skilled insistence. In that other life at which she had hinted so sadly, he would never have dared to touch her, never presumed to raise his eyes to meet hers. She had been a grand lady, he a product of the London gutters, a cly-faker and a sometime highway robber. This knowledge added zest to the conquest, and he lingered over it, teasing and denying her the fulfillment she sought from him, compelling her to plead with him, for, plague take her, had she not denied him in the past?

"Lovely Lady Melia," he whispered, lips pressed to her ear. "You're mine, you're my woman and you want me, don't you?" He let her strain against him, savoring his power over her and deliberately controlling his own desire that he might increase hers. "We could have done this a long while ago but you wouldn't have it . . . because of Jenny. Well, forget Jenny. Say that you want me to take you, Melia!"

"You know I do!" She said it fiercely, the proud restraint of years abandoned at last to a primitive urge she could no longer subdue. There could have been others; when she had worked in the garden with Jenny and Eliza and Charlotte, a score or more of men had made her offers of marriage, and they had included marines, seamen from the *Sirius* and the *Supply*, as well as convicts. But she had waited, wanting an officer like Arnold, a gentleman, and she had waited in vain. Although from one or two of them she had received offers, none had *promised* her marriage. None ever would . . . she bit back a sob.

And here there was only Ned.

Melia's arms went around Ned's waist, her mouth seeking his, and as she gave herself to him with reckless passion, she thrust all thought of Jenny from her mind. . . .

Watt Sparrow passed them, on his way back to the settlement at Parramatta. They were walking toward him, their arms entwined, and they so evidently had eyes only for one another that, he was sure, they did not notice him, crouching down among the shadows of the dusty track he had been following. He recognized Ned Munday without difficulty and guessed the identity of his companion. He swore under his breath, his shrewd eyes taking in the obvious intimacy that existed between them, which left him in no doubt as to the nature of their relationship.

Poor little Jenny would have need of a friend, he thought angrily, if she found out about this betrayal. Well, she had said that she could apply for him to be assigned to her smallholding—he would tell her that he had changed his mind and now wanted to join her. And if Munday raised objections, he could go to the devil, where he rightly belonged.

Within a week of Watt Sparrow's arrival in her household, Jenny was regretting her invitation to him. From the outset Ned had resented his coming, but for some reason which Jenny did not fully understand—after his first furious outburst—he had accepted the little man's presence with sullen resignation, and Melia, more subdued than was her wont, had said nothing.

It was as if they were all in possession of some

secret that they were reluctant to share with her and
Jenny was miserable, intercepting strange, meaningful
glances between Melia and Ned and half-hearing con-
versations among the three of them, which, in her
presence, broke off abruptly and were continued when
she left them.

She got through her usual quota of work, thankful
to escape to the comparative peace and silence of the
newly cleared land beyond the creek, and Ned, to her
relief, toiled from dawn to dusk, digging irrigation
ditches with which to water the six acres of wheat they
had sown in June. Melia also had volunteered to help.

In the cabin, however, when they were all together
in the evenings, the atmosphere was charged with
tension, and attributing this at least in part to Watt
Sparrow's presence, Jenny became increasingly worried about it.

Watt had become someone she could really rely on.
He trudged to Parramatta to pick up their weekly
ration from the government store, dug turnips and
potatoes in the garden plot, cut and carried firewood,
and even, if he thought she was tired, relieved her
of the thankless task of producing an edible meal
from the often putrefying ration meat, which, in
common with the rest of the community, they all
found unpalatable.

Watt was at work on her kitchen table one evening,
some three weeks after he had joined them, when
Jenny returned, weary and disspirited, from her self-
imposed labor on the newly cleared land beyond the
creek. He had been to fetch their rations and, whistling cheerfully, was engaged in cutting bone and
gristle from an unappetizing hunk of salt tack when
she entered the cabin.

"Came from Batavia, this 'ere," he told her. "An

it's bin cured in spices, the way the Dutch folk reckon they like it. 'Orrible stuff—even the flies don't fancy it! But I thought if I boil it fer long enough, it'd maybe do fer—" He broke off, searching her face anxiously. "You look done up, lass. Not ill, are yer?"

"No, of course not," Jenny denied, but he ignored her half-hearted protests and, after making her sit down on Tom's old rocking chair, he brewed sweet tea for her and stood over her while she drank it.

"The word in Parramatta is that the *Atlantic*'s made port," he volunteered. "Sailed wiv' us, she did. An' they say the *Salamander*'s off South 'Ead, with the *William an' Ann* just be'ind 'er. Carryin' sodjers, she is—more o' the New South Wales Corps."

"They're coming to relieve the marines," Jenny said listlessly. She lay back with her eyes closed, feeling suddenly light-headed and nauseated, and Watt, deeply concerned, knelt beside her chair, his hands grasping hers.

"What is it, Jenny love?" he asked. "Somethin's troublin' you, ain't it?"

It all came out then, the words tumbling over each other in her anxiety to make him understand, without hurting his feelings or causing him to take offense. She failed lamentably and knew that she had when Watt Sparrow got to his feet, all the color draining from his gaunt cheeks as he looked down at her with an odd mixture of pity and anger in his eyes.

"You want me ter go, on Ned's account—is that what you're tryin' ter say, Jenny?"

"I . . . yes, I suppose so. *I* want you to stay, Watt, but you—you upset Ned. He hasn't been the same since you came. And I'm afraid that—"

"Afraid that 'e'll walk out on you, is that it?"

Was it? Jenny wondered. Was that her real fear?

She wasn't sure and felt too weary and unhappy to delve deeper. Watt said, his voice clipped, "It'll not be my doin' if 'e goes, lass. You c'n look nearer 'ome for the cause. Your friend Melia—ask 'er."

"*Ask Melia*? But we've been together for years, we've been friends for years! You're not saying that she and Ned—" Jenny broke off, unable to put it into words. "You can't be!"

"That's what I *am* sayin', Jenny. An' I'm not tryin' to hurt you—the last thing I want is to see you hurt, as God's me witness. But you must be blind if you ain't seen what's goin' on between the two of 'em."

Was she blind? Jenny asked herself miserably. Willfully blind? But when had Melia looked at any man, save with cool disdain? And when Ned had mocked her, a few weeks ago, she had been angry, seeing his taunts as the insult they were . . . Watt Sparrow was *wrong*!

She started to repeat her denial, but Watt cut her short. "Jenny love, listen to me—Ned Munday's a bad 'un and 'e'll be the ruin of you if you let 'im."

"But Melia wouldn't . . . she's not like that, Watt. We've been through so much, she and I. When Mam was dying, she helped me take care of her, out of the goodness of her heart. And she—she's a lady, gently born, while Ned—oh, you know what Ned was and she knows that too."

"Watch them when they're together, lass. Maybe she is gently born an' maybe she wouldn't 'ave given Ned the time o' day in the normal way o' things. But things ain't normal in this place, not by a long chalk, are they?" Watt spoke grimly. "I've bin 'ere long enough ter find that out. An' I know what I've seen, Jenny."

"Do you?" she countered, with weary bitterness.

"Aye, that I do. An' I ain't just speakin' up 'cause I want ter stay 'ere—it's for your sake an' 'cause I care about you. I've knew you 'arf yer life an' you're a fine lass, Jenny. But you've gone an' let Ned Munday pull the wool over yer eyes an' make a slave out o' you in the bargain, ain't you?"

Jenny smothered a sigh. Then she remembered something else, the story Ned had poured out in his delirium, the accusations he had made against Watt and Dr. Fry, and her temper flared.

"You got Ned arrested, didn't you, Watt—you and the doctor? It's because of what you did that he's here?"

Watt Sparrow did not deny it. "Yes, but 'e 'ad it comin' to 'im. Doctor Fry wasn't a cruel man but 'e was a just one—'e believed in an eye for an eye, so 'e put the word out on Ned Munday."

"You said it wasn't only on my account?"

"No, it wasn't." Watt shrugged his narrow shoulders, avoiding her gaze. "Look, Jenny, I can't tell you no more, not while you're with 'im. I gave 'im my word I'd keep quiet an' leave 'im ter tell you hisself when—"

"You gave *Ned* your word?" Jenny stared at him in bewilderment, her brief anger fading.

"That's right, lass. Why else d'you s'pose 'e let me stay 'ere? Didn't want me, did 'e—you know that as well as I do."

He was right, she knew. Dear heaven, was there no end to Ned's deviousness?

She looked at Watt, turning over everything he had said to her, searching his eyes for answers.

Watt shuffled his feet uneasily, avoiding her gaze. "I'll pack up me gear termorrer mornin', Jenny love, an' fly the coop. There's your child ter think of, ain't there? Maybe when 'e becomes a father, Ned will learn to be'ave 'imself."

Jenny did not press him to stay, did not even inquire where he would go when he left, an underlying resentment transcending the pity and affection she had felt for him when he had first arrived. The little man flashed a swift, covert glance at her face and went back to his chopping board, whistling with pretended indifference.

"I could do wiv' a few spuds from the pie," he said. "An' maybe a turnip an' some o' that green stuff. Might as well make a good meal, seein' it's ter be me last 'ere."

She went out without replying. Their root vegetables were buried in what in Yorkshire they had called a pie—really a shallow pit with a top covering of light soil—and the first shock came when she found it almost empty. It was the same elsewhere in the garden—virtually everything that was ripe and could be used for barter was gone. Her first thought was that thieves had raided the garden during the night, but then she found the baskets Ned used to carry produce to the store had also vanished, and her heart sank, for the baskets were kept well hidden—no casual garden robber would have found them, without revealing his presence. Even the illicit tobacco, which old Reuben had grown secretly the previous summer and bequeathed to her when he left, was no longer in its place of concealment, and— Jenny looked about her, sickened.

It would have taken two people to carry the laden baskets, and two at least to collect and pack their contents during the time when Watt had been waiting, in the long line outside the government store, for their rations to be distributed, and—she bit back a sob—when she herself had been safely out of sight on the far side of the creek.

Wearily, but with her mouth a tight, resolute line, she trudged to the six-acre plot, where the wheat was showing inch-high green shoots above the still parched earth. There were only two shallow, hurriedly dug irrigation ditches instead of the half-dozen of which, only the previous evening, Ned had proudly boasted —and neither reached the creek, behind its screen of gum and acacia, where the choking mangroves had again taken root. Of Ned and Melia, there was no sign at all.

They did not return that evening. With a grimly silent Watt, Jenny picked apathetically at the good meal he had gone to so much trouble to prepare and sought her bed early, hoping to find oblivion in sleep.

Next day, Watt Sparrow went to Parramatta to glean what information he could concerning the runaways. He was back shortly after noon.

"They went off ter Sydney Cove in the *Lump*, Jenny," he said, his voice carefully controlled. "An' they got clothes an' a dollar or two for the 'baccy an' stuff they knapped from 'ere. It seems Ned got wind o' a ship wantin' men for the whalin'—the *Matilda*, I fancy, 'cause 'er bo'sun was askin' around on the quiet the other day. They say the *Mary Ann* is goin' too, an' they're both short o' crews, so I daresay one of 'em will take 'im, if he says 'is time expired. Masters ain't too fussy when they want men."

"And Melia?" Jenny asked, trying bravely to match his control. "A whaling ship would not take her, surely?"

Watt shrugged. "There's ways—not rightly the ways fer a lady, but it'd be a chance o' gettin' 'ome."

She felt the child move within her and said uncertainly, "We shall have to try and carry on. If you'll help me, Watt, I—I'll be grateful."

He grinned and put a fatherly arm around her. "I'll 'elp, Jenny love. The babby'll 'ave a gran'dad an' a ma—that'll 'ave ter do fer a while, won't it? An' if 'is gran'dad ain't much of an 'and at farmin' yet—well, there's time enough fer 'im ter learn, ain't there? When's the little cuss due ter come into the world, eh?"

"In December, I think," Jenny whispered. "I . . . thank you, Watt. And bless you!"

"We'll get them irrigation ditches dug," he said, smiling at her. "There's plenty o' husky men lookin' fer extra work—government work only takes 'em till midday."

"They have to be paid," Jenny reminded him wryly. "And we've got nothing, Watt."

"That's where you're mistaken, lass." One bright eye closed in an exaggerated wink. "They reckon rum's gettin' ter be the currency 'ere, don't they? Well, Ned's left 'arf a cask be'ind 'im . . . couldn't carry it, I don't suppose, when 'e made 'is flit. We'll use that, Jenny, eh? 'E owes us that much, don't 'e?"

Perhaps he did, Jenny thought wretchedly. She nodded her agreement and went on, dragging her feet, to pick up her hoe. Watt took it from her. "I gotter learn sometime, ain't I? Why not now?"

"Oh, Watt!" Suddenly her control broke. "You're a *good* man, truly you are."

Watt Sparrow held her close, shocked by the intensity of her weeping, and, for the first time in many years, found himself praying. His was a silent prayer, but it came from the heart.

Ten days later a letter from Melia was delivered

to the commissary store. It was addressed to Jenny and she read it, dry-eyed and without emotion.

I am sorry I did not leave you a note to say we were going, but I had neither pen nor paper. I am penning this now, not to ask you to forgive me—I know you cannot do that—but to tell you that Ned has gone.

He signed on as a deckhand in the *Mary Ann*, and I hope, for his sake, that he is not discovered and that he makes his escape.

I am staying here, working again in our old garden. I have petitioned the governor for remission and written to my mother, begging her to send money so that I may pay my passage to England. It will be a long time before I can hope to receive her answer, but I shall wait and pray that she will reply to my plea.

Try not to think too badly of me, Jenny. It was, I think, a sort of madness that overcame me, and I now deeply regret it. We live and learn, do we not?

I sign myself, as I have always been, your loving Melia.

CHAPTER XXVII

The ships—transports with convicts and supplies—
continued to arrive, including the *Queen* from Ire-
land, bearing a hundred fifty unfortunates who had
been sent initially to Newfoundland, where they
had been refused admission. All were emaciated and
sickly, having, the governor suspected, been treated
after the fashion of those who had come out in the
infamous *Neptune*. There had been an attempt at
mutiny on board the *Albemarle*, only just averted by
the decisive action of her master, and in all, two
hundred convicts had died during the passage.

Phillip sent two shiploads of the fittest to Norfolk
Island and, angered by the abuses that had been
practiced, fined one of the masters heavily in the hope
that this might act as a deterrent in the future.

"Although I fear it will not," he confided bitterly

to David Collins, "since they have all brought out goods for private trade, and, damn their eyes, every man jack will, as a result, show a large and totally unmerited profit! Their prices are exorbitant, and they have crammed the wretched convicts into quarters fit only for cattle, in order to allow more space for cargo. But what can we do if the home government permits them to do so?"

To his immense relief the long awaited king's ship *Gorgon*, commanded by Captain John Parker, made her appearance off the Heads on September 21. She had brought six months' provisions for the colony, fruit trees, agricultural seed, and livestock, including sixty-eight sheep and a twenty-strong breeding herd of prime English cattle. In addition her commander delivered the governor's official seal and with it full authority for Phillip, at his discretion, to remit sentences imposed in England—a power which hitherto he had been able only to exercise conditionally.

Most welcome of all to the ailing and overworked governor was the return of Philip Gidley King, now promoted to the rank of commander, with his lieutenant governor's appointment confirmed. King had married during his brief sojourn in England, and his wife, Anna, together with Mrs. Parker—who had accompanied her husband on the voyage—added new luster to the social life of the settlement.

"We will celebrate," the governor decided, after King had given him all the home news he could. "Damme, we'll have the finest dinner party Government House has ever known! The ladies shall feast on emu and duck and kangaroo, and we'll send the fishing boats out too and forget, just for once, what it is to be hungry. Your wife is charming, my dear Philip! My only regret is that all too soon you will have to resume your governorship of Norfolk Island and I shall, in consequence, see all too little of you both."

"That will be to my regret also, sir," King assured him with warm sincerity. He hesitated and then asked, "How has Major Ross acquitted himself as lieutenant governor?"

Phillip's mouth tightened perceptibly. "I am quite positive," he answered with what was obviously restraint, "that the Norfolk Island people, free and convict, will rejoice when you return to them."

"And when *am* I to return to them, sir?" King inquired. "I am entirely at your service, of course, but I'm anxious to get into harness again, and I've told Anna so much about the place that she is eager to take up her abode there."

"It will depend on when I can conclude negotiations for the hire of a ship," the governor told him. "The gallant *Supply* has worn herself out in service to the colony, so I must send her home for a refit and to pay off her people. My intention is to let her sail in company with the *Gorgon*. Captain Parker, as you know, is to give passage to Ross and his marines." He smiled faintly. "My wholly unworthy plan, my dear Philip, is to relieve Ross at so late a juncture that he will virtually step from his transport to the *Gorgon!*"

Philip King nodded in understanding, as the governor went on, "You can count on three or four weeks here. When you go, I will send Captain Paterson, of the New South Wales Corps, and his wife with you —and Surgeon Balmain. Mistress Paterson will be company for your good lady, and young Balmain is an excellent doctor. The chaplain is also anxious to accompany you, for the purpose of performing marriages and baptizing any children who have need of it . . . you now have a community of over eleven hundred souls on Norfolk Island."

"Indeed, sir?" King regarded him with some astonishment. "It has grown—when I left the Island there were about five hundred all told."

"On the latest reckoning we have two thousand eight hundred here on the mainland," Phillip told him. "If only the home government would heed my oft repeated appeals and send me young, healthy convicts with some skills but—Grenville is as bad as Sydney in that respect, alas! You saw his lordship, did you not?"

"Lord Grenville? Yes, sir, I did. Believe me," Philip King spoke earnestly, "I exerted all the powers of oratory I possess to explain our needs to him. He appeared to understand and to be anxious to comply with the requests you have conveyed to him."

"Well, damme, he hasn't done so!" Phillip gave vent to an exasperated sigh. "If fifty farmers and their families were prevailed upon to settle here, they would do more in one year to render us independent than a thousand convicts!"

They talked on far into the night, Phillip finding it a relief to unburden himself to the one man, above all others, who could be expected to understand and sympathize with the despair that was wearing him down. King had experienced on Norfolk Island the same setbacks and problems as he had himself, albeit on a smaller scale and had known the lonely isolation which went with the office of governor.

"You have achieved so much, sir," the younger man said with deep conviction as he prepared at last to take his leave. "Indeed, I would go further and say that you have achieved the impossible."

"We have survived, my dear boy—that in itself is

an achievement the home government did not, perhaps, expect of us. Do you recall"—Arthur Phillip's tired voice was suddenly harsh with bitterness—"that before we sailed from Spithead, I told you I did not think it would cause them undue distress were our entire fleet to vanish without trace before reaching Botany Bay?"

King looked startled. Then he slowly inclined his head. "Yes, sir, I do recall your using those words. At the time I took leave to doubt them." He hesitated and then burst out, "I had not intended to tell you but . . . it came to my knowledge when I was in England that the—er—the expediency of abandoning the colony here and removing its surviving inhabitants to upper Canada was being considered by the home government."

"Because of what we are costing them?" the governor suggested cynically. "Because we are not yet self-supporting and must continue to ask for supplies, as well as people, to be sent to us?"

"Mainly because of the distance they have to travel, sir. Lord Dorchester raised the matter in the House, but his motion was rejected," King answered.

"They are afraid to remove us, Philip. After learning of Lapérouse's visit, they dare not permit the French to replace us. But"—the governor shrugged regretfully—"they will have to replace *me*, and I have told Grenville so. I'm a sick man and in sore need of rest and recuperation." Seeing the expression of shocked dismay on King's face, he laid an affectionate hand on his arm. "It cannot be for quite a long while —a year perhaps. And I am not going for good—I want to return after my leave, if I am fit to do so." He sighed. "I wish some of the others would stay— David Collins in particular, and the splendid Watkin

Tench. Dawes too—his scientific knowledge makes him useful, although I am not enamored of him personally. So far I haven't managed to persuade them but I shall go on trying." He stifled a yawn, and Philip King thought again how strained and ill he looked.

"I must not keep you up, sir," he began apologetically, but the governor cut him short.

"Your return gladdens my heart, Philip—there are so few people to whom I can talk freely of such matters as we have discussed this evening. And . . . there *is* one other matter, a personal and somewhat delicate one, which perhaps we should clear up before you go."

"You mean my two sons, sir, and the convict woman, Ann Inett, who bore them?" King suggested. He was smiling and perfectly at ease, not embarrassed by the question, as the governor had half-expected him to be. "My wife knows of them and of the circumstances of their birth—I told her everything before I asked for her hand. She is a woman of rare understanding, and it is her wish that Norfolk and Sydney should be brought up as members of our family when they are old enough to leave their mother." He saw Phillip's brows rise in astonishment, and his smile widened. "I am the most fortunate of men, sir, and I know it well."

"Indeed you are," the governor agreed, a trifle dryly. "What of Ann Inett? Have you any wishes in respect of her?"

"She is a good woman, sir," King said warmly. "And she deserves remission, which I intended to solicit for her. In due course, I understand that she will marry a sergeant of marines who has decided to settle here."

Phillip nodded his approval. Mrs. King was, he thought, a remarkably understanding and generous young woman but . . . he experienced a momentary pang on behalf of Ann Inett. After four years as ruler of a penal settlement, he knew all too well how difficult it was for any woman, branded with the stigma of conviction as a felon, to remain virtuous and respectable—no matter what she had been prior to transportation. Thinking of the Inett girl, he was reminded of another, who had called herself Amelia Bishop and who had now, in making an appeal for remission, revealed her real name and parentage. She, too, had come out in the hold of a transport of his own first fleet and, like Ann Inett, must on that account be debarred from marriage with her own class and kind as long as she remained here.

He sighed and, rising, poured two glasses of the excellent Madeira that Captain Parker had brought him as a gift. Raising his own glass, he said quietly, "I will give you a toast, Philip, my friend—to the future! And may God help us to make this colony one of which the mother country will one day be proud!"

"I'll drink to that with all my heart, sir," King answered readily. "To the future . . . and be damned to Lord Dorchester!"

The transport *Atlantic* was hired to replace the battered little *Supply*, and on October 26 she sailed for Norfolk Island, taking Philip King and his wife, with Captain and Mrs. Paterson, Assistant Surgeon Balmain, and the chaplain, Reverend Richard Johnson.

The day before she sailed, Governor Phillip gave his promised dinner party, entertaining fifty of his own and the *Gorgon*'s officers to a meal the likes of which had never been seen or contemplated since the founding of the colony. That it would inevitably be followed by shortages, the governor was unhappily aware, for already it was hot, the temperature rising steadily past the eighties, and the threat of a drought once again causing him acute anxiety.

On this account he hired the *Queen* to carry the relief party of the New South Wales Corps to Norfolk Island and bring back Major Ross and his marines, and ordered the master of the *Atlantic* to go on to Calcutta to purchase supplies of flour and peas for the colony, in case no storeships arrived from England.

The *Supply* sailed for home on November 26, and in spite of the blazing heat virtually the entire settlement assembled on the shore to wave her Godspeed. The *Gorgon*, too, was making preparations for departure; she would sail as soon as the *Queen* made port. To Governor Phillip's joy David Collins had decided to remain as judge advocate and relinquish his commission, but the other marine officers, with the exception of George Johnstone, were going . . . the indefatigable explorer Tench with them. Few, even of the rank and file, had elected to stay either as settlers or in the corps, despite the inducements offered to them to do so, and young Lieutenant Dawes, after some indecision, had finally made up his mind to leave.

Captain Tench had been responsible for a great deal of the goodwill now existing between the Indians and the settlers. He had acquired a working knowledge of the aboriginal tongue and— Phillip lowered his glass as the *Supply*'s dingy topsails faded from sight into the heat haze now obscuring the Heads. Since his own fragile health had rendered it inadvisable for him to take part in further exploration, Tench had led the parties which had gone out the previous winter. He, with the surgeons White, Worgan, and Lowes, and latterly with Dawes and the excellent Sergeant Knight, had fought their difficult way through the bush from Botany Bay to Broken Bay, then inland to the edge of the mountain barrier presented by the Carmarthen Range and along the Hawkesbury River. He had extended the hand of friendship to the tribes in these areas and discovered fertile farming land to the north of Rose Hill and on both sides of the Hawkesbury, and had proved, as they had begun to suspect, that it and the Nepean River were one.

But now, alas, Tench was leaving—Knight and Dawes too, and Worgan and Lowes had already gone. John White's health, like his own, was impaired; Nepean had lost interest; and the Carmarthen Mountains were, as yet, unclimbed . . . and likely to remain unclimbed if the officers of the New South Wales Corps were all of the caliber of Macarthur and Paterson. There was Johnstone, of course, but . . . Phillip sighed deeply as he walked slowly back to Government House, very conscious of the pain in his side. There was still so much to do, so much to discover about this land he ruled, and his own days here were numbered.

The transport *Queen* arrived on December 13 with Major Ross and his officers and men, together with the chaplain. Characteristically Ross was full of complaints, but to the governor's relief he went straight on board the *Gorgon*, and paid only one stiff, official call at Government House. He had, apparently, contrived to quarrel with Philip King during the few

days they had been on Norfolk Island together. His
rule, the governor heard, at some length, from Reverend Johnson, had been a far from happy one, in proof
of which the chaplain presented a number of depositions from convicts claiming to have been ill-treated,
which Captain Hill had collected and requested him
to deliver.

"I have to say, sir, in fairness to Major Ross,"
Johnson added, "that agriculture on the island is in
an excellent state, with an extra hundred acres
brought into cultivation as a direct result of his
efforts. Nevertheless, sir, many people spoke to me
of the major's cruelty and oppression, and they were
not all, I assure you, of the convict community."

Phillip thanked him gravely for his report and,
when he had gone, thrust the pile of signed depositions across his desk to Captain Collins.

"I suppose these should be filed, David," he said,
"but clearly no action can be taken now. Mister King
is in command again—he will put matters right, I
don't doubt."

"There is one other thing, sir. One of the escapers
we caught last month—an odd case."

"Oh?" Phillip eyed him expectantly. "What is it?"

"The case of a man named Munday. You may
recall, sir, that he was suspected of stowing away in
the *Waak-sam-heyd* but we gave him the benefit of
the doubt."

The governor inclined his head. "Yes, I remember.
What has the fellow been up to now?"

Collins sorted among his papers. "I took a statement from him this morning, sir. The master of the
Mary Ann handed him over as an attempted escaper
when she returned here from her whaling expedition
a couple of weeks ago. You will remember, her first

rip was extremely successful—she killed nine whales and landed thirty barrels of oil."

David Collins consulted his papers again. "Munday claims to have signed on as a deckhand when the *Mary Ann* came back from Norfolk Island at the end of August, and he says he made both whaling trips with her in that capacity. Captain Jones contradicts that claim—he says Munday attempted to stow away when he was preparing to sail for Peru."

"When does he come up for trial?"

"Tomorrow, sir."

"And what sort of character does he bear?"

Collins shrugged. "Not good, sir. He was working with the Taggart girl on her grant to the north of Rose Hill but he decamped from there in August."

"Then he probably did sign on as a deckhand," Phillip said. "All the same I think we must make an example of him, David, if the court finds against him. We cannot afford to allow ships to come out here short of seamen and procure those they lack from among our convicts, particularly since they take only the young and able. When he has suffered such punishment as the court may impose, Munday should be sent back to the Taggart girl to work in fetters. Her sentence has been remitted from life to seven years. Also, I've granted her ticket of leave. Perhaps he'll set a good example."

The governor rose heavily to his feet, wincing as the pain in his side tore at him without warning. "I'm going to rest for a while—but I'll see you on board the *Gorgon*, shall I not, for the farewell dinner?"

Collins hesitated, wanting to offer him a supporting arm and then decided against it. Arthur Phillip was proud; he did not like attention being drawn to his disability, but it was taking a terrible toll on him.

"Yes, sir, I shall be there," he said.

"And so will Major Ross," Phillip reminded him his grimace not entirely attributable to the pain tha racked him. "But at least it will be the last tim that I shall sit down at table in his company, whic is something to be thankful for. Let us pray Goc David, that Major Grose, when he succeeds him a commandant, will prove more congenial."

"Amen to that, sir."

As her time drew nearer, Jenny came perilousl close to despair. Watt Sparrow was a tower of strengtl but for all his efforts he was no farmer, and the whea of which she had had such high hopes, yielded poor harvest. The convict gang assigned to bring i in worked without enthusiasm and pilfered wheneve opportunity offered, and even when Eliza and he husband, Will Read, hearing of her plight, came ove to give what aid they could, the result was bitterl disappointing.

Eliza herself was with child, Charlotte likewise, an both had their hands full with their own, much large grants, so that the time they could spare was limitec Charlotte and Robert Webb were some distance awa in a recently settled area known as Toongabbe; the came twice, at considerable sacrifice in time and effor and Jenny, feeling for them, begged them not to d so again.

She worked, for as long as she could, but by mid December, even hoeing in the garden had becom almost more than she could cope with, and Watt, witl tears in his eyes, begged her to desist, for the hea was unbearable.

"No use knockin' yerself up, lass," he said. "Besides you gotter think o' the wean, ain't you?" He grinnec and gestured to the crib he had fashioned, with infinite pains, from a log of hardwood. "I want ter see me grandchild occupyin' that work of art, don't I? Pity ter waste it, yer know—even if 'is dad ain't 'ere."

And wasn't likely to be, Jenny thought, with weary resignation, for it was over three months since Ned had made his escape. But, to her shocked surprise, Watt brought news of his recapture when he returned from drawing their rations in Parramatta, a week before Christmas.

"The master 'anded 'im over, when 'is ship come back from the whalin', lass. Must've got on the wrong side o' some of 'em, 'cause there was three others I know of signed on at the same time as 'e did, an' they was still on board when the *Mary Ann* left port fer South America. That's where they've all gone, an' the old *Matilda*, too. Ned could've gone wiv' 'em, if 'e'd played 'is cards right, the stupid glock!"

"Has he been before the court?" Jenny asked, her heart heavy, as the import of Watt's words slowly sank in. "They'll punish him, won't they?"

The little man nodded unhappily. He was reluctant at first to reveal the details of Ned's sentence but it was obvious that he knew, and after some persuasion he told her. "I don't want you gettin' upset, Jenny love, but they ain't let 'im orf lightly—two 'undred lashes, a week on Pinchgut, an' condemned ter work in leg-irons for the next two months." He paused, eyeing her anxiously, and then added, " 'E's ter be sent back 'ere."

Jenny felt the color drain from her cheeks. The last thing she wanted was for Ned to return to her thus, under official compulsion but . . . she looked away quickly, avoiding Watt Sparrow's searching gaze.

In the months that he had been gone, she had resigned herself to his absence, even willed herself to forget him, to plan her life without him but now. . . .

"Perhaps it may bring him to his senses," she managed, her voice flat and devoid of expression. "And we can make use of his help, can't we? You—" She was suddenly uneasy, sensing the little man's resentment. "Oh, Watt, *you* won't go away, will you— even if Ned does come back here?"

His hesitation was barely perceptible, and as if to make amends for it he patted her hand reassuringly. "I'll stick around fer as long as you need me, Jenny," he promised. "Don't you worry your 'ead on my account, lass."

He brewed tea for them both and, as they drank it, he gave her the rest of the news he had gleaned in Parramatta. "They say the *Gorgon's* gone—sailin' 'ome, she is, by the Cape wiv' the marines on board. Only eight of 'em stayed be'ind, an' they've bin given land grants on the north side o' the 'arbor."

Jenny's interest momentarily quickened. "The marines have gone? Did the commandant—did Major Ross go with them?"

"I don't rightly know," Watt confessed. "But I reckon 'e must 'ave, 'cause the word was that the only orficers ter stay was Captain Collins an' Captain Johnstone. Why—did you know any of 'em?"

Jenny shivered, remembering. "I knew Major Ross, I—I'll be glad if he's gone." She offered no explanation, and Watt did not press her for one. He chattered on cheerfully, giving her snippets of overheard gossip and seeking to raise her flagging spirits, but she hardly listened, her thoughts returning to the terrible time when Major Ross had accused her of perjury and sent her to Pinchgut.

So Ned would be going to that same awful place, chained to a rock, with the pitiless sun blazing down on him and only bread and water to sustain him . . . and he would be left there for seven endless days, after having suffered a flogging. Poor Ned—he would be lucky if he survived such a sentence, lucky if— A sharp sensation of pain jabbed at her distended stomach, and she gasped, taken by surprise. It ceased, as unexpectedly as it had begun, and she got up quickly to busy herself with the newly arrived rations, wondering if she had imagined the pain.

She did not want to alarm Watt prematurely. He was anxious enough about her already and would be off, she knew, at the first sign of her baby's impending birth, to fetch the old woman who had agreed to act as midwife from her place of work in Parramatta. The woman, employed as a hutkeeper in the settlement, was unpleasant and grasping, and she had made it plain, on the only occasion when Jenny had spoken to her, that her fee would be doubled if she were compelled to wait more than two hours for the delivery. Her fee—two weeks' ration of flour or half a gallon of rum—was high enough, in all conscience.

But Watt noticed nothing amiss. He set off for his afternoon's work with no more than a mild admonition to her to stay indoors until the heat of the day was over, and went whistling on his way without a backward glance. Jenny experienced another sharp spasm of pain half an hour after he had gone, a third followed and then, seemingly without rhyme or reason, ceased altogether. Dismissing it as imagination, she set herself to cooking the evening meal.

Christmas Day came and went. Whatever celebrations took place in Sydney Cove were not echoed in the settlement at Parramatta; only Reverend Johnson visited them, coming upriver in the *Lump* on Christmas Eve in order to conduct an open-air service early the following morning. Attendance was compulsory for those living in the settlement, and Watt Sparrow trudged over, grumbling mightily at having to leave the cabin in darkness. He returned, just after midday, in better humor, bearing an extra pound of flour, issued on the governor's instructions as a Christmas bonus to every woman, and, to Jenny's surprise, a second letter from Melia.

She read it, moved to tears by the news it contained.

> By the time you receive this, dear Jenny, I shall be on the high seas, a passenger on board His Majesty's ship *Gorgon* and on my way to England.
>
> I can scarcely believe my good fortune, which came about after I had told my circumstances to the good and forever blessed governor and petitioned him for the remission of my sentence.
>
> It seems that a friend of my late father, also in Holy Orders, had made inquiries about me and, having found out that I had been transported to New South Wales, had set matters in train to procure my release. The governor granted me a full pardon and arranged for me to take passage in the *Gorgon*.
>
> I am overwhelmed with joy. We sail tomorrow morning, the eighteenth.
>
> In my newfound happiness, yet still with deep contrition, I sign myself once again your truly loving friend, Melia.

* * *

Beneath this Melia had written: "Amelia Lucinda Marchant, only daughter of Rt. Rev. Stephen John Marchant, late Bishop Suffragan of Bodmin."

Jenny looked up, to meet Watt's bright inquiring gaze. "She's going home, Watt—Melia's on her way back to England! She's been pardoned and. . . ." She started to read the letter aloud, but the little man, hitherto so kindly and uncomplaining, swore aloud, and, head bent, went rushing out of the cabin, his small gnarled hands fiercely clenched into fists at his sides.

"The devil fly away with her!" she heard him mutter. "There's no justice . . . she should be horsewhipped, not pardoned, fer what she done."

Two soldiers of the New South Wales Corps delivered Ned on New Year's Eve. They dumped him unceremoniously at the door of the cabin in the late afternoon and departed without a word, their red coats swiftly lost to sight among the trees at the side of the track.

Ned lay where they had left him, moaning softly, and Jenny saw, as she dropped awkwardly to her knees beside him, that in addition to the leg-irons, they had welded a heavy metal collar about his neck, which had already rubbed the flesh of his neck and shoulders raw. His face was deathly pale, and when, after holding a cup of water to his parched and bloodless lips, she assisted him to rise and stumble into the cabin, she looked with horror at the unhealed pulp to which the flogging had reduced his back and shoulders.

Johnny Butcher had endured two such floggings, she recalled, and would bear the scars of them until the day he died. Ned, too, was marked for life, and her heart went out to him in helpless pity. She uttered no reproach, simply led him to her own rough couch and, when he fell facedown upon it, gently eased the torn and filthy shirt from about his emaciated body and applied the only salve she had—a cloth, wrung out in cold water—to the hideously lacerated skin.

He refused her offer of food but permitted her to spoon a few mouthfuls of oatmeal broth into his mouth, and then, pushing the spoon away, he lapsed into silence, which Jenny made no attempt to break. She went about her preparations for the evening meal with what semblance of calm she could muster, torn by conflicting emotions.

His return could scarcely have been less opportune, with her time so close, she thought, pity giving place to resentment. She did not want him here when her child was born, to remind her of his claim upon her and the babe he had fathered, which, in his absence, she had come to think of solely as her own. He had failed her, so often and so cruelly.

Biting her lower lip, she glanced over at Ned's still form, only to realize that, his chin propped up on one hand, he was awake and had been watching her.

"Isn't it time you were brought to bed?" he demanded, his tone only mildly curious.

Jenny's temper flared. "Is it any concern of yours?" she countered angrily.

"I had supposed it was but—" Meeting her scornful gaze, Ned did not finish what he had been about to say. Instead he told her sullenly, "I did not ask to be sent back here, plague take it!"

"And I did not request it either. Do you imagine I want you back?" Jenny flung at him.

"Not while you have that little swine Sparrow eating

out of your hand . . . the sodding little cly-faker told you, I suppose?"

"He—" The spasm of pain that gripped her was not imagined, Jenny knew. She gasped, clutching the edge of the table for support. Oh, God, she prayed, not now, please God, not now. She straightened her heavy body with infinite effort and moved toward the door, only to be halted by another, much stronger spasm that wrung an involuntary cry from her tightly compressed lips. Watt could not be far away—he had promised to remain without earshot of the cabin, but gaining the open door at last, she could not see him.

Behind her she heard Ned swearing irritably as he lumbered to his feet, impeded by the heavy chain.

"Damn it to hell, Jenny—" He was at her side, gripping her by the shoulders. "I was right, wasn't I? Your time *has* come."

"Yes, I—I think so." She forced the words out from between clenched teeth. "Watt . . . call Watt. He will go for . . . the midwife."

Ned put an arm about her, and with his aid, Jenny reentered the cabin. "Watt," she repeated, her voice thin with urgency. "The . . . midwife. Sarah Burdo . . . she's at the settlement."

She sank down on the couch he had vacated, her whole body damp with perspiration and every muscle contracted, as another pain spasm seized her. Ned pulled the worn coverlet that had been Olwyn Jenkins's over her straining body and said gruffly, "Bide here—I'll find Watt, don't worry."

He stumped outside into the airless heat of the evening, cursing his weakness and the throttling iron collar around his neck. Watt Sparrow came limping slowly up in response to his shout, eyes narrowed and bright with hostility at the sight of him.

"So you're back ter plague us, are yer, yer useless gonif! What's the matter—Jenny thrown yer aht, 'as she?"

"No. She's come to her time," Ned retorted resentfully. "She needs you to fetch the midwife."

Watt paled. "Oh, Gawd!" he exclaimed in dismay. "An I just twisted me ankle—can't 'ardly put one foot in front o' the other." He took in Ned's chains and his gaunt, ashen face and gave vent to a string of exasperated oaths. "But I'll 'ave ter go, seein' you ain't in any state ter crawl four miles, damn your eyes! Always was useless, wasn't you, 'specially when you're needed!"

"I'll fetch the sodding midwife," Ned told him, stung by the little man's contempt. "Hell, Jenny's my woman—it's my place to go! But you told her, didn't you—you broke your word? You told her it was me sold Captain Bloody Wilkes to the Red-breasts!"

Watt Sparrow regarded him in shocked silence for a moment and then shook his head. "No, I never told 'er. I keeps me word when I gives it, Munday."

It was impossible to doubt his vehemence and the honest indignation in his voice, and Ned's brief anger faded. He held up a placatory hand. "All right—you bide with her and I'll be on my way."

Watt gave directions. "Are you sure you can make it?"

"I'll make it, blast you," Ned vowed sulkily. "I'll make it if it kills me. I walked back here, didn't I?"

He thought about Captain Wilkes as he toiled along, shivering involuntarily, despite the heat.

"I forgive all who ever did me an injury," the condemned man had thundered, his voice carrying across the hushed, expectant crowd like the voice of doom.

"Save only one—the Judas who sold me for his own gain. If that man is watching now, let him beware my dying curse! I leave it with him and he must live with it till he, too, meets his end!"

He had lived with it, Ned told himself. Oh, he had lived with it right enough, and it had been his undoing, once Dr. Fry found out at whom the curse had been aimed. The doctor had friends on both sides of the law and he had taken slow and savage vengeance on Harry Wilkes's behalf. Not content with setting the broggers against him, the foul old capon had spread the word farther afield, so that even his own kind had refused him help or sanctuary. He had starved and, driven out of London, had been reduced to begging for crusts and flimping in wretched country towns, where, for a time, he had gone unrecognized . . . until the word caught up with him and he had to move on. And his attempt to sneak back into London had resulted in his arrest, to his getting the boat and being sent out here.

But for what . . . for what *gain*? Ned ground his teeth in impotent fury as the memories came flooding back into his mind, bitter and unpalatable. First the conniving sheriff's officers had reduced his reward to the paltry twenty guineas offered by the mayor of York for Wilkes's capture, and then the Marquis of Danbury's promised payment of a hundred guineas had been withheld. That had been conditional on the recovery of the loot Wilkes had taken from his lordships' guests, they had made out . . . and Wilkes, rot his soul, had disposed of it, almost certainly to Dr. Fry. So it had been heads the cursed doctor won and tails he lost, he reflected aggrievedly.

True, he had paid Harry Wilkes back for the drubbing he had given him in the taproom of the Three

Fools. It had been that that had first prompted him to play the nose, but he wouldn't have done it if they had not offered so high a reward. And, God help him, he would most assuredly not have done it had he realized that it would bring him to his present state, chained and with a heavy, chafing collar round his neck, like some poor dumb animal.

Well, he would go through the motions; he would dig ditches and grub in the soil, as Jenny wanted him to; he would even try to make it up to her, for the sake of the child . . . at least for as long as Watt kept a still tongue in his head and did not tell her the truth about Wilkes and his filthy curse.

Four miles, four sodding miles there and four back . . . added to the four he had walked earlier, that made twelve miles in one day. He halted, breathing heavily. Although the sun had gone down half an hour ago, it was still unbearably hot and he was aching with weariness. He had worked hard enough on the whaler, heaven knew, but that had been work he had enjoyed with plenty of food and drink . . . and no chains, added to the chance of getting to South America or even back to England at the end of it. And he would have been there still if the blasted master had not got his knife into him and accused him of stealing, when all he had done was help himself to a few plugs of tobacco. All the men helped themselves when they thought they could do so undetected, but it had been his bad luck to be caught with the stuff on him . . . his bad luck or Wilkes's infernal curse.

Ned mopped his brow with the sleeve of his shirt and again endeavored to ease the pressure of the iron collar riveted to his neck. He would have to have a drink before he went on any farther—he was parched.

The creek ran somewhere near here, he recalled. He would go down there and sup a few mouthfuls of water—hell, Jenny couldn't begrudge him that, and it wouldn't take long. It stood to reason that he would move a lot faster once his thirst was quenched, and in any case women took quite a long time to give birth when the infant was their first. There was no need for him to knock himself up for the sake of a few minutes.

Ned left the track and, guided by a line of trees, made his way down toward the creekbed at a shambling trot, the leg-irons causing him to stumble as he increased his pace.

The two soldiers who had escorted him to the cabin were making their leisurely way back to their barracks in the Parramatta settlement when they heard the metallic clatter of the chains. They had been visiting one of the emancipated settlers in the area and had been received so hospitably that they had delayed their return until perilously near tap-too. But it *was* New Year's Eve, as Private Henry Daniel had pointed out, and plague take the bloody sergeant if he took their names for reporting in late.

"We can say the sodding prisoner gave us trouble," he suggested for the third time, shaking his companion into wakefulness, "if the sergeant's awkward. Oh, for Gawd's sake, Wallie, pay attention—we gotter tell the same story, don't yer see?"

Walter Cook grinned at him with drunken good humor. "Anythin' you say, Harry boy."

Daniel again became conscious of the clinking of chains. "Hey!" he exclaimed. "You 'ear that?"

"Don't 'ear nuffink," Cook assured him solemnly.

"Well, I can—chains clinkin'. Lissen, an' you'll 'ear 'em too. A con on the runnin' lark, that's what

. . . an' we got orders ter shoot 'em if we catch 'em tryin' to escape, ain't we? Come on, yer soddin' idle man—do yer flamin' duty! Prime yer musket an' let's 'ave a look-see."

Holding his own musket at the ready, Daniel led the way down the slope to where the gleam of water told him the creek was situated. It was dried up in the drought and less than half its normal size, but fresh footprints in the damp mud revealed the probable presence of the fugitive, and he quickened his stride.

Ned rose awkwardly from the water's edge. He saw and recognized the soldiers and raised a hand in greeting. Recognition was mutual, and Daniel yelled to his companion, who was several yards behind him.

"It's that bloody con Munday—the one we 'ad ter escort this mornin'! On the run again, the bastard . . . cover 'im, Wallie! We'll 'ave ter take 'im in or they'll say we never delivered 'im."

Walter Cook caught only a few words, but drunk or sober, he knew his duty.

He leveled his musket, steadied it, and fired, aiming at the runaway's heart from a range of less than a dozen yards.

The ball found its mark. With a strangled cry of anguish Ned fell, and Cook was appalled when Harry Daniel turned on him and cursed him roundly.

"Hell, you told me ter fire," Cook protested indignantly. "An' the bastard was escapin', wasn't 'e?"

"You're a goddamned bloody fool!" Daniel told him. He set down his own musket and sank to his knees beside the motionless form of the convict. The poor devil was trying to speak, trying to tell him something, and he leaned closer, endeavoring to catch the mumbled words.

"Midwife . . . for my woman. Her time's . . . come,

she . . . get Sarah . . . Sarah Burdo." Blood was stain-
ing his lips, a steadily growing pool of it spreading
across the mud, but still he sought to make his meaning clear, raising himself on one arm and bunching
up his fettered legs, as if it an effort to continue on
his errand. An errand he and that great, blundering
idiot Wallie Cook had interrupted . . . Daniel felt
tears stinging his eyes and leaned closer. The woman
in the cabin had been heavy with child, he remembered—he had seen her, when they dumped Munday
at the door.

"You want us ter send Sarah Burdo to your woman
—to the Taggart cabin, friend?" he suggested hoarsely.

Somehow, in spite of the chains and the iron collar
and the blood choking his lungs, Ned Munday got to
his feet. He staggered a few paces, stumbled, and then,
before Daniel could reach out a hand to aid him,
he fell forward and did not speak again.

" 'E's dead, Harry," Cook observed, shaken. He
looked at the smoking musket in his hand and shuddered, quite sober now. "The poor bastard's dead
an' I killed 'im. I ain't never killed anyone before,
I. . . ." His teeth were chattering. "Oh, Gawd! Gawd,
forgive me—'e wasn't escapin', was 'e?"

"No," Daniel confirmed shortly. "But that's 'ow
we'll report it, all the same. Come on!"

"Where're we goin'? For Chrissakes, are we just
ter leave 'im 'ere like this?" Cook questioned. He
passed his tongue nervously over lips that felt suddenly dry. "Shouldn't we bury 'im? Or cover 'im up,
at least?" He made to take off his scarlet jacket,
but Daniel restrained him, a hand gripping his arm.

"Don't be more of a dumb cluck than you can help,
Wallie," he retorted, an edge to his voice. "We'll
bring 'is body in in the mornin' if they want us to.

Right now we're goin' to take the midwife to 'is woman, like 'e asked. I reckon that's the least we can do, so jump to it!"

He strode off, and after a moment of worried indecision Cook followed him.

The midwife reached the cabin a little before midnight. At one o'clock, on the morning of the first day of the year 1792, Jenny Taggart gave birth to a son, and a little later, worn out by her difficult labor, she fell into an exhausted sleep.

It was broad daylight when she awakened, and the sun was streaming into the cabin through the open doorway. Sarah Burdo had taken her fee and gone, but she had washed the baby and laid him in the crib Watt had made for him. The little man was kneeling beside it, making soft, clucking noises to its loudly bawling occupant, and seeing Jenny's eyes open, he lifted the child from the crib and placed his small, swaddling-wrapped body into her arms. His noisy protests instantly ceased, and Watt said proudly, " 'E's a fine, strong boy, Jenny love . . . an' 'e favors you more'n 'e does 'is dad. Real light-colored 'air an' blue eyes . . . a picture, ain't 'e?".

Jenny looked down for the first time at the face of her son, and the face of Johnny Butcher, in miniature, looked back at her. She drew a long, sighing breath and held him to her heart.

"He's beautiful, Watt," she whispered, a catch in her voice. "Oh, he's beautiful!"

"What you goin' ter call 'im?" Watt asked. He added jealously, "Not Edward, I 'ope, 'cause Ned don't deserve that. He ain't come back, you know—gone on the run again, them sodjers reckoned."

Jenny felt tears come to ache in her throat. "I'll

give him a name all his own," she decided. "Justin . . . it's the nicest name I know."

Three weeks later, at a communal service conducted in the open air by Reverend Johnson, with Watt standing as godfather, the boy was christened Justin Angus and his surname registered as Taggart.

EPILOGUE

Governor Phillip sat at his desk, a quill pen in his hand and a small mountain of official papers in front of him.

There was much to arrange before he relinquished the reins of office and set sail, at last, for England. Most of the papers required his approval and signature but . . . he let the quill drop. There was more, so much more to ponder over, assess, and evaluate before he could turn his back on the colony he had founded, five years ago—that Colony of Disgracefuls over whose destiny he had ruled to the best of his honest ability and brought from near starvation to something that now approached prosperity.

He wished, with all his heart, that he could stay, aware that his increasing ill-health precluded it. He had written, in October, to Henry Dundas, the new home secretary, "I believe my returning to England will be the greatest service I can render this colony, independent of any other consideration, for it will put it in my power to shew what may and what may not be expected from it. . . ." Yet he was anxious. The man who would temporarily succeed him was, alas, one he neither liked nor trusted. Major Francis Grose, late of His Majesty's 96th Foot and now commandant of the New South Wales Corps, had reached Sydney on board the *Pitt* in February.

Like Major Ross, he had been officially designated lieutenant governor, and it had been with his connivance and encouragement that the master of the *Pitt* had opened shop and sold—at extremely high prices—£4,000 worth of goods brought out for the specific purpose of private trade. And no doubt, Arthur Phillip thought wryly, the profit made by the *Pitt*'s master had given Major Grose the idea of himself embarking on a similar trading venture . . . certainly he had wasted very little time in putting the idea into practice.

Among the convict transports and storeships that had come out during the year had been the *Britannia,* one of a fleet of three dispatched from Falmouth, which had brought out supplies of meat and flour. He had sent the *Britannia* on to Norfolk Island with provisions of these commodities and, on her return, had discharged her from the government service, on the understanding that her master had instructions from his owners to sail to New Zealand.

It had come as something of a shock to him when he learned that Grose and his officers had chartered her to go to the Cape for the purpose of purchasing supplies and trade goods on their behalf . . . he sighed. Taxed with it, Francis Grose had written him in most insolent terms. He hunted among his papers—the letter, he knew, was one he had retained, with the intention of putting it before Home Secretary Dundas and . . . yes, here it was.

Frowning, Phillip spread out the folded sheet of paper and reread the letter.

> The situation of the soldiers under my command, who at this time have scarcely shoes to their feet and who have no other comforts than the reduced and unwholesome rations served out from the stores, has induced me to assemble the captains of my corps for the purpose of consulting what could be done for their relief and accommodation.
>
> Amongst us we have raised a sufficient sum to take up the *Britannia* and, as all money matters are already settled with the master, who is also an owner, I have now to request you will assist us to escape the miseries of that precarious existence we have hitherto been so constantly exposed to.

He had replied, with some annoyance, that the rations served from the government store, which Major Grose and his officers appeared to find "unwholesome," were the same as he saw daily at his own table, and that as many shoes for his men as had been requisitioned had been issued to them . . . but Grose had been unmoved. His motive—and that of the officers who had supported him in his enterprise—was, undoubtedly, the desire for private profit, however it might be disguised. Against his better judgment, Phillip had had to permit the charter, since the *Britannia* was already under weigh, but he had reported the matter to the home secretary in strong terms stressing that its continuance would be detrimental to the colony's best interests, in that it would open the door to contraband trade by the military.

But would the home government heed his warning? He repeated his sigh. It was they who had selected Francis Grose for his command, they who had ordered the formation of the New South Wales Corps and recruited its rank and file from the scum of the British Army. The men who had enlisted in it were proving themselves a raffish bunch, often superior in infamy and indiscipline to the convicts it was their duty to guard; the officers were, on the whole, below the standard normally prevailing in King's regiments.

And it was into their hands that he would be entrusting his infant colony. He rose and crossed to the window that overlooked the cove and the anchorage, staring out with eyes misted momentarily by tears, as he glimpsed the Indiaman *Atlantic* at her moorings. Boats were plying between her and the shore, carrying Lieutenant Poulden and the last of the marine detachment to join her. Soon, all too soon, he would follow them, and Sydney would know him no more.

Beyond the bluff-bowed *Atlantic*, the smaller *Kitty* lay at anchor, rising and falling on the slight swell. Delayed and badly battered by the storms she had encountered, she had brought mail, provisions, and money—the first received in the colony—to pay the convict superintendents and others in government service. But she had not, alas, brought the free settlers the governor had expected and hoped for or the artisans Dundas had promised . . . there was a slight movement behind him, and Phillip turned, startled out of his reverie, to find David Collins standing at his back.

"Forgive me for disturbing you, sir," the judge advocate said. "But I received a letter from Watkin Tench in the mail the *Kitty* delivered. It was swamped, with the rest, and I've only just managed to dry it out sufficiently to render it legible. I thought it might be of interest to you, sir, as it concerns those people who escaped with Bryant, the fishery superintendent, in your cutter."

Phillip's tired eyes lit up. "Damme, David!" he exclaimed. "You're not going to tell me that they succeeded in reaching Timor, are you?"

Collins smiled. "Indeed I am, sir." He consulted the crumpled sheet of paper in his hand. "They made port in Timor on the fifth of June of last year, without loss of life."

"Incredible!" The governor stared at him. "An incredible feat of navigation in that small cutter. And it took them—what? Nine weeks and immense courage. They are a loss to this colony, David. But how did Tench learn of their achievement? Were they recaptured?"

David Collins nodded, almost with regret. "They were taken to the Cape, sir, and sent on board the *Gorgon* when she reached port. Bryant and his small son died of fever in Batavia; three of the others, Bird, Morton, and Cox, lost their lives on the way to the Cape. But read the letter, if you would care to . . . it supplies all the details."

The governor returned to his desk and settled down to decipher the faded ink of Watkin Tench's missive.

It was my fate to fall in again with part of the little band of adventurers who stole the governor's cutter in March of last year. When I arrived in the *Gorgon* at the Cape of Good Hope, six of them, including the woman, Mary Bryant, and one child, were put on board of us to be carried to England. Four had died and one jumped overboard at Batavia, rather than be taken back to captivity.

On June 5, 1791, they reached Timor and pretended to have been shipwrecked on passage from Port Jackson to India. The Dutch received them with kindness and treated them with hospitality, but one of them, in a moment of intoxication, betrayed the secret. They were immediately secured and committed to prison.

I confess that I could never look at these people without pity or astonishment. They had miscarried in an heroic struggle for liberty, after having combated every hardship and conquered every hazard.

Poor souls! When, as they must, the survivors are brought to trial for escaping from custody, I intend to bring such influence as I possess to bear on their behalf.

"There was a letter enclosed with it, sir," Collins said when the governor came to the end of Watkin Tench's narrative, "addressed to the Taggart girl here, sir, by the prisoner Butcher, with a request that it should be delivered to her. I take it I may have your permission to see that it reaches its destination?"

"Most certainly, David . . . and with the letter you may deliver her remission papers—they are among those I have yet to sign. Dear heaven, how the time is passing! I had best deal with these at once, had I not, so that this desk is left clear for Major Grose." He again picked up his quill and, aided by Collins, dealt swiftly and efficiently with the accumulation of letters, orders, and reports, using the recently delivered seal of his office to stamp those that required it.

The work completed at last, he studied the seal, smiling as he did so. It was of silver, engraved with the motto *Sic Fortis Etruria Crevit* and the royal arms on the obverse. The reverse showed a figure resembling Britannia, surrounded by symbols denoting a bale of wool, a beehive, a pickax, and a shovel, with a ship, a plow, three small figures of laborers, and what appeared to be a town.

"Was he an optimist who designed this, David?" Phillip mused. "Or will these symbols truly represent this colony in days to come?"

"I pray they will, sir," David Collins answered. "I'd have been more certain were you not leaving."

Or if John Hunter or even Philip King were to replace him, Phillip thought, for both were dedicated to their country's service, whereas Grose . . . he studied his loyal young subordinate for a moment with narrowed, speculative eyes. "Much will depend on you, David," he warned. "You must do all in your power to prevent the officers of the New South Wales Corps from enriching themselves by private trade, as would seem to be their present objective. And they must not receive land grants whilst they are still serving in the corps. I have left orders to that effect, as you are aware, duly signed and sealed."

Phillip sighed and placed the seal into Collins's hand.

"Only the governor may use this. Guard it well. And there's this—" He picked up a document from the pile in front of him. "The authority for the chaplain to build a church—poor fellow, survival has had to take precedence, the need for crops has had to be placed before the use of our labor force to build the House of God. But with the town of Sydney now a-building, Mister Johnson must have his Church. You'll see to that for me, will you not, my dear boy?"

"I'll do my utmost, sir," Collins promised with sincerity. He offered his arm. "Dinner is ready to be served, if you have finished."

"Yes, I've finished," Phillip answered, and his eyes suddenly misted, he passed through into his dining room with its assembled guests, leaning heavily on Collins's arm.

Next day the New South Wales Corps paraded to pay him the customary honors, with Major Grose marching arrogantly at its head. At six o'clock on the evening of December 10 Arthur Phillip boarded the *Atlantic*, accompanied by Baneelon and another young aborigine who had served him as hunter and guide, and within an hour the ship weighed anchor to begin the long voyage back to England.

For good or ill, his five years as governor had come to an end.

A small crowd had collected to watch the governor's departure. Among them, standing together on the shore, Jenny and Watt Sparrow saw the boat put off from the landing wharf. Watt lifted the year-old Justin onto his shoulder and said, smiling, "Wave 'im good-bye, me little lad . . . an' wave 'ard, 'cause 'is Excellency's goin' 'ome. An' don't I wish I was goin' wiv' 'im!"

Jenny, her eyes misted, shook her head. "You mustn't speak like that, Watt," she reproached him. "Not to Justin—his home is here, and he'll never know another."

"More's the pity then," Watt retorted as the child obediently waved his small hand in the direction of the departing boat. But Jenny scarcely heard him. Governor Phillip was a good man, she thought, and he had been a good governor—stern, at times, but always fair and just. His going would be the colony's loss, perhaps its greatest loss . . . she glanced uneasily to where the new lieutenant governor stood at the foot of the slope leading up to Government House, surrounded by his officers. She saw Lieutenant Macarthur move to his side, and heard, with an odd sense of foreboding, Major Grose laugh aloud at something the younger officer had said to him.

Governor Phillip's boat went alongside the *Atlantic*; the crew tossed their oars smartly, and the governor's stooping figure could be seen, framed briefly in the entry port, his cocked hat held above his head in salute.

Major Grose gave no sign that he had seen the gesture. Still laughing, he laid his hand on Macarthur's shoulder, and together the two men turned and went toward Government House, to vanish from sight within its portals, talking in low, earnest voices.

"Thick as thieves, them two," Watt Sparrow observed, following the direction of Jenny's gaze.

She nodded, her fingers closing about the two precious sheets of paper in the pocket of her dress. Her pardon and the letter from Johnny Butcher.

At the end of his account Johnny had written:

We made the voyage to Timor, but I'm wishing now that we had not, for we have, it seems, only exchanged one prison for another and lost Will Bryant and his boy, with three of the others, on the way from Batavia to the Cape. A fiend in human form and a disgrace to the noble profession he follows conveyed us here, together with some other poor souls who survived a mutiny on board His Majesty's ship *Bounty*.

Yet I live in the hope of one day seeing you again and, God willing, as a free man, if there is any justice in old England to which I may appeal.

Wait for me, Jenny. . . .

She knew the contents of the letter by heart, she had read it so many times. And she had her pardon . . . Jenny looked at her small golden-haired son with pride and held out her arms to him. She whispered as she held him to her, "One day, Justin, if God is willing, your father will claim you . . . and you'll have no call to be ashamed of him, convict or free."

"What's that?" Watt demanded, puzzled.

Jenny's smile included him in its warmth. "Nothing, really," she answered. "I suppose you'd call it a dream—or perhaps a prayer would be nearer the mark." As she watched the governor's boat being hoisted inboard and heard the first cannon fired in salute, she wondered what the future had in store for them and what her son's heritage would be. Then she added softly, "Governor Phillip's on his way. Let's go home, shall we?"

Watt Sparrow swore under his breath, but after only a brief hesitation he followed her, and they joined a small procession of people making for the *Lump*'s mooring.

The Settlers by William Stuart Long continues the sweeping saga of Jenny, Justin, and the others, both brave and savage, who carve a life for themselves out of the rough and violent new colony that will become Australia, the land of our cousins "down under." The following is an excerpt from *The Settlers* to be published by Dell in August. © 1980 Book Creations, Inc. Produced by Lyle Kenyon Engel

Charles Brace was anxious to engage a suitable young woman to look after his domestic needs, but the ones Foveaux's housekeeper had sent for his inspection had all proved wanting. Several had been prostitutes; two others dumpy country girls, unlettered and bucolic; a third, on her own admission, prone to drink. All offended his fastidious tastes, but perhaps amongst the Irish women . . . he smiled to himself, as he made his way aft, with young Ensign de Catteral at his heels.

The women were under guard, huddled together as if for mutual protection, their faces uniformly sullen and unhappy. But there were a number of pretty faces among them, he saw, and they were clean and wholesome, their hair neatly braided, their clothing feminine. The men on guard duty came to attention as the two officers approached; Brace addressed himself to the sergeant and made their wants known.

"It will be to the advantage of any women to engage themselves as domestic servants in an officer's household," he added, careful to observe the proprieties. "They will receive payment for their services and rations, and a clothing allowance; they will be well treated and comfortably housed. Those engaged in the public service do not fare so well. You are, presumably, well acquainted with these women, Sergeant. Are there any you can recommend?"

To his astonishment, the sergeant answered emphatically, "Nary a one, sir, and that's the gospel truth."

Brace regarded him incredulously. Then, out of the corner of his eye, he caught sight of a slim, dark-haired girl in a striped gingham dress, as she moved across to the taffrail with easy grace, her head held high.

Charles watched the girl in the gingham dress with absorbed attention, taking in her youth and the classic beauty of her profile. His pulse quickened when, sensing his eyes on her, she turned to give him stare for stare, defiant and unafraid.

"Go and report to Captain Foveaux," he snapped at Catteral. . . .

When the boy had gone, he strode purposefully across to the taffrail. There was no cage, no enclosed space for the prisoners to take their exercise, as there usually was on most convict transports. Perhaps Captain Chalmers had treated his unwilling passengers with too much humanity, he thought wryly, and thus invited them to betray his trust.

The girl in the gingham dress observed his approach calmly. She held her ground, making no attempt to avoid him, and when he came to a halt in front of her, Brace found himself at a loss for words. Her eyes, he saw, were of a deep blue, in striking contrast to her shining dark hair, and although she did not smile, she displayed no open sign of hostility. Encouraged by this, he embarked clumsily on the offer of employment he had decided to make her, outlining its advantages in much the same words as he had used to explain them to the sergeant.

She heard him in silence, her lovely face expressionless. When at last she spoke, her voice was educated, with only a faint, musical lilt to it to remind him of her Irish ancestry.

"You're asking me to keep house for you—to cook and clean?"

"Yes. I—"

"And no doubt to be lady's maid to your wife?" the girl pursued.

"No. That is"—Brace could feel himself reddening —"I am not married. I've only been here for just over a month, and my quarters are . . . well, in sore need of a woman's touch."

"And is it the custom here for unmarried officers

to employ young convicted females to keep house for them?"

He looked at her unhappily, not certain whether her questions were intended to discomfit him or whether she genuinely sought answers to them, and finally inclined his head. "Yes, it's quite customary. Conditions are primitive. The houses—"

"I have seen the houses," the girl put in flatly. She leaned back against the taffrail, maintaining the distance between them. "You spoke of public work. Are we required to perform hard labor? Is that the alternative to becoming a maidservant to an officer such as yourself or, perhaps, a married officer?"

The emphasis she had placed on the word *married* left Brace in no doubt that she had seen through his attempt at subterfuge. Unreasonably angered by this and by the thinly veiled disdain with which she was regarding him, he listed the tasks usually allocated to female convicts.

In fact, as he was aware, little or no compulsion was exercised in order to force them to work, but they received no official issues of food or clothing if they did not. For this reason, those who were unable to find a man to provide such necessities for them usually took on some public labor . . . or became prostitutes. . . . If they did not act as hut-keepers for convict-labor gangs or take domestic employment with officers and superintendents, they either worked on the land or made a precarious living on piecework with their needles.

The Irish girl listened to Brace's brusque explanation of the possibilities open to her with growing anger and a sense of outrage. When he came to the end of his recital, she said, in a tone of stinging contempt, "Then I shall work on the land. I would as soon herd hogs as keep house for an English redcoat . . . all of us would!"

"Then I shall wait until you change your mind."